KT-571-304

PENGUIN (🐧) CLASSICS

LOVE-LETTERS BETWEEN
A NOBLEMAN AND HIS SISTER

Little is known about Aphra Behn's early life, from what religious and social background she came or how she obtained her extraordinary education, which allowed her to translate from French with ease, to allude frequently to the classics and to take part in the philosophical, political and scientific debates of her time. She was probably born around 1640 in Kent and in the early 1660s claims to have visited the English colony of Surinam, which forms the setting of her best-known early story, *Oroonoko, or the History of the Royal Slave* (1688), an early discussion of slavery and innate nobility. In 1666 she was employed by Charles II's government as a spy in Antwerp during the Dutch wars; after she received insufficient payment, she turned to literature for a living, writing poetry, political propaganda for the Tory party and numerous short stories, as well as adapting or composing at least nineteen stage plays, many of them extremely successful, such as the comic depiction of Cavalier exile *The Rover* (1677), and the early farce, *The Emperor of the Moon* (1687). During the political upheavals of the end of Charles II's reign and the beginning of James II's she wrote her great amorous and political novel *Love-Letters between a Nobleman and his Sister*, which both satirizes and comments on the turbulent times. Behn had strong sympathy for the culture of Roman Catholicism but was intellectually drawn to the sceptical and materialist philosophy of the libertines with whom she associated. Virginia Woolf acclaimed her as the first woman to earn her living by writing, declaring, 'All women together ought to let flowers fall upon the tomb of Aphra Behn, for it was she who earned them the right to speak their minds.'

JANET TODD is Professor of English Literature at the University of East Anglia. She was formerly a Fellow of Sidney Sussex College, Cambridge, and a Professor at Rutgers University. Her publications include *Women's Friendship in Literature* (1980), *Feminist Literary History* (1988), *The Sign of Angellica: Women, Writing and Fiction* (1989), *Gender, Art and Death* (1933) and, with Marilyn Butler, an edition of Mary Wollstonecraft's work. She has also edited *Oroonoko, The Rover and Other Works* for Penguin Classics. Her biography of Aphra Behn is forthcoming.

APHRA BEHN

Love-Letters between a Nobleman and his Sister

Edited by JANET TODD

PENGUIN BOOKS

PENGUIN BOOKS

Published by the Penguin Group
Penguin Books Ltd, 27 Wrights Lane, London W8 5TZ, England
Penguin Books USA Inc., 375 Hudson Street, New York, New York 10014, USA
Penguin Books Australia Ltd, Ringwood, Victoria, Australia
Penguin Books Canada Ltd, 10 Alcorn Avenue, Toronto, Ontario, Canada M4V 3B2
Penguin Books (NZ) Ltd, 182–190 Wairau Road, Auckland 10, New Zealand

Penguin Books Ltd, Registered Offices: Harmondsworth, Middlesex, England

First published 1684–7
This edition published by Pickering & Chatto (Publishers) Limited 1993
Published with a new Introduction in Penguin Books 1996
1 3 5 7 9 10 8 6 4 2

Text, Appendices and Variants copyright © Pickering & Chatto (Publishers) Limited 1993
Introduction and Notes copyright © Janet Todd, 1993, 1996
All rights reserved

The moral right of the editor has been asserted

Printed in England by Clays Ltd, St Ives plc

Except in the United States of America, this book is sold subject
to the condition that it shall not, by way of trade or otherwise, be lent,
re-sold, hired out, or otherwise circulated without the publisher's
prior consent in any form of binding or cover other than that in
which it is published and without a similar condition including this
condition being imposed on the subsequent purchaser

CONTENTS

ACKNOWLEDGEMENTS

In the preparation of the text and footnotes I have had the help of several institutions and the advice of many scholars. Among the institutions to which I owe gratitude are the Beinecke Rare Book and Manuscript Library of Yale University, the Bodleian Library, Oxford, the British Library, Cambridge University Library, the National Library of Scotland, the Public Record Office, the Special Collections Department of the University of Glasgow, the Library of the University of Texas and Dr Williams's Library, London. I wish to express thanks to Louise Atherton, Virginia Crompton, Maureen Duffy, Paul Jeffreys-Powell, J. R. Jones, Betty Knott, Robert Letellier, Mary Ann O'Donnell, Elizabeth Spearing, David Weston and Melinda Zook. My greatest debt is to the Leverhulme Trust which generously aided my work on an edition of the complete works of Aphra Behn; through its support I have had the assistance of Francis McKee in the preparation of the text.

INTRODUCTION

The Author

Nothing in previous English literature quite prepares the reader for a huge work like *Love-Letters between a Nobleman and his Sister*. Issued anonymously in three parts and running to over one thousand pages, it was the first published prose fiction of the Restoration playwright Aphra Behn. It had all the components of a blockbuster, dealing as it did with an aristocratic scandal and with highly incendiary political events, still unfolding as the parts came out.

When Behn set about writing her first long fiction as a *roman à clef*, in which events and characters were thinly disguised, she was well suited to the task. Born to a humble family in Kent around 1640, she had probably used her connection with Thomas Colepeper (her mother had been his wet-nurse) to make acquaintance with his more extended kin, including the great families of the Sidneys and the Howards. In 1666, during the Second Dutch War between England and Holland, when she was a young woman of twenty-five or so, probably recently widowed, she was sent by the government of Charles II as a secret agent to the Low Countries. Her mission was not regarded as overwhelmingly successful in Whitehall and, when the authorities had had enough of her, Behn found herself stranded in Antwerp with huge debts for accommodation and food, and nothing with which to pay them. She was learning, as she put it, the 'slenderness of . . . rewards' commonly experienced by all 'his Maj[es]tys friends'. The only option for the heroine of *Love-Letters*, left similarly if not so drastically to her own devices in the Low Countries, was, as Behn knew from personal experience, the getting of money.

Returning to England, Behn proceeded to turn herself into a playwright of note; by 1683 she had at least fifteen plays to her credit, making her the most productive dramatist of the time after the Poet Laureate, John Dryden. Many of these plays suggest that, despite her experiences as a secret agent, her loyalty had remained miraculously intact. *The Rover*, *The Roundheads* and *Sir Patient Fancy*, for example, were all plays that mocked the money-grubbing vulgarity of the Whigs, as the party of opposition to the King had come to be called; they also idealized the figure of the Tory courtier or cavalier. Her work fitted the times; literature was politicized during these years and Behn was a professional writer needing to be in vogue.

Once she began writing for the theatre in the early 1670s Behn obtained a wide circle of friends, including authors, actresses and aristocrats: she had some acquaintanceship with the famous rake and poet the Earl of Rochester, and she directed many of her works to the leading politicians of the day. That she achieved her social position over many years is evident from the fact that her early works were not addressed to any great patron. But from 1679, with her dedication of *The Feign'd Curtizans* to Nell Gwyn, she began writing to and for the famous and powerful, such as the King's brother and heir to the throne James Duke of York (later James II), and his illegitimate nephew the Duke of Grafton.

Despite her dedications to royalty and to courtiers, there is no evidence that Aphra Behn was ever quite of the court herself, although some of her plays were acted in the royal theatre before the King. She frequented aristocratic circles and watched the court, and she knew how courtiers and nobles acted and spoke, but she lived and watched as an outsider. This is very much the position of the narrator in the last two parts of *Love-Letters* as she chronicles the antics of the nobly born, if by then debased, protagonists.

In the political fever of the late 1670s and early 80s it was not only the theatre that required the services of a writer. The government wanted an endless stream of pamphlets, lampoons and thinly disguised fictions. Overtly Behn was a Tory and she was becoming a major propagandist, writing eulogistic elegies and panegyrics for court figures, Charles II, Catherine his queen, and most elaborately for James II, with his queen, Mary of Modena. She also probably supplied lampoons, which were published anonymously. In a comic verse address she wrote to a friend in 1683, she described herself going to Charles II to try to get paid for her 'Tory doggerell': her fate with propaganda clearly echoed that with espionage. *Love-Letters*, written during these years, was undoubtedly planned as propaganda. It was also intended as a pot-boiler.

Despite all this political activity Behn was always in need of money. If she had ever been kept by a man – and there is some evidence that she may have lived for a time with a lawyer by the name of John Hoyle in the early 1670s – the period was far in the past. A woman moving on the edge of the court and in theatrical circles had need of considerable upkeep: she required personal servants and messengers, as well as elaborate clothes and money for entertaining in taverns and at home. Since Behn was ailing from at least 1683 onwards she also wanted money for doctors and medicines. In 1685, in the middle of compiling *Love-Letters*, she wrote a letter to the moneylender Zachary Baggs in which she begged a loan of £6.

The Scandal

The most immediate historical inspiration for *Love-Letters* was the scandal involving Ford Lord Grey. Lord Grey had married Lady Mary, daughter of the aristocratic house of Berkeley. She had conceived a passion for the handsome James Scott, Duke of Monmouth, eldest illegitimate son of Charles II and focus of political opposition; their affair was alluded to in lampoons of the time, possibly one by Behn herself since it included references to *The Rover* (see Appendix II). Lord Grey chose to ignore the rumours, but, perhaps out of pique, though perhaps too out of passion, he turned his attentions to his wife's young sister, Lady Henrietta. In the nomenclature of the day she was his sister though she would later be called a sister-in-law. Whether considered incest or adultery, the relationship laid Lord Grey open to a legal charge: Lady Henrietta was still within the guardianship of her father, and it was Lord Berkeley's property that his son-in-law was depreciating.

Grey's seduction of his sister-in-law, and their consequent elopement during a period of high political drama in which Lord Grey was also implicated, was thoroughly entertaining to the nation. But it was less so to the Berkeleys, who had to go through the indignity first of advertising for their daughter in the newspaper (the *London Gazette* for September 1682) and then of bringing a trial to order her return. Five accomplices were tried with Grey and all but one were found guilty as charged.

Shortly after the trial a transcript of the proceedings was published under the title *The Trial of Ford Lord Grey*. It was not common practice to record all trials verbatim at this time, so the appearance of such a detailed account may have been encouraged by the government, which would have found it opportune that Lord Grey, as one of the Duke of Monmouth's most powerful supporters, had become embroiled in scandal. *The Trial* (some of which is printed at the back of this edition) confirms many of the details in the first part of *Love-Letters*, and its glimpses of life in Durdans, the Berkeleys' family seat, may have stimulated the initial idea for the novel.

The lovers' letters and the constant presence of domestic spies to which references were made during the trial were certainly absorbed into the work.

At the trial, the Berkeleys were suing for the return of their daughter. But this was prevented in a dramatic moment when Lady Henrietta, hardly allowed a word in the masculine court in which a woman was either a female child or a *feme covert* (a wife, legally subsumed into her husband), declared she would not return to her father because she was married. This marriage, it turned out, was to a gentleman servant of Lord Grey, a Mr Turner, who was understood to have married her entirely for the convenience of his lord. It was left to Aphra Behn to investigate the inevitable complications of this interesting triangle. In the work Lord Grey becomes Philander, Lady Henrietta becomes Silvia, and Turner becomes Brilljard.

The Historical Background

Although it is not strictly an historical novel, *Love-Letters* takes place against, and dramatizes, the tumultuous political happenings of the early 1680s leading up to and following the death of Charles II in 1685. It was a period that included the end of the Popish Plot, the Rye House Plot, the Exclusion Crisis and, above all, the Monmouth Rebellion, when at King Charles's death the Duke of Monmouth mounted a rebellion against his uncle, the Catholic James II, to secure the throne for himself. In the novel Monmouth appears as Cesario.

Like Dryden and other loyal supporters of James, Behn had long been intrigued by Monmouth, both as a handsome, skittish cavalier and as the dark shadow of legitimate Stuart power, the embodiment of Charles's sexual prowess, which was at once admirable in a monarch and disastrous for a realm. In the closing pages of *Love-Letters* Behn followed history as recorded in pamphlets quite closely: watching the doomed Monmouth/Cesario as he disintegrated under pressure, writing undignified begging letters to his uncle and using his final moments on the scaffold to praise his mistress instead of ensuring his place in history. He died, as Behn recorded, 'more pitied than lamented'.

Although many of the lesser figures in the novel can similarly be identified with actual historical people – Fergusano with Ferguson, for example – Behn also created composite characters from political personages of the time. Tomaso drew on elements of both Sir

Thomas Armstrong, a notable rebel and dissident, and the recently deceased Anthony Ashley Cooper, the first Earl of Shaftesbury, prime mover of the opposition and the main architect of Monmouth as pretender to the throne.

Like people, events appear combined and in code in the novel. The analogy between the Civil Wars of the 1640s and the unrest of the 1680s was a constant in the political pamphlets of both sides, and it was easy enough to make a similar analogy between the tumult in England and the sixteenth- and seventeenth-century religious wars in France. Indeed it was sensible to do so. An author might fall foul of authority quite accidentally or be retrospectively prosecuted if events took an unexpected turn.

From 1678, when the Popish Plot allegations of Titus Oates against the Catholics began in England and Parliament started to consider interfering with the principle of hereditary monarchy by excluding from the throne the Catholic heir, James Duke of York, the nation was in turmoil, a turmoil fomented by the oppositional party of Shaftesbury and Monmouth. The King feared the diminution of his royal prerogative that the exclusion of James indicated, a prerogative for which his father Charles I had gone to the scaffold in 1649. The supporters of Parliament meanwhile feared the twin evils of popery and arbitrary government, which they saw Charles and James introducing into England, and to avoid which they had fought and won the Civil Wars of the 1640s and 50s. The Popish Plot brought this earlier period forcibly to mind and resulted in the deaths of many innocent men, including some whom Behn greatly admired.

The Popish Plot was followed by the more plausible Rye House Plot, an apparent Protestant conspiracy to assassinate Charles II and the Duke of York, as they returned from Newmarket in the spring of 1683. The plan was that the crown would then be offered to the illegitimate but Protestant Duke of Monmouth. In this plot Ford Lord Grey was deeply but obscurely implicated. He was arrested but escaped through the carelessness of a drunken guard.

On the death of Charles II in 1685, Monmouth, in exile in Holland, was urged on by his mistress, Henrietta Wentworth, and Lord Grey, who had joined him immediately after his escape, to rebel against his uncle, King James II. The exiles, now including Lord Grey, the chief aristocrat of the party, returned from Holland under Monmouth's banner, hoping to ignite a popular rebellion against the Catholic James and seize the throne of England for the Protestant cause. The attack proved disastrously mismanaged and misjudged. The survivors of the final battle of Sedgemoor, which ended the Monmouth Rebellion, were ruthlessly dealt with by Judge Jeffries (to whom Behn dedicated a translation in 1688) and Monmouth himself was executed on 15 July 1685. The most famous and extraordinary survivor of the bloody and extensive reprisals was Monmouth's most powerful supporter, Lord Grey. He gained his life, it seems, through his great wealth, for he was forced to pay a bond of £40,000 to the Earl of Sunderland. He was pardoned by James, whom he subsequently abandoned in the final revolution of 1688 which deposed the King and placed his Protestant son-in-law and daughter, William and Mary, on the throne.

The Literary Work

When Part I of *Love-Letters* was published in 1684, Ford Lord Grey, Henrietta Berkeley and the Duke of Monmouth had all taken refuge on the Continent following the Rye House Plot, and the events which inspired the subsequent two volumes had not yet occurred. The ill-fated Monmouth Rebellion took place in the early summer of 1685 and Behn must have been writing at great speed to produce Part II in the same year. She may have made a decision to concentrate on the personal lives of Philander and Silvia in that volume while the events of the Rebellion continued to unfold around her. Part III, *The Amours of Philander and Silvia*, followed in 1687, and it was only then that Behn summarized Monmouth's preparations in Holland for his invasion of England, which must have taken place before she finished Part II.

When Behn was writing the final part of *Love-Letters*, which ended with the failure of the Monmouth Rebellion and the capture of Monmouth and Grey, she already knew of the extra-ordinary pardon of Lord Grey despite his central role in the rebellion. The cynicism of this part, dedicated to the ne'er-do-well Lord Spencer, son of the Earl of Sunderland, suggests some ambiguity of political message. Comparison of the young Spencer and the transgressing Philander was inevitable, as was comparison between Philander/Grey and Spencer's father, the politically slippery Sunderland, the man who saved Grey from the scaffold – a man who, according to some, had himself been a secret dealer with Monmouth.

As a safety measure, *Love-Letters* appeared anonymously. Part of it was brought out by a trade publisher, one who could serve as a front for several probable investors; the identity of these would remain hidden. Perhaps neither they nor Behn herself wished openly to be associated with a work which could potentially be interpreted in embarrassing ways. Consequently, during her lifetime *Love-Letters* was never publicly acknowledged as Aphra Behn's. Sources such as the *Dictionary of National Biography* attribute the novel to the government censor Sir Roger L'Estrange, a man much admired for his staunch royalism. He was a credible candidate since in 1678 he had translated the famous *Lettres portugaises* as *Five love-letters from a nun to a cavalier*, a work that greatly influenced the development of the epistolary genre in English as an investigation of male and female passion. However, by 1691 Gerard Langbaine had firmly ascribed *Love-Letters* to Aphra Behn in *An Account of the English Dramatick Poets*, and some of her later short novels support the ascription. Several, such as *The Fair Jilt*, reveal likenesses in style and content to *Love-Letters*, especially in the development of the sexually manipulative woman. They also resemble the novel in the creation of a spectating narrator, for, in Part II of *Love-Letters*, the narrator emerges from the pretence of the letters to present her story directly.

In its day *Love-Letters* proved to be an immensely popular novel. The Popish Plot had fused politics and erotics in a stream of antipapist pornography from 1678 onwards, and Behn's work plays with this mixture of politics and sex by focusing on the seduction of Henrietta Berkeley – recounted in steamy detail – and on her subsequent progress from aristocratic daughter to wandering whore. A second edition of the full text was printed in 1693 and by the beginning of the eighteenth century it had become the epitome of erotic fiction: a young lady in an Eliza Haywood novel, reading the work, dissolved on her bed in response. The book was serialized in the *Oxford Journal* in 1736, just a year after a verse edition of *The Amours of Philander and Silvia* had been published, and at least another six editions of *Love-Letters* appeared between 1708 and 1765. *The Trial* itself also continued to fascinate the public; a second edition appeared in 1716, thirty-four years after the events had taken place, and it was included in the 1765 edition of *Love-Letters*.

But, by the end of the eighteenth century, both trial and novel had fallen foul of the moral arbiters and *Love-Letters* was rarely mentioned or read. Because of its dubious moral reputation, it was largely ignored by the Victorians. More surprisingly it was also ignored by the late nineteenth- and early twentieth-century critics searching for the origins of the novel and finding them instead in the later, male writers, Richardson and Defoe.

The importance of the lovers' letters as evidence in the trial of Lord Grey may have suggested to Behn the use of the epistolary form for her novel. But no doubt she was also influenced by the contemporary rage for epistolary fiction. Works in letters, translated from French and Spanish, were highly popular in England, among the most influential being *Histoire amoureuse des Gaules* (1665) by Roger de Bussy-Rabutin and Sir Roger L'Estrange's translation of *Lettres portugaises*. The third-person *La Princesse de Clèves* (1679) by Madame de La Fayette, with its focus on the development of character and its dramatic underpinning of lost and counterfeited letters, may also have suggested to Behn some of the physical uses of letters within a fiction that was essentially narrated.

The knowledge that several of these works were thinly disguised accounts of actual events, usually scandalous, can only have added to their popularity. Many of the most influential *romans à clef*, however, were not in the epistolary mode, for example *Hattigé* (1676) by Gabriel de Brémond, which referred to contemporary scandals, and *Les Désordres de l'amour* (1677) by Behn's most obvious French parallel, Madame de Villedieu, which drew on sixteenth-century political events for its plot. Similarly in England Lady Mary Wroth, the aunt of Aphra Behn's foster-brother Thomas Colepeper, had already made scandal her subject in *The Countesse of Montgomerie's Urania* of 1621. None of these works, however, either in French or in English, was on a scale comparable to Aphra Behn's novel.

Love-Letters, her first and longest fictional work, is a heady mixture of history, propaganda, journalism, letters, farce and romance. Through the negotiation of fiction and history, third-person narrative and letter, the novel in its three parts can be seen as a composite text. The real-life character of Henrietta Berkeley is written as Silvia, who is the presumed author of the letters which masquerade as French romantic epistles. Then in Parts II and III Silvia is written as a character in fiction who also continues to write herself within the third-person narrative.

The change in literary genre from a first-person epistolary fiction to a third-person narrative meant a change in vision, and inevitably a reinterpretation of what had gone before. The assumed sincerity of Part I of *Love-Letters* does not merely contrast with the insincerity and artifice of Parts II and III, which deal with 'amours' rather than 'love', but is retrospectively undermined by them: once Philander is proved to be a counterfeiter and a philanderer, something must happen to the reading of his initial love letters which the undiscerning reader had, like Silvia their recipient, taken as sincere.

Beginning as a romantic fiction told in letters, *Love-Letters* mocks that fiction by the presence further on of compromised and coded correspondence and by criticism of it. The novel in the three parts goes on too long and the closure of romance that seemed possible in Part I is rejected by the less firmly constructed or unified Parts II and III. If the original erotic letters were presented as sincere and authentic, the final ones of Silvia are burlesque or pastiche. The literary result of this debasement is as shocking as the scandal on which Part I was based: familial adultery of two aristocratic young people which reduced the lady to a commodity advertised for in the common press, along with runaway servants and horses.

Sexual and State Politics

In politics the libertine creed tended towards the position theoretically outlined by Thomas Hobbes in *Leviathan* (1651), which described a world driven by individual desire and power. 'Whatsoever is the object of any man's appetite or desire, that is it which he for his part calleth good', wrote Hobbes in chapter 6. In sexual and state politics Behn's Philander seems to follow this dictum.

Sexual and state politics were obsessively entwined at the court of Charles II, where private was writ large as public and ambassadors' letters were filled with intrigue, gynaecological detail and notes on royal menstruation. The King's mistress, the Duchess of Portsmouth, was a politician and an agent of Louis XIV, and the identity of Charles's 'engine' with the engine of state was famously declared by another of his mistresses, Nell Gwyn. *Love-Letters* depicts the desire for erotic domination at the heart of aristocratic Restoration culture.

In an early letter of Part I, Philander, who has tried to seduce Silvia through insisting that her image would 'inspirit' him even if all his 'glorious' plans failed, hints that his love affair may cover his treachery. He is in fact declaring the opposite, but the possibility remains: 'our Party fancy I repent my League with 'em, and doubting I'le betray the Cause, grow jealous of me, till by new Oaths, new Arguments I confirm 'em, then they smile all, and cry I am in Love!' (p. 20). This has followed Philander's statement that he is not like other men concerned with his wife's chastity and his own honour. He will not hazard his life for a woman for whom he does not care, nor will he resent the cuckolding of himself by Cesario. Or does he? Could all his acts be fuelled by sexual jealousy? Could politics for him be a subsection of sexuality, not sex of politics?

After all he does remark of Cesario: 'he is so dull as to imagine that for his sake (who never did us service or good, unless Cuckolding us be good) we should venture life and fame to pull down a true Monarch, to set up his Bastard over us', and, more darkly, 'Nor when time comes, shall I forget the ruine of *Mertilla* . . .' (p. 46).

Silvia, who still believes in Philander's political honour, assumes her lover has mistaken his politics. Thus she tries to bring him back to proper royalist sentiments by appealing to his unblemished royalist past: 'Consider my Lord you are born Noble, from Parents of untainted Loyalty, blest with a Fortune few Princes beneath Sovereignty are Masters of; . . . what wou'd you more?' (p. 39). She believes that he is after glory and that she can usefully refer to the good character of the King who has never harmed him:

what has the King, our good, our Gracious Monarch done to *Philander*? how disoblig'd him? or indeed what injury to Mankind? who has he opprest? where play'd the Tyrant; or the Ravisher? what one cruel or angry thing has he committed in all the time of his fortunate and peaceable Reign over us? Whose Ox or whose Ass has he unjustly taken? What Orphan wrong'd, or Widows Tears neglected? but all his Life has been one continu'd Miracle, all Good, all Gracious, Calm and Merciful: and this good, this Godlike King is mark'd out for slaughter, design'd a Sacrifice to the private revenge of a few ambitious Knaves and Rebels, whose pretence is the publick good, and doom'd to be basely Murder'd. (p. 40)

As a description of Charles II this is laughable, but it is not far from the kind of panegyric which Behn herself wrote. The point is not the King's character but his legitimacy. In opposition Cesario, if he were to become king, would be one 'without Law, without right, without consent, without Title, and even without competent parts'. Cesario/Monmouth is here a man who has done no virtuous thing and is nowhere set above others, 'a Prince unfortunate in his Principles and Morals' (p. 42).

As she is about to consummate her love, abandoning thereby her fame and virtue, Silvia realizes that her security cannot rest simply in Philander's vows. She tries in a way to shore these up with her sort of politics. Having given a high royalist picture of the godlike King, she aims to persuade Philander to a loyalty to the royalist cause that should underscore his loyalty to her. But as she goes on, she reveals a kind of erotics of loyalty that argues narcissism rather than fidelity. As she imagines looking at the King in the charged atmosphere before sexual consummation, the plea for loyalty dwindles into a kind of simulation of sex: the glance of the royal eye begets trembling adoration and proximity to the royal person causes the heart to beat, the blood to run cold and the eyes to overflow with tears of joy, while the whole body is suffused with something indefinable. As she experiences copulation and learns its pleasures and drawbacks, so Silvia discovers the rewards and limitations of royalist politics and its involvement in the eroticized person of the King.

Philander shows himself to be far beyond royalist authority and Whig parliamentary desires and to inhabit a cynical world in which all abstract words are meaningless. Long before Behn could have known the outcome of the Monmouth Rebellion, she makes her Philander show his dislike and contempt for Cesario/Monmouth. He had praised Cesario in the early letters to Silvia, but perhaps her reminding him of his cuckolding has made him reveal another view. The majority of people are stupid and are led by whoever will; the others, like himself, use Cesario for self-interest, Cesario being the only fool who cannot see this truth. Philander's proof that Cesario's followers do not wish him well is that they did not prevent him from openly espousing the opposition party (the Whigs) and thus losing all the power he might naturally have had at court with a little deception. He himself continues with Cesario, he insists, because in the vacuum of power that would follow a *coup* there is no reason why he or anyone else should not be the new ruler. This has the ring of the old Commonwealth or Interregnum world where anyone could control. In the implied scheme of the book, when loyalty to the monarch is questioned, all authority is in doubt and God is dethroned. The King, shorn of divine significance, is indeed but a man. In this case any individual could become king if he had enough self-assertiveness, strength and desire:

when Three Kingdoms shall ly unpossest, and be expos'd, as it were, amongst the raffling Crowd, who knows but the chance may be mine, as well as any others, who has but the same hazard, and throw for't; if the strongest Sword must do't, (as they must do't) why not mine still? (p. 45)

The only genuine ruler in this world is individual appetite, as Hobbes had taught. If the word 'King' has no absolute meaning, then neither has 'Husband' or 'Lady' or 'Honour'. It is the Hobbesian world in which words get their value from an association with our 'natural' pursuit of pleasure. Like the 'King', the 'Lady' may be aimed at by anyone who will.

The political constantly impinges on the sexual in lower spheres as well. When the 'husband' Brilljard (Turner) wants to interrupt

Silvia's progress towards a bigamous marriage with her next lover, Octavio, he takes advantage of the political squabbling among the Dutch States to fabricate a story that Octavio is scheming with France (England) and holding converse with French (English) rebels to betray Holland. The French rebels were really spies for France, he claimed. He is the more believed as he is a servant to the rebellious French lord, Philander. After a great furore, Octavio's old uncle, regarding the confusion of events, cries rightly to Briljard, *'Why, what Sir, then it seems all this Noise of betraying the State was but a Cuckold's Dream. Hah! and this wonderful and dangerous Plot, was but one upon your Wife Sir'* (p. 269).

The confusion of politics and sex is neatly caught in one of Philander's fantasies. 'Woman', he claims, was 'born for command and dominion', though custom has given men rule over all. He then imagines Silvia on a throne adorned with crowns and sceptres he has won. Through his power she becomes a kind of Cleopatra driving through the multitude of subject adorers. Masochistically he fantasizes himself as a fettered man at the chariot wheel. Even as he is about to make her the whore who will be scorned by the world if he does not control it, he creates her as the Empress – but the Empress must be his virgin.

Philander sees life solely in terms of conquest, violence and expenditure. Behn, who was translating the maxims of the cynical Duke of La Rochefoucauld at the time she was concluding *Love-Letters*, rendered one of the maxims as: 'Even the most disinterested Love is only commerce in which our self-love always proposes some gain.' Philander's love is far from disinterested. Conquest affirms his existence. Life becomes a hoard of riches needing to be spent. Love may use up one object and require another. Force can gain what diplomacy cannot, and a country conquered and a woman raped are the sweetest possessions.

The early love affair of Silvia and Philander takes place within the context of the political and sexual rivalry between Philander and his prince, Cesario, who has seduced Philander's wife, Mertilla. Immediately after an unexpected display of impotence in Silvia's bed, Philander receives a kind of love letter from Cesario, addressing him as 'my dear' and declaring that the morning should 'find you in my arms'. The eroticism of this politics inspires Philander, who acquits himself with more gusto in the following encounter with Silvia. Silvia, as disguised boy and desirable woman, will link her two lovers, Octavio and Philander, to such an extent that, in almost a case of incestuous voyeurism, Octavio imagines

Philander's ravishing of his sister as the price of his seduction of Philander's 'sister'/mistress.

The political (and sexual) tie between men is mediated by Silvia again when Octavio is thoroughly in her power, swayed to whatever fantastic scenario she creates. This time the tie is between Octavio and his guardian uncle, who together form a shadowy replacement for the Philander–Octavio bond. Silvia is as much a sexual object for the powerful uncle (the first woman he has noticed) as for the less powerful nephew, and she seems to enact again what she partially achieves with the first pair when they duel but do not kill each other; the contest of uncle and nephew is similar but fatal since the old man is accidentally killed by his nephew when he, the paternal figure, finds the nephew–son in bed with his intended wife. What Silvia seeks always to avoid is the apparently inevitable male trajectory: that the contesting men, at the end of their contest, turn their aggressive scorn towards the woman. In the duel between Octavio and Philander, they do; in the death of the uncle through the nephew, the killer remains enthralled.

Philander is the libertine freethinker, the cynic who refuses any authority in love or politics, a picture of the young Earl of Rochester before his deathbed conversion by the cleric Gilbert Burnet (a conversion which Behn pointedly ignored when she came to write her elegiac appreciation of Rochester's life and character). The 'present moment' and the pleasure of the moment matter to him beyond any future over which he has no control, while no fear of an afterlife constrains his movements in this life.

The libertine philosophy which Philander preaches fascinated, attracted and appalled Behn, who investigated it in several of her plays, such as the two parts of *The Rover*. In these she depicted the power and glamour of the egocentricity implicit in the libertine creed so associated with the court of the cynical and pleasure-loving Charles II. At the same time she (lightly) revealed its victims and price: the fallen, bereft and passionate woman, the cradles full of mischief for the sexual woman, the commodification of the self that any sensible woman must accept if she wished to avoid social exile or foolish psychological dependence on a rakish man.

In keeping with his libertinism, Philander abjures the honour code in which honour is signified by the man's physical bravery and the woman's chastity. He denies that his 'Reputation depends on the feeble constancy of a Wife', or that he can be persuaded ''tis Honour to fight for an unretrivable and unvalor'd Prize' (p. 18). It becomes philosophically appropriate, then, that Philander should remain socially and sexually powerful despite proving himself both impotent in the bedroom and cowardly on the battle field. Vows are but words for Philander, who can betray his king, his prince, his wife and his mistress.

The Progress of Silvia

In Silvia, constructed by the author in the first-person letters and then constructed by herself with the author as commentator, *Love-Letters* shows a woman learning with wonder that the femininity of 'softness' and 'trembling doves' she sets out with is a 'fictional' construction and not a natural state. If she wishes to survive outside a protecting family, she must create herself, using her knowledge: she must be hard and calculating while presenting herself as 'feminine', that is, soft and fluttering.

With this knowledge Silvia inevitably travels beyond love and marriage both temperamentally and socially, and she therefore avoids any need for the usual feminine abstractions of virtue, virginity and chastity. It is the extraordinary achievement of Aphra Behn in her novel that the nobly born Silvia brings the reader to the point where it becomes utterly unimportant whether or not she has been bedding her man. (To feel the shock it is only necessary to compare the novel with a later epistolary work, *Clarissa*, in which the heroine, only partially aware of the rape, is still destroyed by it; in *Love-Letters* the body does not even appear to register its own disgrace and undoing, as feminine myths have supposed it should: when Silvia comes round after her swoon on one occasion and finds herself ruffled and disordered, she does not know whether or not she has been raped while unconscious.)

It is fitting that Silvia's tutor in her transformation from naïve girl to self-conscious adult artfully employing the codes of femininity should be a man; the knowledge she requires is bound up with knowledge women must have of men, as well as of her position within the patriarchal structures men create. Philander will teach her that all is 'construction' in language and identity, and that, as 'lover' and 'brother' were not necessarily fixed and incompatible terms, being merely artificial words, so 'lady' and 'whore' could be likewise fluid.

But precisely because of the needs of her sex she will go beyond her mentor. Men can suffer or commit few irrevocable deeds, such as entering a monastery or mounting the scaffold. A man finds many ways back to his starting place in family and society, especially if, like Grey/Philander, he has the gift of language and lacks moral imperatives. For the woman there is no such easy return, however witty and clever she may be. After his sexual escapades Philander will always be a lord, Silvia is no longer a lady. Never an enlightened feminist, Behn notes, but does not repine at, the social distinction between men and women: claims of social equality are as absurd in her world as claims of intellectual inequality.

According to La Rochefoucauld, some would never have been in love if they had not heard love talked of. Philander's first achievement with Silvia will be to raise a desire in her to imitate his self-expressiveness. So Silvia learns to write letters in which she raises desire in the man by relating her own. As she moves further into expressions of herself, the learned repressions of her aristocratic feminine education are undone and sexual display, especially in its literary form, replaces sexual recoil.

Silvia comes to understand that she will flourish only through men and that she can do this by raising desire in them. Her main medium is language. Even in Part I she describes herself as erotically as her lover describes her: she lies 'panting with expectation', all subservient to the man about to undo her. She has understood that for women desire and simulation of desire are interchangeable in their effect of arousing desire in another. This realization allows her to take some control of her sexuality even at this early stage.

Silvia is quick to understand the value of the sexualized body as a commodity. She comes to put 'a price on beauty', not the correct one at first, but she soon understands the market. There is no stress whatever on the female body's physical function of motherhood. The unborn child which is mentioned in the first deceiving interchange of letters between Silvia and Philander is never more than a sign of sex, the 'Pledge of our soft hours'; after her betrayal, it simply becomes an irritating reminder. Later, expecting the birth imminently, Silvia simply looks forward to being 'freed from the only thing that hinder'd her from giving herself entirely to her impatient Lover' (p. 316).

The measure of the distance Silvia's body has travelled since she burnt and blushed for Philander in her father's house is indicated by her last seduction of the hapless Octavio in Part III. Where in the disordered blood, the flushed face and the burning limbs he reveals the sincere responding body associated with femininity, she shows only self-control: her actions become like stage directions, her face is 'set' for seduction, and she falls on his bed 'as' unable to support the sight of his suffering. She even manages to make a tear or two run down her cheek, the seemingly sincere tear that later sentiment would so glorify. When she tries to speak, 'she made her Sobs resist her Words; and left nothing unacted . . .' (p. 359). Despite his knowledge that it was his fortune that 'first won the dear Confession from thee, that drew my Ruin on', Octavio falls a 'shameful Victim to her Flattery'.

In Behn's poem 'To *Lysander*, on some Verses he writ, and asking more for his Heart then 'twas worth', something of Silvia's progress in Parts II and III of *Love-Letters* is succinctly captured and laid at the door of men. In the poem Behn reveals the process by which a woman is forced to play the feminine role, becomes an object, then learns to understand her potentially active role in this economy of desire:

> Take back that Heart, you with such Caution give,
> Take the fond valu'd Trifle back;
> I hate Love-Merchants that a Trade wou'd drive . . .

Neither the speaker of the poem nor Silvia tries to repudiate or retreat from this state of affairs, but understanding allows an ironic response and a knowing delivery of the last lines:

> Let us then love upon the honest Square,
> Since Interest neither have design'd,
> For the sly Gamester, who ne'er plays me fair,
> Must Trick for Trick expect to find.
> *Works* 1, no. 43

By the time Silvia captures and fleeces her last lover, the noble and youthful Alonzo, she has thoroughly adopted Philander's libertine and sceptical views, living for the moment in aristocratic profligacy as perversely as the celebrated Earl of Rochester had done. She becomes aware of the misogyny which tended to mark the Restoration libertine and she counters it not with argument but with imitation: she turns into the female rake, like the Philander of Part II seeking conquest not love.

As Philander and Silvia need to affirm their transgressive existence through sexual conquest, so Silvia needs to affirm her worth through consuming male wealth. Away from the automatic comforts of her parents' aristocratic home, she comes to realize that she is greedy and expensive and that the show of seductive femininity requires constant consumption. When Octavio's elderly uncle makes sexual advances to her, she is revolted by the man and yet his gay jewels sparkle in her eyes, 'so fond is Youth of Vanities, and to purchase an addition of Beauty at any Price'. Wealth is not a means of controlling the environment as much as an addition to the self. When Silvia is about to leave the old man, she lets down to Octavio a night bag containing 'all the Jewels and things of Value she had receiv'd of himself, her Uncle, or any other'; her past is reduced to portable commodities. No wonder Octavio now judges he will soon have 'the Possession of Silvia'.

She needs money partly because she has no status without it. More even than Clarissa, Silvia loses her class when she steps out of her father's house. She moves from being noble daughter to becoming beloved mistress and then betrayed whore, although even at the end of her history she rejects this description as being too constricting and degrading. This is very much the trajectory which Archbishop Tillotson had mapped out for the errant Lady Henrietta Berkeley (see Appendix III).

At the beginning of her story Silvia had assumed that her social position was somehow natural and inalienable and that no action could destroy it. After her seduction, elopement and betrayal, she starts to understand the precariousness of social status for a woman. Once class is destabilized, only gender hierarchy is left and Brilljard, her dominated servant–husband, 'began, from the thoughts she was his wife, to fancy fine enjoyment, to fancy authority . . .' (p. 373).

But, unlike Clarissa, Silvia does not come to realize the untenability of the female identity outside a father's house; instead in the bracing treacherous out-of-doors she grows excited by the possibility of several identities: 'since I have lost my honour, fame and friends, my interest and my Parents, and all for mightier love; I'll stop at nothing now' (p. 108). As she takes on roles, dressing as men and women, and adds more and more men to her plots, Silvia realizes that she has too much knowledge to return to what she was, even if the option were available to her.

Desire

Desire, which in the Hobbesian view everyone tries to fulfil at whatever cost, is the god of *Love-Letters*. He is the sort of tyrant of classical tales that Behn so memorably describes as 'Love' in an early song, 'Love Arm'd'. This tyrant disrupts order and language:

Love in Fantastique Triumph satt
Whilst Bleeding Hearts a round him flow'd,
For whom Fresh paines he did Create,
And strange Tyranick power he show'd;
From thy Bright Eyes he took his fire,
Which round about in sport he hurl'd;
But 'twas from mine, he took desire,
Enough to undo the Amorous World.

From me he took his sighs and tears,
From thee his Pride and Crueltie;
From me his Languishments and Feares,
    And every Killing Dart from thee;
Thus thou and I, the God have arm'd,
And sett him up a Deity;
But my poor Heart alone is harm'd,
Whilst thine the Victor is, and free.

Works 1, no. 18

In the novel desire divides into two main sorts. The first, simpler
sort is associated with the forgetting of the self and self-interest. It
is described as the state of the speaker in Behn's late poem 'Desire',
where, refusing to appear with 'interest', it destroys 'fame and
Honour' and prevents worldly success:

Inform me by what subtil Art,
    What powerful Influence,
You got such vast Dominion in a part
Of my unheeded, and unguarded, heart,
That fame and Honour cannot drive yee hence.

Works 1, no. 77

This sort of desire blurs the everyday ordinary sight, so that the
ideal, not the real, can be contemplated, while discriminating
hearing is overwhelmed by the music of the beloved's voice. Across
genres the poem 'Desire' is the equivalent of Part I of *Love-Letters*.
On the one hand this desire can be praised as romantic; on
the other it can be regarded as a disease, an infection. In *Love-Letters*
it is transgressive, incestuous and illegal; it would serve for a
'poetic spot of time', or it might exist in an atemporal 'golden age'
where there are no physical or social consequences of action, but it is
not suitable for a realistic narrative which necessarily travels
beyond sex into disappointment. In her later career Silvia will act as
a sort of 'fire-ship', the term used in the seventeenth century for a

woman carrying venereal disease to several men. Her disease is not syphilis but the often less curable romantic love or desire; this leads to social and psychological downfall as well as to increasing poverty.

Silvia's own juvenile longing is at first written as virulent disease, 'a strange disorder in my blood, that pants and burns at every Vein . . .' (p. 67), but she will not so suffer once she has learned more about life and herself. Philander, however, achieved the knowledge earlier on: he sees love as a rather trivial ailment for he has run through loves so often that 'I am grown most learn'd and able in the Art: My easie heart is of the Constitution of those whom frequent sickness renders apt to take relapses from every little cause, or wind, that blows too fiercely on 'em' (p. 171).

The second sophisticated sort of erotic desire includes the psychological pleasure of mastering through the manipulation of sexual desire in another. It allows lust but not obsessive romantic love. In Parts II and III of *Love-Letters*, manipulative love is described externally and often condemned by the third-person voice. This method provides a contrast to the plays in which Behn had investigated a similar kind of desire, especially in rakish men, since it can make the psychological analysis the actor fails to give when he or she declaims a speech from a single point of view. By pitting self-gratifying, manipulating desire against a romantic ideal, this voice clarifies the power and insidiousness of the former. When a woman desires mastery the emphasis is on her own body as a valued object. She gets pleasure from it mainly as it is an instrument to arouse interest in another and cause gratification in herself through contemplation and manipulation of that interest. For the man this desire is for a physical and psychological mastering: for rape at its most crude, for domination at its least.

As in *Clarissa*, the act of copulation occurs some way into the narrative and, when it does, it lacks the singularity, distinction and absolute quality of Lovelace's act. But, as with the rape of Clarissa, in which the heroine mostly remembered the bawd and the whores surrounding her, the seduction of Silvia implicates the feminine in the masculine act. Philander arrives to Silvia 'trembling and fainting' and she takes 'his trembling body' in her arms. At which point he faints at her feet. The impotence that follows has an appearance of satiety in the motionless Philander, but it actually denotes shame, the proper response of the female after the successfully accomplished and illicit sexual act. He even sighs like a woman. The scene of impotence significantly concludes with Philander's escape from Silvia's room in female clothes. In these he is met by her lascivious, prowling father who falls on the disguised Philander, now forced to counterfeit the female voice and demeanour. Since he is a 'woman' he must submit to the man who can boast, 'I have my Tools about me' and places a bag of money in one of his hands and a penis in the other.

What appear to have unnerved Philander are the signs of desire in the woman, a kind of sexual violence. The woman must not overpower or dampen desire by her own desire, as the willing lady of Aphra Behn's poem 'The Disappointment' is blamed for doing when the man turns out to be unable to perform at the crucial moment:

> He curs'd his Birth, his Fate, his Stars;
> But more the *Shepherdess's* Charms
> Whose soft bewitching Influence
> Had Damn'd him to the *Hell* of Impotence.
>
> *Works* 1, no. 28

Octavio, the sentimental man who will have his day when the Restoration rakes are attacked after the revolution of 1688, refuses the sexual scheme of manipulative desire, violence, rape and impotence. Sex becomes an attribute of love for him. Yet like all sentimental men, he wants a virgin not a spirited victim. For him real love deifies the female. So, caught in romance, he desires a miracle to make his beloved a maid again. The miracle is his own treatment of her which will make of her an aristocratic virgin, a woman worthy of becoming a wife.

Octavio is not in love with an innocent maid, however; in fact he is actually the first major consumer of Silvia as self-marketer. He believes the signs of the body completely because they are the signs of sentimental romance which assumes the female body to be true. Deeper than his error in misreading the body of his beloved, however, is his misreading of his own desire. Silvia hints at her understanding of this desire, but she does not articulate it: that it is his beloved's cruelty and manipulation that attract him as well as her beauty. The nearest he approaches this realization is his admission that he appreciates Silvia's wit and power. He never quite sees how much he has been paying for and ordering his undoing.

The understanding by Silvia of the nature of male desire is clearest in her use of her final new lover in Part III of *Love-Letters*. Through a clever manoeuvring of her whorish, maidenly, androgynous and homosexual images, Silvia raises a promiscuous desire in the young nobleman, Alonzo. She has, through a piece of cunning ventriloquism with her pen, persuaded Octavio to give her a pension as reward for her reformation. With it she sets herself up as desirable object and arranges for her own celebration by the public. Even Philander, unaware of the original, is 'wholly ravish'd with the Description of the imagined new fair One' and everyone regards her as a 'Wonder'. The rich Alonzo is already 'in Love with what he has not seen' (p. 417); he is captivated by her various forms: as a divine youth, a loose woman in night clothes, a masked lady and a symbol of desire. Her own controlled desire is partly dependent on muddlings of rank and gender and her use of others as conduits of desire. When playing the man before the man she knows desires her, despite her apparent male sex, Silvia lets her amorous page undress her for the shared bed in an inn: 'she was long in undressing, which to colour the Matter, she suffered her Page to do, who, poor Lad, was never in so trembling a condition, as in that manner to be obliged to serve her, where she discovered so many Charms he never before had seen' (p. 394).

Yet desire is never entirely controlled or manipulated. If *Love-Letters* had ended with Part II and its anticipatory paragraph of ills and woes to come, it might have been a Restoration parable about the nature of desire: of romance either giving place to realism when sexual longing is fulfilled, or destroying the romancer by its disjunction from reality. But, despite the anticipatory moral conclusion to Part II, the novel, in its final part, presents not so much a moral tale as a psychological one, portraying an obsession in Silvia beyond lust and self-interest.

Set to marry the rich Octavio and enter a life of ease and restored feminine position, Silvia hears that Philander is in town. Her body makes signs of interest in inadvertent blushes and pantings. Meanwhile Philander, contemplating his leader Cesario's enthrallment to a lady no longer young with whom he had earlier been involved, becomes curious to know whether love can be rekindled. Naturally he thinks of Silvia.

Silvia and Philander are now ready for another encounter in which the desire for mastery and the violence of sexual warfare will be far clearer to both than it was in their earlier relationship. For Silvia, after her experience of controlling Octavio, it is evident that her need is for a subtle sort of dominance even at the expense of feminine dignity and status. She wants both to control and be controlled to affirm her desirability. Simple desire for influence, which had earlier on in her progress been used for self-interest, fades beside a desire to be hurt and have mastery through this pain. The beginning of the process is the reversal of Silvia's progress from marketed woman to marketeer. With Octavio she received money; with Philander she must give up the money she has received from Octavio.

Having realized that she 'had not a Heart that any Love or loss of Honour, or Fortune could break', Silvia ends with a desire for perversity, for transgression, almost for the label of whore, and for what has value only because it will be lost. Her understanding of her own desire, not as sexual longing or interest, but as addiction or obsession, takes her quite outside society with its fixed notions of class and gender. So Silvia's desire to affirm herself and spoil whatever might appear to be to her social advantage has become a drug for which she will pay whatever price. For Philander, the cruellest of the men in the book (whom she thoroughly knows), she 'bends like a Slave for a little Empire over him; and to purchase the Vanity of retaining him, suffers herself to be absolutely undone' (p. 364).

To stress the point of the perverse, antisocial, anarchic nature of desire another character is introduced in the crowded closing pages of the novel: a count's lady, desired in passing by both Philander and Alonzo. She frankly gives her terms for seduction as 500 pistoles and awaits the outcome. But in fact desire finds her in an unexpected way: she is humiliated by the man to whom she had proposed to sell herself when she sees him anticipating their meeting by seducing her maid. The maid has provided her unexpected virginity for a mere 50 pistoles. Only then, in that moment of voyeurism, does she feel desire. Fired by the degradation of desiring a man after her maid, she now genuinely wants Alonzo who, like Philander with Silvia, is not fond of a willing woman and is not impressed when she waives her fee: 'she caressed me with all imaginable fondness; was ready to eat my lips instead of kissing them, and [was] much more forward than I wished' (p. 410). He of course begins to cool.

The Narrator and the Reader

Love-Letters is probably one of Behn's earliest pieces of fictional writing, as opposed to plays for which she was now famous. It was, then, one of the earliest works in which she could create a female character unconstrained by the conventions of the theatre. These constraints are most obviously avoided where she provides a narrator. This narrator is not specifically gendered, but the closeness to the female narrator of the short story *The Fair Jilt* and her proximity to Silvia towards the end make her seem more female than male.

There is an opportunity in novel-writing which does not exist in the theatre for the narrator to treat characters omnisciently, thus determining the reader's response to them, and to provide a moral overview. There *is* a moral discourse in *Love-Letters* which places Silvia as a wicked or manipulative woman, but it is used by the narrator only occasionally. Furthermore this moral discourse is presented as just one among other possible discourses. Inevitably, then, Silvia exists in a context in which the moral placing has no more authority within the text than any other, for example, the self-serving utterances of Silvia or her servants, or the libertine justifications of Philander. In Part II the narrator does not so much take control as imitate the epistolary activity in the book: the narrator's view becomes just one among many views and everything narrated is reduced to a version open to interrogation and dispute by the characters and by the reader.

Most of the time the narrator of Parts II and III seems to hold a traditional view. The liberation of Silvia and Philander from constraints of language and symbol has thrust them into a Hobbesian world, the values of which the narrator will not espouse. In this world, which she presents and intermittently judges, vice travels downwards socially and broken vows corrupt all levels. Vice in high places is copied by the vicious underling: so Cesario seduces Mertilla, Philander follows his prince in seducing Silvia, and Brilljard follows his master in seducing his 'wife'. The narrator exposes the fact that Silvia is diminished by her sexual activity into a whore and that her apparent escape from patriarchy has left her more dependent on men than ever. As in so much traditional literature, from Ariosto to Spenser, desire followed against duty and obligation has resulted not in liberation from the constraints of class and gender but in decline into an inhuman state of selfishness. Discerning readers will know what to make of the marauding Silvia as they will of the forgiven Philander, although the message is not emphasized by the reticent narrator.

Yet, although the novel appears to warn against desire, especially against the manipulative sort, the narrator herself shows for Octavio something of the sort of desire discovered in Silvia at the beginning of Part I. To her eyes Octavio appears 'all rich and gay as a young bridegroom, lovely and young as the morning that flattered him with so fair and happy a day'. In other scenes, too, the voyeurism of the text inevitably becomes the narrator's.

Politically things are just as ambiguous. Behn wrote the last two books in the reign of James II. As in her short novels, there is in *Love-Letters* much concern for vows and loyalty. Her story *The History of the Nun* shows that, however worthy the person, the breaking of a vow can destroy and corrupt. Loyalty even to the wicked or foolish, if it has been vowed, must be held. If Silvia's father is a lecher, it does not, in this configuration, excuse his daughter's failed duty to him. It is the staunch royalist view, which Aphra Behn expressed time and time again in her court poems. But this view is not clearly and repeatedly given to the narrator, and the reader is left to decide the final political effect of *Love-Letters*.

The novel ends unexpectedly, with justification of Philander, whose shallow amorous and political rhetoric has been thoroughly exposed. It is even suggested that Hermione, Cesario's mistress, has been pimping to keep him loyal to her lover and that he (Philander) failed in courage at the fatal battle:

Some Authors in the Relation of this Battle affirm, That *Philander* quitted his Post as soon as the Charge was given, and sheer'd off from that Wing he commanded; but all Historians agree in this Point, that if he did, it was not for want of Courage ... But he disliked the Cause, disapproved of all their Pretensions, ... all the fault his greatest Enemies could charge him with, was, That he did not deal so gratefully with a Prince that loved him and trusted him; and that he ought frankly to have told him, he would not serve him in this Design; and that it had been more Gallant to have quited him that way, than this; but there are so many Reasons to be given for his more Politick and safe Deceit, than are needful in this place ... (p. 433)

The reader of so slippery a text is given little help from the narrator and had better be as professional a decoder as the author is a writer.

Janet Todd
Norwich, 1995

FURTHER READING

EDITIONS OF THE WORKS

The Works of Aphra Behn, ed. Montague Summmers (1915; New York: Phaeton Press, 1967).

The Works of Aphra Behn, ed. Janet Todd (London: Pickering & Chatto; Columbus: Ohio State University Press, 1993–6). This edition is referred to as *Works* in the introduction.

BIBLIOGRAPHY

O'Donnell, Mary Ann, *Aphra Behn: An Annotated Bibliography of Primary and Secondary Sources* (New York: Garland Publishing Inc., 1986).

BIOGRAPHIES

Duffy, Maureen, *The Passionate Shepherdess: Aphra Behn 1640–89* (London: Cape, 1977).

Goreau, Angeline, *Reconstructing Aphra: A Social Biography of Aphra Behn* (New York: Dial, 1980).

Sackville-West, Vita, *Aphra Behn: The Incomparable Astrea* (1927; New York: Russell & Russell, 1970).

CRITICAL WORKS DISCUSSING BEHN

Ballaster, Ros, *Seductive Forms: Women's Amatory Fiction, 1684–1740* (Oxford: Clarendon Press, 1992).

Hobby, Elaine, *Virtue of Necessity: English Women's Writing, 1649–1688* (Ann Arbor: University of Michigan Press, 1988).

MacCarthy, Bridget, *The Female Pen* (1944–47; Cork: Cork University Press, 1994).

Perry, Ruth, *Women, Letters, and the Novel* (New York: AMS, 1980).

Spencer, Jane, *The Rise of the Woman Novelist: From Aphra Behn to Jane Austen* (Oxford: Basil Blackwell, 1986).

Todd, Janet, *The Sign of Angellica: Women, Writing and Fiction 1660–1800* (London: Virago; New York: Columbia University Press, 1989).

CRITICAL WORKS TREATING LOVE-LETTERS

Day, Robert Adams, *Told in Letters: Epistolary Fiction before Richardson* (Ann Arbor: University of Michigan Press, 1966).

Gardiner, Judith Kegan, 'The First English Novel: Aphra Behn's *Love Letters*, the Canon, and Women's Tastes' in *Tulsa Studies in Women's Literature* 8 (Fall, 1989), pp. 201–22.

Novak, Maximilian, 'Some Notes Toward a History of Fictional Forms: From Aphra Behn to Daniel Defoe' in *Novel* 6 (Winter, 1973), pp. 120–33.

Pearson, Jacqueline, 'Gender and Narrative in the Fiction of Aphra Behn' in *Review of English Studies* N.S., Vol. 42 (February 1991), pp. 40–56 and (May 1991), pp. 179–90.

Pollak, Ellen, 'Beyond Incest: Gender and the Politics of Transgression in Aphra Behn's *Love-Letters between a Nobleman and his Sister*' in ed. Heidi Hutner, *Rereading Aphra Behn: History, Theory, and Criticism* (Charlottesville: University of Virginia Press, 1993), pp. 151–86.

Price, Cecil, *Cold Caleb: The Scandalous Life of Ford Grey, First Earl of Tankerville, 1655–1701* (London: Andrew Melrose, 1956).

Todd, Janet, 'Who is Silvia? What is she? Feminine identity in Aphra Behn's *Love-Letters between a Nobleman and his Sister*' in ed. Janet Todd, *Aphra Behn Studies* (Cambridge: Cambridge University Press, 1996).

Wehrs, Donald R., '*Eros*, Ethics, Identity: Royalist Feminism and the Politics of Desire in Aphra Behn's *Love Letters*' in *SEL* 32 (1992), pp. 461–78.

NOTE ON THE TEXT

For this edition the texts of 1684, 1685 and 1687, the three Parts of
Love-Letters between a Nobleman and his Sister, have been set against
variant copies and the results have been collated. Spelling and punctuation have been retained as far as possible and any emendations
that have been made to the text have been listed. The copy-texts
used were taken from University Microfilms Early English Books
1641–1700, 82:10 (Beinecke copies Ij B395 6841 1–3). In the case of
Love-Letters Part I, there is a variant copy of the text in the University of Texas (Aj B396 6841). The Beinecke copy Ij B395 6841 1 has
been set against this text and all variants recorded. Both texts state
that they were 'Printed, and are to be sold by Randal Taylor, near
Stationer's Hall. MDCLXXXIV'; however, it is clear that the text has
been reset in the Beinecke copy. There are no major changes to the
content but a consistent difference in spelling between the two
copies. The Texas copy prefers a more old-fashioned spelling,
giving 'ownes', 'flowres', 'feable' and 'Heroe', for instance, instead
of the Beinecke's 'owns', 'flowers', 'feeble' and 'Hero'. Words such
as 'do' or 'cry' are consistently spelt as 'doe' or 'crie' in the Texas
copy. Such evidence suggests that the text was reset by a new com-
positor, but, as both texts contain numerous printers' errors, it is
impossible to claim one as an improvement on the other or give
either priority. As the Beinecke text is closer to modern spelling
standards it was chosen as the copy-text.

The copy-text of Part II of *Love-Letters* has been placed by a
second copy in the British Library (British Library copy: c.135.e.9.).
Comparison between the two suggests that they both form part of
the same edition although there are some differences and some
variants which indicate that the British Library copy might be a
later issue. Both copies have identical spelling variations and the
same misnumbered pages. Both also have disordered lettering at
points where the type has slipped in the printers' frames; on pages
215 and 229, for example, the slippage is especially severe. However, the British Library copy provides additional errors of its own.
On p. 25, l. 16 the 'l' drops one line in the word 'lowing', and on

p. 278 the 's' in 'sense' which has faded badly in the Beinecke edition has almost completely disappeared, leaving 'sen e'. There are only two variants and they reinforce the idea that the British Library copy is a later issue. On p. 52, l. 22 the word 'POSTSCRIPT' has been added below 'Your PHILANDER', and on p. 115, l. 22 'affectatio n' in the Beinecke copy has been corrected to read 'affectation'. Both corrections, although small, improve the text and suggest that the printer spotted them during the production of the edition.

Part III, *The Amours of Philander and Silvia*, was also set against a British Library copy (British Library copy: c.135.e.9.) and again a comparison of the two suggests that they are both part of the same edition though the evidence of the variants is too slight for any definite identification of an earlier issue. Both copies have identical spelling variants and the disorder of the lettering is similar in both copies, with slipped lettering being common in both. The British Library copy also has extra slippages, on p. 11, where the 't' of the tag-word 'not' has slipped, and on p. 474, where the slipped lettering common to both the Beinecke and the British Library copies on this page is continued for another two lines. There are also two punctuation changes in the British Library copy, both minor: on p. 159 the tag-word 'there' is not followed by a comma as it is in the Beinecke copy, and on p. 192 the comma after the tag-word 'Table' in the Beinecke copy reads as 'Table.' in the British Library copy. Given that some of the differences are improvements, the Beinecke copy may be a later issue of the same edition as the British Library copy, but it is also possible to argue that the additional slippages could indicate further deterioration of the type in the frames for the British Library copy, while the punctuation changes could be two further printing errors.

In the 1680s Protestant countries used the old-style Julian calendar, with the year beginning on 25 March; Roman Catholic countries had been using the reformed Gregorian one from 1582. In England during the Restoration, the year was often shown in both old and new style, between which there was also a ten-day difference. The modern form is used in this edition for dates of performance and publication of plays and novels. Original letters and documents cited in footnotes, however, retain their old style dates.

Love-Letters
between a Nobleman
and his Sister

Love-Letters

Between a

NOBLE-MAN

And his

SISTER.

LONDON,

Printed, and are to be fold by
Randal Taylor, near *Stationer's*
Hall. MDCLXXXIV.

TO

TO

THO. CONDON, Esq;[a]

SIR,

Having when I was at *Paris* last Spring, met with a little Book of Letters, call'd *L' Intregue de Philander & Silvia*,[b] I had a particular fancy, besides my inclinations to translate 'em into English, which I have done as faithfully as I cou'd, only where he speaks of the ingratitude of *Cæsario*[c] to the King, I have added a word or two to his Character that might render it a little more parallel to that of a modern Prince in our Age; for the rest I have kept close to the French.

The Letters art soft and amorous, and besides my esteem and

---

[a] Thomas Condon, a royalist and a firm supporter of James II. He was a Captain in Ferdinando Hastings's regiment in the 1680s. He would become Deputy Lieutenant of the East Riding in 1688 and would stand for parliament for Scarborough in the same year when James II was trying to pack the House of Commons with his supporters.

[b] *The Intrigue of Philander and Sylvia*. No such title exists. Behn's claim that *Love-Letters* is merely a translation of a French novel works on several levels. It points to the French influences on the genre of the 'secret history' such as Bussy-Rabutin's *L'Histoire Amoureuse des Gaules* (1665) while it also introduces the notion of decoding, ciphers and the revelation of secrets. On a more practical level, it also provides a degree of protection for the author who can claim the events described have all taken place in France and no slur has been intended on any public figure in England. In fact, the historical characters intended are frequently clear though no comprehensive key to the work was ever published.

[c] James Scott, Duke of Monmouth. Scott, the illegitimate son of Charles II, became the focus for Whigs worried by the probable succession of James II. In 1669, James had avowed his Catholicism and, during the crisis over popery and arbitrary government in the late 1670s and early '80s, parliament made attempts to pass an Exclusion Bill which would deny James any right to sovereignty. Anthony Ashley Cooper, the Earl of Shaftesbury, who was leader of the exclusionists, backed Monmouth's claims to legitimacy which were apparently verified by a secret marriage contract between Charles II and Monmouth's mother, Lucy Walters. The contract was supposedly locked in a Black Box and would eventually be revealed to the public. Under Shaftesbury's guidance, Monmouth built up national support for his claims by a series of progresses through the English provinces. By 1682, Monmouth was deep in negotiation with several prominent Whigs who were willing to organise a rebellion which would place him on the throne.

obligation to you, I think it no where so proper to address so much tender passion, as to a man whom Heaven and Nature has so well form'd both for dispencing and receiving of Love as your self, you having all in your person that is acceptable to women and desir'd by men, and when you please can make your self as absolutely the joy of the one as the envy of the other; to this is join'd a Vertue, such as I believe the World has rarely produc'd in a Man of your Youth, Fortune and Advantages; you have all the power of the Debauchery of the Age, without the will, you early saw the Follies of the Town, and the greatness of your mind disdaining that common Road of living, shun'd the foppish practice; your well-judging pride chose rather to be singular, and sullenly retire, than heard with that noisie Crowd, that eternally sit out business enough to stock the Town with Wit and Lampoons, and the Stage with Fops, Fools and Cowards: if I might give my real judgment, you are above flattery, and one can almost say no good or generous thing that one cannot justifie in you, no Vertue you cannot lay a claim to; many your modesty hides from the World, and many more you have which envy will not confess; for that just value you set upon your self by shunning the publick haunts, Cabals and Conversations of the Town, in spight of all your Wit and Goodness gives occasion for malice to revenge it self on you a thousand little ways; witness a late mistaken story of an Amour of yours, so often urg'd with heat, and told so much to your disadvantage, by those who have not the happiness of knowing your true principles of honour, your real good nature, your common justice, or sense of Humanity, to be such, as not to be capable of so base, silly and unmanly a practice, and so needless and poor a design: For my part, Sir, I am vain and proud of the belief that I have the capacity and honour to know and understand your Soul, (did I not too well the story also) and am well assur'd it has not a grain, not a thought of so foolish a principle, so unnecessary and dishonest: and I dare affirm that since the imposition of the late Popish Plot[a] upon the Town,

---

[a] In 1678 evidence of a Jesuit-inspired plot to assassinate Charles II was brought to public attention by Israel Tonge and Titus Oates. When Sir Edmund Berry Godfrey, the magistrate who took Oates's deposition, was found murdered the plot appeared to have substance. Parliament's subsequent fears that a successful plot could place the Catholic James, Duke of York on the throne led to the introduction of the first Exclusionist Bill which was intended to deny him sovereignty. Constant discoveries of new evidence of the Popish Plot kept the crisis alive until 1681.

there has not so ridiculous and nonsensical a History past for authentick with unthinking man; but you shou'd give 'em leave to rail, since you have so vast advantages above 'em.

Sir, I wou'd fain think that in the Character of *Philander*[a] there is a great resemblance of your self as to his Person, and that part of his Soul that was possest with Love: he was a French Whigg, 'tis true, and a most apparent Traytor, and there, I confess, the comparison fails extremely; for sure no man was ever so incorrigible so hardned in Torism as your self, so fearless, so bold, so resolute, and confirm'd in Loyalty; in the height of all dangers and threatnings, in the blessed Age of swearing, and the hopeful Reign of evidences,[b] you undaunted held forth for the royal cause, with such force of reason and undeniable sense as those that were not converted, at least were startled, and I shall never forget the happy things I have heard you say on that glorious subject, with a zeal so fervent, yet so modest and gentle your argument, so solid, just, so generous and so very hearty, as has begot you applauses and blessing round the board: a thousand instances, a History I cou'd write of your discourses and acts of Loyalty; but that even your Enemies allow, and I will spare it here, and only say you are an honour and a credit to the Cause that's proud to own you.

In this you are far distant to my amorous Hero; but at least for my own satisfaction, and that I may believe *Silvia*[c] truly happy, give me leave to fansie him such a person as your self, and then I cannot fail of fansying him too, speaking at the feet of *Silvia*, pleading his right of love with the same softness in his eyes and voice, as you can do when you design to conquer; whene'er you

---

[a] Ford Lord Grey of Wark or Werk. Grey was a close friend of Monmouth and may have been involved in the Rye House plot to assassinate Charles II in 1683. He was suspected by the authorities of helping to create support for a new rising against the crown and was imprisoned in the Tower of London. He escaped with the help of one of the guards and made his way to Holland, accompanied by Lady Henrietta Berkeley, his sister-in-law. Earlier in the year he had been tried for kidnapping and seducing her. Cf. Appendix I.

[b] The restoration of Charles II did not immediately remove fears for the safety of the monarchy. In order to secure the government, a wide network of spies was established across Britain and abroad. The secretaries of state were sent a constant stream of intelligence from correspondents in every city and from 'evidences' or informers eager to prove their loyalty, lessen their own punishment or denigrate their personal enemies. Hence the reign of Charles II was sustained by these 'evidences'.

[c] Lady Henrietta Berkeley of Durdans. Her sister, Mary, was married to Lord Grey.

spread your nets for Game, you need but look abroad, fix and resolve, though you, unlike the forward youth of this Age, so nicely pursue the quarry; it is not all, or any Game you fly at, not every Bird that comes to net can please your delicate appetite; though you are young as new desire, as beautiful as light, as amorous as a God, and wanton as a *Cupid*, that smiles, and shoots, and plays, and mischiefs all his fond hours away: Pray Heaven you be not reserv'd like our Hero for some Sister, 'tis an ill sign when so much beauty passes daily unregarded, that your love is reserved to an end as malicious as that of our *Philander's*.

Perhaps you'll be out of humour, and cry, why the Devil did'st thou dedicate the Letters of a Whigg[a] to me, but to make you amends, Sir, pray take notice *Silvia* is true Tory[b] in every part, if but to love a Whigg be not crime enough in your opinion to pall your appetite, and for which even her youth and beauty cannot make an attonement; commodity, which rarely fails in the Trade of love, though never was so low a Market for beauty of both Sexes, yet he that's fortified and stor'd like happy you, need never fear to find his price; for wit and good humour bear still a rate, and have an intrinsick value, while the other is rated by opinion and is at best but a curious picture, where one and the same dull silent Charms make up the day, while the other is always new, and (to use your own expression) is a Book where one turns over a new leaf every minute, and finds something diverting, in eternal new discoveries; it elevates ones Spirits, charms the Soul, and improves ones stock; for every one has a longer date of hearing than seeing, and the eyes are sooner satiated than the ear; therefore do not depend too much on

---

[a] The Whigs were staunchly Protestant and in favour of a system of constitutional monarchy which would limit the king's prerogative and advance the power of parliament. The name derives from the expression 'Whiggamore raid' which was originally applied to a band of Scottish Covenanters who marched on Edinburgh in 1648. Later the term was used for the 'Exclusioners' who opposed the succession of James, Duke of York to the throne because of his Catholicism.

[b] The term covered a wide political spectrum and, like 'Whig', denoted beliefs rather than a party in the modern sense. On the whole, however, someone called a Tory was a royalist and a supporter of the Stuarts in their desire to strengthen the royal prerogative against parliament. A Tory supported the system of absolute monarchy which rested on the belief that the king was God's representative on earth. The name 'Tory' derives from the Irish word 'toraidhe' which was applied to the dispossessed Irish who mounted attacks on English settlers. Later, the term was frequently used to describe anyone who supported the Duke of York's right of succession.

beauty, 'tis but a half conquest you will make when you shew the Man only, you must prove him too; give the soft Sex a sight of your fine Mind as well as your fine Person; but you are a lazy Lover, and ly fallow for want of industry, you rust your stock of hoarded love, while you gaze only and return a single sigher; believe me, Friend, if you continue to fight at that single weapon, there will be no great store of wounds given or taken on either side; you must speak and write if you wou'd be happy, since you can do it so infinitely to purpose; who can be happy without Love? for me, I never numbred those dull days[a] amongst those of my life, in which I had not my Soul fill'd with that soft passion; to Love! why 'tis the only secret in nature that restores Life, to all the felicities and charms of living; and to me there seems no thing so strange, as to see people walk about, laugh, do the acts of Life, and impertinently trouble the world without knowing any thing of that soft, that noble passion, or without so much as having an intreague, or an amusement, (as the French call it) with any dear she, no real Love or Cocettre;[b] perhaps these Letters may have the good fortune to rouse and make you look into your heart, turn o're your store and lavish out a little to divert the toils of life; you us'd to say that even the fatigues of love had a vast pleasure in 'em; *Philander* was of your mind, and I (who advise you like that friend you have honour'd me with the title of) have even preserv'd all the torments of love, before dully living without it; live then and love, thou gay, thou glorious young man, whom Heav'n has blest with all the sweets of life besides; live then and love; and what's an equal blessing, live and be belov'd, by some dear Maid, as nobly born as *Silvia*, as witty and as gay and soft as she, (to you, who know no other want, no other blessing) this is the most advantageous one he can wish you who is,

Sir,

Your obliged and most

humble Servant, &c.

---

[a] Cf. Behn's poem 'To Damon': 'My fancy did no prospect take / Of Conquest's I design'd to make. / But calm and innocent I sate, / Content with my indifferent fate. / (A Medium, I confess, I hate.) / For when the mind so cool is grown / As neither Love nor Hate to own, / The Life but dully lingers on.' [Pickering Masters, *Works of Aphra Behn*, Vol. 1, no. 73, ll.34–43]

[b] *French*: a coquette or flirt.

The ARGUMENT.

*In the time of the Rebellion of the true Protestant Hugonots[a] in Paris,
under the conduct of the Prince of* Condy,[b] *(whom we will call*
Caesario) *many illustrious persons were drawn into the Association,
amongst which there was one, whose Quality and Fortune (join'd with
his Youth and Beauty) rendred him more elevated in the esteem of the
gay part of the World than most of that Age. In his tender years
(unhappily enough) he chanc'd to fall in Love with a Lady, whom we
will call* Mertilla,[c] *who had Charms enough to engage any heart, she
had all the advantages of Youth and Nature, a Shape excellent, a most
agreeable stature, not too tall and far from low, delicately proportion'd,
her face a little inclined to round, soft, smooth and white, her Eyes were
blew, a little languishing, and full of Love and Wit, a Mouth curiously
made, dimpled and full of sweetness; Lips round, soft, plump and red;
white teeth, firm and even; her Nose a little* Roman; *and which gave a
noble grace to her lovely Face, her Hair light brown; a Neck and Bosome
delicately turn'd, white and rising, her Arms and Hands exactly
shap'd; to this a vivacity of Youth ingaging, a Wit quick and flowing,
a Humour gay, and an Air unresistably charming, and nothing was
wanting to compleat the joys of the young* Philander *(so we call our
amorous Hero) but* Mertilla's *heart, which the illustrious* Cæsario *had
before possess'd; however, consulting her Honour and her Interest, and
knowing all the arts as Women do to feign a tenderness, she yields to
marry him: while* Philander, *who scorn'd to owe his happiness to the
commands of Parents, or to chaffer[d] for a Beauty, with her consent*

---

[a] Protestants forced to flee from France owing to the persecution of Louis XIV.
Many of the Huguenots fled to England. Throughout *Love-Letters*, Behn uses France
as a cover for her descriptions of English political life. Paris, therefore, can be read
as London; the Huguenots, as the Protestant supporters of Monmouth; and the
French king, as Charles II.

[b] There may be allusion here to two figures: 'Le Grand Condé' (d. 1686), a French
noble who led the rebel forces in the Fronde against Cardinal Mazarin in the reign
of Louis XIV, and his grandfather, Louis de Bourbon Condé (d. 1569), who led the
Huguenots during their persecution in the religious wars of the sixteenth century
and whose life featured in *The prince of Conde made English* (1675). Dryden drew on
material from the period for his *Duke of Guise* 1683, in which he made political
parallels between the England of the 1680s and sixteenth-century France.

[c] In *The Trial of Ford Lord Grey*, Lady Arabella Berkeley described to the court how
her servant had carried letters between Grey and Henrietta Berkeley. Cf. Appendix I.

[d] To bargain.

steals her away, and marries her; but see how transitory is a violent passion, after being satiated, he slights the prize he had so dearly conquer'd; some say the change was occasion'd by her too visibly continued Love to Cæsario; *but whatever 'twas, this was most certain,* Philander *cast his Eyes upon a young Maid,* Sister *to* Mertilla, *a Beauty whose early bloom promis'd wonders when come to perfection; but I will spare her Picture here,* Philander *in the following Epistles will often enough present it to your view: He lov'd and languish'd long before he durst discover his pain; her being Sister to his Wife, nobly born, and of undoubted fame, rendred his passion too criminal to hope for a return, While the young lovely* Silvia *(so we shall call the noble Maid) sight out her hours in the same pain and languishment for* Philander, *and knew not that 'twas Love, till she betraying it innocently to the o'erjoy'd Lover and Brother, who soon taught her to understand 'twas Love——he persues it, she permits it, and at last yields; when being discover'd in the criminal intrigue, she flies with him; he absolutely quits* Mertilla, *lives some time in a Village near* Paris, *call'd St.* Denice,[a] *with this betray'd unfortunate; till being found out and like to be apprehended, (one for the Rape, the other for the flight) she is forc'd to Marry a* Cadet,[b] *a creature of* Philander's *to bear the name of Husband only to her, while* Philander *had the intire possession of her, Soul and Body: Still the League[c] went forward, and all things were ready for a War in* Paris;[d] *but 'tis not my business here to mix the rough relation of a War with the soft affairs of Love; let it suffice, the Hugonots were defeated and the King got the day, and every Rebel lay at the mercy of his Sovereign;* Philander *was taken Prisoner, made his escape to a little Cottage near his own Palace,[e] not far from* Paris, *writes to* Silvia *to come to him, which she does, and in spight of all the industry to reseize him he got away with* Silvia.

After this flight, these Letters were found in their Cabinets, at their house at St. Denice, *where they both liv'd together for the space of a year, and they are as exactly as possible plac'd in the order they were sent, and were those supposed to be written towards the latter end of their Amours.*

---

[a] Saint-Denis, a suburb to the north of Paris famous for its Gothic Basilica which houses the tombs of many of the French Kings. Behn may also have remembered that Abelard, who fell tragically in love with his pupil, Héloise, became a monk in Saint-Denis. The letters of Abelard and Héloise have remained a popular testimony to their love.

[b] A younger son or a young man who enters military service.

[c] The cabal of Whigs in support of Monmouth.

[d] The rebellion which was allegedly fomenting in London in 1682 at the instigation of Grey, Monmouth and their associates.

[e] Grey's country house at Up Park in Sussex.

LETTERS

To *Silvia.*

Though I parted from you resolv'd to obey your impossible commands, yet know, oh charming *Silvia*! that after a Thousand conflicts between Love and Honour, I found the God (too mighty for the Idol) reign absolute Monarch in my Soul, and soon banish't that Tyrant thence. That cruel Councellor that would suggest to you a Thousand fond Arguments to hinder my noble pursute; *Silvia* came in view! her unresistable *Idea!* with all the charmes of blooming youth, with all the Attractions of Heavenly Beauty! loose, wanton, gay, all flowing her bright hair, and languishing her lovely eyes, her dress all negligent as when I saw her last, discovering a Thousand ravishing Graces, round white small Breasts, delicate Neck, and rising Bosome, heav'd with sighs she wou'd in vain conceal; and all besides, that nicest fancy can imagine surprising——Oh I dare not think on, lest my desires grow mad and raving; let it suffice, oh adorable *Silvia!* I think and know enough to justifie that flame in me, which our weak alliance of Brother and Sister has render'd so criminal; but he that adores *Silvia*, shou'd do it at an uncommon rate; 'tis not enough to sacrifice a single heart, to give you a simple Passion, your Beauty shou'd like it self produce wondrous effects; it shou'd force all obligations, all laws, all tyes even of Natures self: You my lovely Maid, were not born to be obtain'd by the dull methods of ordinary loving; and 'tis in vain to prescribe me measures; and oh much more in vain to urge the nearness of our Relation. What Kin my charming *Silvia* are you to me? No tyes of blood forbid my Passion; and what's a Ceremony impos'd on man by custome? what is it to my Divine *Silvia*, that the Priest took my hand and gave it to your Sister? what Alliance can that create? why shou'd a trick devis'd by the wary old, only to make provision for posterity, tye me to an

11

eternal slavery. No, no my charming Maid, tis nonsense all; let us (born for mightier joys) scorn the dull *beaten road*, but let us love like the first race of men,[a] nearest allied to God, promiscuously they lov'd, and possess'st, Father and Daughter, Brother and Sister met, and reap'd the joys of Love without controul, and counted it Religious coupling, and 'twas encourag'd too by Heav'n it self: Therefore start not (too nice and lovely Maid) at shadows of things that can but frighten fools. Put me not off with these delays! rather say you but dissembl'd Love all this while, than now 'tis born, to let it dy again with a poor fright of nonsense. A fit of Honour! a fantome imaginary and no more; no, no represent me to your soul more favourably, think you see me languishing at your feet, breathing out my last in sighs and kind reproaches, on the pityless *Silvia*; reflect when I am dead, which will be the more afflicting object, the Ghost (as you are pleas'd to call it) of your Murder'd Honour, or the pale and bleeding one of

The lost *Philander*.

I have liv'd a whole day,
and yet no Letter from my Silvia.

To *Philander*.

Oh why will you make me own (oh too importunate *Philander!*) with what regret I made you promise to preferr my Honour before your Love.

I confess with blushes, which you might then see kindling in my face, that I was not at all pleas'd with the Vows you made me, to endeavour to obey me, and I then even wisht you wou'd obstinately have deny'd obedience to my just commands; have pursu'd your criminal flame, and have left me raving on my

---

[a] The offspring of Adam and Eve in the Book of Genesis. Philander is using the biblical precedent to justify his relationship with his sister-in-law despite the Church's disapproval of such ties.

undoing: For when you were gone, and I had leasure to look into my heart, alas! I found whether you oblig'd or not, whether Love, or Honour were prefer'd, I, unhappy I, was either way inevitably lost. Oh what pityless God, fond of his wondrous power, made us the objects of his Almighty vanity? oh why were we two made the first presidents of his new found revenge? for sure no Brother ever lov'd a Sister with so criminal a flame before: At least my unexperienc'd innocence ne're met with so fatal a story: And 'tis in vain (my too charming Brother) to make me insensible of our Alliance; to perswade me I am a stranger to all but your eyes and Soul.

Alas your fatally kind Industry is all in vain. You grew up a Brother with me; the title was fixt in my heart, when I was too young to understand your subtle distinctions, and there it thriv'd and spread; and 'tis now too late to transplant it, or alter its Native Property: Who can graft a flower on a contrary stalk? The Rose will bear no Tulips, nor the Hyacinth the Poppy; no more will the Brother the name of Lover. O spoil not the natural sweetness and innocence we now retain, by an endeavour fruitless and destructive; no, no *Philander*, dress your self in what Charms you will, be powerfull as Love can make you in your soft argument,——yet, oh yet you are my Brother still,-- But why, oh cruel and eternal Powers, was not *Philander* my Lover before you destin'd him a Brother? or why being a Brother did you malicious and spightful powers destine him a Lover! oh take, either title from him, or from me a life which can render me no satisfaction, since your cruel laws permit it not for *Philander*, nor his to bless the now

Unfortunate Silvia.

Wednesday Morning.

To *Philander*.

After I had dismist my Page this morning with my Letter, I walk'd (fill'd with sad soft thoughts of my Brother *Philander*) into the Grove, and commanding *Melinda* to retire, who only attended me, I threw my self down on that bank of grass where we last disputed the dear but fatal business of our souls: Where our prints (that invited me) still remain on the prest greens: There with Ten Thousand sighs, with remembrance of the tender minutes we past then, I drew your last Letter from my Bosome; and often kist and often read it over, but oh, who can conceive my Torment, when I came to that fatal part of it, where you say you gave your hand to my sister, I found my soul agitated with a Thousand different passions, but all insupportable, all mad, and raving; sometimes I threw my self with fury on the ground, and prest my panting heart to the cold earth, then rise in rage and tear my hair, and hardly spare that face that taught you first to love: then fold my wretched Arms to keep down rising Sighs that almost rend my breast, I traverse swiftly the conscious Grove;[a] with my distracted show'ring eyes directed in vain to pityless Heaven, the lovely silent shade favouring my complaints, I cry alowd, oh God! *Philander*'s Married, the lovely charming thing for whom I languish is Married! – That fatal word's enough, I need not add to whom. Married's enough to make me curse my Birth, my Youth, my Beauty, and my eyes that first betrayed me to the undoing object: Curse on the Charms you've flatter'd, for every fancy'd Grace has help'd my ruine on; now like flowers that wither unseen and unpossest in shades, they must dy and be no more, they were to no end created since *Philander*'s Married: Married! oh fate, oh Hell, oh torture and confusion! tell me 'tis to my Sister, that addition's needless, and vain: To make me eternally wretched there needs no more than that *Philander*'s Married! than that the Priest gave your hand away from me; to another and not to me; tir'd out with life I need no other passport than this Repetition, *Philander*'s Married! 'tis that alone is sufficient to lay in her cold Tomb

The wretched and despairing.

SILVIA.

Wednesday night,
  Bellfont.[b]

---

[a] Behn is alluding to the etymology of 'conscious' which is rooted in the Latin 'conscius', meaning 'to know something with other', 'to be privy to' or 'to witness private acts'. Cf. Behn's poem '*The Reflection*: A Song': 'Witness ye Springs, ye Meads and Groves, / Who oft were conscious made / To all our Hours and Vows of Love.' [*Works of Aphra Behn*, Vol. 1, no.32, ll.49–51]

[b] Durdans, near Epsom, the family seat of the Berkeleys.

To *Silvia*.

Twice last night, oh unfaithful and unloving Silvia! I sent my Page, to the old place for Letters, but he return'd the object of my rage, because without the least remembrance from my fickle Maid: In this Torment, unable to hide my disorder, I suffer'd my self to be laid in bed; where the restless torments of the night exceeded those of the day, and are not even by the languisher himself to be exprest; but the returning light brought a short slumber on its Wings; which was interrupted by my attoneing Boy, who brought Two Letters from my adorable *Silvia*: He wak'd me from Dreams more agreeable than all my watchful hours cou'd bring, for they are all tortured——And even the softest mixt with a Thousand despairs, difficulties, and disappointments, but these were all love, which gave a loose to joys undeny'd by Honour! and this way my charming *Silvia* you shall be mind, in spight of all the Tyrannies of that cruel hinderer; Honour appears not my *Silvia* within the close drawn Curtains, in shades and gloomy light the fantom frights not, but when one beholds its blushes, when its attended and adorn'd, and the Sun sees its false Beauties; in silent Groves and grotto's, dark Alcoves, and lonely recesses, all its formalities are laid aside; 'twas then, and there, methought my *Silvia* yielded! with a faint struggle and a soft resistance; I heard her broken sighs, her tender whispering Voice that trembling cry'd—Oh can you be so cruel.——Have you the heart--Will you undo a Maid because she loves you? Oh will you ruine me because you may?—My faithless--My unkind, then sigh't and yielded, and made me happier than a Triumphing God! but this was still a Dream, I wak'd and sigh't and found it vanish all! But oh my *Silvia*, your Letters were substantial pleasure, and pardon your Adorer if he tell you, even the disorder you express, is infinitely dear to him, since he knows it all the effects of Love, Love my soul! which you in vain oppose; pursue it, Dear and call it not undoing, or else explain your fear, and tell me what your soft, your trembling heart gives that cruel title to? is it undoing to Love? and love the Man you say has Youth and Beauty to justifie that Love? a man that adores you with so submissive

15

and perfect a resignation; a man that did not only Love first; but is resolv'd to dy in that agreeable flame; in my Creation I was form'd for Love, and destin'd for my *Silvia*, and she for her *Philander*: And shall we, can we disappoint our Fate, no my soft Charmer, our souls were toucht with the same shafts of Love before they had a being in our Bodies, and can we contradict Divine Decrees?

Or is't undoing, Dear, to bless *Philander* with what you must some time or other sacrifice to some hated loath'd object, (for *Silvia* can never love again) and are those Treasures for the dull conjugal Lover to rifle? was the beauty of Divine shape created for the cold Matrimonial imbrace? and shall the eternal joys that *Silvia* can dispence, be returned by the clumsey Husband's careless forc'd insipid duty's; oh my *Silvia* shall a Husband (whose insensibility will call those Raptures of joy! those Heavenly Blisses! the drudgery of life) shall he I say receive 'em? While your *Philander* with the very thought of the excess of pleasure, the least possession wou'd afford, faints o're the Paper that brings you here his eternal Vows.

Oh where my *Silvia* ly's the undoing then? my Quality and Fortune are of the highest rank amongst men. My youth gay and fond, my Soul all soft, all Love; and all *Silvia*'s! I adore her, I languish for her, I am sick of Love and sick of Life, till she yields she is all mine!

You say my *Silvia* I am Married, and there my happyness is Shipwreck'd; but *Silvia* I deny it, and will not have you think it; no, my Soul was Married to yours in its first Creation; and only *Silvia* is the Wife of my sacred, my everlasting Vows; of my solemn considerate thought, of my ripen'd Judgment, my mature considerations. The rest are all repented and forgot, like the hasty folly's of unsteady Youth, like Vows breath'd in Anger, and dy Perjur'd as soon as vented, and unregarded either of Heav'n or Man. Oh why shou'd my Soul suffer for ever, why eternal pain for the unheedy short-liv'd sin of my unwilling Lips; besides, this fatal thing call'd Wife, this unlucky Sister, this *Mertilla*, this stop to all my Heav'n, that breeds such fatal differences in our soft Affairs, this *Mertilla*[a] I say, first broke

---

[a] It was public knowledge that Monmouth had an affair with Grey's wife, Lady Mary Berkeley. Several satires were published on the subject, including *The Hue and Cry after J——Duke of M——*, which states that to find Monmouth 'be sure to search in the Lady G——ys Placket, and 'tis Ten thousand pound to a Nut-shell but you'll take him napping'. Also cf. Appendix III.

her Marriage Vows to me; I blame her not, nor is it reasonable I shou'd, she saw the young *Cesario*, and Lov'd him. *Cesario*, whom the envying World in spight of prejudice must own, has unresistable Charms, that, Godlike form, that sweetness in his face, that softness in his Eyes and delicate Mouth; and every Beauty besides that Women doat on and Men envy: That lovely composition of Man and Angel! with the addition of his eternal Youth and Illustrious Birth, was form'd by Heav'n and Nature for universal Conquest! and who can love the charming Hero at a cheaper rate than being undone: And she that wou'd not venture Fame, Honour, and a Marriage Vow for the Glory of the young *Cesario*'s heart, merits not the noble Victim; oh wou'd I cou'd say so much for the young *Philander*, who wou'd run a Thousand times more hazards of life and Fortune for the Adorable *Silvia*, than that amorous *Hero* ever did for *Mertilla*, though from that Prince I learn't some of my disguises for my thefts of Love, for he like *Jove* courted in several shapes,[a] I saw 'em all, and suffer'd the delusion to pass upon me; for I had seen the lovely *Silvia*? yes I had seen her, and I lov'd her too. But Honour kept me yet Master of my Vows; but when I knew her false, when I was once confirm'd, – When by my own Soul I found the dissembl'd Passion of her's, when she cou'd no longer hide the blushes or the paleness that seiz'd at the approaches of my disorder'd Rival, when I saw Love dancing in her eyes and her false heart beat with nimble motions, and soft trembling seize every Limb, at the approach or touch of the Royal Lover, then I thought my self no longer oblig'd to conceal my flame for *Silvia*; nay e're I broke silence, e're I discover'd the hidden Treasure of my heart, I made her falshood plainer yet: Even the time and place of the dear assignations I discover'd; certainty! happy certainty! broke the dull heavy chain, and I with joy submitted to my shameful freedome, and caress'd my generous Rival, nay and by Heav'n I lov'd him for't, pleas'd at the resemblance of our Souls, for we were secret Lovers both, but more pleas'd that he Lov'd *Mertilla*, for that made way to my passion for the adorable *Silvia*!

---

[a] Jove was the ruler of the gods. Constantly unfaithful to his wife Hera, he seduced many of his mistresses by first approaching them disguised as another god, mortal or animal.

Let the dull hot-brain'd jealous fool upbraid me with cold Patience: Let the fond Coxcomb whose Honour depends on the frail Marriage Vow, reproach me, or tell me that my Reputation depends on the feeble constancy of a Wife, perswade me 'tis Honour to fight for an unretrivable and unvalor'd Prize, and that because my Rival has taken leave to Cuckold me, I shall give him leave to kill me too: Unreasonable nonsense grown to custome. No by Heav'n! I had rather *Mertilla* shou'd be false, (as she is) than wish and languish for the happy occasion, the Sin's the same, only the Act's more generous: Believe me my *Silvia*, we have all false notions of Virtue and Honour, and surely this was taken up by some despairing Husband in Love with a fair lilting Wife, and then I Pardon him: I shou'd have done as much for only she that has my Soul, can only ingage my Sword, she that I love, and my self only commands and keeps my stock of Honour: For *Silvia*! the Charming the distracting *Silvia*! I cou'd fight for a glance or smile, expose my heart for her dearer fame, and wish no recompence, but breathing out my last gasp into her soft white delicate bosome. But for a Wife! that stranger to my Soul, and whom we Wed for interest and necessity,——A Wife, a light loose unregarding Property, who for a momentary Apetite will expose her fame, without the noble end of loving on, she that will abuse my Bed, and yet return again to the loath'd conjugal imbrace, back to the Armes so hated, that even strong fancy of the absent Youth belov'd, cannot so much as render supportable. Curse on her, and yet she kisses, fawnes and dissembles on, hangs on his Neck, and makes the Sot believe:——Damn her, Brute; I'll whistle her off, and let her down the Wind, as *Othella*[a] says. No I adore the Wife, that when the heart is gone, boldly and nobly pursues the Conqueror, and generously owns the Whore,—Not poorly adds the nautious sin of Jilting to't: That I cou'd have born, at least commended; but this can never Pardon; at worst then the world had said her Passion had undone her, she lov'd and Love at worst is pity. No, no *Mertilla*, I forgive your Love, but never can your poor dissimulation. One drives you but from the heart you value not, but t'other to my eternal contempt. One deprives me but of thee

---

[a] Othello, the moorish hero of Shakespeare's tragedy of the same name. On first hearing of his wife's infidelity he likens her to a hawk, declaring: 'If I do find her haggard, / Though that her jesses were my dear heart-strings, / I'ld whistle her off and let her down the wind / To pray to fortune....' [III.iii.259-64]

Mertilla, but t'other intitles me to a Beauty more surprising, renders thee no part of me; and so leaves the Lover free to *Silvia*, without the Brother.

Thus my excellent Maid I have sent you the sense and truth of my Soul in an affair you have often hinted to me, and I take no pleasure to remember, I hope you will at least think my aversion reasonable, and that being thus undisputably freed from all obligations to *Mertilla* as a Husband, I may be permitted to lay claim to *Silvia* as a Lover, and marry my self more effectually by my everlasting Vows, than the Priest by his common method cou'd do to any other Woman less belov'd, there being no other way at present left by Heav'n, to render me *Silvia's*

Eternal happy Lover and

PHILANDER.

I dy to see you

To *Silvia*.

When I had seal'd the inclos'd, *Brilljard*[a] told me you were this Morning come from *Belfont*, and with infinite impatience have expected seeing you here; which defer'd my sending this to the old place; and I am so vain (oh Adorable *Silvia*!) as to believe my fancy'd silence has given you disquiets, but sure my *Silvia* cou'd not charge me with neglect, no she knows my Soul, and lays it all on chance, or some strange accident, she knows no business cou'd divert me. No were the Nation sinking, the great Senate of the world[b] confounded, our Glorious Designs betray'd and ruin'd, and the vast City all in flame; like *Nero*[c] unconcern'd I'd

---

[a] William Turner, gentleman servant of Lord Grey. Turner married Henrietta Berkeley in order to free his master from charges of kidnapping her. Cf. Appendix I. He then accompanied Grey to Cleve where he quarrelled with him, apparently over Henrietta. Later, reconciled with his master, he fought for Monmouth in 1685, escaped to Holland after the Battle of Sedgemoor and was pardoned in 1686.

[b] Parliament.

[c] Roman emperor from AD 54–68. The adopted son of Claudius, Nero was one of the most notorious rulers in history. Popular legend insists that he fiddled while Rome burned, a myth probably inspired by Nero's love of music and poetry. He was responsible for the death of his own mother and later had his wife killed in order to marry his mistress Poppaea Sabina.

sing my everlasting Song of Love to *Silvia*, which no time or Fortune shall untune. I know my Soul and all its strength and how it's fortify'd, the charming Idea of my young *Silvia* will for ever remain there, the original may fade, time may render it less fair, less blooming in my Arms, but never in my Soul, I shall find thee there the same gay glorious creature that first surptis'd and inslav'd me, believe me Ravishing Maid I shall. Why then, oh why my cruel *Silvia*! are my joys delay'd? why am I by your rigorous commands kept from the sight of my Heav'n my eternal bliss? an Age my fair Tormentor's past, Four tedious live long days are number'd o're, since I beheld the object of my lasting Vows, my eternal wishes, how can you think, oh unreasonable *Silvia*! that I cou'd live so long without you, and yet I am live I find it by my pain, by torments of fears and jealousies insupportable, I languish and go downward to the Earth, where you will shortly see me lay'd without your recalling mercy; 'tis true I move about this unregarded world, appear every day in the great Senate House at Clubs, Caballs, and private consultations (for *Silvia* knows all the business of my Soul, even its politicks of State as well as Love) I say I appear indeed, and give my Voice in publick business, but oh my Heart more kindly is imploy'd, that and my thoughts are *Silvia*'s! Ten Thousand times a day I breath that name my busie fingers are eternally tracing out those Six mystick Letters, a Thousand ways on every thing I touch, form words, and make 'em speak a Thousand things, and all are *Silvia* still; my melancholy change is evident to all that see me, which they interpret many mistaken ways, our Party[a] fancy I repent my League with 'em, and doubting He betray the Cause, grow jealous of me, till by new Oaths, new Arguments I confirm 'em, then they smile all, and cry I am in Love! and this they would believe, but that they see all Women that I meet or converse with are indifferent to me, and so can fix it no where, for none can guess it *Silvia*, thus while I dare not tell my Soul, no not even to *Cesario*, the stifled flame burns inward and torments me so, that (unlike the thing I was) I fear *Silvia* will lose her Love, and Lover too; for those few Charmes she said I had, will fade, and this fatal distance will destroy both Soul and Body too, my very reason will abandon me and I shall rave to see thee; restore me, oh restore me

---

[a] The cabal of Shaftesbury, Sir Thomas Armstrong, Grey and other supporters of Monmouth.

then to *Bellfont* still blest with *Silvia's* presence permit me, oh permit me into those sacred Shades where I have been so often (too innocently) blest! let me survey again the dear characters of *Silvia* on the smooth Birch; oh when shall I sit beneath those Boughs,[a] gazing on the young Goddess of the Grove, hearing her sigh for Love; touching her glowing small white hands, beholding her killing eyes languish, and her Charming bosome rise and fall with short-breath'd uncertain breath; breath as soft and sweet as the restoring breeze that glides or'e the newblown flowers. But oh what is it! what Heav'n of Perfumes, when it inclines to the ravisht *Philander*, and whispers Love, it dares not name aloud!

What power witholds me then from rushing on thee, from pressing thee with Kisses, folding thee in my transported Armes, and following all the dictates of Love without respect of Awe. What is it oh my *Silvia* can obtain a Love so violent and raving, and so wild admit me sacred Maid, admit me again to those soft delights; that I may find if possible, what Devinity (envious of my bliss) checks my eager joys; my raging flame; while you too make an experiment (worth the Tryal) what 'tis makes *Silvia* deny her

Impatient Adorer.

PHILANDER.

My Page is Ill, and I am oblig'd to trust Brilljard *with these to the dear Cottage of their Rendevouz, send me your opinion of his fidelity and ah remember I dy to see you.*

To Philander.

Not yet?——not yet? oh ye dull tedious Hours when will you glide away? and bring that happy moment on, in which I shall at least hear from my *Philander*; Eight and Forty teadious ones

---

[a] This is a familiar trope in Behn's poetry. Cf. 'Song' and 'On *a* Juniper-Tree, *cut down to make* Busks' [*Works of Aphra Behn*, Vol. 1, nos. 2 & 14].

are past, and I am here forgotten still; forlorn, impatient, restless every where; not one of all your little moments (ye un-
diverting hours) can afford me repose; I drag ye on, a heavy
Load; I count ye all; and bless ye when you'r gone; but tremble
at the approaching ones, and with a dread expect you; and
nothing will divert me now, my Couch is tiresome, and my
Glass is vain; my Books are dull, and conversation insupportable, the Grove affords me no relief; nor even those Birds to
whom I have so often breath'd *Philander*'s name, they sing it on
their perching Boughs; no nor the reviewing of his dear Letters,
can bring me any ease. Oh what fate's reserv'd for me; for thus
I cannot live; nor surely thus I shall not dy. Perhaps *Philander*'s
making a tryal of Vertue by this silence. Pursue it, call up all
your reason my lovely Brother to your aid, let us be wise and
silent, let us try what that will do towards the cure of this too
infectious flame; let us, oh let us my Brother sit down here, and
pursue the crime of Loving on no further. Call me Sister——
Swear I am so, and nothing but your Sister: and forbear, oh
forbear my charming Brother to pursue me farther with your
soft bewitching Passion, let me alone, let me be ruin'd with
Honour if I must be ruin'd——For oh! 'twere much happyer I
were no more than that I shou'd be more than *Philander*'s Sister;
or he than *Silvia*'s Brother: Oh let me ever call you by that cold
name, till that of Lover be forgotten: ——Ha!——Methinks on
the suddain a fit of Vertue informs my Soul, and bids me ask
you for what sin of mine my Charming Brother you still persue
a Maid that cannot fly: Ungenerous and unkind! why did you
take advantage of those Freedoms I gave you as a Brother, I
smil'd on you, and sometimes kist you too;——But for my
Sisters sake. I play'd with you, suffer'd your Hands and Lips to
wander were I dare not now; all which I thought a Sister might
allow a Brother and knew not all the while the Treachery of
Love: Oh none, but under that intimate title of Brother, cou'd
have had the opportunity to have ruin'd me, that, that betray'd
me: I play'd away my Heart at a Game I did not understand, nor
knew I when 'twas lost by degrees so subtil, and an authority so
lawful, you won me out of all. Nay then too, even when all was
left, I wou'd not think it Love. I wonder'd what my sleepless
Nights, my waking eternal thoughts, and slumbring Visions of
my lovely Brother meant, I wonder'd why my Soul was continually filled with wishes and new desires; and still concluded
'twas for my Sister all: till I discovered the cheat by jealousie, for

when my Sister hung upon your neck; kist and carrest that face that I ador'd, oh how I found my colour change, my Limbs all trembled, and my blood inrag'd, and I cou'd scarce forbear reproaching you: Or crying out, Oh why this fondness Brother. Sometimes you perceiv'd my concern, at which you'd smile, for you who had been before in Love, (a curse upon the fatal time) cou'd guess at my disorder; then wou'd you turn the wanton play on me: When sullen with my jealousie and the cause, I fly your soft imbrace, yet wish you wou'd pursue and overtake me which you ne're fail'd to do, where after a kind quarrel all was pardon'd, and all was well again: While the poor injur'd innocent my Sister, made her self sport at our delusive Wars. Still I was ignorant, till you in a most fatal hour inform'd me I was a Lover. Thus was it with my heart in those blest days of innocence; thus it was won and lost; nor can all my Stars in Heaven prevent, I doubt prevent my ruine. Now you are sure of the fatal conquest you scorn the trifling Glory you are silent now; oh I am inevitably lost, or with you or without you: And I find by this little silence and absence of yours that 'tis most certain I must either dy or be *Philander*'s.

SILVIA.

If Dorillus *come not with a Letter or that my Page whom I have sent to his Cottage for one bring it not, I cannot support my Life, for oh* Philander *I have a Thousand wild distracting fears, knowing how you are involv'd in the Interest you have espous'd with the young* Cæsario; *how danger surrounds you, how your life and Glory depends on the frail secresie of Villains and Rebels: Oh give me leave to fear eternally your fame and life, if not your Love; if* Silvia *cou'd command,* Philander *shou'd be Loyal as he's Noble; and what generous Maid wou'd not suspect his Vows to a Mistress who breaks 'em with his Prince and Master, Heav'n preserve you and your Glory.*

To Philander.

Another Night oh Heav'ns and yet no Letter come! Where are you my *Philander*? What happy place contains you! if in Heav'n, why do's not some posting Angel bid me hast after you? if on

Earth, why do's not some little God of Love bring the grateful
tidings on his painted Wings! if sick, why does not my own
fond heart by sympathy inform me, but that's all active, vigorous, wishing, impatient of delaying silence, and busie in
imagination; if you are false, if you have forgotten your poor
believing and distracted *Silvia*, why do's not that kind Tyrant
Death, that meager welcome Vision of the desparing, old, and
wretched, approach in dead of Night, approach my restless
Bed, and tole the dismal tidings in my frighted listning ears,
and strike me for ever silent; lay me for ever quiet, lost to the
world, lost to my faithless Charmer: But if a sense of Honour in
you, has made you resolve to prefer mine before your Love,
made you take up a noble fatal resolution never to tell me more
of your Passion, this were a Trial I fear my fond heart wants
courage to bear; or is't a trick, a cold fit only assum'd to try how
much I Love you? I have no Arts Heav'n knows, no guile or
double meaning in my soul, 'tis all plain native simplicity,
fearful and timerous as Children in the Night, trembling as
Doves pursu'd; born soft by Nature, and made tender by Love;
what, oh! what will become of me then! Yet wou'd I were
confirm'd in all my fears: For as I am my condition is yet more
deplorable, for I'm in doubt, and doubt is the worst torment of
the mind: Oh *Philander* be mercyful, and let me know the worst,
do not be cruel while you kill, do it with pity to the wretched
Silvia, oh let me quickly know whether you are at all, or are the
most impatient and unfortunate

Silvia's.

*I rave, I dy for
some Relief.*

To *Philander*.

As I was going to send away this enclos'd: *Dorillus* came with
Two Letters; oh you cannot think *Philander* with how much
reason you call me fickle Maid, for cou'd you but imagine how
I am tormentingly divided, how unresolv'd between violent

Love, and cruel Honour: You would say 'twere impossible to fix me any where; or be the same thing for a moment together, There is not a short hour past through the swift hand of time, since I was all despairing raging Love, jealous, fearful, and impatient; and now, now that your fond Letters have dispers'd those Damons, those tormenting Councellors, and given a little respit, a little tranquility to my Soul; like States luxurious grown with ease, it ungratefully rebells against the Soveraign power that made it great and happy; and now that Traytor Honour heads the mutiners within; Honour whom my late mighty fears had almost famisht and brought to nothing, warm'd and reviv'd by thy new protested flame, makes War against Almighty Love! and I, who but now nobly resolved for Love! by an inconstancy natural to my Sex, or rather my fears, am turn'd over to Honour's side: So the despairing man stands on the Rivers Bank, design'd to plunge into the rapid stream, till coward fear seizing his timerous soul, he views around once more the flow'ry Plains, and looks with wishing eyes back to the Groves, then sighing stops, and cry's I was too rash, forsakes the dangerous shore, and hasts away. Thus indiscreet was I; was all for Love,[a] fond and undoing love! but when I saw it with full Tide flow in upon me, one glance of Glorious Honour, makes me again retreat. I will—I am resolv'd——And must be brave! I can't forget I'm Daughter to the great *Beralti*,[b] and Sister to *Mertilla*, a yet unspotted Maid, fit to produce a race of Glorious Hero's! and can *Philander's* Love set no higher value on me than base poor prostitution! is that the price of his heart?— Oh how I hate thee now! or wou'd to Heav'n I cou'd.——Tell me not thou charming Beguiler, that *Mertilla* was to blame, was it a fault in her, and will it be vertue in me; and can I believe the crime that made her lose your heart, will make me Mistress of it: No, if by any action of her's, the noble House of the *Beralti* be dishonour'd by all the Actions of my Life it shall receive Additions of Luster and Glory! nor will I think *Mertilla's* vertue

---

[a] Dryden's play, *All for Love*, was first performed in 1678 and was an immediate success. Based on Shakespeare's *Antony and Cleopatra*, the play explores the conflict of Anthony's love for Cleopatra and his desire for political power. Behn must have noticed the parallels not only with the lives of Ford Grey and Henrietta Berkeley, but also with the relationship between Monmouth and Henrietta Wentworth.

[b] Behn seems to created the name from *Ber-* the first part of Berkeley and *alti*, the Italian word meaning high or high-ranking.

lessen'd for your mistaken opinion of it, and she may be as much in vain pursu'd perhaps, by the Prince *Cæsario* as *Silvia* shall be by the young *Philander*; the envying world talks loud 'tis true, but oh if all were true that busie babler says, what Lady has her fame? What Husband is not Cuckold? Nay and a friend to him that made him so; and 'tis in vain my too subtil Brother, you think to build the trophies of your Conquests on the ruine of both *Mertilla*'s fame and mine; oh how dear wou'd your inglorious passion cost the great unfortunate house of the *Beralti*, while you poorly ruine the fame of *Mertilla* to make way to the heart of *Silvia*; Remember, oh remember once your Passion was as violent for *Mertilla*, and all the Vows, Oaths, protestations, tears and Prayers you make and pay at my feet, are but the faint repetitions, the feeble eccho's of what you sigh't, out at hers. Nay like young *Paris*,[a] fled with the fair Prize; your fond, your eager Passion made it a Rape: oh perfidious!—Let me not call it back to my remembrance.——Oh let me dy rather than call to mind a time so fatal; when the lovely false *Philander* vow'd his heart, his faithless heart away to any Maid but *Silvia*: —Oh let it not be possible for me to imagine his dear Arms ever grasp'd any body with joy but—*Silvia*'s!—And yet they did, with transports of Love! yes, yes you lov'd! by Heav'n you lov'd this false, this perfidious *Mertilla*; for false she is; you lov'd her, and I'll have it so; nor shall the Sister in me plead her Cause. She's false beyond all Pardon; for you are beautiful as Heav'n it self can render you, a shape exactly form'd, not too low nor too tall, but made to beget soft desire and everlasting wishes in all that look on you; but your face! your lovely face! inclining to round, large piercing languishing black eyes, delicate proportion'd Nose, charming dimpl'd Mouth, plump red Lips, inviting and swelling white Teeth, small and even, fine complexion, and a beautiful turn! all which you had an Art to order in so ingaging a manner that it charm'd all the beholders, both Sexes were undone with looking on you; and I have heard a witty man of your Party swear your face gain'd more to the League and Association than the Cause, and has curst a Thousand times the false *Mertilla* for preferring *Cæsario* (less beautiful) to the adorable

---

[a] In the Greek myth of the Judgment of Paris, Aphrodite offered Helen to Paris as his wife, Athena offered him wisdom and glory, and Hera promised him riches and power. He chose Helen who was already married to Menelaus of Sparta, and by bringing her to Troy he sparked off the Trojan War.

Philander; to add to this, Heav'n! how you spoke, when e're you spoke of Love! in that you far surpast the young *Cæsario*! as young as he, almost as great and Glorious; Oh perfidious *Mertilla*. Oh false, oh foolish and ingrate!——that you abandon'd her was just, she was not worth retaining in your heart, nor cou'd be worth defending with your Sword;——But grant her false; Oh *Philander*! how does her perfidy intitle you to me? false as she is, you still are Married to her; inconstant as she is, she's still your Wife; and no breach of the Nuptial Vow can unty the fatal knot; and that's a Mystery to common sense; sure she was Born for mischief, and Fortune when she gave her you, design'd the ruine of us all, but most particularly

The Unfortunate

Silvia.

To *Silvia*.

My Souls eternal joy, my *Silvia*! what have you done, and oh how durst you knowing my fond Heart try it with so fatal a stroke; what means this severe Letter? and why so eagerly at this time o'th' day, is *Mertilla*'s Vertue so defended; is it a question now whether she is false or not? oh poor, oh frivolous excuse! you love me not, by all that's good you love me not! to try your power you have flatter'd and feign'd, oh Woman! false Charming Woman! you have undone me! I rave, and shall commit such extravagance that will ruine both: I must upbraid you, fickle and inconstant, I must, and this distance will not serve, 'tis too great, my reproaches lose their force, I burst with resentment with injur'd Love, and you are either the most faithless of your Sex, or the most malicious and tormenting: Oh I am past tricks my *Silvia*, your little arts might do well in a beginning flame; but to a settled Fire that is arriv'd to the highest degree, it does but damp its fierceness, and instead of drawing me on, wou'd lessen my esteem, if any such deceit were capable to harbour in the Heart of *Silvia*, but she is all Divine, and I am mistaken in the meaning of what she says: Oh my adorable think no more on that dull false thing a Wife, let

27

her be banisht thy thoughts, as she is my Soul; let her never appear though but in a Dream to fright our solid joys, our true happiness; no, let us look forward to Pleasures vast and un-confin'd, to coming transports: and leave all behind us that contributes not to that Heav'n of Bliss: Remember, oh *Silvia*, that five tedious days are past since I sigh't at your dear feet; and five days to a Man so madly in Love as your *Philander*, is a tedious Age; 'tis now six a Clock in the Morning, *Brilljard* will be with you by Eight, and by Ten I may have your permission to see you, and then I need not say how soon I will present my self before you, at *Bellfont*; for Heaven's sake my eternal Blessing, if you design me this happiness, contrive it so, that I may see no body that belongs to *Bellfont*, but the fair, the lovely *Silvia*; for I must be more moments with you, than will convenient to be taken notice of, lest they suspect our business to be Love, and that discovery, yet, may ruine us. Oh I will delay no longer, my Soul's impatient to see you, I cannot live another Night without it, I dy, by Heav'n! I languish for the appointed hour; you will believe when you see my languld Face and dying Eyes, how much and great a sufferer in Love I am.

My Soul's Delight, You may perhaps deny me from your fear, but oh! do not, though I ask a mighty blessing; *Silvia*'s Company, alone, silent, and perhaps by Dark,—Oh though I faint with the thought only of so blest an opportunity, yet you shall secure me, by what Vows, what imprecautions or ty's you please; bind my busie hands; blind my ravish't eyes; command my Tongue, do what you will; but let me hear your Angels Voice, and have the transported joy of throwing my self at your feet; and if you please give me leave (a man condemn'd eter-nally to Love) to plead a little for my Life and passion; let me remove your fears, and though that mighty Task never make me intirely happy, at least 'twill be a great satisfaction to me to know, that 'tis not through my own fault that I am the

Most Wretched

PHILANDER.

I have order'd Brilljard *to wait your Commands at* Dorillos *his Cottage, that he may not be seen at* Bellfont: *resolve to see me to Night, or I shall come without order and injure both: My dear Damn'd*

28

Wife is dispos'd of at a Ball Cæsario *makes to Night; the opportunity will be luckey, not that I fear her jealousie, but the effects of it.*

To *Philander.*

I tremble with the apprehension of what you ask, how shall I comply with your fond desires? My Soul bodes some dire effect of this bold enterprise, for I must own (and blush while I do own it) that my Soul yields obedience to your soft request, and even whilst I read your Letter, was diverted with the contrivance of seeing you: For though as my Brother you have all the freedoms imaginable at *Bellfont* to entertain and walk with me, yet 'twould be difficult and prejudical to my Honour, to receive you alone any where without my Sister: and cause a suspicion, which all about me now are very far from conceiving, except *Melinda* my faithful confident, and too fatal Councellor: and but for this fear, I know my charming Brother, three little Leagues shou'd not five long days separate *Philander* from his *Silvia*. But my lovely Brother, since you beg it so earnesty, and my heart consents so easily, I must pronounce my own Doom and say, Come my *Philander*, whither Love and soft desire invites you, and take this direction in the management of this mighty affair; I wou'd have you as soon as this comes to your hands, to hast to *Dorillus's* Cottage, without your Equipage, only *Brilljard*, whom I believe you may trust both from his own discretion and your vast bounty's to him; wait there till you receive my commands: and I will retire betimes to my Apartment pretending not to be well, and as soon as the Evenings obscurity will permit, *Melinda* shall let you in at the Garden Gate that is next the Grove, unseen and unsuspected, but oh thou powerful Charmer have a care, I trust you with my all: my dear, dear, my precious Honour, guard it well, for oh I fear my forces are too weak to stand your shock of Beauties; you have Charms enough to justify my yielding, but yet by Heav'n I wou'd not for an Empire: but what's dull Empire to Almighty Love! the God subdues the Monarch! 'tis to your strength I trust, for I am a feeble Woman, a Virgin quite disarm'd by two fair eyes, an Angels Voice and form, but yet I'll dy before I'll yield my Honour; no though our unhappy Family have met reproach

from the imagin'd levity of my Sister; 'tis I'll redeem the bleeding Honour of our Family, and my great Parents Vertues shall
shine in me; I know it, for if it passes this Test, if I can stand this
Temptation, I'm proof against all the World; but I conjure you
aid me if I need it: If I incline but in a Languishing look, if but a
wish appear in my eyes, or I betray consent but in a Sigh; take
not, oh take not the opportunity, lest when you've done I grow
raging mad, and discover all in the wild fit; oh who wou'd
venture on an enemy with such unequal force; what hardy fool
wou'd hazard all at Sea that sees the rising Storm come rouling
on; who but fond Woman, giddy heedless Woman! wou'd thus
expose her Vertue to Temptation, I see, I know my danger, yet
I must permit it; Love soft bewitching Love will have it so, that
cannot deny what my feebler Honour forbids; and though I
tremble with fear, yet Love suggests, 'twill be an Age to Night;
I long for my undoing; for oh I cannot stand the batteries of
your eyes and tongue, these fears, these conflicts I have a
Thousand times a day, 'tis pitiful sometimes to see me, on one
hand a Thousand *Cupids* all gay and smiling present *Philander*
with all the Beauties of his sex, with all the softness in his looks
and Language those Gods of Love can inspire, with all the
Charms of youth adorn'd, bewitching all, and all transporting;
on the other hand, a poor lost Virgin languishing and undone;
sighing her willing rape to the deaf shades and fountains; filling
the Woods with cry's, swelling the Murmering Rivolets with
tears, her noble Parents with a generous Rage reviling her, and
her betray'd Sister loading her bow'd head with curses and
reproaches; and all about her looking forlorn and sad: Judg, oh
Judg my adorable Brother, of the vastness of my courage and
passion, when even this deplorable prospect cannot defend me
from the resolution of giving you admittance into my Apartment this Night, nor shall ever drive you from the Soul of your

SILVIA.

To *Silvia*.

I have obey'd my *Silvia*'s dear commands, and the dictates of
my own impatient Soul, as soon as I receiv'd 'em, I immediately
took Horse for *Bellfont*, though I knew I shou'd not see my

Adorable *Silvia* till Eight or Nine at Night; but oh 'tis wondrous pleasure to be so much more near my eternal joy; I wait at *Dorillus* his Cottage the tedious approaching Night that must shelter me in its kind shades, and conduct me to a pleasure I faint but with imagining; 'tis now my Lovely Charmer Three a Clock, and oh how many tedious hours I am to languish here before the blessed one arrive; I know you Love, my *Silvia*, and therefore must guess at some part of my torment, which yet is mixt with a certain trembling joy not to be imagin'd by any but *Silvia*, who surely loves *Philander*, if there be truth in Beauty, Faith in Youth, she surely loves him much, and much more above her Sex she's capable of Love; by how much more her Soul's form'd of a softer and more delicate composition, by how much more her Wits refin'd and elevated above her duller Sex; and by how much more she is oblig'd if Passion can claim Passion in return, sure no Beauty was ever so much indebted to a slave, as *Silvia* to *Philander*, none ever Lov'd like me! Judg then my pains of Love, my Joys, my fears, my impatience, and desires, and call me to your sacred presence with all the speed of Love; and as soon as 'tis duskish, imagine me in the Meadow behind the Grove, 'till when think me imploy'd in eternal thoughts of *Silvia*; restless, and talking to the Trees of *Silvia*, sighing her charming Name, circling with folded Arms my panting heart, (that beats and trembles the more, the nearer it approaches the happy *Bellfont*) and fortifying the feeble trembler against a sight too Ravishing and surprising. I fear to be sustain'd with Life; but if I faint in *Silvia*'s Arms, it will be happyer far than all the Glories of Life without her.

Send my Angel something from you to make the Hours less tedious, consider me, Love me, and be as impatient as I; that you may the sooner find at your feet your everlasting Lover

PHILANDER.

From *Dorillus*'s Cottage.

To *Philander*.

I have at last recover'd sense enough to tell you, I have receiv'd your Letter by *Dorillus*, and which had like to have been discover'd, for he prudently enough put it under the Strawberys he brought me in a Basket, fearing he shou'd get no other opportunity to have given it me; and my Mother seeing 'em look so fair and fresh, snatcht the Basket with a greediness I have not seen in her before; while she was calling to her Page for a Porcellane Dish to put 'em out, *Dorillus* had opportunity to hint to me what lay at the bottom; Heaven's had you seen my disorder and confusion! what shou'd I do; Love had not one invention in store, and there it was that all the subtilty of Women abandon'd me. Oh Heaven's how cold and pale I grew lest the most important business of my Life shou'd be betray'd and ruin'd, but not to terrify you longer with fears of my danger, the Dish came, and out the Strawberries were powr'd, and the Basket thrown, aside on the Bank where my Mother sat, (for we were in the Garden when we met accidentally *Dorillus* first with the Basket), there were some Leaves of Fern put at the bottom between the Basket and Letter, which by good fortune came not out with the Strawberries, and after a Minute or two I took up the Basket and walking carelessly up and down the Garden, Gather'd her and there a flower, Pinks and Jessamine, and filling my Basket sat down again till my Mother had eat her fill of the Fruit, and gave me an opportunity to retire to my apartment, where opening the Letter, and finding you so near and waiting to see me. I had certainly sunk down on the floor had not *Melinda* supported me, who was only by, something so new, and till now so strange, seiz'd me at the thought of so secret an interview, that I lost all my senses, and Life wholly departing, I rested on *Melinda* without breath or motion, the violent effects of Love and Honour, the impetuous meeting tides of the extreams of joy and fear, rushing on too suddainly, over-whelm'd my senses; and 'twas a pretty while before I recover'd strength to get to my Cabinet, where a second time I open'd your Letter, and read it again with a Thousand changes of Countenance, my whole mass of Blood was in that moment so discompos'd, that I chang'd from Ague to Feaver, several times in a Minute; oh what will all this bring me to? and where will the raging fit end? I dy with that thought, my guilty pen slackens in my trembling hand, and I Languish and fall over the unimploy'd Paper;——Oh help me some Divinity—— Or if you did,—I fear I shou'd be angry! Oh *Philander*! a Thousand Passions and distracted thoughts crowd to get out, and make their soft complaints to thee, but oh they lose them-selves with Mixing; they are blended in a confusion together, and Love nor Art can divide 'em, to deal 'em out in order; sometimes I wou'd tell you of my Joy at your Arrival, and my unspeakable transports at the thought of seeing you so soon, that I shall hear your charming Voice, and find you at my feet making soft Vows a new, with all the Passion of an impatient Lover, with all the eloquence that sighs and Cryes and tears from those lovely eyes can express; and sure that's enough to conquer any where; and to which, course vulgar words are dull: The Rhetorick of Love is half-breath'd, interrupted words, languishing Eyes, flattering Speeches, broken Sighs, pressing the hand, and falling Tears: Ah how do they not perswade; how do they not charm and conquer; 'twas thus with these soft easie Arts, that *Silvia* first was won! for sure no Arts of speaking cou'd have talk'd my heart away, though you can speak like any God! oh whether am I driven, what do I say 'twas not my purpose nor my business here, to give a character of *Philander* no not to speak of Love! but oh like *Cowley*'s Lute,[a] my Soul will sound to nothing but to Love! talk what you will, begin what discourse you please, I end it all in Love! because my Soul is ever fixt on *Philander*; and insensibly its byas leads to that Subject; no, I did not when I began to Write, think of speaking one word of my own weakness; but to have told you with what resolv'd Courage, Honour, and Vertue, I expect your coming; and sure so sacred a thing as Love was not made to ruine these, and therefore in vain my lovely Brother you will attempt it; and yet (oh Heaven's! I give a private Assignation, in my Apartment, alone and at Night; where silence, Love, and shades are all your friends, where opportunity obliges your Passion, while Heav'n knows, not one of all these, nor any kind power is friend to me, I shall be left to you, and all these Tyrants, expos'd without other Guards than this boasted Vertue, which had need be wonderous to resist all these powerful enemies of its purity and repose: Alas I know not its strength, I never try'd it yet; and this will be the first time it has ever been expos'd to your Power; the first time I ever had courage to meet you as a Lover, and let you in by stealth, and put my self unguarded into

---

[a] An allusion to lines from Abraham Cowley's 'Anacreontiques: Or Some Copies of Verses Translated Paraphrastically out of *Anacreon*': 'I'll sing of *Heroes*, and of *Kings*; / In mighty Numbers, mighty things, / Begin, my *Muse*; but lo, the strings / To my great *Song* rebellious prove; / The strings will sound of nought but *Love*... / Farewel then *Heroes*, farewel *Kings*, / And mighty *Numbers*, mighty *Things*; / Love tunes my *Heart* just to my *strings*.' [*Love*, ll.1–17].

your hands; Oh I dy with the apprehension of approaching danger; and yet I have not power to retreat, I must on, Love compells me, Love holds me fast, the smiling flatterer promises a Thousand joys, a Thousand Ravishing Minutes of delight; all innocent and harmless as his Mothers Doves:[a] But oh they Bill and kiss, and do a Thousand things I must forbid *Philander*: for I have often heard him say with sighs, that his complection render'd him less capable of the soft play of Love, than any other Lover: I've seen him fly my very touches, yet swear they were the greatest joy on Earth: I tempt him even with my looks from Vertue; and when I ask the cause, or cry he's cold, he vows 'tis because he dares not indure my Temptations; says his Blood runs hotter and fiercer in his Veins than any others do's; nor has the oft repeated joys reap'd in the Marriage Bed, any thing abated that which he wisht, but he fear'd wou'd ruine me: Thus, thus whole days we have sat and gaz'd and sigh'd; but durst not trust our Vertues with fond Dalliance.

My Page is come to tell me that Madam the Dutchess of——is come to *Bellfont*, and I am oblig'd to quit my Cabinet, but with infinite regret, being at present much more to my Soul's content imploy'd; but Love must sometimes give place to *Devoir*[b] and respect; *Dorillus* too waits, and tells *Melinda*, he will not depart without something for his Lord, to entertain him till the happy hour: The Rustick pleas'd me with the concern he had for my *Philander*; oh my Charming Brother, you have an Art to tame even salvages, a Tongue that wou'd charm and ingage wildness itself, to softness and gentleness, and give the rough unthinking love; 'tis a tedious time to night, how shall I pass the hours?

To *Silvia*.

Say fond Love whither wilt thou lead me? thou hast brought me from the noysey hurry's of the Town, to charming solitude; from Crowded Cabals, where mighty things are resolving to loanly Groves, to thy own abodes, where thou dwell'st, gay

---

[a] Cupid was the son of Venus, to whom doves were sacred.
[b] *French*: Duty.

and pleas'd, amongst the Rural Swains in shady homely Cottages; thou hast brought me to a Grove of flowers, to the brink of Purling Streams, where thou hast laid me down to contemplate on *Silvia*! to think my tedious hours away, in the softest imagination a Soul inspir'd by Love can conceive; to increase my Passion by every thing I behold, for every Sound that meets the sense, is thy proper Musick, oh Love! and every thing inspires thy dictates; the Winds a round me blow soft, and mixing with the wanton Boughs, continually play and Kiss; while those like a coy Maid in Love resist and comply by turns; they like a ravisht vigorous Lover, rush on with a transported violence; rudely imbracing its Spring drest Mistress, ruffling her Native order, while the pretty Birds on the dancing Branches incessantly make Love; upbraiding duller man with his defective want of fire: man the Lord of all! he to be stinted in the most valuable joy of Life! is it not Pity? here's no troublesome Honour, amongst the pretty inhabitants of the Woods and Streams, fondly to give Laws to Nature, but uncontroul'd they play and sing, and Love; no Parents checking their dear delights, no slavish Matrimonial tyes to restrain their Nobler flame. No spyes[a] to interrupt their blest appointments, but every little Nest is free and open to receive the young fletch't Lover; every bough is conscious of their Passion, nor do the generous pair languish in tedious Ceremony, but meeting look, and like, and Love, imbrace with their wingy Arms, and salute with their little opening Bills; this is their Courtship; this the amorous complement, and this only the introduction to all their following happiness; and thus it is with the Flocks and Heards, while scanted man, born alone for the fatigues of Love, with industrious toyl, and all his boasting Arts of Eloquence, his Godlike Image, and his noble form, may labour on a tedious term of years, with pain, expence, and hazard, before he can arrive at happiness, and then too perhaps his Vows are unregarded, and all his Sighs and Tears are vain. Tell me oh you fellow Lovers, yea amorous dear Bruits tell me, when ever you lay Languishing beneath your Coverts thus for your fair she; and durst not approach for fear of Honour? tell me by a gentle bleat ye little butting Rams; do you Sigh thus for your soft white Ewes?

---

[a] *The Trial of Ford Lord Grey* makes it clear that Henrietta Berkeley and Grey were under constant observation by the Berkeley family and their spies. Cf. Appendix I.

do you ly thus conceal'd, to wait the coming shades of Night, till all the curled spyes are folded? no, no, even you are much more blest than Man, who is bound up to rules fetter'd by the nice decencies of Honour.

My divine Maid, thus were my thoughts imploy'd, when from the farthest end of the Grove where I now remain, I saw *Dorillus* approach with thy welcome Letter, he tells you had like to have been surpris'd in making it up; and he receiv'd it with much difficulty, ah *Silvia* shou'd any accident happen to prevent my seeing you to Night, I were undone for ever, and you must expect to find me stretch'd out, dead and cold under this Oak where now I ly Writing on its knotty root; thy Letter I confess is dear, it contains thy Soul and my happiness, but this after story of the surprize I long to be inform'd of, for from thence I may gather part of my Fortune. I rave and dy with fear of a disappointment, not but I wou'd undergo a Thousand Torments and deaths for *Silvia*; but oh consider me, and let me not suffer if possible; for know my charming Angel, my impatient heart is almost broke, and will not contain it self without being nearer my adorable Maid; without taking in at my Eyes a little comfort, no, I am resolv'd! put me not off with tricks, which foolish Honour invents to jilt mankind with; for if you do, by Heav'n I will forget all considerations and respect, and force my self with all the violence of raging Love, into the presence of my cruel *Silvia*, own her mine, and Ravish my delight, nor shall the happy Walls of *Bellfont* be of strength sufficient to secure her, nay, perswade me not, for if you make me mad and raving, this will be the effects on't:—Oh pardon me my sacred Maid, pardon the wildness of my frantick Love. ——I paws'd; took a turn or two in the lone path, consider'd what I had said, and found it was too much; too bold, too rude to approach, my soft, my tender Maid: I am calm my Soul, as thy bewitching smiles; hush as thy secret Sighs, and will resolve to dy rather than offend my adorable Virgin; only send me word what you think of my Fate, while I expect it here on this kind Mossy bed where I now ly; which I wou'd not quit for a Throne, since here I may hope the News may soonest arrive to make me happier than a God! which that nothing on my part may prevent, I here Vow in the face of Heav'n, I will not abuse the freedome my *Silvia* blesses me with; nor shall my Love go beyond the limits of Honour. *Silvia* shall command with a frown, and fetter me with a Smile; prescribe rules to my longing

Ravish't Eyes, and pinion my busie fond Roving hands: and lay at her feet like a tame slave, her adoring

PHILANDER.

To *Philander*.

Approach, approach you sacred Queen of Night,[a] and bring *Philander* Veil'd from all eyes but mine! approach at a fond Lovers call, behold how I ly panting with expectation tir'd out with your tedious Ceremony to the God of day; be kind oh lovely Night, and let the Deity descend to his belov'd *Thetis's*[b] Arms, and I to my *Philander's*; the Sun and I must snatch our joys in the same happy hours! favour'd by thee, oh sacred silent Night! see, see the inamour'd Sun is hasting on apace to his expecting Mistress, while thou dull Night art slowly lingring yet. Advance my Friend! my Goddess! and my confident! hide all my blushes, all my soft confusions, my tremblings, transports, and Eyes all Languishing.

Oh *Philander*! a Thousand things I've done to divert the tedious hours, but nothing can: all things are dull without thee. I'm tir'd with every thing, impatient to end, as soon as I begin 'em, even the Shades and solitary Walks afford me now no ease, no satisfaction and thought, but afflicts me more, that us'd to relieve. And I at last have recourse to my kind Pen: For while I Write methinks I'm talking to thee, I tell thee thus my Soul, while thou methinks art all the while smiling and listening by; this is much easier than silent thought, and my Soul is never weary of this converse, and thus I wou'd speak a Thousand things, but that still, methinks words do not enough express my Soul, to understand that right there requires looks; there is a Rethorick in looks, in Sighs and silent touches that surpasses all! there is an Accent in the sound of words too, that gives a sense and soft meaning to little things, which of themselves are of trivial value, and insignificant; and by the cadence of the

---

[a] Probably Diana, the goddess of the moon.
[b] Behn has probably confused Thetis with Tethys, a deity dwelling in the far west where the sun sets. The same mistake occurs in *A Pindarick Poem on The Happy Coronation Of His most Sacred Majesty James II* . . . [*Works of Aphra Behn*, Vol. 1, no. 67, l. 469].

utterance may express a tenderness which their own meaning does not bear; by this I wou'd insinuate that the story of the heart cannot be so well told by this way as by presence and conversation; sure *Philander* understands what I mean by this? which possibly is nonsense to all but a Lover, who apprehends all the little fond prattle of the thing belov'd, and finds an Eloquence in it, that to a sense unconcern'd wou'd appear even approaching to Folly: But *Philander*, who has the true Notions of Love in him, apprehends all that can be said on that dear Subject; to him I venture to say any thing, whose kind and soft imaginations can supply all my wants in the description of the Soul: Will it not *Philander*, answer me?——But oh where art thou? I see thee not, I touch thee not; but when I hast with transport to imbrace thee, 'tis shadow all, and my poor Arms return empty to my Bosome; why, oh why com'st thou not? why art thou cautious and prudently waitest the slow-pac'd Night. Oh cold, oh unreasonable Lover why?——But I grow wild and know not what I say: Impatient Love betrays me to a Thousand folly's, a Thousand rashnesses: I dy with shame, but I must be undone and 'tis no matter how, whether by my own weakness *Philander*'s Charms, or both; I know not, but so 'tis destin'd,—Oh *Philander*, 'tis two tedious hours Love has counted, since you Writ to me, yet are but a quarter of a Mile distant; what have you been doing all that live-long while? are you not unkind, does not *Silvia* ly neglected and unregarded in your thoughts? hudled up confusedly with your graver business of State, and almost lost in the ambitious crowd? Say, say my lovely Charmer, is she not, does not this fatal Interest you espouse, Rival your *Silvia*, is she not too often remov'd thence to let in that haughty Tyrant Mistress? Alas *Philander* I more than fear she is; and oh my Adorable Lover, when I look forward on our coming happiness, when ever I lay by the thoughts of Honour, and give a loose to Love, I run not far in the pleasing career, before that dreadful thought stop me on my way: I have a fatal prophetick fear, that gives a check to my soft pursuit, and tells me that thy unhappy ingagement in this League, this accursed Association, will one day undo us both, and part for ever thee and thy unlucky *Silvia*; yes, yes my dear Lord; my Soul does presage an unfortunate event from this dire ingagement; nor can your false Reasoning, your fancy'd advantages reconcile it to my honest, good-natur'd heart; and surely the design is inconsistent with Love, for two such mighty contradictions and enemies as Love and ambition, or revenge can never sure abide in one Soul together, at least Love can but share *Philander*'s Heart, when blood and revenge (which he means Glory) Rivals it, and has possibly the greatest part in it, methinks this notice inlarges in me, and every word I speak, and every Minutes thought of it, strengthens its reasons to me, and give me leave (while I am full of the jealousie of it) to express my sentiments, and lay before you those reasons that Love and I think most substantial ones; what you have hitherto desir'd of me, oh unreasonable *Philander*, and what (I out of Modesty and Honour deny'd) I have reason to fear (from the absolute conquest you have made of my Heart) that some time or other the charming thief may break in and rob me of, for fame and Vertue love begins to laugh at. My dear unfortunate condition being thus, 'tis not impossible, oh *Philander*, but I may one day in some unlucky hour in some soft bewitching moment, in some spightful critical ravishing minute, yield all to the Charming *Philander*; and if so where, oh where is my security that I shall not be abandoned by the Lovely Victor, for 'tis not your Vows which you call sacred (and I alas believe so) that can secure me, though I Heav'n knows believe 'em all, and am undone; you may keep 'em all too, and I believe you will, but oh *Philander* in these fatal circumstances you have ingag'd your self in, can you secure me my Lover? your protestations you may, but not the dear Protestor. It is not enough, oh *Philander*, for my eternal unquiet and undoing to know you are Married, and cannot therefore be intirely mine? is not this enough, oh cruel *Philander*? but you must espouse a fatal cause too, more pernicious than that Matrimony, and more destructive to my repose: oh give me leave to reason with you, and since you have been pleas'd to trust and afflict me with the secret; which honest as I am I will never betray yet, yet give me leave to urge the danger of it to you, and consequently to me, if you pursue it, when you are with me, we can think and talk, and argue nothing but the mightier business of Love! and 'tis fit I that so fondly and fatally love you, shou'd warn you of the danger. Consider my Lord you are born Noble, from Parents of untainted Loyalty, blest with a Fortune few Princes beneath Sovereignty are Masters of; blest with all gaining Youth, commanding Beauty, Wit, Courage, Bravery of mind, and all that renders men esteem'd and ador'd, what wou'd you more? what is it oh my Charming Brother then, that you set up for, is it Glory? oh

mistaken lovely Youth, that Glory is but a glittering light that
flashes for a moment, and then it disappears, 'tis a false Bravery, that will bring an eternal blemish upon your honest fame
and house; render your honourable name, hated, detested, and
abominable in story to after Ages, a Traytor? the worst of Titles,
the most inglorious and shameful; what has the King, our good,
our Gracious Monarch done to *Philander*? how disoblig'd him?
or indeed what injury to Mankind? who has he opprest? where
play'd the Tyrant; or the Ravisher? what one cruel or angry
thing has he committed in all the time of his fortunate and
peaceable Reign over us? Whose Ox or whose Ass has he
unjustly taken? What Orphan wrong'd, or Widows Tears neglected? but all his Life has been one continu'd Miracle, all Good,
all Gracious, Calm and Merciful: and this good, this Godlike
King is mark'd out for slaughter, design'd a Sacrifice to the
private revenge of a few ambitious Knaves and Rebels, whose
pretence is the publick good, and doom'd to be basely Murder'd; A Murder! even on the worst of Criminals carries with it
a Cowardise so black and infamous, as the most abject
Wretches, the meanest spirited Creature has an abhorrence for;
what to Murder a Man unthinking, unwarn'd, unprepar'd and
undefended! oh barbarous! oh poor and most unbrave! what
Villain is there so lost to all humanity, to be found upon the face
of the Earth, that when done, dares own so hellish a deed, as
the Murder of the meanest of his Fellow-Subjects, much less the
sacred Person of the King! The Lords Anointed;[a] one whose
awful face 'tis impossible to look without that reverence wherewith one wou'd behold a God! for 'tis most certain, that every
Glance from his piercing wondrous eyes, begets a trembling
Adoration; for my part I Swear to you, *Philander*, I never
approach His Sacred Person, but my Heart beats, my Blood
runs cold about me, and my Eyes o'reflow with Tears of joy,
while an awful confusion seizes me all over, and I am certain
shou'd the most harden'd of your Bloody Rebels look him in the
face, the devilish instrument of Death wou'd drop from his
sacrilegious hand, and leave him confounded at the feet of the
Royal forgiving Sufferer, his eyes have in 'em somthing so

---

[a] The king was held to be God's representative on earth. Monmouth himself
never intended to kill Charles II, although several of his associates – notably Robert
Ferguson – had conspired to assassinate both Charles and James at the Rye House
on the way to Newmarket.

fierce, so Majestick commanding, and yet so good and merciful as wou'd soften Rebellion it self into repenting Loyalty; and like *Cajus Marius*[a] seem to say—Who is't dares hurt the King!—They alone like his Guardian Angels defend his Sacred Person, oh! what pity 'tis, unhappy young man, thy Education was not near the King.

'Tis plain, 'tis reasonable, 'tis honest, Great and Glorious to believe, what thy own sense (if thou wilt but think and consider) wilt instruct thee in, that Treason, Rebellion and Murder are far from the Paths that lead to Glory, which are as distant as Hell from Heav'n. What is it then to advance (since I say 'tis plain, Glory is never this way to be atchiev'd) is it to add more Thousands to those, Fortune has already so lavishly bestow'd on you? oh my *Philander* that's to double the vast crime, which reaches already to Damnation: wou'd your Honour, your Conscience, your Christianity or common humanity suffer you to inlarge your Fortunes at the price of anothers ruine? and make the spoyls of some honest Noble Unfortunate Family, the rewards of your Treachery? wou'd you build your fame on such a Foundation? Perhaps on the destruction of some friend or Kinsman. Oh Barbarous and mistaken Greatness, Thieves and Robbers wou'd scorn such outrages, that had but souls and sense.

Is it for addition of Titles? what elevation can you have much greater than where you now stand fixt, if you do not grow giddy with your fancy'd false hopes, and fall from that glorious height you are already arriv'd to, and which with the honest addition of Loyalty, is of far more value and luster than to arrive at Crowns by Blood and Treason. This will last; to Ages last; in story last. While t'other will be ridicul'd to all posterity, short liv'd and reproachful here, infamous and accurs'd to all eternity.

Is it to make *Cæsario* King? oh what is *Cæsario* to my *Philander*? If a Monarchy you design, then why not this King, this great, this good, this Royal Forgiver?——This who was born a King; and born your King; and holds his Crown by right of Nature, by right of Law, by right of Heav'n it self; Heav'n who has preserv'd him, and confirm'd him ours, by a Thousand miraculous

---

[a] Caius Marius (157–86 BC) was Julius Caesar's uncle by marriage. Plutarch records that Marius was captured while in exile from Rome. His captors, the magistrates of Minturnae, ordered his death but the executioner was unable to fulfil the task. He claimed that Marius's eyes seemed to dart out strong flames and that a voice in the shadows cried 'Do you dare to kill Marius?' The executioner fled and Marius was spared.

escapes and sufferings,[a] and indulg'd him ours by Ten Thousand acts of mercy and indear'd him to us by his wondrous care and conduct, by securing of Peace, plenty, ease and luxurious happiness, o're all the fortunate limits of His Blessed Kingdoms; and will you, wou'd you destroy this wonderous gift of Heaven: this Godlike King,[b] this real good we now possess, for a most uncertain one: and with it the repose of all the happy Nation, to establish a King without Law, without right, without consent, without Title, and indeed without even competent parts[c] for so vast a trust or so Glorious a rule: One who never oblig'd the Nation by one single Act of Goodness, or Valour in all the course of his Life; and who never signaliz'd either to the advantage of one man of all the Kingdom: A Prince unfortunate in his Principles and Morals: And whose sole single Ingratitude to his Majesty, for so many Royal Bounty's, Honours, and Glories heap'd upon him, is of its self enough to set any honest generous heart against him; what is it bewitches you so? is it his Beauty? then *Philander* has a greater Title than *Cæsario*; and not one other merit has he; since in Piety, Chastity, Sobriety, Charity, and Honour, he as little excels as in Gratitude, Obedience, and Loyalty. What then my dear *Philander*! is it his weakness? Ah there's the Argument: You all propose and think to govern so soft a King: But believe me, oh unhappy *Philander*! nothing is more ungovernable than a Fool; nothing more obstinate, willful, conceited and cunning; and for his gratitude, let the world judge what he must prove to his Servants who has dealt so ill with his Lord and Master; how he must reward those that present him with a Crown, who deals so ungraciously with him who gave him Life, and who set him up an happyer object than a Monarch; No, no *Philander*, he that can cabal, and contrive to dethrone a father, will find it easie to discard the wicked

---

[a] Behn is probably referring to Charles II's evasion of commonwealth forces after the royalist defeat at Worcester in 1651. By hiding in Boscobel wood, the king avoided detection and, in a series of further close escapes, reached the safety of France. These events assumed a mythical status when Charles returned to England in the Restoration of 1660 and were celebrated in pamphlets and engravings.

[b] Because the Tories believed that a king was God's representative on earth, rebellion against the monarch was also an attack on God.

[c] Contemporary assessments of Monmouth varied considerably. He was handsome, rakish and a proven soldier. His progresses through the country had strengthened his popularity with the lower classes and it was widely believed he had the healing touch of royalty. Serious politicians such as the Earl of Shaftesbury, however, saw him as a weak figure who could be easily controlled if he were to be placed on the throne.

and hated Instruments that assisted him to mount it; decline him then oh fond and deluded *Philander*, decline him early, for you of all the rest ought to do so; and not to set a helping hand to load him with Honours, that chose you out from all the World to load with infamy: remember that; remember *Mertilla*, and then renounce him; do not you contribute to the adoring of his unfit head with a Diadem, the most glorious of Ornaments, who unadorn'd yours, with the most inglorious of all reproaches.[a] Think of this, oh thou unconsidering Noble Youth, lay thy hand upon thy generous heart, and tell it all the fears, all the reasonings of her that loves thee more than life, a Thousand Arguments I cou'd bring, but these few unstudyed (falling in amongst my softer thoughts) I beg thou wilt accept of, till I can more at large deliver the Glorious Argument to your Soul; let this suffice to tell thee, that like *Cassandria*[b] I rave and prophesie in vain, this Association will be the eternal ruine of *Philander*, for let it succeed or not, either way thou art undone; if thou pursu'st it, and I must infallibly fall with thee, if I resolve to follow thy good or ill Fortune, for you cannot intend Love and Ambition, *Silvia* and *Cæsario* at once: No, perswade me not, the Title to one or t'other must be laid down *Silvia* or *Cæsario* must be abandon'd; this is my fixt resolve, if thy too powerful Arguments convince not in spight of reason; for they can do't, thou hast the tongue of an Angel, and the Eloquence of a God, and while I listen to thy Voice, I take all thou say'st for wondrous sense——Farewell; about. Two hours hence I shall expect you at the Gate that leads into the Garden Grove——Adieu! remember.

SILVIA.

To *Silvia*.

How comes my charming *Silvia* so skill'd in the Mysteries of State? where learnt her tender heart the Notions of rigid business? where her soft Tongue, form'd only for the dear Language

---

[a] A reference to Monmouth's cuckolding of Ford Grey.
[b] Daughter of Priam, king of Troy. Cassandra was loved by Apollo, who gave her the gift of prophecy. When she refused his love, he decreed that she would always prophesy the truth but would be fated never to be believed.

of Love, to talk of the concerns of Nations and Kingdoms? 'tis
true, when I gave my Soul away to my dear Councellor, I
reserv'd nothing to my self, not even that secret that so concern'd my Life, but laid all at her Mercy; my generous Heart
cou'd not Love at a less rate, than to lavish all, and be undone
for *Silvia*; 'tis Glorious ruine, and it pleases me, if it advance
once single joy, or add one demonstration of my Love to *Silvia*;
'tis not enough that we tell those we Love all they love to hear,
but one ought to tell 'em too, every secret that we know; and
conceal no part of that Heart one has made at present to the
person one Loves, 'tis a Treason in Love not to be Pardon'd, I
am sensible that when my story's told (and this happy one of
my Love shall make up the greatest part of my History) that
those that Love not like me, will be apt to blame me, and charge
me with weakness for revealing so great a trust to a Woman;
and amongst all that I shall do to arrive at Glory, that will brand
me with feabless, but *Silvia* when Lovers shall read it, the men
will excuse me, and the Maids bless me! I shall be a fond
admir'd president, for them to point out to their remiss reserving
Lovers, who will be reproached for not persuing my example. I
know not what opinion Men generally have of the weakness of
Women; but 'tis sure a vulgar error, for were they like my
adorable *Silvia*! had they her wit, her vivacity of spirit, her
Courage, her generous fortitude, her command in every graceful look and Action, they were most certainly fit to rule and
Reign, and Man was only born robust and strong to secure 'em
on those Thrones they are form'd (by Beauty, Softness, and a
Thousand Charms which men want) to possess. Glorious
Woman! was born for command and Dominion; and though
custom has usurpt us the name of Rule over all; we from the
beginning found our selves, (in spight of all our boasted prerogative) slaves and Vassals to the Almighty Sex. Take then my
share of Empire ye Gods! and give me Love! let me toyl to gain,
but let *Sylvia* Triumph and Reign, I ask no more! no more than
the led slave at her Chariot Wheels, to gaze on my Charming
Conqueress, and wear with joy her Fetters! oh how proud I
shou'd be to see the dear Victor of my Soul so elevated, so
adorn'd with Crowns and Scepters at her feet, which I had won;
to see her smiling on the adoring Crown, distributing her Glories to young waiting Princes; there dealing Provinces, and there
a Coronet. Heavens! methinks I see the lovely Virgin in this
state, her Chariot slowly driving through the multitude that

press to gaze upon her, she drest like *Venus*[a] richly gay and loose, her Hair and Robe blown by the flying Winds, discovering a Thousand Charms to view, thus the young Goddess look't, then when she drove her Chariot down, descending Clouds to meet the Love-sick God in cooling Shades; and so wou'd look my *Silvia*! ah my soft lovely Maid, such thoughts as these fir'd me with Ambition: For me, I swear by every power that made me Love, and made thee wondrous fair, I design no more by this great enterprize, than to make thee some glorious thing, elevated above what we have seen yet on Earth: to raise thee above Fate or Fortune, beyond that pity of thy duller Sex, who understand not thy Soul, nor can never reach the flights of thy generous Love! no my Soul's joy I must not leave thee lyable to their little natural Malice and scorn, to the impertinence of their reproaches. No my *Silvia* I must on, the great design must move forward; though I abandon it, 'twill advance, and 'tis already too far to put a stop to it, and now I'm enter'd 'tis in vain to retreat, if we are prosperous, 'twill to all Ages be call'd a Glorious enterprize, but if we fail 'twill be base, horrid, and infamous, for the world judges of nothing but by the success; that cause is always good that's prosperous, that is ill that's unsuccessful. Shou'd I now retreat I run many hazards, but to go on I run but one, by the first I shall alarm the whole Cabal with a jealousie of my discovering, and those are persons of too great sense and courage, not to take some private way of revenge, to secure their own stakes; and to make my self uncertainly safe by a discovery indeed, were to gain a refuge so ignoble, as a Man of Honour wou'd scorn to purchase Life at; nor wou'd that baseness secure me. But in going on, oh *Silvia*! when Three Kingdoms[b] shall ly unpossest, and be expos'd, as it were, amongst the raffling Crowd, who knows but the chance may be mine, as well as any others, who has but the same hazard, and throw for't; if the strongest Sword must do't, (as that must do't) why not mine still? why may not mine still? Why may not mine be that fortunate one? *Cæsario* has no more right to it than *Philander*; 'tis true, a few of the Rabble will pretend he has a better title to it, but they are a sort of easy Fools, lavish in nothing but noise and nonsense, true to change and inconstancy, and will abandon him to their own fury for

---

[a] Goddess of Love.
[b] England, Ireland and Scotland.

the next that crys Haloo: Neither is there one part of fifty (of the Fools that cry him up) for his Interest, though they use him for a Tool to work with, he being the only great Man that wants sense enough to find out the cheat, which they dare impose upon. Can any body of reason believe if they had design'd him good, they would let him bare fac'd have own'd a party so opposite to all Laws of Nature, Religion, Humanity and Common gratitude? when his Interest if design'd might have been carry'd on better, if he had still dissembled and stay'd in Court: no believe me, *Silvia*, the Politicians show him[a] to render him odious to all men of tolerable sence of the Party, for what reason soever they have who are disoblig'd (or at least think themselves so) to set up for Liberty, the world knows *Cesario* renders himself the worst of Criminals by it, and has abandon'd an interest more Glorious and Easy than Empire to side with and aid People that never did or ever can oblige him: and he is so dull as to imagine that for his sake (who never did us service or good, unless Cuckolding us be good) we should venture life and fame to pull down a true Monarch, to set up his Bastard over us. *Cesario* must pardon me, if I think his Politicks are shallow as his Parts, and that his own Interest has undone him; for of what advantage soever the design may be to us, it really shocks ones nature to find a Son engag'd against a Father,[b] and to him such a Father: Nor when time comes, shall I forget the ruine of *Mertilla*. But let him hope on—and so will I, as do a thousand more for ought I know; I set out as fair as they, and will start as eagerly; if I miss it now, I have Youth and Vigor sufficient for another Race, and while I stand on Fortunes Wheel[c] as she rouls it round, it may be my turn to be o'th top; for when 'tis set in motion, believe me *Silvia*, 'tis not easily fix't; however let it suffice I'm now in past a retreat, and to urge it now to me, is but to put me into inevitable danger; at best it can but set me where I was, that's worse than death when every fool is aiming at a Kingdom; what man of tolerable Pride and

---

[a] Philander is referring to the Earl of Shaftesbury, who used Monmouth as a political tool.

[b] Cf. Behn's Epilogue to *Romulus* from which the lines, 'of all Treasons, mine was most accurst; /Rebelling 'gainst a King and Father first', probably contributed to Behn's being briefly taken into custody. [*Works of Aphra Behn*, Vol. 1, no. 10, ll.7–8]

[c] Fortuna, goddess of good luck, is usually pictured with a blindfold over her eyes, standing on a wheel and holding a cornucopia. The blindfold emphasises the indiscriminate nature of her gifts, while the wheel indicates the uncertain duration of the luck she bestows.

Ambition can be unconcern'd, and not put himself into a posture of catching, when a Diadem shall be thrown among the Croud? 'twere Insensibility, stupid Dulness, not to lift a hand, or make an effort to snatch it as it flys: though the glorious falling weight should crush me, 'tis great to attempt, and if fortune do not favour Fools, I have as fair a Grasp for't as any other adventurer.

This my *Silvia* is my sense of a business you so much dread, I may rise, but I cannot fall; therefore my *Silvia* urge it no more, Love gave me Ambition, and do not divert the Glorious effects of your wonderous Charms, but let 'em grow and spread and see what they will produce, for my Lovely *Silvia* the advantages will most certainly be hers: —— But no more, how came my Love so Dull to entertain thee so many minutes thus with reasons for an affair which one soft hour with *Silvia* will convince to what she wou'd have it; believe me it will, I will sacrifice all to her repose, nay to her least Command, even the Life of

(*My Eternal Pleasure*)

Your PHILANDER.

I have no longer patience, I must be coming towards the Grove, though 'twill do me no good, more than knowing I am so much nearer my Adorable Creature.

I conjure you burn this, for writing in haste, I have not counterfeited my hand.

To *Silvia*,

Writ in a pair of Tablets.[a]

My Charmer, I wait your Commands in the Meadow behind the Grove, where I saw *Dorinda*, *Dorilus* his Daughter, entring with a Basket of Cowslips for *Silvia*, unnecessarily offering sweets to

---

[a] Sheets of ivory or wood fastened together for writing on.

the Goddess of the Groves[a] from whence they (with all the rest of their gaudy fellows of the Spring) assume their Ravishing Odours. I take every opportunity of telling my *Silvia* what I have so often repeated, and shall be ever repeating with the same joy while I live, that I Love my *Silvia* to Death and Madness, that my soul is on the Wrack, till she send me the happy advancing word! And yet believe me Lovely Maid, I could grow old with waiting here the blessed moment, though set at any distance (within the compass of Life, and impossible to be till then arriv'd to) but when I am so near approach't it; Love from all parts rallies and hastens to my heart for the mighty incounter, till the poor panting overloaded Victim dies with the pressing weight. No more,——You know it, for 'tis and will be eternally *Silvia*'s.

POSTSCRIPT.

Rememer my Adorable, 'tis now seven a Clock,[b] I have my Watch in my hand, waiting and looking on the slow pac'd Minutes, Eight will quickly arrive I hope, and then 'tis dark enough to hide me: think where I am, and who I am, waiting near Silvia, *and her* Philander.

I think my dear Angel you have the other Key of these Tablets, if not they are easily broke open: you have an hour good to write in *Silvia*, and I shall wait unimployed by any thing but thought. Send me word how you were like to have been surpriz'd; it may possibly be of advantage to me in this nights dear adventure. I wonder'd at the Superscription of my Letter indeed, of which *Dorilus* could give me no other account, than that you were surpriz'd, and he receiv'd it with difficulty; give me the story now, do it in charity my Angel. Besides I would imploy all thy moments, for I am jealous of every one that is not dedicated to *Silvia's Philander*.

---

[a] Diana, the virgin goddess of the moon and the hunt, was also associated with groves.
[b] One of the characteristics of the epistolary novel was this ability to describe a moment of consciousness or an action as it actually occurred.

To *Philander*.

I have receiv'd your Tablets, of which I have the Key, and heaven only knows, (for Lovers cannot unless they lov'd like *Silvia* and her *Philander*) what pains and Pantings my heart sustain'd at every thought that brought me of thy near approach; every moment I start, and am ready to faint with joy, Fear, and something not to be exprest that seizes me. To add to this, I have busied my self with dressing my Apartment up with Flowers, so that I fancy the Cermonious business of the night looks like the preparations for the dear joy of the Nuptial Bed, that too is so adorn'd and deck'd with all that's sweet and gay, all which possesses me with so ravishing and solemn a Confusion that 'tis even approaching to the most profound sadness it self. Oh *Philander*, I find I am fond of being undone, and unless you take a more than mortal care of me, I know this night some fatal mischief will befall me; what 'tis I know not, either the loss of *Philander*, my Life, or my Honour, or all together, which a discovery only of your being alone in my Apartment and at such an Hour, will most certainly draw upon us: Death is the least we must expect, by some surprise or other, my Father being rash, and extreamly jealous, and the more so of me, by how much more he is fond of me, and nothing would inrage him like the discovery of an interview like this; though you have Liberty to range the house of *Bellfont* as a Son, and are indeed at home there, but when you come by stealth; when he shall find his Son and Virgin Daughter, the Brother and the Sister so retir'd, so entertain'd.——What but death can insue, or what's worse, eternal shame? eternal confusion on my honour? What Excuse, what Evasions, Vows and Protestations will convince him, or appease *Mertila*'s Jealousy, *Mertilla* my Sister, and *Philander*'s Wife?—Oh God! that cruel thought will put me into ravings; I have a thousand streams of killing reflection that flow from that original Fountain! Curse on the Alliance that gave you a welcome to *Bellfont*. Ah *Philander*, could you not have stay'd ten short years longer? Alas you thought that was an Age in Youth, but 'tis but a day in Love: Ah could not your eager youth have led you to a thousand diversions, a thousand

49

times have baited in the long journey of life without hurrying on to the last Stage, to the last retreat, but the Grave; and to me seem as Irrecoverable as impossible to retrieve thee?——Could no kind Beauty stop thee on thy way, in charity or pity? *Philander* saw me then! and though *Mertila* was more fit for his Caresses, and I but capable to please with Childish prattle. Oh could he not have seen a promising Bloom in my Face, that might have foretold the future Conquests I was born to make? Oh was there no Prophetick Charm that could bespeak your heart, ingage it, and prevent that fatal Marriage? You say my Adorable Brother, we were destin'd from our Creation for one another; that the Decrees of Heaven, or Fate, or both, design'd us for this mutual passion: Why then, oh why did not Heaven, Fate, or Destiny, do the mighty work, when first you saw my infant Charms. But oh *Philander*, why do I vainly rave, why call in vain on time that's fled and gone; why idly wish for Ten years retribution? That will not yield a Day, an Hour, a Minute: No no, 'tis past, 'tis past and flown for ever, as distant as a thousand years to me, as irrecoverable. Oh *Philander*, what hast thou thrown away? Ten glorious years of Ravishing Youth, of unmatch'd Heavenly Beauty, on one that knew not half the value of it; *Silvia* was only born to set a Rate upon't, was alone capable of Love, such love as might deserve it: Oh why was that charming face ever laid on any bosom that knew not how to sigh and pant, and heave at every touch of so much distracting Beauty. Oh why were those dear Arms whose soft pressings that ravish where they circle, destin'd for a Body Cold and Dull, that could sleep insensibly there, and not so much as dream the while what the transporting pleasure signified, but unconcern'd receiv'd the wondrous blessings, and never knew its Price, or thank'd her stars. She has thee all the day, to gaze upon, and yet she lets thee pass her careless sight, as if there were no Miracles in view: she does not see the little Gods of Love that play eternally in thy Eyes; and since she never receiv'd a Dart from thence, believes there's no Artillery there. She plays not with thy Hair, nor Weaves her snowy fingers in thy Curles of Jett, sets it in order, or adores its Beauty: The Fool with flaxen Wigg had done as well for her; a dull white Coxcomb[a] had made as good a Property; a Husband is no more,

---

[a] A wig. A coxcomb was a fool, or a conceited man. The term derives from a pun on Cock's comb and originally described a jester's cap.

at best no more. Oh thou Charming object of my eternal wishes, why wert thou thus dispos'd? Oh save my life, and tell me what indifferent impulse oblig'd thee to these Nuptials: had *Mertila* been recommended or forc'd by the Tyranny of a Father into thy Arms, or for base Lucre thou hast chosen her, this had excus'd thy Youth and Crime; obedience or vanity I could have Pardon'd,——But oh——'Twas Love! Love my *Philander*! thy raving Love, and that which has undone thee was a Rape rather than a Marriage; you fled with her. Oh Heavens, mad to possess you stole the unloving Prise! —— Yes you lov'd her, false as you are you did, perjur'd and faithless. Lov'd her;——Hell and confusion on the World, 'twas so.——Oh *Philander* I am lost—

This Letter was found in pieces torn.

To *Monsieur* the Count of—

My Lord,
These Pieces of Paper which I have put together as well as I could, were writ by my Lady to have been sent by *Dorinda*, when on a sudden she rose in rage from her seat, tore first the Paper, and then her Robes and Hair, and indeed nothing has escap'd the violence of her Passion; nor could my Prayers or Tears retrieve them or calm her: 'tis however chang'd at last to mighty passions of weeping, in which imployment I have left her on her repose, being commanded away. I thought it my duty to give your Lordship this account, and to send the pieces of Paper, that your Lordship may guess at the occasion of the sudden storm which ever rises in that fatal quarter; but in putting 'em in order, I had like to have been surpriz'd by my Lady's Father, for my Lord the Count[a] having long solicited me for favours, and taking all opportunities of entertaining me, found me alone in my Chamber, imployed in serving your Lordship; I had only time to hide the Papers, and to get rid of him) have given him an Assignation to night in the Garden

---

[a] George Berkeley, Earl of Berkeley (1628–98).

Grove to give him the hearing to what he says he has to propose to me: Pray Heaven all things go right to your Lordships wish this Evening, for many ominous things happen'd to day. Madam, the Countess[a] had like to have taken a Letter writ for your Lordship to day; for the Dutchess of——coming to make her a visit, came on a sudden with her into my Lady's Apartment, and surpriz'd her writing in her Dressing Room, giving her only time to slip the Paper into her Comb-box. The first Ceremonies being past, as Madam the Dutchess uses not much, she fell to Commend my Lady's dressing Plate, and taking up the Box and opening it, found the Letter, and Laughing cry'd, Oh have I found you making Love? At which my Lady with an infinite confusion would have retriev'd it,—But the Dutchess not quitting her hold, Cry'd—Nay I am resolved to see in what manner you write to a Lover, and whether you have a Heart tender or cruel; at which she began to read aloud, My Lady to blush and change Colour a Hundred times in a minute; I ready to dye with fear; Madam the Countess in infinite amazement, my Lady interrupting every word the Dutchess read by Prayers and Intreaties, which heighten'd her Curiosity, and being young and airy, regarded not the Indecency, to which she prefer'd her Curiosity, who still Laughing, cry'd she was resolv'd to read it out, and know the constitution of her heart; when my Lady, whose wit never fail'd her, Cry'd, I beseech you Madam, let us have so much complisance for *Melinda* to ask her consent in this affair, and then I am pleas'd you should see what Love I can make upon occasion: I took the hint, and with a real confusion, Cry'd——I implore you Madam not to discover my weakness to Madam the Dutchess; I would not for the World——Be thought to love so passionately as your Ladyship in favour of *Alexis* has made me profess under the name of *Silvia* to *Philander*. This incourag'd my Lady, who began to say a thousand pleasant things of *Alexis*[b] *Dorillus* his Son, and my Lover as your Lordship knows, and who is no inconsiderable fortune for a Maid inrich'd only by your Lordships Bounty. My Lady after this took the Letter, and all being resolv'd it should

---

[a] Elizabeth Massingberd, who married George Berkeley in 1646. Lady Berkeley's account of the discovery of her daughter's letters is given in *The Trial of Ford Lord Grey*. Cf. Appendix I.

[b] Probably Robert Charnock, another of Grey's servants, who constantly accompanied his master to Durdans, the Berkeley family home. Cf. Appendix I.

be read, she her self did it, and turn'd it so prettily into Burlesque Love by her manner of reading it, that made Madam the Dutchess laugh extreamly; who at the end of it cry'd to my Lady — Well Madam I am satisfied you have not a heart wholly insensible of Love, that could so well express it for another. Thus they rallied on, 'till careful of my Lovers repose, the Dutchess urg'd the Letter might be immediately sent away, at which my Lady readily folding up the Letter, writ, for the constant *Alexis* on the out-side: I took it, and beg'd I might leave to retire to write it over in my own hand, they permitted me, and I carried it after sealing it to *Dorillus*, who waited for it, and wondering to find his Sons name on it, Cry'd—Mistress *Melinda*, I doubt you have mistook my present business, I wait for a Letter from my Lady to my Lord, and you give me one from your self to my Son *Alexis*; 'twill be very welcome to *Alexis* I confess, but at this time I had rather oblige my Lord than my Son; I Laughing, reply'd he was mistaken, that *Alexis* at this time meant no other than my Lord, which pleas'd the good man extreamly, who thought it a good omen for his Son, and so went his way satisfy'd; as every body was except the Countess, who fancy'd something more in it than my Lady's inditing for me; and after Madam the Dutchess was gone she went ruminating and pensive to her Chamber, from whence I am confident she will not depart to night, and will possible set Spies in every corner; at least 'tis good to fear the worst, that we may prevent all things that would hinder this nights assignation: As soon as the Coast is clear, I'll wait on your Lordship, and be your Conductor, and in all things else am ready to show my self,

My Lord,

Your Lordships most humble

and most obedient Servant,

MELINDA.

Silvia has order to wait on your Lordship as soon as all is clear.

To *Melinda*.

Oh *Melinda*, what have you told me? Stay me with an immediate account of the recovery and calmness of my Adorable weeping *Silvia*, or I shall enter *Belfont* with my Sword drawn, bearing down all before me 'till I make my way to my Charming Mourner: Oh God! *Silvia* in a rage! *Silvia* in any Passion but that of Love? I cannot bear it, no by Heaven I cannot; I shall do some outrage either on my self or at *Bellfont*. Oh thou dear Advocate of my tenderest Wishes, thou Confident of my never dying flame, thou kind administring Maid, send some relief to my breaking heart—Hast and tell me, *Silvia* is calm, that her bright Eyes sparkle with smiles, or if they languish, say 'tis with Love, with expecting joys; that her dear hands are no more imployed in exercises too rough and unbecoming their native softness. Oh eternal God! taring perhaps her Divine Hair, brighter than the Suns reflecting Beams, injuring the heavenly Beauty of her Charming Face and Bosom, the joy and wish of all Mankind that look upon her: Oh charm her with Prayers and Tears, stop her dear Fingers from the rude assaults, bind her fair hands: Repeat *Philander* to her, tell her he's fainting with the news of her unkindness and outrage on her lovely self, but tell her too, I dye adoring her; tell her I rave, I tear, I curse my self,—For so I do; tell her I would break out into a violence that should set all *Bellfont* in a flame, but for my care of her. Heaven and Earth should not restrain me,—No, they should not,--But her least frown should still me, tame me, and make me a calm Coward: say this, say all, say any thing to charm her rage and tears. Oh I am mad, stark mad, and ready to run on that frantick business I dye to think her guilty of: tell her how 'twould grieve her to see mee torn and mangled; to see that hair she loves ruffl'd and diminisht by rage, violated by my insupportable grief, my self quite bereft of all sense but that of Love, but that of Adoration for my charming, cruel, Insensible, who is possest with every thought, with every imagination that can render me unhapy, born away with every fancy that is in disfavour of the wretched *Philander*. Oh *Melinda*, write immediately, or you will behold me enter a most deplorable object of Pity.

When I receiv'd yours, I fell into such a passion that I forc'd my self back to *Dorillus* his House, lest my transports had hurry'd me to *Bellfont*, where I should have undone all: but as I can rest no where, I am now returning to the Meadow again, where I will expect your aid or dye.

From Dorillus *his Cottage,*
almost nine a Clock.

To *Philander*.

I must own my Charming *Philander*, that my Love is now arriv'd to that excess, that every thought which before but discompos'd me, now puts me into a violence of rage unbecoming my Sex; or any thing but the mighty occasion of it, Love, and which only had power to calm what it had before ruffled into a destructive storm; but like the anger'd Sea, which pants and heaves and retains still an uneasie motion long after the rude winds are appeas'd and hush'd to silence. My heart beats still, and heaves with the sensible remains of the late dangerous tempest of my mind, and nothing can absolutely calm me but the approach of the all-powerful *Philander*; though that thought possesses me with ten thousand fears, which I know will vanish all at thy appearance, and assume no more their dreadful shapes till thou art gone again: bring me then that kind cessation, bring me my *Lysander* and set me above the thoughts of Cares, Frights or any other thoughts but those of tender Love: hast then thou charming object of my eternal wishes, of my new desires, hast to my Arms, my Eyes, my Soul,——But oh be wondrous careful there, do not betray the easie Maid that trusts thee amidst all her sacred store.

'Tis almost dark, and my Mother is retir'd to her Chamber, my Father to his Cabinet, and has left all that Apartment next the Garden wholly without Spies. I have by trusty *Silvia* sent you a Key *Melinda* got made to the Door, which leads from the Garden to the back-Stairs to my Apartment, so carefully lock'd, and the original Key so closely guarded by my jealous Father: that way I beg you to come, a way but too well known to *Lysander*, and by which he has made many an escape to and

55

from *Mertilla*. Oh Damn that thought, what makes it torturing me,——Let me change it for those of *Lysander*, the advantage will be as great as bartering Hell for Heaven; haste then *Lysander*: But what need I bid thee, Love will lend thee his Wings, thou who commandest all his Artillery, put 'em on, and fly to thy Languishing.

SILVIA

O I faint with the dear
thought of thy Approach.

To the Charming Silvia

With much ado, with many a Sigh a panting heart, and many a Languishing look back towards happy *Bellfont*, I have recover'd *Dorillus* his Farm, where I threw me on a Bed, and lay without motion, and almost without life for two hours; 'till at last through all my Sighs, my great Concern, my Torment, my Love and Rage broke silence, and burst into all the different complaints both soft and mad by turns, that ever possest a soul extravagantly seiz'd with frantick Love, Ah *Silvia*, what did I not say? How did I not Curse, and who, except my Charming Maid? For yet my *Silvia* is a Maid; Yes, yes, ye Envying Power she is, and yet the sacred and inestimable treasure was offer'd a trembling victim to the o'rejoy'd and fancy'd Deity, for then and there, I thought my self happier than a triumphing God, but having overcome all difficulties, all the fatigues and toyles of Loves long Sieges, Vanquisht the mighty Fantôm of the fair, the Giant Honour, and routed all the numerous Host of Womens little Reasonings, past all the bounds of peevish Modesty: Nay even all the loose and silken Counterscarps^a that fenc'd the sacred Fort, and nothing stop'd my glorious pursuit: Then, then ye Gods, just then by an over transport, to fall just fainting before the surrendering Gates, unable to receive the

---

^a Outer wall or slope of a ditch in a fortification.

yielding treasure! Oh *Silvia*! what *Demon*, malicious at my Glory, seiz'd my vigor? What God, envious of my mighty joy, render'd me ashameful object of his Raillery? Snatcht my till then) never failing power, and left me dying on thy Charming Bosom. Heavens, how I lay! Silent with wonder, rage and extasy of Love, unable to complain, or rail or storm, or seek for ease but with my sighs alone, which made up all my breath; my mad desires remain'd, but all unactive as Age or Death it self, as cold and feeble, as unfit for joy, as if my Youthful fire had long been past, or *Silvia* had never been blest with Charms. Tell me thou wondrous perfect Creature, tell me, where lay the hidden Witchcraft? Was *Silvia's* Beauty too Divine to mix with Mortal Joys? Ah no, 'twas Ravishing but Humane all. Yet sure 'twas so approaching to Divinity, as chang'd my Fire to Awfull Adoration, and all my wanton heat to reverend Contemplation.—But this is nonsense all, 'twas something more that gave me rage, despair and torments insupportable: No, 'twas no dull Devotion, tame Divinity, but mortal killing Agony, unlucky disappointment, unnatural impotence. Oh I am lost, enchanted by some Magick Spell: Oh what can *Silvia* say? What can she think of my fond passion? She'll swear 'tis all a cheat, I had it not. No, it could not be, such Tales I've often heard, as often laught at too; of disappointed Lovers; wou'd *Silvia* wou'd believe (as sure she may) mine was excess of Passion: What! my *Silvia*! being arriv'd to all the joy of Love, just come to reap the glorious recompence, the full reward, the Heaven for all my sufferings, do I lye grazing only and no more? A dull, a feeble unconcern'd Admirer: Oh my eternal shame!——Curse on my Youth, give me ye Powers Old Age, for that has some excuse, but Youth has none: 'tis Dullness, Stupid Insensibility: Where shall I hide my head, when this lewd Story's told? When it shall be confirm'd, *Philander* the Young the Brisk and Gay *Philander*, who never fail'd the Woman he scarce wisht for; never bauk'd the Amorous conceated Old, nor the ill-favour'd Young; yet when he had extended in his Arms the Young, the Charming Fair and Longing *Silvia*, the untouch'd, unspotted, and till then unwishing Lovely Maid, yielded, defenceless and unguarded all, he wanted power to seize the trembling Prey: Defend me Heaven from Madness. Oh *Silvia*, I have reflected on all the little circumstances that might occasion this disaster, and damn me to this degree of coldness, but I can fix on none: I had 'tis true for *Silvia's* sake some apprehensions of fear of being surpriz'd, for

coming through the Garden, I saw at the farther end a man, at
least I fancy'd by that light it was a man, who perceiving the
glimps of something approach from the Grove made softly
towards me, but with such caution as if he fear'd to be mistaken
in the person, as much as I was to approach him: and reminding what *Melinda* told me of an assignation she had made to
Monsieur the Count—Imagin'd it him; nor was I mistaken when
I heard his voice calling in low tone—*Melinda*.—At which I
mended my pace, and e're he got half way the Garden recover'd the Door, and softly unlocking it, got in unperceiv'd
and fasten'd it after me, well enough assur'd that he saw not
which way I vanisht: however it fail'd not to alarm me with
some fears on your dear account, that disturb'd my repose, and
which I thought then not necessary to impart to you, and which
indeed all vanisht at the sight of my Adorable Maid: When
entering thy Apartment, I beheld thee extended on a Bed of
Roses, in Garments which, if possible, by their wanton loose
negligence and gaiety augmented thy natural Charms: I trembling fell on my Knees by your Bed-side, and gaz'd a while,
unable to speak for transports of joy and love: You too were
silent, and remain'd so, so long that I ventur'd to press your
Lips with mine, which all their eager kisses could not put in
motion, so that I fear'd you fainted; a sudden fright that in a
moment chang'd my Feaver of Love into a cold Ague fit; but
you reviv'd me with a Sigh again, and fired me anew, by
pressing my hand, and from that silent soft incouragement, I by
degrees ravisht a thousand Blisses; yet still between your tempting charming kisses, you would cry—Oh my *Philander* do not
injure me,—Be sure you press me not to the last joys of Love;——
Oh have a care or I am undone for ever; restrain your roving
hands,—Oh whither would they wander,——My Soul, my joy,
my everlasting Charmer, Oh whither would you go.——Thus
with a Thousand Cautions more, which did but raise what you
design'd to calm, you made me but the madder to possess: not
all the Vows you bad me call to mind, could now restrain my
wild and head-strong passion; my raving raging (but my soft)
desire: No *Silvia*, No, it was not in the power of feeble flesh and
blood to find resistance against so many Charms; yet still you
made me swear, still I protested, but still burnt on with the
same torturing flame, till the vast pleasure even became a pain:
To add to this, I saw (Yes *Silvia* not all your Art and Modesty
could hide it) I saw the Ravishing Maid as much inflam'd as I;

she burnt with equal fire, with equal Languishment: Not all her care could keep the Sparks concealed, but it broke out in every word and look; her trembling tongue, her feeble fainting voice betray'd it all, sighs interrupting every syllable; a Languishment I never saw till then dwelt in her Charming Eyes, that contradicted all her little Vows; her short and double breathings heav'd her Breast, her swelling snowy breast, her hands that grasp'd me trembling as they clos'd, while she permitted mine unknown, unheeded to traverse all her Beauties, till quite forgetting all I'd faintly promised, and wholly abandoning my soul to joy, I rusht upon her, who all fainting lay beneath my useless weight, for on a sudden all my power was fled swifter than Lightning hurryed through my infeebled veins, and vanisht all: Not the dear lovely Beauty which I prest, the Dying Charms of that fair face and eyes, the Clasps of those soft Arms, nor the bewitching accent of her voice that murmur'd Love half smother'd in her Sighs, nor all my Love, my vast, my mighty passion, could call my fugitive vigor back again: Oh no, the more I look—The more I touch'd and saw,[a] the more I was undone. Oh pity me my too too lovely Maid, do not revile the faults which you alone create. Consider all your Charms at once expos'd, consider every sense about me ravisht, o'recome with joys too mighty to be supported: No wonder if I fell a shameful sacrifice to the fond Deity, consider how I waited, how I strove, and still burnt on and every tender touch still added fuel to the vigorous Fire; which by your delay consum'd it self in burning. I want Philosophy to make this out, or faith to fix my unhappiness on any chance or natural accident, but this my Charming *Silvia* I am sure, that had I lov'd you less, I'd been less wretched: Nor had we parted *Silvia* on so ill terms, nor had I left you with an opinion so disadvantageous for *Philander*, but for that unhappy noise at your Chamber door, which alarming your fear, occasion'd your recovery from that dear trance, to which Love and soft desire had reduc'd you and me from the most tormenting silent Agony that disappointed joy ever possest a fond expecting heart with. Oh Heavens to have my *Silvia* in my power, Favour'd by silence, night, and safe retreat! then,

---

[a] Cf. Behn's poem on impotence, 'The Disappointment': 'He saw how at her Length she lay, / He saw her rising Bosom bare; / Her loose thin Robes, through which appear / A shape design'd for Love and Play; / ... / A Victim to Loves Sacred Flame; / While the o'er-Ravish'd Shepherd lies / Unable to perform the Sacrifice.' [*Works of Aphra Behn*, Vol. 1, no. 28, ll.61–70]

then, to lye a tame cold sigher only, as if my *Silvia* gave that Assignation alone by stealth, undrest, all loose and languishing, fit for the mighty business of the Night, only to hear me prattle, see me gaze, or tell her what a pretty sight it was to see the Moon shine through the dancing Boughs. O Damn my harden'd dullness,——But no more,——I am all fire and madness at the thought,——But I was saying, *Silvia*, we both recover'd then when the noise alarm'd us. I long to know whether you think we were betray'd, for on that knowledge rests a mighty part of my destiny, I hope we are not, by an accident that befell me at my going away, which (but for my untimely force of leaving my lovely *Silvia*, which gave me pains insupportable) would have given me great diversion. You know our fear of being discover'd occasioned my disguise, for you found it necessary I should depart, your fear had so prevail'd, and that in *Melinda's* Night Gown and Head dress; thus attir'd with much ado, I went and left my soul behind me, and finding no body all along the Gallery, nor in my passage from your apartment into the Garden, I was a thousand times about to return to all my joys; when in the midst of this almost ended dispute, I saw by the light of the Moon (which was by good fortune under a Cloud and could not distinctly direct the sight) a man taking towards me with cautious speed, which made me advance with the more haste to recover the Grove, believing to have escap'd him under the Covert of the Trees; for retreat I could not without betraying which way I went; but just at the entrance of the Thicket, he turning short made up to me, and I perceiv'd it *Monsieur* the Count, who taking me for *Melinda* who it seems he expected, caught hold of my Gown as I would have pass'd him, and Cry'd, Now *Melinda* I see you are a Maid of Honour,—Come retire with me into the Grove where I have a present of a heart and something else to make you, that will be of more advantage to you than that of *Alexis* though something younger.——I all confounded knew not what to reply, nor how, lest he should find his mistake, at least if he he discover'd not who I was: Which silence gave him occasion to go on, which he did in this manner; What not a word *Melinda*, or do you design I shall take your silence for consent? If so, come my pretty Creature, let us not lose the hour Love has given us; at this he would have advanc'd, leading me by the hand which he prest and kist very amorously: Judg my Adorable *Silvia* in what a fine condition your *Philander* was then in. What should I do?

to go had disappointed him worse than I was with thee before; not to go, betray'd me: I had much ado to hold my Countenance, and unwilling to speak, while I was thus imployed in thought, *Monsieur*——Pulling me (eager of joys to come,) and I holding back, he stop'd and cry'd, sure *Melinda* you came not hither to bring me a Denial. I then reply'd whispering,—— Softly, Sir for Heavens sake (sweetning my voice as much as possible) consider I'm a Maid, and would not be discover'd for the world. Who can discover us? reply'd my Lover, what I take from thee shall never be mist, not by *Alexis* himself upon thy Wedding Night;—Come——Sweet Child come:——With that I pull'd back and whisper'd—Heavens, would you make a Mistress of me?——Says he——A Mistress what wouldst thou be a Cherubin? Then I reply'd as before— I am no Whore, Sir,—— No crys he, but I can quickly make thee one, I have my Tools about me Sweet-heart, therefore let's lose no time but fall to work: this last raillery from the brisk old Gentleman had in spight of resolution almost made me burst out into loud Laughter, when he took more gravity upon him, and cry'd——Come, come *Melinda*, why all this foolish argument at this hour in this place, and after so much serious Courtship, believe me I'l be kind to thee for ever; with that he clapt fifty Guinnies in a Purse into one hand, and something else that shall be nameless into the other, presents that had both been worth *Melinda's* acceptance: All this while was I studying an evasion, at last to shorten my pleasant adventure, looking round, I cry'd softly, are you sure, Sir, we are safe—For Heavens sake step towards the Garden door and see, for I would not be discover'd for the world,—Nor I cry'd he——But do not fear, all's safe:—— However see (whisper'd I) that my fear may not disturb your joys. With that he went toward the House, and I slipping into the Grove got immediately into the Meadow, where *Alexis* waited my coming with *Brilljard*, so I left the expecting Lover I suppose ranging the Grove for his fled Nimph, and I doubt will fall heavy on poor *Melinda*, who shall have the Guinneys either to restore or keep as she and the angry Count can agree: I leave the management of it to her wit and conduct.

This account I thought necessary to give my Charmer, that she might prepare *Melinda* for the assault, who understanding all that passed between us, may so dispose of matters, that no discovery may happen by mistake, and I know my *Silvia* and she can find a thousand excuses for the suppos'd *Melinda's* flight. But my Adorable Maid, my business here was not to give an account of my Adventure only, nor of my ravings, but to tell my *Silvia* on what my life depends; which is, in a permission to wait on her again this insuing night; make no excuse, for if you do, by all I adore in Heaven and Earth, I'll end my life here where I receiv'd it. I'll say no more, nor give your Love instructions, but wait impatiently here the Life or Death of your

PHILANDER.[a]

'Tis Six a Clock, and yet my eys have not clos'd themselves to sleep: Alexis *and* Brilljard *give me hopes of a kind return to this, and have brought their Flute and Violin to charm me into a slumber: If* Silvia *love, as I am sure she does, she'll wake me with a dear consent to see me, if not, I only wake to sleep for ever.*

To my fair Charmer.

When I had seal'd the inclos'd, my Page whom I had order'd to come to me with an account of any business extraordinary, is this Morning arriv'd with a Letter from *Cesario*, which I have sent here inclos'd, that my *Silvia* may see how little I regard the world, or the mighty revolution in hand; when set in competition with the least hope of beholding her adorable face, or hearing her Charming Tongue when it whispers the soft dictates of her tender heart into my ravish'd soul; one moments joy like that surmounts an age of dull Empire. No, let the busy unregarded Rout perish, the Cause fall or stand alone for me: Give me but Love, Love and my *Silvia*; I ask no more of Heaven; to which vast joy could you but imagine (Oh wondrous Miracle of Beauty!) how poor and little I esteem the valued trifles of the world, you would in return contemn your part of it, and live with me in silent Shades for ever. Oh! *Silvia*, what hast thou this night to add to the Soul of thy

PHILANDER!

---

[a] In the first edition of *Love-Letters* this letter is signed *Lysander*, a name Behn uses frequently in other works, most notably in her poem 'The Disappointment'.

To the Count of——

I'le allow you, my Dear, to be very fond of so much Beauty as the world must own adorns the Lovely *Silvia*: I'll permit Love too to Rival me in your heart, but not out-rival Glory; hast then my Dear to the advance of that, make no delay, but with the Mornings dawne, let me find you in my Arms, where I have something that will surprize you to relate to you: You were last night expected at——It behoves you to give no Umbrage to Persons who's Interest renders 'em enough jealous. We have two new Advancers come in of Youth and Money, teach 'em not negligence; be careful and let nothing hinder you from taking Horse immediately, as you value the repose and fortune of

> My Dear,

> Your CESARIO.

I call'd last night on you, and your Page following me to my Coach, whisper'd me—if I had any earnest business with you, he knew where to find you; I soon imagin'd where, and bid him call within an hour for this, and post with it immediately, though dark.

To *Philander*.

Ah! what have I done *Philander*, and where shall I hide my guilty blushing face? Thou hast undone my eternal quiet, Oh thou hast ruin'd my everlasting repose, and I must never, never look abroad again: Curse on my face that first debauch'd my Vertue, and taught thee how to Love! Curse on my tempting youth, my shape, my Air, my Eyes, my Voice, my Hands, and every charm that did contribute to my fatal love, a lasting Curse on all—But those of the adorable *Philander*, and those—even in

63

this raging Minute, my furious passion dares not approach with an indecent thought: No, they are sacred all, Madness it self would spare 'em, and shouldst thou now behold me as I sit, my Hair dishevel'd, Ruffl'd and disorder'd, my Eyes bedewing every word I write, when for each Letter I let fall a tear; then (prest with thought) starting, I dropt my Pen, and fall to rave anew, and tear those Garments whose loose negligence help'd to betray me to my shameful ruine, wounding my breast, but want the resolution to wound it as I ought; which when I but propose, Love stays the thought, raging and wild as 'tis, the Conqueror checks it, with whispering only *Philander* to my soul; the dear Name calmes me to an easiness, gives me the Pen into my trembling hand, and I pursue my silent soft complaint: Oh! shouldst thou see me thus, in all these sudden different change of Passions, thou wouldst say *Philander* I were mad indeed; Madness it self can find no stranger motions: And I would calmly ask thee, for I am calm again, how comes it my adorable *Philander*, that thou canst possess a Maid with so much Madness? who art thy self a miracle of softness, all sweet and all serene, the most of Angel in thy composition that ever mingled with humanity; the very words fall so gently from thy tongue, are utter'd with a Voice so ravishingly soft, a tone so tender and so full of Love, 'twould charm even frenzy, calm rude distraction, and wildness wou'd become a silent Listener; there's such a sweet serenity in thy face, such innocence and softness in thy eyes, should desart Savages, but gaze on thee, sure they would forget their native forest wildness, and be inspir'd with easy Gentleness: Most certainly this God-like power thou hast. Why then? Oh tell me in the Agony of my soul, why must those charms that bring Tranquility and peace to all, make me alone a wild, unseemly raver? Why has it contrary effects on me? Oh! all I act and say is perfect madness: Yet this is the least un-accountable part of my most wretched Story;——Oh! I must ner'e behold thy Lovely face again, for if I should, sure I should blush my soul away, no, no, I must not, nor ever more believe thy dear deluding Vows: Never thy charming perjur'd Oaths, after a violation like to this. Oh Heaven, what have I done? Yet by that Heaven I swear I dare not ask my soul, lest it inform me how I was to blame, unless that fatal Minute would instruct me how to revenge my wrongs upon my heart, my fond betraying heart,——Despair and Madness seize me; darkness and horror hide me from humane sight, after an easiness like this;——

What to yield,——To yield my Honour! Betray the secrets of my Virgin wishes——My new desires; my unknown shameful fame,——Hell and Death! Where got I so much confidence? Where learnt the harden'd and unblushing folly? To wish was such a fault, as is a crime unpardonable to own, to shew desire is such a sin in vertue as must deserve reproach from all the world; but I, unlucky I, have not only betray'd all these, but with a transport void of sense and shame, I yield to thy Armes,——I'll not indure the thought,——By Heaven! I cannot; there's something more than rage that animates that thought: some Magick Spell that in the midst of all my sense of Shame keeps me from true repentance; this angers me, and makes me know my Honour but a fantom: Now I could curse again my Youth and Love; but Oh! when I have done, alas *Philander*, I find my self as guilty as before; I cannot make one firm resolve against thee, or if I do, when I consider thee, they weigh not all one lovely Hair of thine. 'Tis all in vain the Charming Cause remains *Philander*'s still as lovely as before, 'tis him I must remove from my fond Eyes and heart, him I must banish from my touch, my smell, and every other sense, by Heaven! I cannot bear the mighty pressure, I cannot see his Eyes, and touch his Hands, smell the perfume every Pore of his breaths forth, tast thy soft kisses, hear thy Charming Voice, but I am all on flame: No, 'tis these I must exclaim on, not my Youth, 'tis they debauch my soul, no natural propensity in me to yield, or to admit of such destructive fires. Fain I would put it off, but 'twill not do, I am the Aggressor still; else, why is not every living Maid undone, that does not touch or see thee? Tell me why? No, the fault's in me, and thou art innocent.——Were but my Soul less delicate, were it less sensible of what it loves and likes in thee, I yet were dully happy; but Oh there is a nicety there so charm'd, so apprehensive of thy Beauties, as has betray'd me to unrest for ever:——Yet something I will do to tame this lewd Betrayer of my right, and it shall plead no more in thy behalf, no more, no more disperse the joys which it conceives through every Vein, (cold and insensible by nature) to kindle new desires there.——No more shall fill me with unknown curiosity; no, I will in spight of all the Perfumes that dwell about thee, in spight of all the Arts thou hast of Looking, of Speaking and of Touching, I will I say assume my native temper, I will be calm, be cold, and unconcern'd, as I have been to all the world,——But to *Philander*,——The Almighty Power he has is unaccountable;——By yonder breaking day that opens in the East, opens to see my shame,——I swear——By that great ruler of the day, the Sun, by that Almighty power that rules them both I swear——I swear *Philander*, Charming Lovely Youth! Thou art the first e're kindl'd soft desires about my soul, thou art the first that ever did inform me that there was such a sort of wish about me. I thought the vanity of being belov'd, made up the greatest part of the satisfaction, 'twas joy to see my Lovers sigh about me, adore and praise me, and increase my Pride by every look, by every word and action; and him I fancy'd best I favour'd most, and he past the happy fortune, him I have suffer'd too, to kiss and press me, to tell me all his Tale of Love, and sigh, which I would listen to with Pride and Pleasure, permitted it, and smil'd him kind returns; nay, by my life, then thought I lov'd him too, thought I could have been content to have past my life at this gay rate, with this fond hoping Lover, and thought no farther than of being great, having rich Coaches, showing Equipage, to pass my hours in dressing, in going to the Operas and the Tower, make Visits where I list, be seen at Balls; and having still the vanity to think the men would Gaze and Languish where I came, and all the Women envy me, I thought no farther on——But thou *Philander* hast made me take new measures, I now can think of nothing but of thee, I loath the sound of Love from any other voice, and Conversation makes my soul impatient, and does not only dull me into Melancholly, but perplexes me out of all humour, out of all patient sufferance, and I am never so well pleas'd when from *Philander*, as when I am retir'd, and curse my Character and Figure in the world, because it permits me not to prevent being visited, one thought of thee, is worth the worlds injoyment, I hate to dress, I hate to be agreable to any Eyes but thine; I hate the noise of Equipage and Crowds, and would be more content to live with thee in some lone shaded Cottage, than be a Queen, and hinder'd by that Grandure one moments conversation with *Philander*: Maist thou despise and loath me, a Curse the greatest that I can invent, if this be any thing but real honest truth. No, no *Philander*, I find I never lov'd till now, I understood it not, nor knew not what those Sighs and Pressings meant which others gave me; yet every speaking glance thy Eyes put on inform my soul what 'tis they plead and languish for: If you but touch my hand, my breath grows faint and short, my blood glows in my face, and runs with an unusual warmth through every vein, and tells my heart what 'tis *Philander* ailes, when he falls sighing on my Bosom; oh then I fear, I answer every look, and every sigh and touch, in the same silent but intelligible Language, and understood I fear too well by thee: 'Till now I never fear'd Love as a Criminal. Oh tell me not mistaken Foolish Maids, true Love is innocent, ye cold, ye dull, ye unconsidering Lovers; though I have often heard it from the Grave and Wise, and preacht my self that Doctrine: I now renounce it all, 'tis false, by Heaven! 'tis false, for now I Love, and know it all a fiction; yes, and love so, as never any Woman can equal me in Love, my soul being all compos'd (as I have often said) of softer Materials. Nor is it fancy sets my Rates on Beauty, there's an intrinsick value in thy Charms, which surely none but I am able to understand, and to those that view thee not with my judging Eyes, ugliness fancy'd wou'd appear the same, and please as well. If all could love or judge like me, why does *Philander* pass so unregarded by a thousand Women, who never sigh'd for him? What makes *Mertilla* who possesses all, looks on thee, feels thy Kisses, hears thee speak, and yet wants sense to know how blest she is; 'tis want of judgment all, and how, and how can she that judges ill, Love well?

Granting my passion equal to its object; you must allow it infinite, and more in me than any other Woman, by how much more my Soul is compos'd of tenderness; and yet I say I own, for I may own it, now Heaven and you are Witness of my shame, I own with all this love, with all this passion, so vast, so true and so unchangeable, that I have Wishes, new unwonted Wishes; at every thought of thee, I find a strange disorder in my blood, that pants and burns in every Vein, and makes me blush, and sigh, and grows impatient, asham'd and angry; but when I know it the effects of Love, I'm reconcil'd, and wish and sigh anew, but when I sit and Gaze upon thy Eyes, thy Languishing thy Lovely dying Eyes; play with thy soft white hand, and lay my glowing Cheek to thine.—Oh God! What Language can express my transport, all that is tender, all that is soft desire seizes every trembling Limb, and 'tis with pain conceal'd.— Yes, yes *Philander*, 'tis the fatal truth, since thou hast found it, I confess it too, and yet I love thee dearly; long, long it was that I essay'd to hide the guilty flame, if Love be guilt; for I confess I did dissemble a coldness which I was not Mistress of: there lyes a Womans Art, there all her boasted Vertue, it is but well dissembling, and no more.—But mine alas is gone, for ever fled; this, this feable guard that should secure my Honour, thou hast betray'd and left it quite defenceless. Ah what's a Womans Honour when 'tis so poorly guarded: No wonder that you conquer with such ease, when we are only safe by the mean arts of base dissimulation, an ill as shameful as that to which we fall. Oh silly refuge! What foolish nonsence, fond custom can perswade; yet so it is, and she that breaks her Laws, loses her fame, her honour and esteem. Oh Heavens! how quickly lost it is! Give me ye Powers, my fame, and let me be a fool; let me retain my vertue and my Honour, and be a dull insensible——But Oh where is it? I have lost it all; 'tis irrecoverably lost: yes, yes, ye charming perjur'd man, 'tis gone, and thou hast quite undone me.——

What though I lay extended on my Bed, undrest, unapprehensive of my fate, my Bosom loose and easie of excess, my Garments ready, thin, and wantonly put on, as if they would with little force submit to the fond straying hand: What then *Philander*, must you take the advantage? Must you be perjur'd because I was tempting? 'Tis true, I let you in by stealth by night, whose silent darkness favour'd your Treachery; but Oh *Philander* were not your Vows as binding by a glimmering Taper, as if the Sun with all his Awful light had been a looker on, I urg'd your Vows as you prest on,——But Oh I fear it was in such a way so faintly and so feebly I upbraided you, as did but more advance your perjuries. Your strength encreas'd, but mine alas declin'd; till I quite fainted in your Arms, left you triumphant Lord of all: No more my faint denials do perswade, no more my trembling hands resist your force, unguarded lay the treasure which you toil'd for, betray'd and yielded to the Lovely Conqueror.——But Oh tormenting,——When you saw the store, and found the Prise no richer, with what contempt, (yes, false dear man.) with what contempt you view'd the unvalu'd Trophy: What! despis'd, was all you call a Heaven of Joy and Beauty expos'd to view, and then neglected? Were all your Prayers heard, your wishes granted, and your toiles rewarded, the trembling Victim ready for the sacrifice, and did you want Devotion to perform it, and did you thus receive the expected blessing——Oh——By Heaven I'll never see the more, and 'twill be charity to thee, for thou hast no excuse in store that can convince my opinion that I am hated, loath'd,——
—I cannot bear that thought,——Or if I do, it shall only serve to fortify my fixt resolve never to see thee more,——And yet I long

to hear thy false excuse, let it be quickly then; 'tis my disdain invites thee——To strengthen which, there needs no more than that you let me hear thy poor defence.——But 'tis a tedious time to that slow hour wherein I dare permit thee, but hope not to incline my soul to love: No I'm yet safe if I can stop but here, but here be wise resolve and be my self.

SILVIA

To *Philander*.

As my Page was coming with the inclos'd he met *Alexis* at the gate with yours, and who would not depart without an answer to it;——to go or stay is the Question. Ah, *Philander*! why do you press a heart too ready to yield to Love and you! alas, I fear you guess too well my answer, and your own Soul might save me the blushing trouble of a reply. I am plung'd in past hope of a retreat, and since my fate has pointed me out for ruine, I cannot fall more gloriously. Take then, *Philander*, to your dear Arms a Maid that can no longer resist, who is disarm'd of all defensive power: She yields, she yields, and does confess it too; and sure she must be more than mortal that can hold out against thy charms and vows. Since I must be undone and give all away, I'll do it generously, and scorn all mean reserves: I will be brave in Love, and lavish all; nor shall *Philander* think I Love him well unless I do. Take, charming Victor, then, what your own merits, and what Love has given you, take, take at last the dear reward of all your sighs and tears, your vows and sufferings. But since, *Philander*, 'tis an Age to night, and till the approach of those dear silent hours, thou knowst I dare not give thee admittance: I do conjure thee go to *Cesario*, whom I find too pressing, not to believe the concerns great; and so jealous I am of thy dear safety, that every thing alarms my fears; oh! satisfie 'em then and go, 'tis early yet, and if you take horse immediately, you will be there by eight this morning; go, I conjure you; for though 'tis an unspeakable satisfaction to know you are so near me, yet I prefer your safety and honour to all considerations else. You may soon dispatch your affairs, and render your self time enough on the place appointed, which is where you last night waited, and 'twill be at least eight at night before 'tis possible to bring you to my arms. Come in your Chariot, and do not heat your self with riding; have a care of me and my life in the preservation of all I love. Be sure you go, and do not, my *Philander*, out of a punctilio[a] of Love, neglect your dear safety——Go then, *Philander*, and all the Gods of Love preserve and attend thee on thy way, and bring thee safely back to

Silvia.

To *Silvia*

Oh, thou most charming of the Sex! thou lovely dear delight of my transported Soul! thou everlasting treasure of my heart! what hast thou done? given me an over joy, that fails but very little of performing what griefs excess had almost finish'd before: Eternal blessings on thee, for a goodness so divine, Oh, thou most excellent and dearest of thy sex! I know not what to do or what to say. I am not what I was, I do not speak, nor walk, nor think as I was wont to do; sure the excess of joy is far above dull sense, or formal thinking, it cannot stay for ceremonious method. I rave with pleasure, rage with the dear thought of coming extasie. Oh *Silvia*, *Silvia*, *Silvia*! my soul, my vital bloud, and without which I could as well subsist——Oh, my adorable, my *Silvia*! methinks I press thee, kiss thee, hear thee sigh, behold thy eyes, and all the wondrous beauty of thy face; a solemn joy has spread it self through every vein, through every sensible artery of my heart, and I can think of nothing but of *Silvia*, the lovely *Silvia*, the blooming flowing *Silvia*; and shall I see thee? shall I touch thy hands, and press thy dear, thy charming body in my arms, and taste a Thousand joys, a thousand ravishments? oh God! shall I? oh *Silvia*, say; but thou hast said enough to make me mad, and I forgetting of thy safety and my own, shall bring thy wild adoring slave to *Bellfont*, and throw him at thy feet, to pay his humble gratitude for this great condescention, this vast bounty.

---

[a] A delicate point of honour or ceremony.

Ah, *Silvia!* how shall I live till night? and you impose too cruelly upon me in conjuring me to go to *Cesario*; alas! does *Silvia* know to what she exposes her *Philander?* whose joy is so transporting great, that when he comes into the grave Cabal he must betray the story of his heart, and in lieu of the mighty business there in hand be raving still on *Silvia*, telling his joy to all the amazed listeners, and answering questions that concern our great affair, with something of my love; all which will pass for madness and undoe me: no, give me leave to rave in silence, and unseen among the trees, they'll humour my disease, answer my murmuring joy, and Echo's flatter it, repeat thy name, repeat that *Silvia's* mine! and never hurt her fame, while the Cabals, business and noisie Town will add confusion to my present transport, and make me mad indeed: no, let me alone, thou sacred lovely creature, let me be calm and quiet here, and tell all the insensibles I meet in the woods what *Silvia* has this happy minute destin'd me: Oh, let me record it on every bark, on every Oak and Beech, that all the world may wonder at my fortune, and bless the generous maid; let it grow up to Ages that shall come, that they may know the story of our loves, and how a happy youth, they call'd *Philander*, was once so blest by Heaven as to possess the charming, the ador'd and lov'd by all, the glorious *Silvia!* a Maid, the most divine that ever grac'd a story; and when the Nymphs would look for an example of love and constancy, let them point out *Philander* to their doubted Swains, and cry, ah! love but as the young *Philander* did, and then be fortunate, and then reap all your wishes: and when the Shepherd would upbraid his Nymph, let him but cry,——see here what *Silvia* did to save the young *Philander*; but oh! there never will be such another Nymph as *Silvia*; Heaven form'd but one to shew the world what Angels are, and she was form'd for me, yes she was——in whom I wou'd not quit my glorious interest to reign a monarch here, or any boasted gilded thing above! take all, take all, ye Gods, and give me but this happy coming night! Oh, *Silvia, Silvia!* by all thy promis'd joys I am undone if any accident should ravish this night from me: this night! no not for a lease of years to all eternity would I throw thee away: Oh! I am all flame, all joyfull fire and softness; methinks 'tis Heaven wheree'er I look around me, air where I tread, and ravishing Musick when I speak, because 'tis all of *Silvia*——let me alone, oh let me cool a little, or I shall by a too excess of joyfull thought lose all my hop'd for bliss. Remove a little from me, go, my *Silvia*, you're so excessive sweet, so wondrous dazling, you press my senses even to pain—— away——let me take air——let me recover breath: oh let me lay me down beneath some cooling shade, near some refreshing crystal murmuring spring, and fan the gentle air about me. I suffocate, I faint, with this close loving, I must allay my joy or be undone——I'll read thy cruel Letters, or I'll think of some sad melancholy hour wherein thou hast dismiss'd me despairing from thy presence: or while you press me now to be gone with so much earnestness, you have some Lover to receive and entertain; perhaps 'tis only for the vanity to hear him tell his nauseous passion to you, breath on your lovely face, and daub your Garments with his fulsome imbrace: but oh, by Heaven, I cannot think that though! and thou has sworn thou canst not suffer it——if I shou'd find thee false—but 'tis impossible—— oh! shou'd I find *Foscario*[a] visit thee, him whom thy Parents favour, I shou'd undo you all, by Heaven I shou'd—but thou hast sworn, what need *Philander* more; yes, *Silvia* thou hast sworn and call'd Heaven's vengeance down whene'er though gavest a look, or a dear smile in love to that pretending Fop; yet from his mighty fortune there is danger in him——what makes that thought torment me now?——begon, for *Silvia* loves me and will preserve my life——

I am not able, my adorable Charmer, to obey your commands of going from the sight of happy *Bellfont*; no, let the great wheel of the vast design roul on——or for ever stand still, for I'll not aid its motion to leave the mightier business of my love unfinish'd: no, let fortune and the duller Fools toil on--for I'll not bate a minute of my joys with thee to save the world, much less so poor a parcell of it; and sure there is more solid pleasure ev'n in these expecting hours I wait to snatch my bliss, than to be Lord of all the universe without it: then let me wait my *Silvia*, in those melancholy shades that part *Bellfont* from *Dorillus* his farm; perhaps my *Silvia* may walk that way so unattended that we might meet and lose our selves for a few moments in those intricate retreats: Ah, *Silvia!* I am dying with that thought——

---

[a] It was rumoured that Henrietta Berkeley had a formal suitor called Forrest. In a letter to her sister the Countess of Rutland, dated August 24, 1682 the Countess of Northampton reports on the scandal, saying that 'sume believes she has drowned her selfe, others thinks she is maryed to on Mr. Foster, but gon she is for sartine'. There is, however, some confusion over the exact role played by Forrest or Foster, as he appears in *The Trial of Ford Lord Grey* as one of Grey's servants.

Oh Heavens! what cruel destiny is mine? whose fatal circumstances do not permit me to own my passion, and lay claim to *Silvia*, to take her without controul to shades or Palaces, to live for ever with her, to gaze for ever on her, to eat, to loll, to rise, to play, to sleep, to act o'er all the pleasures and the joys of life with her—But 'tis in vain I rave, in vain employ my self in the fools barren business, Wishing,——this thought has made me sad as death: Oh, *Silvia*! I can ne'r be truly happy——adieu, employ thy self in writing to me, and remember my life bears date but only with thy faith and Love.

Philander.

Try my Adorable, what you can do to meet me in the Wood this afternoon for there I'll live to day.

To *Philander*.

Obstinate *Philander*, I conjure you by all your vows, by all your sacred love, by those dear hours this happy night design'd in favour of you, to go without delay to *Cesario*; 'twill be unsafe to disobey a Prince in his jealous circumstances. The fatigue of the journey cannot be great, and you well know the torment of my fears; oh! I shall never be happy or think you safe till you have quitted this fatal interest: Go, my *Philander*——and remember whatever toiles you take will be rewarded at night in the Arms of

Silvia.

To Silvia.

Whatever toiles you take shall be rewarded in the arms of *Silvia*!——By Heaven, I am inspired to act wonders: Yes, *Silvia*, yes, my adorable Maid, I am gone, I fly as swift as lightning, or the soft darts of love shot from thy charming eyes, and I can hardly stay to say —adieu.—

73

To the Lady——[a]

Dear Child,

Long foreseeing the misery whereto you must arrive by this
fatal correspondence with my unhappy Lord, I have often, with
tears and prayers, implor'd you to decline so dangerous a passion; I have never yet acquainted our parents with your misfortunes, but I fear I must at last make use of their Authority for
the prevention of your ruine. 'Tis not, my dearest Child, that
part of this unhappy story that relates to me, that grieves me,
but purely that of thine.

Consider, oh young noble Maid, the infamy of being a Prostitute! and yet the act it self in this fatal Amour is not the greatest
sin, but the manner which carries an unusual horrour with it;
for 'tis a Brother too, my Child, as well as a lover, one that has
lain by thy unhappy Sister's side so many tender years, by
whom he has a dear and lovely off-spring, by which he has
more fixt himself to thee by relation and blood: Consider this,
oh fond heedless girl! and suffer not a momentary joy to rob
thee of the eternal fame, me of my eternal repose, and fix a
brand upon our noble house, and so undoe us all.——Alas,
consider after an action so shamefull, thou must obscure thy
self in some remote corner of the world, where honesty and
honour never are heard of: No thou canst not shew thy face, but
'twill be pointed at for something monstrous: for a hundred
ages may not produce a story so lewdly infamous and loose as
thine. Perhaps (fond as you are) you imagin the sole joy of
being belov'd by him, will attone for those affronts and reproaches you will meet with in the censuring world: But Child,
remember and believe me, there is no lasting faith in sin; he that
has broke his Vows with Heaven and me, will be again perjur'd
to Heaven and thee, and all the world!——he once thought me
as lovely, lay at my feet, and sigh'd away his soul, and told such
pityous stories of his sufferings, such sad, such mournfull tales

---

[a] Henrietta Berkeley was approached not only by her sisters but by John Tillotson, later Archbishop of Canterbury who attempted to dissuade her from elopement with Ford Grey. Cf. Appendix III.

of his departed rest, his broken heart and everlasting Love, that sure I thought it had been a sin not to have credited his charming perjuries; in such a way he swore, with such a grace he sigh'd, so artfully he mov'd, so tenderly he look'd. Alas, dear Child, then all he said was new, unusual with him, never told before, now 'tis a beaten road, 'tis learn'd by heart, and easily addrest to any fond believing woman, the tatter'd, worn-out fragments of my Trophies, the dregs of what I long since drain'd from off his fickle heart; then it was fine, then it was brisk and new, now pall'd and dull'd by being repeated often. Think, my Child, what your victorious beauty merits, the victim of a heart unconquer'd by any but your eyes: Alas, he has been my captive, my humble whining slave, disdain to put him on your fetters now; alas, he can say no new thing of his heart to thee, 'tis love at second hand, worn out, and all its gaudy luster tarnish't; besides, my Child, if thou hadst no religion binding enough, no honour that could stay thy fatal course, yet nature should oblige thee, and give a check to the unreasonable enterprise. The griefs and dishonour of our noble Parents, who have been eminent for vertue and piety, oh suffer 'em not to be regarded in this censuring world as the most unhappy of all the race of old nobility; thou art the darling child, the joy of all, the last hope left, the refuge of their sorrow; for they, alas, have had but unkind stars to influence their unadvis'd off-spring: no want of vertue in their education, but this last blow of fate must strike 'em dead: Think, think of this, my Child, and yet retire from ruine; haste, fly from destruction which pursues thee fast; haste, haste, and save thy parents and a sister, or what's more dear, thy fame; mine has already receiv'd but too many desperate wounds, and all through my unkind Lord's growing passion for thee, which was most fatally founded on my ruine, and nothing but my ruine could advance it; and when my Sister, thou hast run thy race, made thy self loath'd, undone and infamous as hell, despis'd, scorn'd and abandoned by all, lampoon'd,[a] perhaps diseas'd; this faithless man, this cause of all will leave thee too, grow weary of thee, nauseated by use, he may perhaps consider what sins, what evils, and what inconveniences and shames thou'st brought him to, and will not be the last shall loath and hate thee: For though youth fansie it

---

[a] There were several broadsides and ballads published on both Henrietta and Mary Berkeley. Cf. Appendix II.

have a mighty race to run of pleasing vice and vanity, the course will end, the goal will be arriv'd to at the last, where they will sighing stand, look back and view the length of pretious time they've fool'd away; when travers'd o'er with honour and discretion, how glorious were the journey, and with what joy the wearied traveller lies down and basks beneath the shades that ends the happy course.

Forgive, dear Child, this advice and persue it, 'tis the effect of my pity, not anger, nor could the name of rival ever yet have power to banish that of sister from my soul——farewell, remember me; pray Heaven thou hast not this night made a forfeit of thy honour and that this which comes from a tender bleeding heart may have the fortune to inspire thee with grace to avoid all temptations for the future, since they must end in sorrow, which is the eternal prayer of,

Dearest Child,
Your affectionate Sister.

To *Philander*.

Ask me not, my dearest Brother, the reason of this sudden change, ask me no more from whence proceeds this strange coldness, or why this alteration; it is enough my destiny has not decreed me for *Philander*: Alas, I see my errour,[a] and looking round about me, find nothing but approaching horrour and confusion in my pursuit of love: Oh whither was I going? to what dark paths, what everlasting shades had smiling love betray'd me had I pursu'd him farther; but I at last have subdu'd his force, and the fond Charmer shall no more renew his arts and flatteries; for I'm resolv'd as Heaven, as fixt as fate and death, and I conjure you, trouble my repose no more, for it you do (regardless of my honour, which if you lov'd you wou'd preserve) I'll do a deed shall free me from your importunities, that shall amaze and cool your vitious flame: no more—— remember you have a noble wife, companion of your vows, and

---

[a] After the discovery of her relationship with Ford Grey, Henrietta Berkeley did claim to regret the affair. Cf. Appendix I.

I have honour, both which are worth preserving, and for which, though you want generous love, you'll find neither that nor courage wanting in

Silvia.

To Silvia.

Yes, my adorable *Silvia*, I will pursue you no farther, only for all my pains, for all my sufferings, for my tormenting sleepless nights, and thoughtfull anxious days; for all my faithless hopes, my tears, my sighs, my prayers and my tears, for my unequall'd and unbound passion, and my unwearied pursuits in love, my never dying flame, and lastly, for my death; I only beg in recompense for all, this last favour from your pity; That you will deign to view the bleeding wound that pierc'd the truest heart that ever fell a sacrifice to love: you'll find my body lying beneath that spreading Oak, so sacred to *Philander*, since 'twas there he first took into his greedy ravish'd soul the dear, the soft confession of thy passion, though now forgotten and neglected all——make what haste you can, you'll find there stretch'd out the mangled carcass of the lost

Philander.

Ah! *Silvia*, was it for this that I was sent in such haste away this morning to *Cesario*? did I for this neglect the world, our great affair, and all that Prince's interest, and fly back to *Bellfont*, on the wings of Love, where in lieu of receiving a dear blessing from thy hand, do I find——never see me more——good Heaven——but, with my life, all my complaints are ended; only 'twould be some ease even in death to know what happy Rival 'tis has arm'd thy cruel hand against *Philander*'s heart.

To Philander.

Stay, I conjure thee stay thy sacrilegious hand; for the least wound it gives the Lord of all my wishes, I'll double on my breast a thousand fold; stay then, by all thy vows, thy love, and all the hopes I swear thou hast this night of a full recompence of all thy pains from yielding *Silvia*; I do conjure thee stay——for when the news arrives thou art no more, this poor, this lost, abandon'd heart of mine shall fall a victim to thy cruelty: no, live, my *Philander* I conjure thee, and receive all thou canst ask, and all that be given by

Silvia.

To Philander.

Oh, my charming *Philander*! how very ill have you recompenc'd my last soft commands? which were that you should live and yet at the same moment, while you were reading of the dear obligation, and while my Page was waiting your kind return, you desperately expos'd your life to the mercy of this innocent Rival, betraying unadvisedly at the same time, my honour and the secret of your love and where to kill or to be kill'd, had been almost equally unhappy: 'twas well my Rage told me you disarm'd him in this rancounter[a]--yet you he says are wounded, some sacred drops of blood are fallen to earth and lost, the least of which are pretious enough to ransom captive Queens: oh! haste *Philander*, to my arms for cure, I dy with fear there may be danger——haste, and let me bath the dear, the wounded part in floods of tears, lay it to my warm lips, and bind it with my torn hair: oh! *Philander*, I rave with my concern for thee, and am ready to break all laws of decency and duty, and fly, without

---

[a] Encounter.

considering, to thy succour, but that I fear to injure thee much more by the discovery, which such an unadvis'd absence would make; pray Heaven the unlucky adventure reach not *Bellfont*; *Foscario* has no reason to proclaim it, and thou art too generous to boast the conquest, and *Silvio* was the only witness, and he's as silent and as secret as the grave; but why, *Philander*, was he sent me back without reply? what meant that cruel silence—— say, my *Philander*, will you not obey me?——will you abandon me? can that dear tongue be perjur'd? and can you this night disappoint your *Silvia* ? what have I done, oh obstinately cruel, irreconcilable——what, for my first offence? a little poor resentment and no more? a little faint care of my gasping honour, cou'd that displease so much? besides I had a cause which you shall see; a Letter that wou'd cool loves honest fires, and turn it to devotion; by Heaven 'twas such a check——such a surprise ——but you your self shall judge if after that, I cou'd say less than bid eternally farewell to love—at least to thee——but I recanted soon; one sad dear word, one soft resenting line from thee, gain'd love the day again, and I despis'd the censures of the duller world: yes, yes, and I confess'd you had o'recome, and did this merit no reply? I asked the Boy a thousand times what you said, how and in what manner you received it, chid him, and laid your silent fault on him, till he with tears convinc'd me, and said he found you hastning to the Grove,—— and when he gave you my commands——you look'd upon him with such a stedfast, wild and fixt regard, surveying him all o're while you were opening it——as argu'd some unusual motion in you, then cried begon——I cannot answer flattery——good Heaven, what can you mean? but e're he got to the farther end of the Grove, where still you walk'd a solemn death-like pace, he saw *Foscario* pass him unattended, and looking back, saw your rancounter, saw all that hapned between you, then ran to your assistance, just as you parted; still you were roughly sullen, and neither took notice of his proffer'd service, nor that you needed it, although you bled apace; he offer'd you his aid to tie your wounds up——but you reply'd——begon, and do not trouble me——Or, cou'd you imagin I cou'd live with this neglect? cou'd you, my *Philander*? Oh, what wou'd you have me do? if nothing but my death or ruin can suffice for my attonement, I'll sacrifice either with joy; yes, I'll proclaim my passion aloud, proclaim it at *Bellfont*, own the dear criminal flame, fly to my *Philander*'s aid and be undone; for thus I cannot, no I will not live, I rave, I languish, faint and dy with pain, say that you live, oh, say but that you love, say you are coming to the Meadow behind the Garden grove in order to your approach to my Arms: Oh, swear that all your Vows are true; oh, swear that you are *Silvia*'s; and in return, I'll swear that I am yours without reserve, whatever fate is destin'd for your

Silvia.

I die with impatience, either to see or hear from you; I fear 'tis yet too soon for the first——oh therefore save me with the last, or I shall rave, and wildly betray all by coming to Dorilus *his Farm, or seeking you where e're you cruelly have hid your self from*

Silvia.

To Silvia.

Ah, *Silvia*, how have you in one day destroy'd that repose I have been designing so many years, oh, thou false—but wondrous fair creature! why did Heaven ordain so much beauty and so much perfidy, so much excellent wit and so much cunning, (things inconsistent in any but in *Silvia*) in one divine frame, but to undo Mankind: yes, *Silvia* thou wert born to Murther more believing men than the unhappy and undone *Philander*. Tell me, thou charming Hypocrite, why hast thou thus deluded me? why, oh, why was I made the miserable object of thy fatal Vow breach? What have I done, thou lovely fickle Maid, that thou should'st be my murtherer? and why dost thou call me from the grave with such dear soft commands, as wou'd awake the very quiet dead, to torture me anew, after my eyes (curse on their fatal sense) were too sure witnesses of thy infidelity? Oh, fickle Maid, how much more kind 't had been to have sent me down to earth, with plain heart-breaking truth than a mean subtile falshood, that has undone thy credit in my soul: truth, Though 'twere cruel, had been generous in thee, though thou wert perjur'd, false, forsworn——thou shou'dst not have added to it that yet baser sin of treachery; you might have been provok'd to

80

have kill'd your friend, but it were base to stab him unawares
defenceless and unwarn'd; smile in my face and strike me to the
heart; sooth me with all the tenderest marks of passion——say
with an invitation too, that wou'd have gain'd a credit in one
that had been jilted o're the world, flatter'd and ruin'd by all thy
cozening sex, and all to send me vain and pleas'd away, only to
gain a day to entertain another Lover in. Oh, fantastick woman!
destructive glorious thing, what needed this deceit? had'st thou
not with unwonted industry perswaded me to have hasted to
Cesario, by Heaven, I'd dully liv'd the tedious day in traversing
the flowry Meads and silent Groves, laid by some murmurring
spring had sigh'd away the often counted hours, and thought
on *Silvia* till the blest minute of my ravishing approach to her,
had been a fond believing and impos'd on Coxcomb, and ne're
had dreamt the treachery, ne're seen the snake that bask'd
beneath the gay, the smiling flowers; securely thou hadst
cozen'd me, reap'd thy new joys, and made my Rival sport at
the expence of all my happiness: Yes, yes, your hasty importunity first gave me jealousie, made me impatient with *Cesario*, and
excuse my self to him by a hundred inventions; neglected all to
hasten back, where all my joys, where all my killing fears and
torments resided—but when came—how was I welcom'd? with
your confirming Billet; yes, *Silvia*, how! let *Dorillus* inform you,
between whose Arms I fell dead, shame on me, dead—and
the first thought my Soul conceiv'd when it return'd, was, not
to dy in jest, I answer'd your commands, and hastned to the
Grove, where——by all that's sacred, by thy self I swear (a
dearer oath than heaven and earth can furnish me with) I did
resolve to die, but oh, how soon my soft my silent passion
turn'd to loud rage, rage easier to be born, to dire despair, to
fury and revenge; for there I saw *Foscario*, my young, my fair,
my rich and powerfull Rival, he hasted through the Grove all
warm and glowing from the fair false ones arms; the blushes
which thy eyes had kindled were fresh upon his cheeks, his
looks were sparkling with the new blown fire his heart so
briskly burnt with, a glad, a peacefull smile drest all his face,
trick'd like a Bridegroom, while he perfum'd the air as he past
through it——none but the man that loves and dotes like me is
able to express my sense of rage: I quickly turn'd the Sword
from my own heart to send it to his elevated one, giving him
only time to——draw——that was the word, and I confess your
Spark was wondrous ready, brisk with success, vain with your

new-given favours, he only cry'd——if *Silvia* be the quarrel—I am prepar'd——and he maintain'd your cause with admirable courage, I confess, though chance or fortune luckily gave me his Sword, which I wou'd have rendred back, and that way wou'd have died, but he refused to arm his hand anew against the man that had not took advantage of him, and thus we parted: Then 'twas that malice supported me with life, and told me I shou'd scorn to dy for so perfidious and so ruinous a creature, but charming and bewitching still, 'twas then I borrow'd so much calmness of my lessening anger to read the Billet o're your Page had brought me, which melted all the rough remaining part of rage away into tame languishment: Ah, *Silvia!* this heart of mine was never form'd by Nature to hold out long in stubborn sullenness; I am already on the excusing part, and fain wou'd think thee innocent and just; deceive me prettily, I know thou canst, sooth my fond heart, and ask how it cou'd harbour a faithless thought of *Silvia*——do——flatter me, protest a little, swear my Rival saw thee not, say he was there by chance——say any thing; or if thou sawst him, say with how cold a look he was receiv'd——oh, *Silvia*, calm my soul, deceive it, flatter it, and I shall still believe and love thee on——yet shoud'st thou tell me truth, that thou art false, by Heaven, I do adore thee so, I still shou'd love thee on; shou'd I have seen thee clasp him in thy arms, print kisses on his cheeks and lips, and more——so fondly and so doatingly I love, I think I shou'd forgive thee, for I swear by all the powers that pity frail mortality, there is no joy, no life, no Heaven without thee! Be false, be cruel, perjur'd, infamous, yet still I must adore thee; my soul was form'd of nothing but of love, and all that love, and all that soul is *Silvia's*, but yet since thou hast fram'd me an excuse, be kind and carry it on—to be deluded well, as thou canst do't, will be the same to innocence as loving; I shall not find the cheat: I'll come then——and lay my self at thy feet, and seek there that repose, that dear content which is not to be found in this vast world besides; though much of my heart's joy thou hast abated, and fixt a sadness in my soul that will not easily vanish——Oh *Silvia*, take care of me, for I am in thy power, my life, my fame, my soul are in thy hands, be tender of the victims, and remember if any action of thy life shou'd shew a fading love, that very moment I perceive the change, you shall find dead at your feet the abandoned

Philander.

Sad as death, I am going towards the Meadow in order to my approach to Silvia, *the World affording no repose to one, but when I am where the dear Charmer is.*

To Philander *in the Meadow.*

And can you be jealous of me, *Philander?* I mean so poorly jealous as to believe me capable of falshood, of vow-breach, and what's worse, of loving any thing but the adorable *Philander?* Oh, I cou'd not once believe so cruel a thought cou'd have entred into the imaginations of a soul so intirely possest with *Silvia,* and so great a judge of Love! Abandon me, reproach me, hate me, scorn me, whenever I harbour any thing in mine so destructive to my repose and thine. Can I *Philander,* give you a greater proof of my passion, of my faithful never-dying passion, than being undone for you? have I any other prospect in all this soft adventure, but shame, dishonour, reproach, eternal infamy, and everlasting destruction, even of soul and body: I tremble with fear of future punishment; but oh, Love will have no devotion (mixt with his ceremonies) to any other Deity; and yet alas, I might have lov'd another and have been sav'd, or any Maid but *Silvia* might have possess'd without damnation. But 'tis a Brother I pursue, it is a Sister gives her honour up, and none but *Cannace*[a] that ever I read in story, was ever found so wretched as to love a Brother with so criminal a flame, and possibly I may meet her fate. I have a Father too as great as *Æolus,*[b] as angry and revengefull where his honour is concern'd; and you found, my dearest Brother, now near you were last night to a discovery in the Garden: I have some reason too to fear this night's adventure, for as ill fate would have it (loaded with other thoughts) I told not *Melinda* of your adventure last night with *Monsieur* the Count, who meeting her early this morning had like to have made a discovery, if he have not

---

[a] Daughter of Aeolus and Enarete. She fell incestuously in love with her brother Macareus and in various legends she was put to death by her father or committed suicide.

[b] Father of Sisyphus, Calyce, Canace and others. Often confused with Aeolus, god of the winds.

really so already; she strove to shun him, but he cried out——
Melinda, you cannot fly me by light, as you did last night in the
dark—she turn'd, and beg'd his pardon for neither coming nor
designing to come, since she had resolv'd never to violate her
vows to *Alexis*; not coming, cried he, not returning again, you
meant *Melinda*, secure of my heart and my purse, you fled with
both: *Melinda*, whose honour was now concern'd and not reminding your escape in her likeness, blushing she sharply denied the fact, and with a disdain that had laid aside all respect,
left him; nor can it be doubted but he fansied (if she spoke
truth) there was some other intrigue of love carried on at *Bellfont*. Judge, my charming *Philander*, if I have not reason to be
fearfull of thy safety and my fame, and to be jealous that so wise
a Man as *Monsieur*, did not take that parly to be held with a
spirit last night, or that 'twas an apparition he courted: But if
there be no boldness like that of love, nor courage like that of a
lover; sure there never was so great a Heroine as *Silvia*. Undaunted, I resolve to stand the shock of all, since 'tis impossible
for me to leave *Philander* any doubt or jealousie that I can
dissipate, and Heaven knows how far I was from any thought
of seeing *Foscario* when I urg'd *Philander* to despair. I have, to
clear my innocence, sent thee the Letter I received two hours
after thy absence, which falling into my Mothers hands, whose
favourite he is, he had permission to make his visit; which
within an hour he did, but how received by me, be thou the
judge, whene're it is thy fate to be oblig'd to entertain some
Woman to whom thy soul has an intire aversion: I forc'd a
complaisance against my nature, endur'd his wrecking courtship with a fortitude that became the great heart that bears thy
sacred image, as Martyrs do, I suffer'd without murmuring or
the least sign of the pain I endur'd——'tis below the dignity of
my mighty passion to justifie it farther, let it plead its own
cause, it has a thousand ways to do't, and those all such as
cannot be resisted, cannot be doubted, especially this last proof
of sacrificing to your repose the never more to be doubted,

Silvia.

About an hour hence I shall expect you to advance.

To the Lady——

Madam,

'Tis not always the divine graces wherewith Heaven has adorn'd your resplendent beauties, that can maintain the innumerable conquests they gain, without a noble goodness, which may make you sensibly compassionate the poor and forlorn captives you have undone. But, most fair of your Sex, 'tis I alone that have a destiny more cruel and severe, and find my self wounded from your very frowns, and secur'd a slave as well as made one; the very scorn from those triumphant stars, your eyes, have the same effects as if they shin'd with the continual splendour of ravishing smiles, and I can no more shun their killing influence, than their all-saving aspects, and I shall expire contented, since I fall by so glorious a Fate; if you will vouchsafe to pronounce my doom from that store-house of perfection, your mouth, from lips that open like the blushing rose, strow'd o're with morning dew, and from a breath sweeter than holy incense; in order to which, I approach you, most excellent beauty with this most humble petition, that you will deign to permit me to throw my unworthy self before the Throne of your mercy, there to receive the sentence of my life or death a happiness though incomparably too great for so mean a Vassal, yet with that reverence and awe I shall receive it, as I wou'd the sentence of the Gods, and which I will no more resist than I wou'd the Thunderbolts of *Jove*,[a] or the revenge of angry *Juno*:[b] For, Madam, my immense passion knows no *medium* between life and death, and as I never had the presumption to aspire to the glory of the first, I am not so abject as to fear I am wholly depriv'd of the glory of the last, I have too long lain convicted, extend your mercy, and put me now out of pain. You have often wreck'd me to confess my Promethian sin;[c]

---

[a] Ruler of the gods.

[b] Sister and wife of Jove and queen of the gods. In Greek and Roman myth she exacts bitter revenge on her husband's lovers.

[c] When Zeus deprived men of fire, Prometheus, a Titan, stole a spark from heaven and brought it to mankind in a stalk of fennel. As punishment Zeus had him chained to a rock where an eagle fed each day on his regenerating liver.

spare the cruel Vulture of despair, take him from my heart in pity, and either by killing woods, or blasting Lightning from those refulgent eyes, pronounce the death of

Madam,

Your admiring slave

Foscario.

To Silvia.

My everlasting Charmer,
I am convinc'd and pleas'd, my fears are vanish't and a Heaven of solid joy is open'd to my view, and I have nothing now in prospect but Angel-Brightness, glittering Youth, dazling Beauty, charming Sounds, and ravishing Touches, and all around me ecstasies of pleasure, unconceivable transports without conclusion; *Mahomet*[a] never fansied such a Heaven, not all his Paradise promis'd such lasting felicity, or ever provided there the recompense of such a Maid as *Silvia*, such a bewitching Form, such soft, such glorious Eyes, where the Soul speaks and dances, and betrays Loves-secrets in every killing glance, a Face, where every motion, every feature sweetly languishes, a Neck all-tempting——and her lovely Breast inviting presses from the eager Lips; such Hands, such clasping Arms, so white, so soft and slender! no, nor one of all his Heavenly enjoyments, though promis'd years of fainting in one continued ecstasie, can make one moments joy with Charming *Silvia*. Oh, I am wrap't (with bare imagination) with much a vaster pleasure than any other dull appointment can dispence——Oh, thou blessing sent from Heaven to ease my toils of life! thou sacred dear delight of my fond doating heart, oh, whither wilt thou lead me, to what vast heights of Love? into extremes as fatal and as dangerous as those excesses were that rendred me so cold in your opinion. Oh, *Silvia, Silvia*, have a care of me, manage my o'rejoy'd Soul and all its eager passions, chide my fond heart, be angry if I

---

[a] Muhammed, (c. AD 570–632), founder of the Muslim religion.

faint upon thy Bosom, and do not with thy tender voice recall me, a voice that kills outright, and calls my fleeting Soul out of its habitation: lay not such charming Lips to my cold Cheeks but let me lie extended at thy feet untouch'd, unsigh't upon, un-press'd with kisses: Oh, change those tender trembling words of Love into rough sounds and noises unconcern'd, and when you see me dying, do not call my Soul to mingle with thy sighs: yet shoud'st thou bate one word, one look or tear, by Heaven, I shou'd be mad; oh, never let me live to see declension in thy love! no, no, my Charmer, I cannot bear the least suppos'd decay in those dear fondnesses of thine; and sure none e're became a Maid so well, nor ever were receiv'd with adorations like to mine!

Pardon, my adorable *Silvia*, the rashness of my passion in this rancounter with *Foscario*; I am satisfied he is too unhappy in your disfavour to merit the being so in mine; but 'twas sufficient I then saw a joy in his face, a pleas'd gayety in his looks to make me think my rage reasonable and my quarrel just; by the style he writes, I dread his Sense less than his Person; but you, my lovely Maid have said enough to quit me of my fears for both——the night comes on——I cannot call it envious though it rob me of the light that shou'd assist me to finish this, since it will more gloriously repay me in a happier place——come on then, thou blest retreat of Lovers, I forgive thy interruptions here, since thou wilt conduct to the Arms of *Silvia*——the adoring

Philander.

If you have any commands for me, this Weeder of the Gardens, whom I met going in thither, will bring it back; I wait in the Meadow, and date this from the dear Primrose bank, where I have sat with Silvia.

To Philander.
After the happy Night.

'Tis done; yes, *Philander*, 'tis done, and after that what will not Love and grief oblige me to own to you? Oh, by what insensible degrees a Maid in love may arrive to say any thing to her Lover without blushing? I have known the time, the blest innocent time when but to think I lov'd *Philander* wou'd have cover'd my face with shame, and to have spoke it wou'd have fill'd me with confusion——have made me Tremble, Blush, and bend my guilty Eyes to Earth, not daring to behold my Charming Conquerour while I made that bashfull confession——though now I am grown bold in Love, and I have known the time when being at Court, and coming from the Presence, being offer'd some officious hand to lead me to my Coach, I have shrunk back with my aversion to your Sex, and have conceal'd my hands in my Pockets to prevent their being touch'd——a kiss wou'd turn my stomack, and amorous looks (though they wou'd make me vain) gave me a hate to him that sent 'em, and never any Maid resolv'd so much as I to tread the paths of honour, and I had many precedents before me to make me carefull: Thus I was armed with resolution, pride and scorn, against all Mankind, but alas, I made no defence against a Brother, but innocently lay expos'd to all his attacks of Love, and never thought it criminal till it kindled a new desire about me. Oh, that I shou'd not dy with shame to own it——yet see (I say) how from one soft degree to another, I do not only confess the shamefull truth, but act it too; what, with a Brother——Oh Heavens! a crime so monstrous and so new——but by all thy Love, by those surprising joys so lately experienc'd——I never will——no, no, I never can——repent it: Oh, incorrigible passion, oh hardned love! at least I might have some remorse, some sighing after my poor departed honour; but why shou'd I dissemble with the Powers divine, that know the secrets of a Soul doom'd to eternal Love? Yet I am mad, I rave and tear my self, traverse my guilty chamber in a disorder'd, but a soft confusion; and often opening the conscious curtains, survey the print where thou and I were last night laid, surveying it with a thousand tender sighs, and kiss and press thy dear forsaken side, imagin over all our solemn joys, every dear transport, all our ravishing repeated blisses, then almost fainting, languishing, cry——*Philander*! oh, my charming little God! then lay me down in the dear place you press'd, still warm and fragrant with the sweet remains that thou hast left behind thee on the Pillow, oh, my Soul's joy! my dear, eternal pleasure! what softness hast thou added to my heart within a few short hours? but oh, *Philander*——if (as I've oft been told) possession, which makes Women fond and doting, shou'd make thee cold and grow indifferent——if nauseated with repeated joy, and having made a full discovery of all that was but once imaginary, when fancy rendred every thing much finer than experience, oh, how were I undone! for me, by all the inhabitants of Heaven I swear, by thy dear charming self, and by thy vows——thou so transcend'st all fancy, all dull imagination, all wondring ideas of what Man was to me, that I believe thee more than humane! some charm divine dwells in thy touches; besides all these, thy charming look thy love, the beauties that adorn thee, and thy wit, I swear there is a secret in Nature that renders thee more dear and fits thee to my Soul; do not ask it me, let it suffice 'tis so, and is not to be told; yes, by it I know thou art the man created for my Soul, and he alone that has the power to touch it; my eyes and fancy might have been diverted, I might have favour'd this above the other, prefer'd that face, that wit, or shape, or air—but to concern my Soul to make that capable of something more than love, 'twas only necessary that *Philander* shou'd be form'd, and form'd just as he is, that shape, that face, that height, that dear proportion; I wou'd not have a feature, not a look, not a hair alter'd, just as thou art, thou art an Angel to me, and I, without considering what I am, what I might be, or ought, without considering the fatal circumstances of thy being married (a thought that shocks my Soul when e're it enters) or whate're other thought that does concern my happiness or quiet, have fixt my Soul to Love and my *Philander*, to love thee with all thy disadvantages, and glory in my ruine; these are my firm resolves——these are my thoughts. But thou art gone, with all the Trophees of my love and honour, gay with the spoils, which now perhaps are unregarded: The mystery's now reveal'd, the mighty secret's known, and now will be no wonder or surprize: But here my vows, by all on which my life depends I swear ——if ever I perceive the least decay of love in thee, if e're thou break'st an Oath, a vow, a word, if e're I see repentance in thy face, or coldness in thy eyes (which Heaven divert) by that bright Heav'n I'll dy: you may believe me, since I had the courage and durst love thee, and after that durst sacrifice my fame, lose all to justifie that love, will when a change so fatal shall arrive, find courage too to die; yes dy *Philander*, assure thy self I will, and therefore have a care of

Silvia.

89

To *Philander*.

Oh, where shall I find repose, where seek a silent quiet, but in my last retreat the Grave! I say not this, my dearest *Philander*, that I do, or ever can repent my love, though the fatal source of all: For already we are betray'd, our race of joys, our course of stoln delight is ended e're begun. I chid, alas, at morning's dawn, I chid you to begon, and yet, Heaven knows, I grasp'd you fast, and rather would have died than parted with you; I saw the day came on, and curst its busie light, and still you cried one blessed minute more, before I part with all the joys of life! and hours were minutes then, and day grew old upon us unawares, 'twas all abroad, and had call'd up all the houshould spies to pry into the secrets of our loves, and thou, by some tale-bearing flatterer, wert seen in passing through the Garden; the news was carried to my Father, and a mighty consult has been held in my Mother's apartment, who now refuses to see me, while I possest with Love, and full of wonder at my new change, lull'd with dear contemplation, (for I am alter'd much since yesterday, however thou hast charm'd me) imagining none knew our theft of love, but only Heaven and *Melinda*: But oh, alas, I had no sooner finish'd this inclos'd, but my Father enter'd my Cabinet,[a] but 'twas with such a look——as soon inform'd me, all was betray'd to him; a while he gaz'd on me with fierceness in his eyes, which so surpriz'd and frighted me, that I, all pale and trembling, threw my self at his feet; he seeing my disorder, took me up, and fixt so stedfast and so sad a look on me, as wou'd have broken any heart but mine, supported with *Philander*'s image; I sigh'd and wept——and silently attended when the storm shou'd fall, which turn'd into a shower so soft and piercing, I almost died to see it; at last delivering me a paper——here, (cried he, with a sigh and trembling interrupted voice) read what I cannot tell thee. Oh, *Silvia*, cried he——thou joy and hope of all my aged years, thou object of my Dotage, how hast thou brought me to the Grave

---

[a] A small room. Cf. Appendix I.

with sorrow? so left me with the Paper in my hand: Speechless unmov'd a while I stood, till he awak'd me by new sighs and cries; for passing through my Chamber by chance, or by design, he cast his melancholy eyes towards my Bed, and saw the dear disorder there, unusual——then cried——Oh, wretched *Silvia*, thou art lost! and left me almost fainting; the Letter, I soon found, was one you'd sent from *Dorillus* his Farm this morning, after you parted from me, which has betray'd us all, but how it came into their hands I since have understood: for, as I said, you were seen passig through the Garden, from thence (to be confirm'd) they dog'd you to the Farm, and waiting there your motions, saw *Dorillus* come forth with a Letter in his hand; which though he soon conceal'd, yet not so soon but it was taken notice of, when hastening to *Bellfont* the nearest way, they gave an account to *Monsieur*, my Father, who going out to *Dorillus*, commanded him to deliver the Letter; his Vassal durst not disobey, but yielded it with such dispute and reluctancy, as he durst maintain with a man so great and powerfull; before *Dorillus* return'd you had taken horse, so that you are a stranger to our misfortune——What shall I do? Where shall I seek a refuge from the danger that threatens us, a sad and silent grief appears throughout *Bellfont*, and the face of all things is changed, yet none knows the unhappy cause by *Monsieur* my Father, and *Madam* my Mother, *Melinda* and my self; *Melinda* and my Page are both dismist from waiting on me, as supposed confidants of this dear secret, and strangers, creatures of *Madam* the Countess, put about me. Oh *Philander*, what can I do? thy advice, or I am lost; but how, alas shall I either convey these to thee, or receive any thing from thee, unless some God of Love in pity of our miseries, shou'd offer us his aid: I'll try to corrupt my new Boy, I see good nature, pity and generosity in his looks, he's well born too, and may be honest.

Thus far, *Philander*, I had writ when Supper was brought me, for yet my Parents have not deigned to let me come into their presence; those that serve me tell me *Mertilla* is this Afternoon arriv'd at *Bellfont*; all's mighty closely carried in the Countesses apartment, I tremble with the thought of what will be the result of the great consultation: I have been tempting of the Boy, but I perceive they are strictly charg'd not to obey me, he says, against his will, he shall betray me, for they will have him search'd, but he has promis'd me to see one of the weeders, who working in the Garden, into which my Window opens, may from thence receive what I shall let down; if it be true I shall get this fatal knowledge to you, that you may not only prepare for the worst, but contrive to set at liberty

the unfortunate

Silvia.

My Heart is ready to break and my Eyes are drowned in Tears: Oh, Philander, *how much unlike the last will prove this fatal night: farewell and think of* Silvia .

This was Writ in the Cover to both the foregoing Letters to Philander.

Philander, all that I dreaded, all that I fear'd is fallen upon me, I have been arraign'd and convicted, three Judges, severe as the three infernal ones, sate in condemnation on me, a Father, a Mother, and a Sister, the fact, alas, was too clearly prov'd, and too many circumstantial truths appear'd against me for me to plead, Not guilty. But, Oh Heavens! had you seen the tears, and heard the Prayers, threats, reproaches and upbraidings——these from an injur'd Sister, those, my heart-broken Parents; a tender Mother here, a railing and reviling Sister there—an angry Father and a guilty conscience——thou woud'st have wondred at my fortitude, my courage and my resolution, and all from Love! For surely I had died, had not thy love, thy powerfull love supported me; through all the accidents of life and fate, that can and will support me; in the midst of all their clamours and their railings I had from that a secret and a soft repose within, that whisper'd me, *Philander* loves me still; discarded and renounc'd by my fond Parents, Love still replies, *Philander* still will own thee; thrown from thy Mother's and thy Sister's arms, *Philander's* still are open to receive thee: And though I rave, and almost dy to see them grieve, to think that I am the fatal cause, who makes so sad confusion in our Family: for, oh 'tis pitious to behold my Sister's sighs and tears, my Mother's sad despair, my Father's raging and his weeping, by melancholy turns: Yet even these deplorable objects, that wou'd move the most obdurate stubborn heart to pity and repentance, render not mine relenting; and yet I'm wondrous pitifull by nature, and I can weep and faint to see the sad effects of my loose wanton love, yet cannot find repentance for the dear charming sin; and yet, shoud'st thou behold my Mother's languishment, no bitter words proceeding from her lips, no tears fall from her down-cast eyes, but silent and sad as death she sits, and will not view the light; shoud'st thou, I say, behold it, thou woud'st if not repent, yet grieve that thou hadst lov'd me: Sure love has quite confounded nature in me, I cou'd not else behold this fatal ruine without revenging it upon my stubborn heart, a thousand times a-day I make new vows against the God of Love, but 'tis too late, and I'm as often perjur'd—— Oh, shou'd the Gods revenge the broken vows of Lovers, what Love-sick man, what maid betray'd like me, but wou'd be damn'd a thousand times for every little love-quarrel, every kind of resentment makes us swear to love no more, and every smile, and every flattering softness from the dear injurer, make us perjur'd: Let all the force of vertue, honour, interest joyn with my suffering Parents to perswade me to cease to love *Philander*, yet let him but appear, let him but look on me with those dear charming eyes, let him but sigh, or press me to his fragrant cheek, fold me——and cry——ah, *Silvia*, can you quit me——no, you must not, you shall not, nay, I know you cannot, remember you are mine——there is such eloquence in those dear words when utter'd with a voice so tender and so passionate, that I believe 'em irresistable——alas, I find 'em so—and easily break all the feebler vows I make against thee; yes, I must be undone, perjur'd, for-sworn, incorrigible, unnatural, disobedient, and any thing rather than not *Philander's* —— turn then, my Soul, from these domestick, melancholy objects, and look abroad, look forward for a while on charming prospects; look on *Philander*, the dear, the young, the amorous *Philander*, whose very looks infuse a tender joy throughout the Soul, and chase all cares, all sorrows and anxious thoughts from thence, whose wanton play is softer than that of young fledg'd Angels, and when he looks and sighs, and speaks, and touches, he is a very God: Where art thou, oh thou miracle of youth, thou charming dear undoer! now thou hast gain'd the glory of the conquest, thou slightest the rifled captive: What, not a line? two tedious days are past and no kind power relieves me with a

93

word, or any tidings of *Philander*——and yet thou mayst have
sent——but I shall never see it, till they raise up fresh witnesses
against me——I cannot think thee wavering, or forgetfull; for if
I did, surely thou knowest my heart so well, thou canst not
think 'twou'd live to think another thought: Confirm my kind
belief, and send to me——

There is a Gate well known to thee through which thou
passest to *Bellfont*, 'tis in the road about half a league from
hence, an old Man opens it, his Daughter weeds in the Garden,
and will convey this to thee as I have order'd her, by the same
messenger thou may'st return thine, and early as she comes I'll
let her down a string, by which way unperceiv'd, I shall receive
'em from her: I'll say no more, nor instruct you how you shall
preserve your

Silvia.

To Silvia.

That which was left in her hands by
Monsieur, *her Father, in*
her Cabinet.

My Adorable Silvia,
I can not more describe to thee the torment with which I part
from *Bellfont*, than I can that Heaven of joy I was rais'd to last
night by the transporting effects of thy wondrous love; both are
to excess, and both killing, but in different kinds. Oh, *Silvia*, by
all my unspeakable raptures in thy arms, by all thy charms of
beauty, too numerous and too ravishing for fancy to imagin——
I swear——by this last night, by this dear new discovery, thou
hast increas'd my love to that vast height, it has undone my
peace——all my repose is gone——this dear, dear night has
ruin'd me, it has confirm'd me now I must have *Silvia*, and
cannot live without her, no, not a day, an hour——to save the
world, unless I had the intire possession of my lovely Maid: Ah,
Silvia, I am not that indifferent dull Lover, that can be rais'd by
one beauty to an appetite, and satisfie it with another, I cannot
carry the dear flame you kindle, to quench it in the imbraces of

Mertilla; no, by the eternal powers, he that pretends to love, and loves at that course rate, needs fear no danger from that passion, he ne're was born to live or dy for love; *Silvia*, *Mertilla*, and a thousand more were all the same to such a dull insensible; no, *Silvia*, when you find I can return back to the once left matrimonial Bed despise me, scorn me, swear (as then thou justly may'st) I love not *Silvia*: Let the hot brute drudge on (he who is fir'd by Nature, not by Love, whom any bodies kisses can inspire) and ease the necessary heats of youth; Love's is a nobler fire, which nothing can allay but the dear she that rais'd it; no, no, my purer stream shall ne're run back to the fountain whence 'tis parted, nay, it cannot, it were as possible to love again where one has ceas'd to love, as carry the desire and wishes back, by Heaven, to me there's nothing so unnatural, no, *Silvia*, it is you I must possess, you have completed my undoing now, and I must dy unless you give me all——but oh, I am going from thee——when are we like to meet——oh, how shall I support my absent hours! thought will destroy me, for 'twill be all on thee, and those at such a distance will be insupportable——what shall I do without thee? if after all the toils of dull insipid life I cou'd return and lay me down by thee, *Herculean* labours[a] wou'd be soft and easie——the harsh fatigues of war, the dangerous hurries of affairs of state, the business and the noise of life, I cou'd support with pleasure, with wondrous satisfaction, cou'd treat *Mertilla* too with that respect, that generous care as wou'd become a Husband, I cou'd be easie every where, and every one shou'd be at ease with me; now I shall go and find no *Silvia* there, but sigh and wander like an unknown thing, on some strange foreign shore; I shall grow peevish as a new-wean'd child, no toys, no bauble of the gaudy world will please my wayward fancy: I shall be out of humour, rail at everything, in anger shall demand, and sullenly reply to every question ask'd and answer'd, and when I think to ease my Soul by a retreat, a Thousand soft desires, a Thousand wishes wreck me, pain me to raving, till beating the senseless floor with my feet——I cry aloud——my *Silvia*!——thus, thus,

---

[a] Hercules, son of Zeus and a mortal, Alcmene. He aroused the jealousy of Zeus's wife, Hera, who punished him with a fit of madness during which he killed his wife and children, thinking they were enemies. The Delphic Oracle declared that he should go to Tiryns and serve King Eurystheus for twelve years, performing the labours he would impose.

my charming dear, the poor *Philander* is employ'd when banish'd from his Heaven! if thus it us'd to be when only that bright outside was ador'd, judge now my pain, now thou hast made known a thousand graces more ——oh, pity me——for 'tis not in thy power to guess what I shall now endure in absence of thee, for thou hast charm'd my Soul to an excess too mighty for a patient suffering: Alas, I dy already——

I am yet at *Dorillus* his Farm, lingring on from one swift minute to the other, and have not power to go; a thousand looks all languishing I've cast from eyes all drown'd in tears towards *Bellfont*, have sight a thousand wishes to my Angel, from a sad breaking heart——Love will not let me go——and Honour calls me——alas, I must away; when shall we meet again? ah when, my *Silvia?*——oh charming Maid——thou'lt see me shortly dead, for thus I cannot live, thou must be mine, or I must be no more——I must away — farewell——may all the softest joys of Heaven attend thee——adieu——fail not to send a hundred times a day, if possible; I've order'd *Alexis* to do nothing but wait for all that comes, and post away with what thou send'st to me—again adieu, think on me—and till thou call'st me to thee, imagin nothing upon earth so wretched as *Silvia*'s own

Philander.

Know, my Angel, that passing through the Garden this Morning, I met Erasto——*I fear, he saw me near enough to know me, and will give an account of it, let me know what happens—adieu half dead, just taking Horse to go from* Silvia.

To *Philander*.

Written in a Leaf of a Table-book.

I have only time to say, on *Thursday* I am destin'd a Sacrifice to *Foscario*, which day finishes the life of

Silvia.

To Silvia.

From Dorillus *his Farm.*

Raving and mad at the News your Billet brought me, I (without considering the effects that wou'd follow) am arriv'd at *Bellfont*; I have yet so much patience about me, to suffer my self to be conceal'd at *Dorillus* his Cottage, but if I see thee not to night, or find no hopes of it——by Heaven I'll set *Bellfont* all in a flame but I will have my *Silvia*; be sure I'll do't— What? to be married ——*Silvia* to be married——and given from *Philander*——Oh, never think it, thou forsworn fair Creature —— What? give *Foscario* that dear charming Body? shall he be grasp'd in those dear naked Arms? taste all thy kisses, press thy snowy Breasts, command thy joys and rifle all thy Heaven? Furies and Hell environ me if he do——Oh, *Silvia*, faithless, perjur'd, charming *Silvia*——and can'st thou suffer it——hear me, thou fickle Angel—— hear my vows, oh faithless Ravisher! that fatal moment that the daring Priest offers to join your hands, and give thee from me, I'll sacrifice your Lover, by Heaven I will, before the Altar stab him at your feet; the holy place, nor the numbers that attend ye, nor all your prayers nor tears shall save his heart; look to't, and be not false——yet I'll not trust thy Faith; no, she that can think but falsely, and she that can so easily be perjur'd——for, but to suffer it is such a sin — such an undoing sin—— ——that thou art surely damn'd! and yet, by Heaven, that is not all the ruin shall attend thee: no, lovely Mischief, no——you shall not scape till the damnation day; for I will rack thee, torture thee and plague thee, those few hours I have to live (if spightfull Fate prevent my just revenge upon *Foscario*) and when I'm dead——as I shall quickly be kill'd by thy cruelty——know, thou fair Murtherer, I will haunt thy sight, be ever with thee, and surround thy bed, and fright thee from the Ravisher; fright all thy loose delights, and check thy joys—— Oh, I am mad!——I cannot think that thought, no, thou shalt never advance so far in wickedness, I'll save thee if I can—— Oh, my adorable, why dost thou torture me? how hast thou sworn so often and so loud that Heaven I am sure has heard thee, and will punish thee? how did'st thou swear that happy blessed night, in which I saw thee last, clasp'd in my arms, weeping with eager love, with melting softness on my bosome —— remember how thou swor'st——oh, that dear night——let me recover strength——and then I'll tell thee more——I must repeat the story of that night, which thou perhaps (oh faithless!) hast forgot——that glorious night when all the Heavens were gay, and every favouring power look'd down and smil'd upon our thefts of love, that gloomy night the first of all my joys, the blessed'st of my life——trembling and fainting I approacht your chamber, and while you met and grasp'd me at the door, taking my trembling body in your arms—remember how I fainted at your feet and what dear arts you us'd to call me back to life—remember how you kiss'd and press'd my face——remember what dear charming words you spoke——and when I did recover, how I ask'd you with a feeble doubtfull voice——Ah, *Silvia*, will you still continue thus, thus wondrous soft and fond? will you be ever mine and ever true——what did you then reply, when kneeling on the carpet where I lay, what, *Silvia*, did you vow? how invoke Heaven? how call its vengeance down if e're you lov'd another man again, if e're you touch'd or smil'd on any other, if e're you suffer'd words or acts of love but from *Philander?* both Heaven and Hell thou did'st awaken with thy oaths, one was an angry listener to what it knew thou'dst break, the other laugh'd to know thou woud'st be perjur'd, while only I, poor I, was all the while a silent fond believer; your vows stopt all my language as your kisses did my lips, you swore and kiss'd and vow'd, and clasp'd my neck——oh charming flatterer! oh artfull dear beguiler! thus into life and peace, and fond security you charm'd my willing Soul! 'Twas then, my *Silvia*, (certain of your heart and that it never cou'd be given away to any other) I press'd my eager joys, but with such tender caution——such fear and fondness, such an awfull passion, as overcame me your faint resistance, my reasons and my arguments were strong, for you were mine by love, by sacred vows, and who cou'd lay a better claim to *Silvia?* how oft I cried——Why this resistance, *Silvia?* my charming dear, whose are you? not *Philander'*s? and shall *Philander* not command his own——you must——ah cruel ——then a soft struggle follow'd with half breath'd words, with sighs and trembling hearts, and now and then——ah cruel and unreasonable was softly said on both sides: thus strove, thus argued——till both lay panting in each others arms, not with the

toil but rapture; I need not say what after follow'd this——
what tender showers of strange indearing mixtures 'twixt joy
and shame, 'twixt love and new surprise, and ever when I dried
your eyes with kisses, unable to repeat any other language than
——oh my *Silvia!* oh my charming Angel! while sighs of joy, and
closely grasping thee——spoke all the rest——while every tender word and every sigh, was Echo'd back by thee; you press'd
me——and you vow'd you lov'd me more than ever yet you did;
then swore anew and in my bosome hid your charming blushing
face, then with excess of love wou'd call on Heaven be witness oh
ye powers (a thousand times ye cried) if ever Maid e're lov'd like
Silvia——punish me strangely, oh eternal powers, if e're I leave
Philander, if e're I cease to love him; no force, no art, not interest,
honour, wealth, convenience, duty, or what other necessary
cause——shall never be of force to make me leave thee——thus
hast thou sworn, oh charming, faithless flatterer, thus 'twixt
each ravishing minute thou wou'dst swear---and I as fast
believ'd---and lov'd thee more——hast thou forgot it all, oh
fickle charmer, hast thou? hast thou forgot between each awfull
ceremony of love how you cried out, farewell the world and
mortal cares, give me *Philander*, Heaven, I ask no more—hast
thou forgot all this? did all the live-long night hear any other
sound but those my mutual vows, of invocations, broken sighs,
and soft and trembling whispers, say had we any other business
for the tender hours? oh, all ye host of Heaven, ye Stars that
shone, and all ye powers the faithless lovely Maid has sworn by,
be witness how she's perjur'd; revenge it all ye injur'd powers,
revenge it, since by it she has undone the faithfullest Youth, and
broke the tenderest heart — that ever fell a sacrifice to love, and
all ye little weeping Gods of love, revenge your murther'd
victim——your

> *Philander*

To *Philander*.

In the Leaves of a Table-Book.

Oh, my *Philander*, how dearly welcome, and how needless were thy kind reproaches? which I'll not endeavour to convince by argument, but such a deed as shall at once secure thy fears now and for the future; I have not a minute to write in, place my dear *Philander*, your Chariot in St. *Vincent*'s Wood, and since I am not able to fix the hour of my flight, let it wait there my coming, 'tis but a little mile from *Bellfont*, *Dorillus* is suspected there, remove thy self to the high-way-gate Cottage---there I'll call on thee-- 'twas lucky that thy fears, or love, or jealousie brought thee so near me, since I'd resolv'd before upon my flight. Parents and honour, interest and fame, farewell —— I leave you all to follow my *Philander*——haste the Chariot to the thickest part of the Wood, for I'm impatient to be gone, and shall take the first opportunity to fly to my *Philander*——Oh, love me, love me, love me!

Under pretence of reaching the Jesamin[a] *which shades my Window, I unperceiv'd let down and receive what Letters you send by the honest Weeder; by her send your sense of my flight, or rather your direction, for 'tis resolv'd already.*

To Silvia.

My lovely Angel,
So carefull I will be of this dear mighty secret, that I will only say *Silvia* shall be obey'd, no more--nay, I'll not dare to think of it, lest in my rapture I shou'd name my joy aloud, and busie

---

[a] Jasmine, a climbing shrub with white or yellow flowers, frequently mentioned in Restoration erotic scenes.

winds shou'd bear it to some officious listener and undo me; no more, no more, my *Silvia*, extremes of joy (as grief) are ever dumb: Let it suffice, this blessing which you proffer. I had design'd to ask, as soon as you'd convinc'd me of your faith; yes, *Silvia*, I had ask'd it, though 'twas a bounty too great for any Mortal to conceive Heaven shou'd bestow upon him; but if it do, that very moment I'll resign the world, and barter all for love and charming *Silvia*. Haste, haste, my life; my arms, my bosome and my Soul are open to receive the lovely fugitive; haste, for this moment I am going to plant my self where you directed.

Adieu.

To *Philander*.

After her Flight.

Ah, *Philander*, how have you undone a harmless, poor unfortunate? alas, where are you? why wou'd you thus abandon me? is this the soul, the bosome, these the arms that shou'd receive me? I'll not upbraid thee with my love, or charge thee with my undoing; 'twas all my own, and were it yet to do, I shou'd again be ruin'd for *Philander*, and never find repentance, no not for a thought, a word or deed of love, to the dear false forsworn; but I can dy, yes, hopeless, friendless——left by all, even by *Philander*——all but resolution has abandon'd me, and that can lay me down whene're I please in safe repose and peace: But oh, thou art not false, or if thou be'st, oh, let me hear it from thy mouth, see thy repented love, that I may know there's no such thing on earth, as faith, as honesty, as love or truth; however be thou true, or be thou false, be bold and let me know it, for thus to doubt is torture worse than death. What accident, thou dear, dear man, has happened to prevent thee from pursuing my directions, and staying for me at the gate? where have I miss'd thee, thou joy of my soul? by what dire mistake have I lost thee? and where, oh where art thou, my charming Lover? I sought thee every where, but like the languishing abandon'd

101

Mistress in the *Canticles*,[a] I sought thee, but I found thee not, no
bed of Roses wou'd discover thee; I saw no print of thy dear
shape, nor heard no amorous sigh that cou'd direct me—I ask'd
the wood and springs, complain'd and call'd on thee through all
the Groves, but they confess'd thee not; nothing but Echo's
answer'd me, and when I cried *Philander*---cried---*Philander*, thus
search'd I till the coming night and my increasing fears made me
resolve for flight, which soon we did, and soon arriv'd at *Paris*,[b]
but whither then to go Heaven knows, I cou'd not tell, for I was
almost naked, friendless and forlorn; at last, consulting *Brilljard*
what to do, after a thousand revolutions he concluded to trust
me with a sister he had who was Married to a *Gidon*[c] of the *Guard
de Core*,[d] he chang'd his name, and made me pass for a Fortune
he had stoln, but oh, no welcomes, nor my safe retreat were
sufficient to repose me all the insuing night, for I had no news of
Philander; no, not a dream inform'd me, a thousand fears and
jealousies have kept me waking, and *Brilljard* who has been all
night in pursuit of thee, is now return'd successless and distracted as thy *Silvia*, for duty and generosity has almost the same
effects in him, with love and tenderness and jealousie in me; and
since *Paris* affords no news of thee, (which sure it wou'd if thou
wert in it, for oh, the Sun might hide himself with as much ease
as great *Philander*) he is resolv'd to search St. *Vincent*'s Wood and
all the adjacent Cottages and Groves; he thinks that you, not
knowing of my escape, may yet be waiting thereabouts, since
quitting the Chariot for fear of being seen you might be so far
advanc'd into the Wood, as not to find the way back to the
Thicket where the Chariot waited: 'tis thus he feeds my hopes
and flatters my poor heart, that fain wou'd think thee true—or if
thou be'st not——but curst be all such thoughts, and far from
Silvia's Soul; no, no, thou art not false, it cannot be, thou art a
God, and art unchangeable; I know by some mistake thou art
attending me, as wild and impatient as I, perhaps thou think'st
me false, and think'st I have not courage to pursue my love and

---

[a] Sacred songs taken from the Bible. *The Song of Solomon* is known as the Canticle of
Canticles and Behn is here alluding to Chapter 3:1 of that book: 'By night on my bed I
sought him whom my soul loveth: I sought him, but I found him not.'

[b] Henrietta Berkeley was moved constantly from one place of hiding to another in
London before the trial. Cf. Appendix I.

[c] Officer who carries the regimental standard.

[d] Dragoon regiment.

fly; and thou perhaps art waiting for the hour wherein thou think'st I'll give my self away to *Foscario*: Oh cruel and unkind! to think I lov'd so lightly, to think I wou'd attend that fatal hour; no, *Philander*, no, faithless, dear inchanter: Last night, the Eve to my intended Wedding-day, having repos'd my Soul by my resolves for flight, and only waiting the lucky minute for escape, I set a willing hand to every thing that was preparing for the ceremony of the ensuing morning; with that pretence I got me early to my Chamber, tried on a thousand dresses, and ask'd a thousand questions, all impertinent, which wou'd do best, which look'd most gay and rich? then drest my Gown with Jewels, deck'd my apartment up, and left nothing undone that might secure 'em both of my being pleas'd and of my stay; nay, and to give the less suspicion, I undress'd my self, even to my under Peticoat and Night-gown; I wou'd not take a Jewel, not a Pistol, but left my Women finishing my work, and carelessly, and thus undrest, walk'd towards the Garden, and while every one was busie in their office, getting my self out of sight, I posted o're the Meadow to the Wood as swift as *Daphne*[a] from the God of day, till I arriv'd most luckily where I found the Chariot waiting, attended by *Brilljard*, of whom, when I (all fainting and breathless with my swift flight) demanded his Lord, he lifted me into the Chariot, and cried, a little farther, *Madam*, you will find him; for he, for fear of making a discovery took yonder shaded path——towards which we went, but no dear vision of my Love appear'd——and thus, my charming Lover, you have my kind adventure; send me some tidings back that you are found, that you are well, and lastly, that you are mine, or this that shou'd have been my wedding day, will see it self that of the death of

Silvia.

Paris, *Thursday, from my Bed, for want of Cloaths*,[b] *or rather, news from* Philander.

---

[a] A nymph and daughter of Peneus, the river-god. Pursued by Apollo, she begged her father to rescue her and he transformed her into a laurel tree.

[b] After Henrietta Berkeley's disappearance, it quickly became common knowledge that she had left Durdans in such haste that she took almost nothing of her wardrobe. In a letter to her sister, the Countess of Rutland, dated August or September, 1682 Bridget Noel writes: 'Concerning grey night clothes which cost 5l. 5s. Lady Harriet Berkeley is said to have gone away with only a night gown and slippers.'

Also cf. Appendix I.

To Silvia.

My life, my *Silvia*, my eternal joy, art thou then safe? and art thou reserv'd for *Philander*? am I so blest by Heaven, by love, and my dear charming Maid? then let me dy in peace, since I have liv'd to see all that my Soul desires in *Silvia*'s being mine; perplex not thy soft heart with fears or jealousies, nor think so basely, so poorly of my love to need more oaths or vows, yet to confirm thee I wou'd swear my breath away; but oh, it needs not here; — take then no care, my lovely dear, turn not thy charming eyes or thoughts back on afflicting objects, oh think not on what thou hast abandoned, but what thou art arriv'd to; look forward on the joys of love and Youth, for I will dedicate all my remaining life to render thine serene and glad; and yet, my *Silvia*, thou art so dear to me, so wondrous pretious to my Soul, that I in my extravagance of love, I fear, shall grow a troublesome and wearying Coxcomb, shall dread every look thou givest away from me——a smile will make me rave, a sigh or touch make me commit a murther on the happy slave, or my own jealous heart, but all the world besides is *Silvia*'s, all but another Lover; but I rave and run too fast away, ages must pass a tedious term of years before I can be jealous, or conceive thou canst be weary of *Philander*---I'll be so fond, so doating, and so playing, thou shalt not have an idle minute to throw away a look in, or a thought on any other; no, no, I have thee now, and will maintain my right by dint and force of love——oh, I am wild to see thee---but, *Silvia*, I am wounded[a]--do not be frighted though, for 'tis not much or dangerous, but very troublesome since it permits me not to fly to *Silvia*, but she must come to me, in order to it, *Brilljard* has a Bill on my Goldsmith in *Paris* for a thousand Pistols to buy thee something to put on; any thing that's ready, and he will conduct thee to me, for I shall rave my self into a feaver if I see thee not to day — I cannot live without

---

[a] Grey does appear to have been involved in a duel at this time. An intelligence report dated June 2 states that 'Mr. Cittell...said he heard a duel was fought between Lord Grey and the Duke of Albemarle and that no great damage was done.'

thee now for thou'rt my life my everlasting charmer: I have order'd *Brilljard* to get a Chariot and some unknown Livery for thee, and I think the continuance of passing for what he has already rendred thee will do very well, till I have taken farther care of thy dear safety, which will be as soon as I am able to rise; for most unfortunately, my dear *Silvia*, quitting the Chariot in the thicket for fear of being seen with it, and walking down a shaded path that suited with the melancholy and fears of unsuccess in thy adventure; I went so far, as e're I cou'd return to the place where I left the Chariot, 'twas gone——it seems with thee; I know not how you mist me —— but possess'd my self with a Thousand false fears, sometimes that in thy flight thou might'st be pursued and overtaken, seiz'd in the Chariot and return'd back to *Bellfont*, or that the Chariot was found and seiz'd on upon suspicion, though the Coach-man and *Brilljard* were disguis'd past knowlege——or if thou wert gone, alas, I knew not whither, but that was a thought my doubts and fears would not suffer me to ease my Soul with; no, I (as jealous lovers do) imagin'd the most tormenting things for my own repose, I imagin'd the Chariot taken, or at least so discover'd as to be forc'd away without thee; I imagin'd that thou wert false ——Heaven forgive me, false, my *Silvia*, and hadst chang'd thy mind; mad with this thought (which I fansied most reasonable and fixt it in my soul) I rav'd about the Wood, making a thousand vows to be reveng'd on all; in order to it I left the Thicket, and betook my self to the high road of the Wood, where I laid me down amongst the fern, close hid, with my Sword ready, waiting for the happy Bridegroom, whom I knew (it being the wedding eve) wou'd that way pass that Evening; pleas'd with revenge which now had got even the place of love; I waited there not above a little hour, but heard the trampling of a horse, and looking up, with mighty joy, I found it *Foscario's*, alone he was, and unattended, for he'd outstrip'd his equipage, and with a lover's haste, and full of joy, was making towards *Bellfont*; but I (now fir'd with rage) leap'd from my covert, cried, stay, *Foscario*, e're you arrive to *Silvia*, we must adjust an odd account between us--at which he stopping, as nimbly alighted ——in fine, we fought, and many wounds were given and received on both sides, till his people coming up parted us just as we were fainting with loss of blood in each others arms; his Coach and Chariot were amongst his equipage, into the first his Servants lifted him, when he cried out with a feeble voice——to have me, who now lay bleeding on the ground put into the Chariot, and to be safely convey'd where ever I commanded, and so in haste they drove him towards *Bellfont*, and me, who was resolv'd not to stir far from it, to the Village within a mile of it; from whence I sent to *Paris* for a Surgeon and dismist the Chariot, ordering in the hearing of the Coachman a Litter to be brought immediately to convey me that night to *Paris*; but the Surgeon coming, found it not safe for me to be removed, and I am now willing to live, since *Silvia* is mine, haste to me then, my lovely Maid, and fear not being discover'd, for I have given order here in the Cabaret[a] where I am, if any enquiry is made after me, to say I went last night for *Paris*: Haste, my love, haste to my arms, as feeble as they are they'll grasp thee a dear wellcome: I'll say no more, nor prescribe rules to thy love, that can inform thee best what thou must do to save the life of thy most passionate adorer,

Philander.

To *Philander*.

I have sent *Brilljard* to see if the Coast be clear that we may come with safety, he brings you instead of *Silvia*, a young Cavalier that will be altogether as wellcome to *Philander*, and who impatiently waits his return at a little Cottage at the end of the Village.

To Silvia.

From the Bastill.[b]

I know my *Silvia* expected me at home with her at dinner to day, and wonders how I cou'd live so long as since morning without the eternal joy of my Soul; but know, my *Silvia*, that a

---

[a] A drinking house or tavern.

[b] The Tower of London. Grey was arrested and placed in the Tower until his trial for the seduction of Henrietta Berkeley who was still missing. In a letter to her sister dated October 24, 1682 the Countess of Northampton writes, "Tis serting he has delewded her and intised her from her father, but wheare she is is not yet knowen ...he must soon produce her, or his Lordship must remaine a prisoner'.

trivial misfortune is now fallen upon me, which in the midst of all our Heaven of joys, our softest hours of life, has so often chang'd thy smiles into fears and sighings, and ruffled thy calm Soul with cares: Nor let it now seem strange or afflicting, since every day for this three months we have been alarm'd with new fears that have made thee uneasie even in *Philander*'s arms, we knew some time or other the storm wou'd fall on us, though we had for three happy months sheltred our selves from its threatning rage; but Love I hope has arm'd us both; for me——let me be depriv'd of all joys, (but those my charmer can dispence) all the false worlds respect, the dull esteem of Fools and formal Coxcombs, the grave advice of the censorious wise, the kind opinion of ill judging Women, no matter, so my *Silvia* remain but mine.

I am, my *Silvia*, arrested at the suit of *Monsieur* the Count, your Father, for a Rape on my lovely Maid: I desire my Soul, you will immediately take Coach and go to the Prince *Cesario*, and he will bail me out; I fear not a fair trial, and *Silvia*, thefts of mutual love were never counted Felony; I may dy for Love, my *Silvia*, but not for loving——go, haste, my *Silvia* that I may be no longer detain'd from the solid pleasure and business of my Soul——haste, my lov'd dear—— haste and relieve

Philander.

Come not to me, lest there should be an order to detain my dear.

To *Philander*.

I am not at all surpriz'd, my *Philander*, at the accident that has befallen thee, because so long expected, and love and that has so well fortified my heart that I support our misfortune with a courage worthy of her that loves and is belov'd by the glorious *Philander*; I am arm'd for the worst that can befall me, and that is my being rendred a publick shame, who have been so in the private whispers of all the Court[a] for near these happy three months, in which I have had the wondrous satisfaction of being retir'd from the World with the charming *Philander*; my Father too knew it long since, at least he cou'd not hinder himself from guessing it, though his fond indulgence suffer'd his Justice and his anger to sleep, and possibly had still slept had not *Mertilla's* spight and rage (I shou'd say just resentment, but I cannot) rouz'd up his drowsie vengeance: I know she has ply'd him with her softning eloquence, her prayers and tears to win him to consent to make a publick business of it; but I am entred, love has arm'd my Soul, and I'll pursue my fortune with that height of fortitude as shall surprise the world; yes *Philander*, since I have lost my honour, fame and friends, my interest and my Parents, and all for mightier love; I'll stop at nothing now, if there be any hazards more to run, I'le thank the spightfull fates that bring 'em on, and will even tire them out with my unwearied passion——Love on, *Philander*, if thou darst, like me; let 'em pursue me with their hate and vengeance, let Prisons, poverty and tortures seize me, it shall not take one grain of love away from my resolv'd heart, nor make me shed a tear of penitence, for loving thee; no, *Philander*, since I know what a ravishing pleasure 'tis to live thine I will never quit the glory of dying also thy

Silvia.

Cesario, *my dear, is coming to be your Bail; with Monsieur the Count of*————*I dy to see you after your suffering for* Silvia.

---

[a] In *The Trial of Ford Lord Grey*, one of the witnesses, a Captain Fitz-Gerrard, stated that

Being in Covent-Garden in Company, there was some discourse about my Lady Harriett Berkeley's being gone from her Father's, as it was the talk of the Town. Evidence that the aristocracy of England were following the scandal closely can be found in a letter to the Countess of Rutland, dated August 25, 1682, from her sister the Countess of Northampton which records that 'There is no newes yett of Lady Haritt Barkely'. Another letter to the Countess of Rutland, dated September 22, 1682, from Viscountess Dursley mentions that 'I cannot yet give you any account of the lost lady. The Berkeley family knows so little what is become of her that they proffer 2001. to whomsoever can discover where she is. . . .'

To Silvia.

Believe me, charming *Silvia*, I live not those hours I am absent from thee, thou art my life, my Soul and my eternal felicity; while you believe this truth, my *Silvia*, you will not entertain a thousand fears, if I but stay a moment beyond my appointed hour, especially when *Philander*, who is not able to support the thought that any thing should afflict his lovely Baby, takes care from hour to hour to satisfie her tender doubting heart. My dearest, I am gone into the City to my Advocates, my Tryal with *Monsieur* the Count, your Father, coming on to morrow, and 'twill be at least two tedious hours e're I can bring my adorable her

Philander.

To Silvia.

I was call'd on my dearest Child, at my Advocates, by *Cesario*, there is some great business this evening debated in the Cabal which is at *Monsieur*——in[a] the City; *Cesario* tells me there is a very diligent search made by *Monsieur* the Count, your Father, for my *Silvia*, I dy if you are taken, lest the fright shou'd hurt thee; if possible, I would have thee remove this evening from those Lodgings, lest the people who are of the Royal party shou'd be induc'd, through malice or gain, to discover thee; I dare not come my self to wait on thee, lest my being seen shou'd betray thee, but I have sent *Brilljard* (whose zeal for thee shall be rewarded) to conduct thee to a little house in the *Fauxburgh S. Germans*,[b] where lives a pretty Woman and Mistress to *Chevalier Tomuso*,[c] call'd

---

[a] The cabal met frequently at the house of Thomas Shepherd, a wine-merchant in Abchurch Lane in London. An intelligence report by one of Sir Leoline Jenkins' informants notes that

ye sd Ld Gray told him also that from Trenchard's Chamber He & sd Sr Thomas Armstrong went to Sheppards, where was likewise the Duke of Monmouth, Ld Russell, Coll: Romsey, Ferguson and Sheppard himselfe

[b] The Faubourg St-Germain was one of the most important streets in Paris at this time and contained the residences of many nobles. In Behn's substitution of Paris for London, the street stands for Charing Cross which was equally important in this period.

[c] Sir Thomas Armstrong. An important member of the Cabal, Armstrong was constantly featured in Tory satires as a lecher.

Belinda, a Woman of wit, and discreet enough to understand what ought to be paid to a Maid of the quality and character of *Silvia*; she already knows the stories of our loves; thither I'll come to thee and bring *Cesario* to supper, as soon as the Cabal breaks up; oh, my *Silvia*, I shall one day recompense all thy goodness, all thy bravery, thy love and thy suffering for thy eternal Lover and Slave,

Philander.

To *Philander*.

So hasty I was to obey *Philander*'s commands, that by the unwearied care and industry of the faithfull *Brilljard*, I went before three a clock disguis'd away to the place whither you order'd us, and was well receiv'd by the very pretty young Woman of the house, who has sense and breeding as well as beauty: But oh, *Philander*, this flight pleases me not: alas, what have I done? my fault is only love, and that sure I shou'd boast, as the most divine passion of the Soul; no, no, *Philander*, 'tis not my love's the criminal, no nor the placing it on *Philander* the crime; but 'tis thy most unhappy circumstances—thy being married, and that was no crime to Heaven till man made laws, and can laws reach to damnation? if so, curse on the fatal hour that thou wert married, curse on the Priest that joyn'd ye, and curst be all that did contribute to the undoing ceremony---except *Philander*'s Tongue, that answer'd yes—oh, Heavens! was there but one dear man of all your whole Creation that could charm the Soul of *Silvia*, and cou'd ye——oh, ye wise all-seeing Powers that knew my Soul, cou'd ye give him away? how had my innocence offended ye? our hearts you did create for mutual love, how came the dire mistake? another wou'd have pleas'd the indifferent *Mertilla*'s Soul as well, but mine was fitted for no other man; only *Philander*, the ador'd *Philander*, with that dear form, that shape, that charming face, that hair, those lovely speaking eyes, that wounding softness in his tender voice, had power to conquer *Silvia*; and can this be a sin? Oh, Heavens can it? must laws which man contriv'd for mere conveniency have power to alter the divine decrees at our Creation---perhaps they argue to

morrow at the bar that *Mertilla* was ordain'd by Heaven for
Philander; no, no, he mistook the Sister, 'twas pretty near he
came, but by a fatal errour was mistaken, his hasty Youth made
him too negligently stop before his time at the wrong Woman,
he shou'd have gaz'd a little farther on—and then it had been
Silvia's lot — 'tis fine divinity they teach that cry--Marriages are
made in Heaven--folly and madness grown into grave custome;
shou'd an unheedy youth in heat of blood take up with the first
convenient she that offers, though he an heir to some grave
Politician, great and rich, and she the outcast of the common
stews, coupled in height of wine, and sudden lust, which once
allay'd, and that the sober morning wakes him to see his errour,
he quits with shame the Jilt, and owns no more the folly; shall
this be call'd a Heavenly conjunction? were I in height of youth,
as now I am, forc'd by my Parents, oblig'd by interest and
honour to marry the old deform'd, diseas'd, decrepid Count
Antonio,[a] whose person, qualities and principles I loath, and
rather than suffer him to consummate his Nuptials, suppose I
shou'd (as sure I shou'd) kill myself, 'twere blasphemy to lay
this fatal marriage to Heavens charge—curse on your nonsense,
ye imposing Gown-men,[b] curse on your holy cant; you may as
well call Rapes and Murthers, Treason and Robbery, the acts of
Heaven; because Heaven suffers 'em to be committed, is it
Heavens pleasure therefore, Heaven's decree? a trick, a wise
device of Priests, no more—to make the nauseated, tir'd out
pair drag on the carefull business of life, drudg for the dull got
family with greater satisfaction, because they'r taught to think
marriage was made in Heaven; a mighty comfort that, when all
the joys of life are lost by it: were it not nobler far that honour
kept him just, and that good nature made him reasonable provision? daily experience proves to us, no couple live with less
content, less ease than those they cry Heaven joins; who is't
loves less than those that marry? and where love is not there is
hate and loathing, at best, disgust, disquiet, noise and repentance: No, *Philander*, that's a heavenly match when two Souls

---

[a] Possibly the Earl of Shaftesbury. Shaftesbury was constantly portrayed as an
aging lecher in Tory propaganda. The most famous of these satiric portraits was
Thomas Otway's character Antonio in *Venice Preserved* (1682). Antonio and his
mistress Aquilina, who is dubbed 'Nicky Nacky', are pictured as debauched creatures engaging in flagellation. Cf. also Behn's poem 'The Cabal at Nickey Nackeys'
[*Works of Aphra Behn*, Vol. 1, no, 48].

[b] Clergymen.

toucht with equal passion meet (which is but rarely seen)--
when willing vows, with serious consideration, are weigh'd
and made; when a true view is taken of the Soul, when no base
interest makes the hasty bargain, when no conveniency or
design of drudge, or slave, shall find it necessary, when equal
judgments meet that can esteem the blessings they possess,
and distinguish the good of eithers love, and set a value on each
others merits, and where both understand to take and pay; who
find the beauty of each others minds, and rate 'em as they
ought, whom not a formal ceremony binds (with which I've
nought to do; but dully give a cold consenting affirmative) but
well considered vows from soft inclining hearts, utter'd with
love, with joy, with dear delight when Heaven is call'd to
witness; She is thy Wife, *Philander*, He is my Husband, this is
the match, this Heaven designs and means, how then, oh, how
came I to miss *Philander?* or he his

Silvia.

*Since I writ this, which I design'd not an invective against Marriage
when I began, but to inform thee of my being where you directed; but
since I writ this, I say the House where I am is broken open*[a] with
Warrants and Officers for me, but being all undrest and ill, the
Officer has taken my Word for my appearance to morrow; it
seems they saw me when I went from my Lodgings and pursued me; haste to me, for I shall need your Counsel.

To Silvia.

My eternal joy, my affliction is inexpressible at the news you
send me of your being surpriz'd; I am not able to wait on thee
yet——not being suffer'd to leave the Cabal, I only borrow this

---

[a] An intelligence report from Roger L'Estrange to the Secretary of State Sir
Leoline Jenkins, dated the 28th of June, gives the following information on Hen-
rietta Berkeley's whereabouts at this time:
    Jones, a milliner, living over against the statue at Charing Cross on the Spring
    Garden side is a great confident of Lord Grey and it was at his house that he and
    Lady Henrietta Berkeley lay when she kept private. If he be near at hand, Jones
    will undoubtedly be with him sometimes and he may be dogged to find out my
    lord, who probably on a point of honour will not forsake his mistress.
Also cf. Appendix I.

minute to tell thee the sense of my Advocate in this case; which was, if thou shoud'st be taken, there was no way, no Law to save thee from being ravisht from my arms but that of marrying thee to some body whom I can trust; this we have often discours'd, and thou hast often vow'd thou'lt do any thing rather than kill me with a separation; resolve then, oh thou charmer of my Soul, to do a deed, that though the name wou'd fright thee, only can preserve both thee and me; it is——and though it have no other terrour in it than the name, I faint to speak it---to marry, *Silvia*; yes, thou must marry;[a] though thou art mine as fast as Heaven can make us, yet thou must marry; I've pitch'd upon the property, 'tis *Brilljard*, him I can only trust in this affair; it is but joining hands ——no more, my *Silvia*—— *Brilljard*'s a Gentleman, though a *Cadet*, and may be supposed to pretend to so great a happiness, and whose only crime is want of fortune; he's handsome too, well made, well bred, and so much real esteem he has for me, and I've so oblig'd him that I'm confident he'll pretend no farther than to the honour of owning thee in Court; I'll tie him from it, nay, he dares not do't, I'll trust him with my life—but oh, *Silvia* is more — think of it, and this night we will perform it, there being no other way to keep *Silvia* eternally

Philander's.

---

[a] The sensational ending to the trial of Ford Grey was recorded in the contemporary diary of Sir Roger Morrice. On Thursday Nov 23, 1682, he notes that

This day my Lord Greys business came to a Tryall, a great many things were laid open by the parties concerned, that it had been much for the honour of them all to have had them buried in perpetuall oblivion. The Lady Henrietta did in Court own her selfe to be marryed to the Son of Sr William Turner the Civillian, who was also in Court & averred his Mariag wth her…. In the Lord Grey's Tryall above mentioned, The Jury late in the evening found the Bill against the Lord Grey, who is at liberty upon Bayle on her appearance in Court, and is discharged from his imprisonment upon the Capias in Withernam.

Two days later, Morrice notes that 'The Lady Henrietta and Mr. Turner her husband are both committed Prisoners to the Kings Bench.' The following week, on the 20th, he also records that 'Mr. Turner and his wife the Lady Henrietta upon proofe of their Marriage are set at liberty' and, on the 22nd, he writes that

All the matters betwixt the Lord Grey Earle of Berkley Lady Henrietta &c are Compremised betweene themselves, and so no Judgment was this Term nor is to be given against the said Lord Grey.

To Silvia.

Now, my adorable *Silvia*, you have truly need of all that heroick bravery of mind I ever thought thee Mistriss of; for *Silvia*, coming from thee this morning, and riding full speed for *Paris*, I was met, stopt and seiz'd for high Treason,[a] by the King's messengers, and possibly may fall a sacrifice to the anger of an incens'd Monarch; my *Silvia*, bear this last shock of fate with a courage worthy thy great and glorious Soul; 'tis but a little separation, *Silvia*, and we shall one day meet again; by Heaven, I find no other sting in death but parting with my *Silvia*, and every parting wou'd have been the same; I might have died by thy disdain, thou might'st have grown weary of thy *Philander*, have lov'd another, and have broke thy vows, and tortur'd me to death these crueller ways; but fate is kinder to me, and I go blest with my *Silvia*'s love, for which Heaven may do much, for her dear sake, to recompence her faith, a Maid so innocent and true to sacred love; expect the best, my lovely dear, the worst has this comfort in't, that I shall die my charming *Silvia*'s

Philander.

To Philander.

I'll only say, thou dear supporter of my Soul, that if *Philander* dies, he shall not go to Heaven without his *Silvia*—by Heaven and earth I swear it. I cannot live without thee, nor shalt thou die without thy

Silvia.

---

[a] Six months after the trial of Ford Grey, Sir Roger Morrice records the following entry in his diary on May 10, 1683.

On Tuesday May the 8th at Guildhall 21 were Indicted for a Riot about the choice of the Sheriffs. The Lord Grey The two Sheriffs, Mr [Shute?] and Mr Pilkington Sr Tho. Player Mr John Jekel Mr Degle Mr Freeman Mr Swinock and as many more as to make them 14 were found guilty.

Morrice later notes that they were all freed upon bail and that on May 19th Grey was bound to the peace for a year. A month later, however, Grey was arrested again on charges relating to bundles of muskets found at his house in London.

To Silvia.

See, see, my adorable Angel, what cares the powers above take of divine innocence, true love and beauty, oh, see what they have done for their darling *Silvia*; cou'd they do less?

Know, my dear Maid, that after being examined before the King, I was found guilty enough to be committed to the *Bastile*,[a] (from whence, if I had gone, I never had return'd, but to my death) but the Messenger into whose hands I was committed refusing other Guards, being alone with me, in my own Coach, I resolv'd to kill if I cou'd no other way oblige him to favour my escape; I tried with Gold before I shew'd my dagger, and that prevail'd, a way less criminal, and I have taken sanctuary in a small Cottage near the Sea shore,[b] where I wait for *Silvia*; and though my life depend upon my flight, nay, more, the life of *Silvia*, I cannot go without her; dress your self then, my dearest, in your Boys cloaths, and haste with *Brilljard*, whither this

---

[a] On Thursday June 28, 1683 Sir Roger Morrice notes that

On Tuesday night the 26 my Lord Grey was examined and committed to the Tower, but made an escape at the Tower gate out of the Coach, the Serjeant at Armes (Mr. Dearham) that apprehended him being fallen a sleepe, who is committed and put into (I thinke) the hole in the Tower.

An intelligence report dated June 27 gives an account of the escape:

He, being brought this morning in a coach to the Tower by Sergeant Deerham, the coach stopping at the Bulwark Gate, found the Serjeant asleep, who not waking on his jogging him, the coachman not knowing any thing suffered him to come out of the coach and walk away, leaving the serjeant sleeping and a servant or two of his standing by the coach. He took water near the Customhouse and was landed at Pickled Herring on the other side. Before they landed him, they were followed by a soldier in a boat, who called them Stop a traitor, on which the waterman stopped till he came up but immediately the soldier said it was not the man and after whispering a little with him they went off together.

[b] A report to Sir Leoline Jenkins, dated July 4th notes that

Intelligence came to Portsmouth that four men and a woman in disguise came to a small creek near Chichester, where a vessel lay ready, which presently put to sea. On notice hereof a little yacht and the guard boats sailed to Spithead, hoping to have seized the passengers, but they are returned without any tidings of them.

A report submitted on the 3rd of July could not accurately identify the passengers on the ship but records that

they mistook the time and were forced to ride up and down by the shore six hours before the ferryman could carry them over, so that had the Sheriff been in the county to have secured the place, not one of them could have escaped.

Seaman[a] will conduct thee, whom I have hir'd to set us on some shore of safety;[b] bring what news you can learn of *Cesario*; I wou'd not have him die poorly after all his mighty hopes nor be conducted to a scaffold with shouts of joy, by that uncertain beast the Rabble, who us'd to stop his Chariot wheels with a fickle adorations whene're he look'd abroad——by Heaven, I pity him, but *Silvia*'s presence will chase away all thoughts, but those of love, from

Philander.

I need not bid
thee haste.

La Fin.

---

[a] By the 8th of July Sir Richard May had obtained more accurate information on the ship that had ferried Grey and Henrietta Berkeley to Holland:
I conclude that no persons mentioned in the proclamation escaped from this port, save Lord Grey, for but five persons went on board the Hare Pink, three whereof were Lord Grey, Madame Turner and Everest, the other two supposed to be Lord Grey's servants. The master is a Isle of Wight man with a wooden leg, a conventicle preacher having a pension for loss of his leg in his Majesty's service. The chief part owner of the pink is Thomas Hurst, commonly called Major Hurst, an active Independent of this place, formerly a soldier or officer against the late King, pardoned as Major Braman and many more of them were, without repentance
[b] An informer's deposition later clarified the events leading up to the escape of Grey and Henrietta Berkeley:
The sayd William Smith being sent by the Lord Gray to tell this Informant his condition & to desire him to get a Vessell ready to transport the said Lord Gray beyond sea. This Informant...went and spoke wth a certain wooden-leggd Master of a Vessell to sett a friend of his over...this Informant appointing the Sd master to take him and his friends on board ye next day at eleven a clock in the morning, at a place call'd the Mine-House, near ye mouth of Chichester Harbor. This Informant further Deposeth that he went to Up Park that night where he found ye foresd Lord Gray ... in the midst of a great wood in his Park where he had noe body with him save ye soldier that had run away with him from the Tower...and did thereupon convey ye said Ld Gray, ye Lady Henrietta Bartlett, Mr Turner her husband, ye soldier aforesaid, and 2 servants to ye mine-house abovementioned the place design'd to take them on board. This Deponent adds also, that they all lay in a wood near the water side till the time of their imbarking which was ye next day (being fryday) between ye hours of 12 & one at which time they did sett saile immediately to sea ye wind being at North West

Love Letters

FROM A

NOBLE MAN

TO HIS

SISTER:

Mixt With the

HISTORY

OF THEIR

ADVENTURES.

The Second Part by the
fame Hand.

LONDON,

Printed for the Author, and are to be fold
by the Bookfellers of *London*, 1685.

Lemuel Kingdon, *Esq;*[a]

SIR,

*I beg you will give me leave to express my gratitude in some measure,
for the favours I have receiv'd of you, and to make an acknowledgment
where I cannot pay a debt. 'Tis only what was long since design'd you,
when possibly it might have found something a better wellcome, by its
having made (as then it must have done) a voyage to have kist your
hands, and might perhaps then have contributed in some small degree
to your diversion, in a place where there is found so little — In order to
it I sent you the first part by one of your Officers, of which this is a
continuation. But being oblig'd to lay it by for other more material
business,[b] it has had the misfortune not to approach you till now, and
to which honour it has nothing to intitle it, but that of bearing your
Name before it, which will put a value upon it to the World. And since
I never was of a nature to hord any good to my peculiar use, 'tis with
great satisfaction I am, by this short character of you, distributing a
blessing to that part of Mankind who have not that of knowing you. For
there is an unspeakable pow'r and pleasure in obliging, and 'tis a pain
to the good natur'd to conceal any thing, whose communication may
gratify the world, and I am uneasie when a good man is not as well*

---

[a] Kingdon had been paymaster general of the forces in the 1670s. By 1685,
however, when Behn sent him a copy of the first part of *Love-Letters*, he was in
Ireland as commissioner of the revenue. In the same year he returned to stand as
MP for Bedwyn in James's first parliament.

[b] There is evidence that Behn was in financial difficulties in 1685. A letter to
Zachary Baggs, son of a gold merchant, suggests she had been forced to borrow
money:

Whereas I am indebted to Mr baggs the sum of six pound for the payment of
which Mr Tonson has obliged himself. Now I do hereby empower Mr Zachary
Baggs, in case the said debt is not fully discharged before Michaelmas next to stop
what money he shall hereafter have in his hands of mine, upon the playing my
first play till this aforesaid debt of six pound be discharged. Witness my hand this
1st August, ———85

117

understood by every body as by myself, and I boast that honour here, with more vanity than of any other happyness. Tho I know, I shall be censur'd by your lovers for saying so little where so much is due: But since I write to the number that do not know you, rather than those that do, this will at least suffice to shew how fine a thing man can be, so qualify'd and set out by nature for eternal esteem. For, Sir, there is in you something, besides the common vertues of your Sex, so ingaging, some Art in Nature so peculiar to your self, so insinuating into the soul, that there is not found any thing so dull in Humankind as not to love, Honour and value you: Nor is that man born that is your Enemy, no not even amongst those Phanatical dispositions,[a] whose principles and opinions are so distant from those Honest and Generous ones of yours; at least they love the Man tho they raile at his notions, esteem the person tho they abominate the loyallist; nor can I reflect on the excellency of your temper, but I think you born to put the ill natur'd world in to good Humour. You are all ways easie without affectation, merry without extravigance, generous, liberal, and good without vanity, sedate and even without constraint, cheerful and calme as innocence, tho the World storm and reel with mad confusion, still from the serenity of your looks we read the fair weather in your mind, which times or seasons can never discompose, while all goes well with your King and Country. You have a greatness of Soul which it seemes as if fate durst not oppress, and he who is so truly magnificent within, needs not trouble the World for elbow room, and who is ambitions of more than you possess, does but purchase an empty name at the expence of his repose and sense, and lessens his Glory by equalling it to a Title. The Sun at noon is no wonder, but to see as great an Illumination in a Star tho of the first magnitude, we gaze at with admiration. Title (that trifle which you can command when you please, and which 'tis far greater to merit than to wear,) serves rather to render vice more apparent than to elivate the vertues. Heav'n has made you more truly happy, and has set no blessing at too vast a distance for your reach; but has subdued even all your wishes to your pow'r, and left you almost nothing to ask: having suted your fame and fortune to the greatness of your mind

How soon at the choice of the most glorious Senate,[b] that ever blest

---

[a] Extreme Whigs and the supporters of the Monmouth Rebellion. By the time of the publication of *Love-Letters*, Part II, the rebellion was over and Monmouth had been executed.

[b] James II's first parliament, which he assembled in 1685.

the Land, was your vallu'd name snatch'd by every glad and giving voice, and made the Musick of the happy day, when black exclusioners[a] *were justly damn'd from the field, and only such untainted Supporters of the Royal cause, thought worthy to bear apart in so glorious a Concerne, as* Giving Cæsar[b] *his due! Here, Sir, you appear'd in your proper sphere dispersing that darling vertue of your Soul, lavishly giving, generously disposing and dealing out according to your mighty mind, and had the glory even of obliging a Monarch, than which nothing could be a greater satisfaction to you. But, Sir, you do all things with a perfect good grace, and even business, that toyle of Life, you render soft and easie, and as if you alone were created to manage the concernes of the World you make business your pleasure and diversion, and laugh at those that fatigue them selves with mighty affairs, and who assume like* Trincilo,[c] *a dull Gravity, to be esteem'd great, wise, and busie, while you discover only the best and noblest part of business, the effects of it, the rest, the Gentleman so handsomly conceals, we perceive no more than Fairy Huswifry, which is still acted in the shades and silence of the night, when Mortals are a sleep, and who find all fair and clean in the morning, but cannot guess at the invisible hand that did it. I am so good a subject that I wish all his Majesties work done by such hands, heads and heart, so effectual and so faithful, and than we shall fear no more Rebellions, but every man shall bask securely under his own Vine, that has one.—For my part I have only escap'd fleaing by the Rebels to starve more securely in my own native Province of Poetry, tho I am as well pleas'd at our late Victory,[d] and the Growing Glories of my King, as he that has got a Commission by it, if I may have this*

---

[a] Those Whigs who had supported the Exclusion Bills in the early 1680s demanding the exclusion of James, Duke of York, from the succession to the throne because of his Catholicism.

[b] Gaius Julius Caesar (102–144 BC), the politician who emerged from the struggles which destroyed the Roman republic and eventually became the first Roman emperor. Behn is here referring to James II who was crowned King of England in 1685. In *A Pindarick on the Death of Our Late Sovereign*, she also equates Charles II with Caesar [*Works of Aphra Behn*, Vol. 1, no. 65] and, in *Oroonoko*, the African king is given the name Caesar by the slave-masters.

[c] A minor character in Shakespeare's *The Tempest*. Behn is here referring to John Dryden and Charles Davenant's adaptation of the play as *The Tempest or The Enchanted Island* (1670) which had a modified subplot in which royalist and republican themes were prominent. Trinculo, having married Sycorax, states 'you are in a high place, Spouse, and must give good Example. Here they come, we'll put on the gravity of Statesmen, and be very dull, that we may be held wise.' [IV.ii.12–15]

[d] The defeat of the Duke of Monmouth's rebel forces. The rebellion was effectively ended at the Battle of Sedgemoor in July, 1685.

by it, if I may have this happyness added to it, of still retaining the
Honour of your friendship, and be still number'd in the Crowd of

SIR,

Your most Oblig'd
humble Servant,

A. B.

LETTERS

FROM A

NOBLE MAN

TO HIS

SISTER:

The Second Part by the same hand.

The ARGUMENT.

At the end of the first Part of these Letters, we left *Philander*
impatiently waiting on the Sea shore for the approach of the
lovely *Silvia*; who accordingly came to him drest like a youth, to
secure her self from a discovery. They staid not long to caress
each other, but he taking the welcome Maid in his Arms, with a
transported joy bore her to a small Vessel, that lay ready near
the *Beach*, where with only *Brilljard* and two Men Servants, they
put to Sea, and past into *Holland*, landing at the nearest Port;[a]
where after having refresht themselves for two or three days,
they past forward towards the *Brill*.[b] *Silvia* still remaining under
that amiable disguise; but in their passage from Town to Town,
which is sometimes by Coach, and other times by Boat, they
chanc'd one day to incounter a young *Hollander*[c] of a more than
Ordinary Gallantry, (for that Country so degenerate from good
manners and almost common Civility, and so far short of all the

---

[a] An intelligence report informed Sir Leoline Jenkins that Grey and his associates
'were at sea from fryday till Munday night at which time they arriv'd in Flushing
Harbour from whence they went in the ships boat up to Middleburgh'.

[b] Brielle, a Dutch port.

[c] In the late seventeenth century, Holland was one of seven provinces united for
their own defence by the Union of Utrecht in 1579.

good qualities that made themselves appear in this young Noble Man. He was very hansom, well made, well drest, and very well attended; and whom we will call *Octavio*,[a] and who, young as he was, was one of the States of *Holland*;[b] he spoke admirable good French, and had a vivacity and quickness of Wit unusual with the Natives of that part of the World, and almost above all the rest of his Sex: *Philander* and *Silvia* having already agreed for the Cabin of the Vessel that was to carry them to the next Stage, *Octavio* came too late to have any place there but amongst the common crow'd; which the Master of the Vessel,[c] who knew him was much troubl'd at, and addrest himself as civilly as he cou'd to *Philander* to beg permission for one Stranger of quality to dispose of himself in the Cabin for that day: *Phillander* being well enough pleas'd, so to make an acquaintance with some power of that Country, readily consented, and *Octavia* enter'd with an address so graceful and obliging, that at first sight he inclin'd *Phillanders* heart to a friendship with him, and on the other side the lovely person of *Phillander*, the quality that appear'd in his face and mein oblig'd *Octavio* to become no less

---

[a] In his confession, later published as *The Secret History of the Rye House Plot*, Grey says that while in Cleve

I laid aside all thoughts of England, but such as were for my support, and held no correspondence with any in it, but about my own private affairs, till such time as monsieur Fuchs was sent Ambassador, by his master the elector of Brandenburgh, to the States of Holland; who in his way thither rested some days at Cleve, where by the means of some friends I became acquainted with him (which to the best of my remembrance was the next spring after my coming over.) Our acquaintance in a short time grew to so great a friendship, that I received many proof of his...

It is also possible that Octavio is based on Hermanus de Bressaw, the merchant who helped Grey and his companions to settle in Cleve. However, while there may be some historical basis for the characters of Octavio, his sister Calista and her husband, the Count of Clarinau, Behn uses them primarily to construct more traditional romantic plots which parallels the story of Philander and Silvia.

[b] The United Provinces, of which Holland was just one, were also known as the States of Holland. Each was virtually a sovereign state and they were linked together as a republican federation rather than by the authority of one central monarch.

[c] An intelligence report notes that

ye Lord Gray aforesaid had had some small direction from the master of the Vessell to one Mr Washington a Merchant at Rotterdam, who lives upon the new Haven, and did formerly lodge the Earle of Shaftesbury...ye sd Mr Washington did kindly entertain the foremention'd Lord Gray (tho' a person to him unknown) for ye space of 3 weekes or thereabouts, being the time that the sd Lady H. Bartlett [Berkeley] stay'd ill with the Deponent at Middleburgh.

The report goes on to state that another reason for leaving Henrietta Berkeley in Middelburg was a report in a Dutch gazette that Lord Grey was travelling in the company of his sister-in-law.

his admirer. But when he saluted *Silvia*, who appear'd to him a youth of quality, he was extreamly charm'd with her pretty gayety, and an unusual Air and life in her address and motion, he felt a secret joy and pleasure play about his Soul he knew not why; And was almost angry that he felt such an emotion for a youth, tho the most lovely that he ever saw: After the first complyments, the fell into discourse of a thousand indifferent things; and if he were pleas'd at first sight with the two Lovers, he was wholly charm'd by their conversation; especially that of the amiable youth; who well enough pleas'd with the young Stranger, or else hitherto having met nothing so accomplisht in her short Travels, and indeed despairing to meet any such; she put on all her gayety and charms of Wit, and made as absolute a Conquest as 'twas possible for her suppos'd Sex to do over a man, who was a great admirer of the other; and surely the lovely Maid never appear'd so charming and desirable as that day; they din'd together in the Cabin, and after dinner repos'd on little Matresses by each others side, where every motion, every Limb as carelessly she lay, discover'd a thousand Graces and more and more inflam'd the now beginning Lover; she cou'd not move, nor smile, nor speak, nor order any charm about her, but had some peculiar Grace that begun to make him uneasie; and from a thousand little Modesties both in her blushes and motions he had a secret hope she was not what she seem'd, but of that Sex whereof she discovered so many softnesses and beauties; tho to what advantage that hope wou'd amount to his repose, was yet a disquiet he had not consider'd nor felt: Nor cou'd he by any fondness between them or indiscretion of love, conceive how the lovely Strangers were allied; he only hop'd, and had no thoughts of fear, or any thing that cou'd check his new beginning flame. While thus they past the after-noon, they ask'd a thousand questions. Our Lovers of the Country and manners, and their security and civility to Strangers; to all which *Octavio* answer'd as a man, who wou'd recommend the place and persons purely to oblige their stay; for now self interest makes him say all things in favour of it; and of his own friendship, offers them all the service of a Man of power, and who cou'd make an interest in those that had more than himself; much he protested, much he offer'd, and yet no more than he design'd to make good on all occasions, which they receiv'd with an acknowledgment, that plainly discover'd a generosity and quality above the common rate of Men; so that finding in each other occasions for Love and friendship, they mutually protest it, and nobly entertain'd it. *Octavio* told his Name and quality, left nothing unsaid that might confirm the Lovers of his sincerity. This begot a confidence in *Phillander*, who in return told him so much of his Circumstances as suffic'd to let him know he was a person so unfortunate to have occasion'd the displeasure of his King against him, and that he cou'd not continue with any repose in that Kingdom, whose Monarch thought him no longer fit for those honours he had before receiv'd; *Octavio* renew'd his protestations of serving him, with his interest and fortune, which the other receiving with all the Gallant modesty of an unfortunate Man, they came a shore where *Octavio*'s Coaches and Equipage waiting his coming to conduct him to his house, he offer'd his new friends the best of 'em to carry them to their lodging, which he had often prest might be his own Pallace, but that being refus'd as too great an honour, he wou'd himself see them plac'd in some one, which he thought might be most sutable to their quality; they excus'd the trouble, but he prest too eagerly to be deny'd and he conducted them to a Merchants house[a] not far from his own, so Love had contriv'd for the better management of this new affair of his heart, which he resolv'd to persue, be the fair object of what sex soever; but after having well enough recommended em to the care of the Merchant he thought it justice to leave em to their rest, tho with abundance of reluctancy. So took his leave of both the Lovely Strangers and went to his own home: and after a hasty supper got himself put to bed: not to sleep; for now he had other business: Love took him now to task, and ask'd his heart a thousand questions. Then 'twas he found the Idea of that fair unknown had absolute possession there: Nor was he at all displeas'd to find he was a captive; his

---

[a] Little is known of 'Mr Washington' except that he was an English merchant with a house on the new haven in Rotterdam. The Earl of Shaftesbury and Robert Ferguson, his secretary, had lodged with Washington in November 1682, shortly before the Earl's death. Since Washington was a strong supporter of the Whig cause, it was natural that Ford Grey should have sought help from him. Contemporary reports to Secretary of State Jenkins record that

ye forsaid Lady [Henrietta Berkeley]...came to Rotterdam to the sd Lord Gray after some 3 weekes stay (as it is said before) at Middleburgh but not tarrying longer than ye next day (after their arrivall) at Rotterdam...My Lord Mr Turner and this Informant went forwards by Waggons to Cleve, where they had Letters of Recommendation from Mr Washington to one Myn Heere Harmanus de Bressaw who recd them all very kindly.

youth and quality promise his hopes, a thousand advantages above all other men: but when he reflected on the Beauty of *Phillander*, on his Charming youth and Conversation, and every Grace that adorns a Conqueror, he grew inflam'd, disorderd, restless, angry, and out of Love with his own attractions; consider'd every Beauty of his own person and found 'em, or at least thought 'em infinitly short of those of his now Fancy'd Rival, yet 'twas a Rival that he cou'd not hate nor did his passion abate one thought of his Friendship for *Phillander*, but rather more increas'd it, insomuch that he once resolv'd it shou'd surmount his Love if possible, at least he left it on the upper hand, till time shou'd make a better discovery. When tir'd with thought we'l suppose him a sleep, and see how our Lovers far'd. Who being lodg'd all on one Stair Case (that is *Phillander*, *Silvia*, and *Brilljard*) it was not hard for the Lover to steal into the longing Arms of the expecting *Silvia*; no fatigues of tedious journeys and little voyages had a bated her fondness or his vigour, the night was like the first, all joy! all transport! *Briljard* lay so near as to be a witness to all their sighs of Love, and little soft murmurs, who now began from a servant to be permitted as an humble companion; since he had had the Honour of being marry'd to *Silvia*, who yet he durst not lift his eyes or thoughts that way: yet it might be perceiv'd he was melancholy and sullen, when e're he saw their daliances, nor cou'd he know the joys his Lord nightly stole, without an impatience, which if but minded or known perhaps had cost him his life: he began from the thoughts she was his wife, to fancy fine injoyment, to fancy Authority which he durst not asume. And often wisht his Lord wou'd grow cold as possessing Lovers do; that then he might advance his hope, when he shou'd ever abandon or slight her: he cou'd not see her kist without blushing with resentment, but if he has assisted to undress him for her bed, he was ready to dy with anger, and wou'd grow sick and leave the office to himself, he cou'd not see her naked charmes, her armes streatcht out to receive a Lover with impatient joy without madness. To see her clasp him fast when he threw himself into her soft white bosom, and smother him with kisses: No, he cou'd not bear it now, and almost lost his respect when he beheld it, and grew sawcy unperceiv'd. And 'twas in vain that he look'd back upon the reward he had to stand for that necessary Cypher a Husband, in vain he consider'd the reasons why, and the occasion wherefore; he now seeks for presidents of

125

usurp'd dominion, and thinks she is his Wife, and has forgot
that he's her creature, and *Phillanders* Vassal. These thoughts
disturb'd him all the night, and a certain jealousie, or rather
curiosity to listen to every motion of the Lovers, While they
were imploy'd after a different manner.

Next day it was debated what was best to be done as to their
conduct in that place: or whether *Silvia* shou'd yet own her Sex
or not, but she pleas'd with the Cavalier in her self: beg'd she
might live under that disguise. Which indeed gave her a
thousand charms to those which nature had already bestow'd
on her Sex, and *Philander* was well enough pleas'd she shou'd
continue in that agreable dress, which did not only add to her
beauty, but gave her a thousand little Priviledges, which otherwise wou'd have been deny'd to Women. Tho in a Country of
much Freedom. Every day she apear'd in the Toure, she fail'd
not to make a conquest on some unguarded heart of the fair
Sex, nor was it long ere she receiv'd *Billet Deux* from most of the
most accomplish'd who could speak and write *French*. This gave
them a pleasure in midst of their unlucky exile; and she fail'd
not to boast her conquests to *Octavio*, who every day gave all his
hours to Love, under the disguise of Friendship, and every day
receiv'd new wounds, both from her conversation and beauty,
and every day confirm'd him more in his first belief, that she
was a Woman: and that confirm'd his Love. But still he took
care to hide his passion with a gallantry that was natural to him,
and to very few besides; and he manag'd his eyes, which were
always full of Love so equally to both, that when he was soft
and fond it appear'd more his natural humour than from any
particuler cause, and that you may believe that all the arts of
gallantry, and graces of good managment were more peculiarly
his, than anothers, his Race was illustrious, being descended,
from that of the Princes of *Orange*,[a] and great birth will shine
through, and shew it self in spight of education and obscurity,
but *Octavio* had all those additions that render a man truly great

---

[a] The House of Orange occupied an ambiguous place in the political structure of
the States of Holland. The Prince of Orange was the 'Stadholder' of the republic.
The position was not that of a monarch, rather one of president or patriarch. In
wartime, the Stadholder would take on the role of uniting the armed forces and
leading them into battle. Throughout the seventeenth century, the members of the
House of Orange did try to move further towards the monarchical structure of
families such as the Stuarts but anti-Orangist forces in the Dutch Republic kept
these efforts in check.

and brave, and this is the character of him that was next undone by our unfortunate and fatal Beauty. At this rate for sometime they liv'd thus disguis'd under feign'd names. *Octavio* omitting nothing that might oblige 'em in the highest degree, and hardly any thing was talk'd of but the new and beautiful Strangers; whose conquest in all places over the Ladys are well worthy, both for their rarity and comedy to be related intirely by themselves in a Novel. *Octavio* every day saw the abundance of pleasure the little revenges of Love on those Womens hearts who had made before little conquests over him, and strove by all the gay presents he made young *Fillmond*[a] (for so they call'd *Silvia*,) to make him appear unresistable to the Ladies, and while *Silvia* gave them new wounds, *Octavio* fail'd not to receive 'em too among the crow'd, till at last he became a confirm'd slave to the lovely unknown; and that which was yet more strange she captivated the Men no less than the Women, who often gave her *Serinades* under her Window with Songs fitted to the Courtship of a Boy, all which added to their diversion; but fortune had smil'd long enough and now grew weary of obliging, she was resolved to undeceive both Sexes and let 'em see the Errors of their love; for *Silvia* fell into a Feaver[b] so violent that *Phillander* no longer hop'd for her recovery, insomuch that she was oblig'd to own her Sex and take Women Servants out of decency, this made the first discovery of who and what they were, and for which every body languisht under a secret grief. But *Octavio* who now was not only confirm'd she was a Woman, but that she was neither wife to *Phillander*, nor cou'd in almost all possibility ever be so: That she was his Mistress, gave him hope that she might one day as well be conquer'd by him; and he found her youth, her Beauty, and her quality, merited all his pains of lavish Courtship: And now there remains no more than the fear of her dying to oblige him immediately to a discovery of his passion, too violent now by his new hope to be longer

---

[a] Behn has perhaps chosen the name for its echoes of the French words *fille du monde* which translate as 'worldly woman'.

[b] Intelligence reports confirm that Henrietta Berkeley fell ill shortly after her arrival at Middelburg:

they layd that night in an Inn upon the Market place, & there the Lady Henrietta Bartlett happening to be very sick with her sea-voyage the said Ld Gray thought fitt to stay till Wednesday morning, and then went for Rotterdam with ye foresd 2 persons – Mr Turner & the soldier leaving the Informt to take care of the said Lady at Middleburgh.

conceal'd, but decency forbids he shou'd now persue the dear design; he waited and made Vows for her recovery; visited her and found *Phillander* the most deplorable object that despair and love cou'd render him, who lay eternally weeping on her bed, and no Counsel or perswasion cou'd remove him thence; but if by chance they made him sensible 'twas for her repose, he wou'd depart to ease his mind by new torments, he wou'd rave and tear his delicate hair, sigh and weep upon *Octavio's* bosome, and a thousand times begin to unfold the story already known to that generous Rival; despair, and hopes of pitty from him, made him utter all; and one day, when by the advice of the Physitian he was forc'd to quit the Chamber to give her rest, he carried *Octavio* to his own, and told him from the beginning all the story of his Love with the charming *Silvia*; and with it all the story of his Fate: *Octavio* sighing (tho glad of the opportunity) told him his affairs were already but too well known, and that he fear'd his safety from that discovery, since the States had oblig'd themselves to harbour no declar'd Enemy to the French King: At this news our young unfortunate shew'd a resentment that was so moving, that even *Octavio*, who felt a secret joy at the thoughts of his departure, cou'd no longer refrain from pity and tenderness, even to a wish that he were less unhappy and never to part from *Silvia*; but soon love grew again triumphant in his heart, and all he cou'd say was that he wou'd afford him the aids of all his power in this incounter, which with the acknowlegments of a Lover, whose life depended on it, he receiv'd and parted with him, who went to learn what was decreed in Councel concerning him. While *Phillander* return'd to *Silvia* the most dejected Lover that ever Fate produc'd; where he had not sigh'd away above an hour but he receiv'd a Billet by *Octavio's* Page from his Lord; he went to his own apartment to read it, fearing it might contain something too sad for him to be able to hold his temper at the reading of, and which wou'd infallibly have disturb'd the repose of *Silvia*, who shar'd in every cruel thought of *Phillanders*; when he was alone he open'd it, and read this.

Octavio *to* Phillander.

My Lord,
I had rather dy then be the ungrateful messenger of news, which I am sensible will prove so fatal to you, and which will be best exprest in fewest words, 'tis decreed, that you must retire from the United Provinces in Four and Twenty hours, if you will save a life that is dear to me and *Silvia*, there being no other security against your being render'd up to the King of *France*. Support it well, and hope all things from the assistance of,

Your Octavio.

From the Council
Wednesday.

Phillander having finisht the reading of this, remain'd a while wholly without life or motion, when coming to himself he sigh'd and cryd, —— Why——farewel trifling life —— If of the two extreames one must be chosen, rather than I'le abandon *Silvia*, I'le stay and be deliver'd up a Victim to incensed *France*——'Tis but a life——At best I never Vallu'd thee——And now I scorn to preserve thee at the Price of *Silvias* teares! Then taking a hasty turn or two about his chamber, he pawsing cryd——But by my stay I ruine both *Silvia* and my self, her life depends on mine, and 'tis impossible hers can be preserv'd when mine is in danger, by retiring I shall shortly again be blest with her sight in a more safe security; by staying I resign my self poorly to be made a publick scorn to *France*, and the cruell Murderer of *Silvia*; now 'twas, after an hundred turns and pawses intermixt which sighs and raveings, that he resolv'd for both their safeties to retire, and having a while longer debated within himself how and where; and a little time ruminated on his hard persuing fate, grown to a calm of grief (less easy to be born than rage) he hastes to *Silvia*, whom he found something more cheerful than before, but dares not aquaint her with the commands he had to depart —— But silently he views her, while teares of Love and grief glide unperceivably from his fine eyes, his soul grows tenderer at every look, and pity and compassion joyning to his

Love, and his despairs, set him on the wrack of Life, and now believing it less pain to dy than to leave *Silvia*; resolves to disobey and dare the worst that shall befall him, he yet had some glimmering hope, as Lovers have, that some kind chance will prevent his going or being deliver'd up, he trusts much to the Friendship of *Octavio*, whose power joyn'd with that of his Unkle. (Who was one of the States also, and whom he had an ascendant over, as his Nephew and his heir,) might serve him; he therefore ventures to move him to compassion, by this following Letter.

Phillander *to* Octavio.

I know, my Lord, that the Exercise of Vertue and Justice is so innate to your soul, and so fixt to the very Principle of a generous Commonwealths man,[a] that where those are in competition 'tis neither birth, wealth, or Glorious merit, that can render the unfortunate condemn'd by you, worthy of your pity or pardon: your very Sons and fathers fall before your justice, and 'tis crime enough to offend, (tho innocently,) the least of your wholsom laws, to fall under the extremity of their rigor. I am not ignorant neither how flourishing this necessary Tyranny,[b] this lawful oppression, renders your State; how safe and glorious; how secure from Enemies at home, (those worst of foes) and how fear'd by those abroad; pursue then, Sir, your justifiable method, and still be high and mighty, retain your ancient Roman vertue,[c] and still be great as *Rome* her self in her height of glorious Commonwealths; rule your stubborn Natives by her

---

[a] During the Interregnum in England, the state was known as 'the Commonwealth'. With the restoration of Charles II, 'commonwealthmen' became the term for the Whigs who derived their beliefs from the republican ideology of that period.

[b] As in Commonwealth England, the government of the States of Holland was influenced by strict religious principles. The judicial system was known internationally for its harshness and foreign travellers frequently recorded their visits to the Amsterdam prisons which the Dutch liked to exhibit as models for other institutions.

[c] Both commonwealthmen and monarchists employed the concept of Roman-Machiavellian 'virtù'. For the republicans, it described a devotion to the public good and the relationship of equality between those who are ruled and their rulers. For the monarchists, it had a narrower definition in which the absolute right of a sovereign could not be opposed by the rights of a subject.

excellent examples, and let the height of your ambition be only to be as severely just, as rigidly good as you please, but like her too, be pitiful to Strangers, and dispence a Noble Charity to the distress'd, compassionate a poor wandring young Man, who flies to you for refuge, lost to his Native home, lost to his fame, his fortune, and his Friends; and has only left him the know-ledge of his innocence to support him from falling on his own Sword, to end an unfortunate life, persu'd every where, and safe no where, a Life whose only refuge is *Octavio*'s goodness, nor is it barely to preserve this life, that I have recourse to that only as my Sanctuary; and like an humble Slave implore your pity: Oh, *Octavio* pity my Youth; and interceed for my stay yet a little longer, Your self makes one of the illustrious Number of the Grave, the Wise, and mighty Councel, your Unkle and Relations make up another considerable part of it, and you are too dear to all, to find a refusal of your just and compassionate application. Oh! what fault have I committed against you, that I shou'd not find a safety here, as well as those charg'd with the same Crime with me, tho of less quality? Many I have incoun-ter'd here of our unlucky party,[a] who find a safety among you; is my birth a Crime? Or does the greatness of that augment my guilt? Have I broken any of your Laws, committed any outrage? Do they suspect me for a spie to *France*?[b] Or do I hold any Corrispondence with that ungrateful Nation? Does my Reli-gion, Principle, or Opinion differ from yours? Can I design the subversion of your Glorious State? Can I plot, cabal, or mutiny alone? Oh charge me with some offence, or your selves of injustice. Say, why I am deny'd my length of earth amongst you, if I dy? Or why to breath the open Air, if I live, since I shall neither oppress the one, nor infect the other; but on the con-trary am ready with my sword, my youth, and Blood to serve you, and bring my little aids on all occasions to yours: and shou'd be proud of the Glory to dy for you in Battle, who wou'd

---

[a] The States of Holland were the most frequent refuge for English Whig extrem-ists or commonwealthmen fleeing the king. The States were Protestant and republi-can, offering these English exiles a sympathetic alternative to Restoration Britain. The aim of Behn's own spying mission in Antwerp in 1666 was to infiltrate the exiled English community in the neighbouring States of Holland.

[b] It was common for English exiles in the States of Holland to be recruited by England's Secretaries of State as spies against the Dutch. In 1666, Behn herself succeeded in recruiting William Scot as a spy against his own regiment of English exiles and their Dutch allies.

deliver me up a Sacrifice to *France*. Oh! where *Octavio* is the glory or vertue of this *Punctilio*, for 'tis no other? There are no Laws that bind you to it, no obligatory Article of Nations, but an unnecessary complyment made a *nemini contradicente*[a] of your Senate, that argues nothing but ill nature, and cannot redound to any one advantage. An Ill nature that levell'd at me alone; for many I found here, and many shall leave under the same circumstances with me; 'tis only me whom you have mark'd out the victim to atone for all: Well then, my Lord, if nothing can move you to a safety for this unfortunate, at least be so merciful to suspend your cruelty a little, yet a little, and possible I shall render you the body of *Phillander*, tho dead, to send into *France*, as the trophy of your fidelity to that Crown: Oh yet a little stay your cruel sentence, till my lovely Sister, who pursu'd my hard fortunes, declare my Fate by her life or death: Oh my Lord, if ever the soft passion of Love have touch'd your soul, if you have felt the unresistable force of young charms about your heart, if ever you have known a pain and pleasure from fair eyes, or the transporting Joyes of Beauty. Pity a youth undone by Love and ambition, those powerful conquerours of the young. —— Pity, oh Pity a youth that dies, and will ere long no more complain upon your Rigours. Yes, my Lord, he dies without the force of a terrifying Sentence, without the grim reproaches of an angry Judg, without the soon consulted Arbitrary—— Guilty! of a severe and hasty Jury, without the ceremony of the Scaffol'd, Ax, and Hang man, and the clamours of inconsidering Crowds. All which melancholy ceremonies render death so terrible, which else wou'd fall like gentle slumbers upon the eye-lids. And which in field I wou'd incounter with that joy I wou'd the sacred thing I Love! But oh, I fear my fate is in the lovely *Silvia*, and in her dying eyes you may read it, in her languishing face you'le see how near it is aproacht. Ah! will you not suffer me to attend it there? by her dear side I shall fall as calmly as flowers from their stalks, without regret or pain: Will you by forcing me to dy from her, run me to a madness? To wild distraction? Oh think it sufficient that I dy here before half my race of youth be run, before the light be half burnt out, that might have conducted me to a world of Glory! Alas, she dies —— The Lovely *Silvia* dies, she is sighing out a soul to which mine is so intirely fixt, that they

---

[a] *Latin*: to be contradicted by no-one.

must go upward together. Yes, yes, she breaths it sick into my bosom, and kindly gives mine its disease of death; let us at least then dy in silence, quitted; and if it please Heaven to restore the languish'd Charmer, I will resign my self up to all your Rigorous honour, only to let me bear my treasure with me, while we wander o're the world to seek us out a safety in some part of it, where pity and compassion is no crime. Where men have tender hearts, and have heard of the God of Love; where Politicks are not all the business of the powerful, but where civillity and good nature reign.

Perhaps, my Lord, you'l wonder I plead no weightier Argument for my stay than Love, or the griefs and tears of a languishing Maid: But oh! they are such tears as every drop wou'd ransom lives, and nothing that proceeds from her charming eyes can be valu'd at a less rate! In Pity to her, to me, and your Amorous youths, let me bear her hence. For shou'd she look abroad as her own Sex, shou'd she appear in her natural and proper beauty, alas they were undone. Reproach not (my Lord) the weakness of this confession, and which I make with more Glory than cou'd I boast my self Lord of all the Universe: if it appear a fault to the more grave and wise, I hope my youth will plead something for my excuse. Oh say, at least, 'twas Pity that Love had the ascendent over *Phillanders* soul, say 'twas his Destiny, but say withal, that it put no stop to his advance to Glory; rather it set an edg upon his Sword, and gave wings to his ambition! — Yes, try me in your Councells, prove me in your Camps, place me in any hazard ——But give me Love! and leave to wait the life or death of *Silvia*, and then dispose as you please,

My Lord

Of Your unfortunate, Philander.

Octavio *to* Philander.

My Lord,
I am much concern'd that a Request so reasonable as you have made, will be of so little force with these arbitrary Tyrants of State, and tho you have addrest and appeal'd to me as one of

that grave and rigid number, (tho without one grain of their formalities, and I hope age, which renders us less Gallant, and more envious of the joys and liberties of youth, will never reduce me to so dull and thoughtless a member of State) yet I have so small and single a portion of their power, that I am asham'd of my incapacity of serving you in this great affair. I bear the Honour and the name 'tis true, of Glorious sway; but I can boast but of the worst and most impotent part of it, the Title only; but the busie, absolute, mischievious Politician, finds no room in my Soul, my humour, or constitution: And Ploding restless power I have made so little the business of my gayer, and more careless youth, that I have even lost my right of rule, my share of Empire amongst them. That little power (whose unregarded losse I never bemoan'd till it render'd me uncapable of serving *Phillander*,) I have stretch'd to the utmost bound for your stay; insomuch that I have receiv'd many reproaches from the wiser Coxcombs; have had my youths little debauches hinted on, and Judgments made of you (disadvantagious) from my Friendship to you; a Friendship, which, my Lord, at first sight of you, found a being in my soul, and when your wit, your goodness, your greatness, and your misfortunes has improv'd to all the degrees of it: Tho I am infinitely unhappy that it proves of no use to you here, and that the greatest testimony I can now render of it, is to warn you of your aproaching danger. And hasten your departure, for there is no safety in your stay. I just now heard what was decreed against you in councel, which no pleading nor Eloquence of Friendship had force enough to evade. Alass, I had but one single voyce in the number, which I sullenly and singly gave, and which unregarded past. Go then, my Lord, haste to some place where good breeding and humanity reigns. Go and preserve *Silvia*, in providing for your own safety; and believe me, till she be in a Condition to persue your Fortunes, I will take such care that nothing shall be wanting, either to recovery here, in order to her following after you. I am, alas but too sensible of all the pains you must indure by such a separation, for I am neither insensible, nor uncapable of love, or any of its violent effects: Go then, my Lord, and preserve the lovely Maid in your flight, since your stay and danger will serve but to hasten on her death: Go, and be satisfied she shall find a protection sutable to her Sex, her innocence, her Beauty, and her quality, and that where-ever you fix your stay, she shall be resign'd to your Arms by my Lord,

> Your Eternal Friend
> and humble Servant,
> Octavio.

Least in this sudden remove you shou'd want Mony, I have sent you several Bills of Exchange to what place soever you arrive, and what you want more (make no scruple to use me as a friend) and command.

After this Letter, finding no hopes, but on the contrary a dire necessity of departing, he told *Briljard* his misfortune, and ask'd his Counsel in this extremity of affairs. *Brilljard* (who of a Servant was become a Rival) you may believe, gave him such advice as might remove him from the object he ador'd. But after a great deal of dissembl'd trouble, the better to hide his joy, he gave his advice for his going with all the arguments that appear'd reasonable enough to *Philander*. And at every period urg'd that his life being dear to *Silvia*, and on which hers so immediately depended, he ought no longer to debate but haste his flight, to all which councell or Amorous *Hero*, with a soul ready to make its way thro' his trembling body, gave a sighing unwilling assent. 'Twas now no longer a dispute, but was concluded he must go, but how was only the question. How shou'd he take his farewel, how shou'd he bid adieu, and leave the dear object of his soul in an estate so hazardous, he form'd a thousand sad Ideas to torment himself with: fancying he shou'd never see her more, that he shou'd hear that she was dead, tho now she appear'd on this side of the Grave, and had all the signs of a declining disease. He fancy'd absence might make her cold and abate her passion to him, that her powerful beauty might atract adorers, and she being but a Woman, and no part Angel, but her form, 'twas not expected she shou'd want her Sexes frailties. Now he cou'd consider how he had won her, how by importunity and opportunity she had at last yielded to him, and therefore might to some new Gamster, when he was not by to keep her heart in continual play: Then 'twas that all the despair of jealous love, the throbs and piercing of a violent passion seiz'd his timorous and tender heart, he fancy'd her already in some new Lovers Arms, and ran o're all the soft enjoyments he had had with her; and fancy'd with tormenting thought, that so another wou'd possess her: till rackt with tortures he almost fainted on the *Repose* on which he was set: But *Brilljard* rous'd and indeavour'd to convince him: Told him he hop'd his fear was needless, and that he wou'd take all the watchful care imaginable of her conduct, be a spy upon her vertue, and from time to time give notice of all that shou'd pass: Bid him consider her quality, and that she was no common Mistress whom hire cou'd lead astray, and that if from the violence of her passion, or her more severe fate she had yeilded to the most Charming of men, he ought as little to imagine she cou'd be again a Lover, as that she cou'd find an object of equal beauty with that of *Phillander*. In fine, he sooth'd and Flatter'd him into so much ease, that he resolves to take his leave for a day or two under pretence of meeting and consulting with some of the rebell party; and that he wou'd return again to her by that time it might be imagin'd her feaver might be abated, and *Silvia* in a condition to receive the news of his being gone for a longer time, and to know all his affairs. While *Brilljard* prepar'd all things necessary for his departure, *Phillander* went to *Silvia*. From whom, having been absent two tedious hours; she caught him in her Arms with a transport of joy; reproach'd him with want of Love, for being absent so long. But still the more she spoke soft sighing words of Love, the more his Soul was seiz'd with melancholy. His sighs redoubl'd and he cou'd not refrain from leting fall some tears upon her bosom—— Which *Silvia* perceiving with a look and a trembling in her voyce, that spoke her fear, she cry'd, oh *Phillander*! these are unusual marks of your tenderness. Oh tell me, tell me quickly, what they mean. He answer'd with a sigh, and she went on ——'Tis so, I am undone, 'tis your lost vows, your broken faith you weep, Yes, *Phillander*, you find the flower of my beauty faded, and what you lov'd before you pity now, and these be the effects of it. Then sighing, as if his Soul had been departing on her neck, he cry'd by heaven, by all the powers of Love, thou art the same dear charmer that thou wert, then pressing her body to his bosom, he sigh'd a new as if his heart were breaking —— I know (says she) *Phillander* there's some hidden cause that gives these sighs their way, and that dear face a paleness. Oh tell me all; for she that cou'd abandon all for thee, can dare the worst of Fate, If thou must quit me —— Oh *Phillander*, if it must be so, I need not stay the lingering death of a feable Feaver: I know a way more noble and more sudden.

136

Pleas'd at her resolution, which all most destroy'd his jealousie and fears, a thousand times he kist her, mixing his grateful words and thanks with sighs, and finding her fair hands (which he put often to his mouth) to increase their fires, and her pulse to be more high and quick, fearing to relapse her into her (abating) feaver he forc'd a smile, and told her, he had no griefs, but what she made him feel, no torments but her sickness, nor sighs but for her pain, and left nothing unsaid, that might confirm her he was still more and more her Slave; and concealing his design in favour of her health, he ceas'd not vowing and protesting till he had settled her in all the tranquillity of a recovering beauty. And, as since her first Illness he had never departed from her Bed, so now this night he strove to appear in her Arms with all that usual Gayety of Love that her condition wou'd permit, or his circumstances cou'd feign, and leaving her a sleep at day-break (with a force upon his Soul that cannot be conceiv'd) but by parting Lovers, he stole from her Arms and retiring to his chamber he soon got himself ready for his flight and departed. We will leave *Silvia*'s ravings to be exprest by none but her self, and tell you that after about Fourteen days absence *Octavio* receiv'd this Letter from *Phillander*:

Phillander *to* Octavio.

Being safely arriv'd at *Collen*,[a] and by a very pretty and lucky adventure lodg'd in the house of the best quallity in the Town, I find my self much more at ease then I thought it possible to be without *Silvia*, from whom I am nevertheless impatient to hear, I hope absence appears not so great a Bugbear to her as 'twas imagin'd. For I know not what effects it wou'd have on me to hear her griefs exceeded a few sighs and tears. Those my kind absence has taught me to allow and bear without much pain,

---

[a] Cologne. There is no evidence that Grey himself ever went to Cologne at this time. In his confession, he mentions visits to Brussels and Amsterdam and describes his attempts to raise a regiment of horse in Berlin under the Elector of Brandenburg.

but shou'd her Love transport her to extreams of rage and despair, I fear I shou'd quit my safety here, and give her the last proof of my Love and my compassion: throw my self at her Feet, and expose my life to preserve hers, Honour wou'd oblige me to't. I conjure you, my dear *Octavio*, by all the Friendship you have vow'd me, (and which I no longer doubt,) let me speedily know how she bears my absence, for on that knowledg depends a great deal of the satisfaction of my life, carry her this inclos'd which I have writ her, and soften my silent departure, which possibly may apear rude and unkind, plead my pardon, and give her the story of my necessity of offending, which none can so well relate as your self. And from a mouth so eloquent, to a Maid so full of Love, will soon reconcile me to her heart. With her Letter I send you a Bill to pay her 2000 Patacons,[a] which I have paid *Vander Hanskin*[b] here, as his Letter will inform you, as also those Bills I receiv'd of you at my departure, having been supply'd by an *English* Merchant here, who gave me credit. 'Twill be an Age till I hear from you, and receive the news of the health of *Silvia*. Than which two blessings nothing will be more wellcom to,

Collen.

Generous Octavio,
Your PHILANDER.

Direct your Letters for me to your Merchant *Vander Hanskin*.

---

[a] A Portugese or Spanish silver coin.

[b] The English merchant may be based on Israel Hayes, who traded out of Amsterdam. An intelligence report from this period informed the Secretary of State, Leoline Jenkins, that

the chief persons that conveyed money to the said Lord Gray since his escape…is the Lady Gray ye foresd Lord Gray's wife and Mr Ralph Gray his brother who in about the latter end of July or ye being of August return'd the sd Lord Gray 300l by a Bill procur'd and drawn upon one Mr Israel Hayes Mercht of Amsterdam (who is Alderman Hayes His son of London…yt 150l was return'd ye sd Lord Gray…from Mr John Archer a Merchant of London about the end of October or the beginning of November. … & lastly that 150l was return'd ye sd Lord Gray in Dec. last …payable to Mr Washington for the use of ye sayd Lord Ld Gray

Philander *to* Silvia.

There is no way left to gain my *Silvia's* pardon, for leaving her, and leaving her in such circumstances, but to tell her 'twas to preserve a life, which I believ'd intirely dear to her, but that unhappy crime is too severely punisht by the cruelties of my absence. Believe me, Lovely *Silvia*, I have felt all your pains, I have burnt with your feaver, and sigh'd with your oppressions; Say, has my pain abated yours? Tell me! and hasten my health by the assurance of your recovery, or I have fled in vain from those dear Arms to save a life, of which I know not what account to give you, till I receive from you the knowledg of your perfect health, the true state of mine. I can only say I sigh, and have a sort of a being in *Collen*, where I have some more assurance of protection than I cou'd hope from those int'rested Bruits,[a] who sent me from you, yet Bruitish as they are, I know thou art safe from their Clownish outrages. For were they sensless as their Fellow Monsters of the sea, they durst not prophane so pure an excellence as thine, the sullen Boors wou'd jouder[b] out a wellcom to thee, and gape, and wonder at thy awful beauty, tho they want the tender sense to know, to what use 'twas made. Or if I doubted their Humanity, I cannot the Friendship of *Octavio*, since he has given me too good a proof of it to leave me any fear, that he has not in my absence persu'd those generous sentiments for *Silvia* which he vow'd to *Philander*, and of which the first proof must be his relating the necessity of my absence, to set me well with my adorable Maid. Who, better than I, can inform her: and that I rather chose to quit you only for a short space, than reduce my self to the necessity of losing you eternally. Let the satisfaction this ought to give you, retrieve your health and beauty, and put you into a condition of restoring to me all my joys. That by persuing the dictates of your Love, you may again bring the greatest happyness on earth to the Arms of

Your PHILANDER.

---

[a] Brutes.
[b] Grunt, speak rudely.

My affairs here are yet so unsettl'd, that I can take no order for your coming to me but, as soon as I know where I can fix with safety, I shall make it my business and my happyness: Adieu. Trust *Octavio* with your Letters only.

This Letter *Octavio* wou'd not carry himself to her, who had omitted no day, scarce any hour, wherein he saw not or sent not to the charming *Silvia*, but he found, in that which *Philander* had writ to him, an Aire of coldness altogether unusual with that passionate Lover, and infinitely short in point of tenderness to those he had formerly seen of his, and from what he had heard him speak; so that he no longer doubted (and the rather because he hop'd it) but that *Philander* found an abatement of that heat, which was wont to inspire at a more Amorous rate; this appearing declension he cou'd not conceal from *Silvia*, at least to let her know he took notice of it; for he knew her Love was too quick sighted and sensible to pass it unregarded, but he with reason thought, that when she shou'd find others observe the little flight she had put on her, her pride (which is natural to women in such cases) wou'd decline and lessen her Love, for his Rival. He therefore sent his Page with the Letters inclos'd in this from himself.

Octavio *to* Silvia.

Madam,

From a little necessary debauch I made last night with the Prince, I am forc'd to imploy my Page in those duties I ought to have perform'd my self: He brings you, Madam, a Letter from *Philander*, as mine which I have also sent you informes me; I shou'd else have doubted it; 'tis, I think, his character, and all he says of *Octavio* confesses the Friend, but where he speaks of *Silvia* sure he disguises the Lover: I wonder the mask shou'd be put on now to me, to whom before he so frankly discover'd the secrets of his Amorous heart. 'Tis a mistery I wou'd fain perswade my self he finds absolutely necessary to his interest, and I hope you will make the same favorable constructions of it, and not impute the lessen'd zeal wherewith he treats the charming *Silvia* to any possible change or coldness, since I am but too

140

fatally sensible, that no man can arrive at the Glory of being belov'd by you, that had ever power to shorten one link of that dear chain, that holds him, and you need but survey that adorable face, to confirm your tranquillitie, set a just value on your charmes, and you need no arguments to secure your everlasting Empire, or to establish it in what heart you please, this fatal truth I learnt from your fair eyes, e're they discover'd to me your Sex, and you may as soon change to what I then believ'd you, as I from adoring what I now find you; if all then, Madam, that do but look on you become your Slaves, and languish for you, love on, even without hope, and die, what must *Phillander* pay you, who has the mighty blessing of your Love, your Vows, and all that renders the hours of amorous Youth sacred, glad, and Triumphant? But you know the conquering power of your charmes too well to need either this daring confession, or a defence of *Phillanders* vertue from,

Madam,

Your obedient Slave,

Octavio.

Silvia had no sooner read this with blushes, and a thousand fears, and trembling of what was to follow in *Phillander*'s Letters both to *Octavio* and to her self, but with an Indignation agreeable to her haughty Soul she cry'd —— *How,---slighted! and must* Octavio *see it too: By Heaven if I shou'd find it true he shall not dare to think it*; then with a generous rage she broke open *Phillanders* Letter; and which she soon perceiv'd did but too well prove the truth of *Octavio*'s suspition, and her own fears. She repeated it again and again, and still she found more cause of grief and anger; Love occasion'd the first, and Pride the last: And, to a Soul perfectly haughty, as was that of *Silvia* 'twas hard to guess which had the assendant: She consider'd *Octavio* to all the advantages that thought cou'd conceive in one who was not a Lover of him; she knew he merited a heart tho she had none to give him, she found him charming without having a tenderness for him, she found him young and amorous without desire towards him, she found him great, rich, powerful, and generous, without designing on him, and tho she knew her Soul free from all Passion, but that for *Philander*; nevertheless she blusht and was angry, that he had thoughts no more advantagious to the power of those charmes, which she wisht might appear to him above her Sex: It being natural to Women to desire Conquests, tho they hate the conquer'd; to glory in the tryumph, tho they despise the Slave. And believ'd, while *Octavio* had so poor a sense of her beauty as to believe it cou'd be forsaken, he would adore it less; And first to satisfie her pride she left the softer business of her heart to the next tormenting hour, and sent him this careless answer by his Page, believing if she appear'd too angry it might look as if she valu'd his opinion, and therefore dissembled her thoughts, as women in those cases ever do, who when most angry seem the most Galliard,[a] especially when they have need of the friendship of those they flatter.

Silvia *to* Octavio.

Is it indeed *Octavio*, that you believe *Philander* cold, or wou'd you make that a pretext to the declaration of your own passion, we French Ladies are not so nicely ty'd up to the formalities of vertue, but we can hear Love at both ears, and if we receive not the addresses of both, at least we are perhaps vain enough, not to be displeas'd, to find we make new conquests. But you have made your attacque with so ill conduct, that I shall find force enough without more aids to repulse you. Alas, my Lord! did you believe my heart was left unguarded when *Philander* departed? No, the careful charming Lover left a thousand little gods to defend it, of no less power than himself. Young Deities, who laugh at all your little arts and treacheries, and scorn to resign their Empire to any feable Cupids you can draw up against 'em. Your thick foggy air breeds *Loves* too dull and heavy for noble flights, nor can I stoop to them. The Flemish Boy[b] wants arrows keen enough for hearts like mine, and is a

---

[a] Full of high spirits.
[b] Cupid, the god of love. Behn refers to him as the Flemish boy because he was a favourite subject in the large numbers of emblem books produced in the Low Countries at this time.

Bungler in his Art, too lasie and remiss, rather a heavy *Bachus*[a] than a *Cupid*,[b] a Bottle sends him to his Bed of Moss, where he sleeps hard, and never dreams of *Venus*.[c]

How poorly have you paid your self, my Lord, (by this pursuit of your discover'd Love) for all the little friendship you have rendred me? How well you have explain'd, you can be no more a Lover than a Friend, if one may judg the first by the last: Had you been thus obstinate in your passion before *Philander* went, or you had believ'd me abandon'd, I should perhaps have thought, that you had lov'd indeed, because I should have seen you durst, and should have believ'd it true, because it ran some hazards for me, the resolution of it would have reconcil'd me then to the temerity of it, and the greatest demonstration you cou'd have given of it, woud have been the danger you wou'd have ran and contemned; and the preferance of your passion above any other consideration. This, my Lord, had been generous, and like a Lover, but poorly thus to set upon a single Woman in the disguise of a Friend, in the dark silent melancholy hour of absence from *Philander*, then to surprise me, then to bid me deliver! to pad for hearts! it was not like *Octavio*. That *Octavio*, *Philander* made his Friend, and for whose dear sake, my Lord, I will no further reproach you, but from a goodness, which, I hope, you will merit, I will forgive an offence, which your ill timing has render'd almost inexcusable; and expect you will for the future consider better how you ought to treat

SYLVIA.

As soon as she had dismist the Page, she hasted to her business of Love, and again read over *Philanders* Letter, and finds still new occasion for fear; she had recourse to pen and paper for a relief of that heart which no other way cou'd find it; and after, having wip'd the tears from her eyes, she writ this following Letter.

---

[a] Latin form of Dionysus, god of wine and ecstasy.
[b] The boy-god of love and son of Venus.
[c] Goddess of love and mother of Cupid.

Silvia *to* Philander.

Yes, *Philander*, I have received your Letter, and but I found my name there, shou'd have hop'd it was not meant for *Silvia*: Oh! 'tis all cold —— Short — Short and cold as a dead Winters day. It chill'd my blood, it shiver'd every vein. Where, oh where hast thou lavish'd out all those soft words so natural to thy Soul, with which thou us'd to charm; so tun'd to the dear musick of thy voice? What is become of all the tender things, which, as I us'd to read, made little nimble pantings in my heart, my blushes rise, and tremblings in my bloud, adding new fire to the poor burning Victim! Oh where are all thy pretty flatteries of Love, that made me fond, and vain, and set a value on this trifling Beauty? Hast thou forgot thy wondrous Art of loving? Thy pretty cunings, and thy soft deceivings? Hast thou forgot 'em all? Or hast forgot indeed to love at all? Has thy industrious passion gather'd all the sweets, and left the rifled flower to hang its wither'd head, and die in shades neglected, for who will prize it now, now, when all its perfumes fled. Oh my *Philander*, oh my charming Fugitive! wast not enough, you left me like false *Theseus*[a] on the shore, on the forsaken shore, departed from my fond my clasping Arms; where I believ'd you safe, secure, and pleas'd; when sleep and night, that favour'd you and ruin'd me, had render'd 'em incapable of their dear loss? Oh was it not enough, that when I found 'em empty and abandon'd, and the place cold where you had lain, and my poor trembling bosom unpossest of that dear load it bore, that I almost expired with my first fears; Oh if *Philander* lov'd he wou'd have thought that cruelty enough, without the sad addition of a growing coldness: I wak'd, I mist thee, and I call'd aloud, *Philander!* my *Philander*! But no *Philander* heard; then

---

[a] Greek hero who freed Athens of its yearly tribute of six boys and six girls to King Minos of Crete. Minos sacrificed the youths to the Minotaur, a monster which roamed a labyrinth created to hold him by Daedalus. Theseus was guided through the labyrinth by a ball of thread given to him by Ariadne, daughter of Minos. When he had killed the Minotaur, Theseus took Ariadne with him on his journey home, but then abandoned her at Naxos. She was later rescued by Dionysus, who married her and granted her immortality.

drew the close drawn Curtains, and with a hasty and busie view, survey'd the Chamber over, but Oh! in vain I view'd, and call'd yet louder, but none appear'd to my assistance, but *Antonet*[a] and *Briljard* to torture me with dull excuses, urging a thousand feign'd and frivolous reasons to satisfie my fears: But I, who lov'd, who doated even to madness, by nature soft, and timerous as a Dove, and fearful as a Criminal escap'd, that dreads each little noise, fancy'd their eyes and guilty looks confest the treasons of their hearts and tongues, while they, more kind than true, strove to convince my killing doubts: Protested, that you would return by night, and feign'd a likely story to deceive, Thus between hope and fear I languisht out a day, Oh Heavens! a tedious day without *Philander*, who wou'd have thought, that such a dismal day shou'd not with the end of its reign have finish'd that of my life, but then *Octavio* came to visit me, and who till then I never wisht to see, but now I was impatient for his coming, who by degrees told me that you were gone — I never ask'd him where, or how, or why, that you were gone was enough to possess me of all I fear'd, your being apprehended, and sent into *France*, your delivering your self up, your abandoning me; all, all, I had an easie faith for, without consulting more than That, Thou wert gone, — that very word yet strikes a terrour to my Soul, disables my trembling hand, and I must wait for reinforcements from some kinder thoughts. But, Oh! from whence shou'd they arrive? from what dear present felicity, or prospect of a future, tho never so distant, and all those past ones, serve but to increase my pain; they favour me no more, they charm and please no more, and only present themselves to my memory to compleat the number of my sighs and tears, and make me wish that they had never been, tho even with *Philander*! Oh, say, thou Monarch of my panting Soul, How hast thou treated *Silvia*, to make her wish, that she had never known a tender joy with thee: Is't possible she shou'd repent her loving thee, and thou shou'dst give her cause! Say, dear false Charmer, is it? But O, there is no lasting Faith in sin! — Ah — What have I done? How dreadful is the Scene of my first debauch, and how glorious that never to be regain'd prospect of my Virgin innocence, where I sate inthron'd

---

[a] *The Trial of Ford Lord Grey* mentions that Henrietta Berkeley did have a French maid in England and intelligence reports confirm that maids were sent from England to assist Henrietta at her lying-in. Cf. Appendix I.

in awful vertue, crown'd with shining honour, and adorn'd with unsullied reputation, till thou, O Tyrant *Love!*[a] with a charming usurpation, invaded all my glories; and which I resign'd with greater pride and joy than a young Monarch puts 'em on. Oh, why then do I repent? as if the vast, the dear expence of pleasures past were not enough to recompence for all the pains of Love to come? But why, O why do I treat thee as a Lover lost already. Thou art not, canst not, no, Ile not believe it, till thou thy self confess it. Nor shall the omission of a tender word or two make me believe thou hast forgot thy vows. Alas it may be I mistake thy cares, thy hard fatigues of Life, thy present ill circumstances (and all the melancholy effects of thine and my misfortunes) for coldness and declining Love. Alas, I had forgot my poor, my dear *Philander* is now oblig'd to contrive for Life, as well as Love; thou perhaps (fearing the worst) art preparing Eloquence for a Council Table, and in thy busie and guilty imaginations, haranguing it to the grave Judges, defending thy innocence, or evading thy guilt: Feeing Advocates, excepting Juries, and confronting Witnesses, when thou shou'dst be giving satisfaction to my fainting love sick heart: Sometimes in thy labouring fancy the horrour of a dreadful Sentence for an ignominious death strikes upon thy tender Soul with a force that frights the little God from thence, and I am perswaded there are some moments of this melancholy nature, wherein your *Silvia* is even quite forgotten, and this too she can think just and reasonable, without reproaching thy heart with a declining passion, especially when I am not by to call thy fondness up, and divert thy more tormenting hours: But Oh, for those soft minutes thou hast design'd for Love, and hast dedicated to *Silvia, Philander* shou'd dismiss the dull formalities of rigid business, the pressing cares of dangers, and have given a loose to softness. Cou'd my *Philander* imagine this short and unloving Letter sufficient to atone for such an absence? And has *Philander* then forgotten the pain with which I languish'd, when but absent from him an hour; how then can he imagine I can live, when distant from him so many Leagues, and so many days? while all the scanty comfort I have for life is, that one day we might meet again; but

---

[a] Love is frequently perceived as a tyrant in Restoration tragedy and Behn uses the metaphor again in a song at the beginning of *Abdelazer, or The Moor's Revenge*, Act I, i: '*Love in fantastick Triumph sat, / Whilst bleeding Hearts around him flow'd, / For whom fresh Pains he did create, / And strange Tyrannick Pow'r he shew'd.*'

where, or when, or how – thou hast not love enough so much as to divine; but poorly leavest me to be satisfied by *Octavio*, committing the business of thy heart, the once great importance of thy Soul, the most necessary devoires of thy life, to be supply'd by another. Oh *Philander*, I have known a blessed time in our reign of Love, when thou wou'dst have thought even all thy own power of too little force to satisfie the doubting Soul of *Silvia*: Tell me, *Philander*, hast thou forgot that time? I dare not think thou hast, and yet (O God) I find an alteration, but Heaven divert the Omen: Yet something whispers to my Soul, I am undone! Oh where art thou my *Philander*? Where's thy heart? And what has it been doing since it begun my Fate? How can it justifie thy coldness, and thou this cruel absence, without accounting with me for every parting hour? My Charming Dear was wont to find me business for all my lonely absent ones? and writ the softest Letters — Loading the Paper with fond Vows and Wishes, which e're I had read o're, another wou'd arrive, to keep Eternal warmth about my Soul; nor wert thou ever wearied more with writing, than I with reading or with sighing after thee; but now — Oh! there's some Mystery in't I dare not understand. Be kind at least and satisfie my fears, for 'tis a wonderous pain to live in doubt, if thou still lov'st me, swear it o're a new! and curse me if I do not credit thee. But if---thou art declining,---or shou'dst be sent a shameful Victim into *France*---- Oh thou deceiving Charmer, yet be just and let me know my Doom; By Heaven this last will find a welcome to me, for it will end the torment of my doubts, and fears of losing thee another way, and I shall have the Joy to dye with thee; dye belov'd, and dye

Thy SILVIA.

Having read over this Letter she fear'd she had said too much of her doubts, and apprehensions of a change in him; for now she flies to all the little Stratagems and artifices of Lovers, she begins to consider the worst, and to make her best of that, but quite abandon'd she cou'd not believe her self without flying into all the rage that disappointed Women cou'd be possest with, she calls *Briljard* shews him his Lords Letters, and told him (while he read) her doubts and fears; he being thus instructed by her self in the way how to deceive her on, like Fortunetellers who gather peoples Fortune from themselves and then return it back for their own Divinity; tells her he saw

indeed a change! glad to improve her fear, and feigns a sorrow
almost equal to hers: *'Tis evident*, says he, *'Tis evident, that he's
the most ungrateful of his Sex! Pardon Madam* (continued he, bowing) *If my Zeal for the most Charming Creature on Earth make me
forget my duty to the best of Masters and Friends, Ah* Brilljard, cry'd
she, with an Air of languishment that more inflam'd him, *have a
care least that mistaken Zeal for me shou'd make you prophane a
Vertue, which has not, but on this occasion shew'd that it wanted
Angels for its guard. Oh,* Brilljard, *if he be false----If the dear Man be
perjur'd, take, take kind Heaven! the life you have preserv'd, but for a
greater proof of your revenge* — And at that word she sunk into his
Arms, which he hastily extended as she was falling, both to
save her from harm and to give himself the pleasure of grasping
the lovely'st body in the World to his Bosome, on which her fair
face declin'd cold, dead and pale, but so transporting was the
pleasure of that dear burden, that he forgot to call for, or to use
any aid to bring her back to life, but trembling with his love and
eager passion he took a thousand joys, he kist a thousand times
her Luke-warm lips, suckt her short sighs, and ravisht all the
sweets her Bosome (which but guarded with a loose Night
Gown) yielded his impatient touches. Oh, Heaven who can
express the pleasures he receiv'd, because no other way he ever
cou'd arrive to so much dareing, 'twas all beyond his hope,
loose were her Robes, insensible the Maid, and love had made
him insolent, he rov'd, he kist, he gaz'd, without controul,
forgetting all respect of persons or of place, and quite despairing by fair means to win her, resolves to take this luckey opportunity; the door he knew was fast, for the Counsel she had to
ask him admitted of no lookers on, so that at his enterance she
had secur'd that pass for him her self, and being near her Bed,
when she fell into his Arms, at this last daring thought, he lifts
her thither and lays her gently down, and while he did so, in
one Minute, ran o're all the killing joys he had been witness to,
which she had given *Philander*; on which he never paws'd but
urg'd by a *Cupid* altogether malicious and wicked, he resolves
his cowardly Conquest, when some kinder God awaken'd *Silvia*,
and brought *Octavio* to the Chamber door, who having been
us'd to a freedom which was permitted to none but himself
with *Antonett* her woman, waiting for admittance, after having
knockt twice softly, *Brilljard* heard it, and redoubl'd his disorder, which from that of Love grew to that of surprise; he
knew not what to do, whether to refuse answering or to

re-establish the reviving sense of *Silvia*; in the moment of perplexing thought, he fail'd not however to set his hair in order,
and ajust him, tho there were no need of it, and steping to the
door (after having rais'd *Silvia*, leaning her head on her hand on
her bed side,) he gave admittance to *Octavio*; but oh Heaven,
how was he surpriz'd when he saw it was *Octavio*? his heart
with more force than before redoubl'd its beats, that one might
easily perceive every stroke by the motion of his Cravate, he
blusht, which to a complexion perfectly fair, as that of *Briljard*
(who wants no Beauty either in face or person) was the more
discoverable, add to this his trembling, and you may easily
imagine what a fuger he represented himself to *Octavio*: Who
almost as much surpriz'd as himself to find the Goddess of his
Vows and Devotions with a young *Endimion*[a] a lone, a door shut
too, her Gown loose (which from the late fit she was in and
Briljards rape upon her Bosom) was still open and discover'd a
World of unguarded Beauty, which she knew not was in view,
with some other disorders of her head Cloaths, gave him in a
moment of thousand false apprehensions, *Antonett* was no less
surpriz'd, so that all had their part of amazement, but the
innocent *Silvia*, whose Eyes were beautiful with a melancholly
calm, which almost set the generous Lover at ease, and took
away his new fears, however he cou'd not chuse but ask *Briljard*
what the matter was with him, he lookt so out of countenance,
and trembled so, he told him, how *Silvia* had been, and what
extream frights she had possest him with, and told him the
occasion, which the lovely *Silvia* with her eyes and sighs
assented to, and *Brilljard* departed; how well pleas'd you may
imagine, or with what gusto he left her with the lovely *Octavio*,
whom he perceiv'd too well was a Lover in the disguise of a
Friend: But there are in love those wonderful Lovers who can
quench the Fire one Beauty kindles, with some other Object,
and as much in Love as *Brilljard* was he found *Antonett* an
Antidote that dispell'd the grosser part of it, for she was in Love
with our Amorous friend, and courted him with that passion
those of that Country do almost all handsom Strangers, and
one convenient principle of the Religion of that Country is to

---

[a] Greek youth beloved by Selene, goddess of the Moon. Selene came upon the
sleeping Endymion on Mt Latmus and blest him with eternal sleep so that she could
visit him nightly without being observed.

think it no sin to be kind while they are single Women, tho otherwise (when Wives) they are just enough, nor does a Woman that manages her affairs thus discreetly meet with any reproach, of this humour was our *Antonett* who persu'd her Lover out half jealous there might be some amarous intrigue between her Lady and him, which she sought in vain by all the feable Arts of her Countries Sex to get from him, while on the other side, he believing she might be of use in the farther discovery he desir'd to make between *Octavio* and *Silvia*; not only told her she her self was the Object of his wishes, but gave her a substantial proof on't, and told her his design, after having her Honour for security that she wou'd be secret, the best Pledge a man can take of a Woman: After she had promis'd to betray all things to him she departed to her affairs, and he to giving his Lord an account of *Silvia*, as he desir'd in a Letter which came to him with that of *Silvia*, and which was thus,

Philander *to* Briljard.

I Doubt not but you will wonder that all this time you have not heard of me, nor indeed can I well excuse it, since I have been in a place, whence with ease I cou'd have sent every Post, but a new affair of Gallantry has engag'd my thoughtful hours, not that I find any passion there that has abated one sigh for *Silvia*, but a mans hours are very dull, when undiverted by an intrigue of some kind or other, especially to a heart young and gay as mine is, and which would not if possible bend under the fatigues of more serious thought and business; I shou'd not tell you this, but that I wou'd have you feign all the dilatory excuses that possible you can to hinder *Silvia*'s coming to me, while I remain in this Town, where I design to make my abode but a short time, and had not staid at all, but for this stop to my journey, and I scorn to be vanquish'd without taking my revenge, 'tis a sally of Youth, no more — a flash that blazes for a while, and will go out with enjoyment. I need not bid you keep this knowledge to your self, for I have had too good a confirmation of your faith and friendship to doubt you now, and believe you have too much respect for *Silvia* to occasion her any disquiet. I long to know how she takes my absence, send me at large of all that passes, and give your Letters to *Octavio*, for none else shall know where I am, or how to send to me: Be careful of *Silvia*, and observe her with diligence, for possibly I should not be extravagantly afflicted to find she were inclin'd to love me less for her own ease and mine, since Love is troublesome when the height of it carries it to jealousies, little quarrels, and eternal discontents, all which beginning Lovers prize, and pride themselves on every distrust of the fond Mistress, since 'tis not only a demonstration of love in them, but of power and charmes in us, that occasion it, but when we no longer find the Mistress so desirable, as our first wishes form her, we value less their opinion of our persons, and only endeavour to render it agreeable to new Beauties, and adorn it for new Conquests, but you *Briljard*, have been a Lover, and understand already this Philosophy. I need say no more then, to a man who knows so well my Soul but to tell him I am

His constant Friend

Philander.

This came as *Briljards* Soul cou'd wish, and had he sent him word he had been chosen King of *Poland*[a] he cou'd not have receiv'd the news with so great joy, and so perfect a welcom. How to manage this to his best advantage was the business he was next to consult, after returning an answer; now he fancied himself sure of the lovely prize, in spight of all other oppositions: *For* (says he, in reasoning the case) *if she can by degrees arrive to a coldness to* Philander, *and consider him no longer as a Lover, she may perhaps consider me as a Husband, or shou'd she receive* Octavio's *addresses, when once I have found her feable I will make her pay me for keeping of every secret.* So either way he

---

[a] A glancing attack on the Earl of Shaftesbury. It was stock Tory propaganda that the Earl had hoped to be given the throne of Poland to which Sobieski was elected in 1674. Several satirical poems were pubished on the subject including 'The Last Will and Testament of Anthony, King of Poland' in 1682. Thomas Otway makes reference to it in the same year when he satirized Shaftesbury as Antonio in *Venice Preserv'd*. Behn also refers to the Poland in Act III of *The City Heiress* when Sir Timothy Treat-all, a caricature of Shaftesbury, is told that 'The Polanders by me salute you, Sir, and have in the next new Election, prick'd ye down for their succeeding King.'

entertain'd a hope, tho never so distant from Reason and probability: but all things seem possible to longing Lovers, who can on the least hope resolve to out wait even Eternity (if possible) in expectation of a promis'd blessing, and now with more than usual care he resolv'd to dress and set out all his Youth and Beauty to the best advantage, and being a Gentleman well born, he wanted no Arts of dressing, nor any advantage of shape or Mein, to make it appear well: Pleas'd with this hope, his art was now how to make his advances without appearing to have design'd doing to. And first to act the Hypocrite with his Lord was his business; for he consider'd rightly, if he should not represent *Silvia*'s sorrows to the life, and appear to make him sensible of 'em, he shou'd not after be credited if he related any thing to her disadvantage; for to be the greater Enemy you ought to seem to be the greatest Friend. This was the policy of his heart, who in all things was inspir'd with phanatical notions. In order to this, being alone in his Chamber, after the defeat he had in that of *Silvia*'s, he writ this Letter.

Briljard to *Philander*.

My Lord,

You have done me the honour to make me your Confident in an affair, that does not a little surprize me: Since I believ'd, after *Silvia*, no mortal Beauty cou'd have touch'd your heart, and nothing but your own excuses could have suffic'd to have made it reasonable: and I only wish, that when the fatal news shall arrive to *Silvia*'s ear (as for me it never shall) the she may think it as pardonable as I do; but I doubt 'twill add abundance of grief, to what she is already possest of, if but such a fear shou'd enter in her tender thoughts. But since 'tis not my business, my Lord, to advise or counsel, but to obey, I leave you to all the success of happy Love, and will only give you an account how affairs stand here, since your departure.

The Morning you left the *Brill*, and *Silvia* in Bed, I must disturb your more serene thoughts with telling you, that her first surprise and griefs at the news of your departure, were most deplorable, where raging madness and the softer passion of Love, complaints of grief and anger, sighs, tears, and cries were so mixt together, and by turns so violently seiz'd her, that all about her wept and pitty'd her; 'twas sad, 'twas wonderous sad my Lord to see it: Nor cou'd we hope her Life, or that she wou'd preserve it if she cou'd, for by many ways she attempted to have releas'd her self from pain by a violent Death, and those that strove to preserve that, cou'd not hope she wou'd ever have return'd to sense again, sometimes a wild extravagant Raving wou'd require all our aid, and then again she would talk and rail so tenderly——and express her resentment in the kindest softest words that ever madness utter'd, and all of her *Philander*, till she has set us all a weeping round her, sometimes she'd sit as calm and still as death, and we have perceiv'd she liv'd only by sighs and silent Tears that fell into her bosom, then on a suddain wildly gaze upon us with Eyes that even then had wonderous Charms, and frantickly survey us all, then cry aloud, where is my Lord *Philander*?——Oh, bring me my *Philander*, *Brilljard*, Oh *Antonett*, *where have you hid the Treasure of my Soul*, then weeping floods of Tears, wou'd sink all fainting in our Arms. Anon with trembling words and sighs she'd cry,—— *but Oh my dear* Phillander *is no more, you have surrendered him to* France——*Yes, yes, you've given him up, and he must dye, Publickly dye, be led a sad Victim thro the joyful crowd---reproacht and fall ingloriously* —— Then rave again and tear her lovely hair, and Act such wildness,---so moving and so sad, as even infected the pittying beholders, and all we cou'd do was gently to perswade her grief, and sooth her raveing Fits, but so we swore, so heartily we vow'd that you were safe, that with the aid of *Octavio*, who came that day to visit her, we made her capable of hearing a little reason from us: *Octavio* kneel'd and beg'd she wou'd but calmly hear him speak, he pawn'd his Soul, his honour, and his life *Philander* was as safe from any injury either from *France* or any other Enemy as he, as she, or Heaven it self; in fine, my Lord, he Vow'd, he swore, and pleaded till she with patience heard him tell your Story, and the necessity of your absence, this brought her temper back and dry'd her Eyes, then sighing answer'd him – *that if for your safety you were fled, she wou'd forgive your cruelty and your absence, and indeavour to be her self again*: But then she wou'd a thousand times conjure him not to deceive her faith, by all the friendship that he bore *Philander*, not to possess her with false hopes, then wou'd he swear a new, and as he swore, she wou'd behold him with such charming sadness in her Eyes, the he almost forgot what he wou'd

say, to gaze upon her and to pay his Pitty? But if with all his
power of Beauty and of Rhetorick he left her Calm, he was no
sooner gone, but she return'd to all the Tempests of despairing
Love, to all the unbelief of faithless passion, wou'd neither
sleep, nor eat nor suffer, day to enter; but all was sad and
gloomy as the vault that held the *Ephesian*[a] Matron, nor suffer'd
she any to approach her but her Page, and Count *Octavio*, and
he in midst of all was well receiv'd, not that I think my Lord she
feigned any part of that close retirement to entertain him with
any freedom, that did not become a Woman of perfect Love and
Honour, tho' I must own, my Lord, I believe it impossible for
him to behold the Lovely *Silvia* without having a passion for
her, what restraint his Friendship to you may put upon his
heart or Tongue, I know not, but I conclude him a Lover, tho
without success, what effects that may have upon the heart of
Silvia only time can render an account of: And whose conduct I
shall the more particularly observe from a curiosity natural to
me, to see, if it may be possible for *Silvia* to love again after the
adorable *Phillander*, which levity in one so perfect wou'd cure
me of the Disease of Love, while I liv'd amongst the fickle Sex:
But since no such thought can yet get possession of my belief I
humbly beg your Lordship wou'd entertain no jealousie that
may be so fatal to your repose and to that of *Silvia*, doubt not
but my fears proceed perfectly from the zeal I have for your
Lordship, for whose Honour and tranquillity none shall venture so far as,

> My Lord,
> *Your Lordships most humble*
> *and Obedient Servant.*
> Brilljard.

---

[a] The Story of the Ephesian Matron is told in Petronius's *Satyricon* and in La
Fontaine's *Fables*. Bk 12. A widow decides to die in the tomb where her husband is
laid to rest. After fasting for several days, she accepts food from a soldier guarding
crucified corpses which are on public view. She eventually becomes the soldier's
mistress and gives him her husband's body to replace that of one of the criminals
which had been removed by relatives. In Otway's *Venice Preserv'd* II.i Antonio's
mistress, Aquilina, is also compared to the Ephesian matron.

POSTSCRIPT.

My Lord the Groom shall set forward with your Coach Horses to morrow Morning according to your Order.

Having writ this, he read it over; not to see whether it were wity or Eloquent, or writ up to the fence of so good a Judge as *Philander*, but to see whether he had cast it for his purpose; for there his Master-piece was to be shewn; and having read it, he doubted whether the relation of *Silvia's* griefs were not too moving, and whether they might not serve to revive his fading love which were intended only as a demonstration of his own pitty, and compassion, that from thence the deceiv'd Lover might with the more ease entertain a belief in what he hinted of her Levity when he was to make that out, as he now had but toucht upon it, for he wou'd not have it thought the business of malice to *Silvia*, but duty and respect to *Philander*: That thought reconcil'd him, to the first part without alteration, and he fancy'd he had said enough in the latter, to give any man of Love and Sence a Jealousie which might inspire a young Lover in persute of a new Mistress, with a revenge that might wholly turn to his advantage, for now every ray gave him light enough to conduct him to hope, and he believe'd nothing too difficult for his Love, nor what his invention cou'd not conquer, he fancy'd himself a very *Machiavel*[a] already, and almost promis'd himself the Charming *Silvia*, with these thoughts he seals up his Letters and hastes to *Silvia's* Chamber for her Further commands, having in his politick transports forgotten he had left *Octavio* with her. *Octavio*, who no sooner had seen *Brilljard* quit the Chamber all trembling and disorder'd, after having given him enterance, but the next step was to the Feet of the newly recover'd languishing Beauty, who not knowing any thing of the freedom the daring Husband-Lover had taken, was not at all surpriz'd to hear *Octavio* cry (kneeling before her) *Ah Madam, I no longer wonder you use* Octavio *with such rigour*, then sighing

---

[a] Niccolò Machiavelli (1469–1527), political theorist in the Florentine republic. His most famous work, *Il Principe* (*The Prince*) was written in 1513 and it argued that a ruler must sometimes employ unethical means to govern effectively. Subsequently, the term 'Machiavellian' became synonymous with deviousness.

declin'd his Melancholly Eyes, where love and jealousie made themselves too apparent, while she believing he had only reproach'd her want of Ceremony at his entrance, checking her self, she started from the Bed and taking him by the hands to raise him, she cry'd, *Rise, my Lord, and pardon the omission of that respect which was not wanting but with even life it self* Octavio answer'd, *Yes Madam, but you took care not to make the World absolutely unhappy in your Eternal loss, and therefore made choice of such a time to dye in when you were sure of a skilful person at hand to bring you back to life – My Lord –* said she (with an innocent wonder in her Eyes, and an ignorance that did not apprehend him) *I mean Briljard,* said he, *whom I found sufficiently disorder'd to make me believe he took no little pairs to restore you to the World again.* This he spoke with such an Air as easily made her imagine he was a Lover to the degree of jealousie and therefore behold him with a look that told him her disdain before she spoke) she reply'd hastily, *My Lord if* Brilljard *have exprest by any disorder or concern of his kind sense of my sufferings I am more oblig'd to him for it then I am to you for your opinion of my vertue, and I shall hereafter know how to set a value both on the one and on the other, since what he wants in quality and ability to serve me, he sufficiently makes good with his respect and Duty.* At that she wou'd have quitted him, but he (still kneeling) held her Train of her Gown, and besought her with all the Eloquence of moving and petitioning Love. *That she wou'd Pardon the effect of a Passion, that cou'd not run into less extravagancy at a sight so new and strange, as that she shou'd in a morning with only her Night Gown thrown loosely about her lovely body, and which left a thousand Charms to view, alone receive a man into her Chamber, and make fast the door upon 'em, which when (from his importunity) was open'd he found her all ruffled, and almost fainting on her Bed, and a young blushing youth start from her Arms with trembling Limbs, and a heart that beat time to the Tune of active love, faultering in his speech, as if scarce yet he had recruited the sense he had so happily lost in the Amorous incounter:* With that surveying of her self, as she stood, in a great Glass, which she cou'd not hinder her self from doing, she found indeed her Night Linnen, her Gown, and the bosome of her Shift in such disorder, as if at least she had yet any doubt remaining that *Briljard* had not treated her well; she however found cause enough to excuse *Octavio's* opinion, weighing all the circumstances together, and adjusting her Linnen and Gown with blushes that almost appear'd criminal, she turn'd to *Octavio*, who still held her, and still beg'd her Pardon, assuring him upon her Honour, her love to *Philander*, and her friendship for him, that she was perfectly innocent, and that *Brilljard*, tho' he shou'd have quality and all other advantages which he wanted to render him acceptable, yet that there was in Nature something which compell'd her to a sort of coldness and disgust to his person for she had so much the more abhorrance to him as he was a Husband, but that was a secret to *Octavio*, but she continu'd speaking——*And cry'd no, cou'd I be brought to yield to any but* Philander, *I own I find Charms enough in* Octavio *to make a conquest, but since the possession of that dear man is all I ask of Heaven, I charge my Soul with a Crime, when I but hear love from any other, therefore I conjure you, if you have any satisfaction in my conversation, never to speak of Love more to me, for if you do, Honour will oblige me to make vows against seeing you: All the freedoms of friendship I'le allow: Give you the Liberties of a Brother, admit you alone by Night, or any way but that of Love; but that's a reserve of my Soul which is only for* Philander, *and the only one that ever shall be kept from* Octavio. She ended speaking and rais'd him with a smile; and he with a sigh, told her she must command; then she fell to telling him how she had sent for *Briljard*: and all the Discourse that past; with the reason of her falling into a swound, in which she continu'd a moment or two, and while she told it she blusht with a secret fear, that in that Trance some freedoms might be taken which she durst not confess, but while she spoke our still more passionate Lover devour'd her with his eyes, fixt his very Soul upon her Charms of speaking and looking, and was a thousand times (urg'd by transporting passion) ready to break all her dictates, and vow himself her Eternal Slave, but he fear'd the result, and therefore kept himself within the bounds of seeming friendship, so that after a thousand things she said of *Philander*, he took his leave to go to Dinner, but as he was going out he saw *Brilljard* enter; who, as I said, had forgot he left *Octavio* with her, but in a moment recollecting himself, he blusht at the apprehension, that they might make his disorder, the subject of their Discourse, so what with that, and the sight of the dear object of his late disappointed pleasures, he had much ado to assume an assurance to approach; But *Octavio* past out and gave him a little release. *Silvia's* confusion was almost equal to his, for she lookt on him as a Ravisher, but how to find that Truth, which she was very curious to know, she call'd up all the Arts of Women to instruct her in, by threats she knew 'twas vain, therefore she assumed an Artifice, which indeed was almost a stranger to her heart, that of gilting him out of a secret which she knew he wanted generosity to give handsomely, and meeting him with a smile, which she forc'd she cry'd, *How now* Briljard, *are you so faint hearted a Souldier, you cannot see a Lady dye without being terrifi'd. Rather Madam,* (replyed he blushing a new) *so soft hearted I cannot see the loveliest person in the World fainting in my Arms, without being disorder'd with grief and fear, beyond the power of many days to resettle again.* At which she approacht him, who stood near the door, and shutting it, she took him by the hand and smiling cry'd, *And had you no other business for your heart but grief and fear, when a fair Lady throws her self into your Arms, it ought to have had some kinder effect on a person of* Brilljards *youth and complexion.* And while she spoke this she held him by the wrist, and found on the suddain his pulse to beat more high, and his heart to heave his bosom with sighs, which now he no longer took care to hide; but with a transported joy he cry'd *Oh Madam do not urge me to a confession that must undo me, without making it criminal by my discovery of it, you know I am your slave* – when she with a pretty wondering smile cry'd – *what a Lover too and yet so dull! Oh Charming* Silvia, says he (and falling on his knees) *give my profound respect a kinder Name,* to which she answer'd – *You that know your sentiments may best instruct me by what Name to call em, and you* Brilljard *may do it without fear, – You saw I did not struggle in your Arms, nor strove I to defend the kisses which you gave – Oh Heavens* cry'd he transported with what she said, *is it possible that you cou'd know of my presumption and favour it too? I will no longer then curse those unlucky Stars that sent* Octavio *just in the blessed Minute to snatch me from my Heav'n, the lovely Victim lay ready for the Sacrifice, all prepared to offer, my lands, my eyes, my Lips, were tir'd with pleasure, but yet they were not satisfied, oh there was joys beyond those ravishments of which one kind Minute more had made me absolute Lord: Yes and the next* said she, *had sent this to your heart* – Snatching a Penknife that lay on her Toylite, where she had been writing, which she offered so near to his bosome that he believ'd himself already pierc'd, so sensibly killing were her words, her motion, and her look, he started from her and she threw away the Knife, and walking a turn or two about the Chamber, while he stood immovable with his eyes fixt to earth, and his thoughts on nothing but a wild confusion, of which he vow'd afterwards he cou'd give no account of: But as she turn'd she beheld him with some compassion, and remembering how he had it in his power to expose her in a strange Country, and own her for a wife, she believ'd it necessary to hide her resentments; and cry'd, Brilljard *for the friendship your Lord has for you, I forgive you, but have a care you never raise your thoughts to a presumption of that Nature more: Do not hope I will ever fall below* Philanders *Love; go and repent your Crime – and expect all things else from my favour* – At this he left her with a bow that had some malice in it, and she return'd into her dressing Room – After dinner *Octavio* writes her this Letter, which his Page brought.

Octavio *to* Silvia.

Madam,

'Tis true, that in obedience to your commands, I begg'd your pardon for the confession I made you of my passion. But since you cou'd not but see the contradiction of my tongue in my eyes, and hear it but too well confirm'd by my sighs, why will you confine me to the formalities of a silent languishment, unless to increase my flame with my pain.

You conjure me to see you often, and at the same time forbid me speaking of my passion, and this bold intruder comes to tell you now, that 'tis impossible to obey the first, without disobliging the last, and since the crime of adoring you exceeds my disobedience in not waiting on you, be pleas'd at least to pardon that fault, which my profound respect to the lovely *Silvia* compells me to commit; for 'tis impossible to see you, and not give you an occasion of reproaching me: If I cou'd make a truce with my eyes, and like a mortifi'd Capuchion,[a] look alwayes downwards, not daring to behold the glorious temptations of your Beauty, yet you wound a thousand wayes besides; your touches inflame me, and your voice has musick in't, that strikes upon my Soul with ravishing tenderness; your Wit is unresistable and peircing; your very sorrows and complaints have charms, that make me soft without the aid of Love: But Pity joyn'd with Passion raises a flame too mighty for my conduct!

---

[a] Member of an order founded by Matteo di Bassi of Urbino as an offshoot of the Franciscans; its rule was drawn up in 1529. It was called capuchin because of the hooded habit worn by members of the order.

And I in transports every way confess it! Yes, yes, Upbraid me!
Call me Traytor and ungrateful! Tell me my friendships fals! But
Silvia, yet be just, and say my love was true. Say only he had
seen the charming *Silvia*; and who is he, that after that wou'd
not excuse the rest in one so absolutely born to be undone by
Love! as is

Her destin'd Slave

Octavio.

Postscript.

Madam: *Among some Rarities. I this Morning saw, I found these
Trifles* Florio *brings you, which be cause uncommon I presume to send
you.*

Silvia, notwithstanding the seeming severity of her Commands, was well enough pleas'd to be disobey'd, and Women
never pardon any fault more willingly, than one of this nature,
where the Crime gives so infallable a demonstration of their
power and Beauty; nor can any of their Sex be angry in their
hearts for being thought desirable; and 'twas not with pain, that
she saw him obstinate in his passion, as you may believe by her
answering his Letters, nor ought any Lover to despair, when he
receives denial under his Mistresses own hand, which she sent
in this to *Octavio*.

Silvia *to* Octavio.

You but ill judge of my Wit, or Humour, *Octavio*, when you
send me such a Present, and such a Billet, if you believe I either
receive the one, or the other as you design'd. In obedience to
me you will no more tell me of your Love, and yet at the same
time you are breaking your word from one end of the Paper to
the other. Out of respect to me you will see me no more, and
yet are bribing me with presents; believing you have found out
the surest way to a Womans heart. I must needs confess,

Octavio, there is great eloquence in a pair of Bracelets of five thousand Crowns: 'Tis an Argument to prove your Passion, that has more prevailing reason in't, than either *Seneca*[a] or *Tully*[b] cou'd have urg'd, nor can a Lover write or speak in any Language so significant, and very well to be understood, as in that silent one of presenting. The malicious World has a long time agreed to reproach poor Women with cruel, unkind, insensible, and dull; when indeed 'tis those men that are in fault, who want the right way of addressing, the true and secret Arts of moving; that sovereign Remedy against disdain. 'Tis you alone, my Lord, like a young *Columbus*,[c] that have found the direct, unpractic'd way to that little and so much desir'd World the favour of the Fair, nor cou'd Love himself have pointed his Arrows with any thing more successful, for his conquest of hearts: But mine, my Lord, like *Scaeva*'s Sheild,[d] is already so full of Arrows shot from *Philanders* eyes, it has no room for any other darts! Take back your presents then, my Lord, and when you make 'em next, be sure you first consider the Receiver; for know, *Octavio*, Maids of my Quality, ought to find themselves secure from addresses of this nature, unless they first invite; you ought to have seen advances in my freedoms, consenting in my eyes, or (that usual vanity of my Sex) a thousand little trifling Arts of affectation, to furnish out a conquest, a forward complysance, to every Gawdy Coxcombe, to fill my train with amorous Cringing Captives, this might have justified your pretensions, but on the contrary my Eyes and thoughts which never stray'd from the dear man I love, were always bent to earth, when gaz'd upon by you, and when I did but fear you lookt with love, I entertain'd you with *Phillanders* praise, his wondrous Beauty and his wondrous Love! and left nothing

[a] The Roman writer and philosopher, Lucius Annaeus Seneca (c.4 BC–AD 65), stoic philosopher, teacher of rhetoric and advisor to the Emperor Nero.

[b] The Roman writer and politician, Marcus Tullius Cicero (106–43 BC). Having supported the senators who assassinated Julius Caesar, Cicero was put to death for his speeches attacking Mark Antony.

[c] Cristoforo Colon, (1451–1506). A Genoese geographer and explorer, Columbus with his voyages confirmed the existence of the Americas. His venture was funded by the Spanish when he argued that he had discovered a direct route to Asia.

[d] Gaius Mucius Scaevola, legendary Roman hero. When threatened with torture after an unsuccessful assassination attempt on the beseiging king, Porsena, Gaius thrust his right hand into an altar fire and allowed it to be completely consumed in order to demonstrate his determination. Porsena was impressed by the youth's courage and withdrew his forces. Gaius was henceforth known as Scaevola, meaning 'left-handed'. The shield full of arrows indicated his bravery during the siege of Rome.

161

untold that might confirm you how much impossible it was I
e're shou'd love again, that I might leave you no room for hope,
and since my story has been so unfortunate to alarm the whole
world with a conduct so fatal, I made no scruple of telling you
with what joy and pride I was undone; if this incourage you; if
Octavio have sentiments so meanly poor of me, to think because
I yielded to *Philander*, his hopes shou'd be advanc'd? I banish
him for ever from my sight, and after that disdain the little
service, he can render the

Never to be alter'd Silvia

This Letter, she sent him back by his Page, but not the
Bracelets which were indeed very fine, and very considerable,
at the same time she threatned him with banishment, she so
absolutely expected to be disobey'd in all things of that kind,
that she drest her self that day to advantage, which since her
arrival she never had done in her own habits; what with her
illness and *Philanders* absence a careless negligence had seiz'd
her, till rous'd and waken'd to the thoughts of Beauty by *Octavio's* Love, she began to try its force, and that day drest: while
she was so imploy'd the Page hastes with the Letter to his Lord,
who chang'd Colour at the sight of it e're he receiv'd it, not that
he hop'd it brought love, 'twas enough she wou'd but answer,
tho she rail'd; let her (said he in opening it) vow she hates me:
*Let her call me Traytor and unjust, so she take the pains to tell it this
way*, for he knew well those that argue will yield, and only she
that sends him back his own Letters without reading em can
give dispair. He read therefore without a sigh, nor complained
he on her rigours, and because it was too early yet to make his
Visit, to shew the impatience of his Love, as much as the reality
and resolution of it, he bid his Page wait and sent her back this
answer.

Octavio *to* Silvia.

Fair angry *Silvia*, how has my Love offended? Has its excess
betray'd the least part of that respect due to your Birth and
Beauty? Tho I am young as the Gay rudy Morning, and vigorous

as the guilded Sun at Noon, and Amorous as that God when with such haste he chas'd young *Daphne*[a] o're the flowrr'y Plain! it never made me guilty of a thought that *Silvia* might not Pitty, and allow. Nor came that trifling present to plead for any wish, or mend my Eloquence, which you with such disdain upbraid me with, the Bracelets came not to be rafl'd for your Love, nor Pimp to my desires, Youth scorns those common aids; No, let dull Age pursue those ways of merchandize, who only buy up hearts at that vain price, and never make a Barter, but a Purchase. Youth has a better way of trading in Loves Markets, and you have taught me too well to judge of, and to value Beauty, to dare to bid so cheaply for it; I found the toy was gay, the work was neat, and fancy new; and know not any thing they wou'd so well adorn as *Silvia's* lovely hands: I say, if after this, I should have been the mercenary fool to have dunn'd you for return, you might have us'd me thus;——Condemn me e're you find me sin in thought; that part of it was yet so far behind 'twas scarce arriv'd in wish. You shou'd have staid till it approacht more near, before you damn'd it to eternal silence. To love, to sigh, — to weep, to pray, and to complain; why one may be allow'd it in Devotion; but you, nicer than Heaven it self, makes that a Crime, which all the powers Divine have ne're decreed one I will not plead, nor ask you leave to love; Love is my right, my business, and my Province; the Empire of the young, the vigorous, and the bold; and I will claim my share; the Air, the Groves, the Shades, are mine to sigh in, as well as your *Philanders*, the Eccho's answer me as willingly, when I complain or Name the cruel *Silvia*; Fountains receive my Tears, and the kind Springs reflection agreeably flatters me to hope: and makes me vain enough to think it just and reasonable I shou'd pursue the Dictates of my Soul—Love on in spight of opposition, because I will not lose my Priviledge, you may forbid me naming it to you, in that I can obey, because I can; but not to love! not to adore the fair! and not to languish for you, were as impossible as for you not to be lovely, not to be the most charming of your Sex. But I am so far from a pretending

---

[a] Behn often employs allusions to the myth of Daphne fleeing the advances of Apollo. In her poem, 'The Disappointment', she refers ironically to the story when Chloris flees her impotent lover: 'Finding that God of her desire / Disarm'd of all his Awful fires… / Like Lightning through the Grove she hies, / Or Daphne from the Delphick God / No Print upon the grassey Road / She leaves, t'instruct pursuing Eyes.' [*Works of Aphra Behn*, Vol. 1, no.28, ll.112–124]

fool, because you've been possest, that often that thought
comes cross my Soul, and checks my advancing Love! and I
wou'd buy that thought off with all most all my share of future
bliss! Were I a God, the first great Miracle shou'd be to form you
a Maid again! For oh, what ever reasons flattering Love can
bring to make it look like just, the World! the World fair *Silvia*,
still will censure, and say — you were to blame, but 'twas that
fault alone that made you mortal, we else shou'd have ador'd
you as a Deity, and so have lost a generous race of young
succeeding *Hero's*, that may be born of you! yet had *Philander*
lov'd but half so well as I, he wou'd have kept your glorious
Fame intire, but since alone for *Silvia*, I love *Silvia!* let her be
false to honour, false to Love! wanton and proud, ill natur'd,
vain, fantastique; or what is worse — let her pursue her Love,
be constant and still dote upon *Philander* —— Yet still she'l be
the *Silvia* I adore, that *Silvia* born eternally to inslave.

Octavio.

This he sent by *Florio* his Page at the same time that she
expected the Visit of his Lord, and blusht with a little anger and
concern at the disappointment; however she hasted to read the
Letter, and was pleas'd with the haughty resolution he made,
in spight of her, to love on as his right by birth; and she was
glad to find from these positive resolves, that she might the
more safely disdain, or at least assume a Tyranny which might
render her vertue Glorious, and yet at the same time keep him
her slave on all occasions when she might have need of his
service, which in the circumstances she was in, she did not
know of what great use it might be to her, she having no other
design on him, bating the little Vanity of her Sex, which is an
ingredient so intermixt with the greatest vertues of Women
kind, that those who indeavour to cure 'em of that disease, robs
'em of a very considerable pleasure, and in most, 'tis incurable:
Give *Silvia* then leave to share it with her Sex, since she was so
much the more excusable by how much a greater portion of
Beauty she had than any other, and had sense enough to know
it too; as indeed whatever other Knowledge they want, they
have still enough to set a price on beauty, tho they do not
always rate it, for had *Silvia* done that, she had been the happiest of her Sex! but as she was, she waited the coming of
Octavio, but not so as to make her quit one sad thought for

Philander. Love and vanity, tho they both reign'd in her Soul, yet the first surmounted the last, and she grew to impatient ravings when ever she cast a thought upon her fear that *Philander* grew cold; and possibly pride and vanity had as great a share in that concern of hers as Love it self, for she wou'd oft survey her self in her Glass, and cry! *Gods! can this Beauty be despis'd! this Shape, this Face, this Youth, this Air, and what's more obliging yet, a heart that adores the fugitive, that languish and sighs after the dear Runaway: Is is possible he can find a Beauty,* added she, *of greater perfection — But oh 'tis fancy sets the rate on Beauty; and he may as well love a third time as he has a Second: For in Love those that once break the rules and Laws of that Deity set no bounds to their Treasons, and disobedience. Yes yes* wou'd she cry, *he that cou'd have* Mertilla *the fair, the young, the Noble, Chast and fond* Mertilla, *what after that may he not do to* Silvia, *on whom he has less tyes, less obligations: Oh wretched Maid — what has thy fondness done! he's satiated now with thee, as before with* Mertilla, *and carries all those dear, those charming joys, to some new Beauty, whom his looks have Conquer'd, and whom his soft bewitching Vows will ruin!* with that she rav'd and stampt, and cry'd aloud! *Hell — Fires — Tortures — Dagers — Racks and Poyson — come all to my relief! Revenge me on the perjur'd lovely Divel —— But I'le be brave — — I will be brave and hate him —* This she spoke in a tone less fierce, and with great Pride, and had not paws'd and walk'd above a hasty turn or two, but *Octavio* as impatient as love cou'd make him, enter'd the Chamber, so drest; so set out for Conquest, that I wonder at nothing more than that *Silvia* did not find him altogether Charming, and fit for her revenge who was form'd by Nature for Love: And had all that cou'd render him the Dotage of Women; but where a heart is pre-possest, all that is Beautiful in any other Man serves but as an ill comparison to what it loves, and even *Philanders* likeness, that was not indeed *Philander*, wanted the secret to charm. At *Octavio's* enterance she was so fixt on her Revenge of Love, that she did not see him who presented himself as so proper an Instrument, till he first sighing, spoke, *Ah Silvia, shall I never see that Beauty easie more? Shall I never see it reconcil'd to content, and a soft calmness fixt upon those Eyes, which were form'd for looks all tender and serene, or are they resolv'd* (continued he sighing) *never to appear but in storms when I approach? Yes,* replyed she, *when there's a Calm of Love in yours that raises it. Will you confine my Eyes* (said he) *that are by Nature soft? May not their silent Language tell you my hearts sad*

Story? But she reply'd with a sigh, *it is not generously done* Octavio, *thus to pursue a poor unguarded Maid, left to your Care, your promises of Friendship.* Ah will you use Philander *with such treachery?* Silvia, said he, *my Flame's so just and reasonable, that I dare even to him pronounce I love you, and after that dare love you on —— And wou'd you* (said she) *to satisfie a little short liv'd passion, forfeit those vows you've made of Friendship to* Philander? *That heart that loves you* Silvia (he replyed) *cannot be guilty of so base a thought,* Philander *is my Friend, and as he is so, shall know the dearest secrets of my Soul. I shou'd believe my self indeed ungrateful* (continued he) *where e're I lov'd, shou'd I not tell* Philander, *he told me frankly all his Soul, his loves, his griefs, his Treasons, and escapes, and in return I'le pay him back with mine, and do you Imagine* (said she) *that he wou'd permit your love, how shou'd he hinder me* (re-ply'd he.) *I do believe* (said she) *he'd forfeit all his safety and his friendship and fight ye, then I'd defend my self,* said he, *if he were so ungrateful.* While they thus argued *Silvia* had her thoughts a part, on the little stratagems that Women in love sometimes make use of, and *Octavio* no sooner told her he would send *Philander* word of his Love, but she imagin'd that such a know-ledge might retrieve the heart of her Lover, if indeed it were on the wing, and revive the dying Embers in his Soul, as usually it does from such occasions, and on the other side she thought that she might more allowably receive *Octavio*'s addresses, when they were with the permission of *Philander*, if he cou'd love so ill as to permit it, and if he cou'd not, she shou'd have the joy to undeceive her fears of his inconstancy tho she banisht for ever the agreeable *Octavio*, so that on *Octavio's* farther urging the necessity of his giving *Philander* that sure mark of his friend-ship, she permitted him to write, which he immediately did on her Table where there stood a little Silver Scrutore[a] which con-tain'd all things for his purpose.

---

[a] Escritoire, a writing desk.

Octavio *to* Philander.

My Lord

Since I have vow'd you my Eternal friendship, and that I absolutely believe my self honour'd with that of yours, I think my self oblig'd by those powerful tyes to let you know my heart, not only now as that friend from whom I ought to conceal nothing, but as a Rival too, whom in honour I ought to treat as a generous one; perhaps you will be so unkind as to say I cannot be a friend and a Rival at the same time, and that almighty love that sets the world at odds, chases all things from the heart, where that reigns, to establish it self the more absolutely there, but, my lord, I avow mine a Love of that good Nature, that can indure the equal sway of friendship, where like two perfect Friends they support each others Empire there, nor can the glory of one Eclipse that of the other, but both like the notion we have of the Deity, tho two distinct passions make but one in my Soul, and tho friendship first enter'd 'twas in vain I call'd it to my aid, at the first soft invasion of *Silvia's* power; and you my charming friend, are the most oblig'd to, pitty me, who already knows so well the force of her beauty I wou'd fain have you think, I strove at first with all my reason against the irrisistible lustre of her eyes. And at the first assaults of Love, I gave him not a welcome to my bosome, but like slaves unus'd to fetters, I grew sullen with my chains, and wore 'em for your sake uneasily. I thought it base to look upon the Mistress of my friend with wishing eyes; but softer Love soon furnisht me with arguments to justifie my claim, since Love is not the choice but the face of the Soul, who seldom regards the object lov'd as 'tis, but as it wishes to have it be, and then kind fancy makes it soon the same. Love that Almighty Creator of somthing from nothing, forms a Wit, a Hero, or a Beauty, Vertue, good Humour, Honour, any excellence, when oftentimes there's neither in the Object, but where the agreeing world has fixt all these, and 'tis by all resolv'd, (whether they love or not) that this is she, you ought no more *Philander* to upbraid my Flame; than to wonder at it; it is enough I tell you that 'tis *Silvia*, to justifie my passion! nor is't a Crime that I confess, I love!

167

since it can never rob *Philander* of the least part of what I've vow'd him, or if his nicer Honour will believe me guilty of a fault, let this attone for all; that if I wrong my friend in loving *Silvia*, I right him in despairing, for oh I am repuls'd with all the Rigour of the coy, and fair, with all the little Malice of the wity Sex! and all the Love of *Silvia* to *Philander*, — There, there's the stop to all my hopes, and happiness, and yet by Heaven, I love thee, oh thou favour'd Rival!

After this frank Confession, my *Philander*, I shou'd be glad to hear your sentiment, since yet in spight of Love, in spight of Beauty I am resolv'd

To dy Philanders

Constant Friend, Octavio.

After he had writ this, he gave it *to Silvia. See Charming Creature* (said he in delivering it) *if after this you either doubt my Love or what I dare for* Silvia. *I neither receive it* (said she) *as a proof of the one or the other; but rather that you believe by this frank Confession, to render it as a piece of Gallantry and diversion to* Philander; *for no Man of sense will imagine that, love, true, or arriv'd to any height, that makes a publique confession of it to his Rival. Ah* Silvia answer'd he, *how malicious is your Wit, and how active to turn its pointed mischief on me, had I not writ, you wou'd have said I durst not, and when I make a declaration of it, you call it only a slight piece of Gallantry! but* Silvia *you have wit enough to try it a thousand ways, and power enough to make me obey; use the extremity of both; so you recompence me at last with a confession that I was at least found worthy to be numbred in the crowd of your adorers* Silvia reply'd, *he were a dull Lover indeed, that wou'd need instructions from the Wit of his Mistress to give her proofs of his passion, what ever opinion you have of my sense, I have too good a one of* Octavio's *to believe that when he's a Lover he'le want aids to make it appear, till then we'le let that argument alone and consider his address to* Philander. She then read over the Letter he had writ, which she lik'd very well for her purpose, for at this time our young Dutch *Hero* was made a property of, in order to her revenge on *Philander*. She told him *he had said too much both for himself and her.* He told her, *he had declar'd nothing with his Pen; that he wou'd not make good with his Sword. Hold Sir*, said she, *and do not imagine from the freedom you have taken in owning your passion to* Philander, *that I shall allow it here; what you declare to the world is your own Crime, but when I hear it, 'tis no longer yours but mine, I therefore conjure you, my Lord, not to charge my Soul with so great a sin against* Philander, *and I confess to you I shall be infinitely troubl'd to be oblig'd to banish you my sight for ever.* He heard her and answer'd with a sigh, for she went from him to the Table and seal'd her Letter and gave it him to be inclos'd to *Philander,* and left him to consider on her last words which he did not lay to heart, because he fancy'd she spoke this as women do that will be won with industry, he in standing up as she went from him, saw himself in the great glass, and bid his person answer his heart, which from every view he took, was reinforc'd with new hope, for he was too good a judge of Beauty not to find it in every part of his own Amiable person, nor cou'd he imagine from *Silvia*'s eyes, (which were naturally soft and languishing, and now the more so from her fears and jealousies) that she meant from her heart the rigours she exprest: Much he allow'd for his short time of Courtship, much to her Sexes modesty, much from her quality, and very much from her Love, and imagin'd it must be only time and assiduity, opportunity, and obstinate passion, that was only capable of reducing her to break her faith with *Philander,* he therefore indeavour'd by all the good dressing, the advantage of lavish gayety, to render his person agreeable and by all the Arts of Gallantry to charm her with his conversation, and when he cou'd handsomly bring in love, he fail'd not to touch upon it as far as it wou'd be permitted, and every day had the vanity to fancy he made some advances, for indeed every day more and more she found she might have use for so considerable a Person, so that one may very well say, never any past their time better than *Silvia* and *Octavio,* tho with different ends, all he had now to fear was from the answer *Philanders* Letter shou'd bring for whom he had in spight of Love, so intire a friendship that he even doubted whether, (if *Philander* cou'd urge reasons potent enough) he shou'd not chuse to dye and quit *Silvia* rather then be false to friendship; one Post past, and another, and so eight successive ones, before they receiv'd one word of answer to what they sent, so that *Silvia,* who was the most impatient of her Sex, and the most in Love, was raving and acting all the extravagance of despair, and even *Octavio* now became less pleasing, yet he fail'd not to Visit her every day to send her rich presents and to say all that a fond Lover or a faithful friend

might urge for her relief: at last *Octavio* receiv'd this following
Letter.

Philander *to* Octavio.

You have shew'd *Octavio* a freedom so generous, and so beyond
the usual Measures of a Rival, that 'twere almost injustice in me
not to permit you to love on, if *Silvia* can be false, to me and all
her vows, she is not worth preserving, if she prefer *Octavio* to
Philander, then he has greater merit and deserves her best; but if
on the contrary she be just, if she be true and constant. I cannot
fear his Love will injure me, so either way *Octavio* has my leave
to Love the Charming *Silvia*: alas I know her power, and do not
wonder at thy fate! for 'tis as natural for her to Conquer, as 'tis
for youth to yield, oh she has fascination in her Eyes! a spell
upon her tongue, her Wit's a Philter,[a] and her air and motion all
snares for heedless hearts; her very faults have Charmes, her
pride, her peevishness, and her disdain, have unresisted
power. Alas you find it every day——and every Night she
sweeps the Toore[b] along, and shews the Beauty, she inslaves
the Men, and Rivals all the Women! how oft with Pride and
Anger I have seen it, and was the inconsidering Coxcombe
then, to rave and rail at her; to curse her Charms, her fair
inviting and perplexing Charmes, and bullyed every Gazer; by
Heaven I cou'd not spare a smile, a look! and she has such a
lavish freedom in her humour, that if thou chance to love as I
have done—'twil surely make thee mad, if she but talkt aloud,
or put her little affectation on, to shew the wondering crowd
what she cou'd do, if she design'd to shew the force of Beauty;
oh God! how lost in rage, how mad with jealousie, was my fond
breaking heart, my eyes grew fierce, and Clamorous my Tongue! and I have scarce contain'd my self from hurting, what I so
much ador'd! but then the subtil Charmer, had such Arts to
flatter me to peace again — to clasp her lovely arms about my
neck—to sigh a thousand dear confirming vows into my
Bosom, and kiss, and smile, and swear——and talk away my

---

[a] A drink that is meant to stimulate desire in anyone who consumes it.
[b] A regular walk through the town.

rage,——and then — Oh my *Octavio!* no humane fancy can present the joy of the dear reconciling moment, where little quarrels rais'd the rapture higher, and she was always new. These are the wondrous pains, and wondrous pleasures, that Love by turns inspires; till it grows wise by time and repetition, and then the God assumes a serious gravity, injoyment takes off the uneasie keeness of the passion, the little jealous quarrels raise no more, quarrels the very Feathers of Loves darts, that send 'em with more swiftness to the heart; and when they cease, your transports lessen too, then we grow reasonable, and consider; we love with prudence then; as Fencers fight with foyls; a sullen brush perhaps sometimes or so; but nothing that can touch the heart, and when we are arriv'd to love at that dull easie rate, we never die of that Disease, then we've recourse to all the little Arts, the aids of flatterers, and dear dissimulation (that help meet to the luke warme lover) to keep up a good Character of constancy and a right understanding.

Thus, *Octavio,* I have ran thro' both the degrees of Love; which I have taken so often, that I am grown most learn'd and able in the Art: My easie heart is of the Constitution of those whom frequent sickness renders apt to take relapses from every little cause, or wind, that blows too fiercely on 'em it renders it self to the first effects of new surprizing Beauty, and finds such pleasure, in beginning passion, such dear delight of fancying new injoyment, that all past loves, past Vow, and obligations, have power to bind no more; no pitty, no remorce, no threatning danger, invades my amorous course; I scowre along the flow'ry plains of Love, view all the charming prospect at a distance, which represents it self all gay and glorious! and long to lay me down, to stretch and bask in those dear joys that fancy makes so ravishing; nor am I one of those dull whining slaves, whom quallity or my respect can awe into a silent Cringer, and no more! no Love, Youth, and oft success has taught me boldness and Art, desire and cunning to attaque, to search the feeble side of female weakness, and there to play loves Engines, for Women will be won, they will *Octavio!* if Love and wit find any opportunity,

Perhaps, my friend, you're wondring now, what this discourse, this odd discovery of my own inconstancy tends to? Then since I cannot better pay you back the secret you have told me of your Love, than by another of my own, take this confession from thy Friend——I love! — I languish, and am dying, —

for a new Beauty. To you, *Octavio*, you that have liv'd twenty dull tedious years, and never understood the Mystery of Love, till *Silvia* taught you to adore; this change may seem a wonder, you that have lasily run more than half your youths gay course of life away; without the pleasure of one nobler hour of mine! who like a Miser hoord your sacred store, or scantily have dealt it but to one, think me a lavish prodigal in love, and gravely will reproach me with inconstancy,——but use me like a friend and hear my story.

It happen'd in my last days journey, on the road I overtook a man of quality, for so his Equipage confest, we joyn'd and fell into discourse of many things indifferent, till from a Chain of one thing to another, we chanc'd to talk of *France*, and of the Factions there, and I soon found him a *Cæsarian*; for he Grew hot with his concern for that Prince, and fiercely own'd his int'rest, this pleas'd me, and I grew familier with him; and I pleas'd him so well, in my Devotion for *Cæsario*, that being arriv'd at *Collen*, he invites me home to his Pallace, which he beg'd I would make use of as my own, during my stay at *Collen*. Glad of the opportunity I obey'd; and soon inform'd my self by a Spanish Page (that waited on him) to whom I was oblig'd, he told me it was the Count of *Clarinau*,[a] a Spaniard born and of quality, who for some disgust at Court retir'd hither; that he was a person of much gravity a great polititian, and very rich; and tho well in years was lately married to a very Beautiful young Lady, and that very much against her consent: A Lady whom he had taken out of a Monastery, where she had been pentioned from a Child, and of whom he was so fond and jealous, he never wou'd permit her to see or be seen by any Man, and if she took the Air in her Coach, or went to Church, he oblig'd her to wear a Veil. Having learnt thus much of the Boy, I dismiss'd him with a present; for he had already inspir'd me with curiosity, that prologue to love, and I knew not of what use he might be hereafter; a curiosity that I was resolv'd to satisfie, tho I broke all the laws of hospitality, and even that first Night I felt an impatience that gave me some wonder; in fine, three days I languisht out in a disorder that was very near allied to that of Love. I found my self magnificently lodg'd, attended

---

[a] As Spain controlled part of the Netherlands at this time, many Spanish nobles were resident there. As with Octavio, Behn places the Count of Clarinau in a more traditional romantic plot than Silvia and Philander. Throughout Part II of *Love-Letters*, the events in Philander's letters are paralleled by the similar picaresque and romantic events of Octavio and Silvia.

with a formal Ceremony, and indeed all things were as well as I cou'd imagine, bating a kind opportunity to get a sight of this young Beauty: now half a Lover grown, I sight and grew opprest with thought, and had recourse to Groves, to shady walks and Fountains, of which the delicate Gardens aforded variety, the most resembling nature, that ever Art produc'd, and of the most Melancholly recesses, fancying there in some lucky hour, I might incounter what I already so much ador'd in *Idea*: Which still I form'd just as my fancy wisht, there, for the first two days, I walkt, and sight, and told my new born passion to every gentle Wind that play'd among the boughs, for yet no Lady bright appear'd beneath 'em, no Visionary Nymph the Groves afforded, but on the third day, all full of Love and Stratagem in the cool of the Evening, I past into a Thicket near a little Rivulet, that purl'd and murmur'd thro the glade, and past into the Meads, this pleas'd and fed my present Amorous humour, and down I laid myself on the shady brink, and listen'd to its melancholly glidings, when from behind me, I heard a sound more ravishing, a Voice that sung these Words,

> Alas, in vain, you *Powers* above,
>   You gave me youth, you gave me Charms,
> And every tender sense of Love;
>   To destin me to old Phileno's Arms,
> Ah how can youths gay spring allow,
> The chilling kisses of the Winter's Snow.

> All Night I languish by his side,
>   And fancy of joys I never taste,
> As men in Dreams a Feast provide,
>   And waking find with grief they fast.
> Either ye Gods my Youthful fires alay.
> Or make the old Phileno, young and Gay.

> Like a fair flower in shades obscurity,
>   Tho every sweet adorns my head,
> Ungather'd, unadmir'd I lie.
>   And wither on my silent gloomy Bed,
> While no kind aids to my relief appear,
> And no kind Bosom makes me Triumph there.[a]

---

[a] No other printing of this poem has been found.

By this you may easily guess, as I soon did, that the Song was sung by Madam the Countess of *Clarinau*, as indeed it was; at the very beginning of her Song my joyful Soul divin'd it so! I rose and advanc'd by such slow degrees as neither alarm'd the fair Singer, nor hinder'd me the pleasure of hearing any part of the Song, till I approacht so near as (behind the shelter of some jesimin that divided us) I unseen, compleated those wounds at my Eyes, which I had receiv'd before at my Ears. Yes, *Octavio*, I saw the lovely *Clarinau!* leaning on a Pillow made of some of those Jesimins, which favour'd me, and serv'd her for a Canopy. But, Oh my Friend! how shall I present her to thee in that Angel form, she then appear'd to me? all young! all ravishing as new born light to lost benighted Travellers; her Face, the fairest in the World was adorn'd with Curls of shining jett ty'd up — I know not how, all carelessly with Scarlet Ribbon mixt with pearls; her Robe was gay and rich, such as young Royal Brides put on when they undress for joys! her Eyes were black, the softest Heaven e're made, her mouth was sweet, and form'd for all delight, so red her Lips, so round, so grac'd with dimples, that without one other Charm, that was enough to kindle warm desires about a frozen heart! a sprightly air of Wit compleated all, increas'd my Flame, and made me mad with love! endless it were to tell thee all her Beauties, Nature all o're, was lavish and profuse, let it suffice her face, her shape, her mien, had more of Angel in 'em than humanity! I saw her thus all Charming! thus she lay! a smiling melancholly drest her Eyes, which she had fixt upon the Rivulet, near which I found her lying: just such I fancy'd fam'd *Lucretia*[a] was, when *Tarquin* first beheld her, nor was that Royal Ravisher more inflam'd than I! or readier for th'incounter. Alone she was which heighten'd heighten'd my desires! Oh Gods! alone lay the young lovely Charmer, with wishing Eyes, and all prepar'd for Love! the shade was gloomy, and the tell tale leaves combin'd so close, they must have given us warning, if any had approacht from either side! all favour'd my design and I advanc'd! but with such caution as not to inspire her with a fear, instead of that of Love! a slow, uneasie pace, with folded Arms, Love in

---

[a] Lucretia was the wife of Tarquinius Collatinus, here referred to as '*Tarquin*'. After being raped by Sextus, son of Tarquin the Proud, ruler of Rome, Lucretia told her husband what had happened and then took her own life. The rape and death of Lucretia sparked a rebellion by Junius Brutus and the Tarquins were expelled from Rome.

my Eyes, and burning in my heart.———At my approach she scarce contain'd her cries, and rose surpriz'd and blushing, discovering to me such proportion'd height———so lovely and Majestick———that I stood gazing on her, all lost in Wonder, and gave her time to dart her Eyes at me, and every look pierc'd deeper to my Soul, and I had not sense but love, silent admiring Love! Immoveable I stood, and had no other motion but that of a heart all panting, which lent a feeble trembling to my Tongue, and even when I wou'd have spoke to her, it sent a sigh up, to prevent my boldness: and, oh *Octavio*, tho I have been bread in all the sawcy daring of a forward Lover, yet now I wanted a convenient impudence, aw'd with a haughty sweetness in her look, like a Fauxbrave[a] after a vigorous on set, finding the danger fly so thick around him, sheers off and dares not face the pressing Foe, struck with too fierce a lightening from her eyes, whence the God sent a thousand winged Darts, I veil'd my own and durst not play with Fire; while thus she hotly did pursue her Conquest, and I stood fixt on the defensive part, I heard a rusling amongst the thick Grown Leaves, and thro' their Mystick windings soon perceiv'd the good old Count of *Clarinau*, approaching, Muttering and mumbling to old *Dormina*, the Dragon appointed to guard this lovely Treasure, and which, she having left alone in the Thicket, and had retir'd but at an awful distance had most extreamly disoblig'd her Lord. I only had time enough in this little moment, to look with eyes that ask'd a thousand pitties, and told her in their silent Language how loath they were to leave the Charming Object, and with a sigh———I vanisht from the wondering fair One, nimble as lightening, silent as a shade: To my first post behind the Jesimins, that was the utmost that I cou'd perswade my heart to do; you may believe my dear *Octavio*. I did not bless the Minute that brought old *Clarinau* to that dear recess, nor him, nor my own fate, and to compleat my torment I saw him (after having gravely reproach'd her for being alone without her Woman) yes I saw him, fall on her neck, her lovely Snowy neck, and loll, and kiss, and hang his tawny wither'd Arms on her fair Shoulders, and press his nauscious load upon *Calista's* Body, (for so I heard him name her) while she was gazing still upon the empty place, whence she had seen me vanish, which he perceiving cry'd, ——

---

[a] A coward or false hero.

My little Fool, what is't thou gazest on, turn to thy none old man and buss him soundly——when putting him by with a disdain, that half made amends for the injury he had done me by coming. *Ah my Lord*, cry'd she; *even now, just there I saw a lovely vision, I ne're beheld so excellent a thing; How*, cry'd he, *a vision, a thing* —— *what Vision what thing, where, how, and when--Why there*, said she, *with my eyes, and just now, it vanisht behind yon Jesamins*: With that I drew my Sword---for I dispair'd to get off unknown, and being well enough acquainted with the jealous nature of the Spaniards, which is no more then see and stab, I prepar'd to stand on my defence; till I cou'd reconcile him if possible to reason; yet even in that moment I was more afraid of the injury he might do the innocent fair One then of what he cou'd to me, but he not so much as dreaming she meant a Man by her lovely Vision, fell a kissing her a new, and beckoning *Dormina* off to pimp at distance, told her, *The Grove was too sweet, the Rivers Murmurs too delicate, and she was so curiously drest, that altogether had inspir'd him with a love fit*, and then assaulting her a new withe Sneere which you have seen a Satyr make in Pictures, he fell to act the little tricks of youth, that lookt so goatish in him——
——instead of kindling 'twou'd have dampt a flame, which she resisted with a scorn so charming gave me new hope and fire, when to oblige me more, with Pride, disdain, and loathing in her Eyes, she fled like *Daphne* from the Ravisher, he being bent on love persu'd her, with a feeble pace, like an old Wood God chacing some coy Nimph, who wing'd with fear out strips the flying Wind, and tho a God he cannot overtake her; and left me fainting with new love, new hope, new jealousie, impatience, sighs, and wishes, in the abandon'd Grove. Nor cou'd I go without another view of that dear place in which I saw her lie, I went — and laid me down just on the print which her fair body made, and prest, and kist it o're a thousand times, with eager transports, and even fancy'd fair *Calista* there; there 'twas I found the paper with the Song which I have sent you; there I ran o're a thousand Stratagems to gain another view, no little States men had more Plots and Arts, than I to gain this. Object I ador'd, the soft Idea of my burning heart, now raging wild, abandon'd all to Love and loose desire, but hitherto my industry is vain, each day I haunt the thickest Groves and Springs, the flow'ry Walks, close Arbors, all the day my busie Eyes and heart are searching her, but no intelligence they bring me in; in fine *Octavio*, all that I can since learn is, that the bright *Calista*

had seen a Vision in the Garden, and ever since was so possest with melancholy, that she had not since quited her Chamber, she is daily pressing the Count to permit her to go into the Garden to see if she can again incounter the lovely *Phantom*, but whether from any Description she have made of it, (or from any other cause) he imagines who it was, I know not, but he indeavours all he can to hinder her, and tells her 'tis not lawful to tempt heaven by invoking an apparition, so that till a second view eases the torments of my mind there is nothing in nature to be conceiv'd so raving mad as I: as if my despairs of finding her again increas'd my impatient flame instead of lessening it.

After this declaration judge *Octavio*, who has given the greatest proofs of his friendship, you or I: You being my Rival trust me with the Secret of loveing my Mistress, which can no way redound to your disadvantage, but I by telling you the secrets of my Soul, put it into your power to ruin me with *Silvia*, and to establish your self in her heart? a thought I yet am not willing to bear, for I have an ambition in my love, that wou'd not while I am toyling for Empire here, lose my dominion in another place; but since I can no more rule a Womans heart, than a Lovers Fate, both you and *Silvia*, may deceive my opinion in that, but shall never have power to make me believe you less my friend, than I am

Your Philander.

POSTSCRIPT.

The inclos'd I need not oblige you to deliver: You see I give you opportunity.

Octavio no sooner arriv'd to that part of the Letter which nam'd the Count of *Clerinau*, but he stop'd and was scarce able to proceed, for the Charming *Calista* was his Sister, the only one he had who having been bred in a Nunnery was taken thence to be married to this old rich Count, who had a great Fortune: Before he proceeded, his Soul divin'd this was the new Amour that had ingag'd the heart of his Friend, he was afraid to be farther convinc'd, and yet a curiosity to know how far he had proceeded made him read it out with all the disorder of a man jealous of his Honour, and nicely careful of his Fame; he consider'd her young about eighteen, married to an Old ill favour'd jealous Husband, no Parents but himself to right her wrongs, or revenge her levety, he knew tho she wanted no Wit she did Art, for being bred without the Conversation of Men she had not learnt the little cunnings of her Sex, he guest by his own Soul that hers was soft and apt for impression, he judg'd from her Confession to her Husband of the Vision, that she had a simple Innocence, that might betray a young Beauty under such Circumstances; to all this he consider'd the Charms of *Philander* unresistable, his unwearied industry in love, and concludes his Sister lost. At first he upbraids *Philander*, and calls him ungrateful, but soon thought it unreasonable to accuse himself of an injustice, and excus'd the frailty of *Philander*, since he knew not that she whom he ador'd was Sister to his friend; however it fail'd not to possess him with inquietude that exercis'd all his Wit, to consider how he might prevent an inseparable injury to his Honour, and an intrigue that possibly might cost his Sister her Life, as well as Fame: In midst of all those torments he forgot not the more important Business of his Love. For to a Lover, who has his Soul perfectly fixt on the fair object of its adoration, what ever other thought, fatigue, and cloud, his mind, that like a soft Gleam of new sprung light, darts in and spreads a glory all around, and like the God of day chears every drooping vital, yet even these dearer thoughts wanted not their torments. At first he strove to attone for the fears of *Calista*, with those of imagining *Philander* false to *Silvia*. Well, cry'd he; — *If thou beest lost* Calista, *at least thy ruin has laid a foundation for my happiness, and every Triumph* Philander *makes of thy Vertue, it the more secures my Empire over* Silvia, *and since thy Brother cannot be happy: but by the Sisters being undone, yield thou, oh faithless fair one, yield to* Philander *and make me blest in* Silvia! *And thou* (continued he) *Oh perjur'd Lover and inconstant Friend, glut thy insatiate flame* —— *rifle* Calista *of every Vertue Heaven and Nature gave her, so I may but revenge it on thy* Silvia! Pleas'd with this joyful hope he traverses his Chamber glowing and blushing with new kindling fire, his heart that was all gay, defus'd a gladness, that exprest it self in every Feature of his lovely face, his eyes that were by nature languishing, shone now with an unusual Air of briskness, Smiles grac'd his mouth, and dimples drest his face, insensibly his busie fingers trick and dress, and set his hair, and without designing it, his feet are bearing him to *Silvia*, till he slept short and wonder'd whither he was going, for yet it was not time to make his Visit *Whither fond Heart*, (said he) *O whither wou'dst thou hurry this Slave to thy soft fires*! And now returning back he paws'd and fell to thought — He remember'd how impatiently *Silvia* waited the return of the answer he writ to him, wherein he own'd his passion for that Beauty. He knew she permitted him to write it, more to raise the little brisk fires of Jealousie in *Philander*, and to set an edge on his blunted love, than from any favours she design'd *Octavio*: And that on this answer depended all her happiness, or the confirmation of her doubts, and that she wou'd measure *Philanders* love by the effects she found there of it. So that never Lover had a game to play as our new one. He knew he had it now in his power to ruin his Rival, and to make almost his own terms with his fair Conqueress, but he consider'd the secret was not render'd him for so base an end, nor cou'd his love advance it self by wayes so false, dull, and criminal,—between each thought he paws'd, and now resolves she must know he sent an answer to his Letter, for shou'd she know he had, and that he shou'd refuse her the sight of it, he believ'd with reason she ought to banish him for ever her presence, as the most disobedient of her Slaves. He walks and pawses on—but no kind thought presents it self to save him; either way he finds himself undone, and from the most gay, and most triumphing Lover on the Earth, he now, with one serious thought of right reasoning, finds he is the most miserable of all the Creation! He reads the Superscription of that *Philander* writ to *Silvia*, which was inclos'd in his, and finds it was directed only —— For *Silvia*, which wou'd plainly demonstrate it came not so into *Holland*, but that some other cover secur'd it; so that never any, but *Octavio* the most nice in Honour, had ever so great a contest with Love and Friendship: for his Noble temper was not one of those that cou'd Sacrifice his friend to his little Lusts, or his more solid passion, but truly brave, resolves now rather to die than to confess *Philanders* Secret, to evade which he sent her Letter by his Page, with one from himself, and commanded him to tell her that he was going to receive some Commands from the Prince of *Orange*, and that he wou'd wait on her himself in the Evening. The Page obeys, and *Octavio* sent him with a sigh and Eyes, that languishingly told him, he did it with regreet.

The Page hasting to *Silvia*, finds her in all the disquiet of an expecting Lover, and snatching the Papers from his hand, the first she saw was that from *Philander*, at which she trembl'd with fear and joy, for Hope, Love and Despair at once seiz'd her, and hardly able to make a sign with her hand for the Boy to withdraw, she sunk down into her Chair all pale, and almost fainting, but reassuming her Courage, she open'd it, and read this.

Philander *to* Silvia.

Ah *Silvia*! Why all these Doubts and Fears? Why at this distance, do you accuse your Lover, when he's uncapable to fall before you, and undeceive your little jealousies. Oh *Silvia*, I fear this first reproaching me, is rather the effects of your own guilt, than any that love can make you think of mine, Yes, yes, my *Silvia*, 'tis the Waves that roul, and glide away, and not the steady shore. 'Tis you begin to unfasten from the Vows that hold you, and float along the flattering Tide of Vanity. 'Tis you, whose Pride and Beauty scorning to be confin'd, gives way to the admiring Croud, that sigh for you. Yes, yes, you, like the rest of your fair glorious Sex, love the admirer tho you hate the Coxcomb. 'Tis vain! 'tis great! and shews your Beauties Power! — Is't possible, that for the safety of my Life, I cannot retire but you must think I'm fled from Love and *Silvia*! or is it possible that pitying tenderness that made me uncapable of taking leave of her shou'd be interpreted as false—— And base, —— and that an absence of thirty days, so forc'd, and so compell'd must render me inconstant, —— lost —— ungrateful—— as if that after *Silvia* heaven e're made a Beauty that cou'd Charm me?

You charge my Letter with a thousand faults, 'tis short, 'tis cold, and wants those usual softnesses that gave 'em all their welcom, and their Graces. I fear my *Silvia* loves the flatterer, and not the Man, the Lover only, not *Philander*: And she considers him not for himself, but the gay glorious thing he makes of her! Ah! too self int'rested! Is that your Justice? You ne'r allow for my unhappy circumstances, you never think how care oppresses me: Nor what my Love contributes to that care. How business, danger, and a thousand ills, takes up my harass'd mind; by every power I love thee still, my *Silvia*, but time has

made us more familiar now, and we begin to leave off Ceremony, and come to closer joys, to joyn our int'rest now, as
people fixt, resolv'd to live and die together; to weave our
thoughts, and be united stronger. At first we shew the gayest
side of Love, dress and be nice in every word and look, set out
for conquest all; spread every Art, use every Stratagem ——but
when the toyl is past, and the dear Victory gain'd, we then
propose a little idle rest, a little easie slumber; We then
embrace, lay by the Gawdy shew, the Plumes and guilded
Equipage of Love, the trappings of the Conqueror, and bring
the naked Lover to your Arms; we shew him then uncas'd with
all his little disadvantages; perhaps the flowing hair, (those
Ebon[a] Curles you have so often comb'd, and drest, and kist) are
then put up and shew a fiercer Air, more like an Antique
Roman than *Philander*, and shall I then, because I want a Grace
be thought to love you less; because the embroider'd Coat, the
Point,[b] and Garniture's laid by, must I put off my Passion with
my Dress? No, *Silvia*, love allows a thousand little freedoms:
Allows me to unbosom all my Secrets; tell thee my wants, my
Fears, complaints and dangers, and think it great relief, if thou
but sigh and pitty me: And oft thy Charming wit has aided me,
but now I find thee adding to my pain. Oh where shall I unload
my weight of cares, when *Silvia*, who was wont to sigh, and
weep, and suffer me to ease the heavy Burden, now grows
displeas'd and peevish with my moans, and calls 'em the effects
of dying love! instead of those dear smiles, that fond bewitching
prattle, that us'd to calm my roughest storm of Grief, she now
reproaches me with coldness, want of concern and Lovers
Rethorick: And when I seem to beg relief, and shew my Souls
resentment, 'tis then I'm false; 'tis my aversion! or the effects of
some new kindling Flame! Is this fair dealing *Silvia*? can I not
spare a little sigh from love, but you must think I rob you of
your due? If I omit a tender Name by which I us'd to call you,
must I be thought to lose that passion that taught me such
indearments? And must I ne're reflect upon the ruin both of my
fame and Fortune, but I must run the risk of losing *Silvia* too?
Oh cruelty of Love! Oh too, too fond and jealous Maid, what
Crimes thy innocent passion can create, when it extends
beyond the bounds of reason: Ah too, too nicely tender *Silvia*,

---

[a] Ebony.
[b] Thread lace.

that will not give me leave to cast a thought back on my former glory; yet even that loss I cou'd support with tameness and content, if I believ'd my suffering reach'd only to my heart, but *Silvia*, if she love, must feel my torments too, must share my loss, and want a thousand Ornaments, my sinking Fortune cannot purchase her; believe me Charming Creature, if I shou'd love you less, I have a sense so just of what you've suffer'd for *Philander*, I'd be content to be a Galley Slave, to give thy Beauty, Birth and Love their due, but as I am thy Faithful Lover still, depend upon that Fortune Heaven has left me; which if thou canst (as thou hast often sworn) then thou wou'dst submit to be cheerful still, be gay and confident, and do not judge my heart by little words, my heart — too great and fond for such poor demonstrations.

You ask me *Silvia* where I am, and what I do; all I can say is that at present I am safe from any fears of being deliver'd up to *France*, and what I do, is sighing, dying, grieving; I want my *Silvia*: But my Circumstances, yet have nothing to incourage that hope, when I resolve where to settle, you shall see what haste I will make to have you brought to me: I am impatient to hear from you, and to know how that dear pledge of our soft hours advances. I mean what I believe I left thee possest of, a young *Philander*: Cherish it *Silvia*, for that's a certain Obligation, to keep a dying fire alive, be sure you do it no hurt by your unnecessary grief, tho there needs no other tie but that of Love to make me more intirely

Your Philander.

If *Silvia*'s Fears were great before she open'd the Letter, what were her pains when all those fears were confirmed from that never failing mark of a declining Love, the coldness and alteration of the Stile of Letters, that first Symptom of a dying flame? *Oh where*, said she, *where, Oh perjur'd Charmer, is all that ardency that us'd to warm the Reader, where is all that Natural Innocence of Love that cou'd not, even to discover and express a Grace in Eloquence, force one soft word, or one Passion. Oh*, continued she, *he is lost and gone from* Silvia *and his Vows; some other has him all, Clasps that dear body, hangs upon that face, gazes upon his Eyes, and listens to his Voyce, when he is looking, sighing, swearing, dying, lying and damning of himself for some new Beauty*——*He is, I'le not indure it, aid me*

Antonett, Oh where's the perjur'd Traytor! Atonett who was waiting on her seeing her rise on the suddain in so great a fury wou'd have staid her hasty turns and ravings, beseeching her to tell her what was the occasion, and by a discovery to ease her heart, but she with all the fury imaginable, flung from her Arms, and ran to the Table, and snatching up a Penknife, had certainly sent it to her heart had not *Antonett* stept to her and caught her hand, which she resisted not, but blushing resign'd with telling her she was asham'd of her own Cowardize, *for*, said she, *if I had design'd to have been brave, I had sent you off and by a Noble resolution have freed this slave within* (striking her Breast) *from a Tyranny which it shou'd disdain to suffer under*: With that she rag'd about the Chamber with broken words and imperfect threatnings, unconsider'd imprecations, and unheeded Vows and Oaths: at which *Antonett* redoubl'd her Petition to know the cause; and she reply'd—Philander! *the dear, the soft, the fond and Charming* Philander *is now no more the same. Oh* Antonett said she, *didst thou but see this Letter compar'd to those of heretofore, when Love was gay and young, when new desire drest his soft Eyes in tears, and taught his tongue the Harmony of Angels; when every tender word had more of passion then Volumes of this forc'd this trifling business. Oh thou woud'st say I were the wretch'dst thing that Nature ever made——Oh thou wou'dst curse as I do——Not the dear Murderer, but thy Franctick self, thy mad, deceiv'd, believing, easie self; if thou wert so undone ——* Then while she wept she gave *Antonett* liberty to speak, which was to perswade her, her fear were vain; she urg'd every argument of Love she had been Witness too, and cou'd not think it possible he cou'd be false: To all which the still weeping *Silvia* lent a willing ear: For Lovers are much inclin'd to believe every thing they wish. *Antonett* having a little calm'd her, continu'd telling her that to be better convinc'd of his Love or his perfidy, she ought to have Patience till *Octavio* shou'd come to visit her, *For have you forgotten, Madam*, said she, *that that generous Rival has sent him word he is your Lover*: For *Antonett* was waiting at reading of that Letter, nor was there any thing the open hearted *Silvia* conceal'd from that Servant; and Women, who have made a breach in their Honour, are seldom so careful of their rest of Fame, as those who have a Stock intire; and *Silvia* believ'd after she had trusted the Secret of one Amour to her discretion, she might conceal none. *See Madam*, says *Antonett, here is a Letter yet unread: Silvia* who had been a great while impatient for the return of *Octavio*'s answer from *Philander*, expecting from thence the confirmation of all her doubts: Hastily snatch'd the Letter out of *Antonetts* hand, and read it, hoping to have found something there to have eas'd her Soul one way or other: a Soul the most raging and haughty by Nature, that ever possest a Body, the Words were these.

Octavio *to* Silvia.

At least you'l pity me, Oh Charming *Silvia*, when you shall call to mind the cruel services, I am oblig'd to render you; to be the Messenger of love from him, whom Beauty and that God plead so strongly for already in your heart.

If after this, you can propose a torture, that yet may speak my passion and obedience in any higher measure, command and try my fortitude, for I too well divine, Oh rigorous Beauty, the business of your love sick Slave will be, only to give you proofs how much he does adore you, and ne're to taste a joy, even in a distant hope, like Lamps in Urns my lasting Fire must burn; without one kind material to supply it. Ah *Silvia*, if e're it be your wretched fate to see the Lord of all your Vows given to anothers Arms — When you shall see in those soft eyes that you adore a languishment and joy, if you but name another Beauty to him:—— When you behold his blushes fade and rise at the approaches of another Mistress. — Hear broken sighs and unassur'd replys, when e're he answers some new con-queress: tremblings, and pantings seizing every part at the warm touch as of a second Charmer. Ah *Silvia* do but do me justice then, and sighing say — I pitty poor *Octavio*.

Take here a Letter from the blest *Philander*, which I had brought my self, but cannot bear the torment of that joy, that I shall see advancing in your eyes when you shall read it o're — no — 'tis too much that I imagine all! yet bless that patient fondness of my Passion that makes me still

Your Slave, and
Your Adorer.

Octavio.

At finishing this, the jealous fair One redoubl'd her tears with such violence that 'twas in vain her Woman strove to abate the flowing Tide by all the reasonable arguments she cou'd bring to her aid, and *Silvia* to increase it, read again the latter part of the ominous Letter, which she wet with the tears that stream'd from her bright eyes, *Yes, yes,* cry'd she laying the Letter down) *I know* Octavio *this is no Prophesie of yours, but a known truth; alas, you know too well the fatal time's already come when I shall find these changes in* Philander! *Ah Madam* reply'd Antonett, *how curious are you to search out torments for your own heart, and as much a Lover as you are, how little do you understand the Arts and Politicks of Love: Alas, Madam,* continu'd she, *you your self have arm'd my Lord* Octavio *with those Weapons that wound you: The last time he writ to my Lord* Philander, *he found you possest with a thousand fears and jealousies; of these he took advantage to attaque his Rival, for what man is there so dull that wou'd not assault his Enemy in that part where the most considerable mischief may be done him; 'tis now* Octavio's *Int'rest and his business to render* Philander *false, to give you all the umbrage that is possible of so powerful a Rival, and to say any thing that may render him hateful to you, or at least to make you love him less. Away,* reply'd *Silvia* (with an uneasie smile) *how foolish are thy reasonings, for were it possible I cou'd Love* Philander *less, is it to be imagin'd, that shoud make way for* Octavio *in my heart, or any, after that dear deceiver? No doubt of it,* reply'd Antonett, *but that very effect it wou'd have on your heart, for Love in the Soul of a witty person is like a scain of Silk;[a] to unwin'd it from the Bottom, you must wind it on another or it runs into confusion and becomes of no use, and then of course, as one lessens the other increases, and what* Philander *loses in Love,* Octavio *or some one industrious Lover will most certainly gain: Oh* reply'd Silvia *you are a great Phylosopher in Love. I shou'd be Madam,* cry'd Antonett, *had I but had a good Memory, for I had a young Church man once in love with me, who has read many a Philosophical Lecture to me upon Love; among the rest he us'd to say the soul was all compos'd of Love. I us'd to ask him then if it were form'd of so soft Materials, how it came to pass that we were no oftner in love, or why so many were so long before they lov'd, and others who never lov'd at all? No queston but he answer'd you wisely,* said Silvia carelessly and sighing, with her thoughts but half attentive. *Marry and so he did,* cry'd Antonett, *at least I thought so then,*

---

[a] Skein.

because I loved a little. He said, *Love of it self was unactive, but 'twas inform'd by Object, and then too that Object must depend on fancy (for souls, tho all love, are not to love all) now fancy,* he said, *was sometimes nice, humourous, and fantastick, which is the reason we so often love those of no merit, and despise those that are most excellent; and sometimes fancy guides us to like neither,* he us'd to say *Women were like Misers, tho they had always love in store, they seldom car'd to part with it, but on very good int'rest and security,* Cent per Cent, *most commonly heart for heart at least, and for security he said we were most times too unconscionable, we ask'd Vows at least, at worst Matrimony——* Half angry, *Silvia* cry'd, *— and what's all this to my loving against? Oh* Madam, reply'd Antonett, *he said a Woman was like a Gamester, if on the winning hand, hope, int'rest, and vanity made him play on, besides the pleasure of the play it self; if on the losing, then he continu'd throwing at all to save a stake at last, if not to recover all; so either way they find occasion to continue the game. But oh,* said *Silvia* sighing, *what shall that Gamester set, who has already play'd for all she had, and lost it at a cast? Oh* Madam, reply'd Antonett, *The young and fair find Credit every where, there's still a prospect of a return, and that Gamester that plays thus upon the tick is sure to lose but little, and if they win, 'tis all clear gains. I find,* said Silvia, *you are a good manager in love; you are for the frugal part of it. Faith Madam,* said Antonett, *I am indeed of that opinion, that love and int'rest always do best together, as two most excellent ingredients in that rare Art of preserving of Beauty. Love makes us put on all our Charms, and int'rest gives us all the advantage of dress, without which Beauty is lost, and of little use. Love wou'd have us appear always new, always gay, and magnificent, and money alone can render us so, and we find no Women want Lovers so much as those who want Petticoats, Jewels, and all the necessary trifles of Gallantry. Of this last opinion I find you your self to be; for even when* Octavio *comes, on whose heart you have no design, I see you dress to the best advantage, and put on many, to like one: Why is this but that, even unknown to your self, you have a secret joy and pleasure in gaining Conquests and of being ador'd and thought the most Charming of your Sex. That is not from the inconstancy of my heart,* cry'd Silvia, *but from the little vanity of our Natures. Oh* Madam, reply'd Antonett, *there is no friend to Love, like Vanity; it is the falsest betrayer of a Womans heart, of any Passion or humour she can be guilty of, not Love it self betrays her sooner to Love than Vanity or Pride, and, Madam, I wou'd I might have the pleasure of my next wish, when I find you not only list'ning to the love of* Octavio, *but even approving it too. Away,* reply'd *Silvia* in frowning, *your mirth grows rude and troublesome,—Go bid the Page wait, while I return an answer to what his Lord has sent me.* So sitting at the Table she dismist *Antonett*, and writ this following Letter.

Silvia *to* Octavio.

I find *Octavio* this little Gallantry of yours, of shewing me the Lover, stands you in very great stead, and serves you upon all occasions for abundance of uses, amongst the rest, 'tis no small obligation you have to't, for furnishing you with handsom pretences to keep from those who importune you, and from giving 'em that satisfaction by your Council and Conversation which possibly the unfortunate may need of sometimes; and when you are prest and oblig'd to render me the friendship of your Visits, this necessary ready love of yours, is the only evasion you have for the answering a thousand little questions I ask you of *Philander*; whose heart I am afraid you know much better than *Silvia* does, I cou'd almost wish *Octavio*, that all you tell me of your passion were true, that my commands might be of force sufficient to compel you, to resolve my heart in some doubts that oppress it, and indeed if you wou'd have me believe the one, you must obey me in the other, to which end I conjure you to hasten to me, for something of an unusual coldness in *Philanders* Letter, and some ominous divinations in yours, have put me on the rack of thought, from which nothing but Confirmation can relieve me, this you dare not deny if you value the repose

Of Sllvia.

She read it over, and was often about to tear it, fancying it was too kind: But when she consider'd 'twas from no other inclination of her heart than that of getting the secrets out of his, she pardon'd her self the little levity she found it guilty of, all which considering as the effects of the violent Passion she had for *Philander*, she found it easie to do, and sealing it she gave to to *Antonett* to deliver to the Page, and set herself down to ease her soul of its heavy weight of grief, by her complaints

to the dear Author of her pain; for when a Lover is insupport-
ably afflicted there is no ease like that of writing to the person
lov'd: And that all that comes uppermost in the Soul, for true
love is all unthinking artless speaking, incorrect disorder, and
without Method, as 'tis without bounds or rules, such were
Silvia's unstudy'd thoughts, and such her following Letter.

Silvia *to* Philander.

Oh my *Philander*, how hard it is to bring my Soul to doubt,
when I consider all thy past tender vows, when I reflect how
thou hast lov'd and sworn. Methinks I hear the Musick of thy
voice still whispering in my bosom; methinks the Charming
softness of thy words remain like lessening Eccho's on my Soul,
whose distant Voyces by degrees decay, till they be heard no
more! Alas I've read thy Letter o're and o're and turn'd the
sense a thousand several ways, and all to make it speak and
look like Love——Oh I have flatter'd it with all my Art. Sometimes I fancy'd my ill reading spoil'd it, and then I tun'd my
Voice to softer Notes, and read it o're again; but still the words
appear'd too rough and harsh for any moving Air, which way
so e're I chang'd, which way so e're I question'd it of love, it
answer'd in such Language—as others wou'd perhaps interpret
love, or something like it; but I who've heard the very God
himself speak from thy wondrous Lips, and known him guide
thy Pen when all the eloquence of moving Angels flow'd from
thy charming Tongue! when I have seen thee fainting at my
feet, (whil'st all Heaven open'd in thy glorious face) and now
and then sigh out a trembling word; in which there was contain'd more love, more Soul, than all the Arts of speaking ever
found. What sense! Oh what reflections must I make on this
decay, this strange — this suddain alteration in thee? But that
the cause is fled, and the effect is ceas'd, the God retir'd, and all
the Oracles[a] silenc'd! Confess — oh thou eternal Conqueror of
my Soul, whom every hour, and every tender joy, renders more

---

[a] The prophecies of the gods. Priests interpreted the words or signs given by the
gods to those who came to the oracle for advice.

188

dear and lovely———Tell me why (if thou still lov'st me, and lov'st as well) does love not dictate to thee as before! Dost thou want words? Oh then begin again, repeat the old ones o're ten thousand times, such repetitions are loves Rethorick! how often have I ask'd thee in an hour, when my fond Soul was doating on thy Eyes, when with my Arms, clasping thy yielding Neck, my lips imprinting kisses on thy cheeks, and taking in the breath, that sight from thine, how often have *I* ask'd this little but important question of thee? *Does my* Philander *Love me?* then kiss thee for thy *Yes* and sighs, and ask again, and still my Soul was ravisht with new joy, when thou woud'st answer, *Yes; I love thee dearly*! and if *I* thought you spoke it with a tone that seem'd less soft and fervent than *I* wisht, *I* ask'd so often till *I* made thee answer in such a voice as I wou'd wish to hear it; all this had been impertinent and foolish in any thing but love, to any but a Lover: But oh—give me the impertinence of love! talk little nonsense to me all the day, and be as wanton as a playing *Cupid*, and that will please and Charm my love sick heart better than all fine sense and reasoning.

Tell me, *Philander*, what new accident, what powerful misfortune has befallen thee, greater than what we have experienc'd yet? cou'd drive the little God out of thy heart, and make thee so unlike my soft *Philander*? What place contains thee, or what pleasures ease thee, that thou art now contented to live a tedious day without thy *Silvia*. How then the long long Age of forty more, and yet thou liv'st, art patient, tame, and well; thou talk'st not now of ravings, or of dying, but lookst about thee like a well pleas'd Conqueror after the toyls of Battel——Oh *I* have known a time——but let me never think about it more! it cannot be remembered without madness! What think thee fallen from love! to think that I must never hear thee more pouring thy Soul out in soft sighs of love? A thousand dear expressions by which I knew the Story of thy heart, and while you tell it, bid me feel it panting —— Never to see thy Eyes fixt on my face——till the soft showres of joy wou'd gently fall and hang their shining dew upon thy looks, then in a Transport snatch me to thy bosom, and sigh a thousand times e're thou cou'dst utter—— *Ah* Silvia *how I love thee*——Oh the dear Eloquence, those few short words contain; when they are sent with Lovers accents, to a Soul all languishing! but now —— alass, thy love is more familiar grown ——Oh take the other part o'th' Proverb too and say 't has bred contempt, for nothing less than that your Letter shews, but more it does, and that's indifference, less to be born than hate or any thing—

At least be just and let me know my doom; do not deceive the heart that trusted all thy Vows, if thou be'st generous —— if thou let'st me know — —thy date of Love——is out (for love perhaps as life has dates) and equally uncertain, and thou no more canst stay the one than t'other, yet if thou art so kind for all my honour lost; my youth undone, my Beauty tarnisht, and my lasting vows to let me fairly know thou art departing, my worthless Life will be the only loss; But if thou still continuest to impose, upon my easie Faith, and I shou'd any other way learn my approaching Fate——Look to't *Philander*——She that had the courage t'abandon all for Love, and faithless thee, can when she finds her self betray'd and lost, Nobly revenge the ruin of her fame, and send thee to the other World with,

Silvia

She having writ this, read it over, and fancy'd she had not spoke half the sense of her Soul — Fancy'd if she were again to begin she cou'd express her self much more to the purpose she design'd, than she had done. She began again and writ two or three new ones, but they were either too kind or too rough, the first she fear'd wou'd shew a weakness of Spirit, since he had given her occasion of jealousie, the last she fear'd wou'd disoblige if all those jealousies were false, she therefore tore those last she had writ, and before she seal'd up the first she read *Philanders* Letter again, but still ended it with fears that did not lessen those she had first conceiv'd; still she thought she had more to say as Lovers do, who never are weary of speaking or writing to the dear object of their Vows, and having already forgotten what she had said just before——and her heart being by this time as full as e're she began she took up her complaining Pen, and made it say this in the Covert of the Letter.

Oh *Philander!* Oh thou eternal Charmer of my Soul, how fain I wou'd repent me of the cruel thoughts I have of thee; when I had finisht this inclos'd I read again thy chilling Letter, and strove with all the force of Love and soft imagination to find a dear occasion of asking Pardon for those fears, which press my breaking heart: but Oh the more I read, the more they strike upon my tenderest part,——something so very cold, so careless,

and indifferent you end your Letter with——I will not think of
it—by Heaven it makes me rave—and hate my little power, that
cou'd no longer keep thee soft and kind. Oh if those killing
fears (bred by excess of Love) are vainly taken up in pity my
adorable — in pity to my tortur'd Soul convince 'em. Redress
the torment of my jealous doubts, and either way confirm me;
be kind to her that dyes and languishes for thee, return me all
the softness that first Charm'd me, or frankly tell me my
approaching Fate. Be generous, or be kind, to the unfortunate
and undone.

Silvia.

She thought she had ended here, but here again she read
Philanders Letter, as if on purpose to find new torments out for
a heart too much prest already; a sowre that is always mixt with
the sweets of Love, a pain that ever accompanies the pleasure.
Love else were not to be number'd among the passions of men,
and was at first ordain'd in Heaven for some divine motion of
the Soul, till *Adam* with his loss of *Paradise* debaucht it, with
jealousies fears, and curiosities, and mixt it with all that was
afflicting;[a] but you'l say he had reason to be jealous, whose
Woman for want of other Seducers listen'd to the Serpent, and
for the Love of change wou'd give way even to a Devil, this little
Love of Novelty and knowledge has been intail'd upon her
daughters ever since, and I have known more Women rendered
unhappy and miserable from this torment of curiosity, which
they bring upon themselves, than have ever been undone by
less villainous Men. One of this humour was our haughty and
Charming *Silvia*, whose Pride and Beauty possessing her with a
belief that all Men were born to dye her Slaves made her uneasie at every action of the Lover (whether belov'd or not) that
did but seem to slight her Empire; but where indeed she lov'd
and doated, as now on *Philander*, this humour put her on the
rack at every thought or fancy that he might break his Chains
and having laid the last Obligation upon him, she expected him
to be her Slave for ever, and treated him with all the haughty
Tyranny of her Sex, in all those moments when softness was

---

[a] Milton's *Paradise Lost* was published in 1667 and it inspired a constant stream of
poems discussing the Genesis myth and assessing the relationship between men
and women in this period.

not predominate in her Soul. She was shagrien at every thing if but displeas'd with one thing, and while she gave torments to others she fail'd not to feel 'em the most sensibly her self; so that still searching for new occasion of quarrel with *Philander* she drew on her self most intollerable pains, such as doubting Lovers feel after long hopes and confirm'd joys, she reads and weeps, and when she came to that part of it that inquir'd of the health and being of the pledge of Love——she grew so tender that she was almost fainting in her Chair, but recovering from the soft reflection, and finding she had said nothing of it already she took her Pen again and writ.

You ask me, Oh Charming *Philander* how the Pledge of our soft hours thrives? Alas, as if it meant to brave the worst of fate! it does advance, my sorrows and all your cruelties have not destroy'd that. But I still bear about me the destiny of many a sighing Maid, that this (who will I am sure be like *Philander*) will ruin with his looks.

Thou Sacred Treasure of my Soul forgive me, if I have wrong'd thy love; adieu.

She made an end of writing this, just when *Antonett* arriv'd, and told her *Octavio* was alighted at the Gate, and coming to visit her, which gave her occasion to say this of him to *Philander*,

I think I had not ended here but that *Octavio* the bravest and the best of friends is come to visit me. The only Satisfaction I have to support my life in *Philanders* absence, pay him those thanks that are due to him from me, pay him for all the generous cares he has taken of me; beyond a friend! almost *Philander* in his blooming Passion when 'twas all new and young, and full of duty, cou'd not have render'd me his service with a more awful industry: sure he was made for love and glorious friendship. Cherish him them, preserve him next your Soul, for he's a Jewel, fit for such a Cabinet: His form, his parts, and every Noble action, shews us the Royal Race from whence he sprung, and the Victorious *Orange*[a] confesses him his own in every Vertue, and in every Grace, nor can the illigitimacy eclips him; sure he was got in the first heat of Love, which form'd him so a Hero——But no more. *Philander* is as kind a Judge as

Silvia.

---

[a] William, Prince of Orange, who would later become king of England in 1688.

She had no sooner finisht this and seal'd it, but *Octavio* came into the Chamber, and with such an Air, with such a Grace, and mien he approach'd her — with all the languishment of soft trembling Love in his face, which with the addition of the dress he was that day in, (which was extreamly rich and advantagious, and altogether such as pleases the Vanity of Women.) I have since heard the Charming *Silvia* say, in spight of all her tenderness for *Philander*; she found a soft emotion in her Soul, a kind of pleasure at his approach, which made her blush with some kind of anger at her own easiness. Nor cou'd she have blusht in a more happy season; for *Octavio* saw it, and it serv'd at once to add a Luster to her paler Beauty, and to betray some little kind sentiment, which possest him with a joy that had the same effects on him: *Silvia* saw it; and the care she took to hide her own, serv'd but to increase her blushes, which put her into a confusion she had much ado to reclaim; she cast her Eyes to Earth, and leaning her Cheek on her hand, she continu'd on her seat without paying him that usual Ceremony she was wont to do. While he stood speechless for a moment gazing on her with infinite satisfaction, when she to assume a formality as well as she cou'd, rose up and cry'd (fearing he had seen too much) Octavio *I have been considering after what manner I ought to receive you, and while I was so, I left those Civillities unpaid which your quality, and my good manners ought to have render'd you.* Ah Madam, reply'd he sighing, *if you wou'd receive me as I merited and you ought, at least you wou'd receive me as the most passionate Lover that ever Ador'd you. I was rather believing,* said *Silvia, that I ought to have receiv'd you as my Foe: Since you conceal from me so long what you cannot but believe I am extreamly impatient of hearing, and what so neerly concerns my repose.* At this he only answering with a sigh, she pursu'd. *Sure,* Octavio, *you understand me:* Philanders *answer to the Letter of your confessing Passion has not so long been the subject of our discourse and expectation, but you guess at what I mean?* *Octavio,* who on all Occasions wanted not wit, or reply, was here at a loss, what to answer: Notwithstanding he had consider'd before what he wou'd say: but let those in love fancy, and make what fine speeches they please, and believe themselves furnisht with abundance of eloquent Harangues at the sight of the dear Object they lose 'em all, and love teach 'em a dialect much more prevailing without the expence of duller thought: And they leave unsaid all they had so floridly form'd before, and sigh a thousand things with more success: Love like

Poetry cannot be taught, but uninstructed flows without painful study, if it be true; 'tis born in the Soul, a Noble inspiration not a Science! such was *Octavio*'s, he thought it dishonourable to be guilty of the meaness of a Lye, and say he had no answer: He thought it rude to say he had one and wou'd not shew it *Silvia*: And he believ'd it the height of ungenerous baseness to shew it, while he remain'd this moment silent; *Silvia*, who's love, jealousie, and impatience indur'd no delay, with a malicious half smile, and a tone all angry, scorn in her Eyes, and passion on her Tongue, she cry'd——*'Tis, well* Octavio, *that you so early let me know you can be false, unjust, and faithless, you knew your power, and in pitty to that Youth and easiness you found in me, have given a Civil warning to my heart. In this I must confess,* continu'd she, *you have given a much greater testimony of your friendship for* Philander, *than your Passion for* Silvia; *And, I suppose, you came not here to resolve your self of which you should prefer, that was decided e're you arriv'd, and this visit I imagine was only to put me out of doubt: A piece of Charity you might have spar'd.* She ended this with a scorn, that had a thousand Charmes, because it gave him a little hope; and he answer'd with a sigh, *Ah Madam, how very easie you find it to entertain thoughts disadvantagious of me: And how small a fault your Wit and cruelty can improve to a Crime. You are not offended at my friendship for* Philander. *I know you do not Vallue my Life, and my repose so much, as to be concern'd who, or what, shares this heart, that adores you; No, it has not merited that Glory; Nor dare I presume to hope, you shou'd so much as wish my Passion for* Silvia, *shou'd surmount my Friendship to* Philander. *If I did,* reply'd she with a scorn, *I perceive I might wish in vain:* Madam, answer'd he, *I have too Divine an opinion of the justice of the Charming* Silvia *to believe I ought, or cou'd make my approaches to her heart by ways so base and ungenerous, the result of even tollerated Treason is to hate the Traytor. Oh, you are very nice,* Octavio, replyed Silvia, *in your Punctilio to* Philander, *but I perceive you are not so tender in those you ought to have for* Silvia? *I find Honour in you men, is only what you please to make it, for at the same time you think it ungenerous to betray* Philander, *you believe it no breach of* Honour *to betray the eternal repose of* Silvia? *You have promis'd* Philander *your friendship, you have avow'd your self my Lover, my Slave, my Friend, my every thing, and yet not one of these has any tye, to oblige you to my interest, pray tell me,* continued She, *when you last writ to him, was it not in order to receive an answer from him? And was not I to see that answer? And here you think it no dishonour to break your word or promise; by which I find your false Notions, of Vertue and Honour, with which you serve your selves, when int'rest, design, or self Love makes you think it necessary.* Madam, replyed Octavio, *you are pleas'd to persue your anger, as if indeed I had disobeyed your command, or refus'd to shew you what you Imagine I have from* Philander: Yes, I do replyed she hastily; *and wonder why you shou'd have a greater friendship for* Philander, *than for* Silvia, *especially if it be true that you say, you have joyned Love to friendship; or are you of the opinion of those that cry they cannot be a Lover and a friend of the same Object. Ah Madam,* cry'd our perplext Lover, *I beg you to believe, I think it so much more my Duty and inclination to serve and obey* Silvia *than I do* Philander *that I swear to you Oh, Charming Conqueress of my Soul, if* Philander *have betrayed* Silvia, *he has at the same time betray'd* Octavio, *and that I wou'd revenge it with the loss of my Life: In injuring the adorable* Silvia, *believe me, lovely Maid, he injures so much more than a Friend, as Honour is above the inclination; if he wrong you, by Heaven he cancels all! he wrongs my Soul, my Honour, Mistress and my Sister:* Fearing he had said too much, he stopp'd and sight at the word Sister, and casting down his Eyes, blushing with shame and anger, he continu'd, *Oh, give me leave to say a Sister, Madam, least Mistress had been too daring and presumptious, and a Title that wou'd not justifie my quarrel half so well, since 'twould take the Honour from my just resentment and blast it with the scandal of self int'rest or jealous revenge. What you say* replyed she, *deserves abundance of acknowledgement; but if you wou'd have me believe you, you ought to hide nothing from me, and he methinks that was so daring to confess his Passion to* Philander, *may, after that, venture on any discovery: In short* Octavio, *I demand to see the return you have from* Philander, *for possibly*—said the, sweet'ning her Charming face into a Smile design'd, *I shou'd not be displeas'd to find I might with more freedom receive your Addresses, and on the coldness of* Philanders *reasoning may depend a great part of your Fate, or Fortune: Come, come, produce your credentials, they may recommend your heart more effectually than all the fine things you can say, you know not how the least appearance of a slight from a Lover, may advance the Pride of a Mistress, and Pride in this affair will be your best Advocate.* Thus she insinuated with all her female Arts, and put on all her Charms of Looks and smiles, sweetned her mouth, soften'd her Voyce and Eyes, assuming all the tenderness and little affectations her subtil Sex was capable of, while he lay all ravisht and almost expiring at her Feet; sometimes transported with imagin'd Joys in the possession of the dear flattering Charmer, he was ready to unravel all the Secrets of *Philanders* letter; but Honour yet was even above his Passion and made him blush at his first hasty thought; and now he strove to put her off, with all the Art he cou'd, who had so very little in his Nature, and whose real Love and perfect Honour had set him above the little evasions of Truth, who scorn'd in all other cases the baseness and cowardize of a Lye: and so unsuccessful now was the little honest cheat, which he knew not how to manage well, that 'twas soon discover'd to the Wity, jealous, and angry *Silvia*: So that after all the rage a passionate Woman cou'd express, who believ'd her self injur'd by the only two persons in the World from whom she expected most Adoration? she had recourse to that Natural and softning aid of her Sex, her Tears, and having already reproach'd *Octavio* with all the malice of a defeated Woman, she now continued it in so moving a manner, that our *Hero* cou'd no longer remain unconquer'd by that powerful way of Charming, but unfixt to all he had resolv'd gave up, at least, a part of the secret, and own'd he had a Letter from *Philander*; and after this confession knowing very well he cou'd not keep her from the sight of it; no tho an Empire were render'd her to buy it off; his Wit was next imploy'd how he shou'd defend the sense of it, that she might not think *Philander* false. In Order to this, he, forcing a Smile, told her, that *Philander* was the most malicious of his Sex, and had contriv'd the best Stratagem in the world to find whether *Silvia* still lov'd, or *Octavio* retain'd his friendship for him; *And but that,* continued he, *I know the Nature of your curious Sex to be such, that if I shou'd perswade you not to see it, it wou'd but the more inflame your desire of seeing it, I wou'd ask no more of the Charming* Silvia, *than that she wou'd not oblige me to shew, what wou'd turn so greatly to my own advantage: if I were not too sensible, 'tis but to intrap me, that* Philander *has taken this method in his answer. Believe me Adorable* Silvia, *I plead against my own Life, while I beg you not to put my honour to the test, by commanding me to shew this Letter, and that I joyn against the int'rest of my own Eternal repose while I plead thus:* she hears him with a hundred changes of countenance. Love, rage, and Jealousie swell in her fiercer Eyes, her breath beats short, and she was ready to burst into speaking before he had finisht what he had to say; she calls up all the little discretion and Reason Love had left her to manage her self as she ought in this great occasion; she bit her Lips and swallow'd her rising sighs; but he soon saw the storm he had rais'd and knew not how to stand the shock of its fury; he sighs, he pleads in vain, and the more he indeavours to excuse the Levity of *Philander*, the more he rends her heart, and sets her on the Rack; and concluding him false, she cou'd no longer contain her rage, but broke out into all the fury that madness can inspire, and from one degree to another wrought her Passion to the height of Lunacy: She tore her Hair and bit his hands, that indeavour'd to restrain hers from violence, she rent the Ornaments from her fair Body, and discover'd a thousand Charms and Beauties, and finding now that both his strength and reason was too weak to prevent the mischiefs he found he had brought on her, he calls for help; When *Briljard* was but too ready at hand; with *Antonett* and some others, who came to his assistance; *Briljard* who knew nothing of the occasion of all this, believ'd it second part of his own late adventure, and fancy'd that *Octavio* had us'd some violence to her, upon this he assumes the Authority of his Lord, and secretly that of a Husband or Lover, and upbraiding the innocent *Octavio* with his brutallity they fell to such words as ended in a challenge the next morning, for *Briljard* appear'd a Gentleman, Companion to his Lord; and one whom *Octavio* cou'd not well refuse, this was not carried so silently but *Antonett* busie as she was about her raving Lady heard the appointment, and *Octavio* quitted the Chamber almost as much disturb'd as *Silvia*, whom, with much ado, they perswaded him to leave, but before he did so he on his knees offer'd her the Letter and implor'd her to receive it. So absolutely his Love had vanquisht his Nobler part, that of honour; but she attending no motions but those of her own Rage, had no regard either to *Octavio*'s proffer or his Arguments of Excuse, so that he went away with the Letter, in all the extremity of disorder; this last part of his submission was not seen by *Briljard*; who immediately left the Chamber, upon receiving *Octavio*'s answer to his Challenge; so that *Silvia* was now left with her Woman only, who by degrees brought her to more calmness; and *Briljard* impatient to hear the reproaches, he hop'd she wou'd give *Octavio* when she was return'd to reason, being curious of any thing that might redound to his disadvantage, whom he took to be a powerful Rival, return'd again into her Chamber: But in lieu of hearing what he wisht; *Silvia* being recover'd from her passion of madness, and her Soul in a state of thinking a little with reason; she misses *Octavio* in the crow'd, and with a Voyce, her rage had infeebl'd to a Languishment, she cry'd — surveying carefully those about her, *Oh where's* Octavio? *Where is that Angel man? he who of all his kind can give comfort.* Madam, replyed Antonett, *he is gone, while he was here, he kneel'd and pray'd in vain, but for a word, or look, his Tears are yet remaining wet upon your Feet, and all for one sensible reply, but rage had deafen'd you: what has he done to merit this?* Oh Antonett cry'd Silvia — *'Twas what he wou'd not do that makes me rave, run, hast and fetch him back — But let him leave his Honour all behind; Tell him he has too much consideration for* Philander, *and none for my repose. Oh, fly* Briljard—*Have I no friend in view, dares carry a Message from me to* Octavio? *Bid him return, oh instantly return — I dye, I languish for a sight of him — Descending Angels wou'd not be so welcome — Why stand ye still, have I no power with you—Will none obey*—Then running hastily to the Chamber Door, she call'd her Page to whom she cry'd——*Hast, hast, dear youth, and find* Octavio *out, and bring him to me instantly: Tell him I dye to see him.* The Boy glad of so kind a Message, to so liberal a Lover, runs on his Errant while she returns to her Chamber, and indeavours to recollect her senses against *Octavio's* coming as much as possible she cou'd: She dismisses her Attendant with different apprehensions; sometimes *Briljard* believ'd this was the second part of her first raving, and having never seen her thus, but for *Philander* concludes it the height of tenderness and Passion for *Octavio*, but because she made so publique a Declaration of it he believ'd he had given her a Philter, which had rais'd her flame so much above the bounds of modesty and discretion; concluding it so, he knew the usual effects of things of that Nature, and that nothing cou'd allay the heat of such a love but possession, and easily deluded with every fancy that flatter'd his love; mad, starke mad by any way to obtain the last blessing with *Silvia*, he consults with *Antonett* how to get one of *Octavio's* Letters out of her Ladies Cabinet, and feigning many frivolous reasons, which deluded the Amorous Maid; he perswaded her to get him one, which she did in half an hour after; for by this time *Silvia* being in as much tranquillity as 'twas possible a Lover cou'd be in, who had the hopes of knowing all the Secrets of the false betrayer, she had call'd *Antonett* to dress her; which she resolved shou'd be in all the careless magnificence that Art or Nature cou'd put on; to Charm *Octavio* wholly to Obedience; whom she had sent for, and whom she expected; but she was no sooner set to her Toylight, but *Octavio's* Page arriv'd with a Letter from his Master, which she greedily snacht; and read this.

Octavio *to* Silvia.

By this time, oh Charming *Silvia* give me leave to hope your Rage is abated, and your reason return'd, and that you will hear a little from the most unfortunate of men, whom you have reduc'd to this miserable Extremity of losing either the Adorable Object of his Soul, or his Honour: If you can prefer a little curiosity that will serve but to afflict you before either that or my repose. What esteem ought I to believe you have for the unfortunate *Octavio*; and if you hate me, as 'tis evident if you compel me to the extremity of losing my repose or honour, what reason or argument have I to prefer so careless a Fair One above the last. 'Tis certain you neither do nor can love me now; and how much below that hope shall the expos'd and abandon'd *Octavio* be, when he shall pretend to that Glory without his Honour: Believe me, Charming Maid, I wou'd Sacrifice my life, and my intire Fortune at your least command to serve you; but to render you a devoyr[a] that must point me out the basest of my Sex, is what my temper must resist in spight of all the violence of my Love, and I thank my happyer Stars that they have given me resolution enough rather to fall a Sacrifice to the last, than be guilty of the breach of the first: This is the last and present thought and pleasure of my Soul, and least it shou'd by the force of those Divine Ideas which Eternally surround it, be sooth'd and flatter'd from its Noble Principles, I will to morrow put my self out of the hazard of Temptation, and divert if possible by absence to the Compagne, those soft importunate betrayers of my Liberty; that perpetually solicit in favour of you: I dare not so much as bid you adieu, one sight of that bright Angels face, wou'd undo me, unfix my Nobler resolutions, and leave me a despicable Slave, sighing my unrewarded Treason at your insensible Feet: My Fortune I leave to be dispos'd by you; but the more useless necessary I will for ever take from those lovely Eyes, who can look on nothing with joy, but the happy *Philander*: If I have denied you one satisfaction, at least I have

---

[a] *French*: duty.

given you this other of securing you Eternally from the trouble and importunity of

Madam your Faithful

Octavio.

This Letter to any other less secure of her own power than was our fair Subject, wou'd have made them impatient and angry: But she found that there was something yet in her power, the dispensation of which cou'd soon recall him from any resolution he was able to make of absenting himself: Her Glass stood before her, and every glance that way was an assurance and security to her heart; she cou'd not see that Beauty and doubt its power of perswasion; She therefore took her Pen, and writ him this answer, being in a moment furnisht with all the Art and subtilty that was necessary on this occasion.

Silvia *to* Octavio.

My Lord,
Tho I have not Beauty enough to command your heart; at least allow me sense enough to oblige your belief, that I fancy and resent all that the letter contains which you have deny'd me, and that I am not of that sort of Women, whose want of youth or Beauty renders so constant to pursue the Ghost of a departed Love: It is enough to justifie my Honour, that I was not the first Agressor. I find my self persu'd by too many Charmes of Wit, Youth, and Gallantry, to bury my self beneath the willows, or to whine away my youth by murmuring Rivers, or betake me to the last refuge of a declining Beauty, a Monastary: no my Lord, when I have reveng'd and recompenc'd my Self for the injuries of one inconstant, with the joys a thousand imploring Lovers offer, it will be time to be weary of a world which yet every day presents me new joys; and I swear to you, *Octavio,* that it was more to recompence what I ow'd your passion that I desir'd a convincing proof of *Philanders* false-hood, than for any other reason, and you have too much Wit not to know it; for what

other use cou'd I make of the Secret; if he be false he's gone, unworthy of me, and impossible to be retriev'd, and I wou'd as soon dye my sullied Garments and wear them over again, as take to my imbraces a reform'd Lover, the Native first Luster of whose passion is quite extinct, and is no more the same; no, my Lord, she must be poor in Beauty that has recourse to shifts so mean; if I wou'd know the Secret by all that's good it were to hate him heartily, and to dispose of my Person to the best advantage; which in honour I cannot do, while I am uncon-vinc'd of the falseness of him with whom I have exchang'd a thousand Vows of fidellity, but if he unlink the Chain I am at perfect liberty, and why by this delay you shou'd make me lose my time, I am not able to conceive unless you fear I shou'd then take you at your word, and expect the performance of all the Vows of Love you have made me. — If that be it — My Pride shall be your security, or if other recompence you expect, set the Price upon your Secret, and see at what rate I will purchase the liberty it will procure me, possibly it may be such as may at once infranchize me, and revenge me on the perjur'd ingrate, than which nothing can be a greater Satisfaction to

Silvia,

She Seals this Letter with a wafer, and giving it to *Antonett* to give the Page, believing she had writ what wou'd not be in vain to the quick sighted *Octavio*: *Antonett* takes both that and the other which *Octavio* had sent and left her Lady busie in dressing her head, and went to *Briljards* Chamber, who thought every moment an Age till she came; so vigorous he was on his new design: That which was sent to *Octavio* being seal'd with a wet Wafer he neatly opens, as 'twas easie to do, and read and Seal'd again, and *Antonett* deliver'd it to the Page. After receiving what pay *Briljard* cou'd force himself to bestow upon her; some flat-teries of dissembl'd love; and some cold Kisses, which even imagination cou'd not render better, She return'd to her Lady, and he to his Stratagem, which was to counterfeit a Letter from *Octavio*: She having in hers given him a hint, by bidding him set a price upon the Secret, which he had heard was that of a Letter from *Philander*, with all the Circumstances of it, from the faith-less *Antonett* whom Love had betray'd and after blotting much paper to try every Letter through the Alphabet, and to produce them like those of *Octavio*, which was not hard for a Lover of ingenuity; he fell to the business of what he wou'd write, and having finisht it to his liking, his next trouble was how to convey it to Her; for *Octavio* always sent his by his Page, whom he cou'd trust. He now was certain of love between 'em? For tho he often had perswaded *Antonett* to bring him Letters, yet she cou'd not be wrought on till now to betray her trust: And what he long apprehended, he found too true on both sides, and now he waited but for an opportunity to send it seasonably, and in a lucky minute. In the mean time *Silvia* adorns her self for absolute conquest and disposing her self in the most charming, careless, and tempting manner she cou'd devise, she lay expecting her coming Lover, on a repose of rich Embroidery of Gold on blew Sattin, hung inside with little Amorous Pictures of *Venus* descending in her Chariot naked to *Adonis*,[a] she imbracing, while the youth more eager of his rural sports turns half from her, in a posture of pursuing his Dogs, who are on their Chace: Another of *Armida*[b] who is dressing the sleeping warrior up in wreaths of Flowers, while a hundred little Loves are playing with his guilded Armour; this puts on his Helmet too big for his little head that hides his whole face; another makes a Hobby horse of Sword and Lance, another fits on his breast piece, while three or four little *Cupids* are seeming to heave and help him to hold it an end, and all turn'd the Emblemes of the *Hero* into ridicule. These and some other of the like nature adorn'd the Pavillion of the languishing Fair One, who lay carelessly on her side; her Arm leaning on little Pillows, of Point of *Venice*,[c] and a Book of Amours in her other hand. Every noise alarm'd her with trembling hope that her Lover was come, and I have heard she said she verily believ'd that acting and feigning the Lover possest her with a tenderness against her knowledge and Will; and she found something more in her Soul than a bare curiosity of seeing *Octavio* for the Letters sake:

---

[a] God of vegetation and fertility. Venus met and fell in love with Adonis when he was out hunting one day. He continued his hunt, was killed by a wild boar and roses sprang from his blood.

[b] In Tasso's *Jerusalem Delivered*, Armida is the niece of the king of Damascus. When Jerusalem is besieged by Christians, she helps to defend the city by luring Christian knights to a garden of indolence.

[c] Venetian thread lace was known for its high quality.

But in Lieu of her Lover, she found her self once more approacht with a Billet from him; which brought this.

Octavio *to* Silvia.

Ah *Silvia*, he must be more than humane, that can withstand your Charms, I confess my frailty, and fall before you, the weakest of my Sex, and own I am ready to believe all your dear Letter contains, and have vanity enough to wrest every hopeful word to my own int'rest, and in favour of my own Heart: What will become of me, if my easie faith shou'd only flatter me, and I with shame shou'd find it was not meant to me, or if it were, 'twas only to draw me from a Virtue which has been hitherto the Pride and Beauty of my youth, the Glory of my name, my Comfort and refuge in all extreams of Fortune: The eternal Companion, Guide and Counsellor of all my actions: Yet this good you only have power to rob me of, and leave me expos'd to the scorn of all the laughing World: Yet give me Love! give me but hope in lieu of it, and I am content to devest my self of all besides.

Perhaps you will say *I* ask too mighty a rate for so poor a secret? But even in that, there lies one of my own, that will more expose the feebleness of my Blood and Name, than the discovery will me in particular, so that I know not what I do, when I give you up the knowledge you desire. Still you will say all this is to inhaunce its value, and raise the Price: And oh, I fear you have taught my soul every quality, it fears and dreads in yours, and learnt it to chaffer for every thought, if I cou'd fix upon the rate to sell it at: And I with shame confess I wou'd be Mercenary, cou'd we but agree upon the Price: But my respect forbids me all things, but silent hope, and that in spight of me, and all my reason, will predominate? for the rest I will wholly resign my self and all the faculties of my Soul to the Charming Arbitrator of my peace, the powerful Judge of Love, the adorable *Silvia*; And at her Feet render all she demands; yes, she shall find me there to justifie all the weakness this proclaims, for I confess, oh too too powerful Maid, that you have absolutely subdu'd.

Your Octavio.

She had no sooner read this Letter, but *Antonett* instead of laying it by, carried it to *Briljard*, and departed the Chamber to make way, for *Octavio*, who she imagin'd was coming to make his visit, and left *Silvia* considering how she shou'd manage him to the best advantage, and with most honour acquit her self, of what she had made him hope, but instead of his coming to wait on her; an unexpected accident arriv'd to prevent him, for a messenger from the Prince came with commands that he shou'd forthwith come to his Highness, the messenger having command to bring him along with him; So that not able to disobey he only beg'd time to write a note of business, which was a Billet to *Silvia*, to excuse himself till the next day, for it being five Leagues, to the Village where the Prince waited his coming, he cou'd not return that night: which was the business of the Note, with which his Page hasted to *Silvia*: *Briljard* who was now a vigilent Lover, and waiting for every opportunity that might favour his design: Saw the Page arrive with the Note; and as 'twas usual he took it to carry to his Conqueress, but meeting *Antonett* on the Stayers, he gave her what he had before counterfeited with such Art, after he had open'd what *Octavio* had sent, and found Fortune was wholly on his side, he having learn'd from the Page, besides that his Lord had taken Coach with Monsieur——to go to his Highness, and wou'd not return that night: *Antonett* not knowing the deceit carried her Lady the forg'd Letter, who open'd it with eager hast, and read this.

TO THE
CHARMING SILVIA.

Madam,

Since I have a secret which none but I can unfold; and that you have offer'd at any rate to buy it of me: Give me leave to say that you fair Creature have another secret, a joy to dispence, which none but you can give the languishing *Octavio*: If you dare purchase this of mine, with that infinitely more valuable one of yours: I will be as secret as death, and think my self happier than a fancy'd God! Take what Methods you please for the payment, and what time, order me, command me, conjure me,

I will wait, watch, and pay my Duty at all hours, to snatch the most convenient one to reap so ravishing a blessing I know you will accuse me with all the confidence and rudeness in the world; but, oh! to consider lovely *Silvia*, that that passion, which cou'd change my Soul from all the Course of Honour, has power to make me forget that nice respect your Beauty aws me with, and my passion is now arriv'd at such a height, it obeys no Laws but its own; and I am obstinately bent on the pursuit of that vast pleasure, I fancy to find in the dear, the ravishing Arms of the Adorable *Silvia*: Impatient of your answer, I am as love compels me.

> *Madam your Slave,*
>
> Octavio.

The Page, who waited no answer was departed; but *Silvia* who believ'd he attended it, was in a thousand minds what to say or do: She blush'd as she read, and then lookt pale, with anger and disdain, and but that she had already given her Honour up, it wou'd have been something more surprising: But she was us'd to questions of that Nature, and therefore receiv'd this so much the less concern; nevertheless 'twas sufficient to fill her Soul with a thousand agitations, but when she wou'd be angry the conclusion of what she had writ to him, to incourage him to this boldness stop'd her rage: When she wou'd take it ill, she consider'd his knowledge of her lost fame, and that took off a great part of her resentment on that side; and in midst of all she was raving for the knowledge of *Philanders* secret. She rose from the Bed, and walk'd about the room in much disorder, full of thought and no consideration; she is asham'd to consult of this affair with *Antonett*, and knows not what to fix on: The only thing she was certain of, and which was fully and undisputably resolv'd in her Soul, was never to consent to so false an Action, never to buy the secret at so dear a rate; she abhors *Octavio*, whom she regards no more as that fine thing which before she thought him, and a thousand times she was about to write her despight and contempt, but still the dear secret staid her hand, and she was fond of the torment: At last *Antonett*, who was afflicted to know the cause of this disorder, ask'd her Lady if *Octavio* wou'd not come: *No* replyed *Silvia* blushing at the

Name, *nor never shall the ungrateful man dare to behold my face any more. Jesu,* replyed *Antonett, what has he done Madam, to deserve this severity? For he was a great benefactor to* Antonett, *and had already by his gifts and presents made her a Fortune for a Burgomaster:*[a] He has, said *Silvia, committed such an impudence, as deserves death from my Hand:* This she spoke in rage, and walk'd away cross the Chamber. *Why Madam,* cry'd *Antonett, does he denie to give you the Letter: No* replyed *Silvia, but askes me such a price for it, as makes me hate my self, that am reduc'd by my ill conduct, to Addresses of that Nature: Heavens, Madam, what can he ask you, to afflict you so; the presumptuous man,* said she (in rage) *has the impudence to ask what never man, but* Philander *was ever possest of* — At this *Antonett* laught——*Good Lord, Madam,* said she, *and are you angry at such desires in men toward you? I believe you are the first Lady in the World, that was ever offended for being desirable: Can any thing proclaim your Beauty more, or your youth or Wit? marry Madam, I wish I were worthy to be ask'd the question by all the fine dancing, dressing, Song-making Fops in Town: And you wou'd yield,* replyed *Silvia, not so neither* replyed *Antonett, but I wou'd spark my self, and value my self the more upon't. Oh,* said *Silvia, she that is so fond of hearing of Love, no doubt but will find some one to practice it with. That's as I shou'd find my self inclin'd,* replyed *Antonett: Silvia* was not so intent on *Antonett's* rail'ery, but she imploy'd all her thought the while, on what she had to do; and those last words of *Antonett's* jogg'd a thought that ran on to one very advantagious, at least her present and first apprehension of it was such: And she turn'd to *Antonett* with a face more gay than it was the last minute, and cry'd, *Prithee good Wench tell me, what sort of man wou'd soonest incline you to a yielding? if you command me Madam, to be free with your Lordship,* reply'd *Antonett, I must confess there are too sorts of men that wou'd most villainously incline me; the first is he that wou'd make my fortune best. The next her wou'd make my pleasure; the young, the handsome, or rather the well bread, and good humour'd: But above all the Man of Wit: But what wou'd you say* Antonett, replyed *Silvia, if all these made up in one man shou'd make his Addresses to you? Why then most certainly Madam,* replyed *Antonett; I shou'd yield him my Honour, after a reasonable siege.* This tho' the wanton young maid spoke possibly at first more to put her Lady in good humour than from any inclination she had to

----

[a] Mayor of a town in the Low Countries.

what she said, yet after many arguments upon that subject, *Silvia* cunning enough to pursue her design, brought the business more home, and told her in plain terms that *Octavio* was the man who had been so presumptious as to ask so great a reward as the possession of her self for the secret she desir'd; and after a thousand little subtilties, having made the forward Girle confess with blushes, she was not a Maid; she insinuated into her an opinion that what she had done already (without any other motive than that of Love, as she confest in which int'rest had no part,) wou'd make the trick the easier to do again, especially if she brought to her Arms a person of Youth, Wit, Gallantry, Beauty, and all the Charming qualities that adorn a man, and that besides she shou'd find it to good account, and for her secresies, she might depend upon it, since the person to whose imbraces she shou'd submit her self, shou'd not know but that she her self was the Woman, so that says *Silvia, I will have all infamy, and you the reward every way with unblemisht Honour*, while she spoke the willing Maid gave an inward pleasing attention, tho at first she made a few faint modest scruples; Nor was she less joy'd to hear it shou'd be *Octavio*, whom she knew to be rich, and very handsome, and she immediately found the humour of inconstancy cease her, and *Briljard* appear'd a very Husband Lover in comparison of this new Brisker man of quality; so that after some pro's and Con's the whole matter was thus concluded on between these two young persons; who neither wanted Wit, nor Beauty; and both cro'd over the contrivance, as a most diverting piece of little Malice, that shou'd serve their present turn, and make 'em sport for the future. The next thing that was consider'd, was a Letter which was to be sent in answer, and that *Silviu* being to write with her own hand, begot a new doubt, in so much as the whole business was at a stand: For when it came to that point that she her self was to consent, she found the project look with a face so foul, that she a hundred times resolv'd and unresolv'd. But *Philander* fill'd her Soul, revenge was in her view, and that one thought put her on new resolves to pursue the design, let it be never so base and dishonourable: *Yes*, cry'd she ast last, *I can commit no action, that is not more just, excusable, and honourable, than that which* Octavio *has done to me, who uses me like a common Mistris of the Town, and dares ask, me that which he knows, he durst not do if he had not mean, and abject thoughts of me; his baseness deserves death from my hand if I had courage to give it him, and the least I can do is to deceive the deceiver, Well then give me my Scrutore,* says she, so sitting down she writ this, not without abundance of guilt and confusion, for yet a certain Honour, which she had by birth check'd the cheat of her Pen.

Silvia

Silvia *to* Octavio.

The price *Octavio*, which you have set upon your secret, I (more generous than you) will give your merit; to which alone 'tis due, if I shou'd pay so high a price for the first, you wou'd believe I had the less esteem for the last, and I wou'd not have you think me so poor in spirit to yield on any other terms: If I valued *Philander* yet—after his confirm'd inconstancy, I wou'd have you think I scorn to yield a Body where I do not give a Soul, and am yet to be perswaded there are any such Brutes amongst my Sex, but as I never had a wish but where I lov'd, so I never extended one till now, to any but *Philander*, yet so much my sense of shame is above my growing tenderness that I cou'd wish you wou'd be so generous to think no more of what you seem to pursue with such earnestness and haste: But least I shou'd retain any sort of former love for *Philander*, whom I am impatient to race wholly from my Soul. I grant you all you ask provided you will be discreet in the management: *Antonett* therefore shall only be trusted with the secret, the outward gate you shall find at twelve only shut too, and *Antonett* wait you at the Stairs foot to conduct you to me; come alone. I blush and guild the Paper with their reflections, at the thought of an incounter like this before I am half enough secur'd of your heart? And that you may be made more absolutely the master of mine, send me immediately *Philanders* Letter inclos'd, that if any remains of shagrien[a] possess me, they may be totally vanquisht by twelve a Clock.

Silvia

---

[a] Chagrin.

She having with much difficulty writ this, read it to her trusty confident; for this was the only secret of her Ladys she was resolv'd never to discover to *Briljard*, and to the end he might know nothing of it, she seal'd the Letter with Wax; But before she seal'd it, she told her Lady, she thought she might have spar'd abundance of her blushes, and have a writ a less kind Letter, for a word of invitation or consent, wou'd have serv'd as well: To which *Silvia* replyed, her anger against him was too high, not to give him all the defeat imaginable, and the greater the Love appear'd, the greater wou'd be the revenge, when he shou'd come to know (as in time he shou'd) how like a false friend she had treated him: This reason or any at that time wou'd have serv'd *Antonett*, whose heart was set upon the new adventure, and in such haste she was (the night coming on a pace) to know how she shou'd dress, and what more was to be done, that she only went out to call the Page, and meeting *Briljard*, (who watcht every bodies motion) on the Stair-Case, he asked her what that was, and she said to send by *Octavio*'s Page: *You need not look in it* said she (when he snatcht it hastily out of her hand): *For I can tell you the contents, and 'tis seal'd so it must be known if you unrip it: Well, well*, said he, *if you tell it me it will satisfie my curiosity as well; therefore I'le give it the Page.* She returns in again to her Lady, and he to his own Chamber to read what answer the dear Object of his desire had sent to his forg'd one. So opening it, he found it such as his Soul wisht: and was all joy and extasie, he views himself a hundred times in the glass, and set himself in Order with all the Opinion and pride, as if his own good parts had gain'd him the blessing; he inlarg'd himself as he walkt, and knew not what to do, so extreamly was he ravisht with his coming Joy, he blest himself, his Wit, his Stars his Fortune, then read the dear obliging Letter, and kist it all over, as if it had been meant to him, and after he had torc'd himself to a little more serious consideration, he bethought himself of what he had to do in Order to this dear appointment: He finds in her Letter, that in the first place he was to fend her the Letter from *Philander*: I told you before he took *Octavio*'s Letter from the Page; when he understood his Lord was going five Leagues out of Town to the *Prince*. *Octavio* cou'd not avoid his going and write to *Silvia*; in which he sent her the Letter *Philander* writ, wherein was the first part of the confession of his love to Madam the Countess of *Clarinau*: Generously *Octavio* sent it without terms; but *Briljard* slid his own forg'd one into

Antonetts hand, in Lieu of it, and now he read that from *Philander*, and wonder'd at his Lords inconstancy, yet glad of the opportunity to take *Silvia's* heart a little more off from him, he soon resolv'd she shou'd have the Letter, but being wholly mercenary, and fearing, that either when once she had it, it might make her go back from her promis'd assignation, or at least put her out of humour, so as to spoil a great part of the entertainment he design'd: He took the pains to counterfeit another Billet to her, which was this,

To Silvia.

Madam,
Since we have began to chaffer, you must give me leave to make the best of the advantage I find I have upon you; and having violated my Honour to *Philander*, allow the breach of it in some degree on other occasions; not but I have all the obedience and Adoration for you that ever possest the Soul of a most passionate and languishing Lover: But fair *Silvia*, I know not whether, when you have seen the secret of the false *Philander*, you may not think it less valuable than you before did, and so defraud me of my due. Give me leave, oh wonderous Creature! to suspect even the most perfect of your Sex; and to tell you that I will no sooner approach your presence, but I will resign the paper you so much wish; if you send me no answer, I will come according to your Directions; if you do, I must obey and wait, tho with that impatience that never attended a suffering Lover, or any, but,

Divine Creature, your

Octavio.

This he seal'd and after a convenient distance of time, carried as from the Page to *Antonett*, who was yet contriving with her Lady, to whom she gives it, who read it with abundance of impatience, being extreamly angry at the rudeness of the stile, which she fancy'd much alter'd from what it was, and had not her rage blinded her, she might easily have perceiv'd the difference too of the Character, tho it come as near to the like as possible so short a practice cou'd produce: She took it with the other, and tore it in pieces; with rage, and swore she wou'd be reveng'd; but after calmer thoughts she took up the pieces to keep, to upbraid him with, and fell to weeping, for anger, defeat, and shame; but the *April* show'r being past, she return'd to her former resentment, and had some pleasure amidst all her torment of fears, jealousies, and sense of *Octavio's* disrespect, in the thoughts of revenge; in Order to which she contrives how *Antonett* shall manage her self, and commanding her to bring out some fine point Linnen, she drest up *Antonett's* head with them, and put her on a Shift lac'd with the same; for tho she intended no Light shou'd be in the Chamber, when *Octavio* shou'd enter; she knew he understood by his touch the difference of fine things from other, in fine having drest her exactly, as she felt her self us'd to be, when she receiv'd *Octavio's* Visits in Bed, she imbrac'd her, and fancy'd she was much of her own shape and bigness, and that 'twas impossible to find the deceit; and now she made *Antonett* dress her up in her Cloaths, and mobbing her Sarcenet[a] hood about her head, she appear'd so like *Antonett* (all but the face) that 'twas not easie to distinguish 'em; And Night coming on they both long for the hour of twelve, tho with different designs; and having before given notice that *Silvia* was gone to Bed, and wou'd receive no Visit that Night, they were alone to finish all their business, this while *Briljard* was not idle, but having a fine Bath made he washt and perfum'd his Body and after drest himself in the finest Linnen perfum'd, that he had, and made himself as fit as possible for his design, nor was his shape which was very good, or his stature unlike to that of *Octavio*: And ready for the approach, he conveys himself out of the house telling his footman, he wou'd put himself to Bed after his Bathing, and locking his Chamber door, stole out, and it being dark many a longing turn he walk'd impatient till all the Candles were out in every Room of the House; in the mean time he imploy'd his thoughts on a thousand things, but all relating to *Silvia*; sometimes the Treachery he shew'd in this Action to his Lord, caused short liv'd blushes in his Face, which vanish as soon, when he

---

[a] A fine silk used for linings.

consider'd his Lord false to the most beautiful of her Sex: Sometimes he accus'd and curst the Levity of *Silvia*, that cou'd yield to *Octavio*, and was as jealous as if she had indeed been to have receiv'd that Charming Lover, but when his thought directed him to his own happiness, his Pulse beat high, his blood flasht apace in his Cheeks, his eyes languisht with Love; and his Body with a feverish fit. In these extreams by turns he past at least three teadious hours, with a strikeing watch in his hand; and when it told 'twas twelve, he advanc'd nearer the door, but finding it shut walk'd yet with greater impatience every half minute going to the door; at last he found it yield to his hand that pusht it: But oh, what mortal can express his Joy, his heart beats double, his knees tremble, and a feebleness seizes every Limb, he breaths nothing but short sighs, and is ready in the dark hall to fall on the Floor, and was forc'd to lean on the rail that begins the Stairs to take a little Courage: While he was there recruting himself, intent on nothing but his vast joy; *Octavio* who going to meet the *Prince*, being met half way by that young *Hero* was dispatched back again without advancing to the end of his five Leagues, and impatient to see *Silvia*, after *Philanders* Letter that he had sent her, or at least impatient to hear how she took it, and in what condition she was, he, as soon as he alighted, went towards her house in hope to have met *Antonett*, or her Page, or some that cou'd inform him of her welfare; tho 'twas usual for *Silvia* to set up very late, and he had often made her Visits at that hour: And *Briljard* wholly intent on his adventure, had left the door open, so that *Octavio* perceiving it, believ'd they were all up in the back rooms where *Silvia*'s apartment was towards a Garden, for he saw no light forward; but he was no sooner enter'd (which he did without noise) but he heard a soft breathing, which made him make a stand in the Hall: And by and by he heard the soft tread of some body descending the Stairs: At this he approaches near, and the Hall being a Marble floor, his tread was not heard: When he heard one cry with a sigh——*Whose there*? And another reply, *'tis I, who are you*? The first reply'd, *a faithful and an impatient Lover. Give me your hand then*, reply'd the female voice, *I will conduct you to your happiness*; you may imagine in what surprize *Octavio* was, at so unexpected an adventure, and like a jealous Lover did not at all doubt but the happiness expected was *Silvia*, and the impatient Lover some one whom he cou'd not imagine, but rav'd within to know, and in a moment ran over in his thoughts

all the men of quallity or celibrated Beauty, or Fortune in the
Town but was at as great a loss, as at first thinking: *But be thou,
who thou wilt*, cry'd he to himself, *Traytor as thou art, I will by thy
death revenge my self on the faithless Fair One*; and taking out his
Sword, he advanc'd toward the Stairs foot, when he heard
them both softly ascend; but being a man of perfect good Nature, as all the brave and witty are, he reflected on the severe
usage he had had from *Silvia*, notwithstanding all his industry,
his vast expence, and all the advantages of Nature. This
thought made him in the midst of all his jealousie and haste,
pawse a little moment, and fain he wou'd have perswaded
himself, that what he heard was the Errors of his sense; or that
he dream'd, or that it was at least not to *Silvia*, to whom this yet
ascending Lover was advancing; but to undeceive him of that
favourable imagination, they were no sooner on the top of the
Stairs, but he not being many steps behind cou'd both hear and
see by the ill light of a great Sash window on the Stair Case: The
happy Lover enter the Chamber door of *Silvia*, which he knew
too well to be mistaken, not that he cou'd perceive who or what
they were, but two persons not to be distinguisht. Oh what
human fancy (but that of a Lover to that degree that was our
young *Hero*,) can imagine the amazement and torture of his
Soul, wherein a thousand other passions reign'd at once, and
maugre all his Courage and resolution forc'd him to sink beneath their weight, he stood holding himself up by the rails of
the Stair Case, without having the power to ascend farther, or
to shew any other signs of life, but that of sighing, had he been
a favour'd Lover, had he been a known declar'd Lover, to all the
World, had he but hop'd he had had so much int'rest with the
false Beauty, as but to have been design'd upon for a future love
or use, he wou'd have rusht in, and have made the guilty Night
a Covert to a Scene of Blood; but even yet he had an awe upon
his Soul for the perjur'd Fair One, tho at the same time he
resolv'd she shou'd be the object of his hate; for the Nature of
his honest Soul abhor'd an Action so treacherous and base: He
begins in a moment from all his good thoughts of her, to think
her the most Jilting of her Sex, he knew if int'rest cou'd oblige
her, no man in *Holland* had a better pretence to her than himself, who had already without any return even so much as
hope, presented her the vallue of eight or ten thousand pound,
in fine Plate and Jewels: If it were looser desire he fancy'd
himself to have appear'd as capable to have serv'd her as any

man, but oh he considers there is a fate in things, a destiny in Love that elevates and advances the most mean, deform'd, or abject, and debases and contemns the most worthy and magnificent: Then he wonders at her excellent art of dissembling for *Philander*, he runs in a minute over all her Passions of rage, jealousie, tears and softness, and now he hates the whole Sex, and thinks 'em all like *Silvia*, than which nothing cou'd appear more despicable to his present thought, and with a smile (while yet his heart was insensibly breaking, he fancies himself a very Coxcomb, a Cully,[a] an impos'd on Fool, and a conceited Fop; Value's *Silvia* as a common fair Jilt, whose whole design was to deceive the World and make her self a Fortune, at the price of her Honour, one that receives all kind bidders, and that he being too lavish, and too modest was reserv'd the Cully on purpose to be undone and Jilted out of all his fortune; This thought was so perfectly fixt in him that he recover'd out of his excess of pain, and fancy'd himself perfectly cur'd of his blind passion, resolves to leave her to her beastly entertainment, and to depart; but before he did so, *Silvia* (who had conducted the Amorous Spark to the Bed where the expecting Lady lay drest rich and sweet to receive him) return'd out of the Chamber, and the light being a little more favourable to his eyes, by his being so long in the dark, he perceiv'd it *Antonett*, at least such a sort of figure, as he fancy'd her, and to conform him saw her go into that Chamber where he knew she lay; he saw her perfect dress, and all confirm'd him; this brought him back almost to his former confusion, but yet he commands his passion, and descended the Stairs, and got himself out of the Hall into the Street; and *Silvia* having forgot the street door was open, went and shut it, and return'd to *Antonett*'s Chamber with the Letter, which *Briljard* had given to *Antonett*, as she lay in the Bed, believing it *Silvia*, for that trembling Lover was no sooner enter'd the Chamber and approacht the Bed side, but he kneel'd before it and offer'd the price of his happiness, this Letter; which she immediately gave to *Silvia* unperceiv'd, who quitted the Room; and now with all the eager hast of impatient love, she strikes a Light and falls to reading the sad contents; but as she read she many times fainted over the Paper, and as she has since said 'twas a wonder she ever recover'd, having no body

---

[a] A fool or a dupe.

214

with her, by that time she had finisht it, she was so ill she was
not able to get her self into Bed, but threw her self down on the
place where she sate which was the side of it, in such agonies of
grief and despair, as never any Soul was possest of; but *Silvia's*
wholly abandon'd to the violence of Loves and despair: it is
impossible to paint a torment to express hers by, and tho' she
had vow'd to *Antonett* it shou'd not at all effect her, being so
prepossest before; yet when she had the confirmation of her
fears, and heard his own dear soft words addrest to another
object, saw his transports, his impatience, his languishing, industry; and indeavour to obtain the new desire of his soul; she
found her resentment above rage, and given over to a more
silent and less supportable torment, brought her self into a high
Fever; where she lay without so much as calling for Aid in this
extremity, not that she was afraid the cheat she had put on
Octavio would be discover'd, for she had lost the remembrance
that any such prank was plaid; and in this multitude of
thoughts of more concern, had forgot all the rest of that Nights
action.

Octavio this while was traversing the street wrapt in his Cloke
just as if he had come from Horse, for he was no sooner gone
from the door, but his resenting passion return'd, and he resolv'd to go up again, and disturb the Lovers, tho it cost him his
life and fame: But returning hastily to the door he found it shut;
at which being inrag'd he was often about to break it open, but
still some unperceivable respect for *Silvia* prevented him, but he
resolv'd not to stir from the door, till he saw the fortunate rogue
come out, who had given him all this torment. At first he curst
himself for being so much concern'd for *Silvia* or her actions, to
waste a minute, but flattering himself that it was not love to her,
but pure curiosity to know the man, who was made the next
fool to himself, tho the more happy one, he waited all Night,
and when he began to see the day break, which he thought a
thousand years; his Eye was never off from the door, and
wonder'd at their confidence, who wou'd let the day break
upon them, *but the Close drawn Curtains there,* cry'd he, *favours
the happy Villainy:* Still he walk'd on, and still he might for any
Rival that was to appear for a most unlucky accident prevented
Briljard's coming out, as he doubly intended to do, first for the
better carrying on of his cheat of being *Octavio*; and next that he
had challenged *Octavio* to fight, and when he knew his Error,
design'd to have gone this morning and ask'd him pardon if he

had been return'd; but the Amorous Lover over Night, ordering himself, for the incounter to the best advantage had sent a Note to a Doctor, for something that wou'd incourage his spirits, the Doctor came, and opening a little Box, wherein was a powerful Medicine: He told him that a Dose of those little flies[a] wou'd make him come off with wonderous Honour in the Battail of Love, and the Doctor being gone to call for a glass of Sack,[b] the Doctor having laid out of the Box what he thought requisite on a piece of Paper, and leaving the Box open; our Spark thought if such a Dose wou'd incourage him so, a greater wou'd yet make him do greater Wonders, and taking twice the quantity out of the Box, puts 'em into his pocket, and having drunk the first with full directions, the Doctor leaves him, who was no sooner gone, but he takes those out of his pocket, and in a glass of Sack drinks 'em down; after this he bathes and dresses, and believes himself a very *Hercules*[c] that cou'd have got at least twelve Sons that happy Night; But he was no sooner laid in Bed with the Charming *Silvia* as he thought, but he was taken with intollerable gripes and pains, such as he had never felt before, insomuch as he was not able to lie in the bed, this enrages him, he grows mad and asham'd, sometimes he had little intermissions for a moment of ease, and then he wou'd plead softly by her Bed side, and ask ten thousand pardons, which being easily granted he wou'd come into bed again, but then the pain wou'd seize him anew, so that after two or three hours of distraction he was forc'd to dress and retire; but instead of going down he went softly up to his own Chamber, where he sate him down and curst the World himself and his hard fate; and in this extremity of pain, shame and grief, he remain'd till break of day: By which time *Antonett* who was most violently afflicted, got her Coats on, and went to her own Chamber, where she found her Lady more dead than alive: She immediately shifted her bed Linnen, and made her Bed, and conducted her to it; without indeavouring to divert her with the History of her own misfortune; and only ask'd her many questions concerning her being thus ill, to which the wretched *Silvia* only answer'd with

---

[a] Spanish fly, or Cantharides – a bright green beetle which was dried and mixed with food or drink to act as a potent aphrodisiac.
[b] Dry white wine from Spain or the Canary Islands.
[c] Hercules, son of Zeus and a mortal, Alcmene. Celebrated in Greek and Roman myth for his heroic deeds.

sighs, so that *Antonett* perceiv'd 'twas the Letter that had disorder'd her, and begg'd she might be permitted to see it; she gave her leave and *Antonett* read it, but no sooner was she come to that part of it, which nam'd the Countess of *Clarinau*, but she ask'd her Lady if she understood who that person was, with great amazement: At this *Silvia* was content to speak, pleas'd a little that she shou'd have an account of her Rival. *No*, said she, *Dost thou know her, Yes Madam*, replyed *Antonett particularly well, for I have serv'd her ever since I was a Girle of five years old; she being of the same Age with me, and sent at six years old both to a Monastery; for she being fond of my play, her Father sent me at that Age with her, both to serve and to divert her with Babies and Baubles, there we liv'd seven years together, when an old rich Spaniard the Count of* Clarinau, *fell in love with my Lady, and married her from the Monastery, before she had seen any part of the World beyond those sanctified Walls. She cry'd bitterly to have had me to* Collen *with her, but he said I was too young now for her service, and so sent me away back to my own Town, which is this, and here my Lady was born too, and is Sister to* —— Here she stopt, fearing to tell; which *Silvia* perceiving, with a briskness (which her indisposition one wou'd have thought cou'd not have allow'd sate up in her Bed and cry'd. *Hah Sister to whom? Oh, how thou wou'dst please me to say, to* Octavio, *why Madam wou'd it please you* said the blushing Maid. *Because* said *Silvia, 'twou'd in part revenge me on his bold Addresses to me, and he wou'd also be oblig'd in honour to his Family, to revenge himself on* Philander. *Ah Madam* said she, *as to his presumption towards you, fortune has sufficiently reveng'd it*; at this she hung down her head and look'd very foolishly: *How*, said *Silvia* smiling and rearing her self yet more in her Bed, *is any misfortune arriv'd to* Octavio. *Oh how I will triumph and upbraid the daring man* —— *tell me quickly what it is? for nothing wou'd rejoyce me more than to hear he were punisht a little*; Upon this *Antonett* told her what an unlucky Night she had, how *Octavio* was seiz'd, and how he departed, by which *Silvia* believ'd he had made some discovery of the cheat that was put upon him, and that he only feign'd illness to get himself loose from her imbraces; and now she falls to considering how she shall be reveng'd on both her Lovers: And the best she can pitch upon is that of setting them both at odds, and making 'em fight and revenge themselves on one another; but she like a right Woman, cou'd not dissemble her resentment of jealousie, what ever art she had to do so in any other point; but mad to ease her Soul that was full; and to upbraid *Philander*, she

writes him a Letter, but not till she had once more, to make her
stark mad, read his over again; which he sent *Octavio*.

Silvia *to* Philander.

Yes perjur'd Villain, at last all thy perfidy is arriv'd to my
knowledge; and thou hadst better have been damn'd, or have
fall'n, like an ungrateful Traytor as thou art, under the publique
shame of dying by the common Executioner, than have fall'n
under the grasp of my revenge, insatiate as thy Lust, false as
thy Treasons to thy Prince, fatal as thy destiny, lowd as thy
infamy,[a] and bloody as thy party. Villain, Villain, where got
you the courage to use me thus, knowing my injuries, and my
Spirit; thou seest base Traytor, I do not fall on thee with
treachery, as thou hast on thy King and Mistress, to which thou
has broke thy Holy vows of allegiance and Eternal Love! but
thou that hast broke the Laws of God and Nature! What cou'd I
expect, when neither Religion, Honour, common Justice, nor
Law cou'd bind thee to humanity; thou that betray'd thy Prince,
abandon'd thy Wife, renounc'd thy Child, kill'd thy Mother,
ravisht thy Sister, and art in open Rebellion against thy Native
country, and very Kindred, and Brothers. Oh alter this what
must the Wretch expect, who has believ'd thee, and follow'd
thy abject fortunes, the miserable outcast Slave, and contempt
of the World; what cou'd she expect, but that the Villain is still
potent in thee unrepented, and all the Lover dead and gone,
the Vice remains and all the Virtue vanisht. Oh, what cou'd I
expect from such a Divel, so lost in sin and wickedness, that
even those, for whom he ventur'd all his Fame, and lost his
Fortune, lent like a State Cully upon the publique Faith, on the
security of Rogues, Knaves and Traytors; even those I say
turn'd him out of their Councels, for a reprobate too lewd for
the villainous society: Oh, curst that I was by Heaven and Fate,
to be blind and deaf to all thy infamy, and suffer thy adorable

---

[a] Grey was by now notorious both for the scandal of his elopement with his
sister-in-law and for his involvement with the Rye-House Plot and the Duke of
Monmouth. In England, he was the constant butt of satires and lampoons and his
name was synonymous with deviousness.

bewitching face Face and Tongue to charm me to madness and undoing, when that was all thou hadst left thee thy false person, to cheat the silly, easie, fond, believing World, into any sort of opinion of thee, for not one good principle was left; not one poor vertue to guard thee from Damnation, thou hadst but one friend left thee, one true, one real Friend, and that was wretched *Silvia*, she, when all abandon'd thee but the Executioner, fled with thee, suffer'd with thee, starv'd with thee, lost her Fame and Honour with thee, lost her friend, her Parents, and all her Beauties hopes for thee, and in lieu of all, found only the accusation of all the good, the hate of all the Virtuous, the reproaches of her kindred, the scorn of all chast Maids, and curses of all honest Wives; and in requital had only thy false Vows, thy empty love, thy faithless imbraces, and cold dissembl'd kisses. My only comfort was, (ah miserable comfort) to fancy they were true; now that's departed too, and I have nothing but a brave revenge left in the room of all! in which I'le be as merciless and irreligious as even thou hast been in all thy Actions; and there remains about me only this sense of Honour yet; that I dare tell thee of my bold design; a bravery thou hast never shew'd to me, who takest me unawares, stab'st me without a warning of the blow; so wou'd thou serve thy King hadst thou but power; and so thou serv'st thy Mistress; when I look back even to thy infancy, thy life has been but one continu'd race of treachery, and I (destin'd thy evil genius) was born for thy tormentor, for thou hast made a very Fiend of me, and I have Hell within; all rage, all torment, fire, distraction, madness; I rave, I burn, I tear my self and faint, am still a dying, but can never fall, till I have graspt thee with me: Oh, I shou'd laugh in flames to see thee howling by: I scorn thee, hate thee, loath thee more than ever I have lov'd thee, and hate my self so much for ever loving thee, (to be reveng'd upon the filthy, Criminal) I will expose my self to all the World, Cheat, Jilt, and flatter all as thou hast done, and having not one sense or grain of Honour left, will yield the abandon'd body, thou hast rifl'd to every asking Fop: Nor is that all, for they that purchase this, shall buy it at the price of being my *Bravos*:[a] And all shall aid in my revenge on thee; all merciless and as resolv'd as I; as I! The injur'd

Silvia

---

[a] Ruffians hired for either protection or assault.

Having shot this flash of the lightning of her Soul, and finisht her rant, she found her self much easier in the resolves on revenge, she had fix'd there? she scorn'd by any vain indeavour to recal him from his passion, she had wit enough to have made those eternal observations, that love once gone is never to be retriev'd, and that it was impossible to cease loving, and then again to love the same person, one may believe for sometime ones love is abated, but when it comes to a tryal, it shews it self as vigorous as in its first shine; and finds its own Error, but when once one comes to love a new Object, it can never return with more than pity, compassion, or civility for the first: This is a most certain truth which all Lovers will find, as most Wives may experience, and which our *Silvia* now took for granted, and gave him over for dead to all but her revenge. Tho Fits of softness, weeping, raving, and tearing, wou'd by turns seize the distrasted abandon'd Beauty; in which extremities she has recourse to scorn and Pride, too feeble to aid her too often: The first thing she resolv'd on by the advice of her reasonable Councellor, was to hear Love at both her ears, no matter whether she regard it or not, but to hear all as a remedy against loving one in particular, for 'tis most certain that the use of hearing Love, or of making Love (tho' at first without design) either in Women or men, shall at last unfix the most confirm'd and constant resolution. *And since you are assur'd continued Antonett, that sighs nor tears brings back the wander'd Lover, and that dying for him will be no revenge on him, but rather a kind assurance that you will no more trouble the man, who is already weary of you, you ought with all your power, industry, and Reason rather to seek the preservation of that Beauty, and fine humour to serve you on all occasions, either for revenge or love, than by a foolish and insignificant Concern and Sorrow reduce your self to the condition of being scorn'd by all, or at best but pitty'd*: How pity'd cry'd the haughty *Silvia*, is there any thing so insupportable to our Sex as pity! No surely reply'd the Servant, when 'tis accompany'd by Love; Oh what blessed comfort 'tis to hear people cry —— She was once Charming, once a Beauty; is any thing more grating Madam? At this rate she ran on, and left nothing unsaid that might animate the Angry *Silvia* to love a new, or at least to receive and admit of love, for in that Climate, the Air Naturally breeds Spirits avaritious, and much inclines 'em to the Love of Mony, which they will gain at any price or hazard, and all this discourse to *Silvia* was but to incline the revengeful listening Beauty to admit of the Addresses of *Octavio*, because she knew he wou'd make her fortune. Thus was the unhappy Maid, left by her own unfortunate conduct, incompass'd in on every side with distraction; and she was pointed out by fate to be made the most wretch'd of all her Sex, nor had she left one faithful friend to advise or stay her youth in its hasty advance to ruin; she hears the perswading Eloquence of the flattering Maid, and finds now nothing so prevailent on her Soul as revenge, and nothing sooths it more? and amongst all her Lovers, or those at least that she knew ador'd her, none was found so proper an instrument as the Noble *Octavio*, his youth, his Wit, his Gallantry, but above all his fortune pleads most powerful with her; so that she resolves upon the Revenge and fixes him the man; whom she now knew by so many Obligations was oblig'd to serve her turn on *Philander*: Thus *Silvia* found a little tranquillity, such as it was, in hope of revenge, while the passionate *Octavio* was wreck'd with a thousand pains and torments, such as none but Jilted Lovers can imagine, and having a thousand times resolv'd to hate her, and as often to love on, in spight of all – after a thousand arguments against her, and as many in favour of her, he arriv'd only to this knowledge, that his love was extream, and that he had no power over his heart, that Honour, Fame, Int'rest, and whatever else might oppose his Violent flame, were all too weak to extinguish the least spark of it, and all the Conquest he cou'd get of himself was, that he suffer'd all his torment, all the Hell of raging Jealousie grown to Confirmation, and all the pangs of absence for that whole day, and had the Courage to live on the Rack without easing one moment of his Agony by a Letter or Billet; which in such cases discharges the burthen and pressures of the love sick heart; and *Silvia* who drest, and suffer'd her self wholly to be carry'd away by her Vengeance, expected him with as much impatience as ever she did the coming of the once adorable *Philander*, tho with a different passion; but all the live long day past in expectation of him, and no Lover appear'd; not not so much as a Billet, nor page at her uprising to ask her health, so that believing he had been very ill indeed, from what *Antonett* told her of his being so all Night, and fearing now that it was no discovery of the cheat put upon him by the exchange of the Maid for the Mistress, but real sickness, she resolv'd to send to him, and the rather because *Antonett* assur'd her he was really sick, and in a cold damp sweat all over his face and hands which she toucht, and that from his infinite concern at the defeat, the extreme respect he shew'd her in midst of all, the rage at his own disappointment, and every Circumstance, she knew it was no feign'd thing for any discovery he had made: On this confirmation, from a Maid cunning enough to distinguish truth from flattery, she write *Octavio* this letter at Night.

Silvia *to* Octavio.

After such a parting from a Maid so intirely kind to you; she might at least have hop'd the favour of a Billet from you, to have inform'd her of your health; unless you think that after we have surrender'd all we are of the Humour of most of your Sex, who despise the obliger, but I believ'd you a man above the little Crimes and Levities of your race, and I am yet so hard to be drawn from that opinion; I am willing to flatter my self, that 'tis yet some other reason that has hinder'd you from visiting me since, or sending me an account of your recovery, which I am too sensible of to believe was feign'd, and which indeed has made me so tender, that I easily forgive all the disappointment I receiv'd from it; and beg you will not afflict your self at any loss, you sustain'd by it, since I am still, so much the same I was, to be as sensible as before of all the obligations I have to you, send me word immediately how you do, for on that de-pends a great part of the happiness of

Silvia

You may easily see by this Letter she was not in a humour of either writing love or much flattery, for yet she knew not how she ought to resent this absence in all kinds from *Octavio*, and therefore with what force she cou'd put upon a Soul too wholly taken up with the thoughts of another, more dear and more afflicting, she only writ this to fetch one from him, that by it she might learn part of his sentiment of her last Action, and sent her Page with it to him; who, as was usual, was carried directly up to *Octavio*, whom he found in a Gallery walking in a most dejected posture without a Hat, unbrac'd, his Arms a cross his open breast; and his eyes bent to the Floor; and not taking any notice when the Pages enter'd, his own was forc'd to pull him by the Sleeve, before he wou'd look up, and starting from a thousand thoughts that opprest him almost to death, he gaz'd wildly about him and ask'd their business: When the Page delivered him the Letter; he took it, but with such confusion as he had much a do to support himself, but resolving not to shew his feebleness to her Page he made a shift to get to a Wax Light, that was on the Table and read it; and was not much amaz'd at the contents, believing she was persuing the business of her Sex and Life, and Jilting him on;·(for such was his opinion of all Women now) he forc'd a smile of scorn, tho' his Soul were bursting, and turning to the Page gave him a liberal reward, as was his daily use when he came, and Muster'd up so much Courage as to force himself to say – *Child tell your Lady it requires no answer, you may tell her too, that I am in perfect good Health* —— He was opprest to speak more, but sighs stopp'd him, and his former resolution, wholly to abandon all corrispondence with her, check'd his forward Tongue; and he walk'd away to prevent himself from saying more: While the Page, who wonder'd at this turn of Love, after a little waiting, departed, and when *Octavio* had ended his walk, and turn'd, and saw him gone, his heart felt a thousand pangs not to be born or supported; he was often ready to recal him, and was angry the Boy did not urge him for an answer, he read the Letter again, and wonders at nothing now after her last nights Action, tho all was riddle to him; he found 'twas writ to some happier man than himself, however he chanc'd to have it by mistake, and turning to the outside, view'd the superscription; where there happen'd to be none at all, for *Silvia* writ in haste and when she did it 'twas the least of her thoughts: And now he believ'd he had found out the real Mystery, that it was not meant to him; he therefore calls his Page, whom he sent immediately after that of *Silvia*, who being yet below (for the Lads were laughing together for a moment) he brought him to his distracted Lord; who nevertheless assum'd a mildness to the innocent Boy, and cry'd *My Child thou hast mistaken the person to whom thou shou'dst have carried the Letter, and I am sorry I open'd it; pray return it to the happy Man 'twas meant to*, giving him the Letter; *My Lord* reply'd the Boy, *I do not use to carry Letters to any but your Lordship: 'Tis the footmens business to do that to other persons: 'Tis a mistake, where ever it lies*, cry'd *Octavio* sighing, *whether in thee or thy Lady* – So turning from the wondering Boy he left him to return with his Letter to his Lady, who grew mad at the relation of what she heard from the Page, and notwithstanding the torment she had on her Soul occasioned by *Philander*, she now found she had more to indure, and that in spight of all her love Vows and resentments, she had something for *Octavio* to which she cou'd not give a Name, she fancies it all pride, and concern for the indignity put on her Beauty? but what ever it was this flight of his so wholly took up her Soul, that she had for sometime quite forgot *Philander*, or when she did think on him 'twas with less resentment than of this affront; she considers *Philander* with some excuse now; as haveing long been possest of a happiness he might grow weary off; but a new Lover, who had for six months incessantly lain at her feet, imploring, dying, vowing, weeping, sighing, giving, and acting all things the most passionate of men was capable of, or that love cou'd inspire, for him to be at last admitted to the possession of the ravishing Object of his Vows and Soul, to be laid in her Bed; nay in her very Arms (as She imagin'd he thought) and then, even before gathering the Roses he came to pluck, before he had begun to compose, or finisht his Nosegay: To depart the happy Paradise with a disgust, and such a disgust, as first to oblige him to dissemble sickness, and next fall even from all his Civilities: Was a contempt she was not able to bear: especially from him who of all men living she design'd to make the greatest property of, as most fit for her revenge, of all degrees and sorts: But when she reflected with reason, (which she seldom did, for either Love or rage blinded that) she cou'd not conceive it possible that *Octavio* cou'd be fall'n so suddenly from all his Vows and professions, but on some very great provocation: Sometimes she thinks he tempted her to try her Vertue to *Philander*, and being a perfect Honourable friend, hates her for her Levity, but she considers his presents, and his unwearied industry, and believes he wou'd not at that expence have bought a knowledg which cou'd profit neither himself or *Philander*; then she believes some disgustful Scent or something about *Antonett* might disoblige him; but having call'd the Maid conjuring her to tell her whether any thing past between her and *Octavio*; she again told her Lady the whole truth, in which there cou'd be no discovery of infirmity there; she imbrac'd her, she kiss'd her bosom, and found her touches soft, her breath and Bosom sweet as any thing in Nature cou'd be; and now lost almost in a Confusion of thought, she cou'd not tell what to imagine; at last she being wholly possest that all the fault was not in *Octavio*, (for too often

we believe as we hope) she concludes that *Antonett* has told him
all the cheat she put upon him: This last thought pleas'd her,
because it seem'd the most probable, and was the most favourable to her self; and a thought, that if true cou'd not do her any
injury with him. This set her heart a little to rights, and she
grew calm with a belief, that if so it was, as now she doubted
not, a sight of her, or a future hope from her, wou'd calm all his
discontent, and beget a right understanding: She therefore resolves to write to him and own her little fallacy: But before she
did so; *Octavio* whose passion was as violent as ever in his Soul,
tho 'twas opprest with a thousand torments, and languisht
under as many feeble resolutions, burst at last into all its former
softness, and he resolves to write to the false Fair One, and
upbraid her with her last Nights infidelity: Nor cou'd he sleep
till he had that way Charm'd his senses, and eas'd his sick
afflicted Soul: It being now ten at Night: and he retir'd to his
Chamber, he set himself down, and writ this.

Octavio *to* Silvia.

Madam,
You have at last taught me a perfect knowledge of my self; and
in one unhappy Night, made me see all the follies and Vanities
of my Soul, which self Love and fond imagination had too long
render'd that way guilty; long, long! I've play'd the Fop as
others do, and shew'd the gaudy Monsieur, and set a Value on
my worthless person for being well drest, as I believ'd, and
furnisht out for Conquest, by being the gayest Coxcombe in the
Town, where even as I past perhaps I fancy'd, I made advances
on some wishing hearts, and vain, with but imaginary Victory,
I still fool'd on.——And was at last undone; for I saw *Silvia*, the
Charming faithless *Silvia*; a Beauty that one wou'd have
thought had had the power to have cur'd the fond disease of
self conceit and foppery, since love they say's a remedy against
those faults of youth, but still my vanity was powerful in me,
and even this Beauty too: I thought it not impossible to vanquish, and still drest on, and took a mighty care to shew my
self——a Blockhead, curse upon me, while you were laughing
at my industry, and turn'd the fancying fool to ridicule: Oh, he

deserv'd it well; most wondrous well; for but believing any thing about him, cou'd merit but a serious thought from *Silvia*. *Silvia*! whose business is to laugh at all; yet Love, that is my sin, and punishment, reigns still as absolutely in my Soul, as when I wisht, and hop'd, and long'd for mighty blessings you cou'd give; yes I still love! only this wretchedness is fix'd to it, to see those Errors which I cannot shun; my love's as high, but all my wishes gone; My Passion still remains entire and raving, but no desire, I burn, I dye, but do not wish to hope, I wou'd be all despair, and like a Martyr, am vain and proud even in suffering. Yes, *Silvia*——When you made me wise, you made me wretch'd too; before, like a false Worshipper, I only saw the Gay, the gilded side of the deceiving Idol, but now 'tis fall'n— discovers all the cheat and shews a God no more: and 'tis in Love as in Religion too, there's nothing makes their voteries truly happy but being well deceiv'd: For even in love it self, harmless, and innocent, as 'tis by Nature, there needs a little Art to hide the daily discontents and torments, that fears distrusts, and Jealousies create; a little soft dissimulation's needful, for where the Lover's easie, he's most constant. But oh, when love it self's defective too, and manag'd by design and little int'rest, what cunning, oh what cautions ought the fair designer then to call to her defence; yet I confess your Plot—Still Charming *Silvia*! Was subtilly enough contriv'd, discreetly carry'd on—The shades of Night, the happy Lovers Refuge, favour'd you too: 'twas only fate, was cruel, fate that conducted me, in an unlucky hour, dark as it was, and silent too the Night, I saw,——Yes, faithless Fair, I saw, I was betray'd; by too much faith, by too much love undone, I saw my fatal ruin and your perfidy: And like a tame ignoble sufferer left you without revenge!

I must confess, oh thou deceiving Fair One, I never cou'd pretend to what I wisht; and yet methinks, because I know my heart, and the entire Devotion that it paid you; I merited at least not to have been impos'd upon; but after so dishonourable an Action, as the betraying the Secret of my friend, it was but just that I shou'd be betray'd, and you have paid me well; deserv-'dly well, and that shall make me silent; and what so e're I suffer, how e're I dye, how e're I languish out my wretch'd life, I'le bear my sighs where you shall never hear 'em, nor the reproaches my complaints express: Live thou a punishment to vain fantastick hoping youth, live and advance in cunning and deceit, to make the fond believing men more wise, and teach the Women newer Arts of falshood, till they deceive so long, that man may hate and set as vast a distance between Sex and Sex, as I've resolv'd (oh *Silvia*) thou shalt be, for ever from

Octavio.

This letter came just as *Silvia* was going to write to him; of which she was extreamly glad, for all along there was nothing exprest that cou'd make her think he meant any other than the cheat she put upon him in *Antonett* instead of her self: And it was some ease to her mind to be assur'd of the cause of his anger and absence, and to find her own thought confirm'd, that he had indeed discover'd the truth of the matter: she knew since that was all she cou'd easily reconcile him by a plain confession, and giving him new hopes; she therefore writes this answer to him, which she sent by his Page, who waited for it.

Silvia *to* Octavio.

I own too angry, and too nice *Octavio*, the Crime you charge me with; and did believe a person of your Gallantry, Wit, and Gayety wou'd have past over so little a fault, with only reproaching me pleasantly, I did not expect so grave a reproof, or rather so serious an accusation, youth has a thousand follies to answer for, and cannot *Octavio*, pardon one sally of it, in *Silvia*; I rather expected to have seen you early here this morning pleasantly rallying my little perfidy, than to find you railing at a distance at it; calling it by a thousand names that does not merit half this malice: And sure you did not think me so poor in good, Nature but I cou'd some other coming hour have made you amends for those you lost last Night, possibly I cou'd have wisht my self with you at the same time; and had I perhaps follow'd my inclination I had made you happy as you wisht, but there were powerful reasons, that prevented me, I conjure you to let me see you, where I will make a confession of my last nights sin, and give you such arguments to convince you of the necessity of it, as shall absolutely reconcile you to love, hope, and——

SILVIA.

It being late, she only sent this short Billet: And not hoping that Night to see him, she went to bed, after having inquir'd the health of *Briljard* whom she heard was very ill; and that young defeated Lover finding it impossible to meet *Octavio* as he had promis'd, not to fight him but to ask his pardon for his mistake, he made a shift with much ado to write him a Note, which was this:

My Lord,
I confess my yesterdays rudeness, and beg you will give me a Pardon before I leave the World, for I was last Night taken violently ill, and am unable to wait on your Lordship, to beg what this most earnestly does for

Your Lordships most Devoted
Servant, Briljard

This Billet, tho it signifi'd nothing to *Octavio*, it serv'd *Silvia* afterwards to a very good use and purpose, as a little time shall make appear: And *Octavio* receiv'd these Notes from *Briljard* and *Silvia*, at the same time; the one he flung by regardless, the other he read with infinite pain, scorn, hate, indignation, all at once storm'd in his heart, he felt every passion there but that of Love, which caus'd 'em all, if he thought her false and ungrateful before, he now thinks her fall'n to the lowest degree of lewdness, to own her Crime with such impudence; he fancies now he's cur'd of Love, and hates her absolutely, thinks her below even his scorn, and puts himself to bed, believing he shall sleep as well as before he saw the Light, the foolish *Silvia*: But oh he boasts in vain, the Light, the foolish *Silvia* was Charming still; still all the Beauty appear'd, even in his slumbers the Angell dawn'd about him, and all the Fiend was laid: He sees her lovely Face, but the false heart is hid; he hears her Charming Wit, but all the cunnings husht; he views the motions of her delicate Body, without regard to those of her mind, he thinks of all the tender words she has given him, in which the Jilting part is lost, and all forgotten, or if by chance it crost his happier thought, he rowls and tumble in his Bed, he raves and calls upon her charming Name, till he have quite forgot it, and takes all the pains he can to deceive his own heart:

Oh 'tis a tender part; and can indure no hurt; he sooths it therefore, and at the worst resolves, since the vast blessing may be purchas'd, to revel in delight; and cure himself that way: These flattering thoughts kept him all night waking, and in the Morning he resolves his Visit; but taking up her Letter which lay on the Table, he read it o're again, and by degrees, wrought himself up to madness, at the thought that *Silvia* was possest; *Philander* he cou'd bear with little patience, but that because before he lov'd or knew her, he cou'd allow; but this—This wrecks his very Soul; and in his height of fury writes this Letter without consideration.

Octavio *to* Silvia.

Since you profess your self a common Mistress, and set up for the Glorious trade of sin; send me your price, and I perhaps may purchase Damnation at your rate; may be you have a Method in your dealing, and I've mistook you all this while, and dealt not your way: Instruct my youth, great Mistress of the Art, and I shall be obedient; tell me which way I may be happy too, and put in for an adventurer; I have a stock of ready youth and mony, pray name your time and sum for hours, or Nights, or months; I will be in at all, or any, as you shall find leasure to receive the

Impatient Octavio.

This in a Mad moment he writ, and sent it e're he had consider'd farther, and *Silvia* who expected not so course and rough a return, grew as mad as he in reading it; and she had much ado to hold her hands off from beating the innocent Page that brought it: To whom she turn'd with fire in her Eyes, flames in her Cheeks, and Thunder on her Tongue, and cry'd, *Go tell your Master, that he is a Villain! and if you dare approach me any more from him, I'le have my Footmen whip you!* and with a scorn that discover'd all the indignation in the World she turn'd from him and tearing his Note, threw it from her and walk'd her way: And the Page thunderstruck return'd to his Lord, who

by this time was repenting he had manag'd his passion no
better; and at what the Boy told him, was wholly convinc'd of
his Error, he now consider'd her Character and quallity; and
accus'd himself of great indiscretion; and as he was sitting the
most dejected melancholly man on Earth, reflecting on his misfortune, the Post arriv'd with Letters from *Philander*, which he
open'd and laying by that which was inclos'd for *Silvia* he read
that from *Philander* to himself:

Philander *to* Octavio.

There is no pain, my dear *Octavio*, either in Love or friendship
like that of doubt; and I confess my self guilty of giving it you in
a great measure by my silence the last Post, but having business
of so much greater concern to my heart than even writing to
Octavio, I found my self unable to pursue any other, and I
believe you cou'd too with the less impatience bear with my
neglect having affairs of the same nature there; our circumstances and the business of our hearts then being so resembling, methinks, I have as great an impatience to be recounting to
you the story of my Love and Fortune, as I am to receive that of
yours, and to know what advances you have made in the heart
of the still charming *Silvia!* tho there will be this difference in
the relations; mine, when ever I recount it, will give you a
double satisfaction, first from the share your friendship makes
you have in all the pleasures of *Philander*, and next that it
excuses *Silvia* if she can be false to me, for *Octavio*; and still
advances his design on her heart: but yours, when ever I receive it, will give me a thousand pains which 'tis however, but
just I should feel, since I was the first breaker of the solemn
League and Covenant made between us: which yet I do by all
that's sacred with a regret, that makes me reflect with some
repentance in all those moments wherein I do not wholly give
my soul up to Love, and the more beautiful *Calista*; yes more,
because new.

In my last, my dear *Octavio*, you left me pursuing, like a
Knight Errant, a Beauty inchanted, within some invisible Tree,
or Castle, or Lake, or any thing inaccessable, or rather wandering in a Dream after some glorious disappearing fantom: and

for some time indeed, I knew not whether I slept or wak'd, I saw daily the good old Count of *Clarinau*; to whom I durst not so much as ask a civil question towards the satisfaction of my soul; the Page was sent into *Holland* (with some Express to a Brother in Law of the Counts) of whom before I had the intelligence of a fair young wife to the old Lord his Master, and for the rest of the Servants they spoke all Spanish, and the devil a word we understood each other so that 'twas impossible to learn any thing farther from them: and I found I was to owe all my good Fortune to my own industry, but how to set it a working, I cou'd not devise; at last it happen'd, that being walking in the Garden which had very high Walls on three sides, and a large fine apartment on the other, I concluded, that 'twas in that part of the house, my fair new Conqueress resided, but how to be resolv'd I cou'd not tell, nor which way the Windows lookt that were to give the light, towards that part o'th' Garden there was none, at last I saw the good old Gentleman man come trudging through the Garden fumbling out of his Pocket a Key, I stept into an Arbor to observe him, and saw him open a little door that led him into another Garden, and locking the door after him vanisht; and observing how that side of the Apartment lay, I went into the street and after a large compass, found that which fac'd that Garden, which made the fore part of the Apartment. I made a story of some occasion I had for some upper rooms and went into many houses, to find which fronted best the Apartment, and still dislik'd something till I met with one so directly to it, that I cou'd, when I got a story higher, look into the very Rooms, which only a delicate Garden parted from this by street: there 'twas I fixt, and learnt from a young Dutch woman that spoke good France, that, that was the very place I lookt for; the Apartment of Madam, the Countess of *Clarinau*: She told me too, that every day after Dinner the old Gentleman came thither, and sometimes a nights: and bewail'd the young Beauty, who had no better entertainment than what an old wither'd Spaniard of threescore and ten, cou'd give her: I found this young woman apt for my purpose, and having very well pleas'd her with my conversation, and some little presents I made her, I left her in good humour, and resolv'd to serve me on any design, and returning to my lodging I found old *Clarinau* return'd, as brisk and gay as if he had been carest by so fair and young a Lady, which very thought made me rave, and I had abundance of pain to withhold my rage from breaking out upon him, so jealous and envious I was of what now I lov'd and desir'd, a thousand times more than ever; since the relation my new young female friend had given me: who had wit and beauty sufficient to make her judgment impartial: however I contain'd my jealousie with the hopes of a suddain revenge, for I fancy'd the business half accomplisht in my knowledg of her residence. I feign'd some business to the old Gentleman, that wou'd call me out of town for a week to consult with some of our party, and taking my leave of him he offer'd me the Complement of Money, or what else I should need in my affair, which at that time was not unwelcome to me, and being well furnisht for my enterprise. I took Horse without a Page or Footman to attend me, because I pretended my business was a secret, and taking a turn about the Town in the Evening, I left my horse without the gates and went to my secret new quarters, where my young Friend receiv'd me with the joy of a Mistress, and with whom indeed I cou'd not forbear entertaining my self very well, which ingag'd her more to my service, with the aid of my liberallity; but all this did not allay one spark of the fire kindled in my Soul for the lovely *Calista*; and I was impatient for Night, against which time I was preparing an Ingine to mount the Battlement, for so it was that divided the Garden from the Street, rather than a Wall: All things fitted to my purpose, I fixt my self at the Window that lookt directly towards her Sashes; and had the satisfaction to see her leaning there, and looking on a Fountain that stood in the midst of the Garden, and cast a thousand little streams into the Air, that made a melancholly noise in falling into a large Alabaster Cistern beneath: Oh how my heart danc'd at the dear sight, to all the tunes of Love; I had not power to stir or speak, or to remove my eyes, but languisht on the window where I leant half dead with Joy and transport; for she appear'd more Charming to my view: undrest and fit for Love! Oh, my *Octavio*, such are the pangs which I believe thou felt at the approach of *Silvia*, so beats thy heart, so rise thy sighs, and Wishes; so trembling, and so pale at every view, as I was in this lucky Amorous moment! and thus I fed my Soul till Night came on, and left my Eyes no Object, but my heart,——a thousand dear Idea's: And now I sally'd out, and with good success, for with a long engine which reacht the top of the Wall I fixt the end of my Ladder there, and mounted it, and sitting on the top brought my Ladder easily up to me, and turn'd it over to the other side;

and with abundance of ease descended into the Garden which was the finest I had ever seen; for now as good luck wou'd have it, who was design'd to favour me: The Moon begun to shine so bright as even to make me distinguish the Colours of the Flowers that drest all the Banks in ravishing order, but these were not the Beauty I came to possess, and my new thoughts of disposing my self and managing my matters, now took off all that admiration that was justly due to so delightful a place, which art and Nature had a greed to render Charming to every sense, thus much I consider'd it, that there was nothing that did not invite to love; a thousand pretty recesses of Arbours, Grotts[a] and little Artificial Groves; Fountains inviron'd with Beds of flowers and little Rivulets, to whose dear fragrant Banks, a wishing Amorous God wou'd make his soft retreat, after having ranged about rather to seek a Covert on occasion, and to know the passes of the Garden, which might serve me in any Extreamity of surprize that might happen. I return'd to the fountain that fac'd *Calista's* Window, and leaning on its brink view'd the whole apartment, which appear'd very magnificent: Just against me I perceiv'd a Door that went into it; which while I was considering how to get open, I heard it unlock, and skulking behind the large Bason of the Fountain, (yet so as to mark who came out) I saw to my unspeakable transport the Fair, the Charming *Calista*, dress just as she was at the Window, a loose gown of Silver stuff lapt about her delicate Body, her Head in fine night Cloaths, and all careless as my Soul cou'd wish; she came and with her the old Dragon; and I heard her say in coming out, — *This is too fine a Night to sleep in: Prethee* Dormina *do not grudge me the pleasure of it, since there are so very few, that entertain* Calista. This last she spoke with a sigh, and a languishment in her Voice, that shot new flames of Love into my panting heart, and trill'd through all my vains; while she persu'd her walk with the old Gentle woman; and still I kept my self at such a distance, to have 'em in my sight, but slid along the shady side of the walk where I cou'd not be easily seen, while they kept still on the shiny part: She led me thus through all the Walks, through all the Maze of Love; and all the way I fed my greedy Eyes upon the melancholy Object of my raving desire; her shape, her gate, her motion, every step, and every

---

[a] Grottoes.

movement of hand and head, had a peculiar grace; a thousand times I was tempted to approach her, and discover my self, but I dreaded the fatal consequence, the old Woman being by, not knew I whether they did not expect the Husband there; I therefore with impatience waited when she wou'd speak, that by that I might make some discovery of my destiny that Night; and after having tir'd her self a little with walking, she sate down on a fine seat of White Marble, that was plac'd at the end of a grassie walk: And only shadow'd with some tall Trees that rank'd themselves behind it, 'gainst one of which I lean'd: There for a quarter of an hour they sate as silent as the Night, where only soft breath'd Winds were heard amongst the bows, and softer sighs from fair *Calista*; at last the old thing broke silence, who was almost a Sleep while she spoke. *Madam if you are weary, let us retire to Bed, and not sit gazing here at the Moon; to bed,* reply'd *Calista, what shou'd I do there? marry sleep,* quoth the old Gentlewoman, *what shou'd you do? Ah* Dormina (sight *Calista) wou'd Age wou'd seize me too, for then perhaps I shou'd find at least the Pleasure of the old: be dull and Lazy; Love to Eat and Sleep not, have my slumbers undisturb'd with Dreams more insupportable than my waking wishes; for reason, then suppresses rising thoughts, and the impossibility of obtaining keeps the fond soul in order, but Sleep—Gives an unguarded loose to soft desire, it brings the lovely fantom to my view, and tempts me with a thousand Charms to Love; I see a Face, a Myne, a Shape, a look! such as Heaven never made or any thing, but fond imagination! Oh 'twas a wondrous Vision! for my part,* reply'd the old One, *I am such a Heathen Christian, Madam, as I do not believe there are any such things as Visions, or Ghosts, or fantoms: But your head runs of a young man, because you are married to an old one; such an Idea as you fram'd in your wishes, possest your fancy, which was so strong (as indeed fancy will be sometimes,) that it perswaded you, 'twas a very fantom or Vision. Let it be fancy or Vision, or what ever else you can give a Name, to,* reply'd *Calista* still *'tis that, that never ceas'd since to torture me with a thousand pains, and prithee why* Dormina *is not fancy since, as powerful in me as it was before (fancy has not been since so kind; yet I have given it room for thought, which before I never did, I set whole hours and days, and fix my soul upon the lovely Figure, I know its stature to an Inch; tall and Divinely made, I saw his hair long, Black, and Curling to his wast all loose and flowing, I saw his eyes where all the Cupids play'd, black, large and sparkling piercing, loveing, languishing. I saw his Lips sweet, dimpl'd red, and soft, a youth compleating all, like early* May;

234

that looks and smels, and cheers above the rest: In fine, I saw him such
as nothing but the nicest fancy can imagine, and nothing can describe,
I saw him such as robs me of my rest, as gives me all the raging pains
of love (Love I believe it is) without the joy of any single hope: Oh
Madam said Dormina, *that Love will quickly die, which is not nurst*
with hope, why, that's its only Food. Pray Heaven I find it so, reply'd
Calista. At that she sight as if her heart had broken, and lean'd
her Arm upon a rail of the end of the Seat, and laid her lovely
Check upon her hand, and so continu'd sighing without speaking. While I who was not a little transported with what I heard
with infinite pain, withheld my self from kneeling at her Feet,
and prostrating before her that happy fantom of which she had
spoke so favourably; but still I tear'd my Fate: And to give any
offence; while I was amidst a thousand thoughts considering
which to pursue, I cou'd hear *Dormina* snoring as fast as cou'd
be, leaning at her ease on the other end of the Seat, supported
by a white Marble rail, which *Calista* hearing also turn'd, and
look't on her, then softly rose, and walk'd away to see how long
she wou'd sleep there, if not wak'd! Judge now, my dear *Octa-*
vio, whether Love and Fortune were not absolutely subdu'd to
my int'rest, and if all things did not favour my design: The very
thought of being alone with *Calista;* of making my self known to
her, of the oppertunity she gave me by going from *Dormina* into
a by Walk, the very joy of ten thousand hopes, that fill'd my
Soul in that happy moment, which I fancy'd the most blest of
my life, made me tremble all over, and with unassur'd steps, I
softly persu'd the Object of my new desire: Sometimes I even
overtook her, and fearing to fright her, and cause her to make
some noise that might alarm the sleeping *Dormina,* I slackt my
pace, till in a Walk, at the end of which she was oblig'd to turn
back, I remain'd; and suffer'd her to go on, 'twas a Walk of
Grass, broad and at the end of it a little Arbour of Greens, into
which she went and sate down, looking towards me, and
methought she look't full at me; so that finding she made no
noise, I softly approach'd the door of the Arbour, at a convenient distance, she then stood up, in great amaze as she after
said, and I kneeling down in an humble posture; cry'd,——
Wonder not, oh Sacred Charmer of my Soul, to see me at your
Feet; at this late hour, and in a place so inaccessible, for what
attempt is there so hazardous, despairing Lovers dare not
undertake, and what impossibility almost, can they not overcome; remove your fears, oh Conqueress of my Soul, for I am

an humble Mortal that Adores you; I have a thousand Wounds, a thousand pains that proves me flesh and Blood, if you wou'd hear my story: Oh give me leave to approach you with that Awe, you do the sacred Altars; for my Devotion is as pure as that which from your Charming Lips ascends the Heavens:——— With such Cant and stuff, as this, which Lovers serve themselves with, on occasion, I lessen'd the terrors of the frighted Beauty, and she soon saw with Joy in her Eyes, that I was both a mortal, and the same she had before seen in the outward Garden: I rose from my knees then, and with a Joy that wander'd all over my body, trembling and panting I approach'd her, and took her hand and kist it with a transport that was almost ready to lay me fainting at her Feet; nor did she answer any thing to what I had said, but with sighs suffer'd her hand to remain in mine; her Eyes she cast to Earth, her Breast heav'd with nimble motions, and we both unable to support our selves, sate down together on a Green Bank in the Arbour, where by that Light we had, we gaz'd at each other unable to utter a syllable on either side. I confess, my dear *Octavio*, I have felt Love before, but do not know, that ever I was possest with such pleasing pain, such agreeable languishment in all my life, as in those happy moments, with the fair *Calista*: And on the other, I dare answer for the soft Fair One; she felt a passion as tender as mine; which, when she cou'd recover her first transport, she exprest in such a manner, as has wholly Charm'd me: For with all the Eloquence of young Angels, and all their innocence too, she said, she whisper'd, she sight, the softest things that ever Lover heard. I told you before she had from her infancy been bred in a Monastery, kept from the sight of men, and knew no one art or subtilty of her Sex: But in the very purity of her innocence, she appear'd like the first born Maid in Paradice, generously giving her Soul away to the great Lord of all, the new form'd man, and nothing of her hearts dear thoughts did she reserve, (but such as modest Nature shou'd conceal) yet, if I touch't but on that tender part where Honour dwelt; she had a sense to nice, as 'twas a Wonder, to find so vast a store of that mixt with so soft a passion. Oh what an excellent thing a perfect Women is, e're man has taught her Arts to keep her Empire, by being himself inconstant? all I cou'd ask of Love she freely gave, and told me every sentiment of her heart, but 'twas in such a way; so innocently she confest her passion that every word added new flames to mine, and made me raging mad; at last she suffer'd me to kiss, with caution; but one begat another,—that, a Number——And every one was an advance to happiness, and I, who knew my advantage, lost no time, but put each Minute to the properest use, now I imbrace, Clasp her Fair Lovely Body close to mine, which nothing parted but her shift and Gown, my busie hands find passage to her Breasts, and give, and take a thousand nameless Joys; all but the last, I rcapt; that heaven was still deny'd; tho she were fainting in my trembling Arms, still she had watching sense to guard that Treasure: Yet in spight of all, a thousand times I brought her to the very point of yielding, but oh she begs and pleads with all the Eloquence of love! tells me that what she had to give she gave, but wou'd not violate her Marriage Vow: No, not to save that life she found in danger with too much Love, and too extream desire; she told me that I had undone her quite, she sight and wisht, that she had seen me sooner, e're Fate had render'd her a Sacrifice to the imbraces of old *Clarinau*, she weept with Love, and answer'd with a sob, to every Vow I made: thus by degrees she wrought me to undoing, and made me mad in Love: 'Twas thus we past the Night; we told the hasty hours and curst their coming: we told from ten to three, and all that time seem'd but a little Minute: Nor wou'd I let her go, who was as loath to part, till she had given me leave to see her often there; I told her all my story of her Conquest, and how I came into the Garden: She ask'd me pleasantly if I were not afraid of old *Clarinau*, I told her no, of nothing but of his being happy with her, which thought I cou'd not bear; she assur'd me I had so little reason to envy him, that he rather deserv'd my compassion, for that her aversion was so extream to him; his person, years, his temper, and his diseases were so disagreeable to her, that she cou'd not dissemble her disgust, but gave him most evident proofs of it too frequently; ever since she had the misfortune of being his Wife; but that since she had seen the Charming *Philander*, (for so we must let her call him too) his Company and Conversation was wholly insupportable to her; and but that he had ever us'd to let her have four Nights in the Week her own, wherein he never disturb'd her repose, she shou'd have been dead with his nasty entertainment; She vow'd she never knew a soft desire, but for *Philander* she never had the least concern for any of his Sex besides, and till she felt his touches — took in his kisses, and suffer'd his dear imbraces; she never knew that Woman was ordain'd for any Joy with man, but fancy'd it design'd in its Creation for a poor Slave to be opprest at pleasure by the Husband, dully to yield obedience and no more: But I had taught her now she said to her Eternal ruin, that there was more in Nature than she knew, or ever shou'd, had she not seen *Philander*; she knew not what dear name to call it by, but something in her Blood; something that panted in her heart, glow'd in her Cheeks and languisht in her looks, told her she was not born for *Clarinau*; or love wou'd do her wrong: I sooth'd the thought, and urg'd the Laws of Nature, the power of Love, necessity of Youth,——And the wonder that was yet behind, that ravishing somthing, which not love or kisses cou'd make her guess at; so beyond all soft imagination that nothing but a tryal cou'd convince her; but she resisted still, and still I pleaded with all the subtillest Arguments of Love, words mixt with kisses: sighing mixt with Vows, but all in vain, Religion was my Foe, and Tyrant Honour guarded all her Charms; thus did we pass the Night till the young Morn advancing in the East forc'd us to bid adieu: Which oft we did, and oft we sigh'd and kist, oft parted and return'd, and sigh'd again, and as she went away, she weeping cry —— wringing my hand in hers, pray Heav'n *Philander*, this dear interview, do not prove fatal to me, for, oh, I find frail Nature weak about me, and one dear minute more wou'd forfeit all my Honour. At this she started from my trembling hand, and swipt the Walk like Wind so swift and suddain, and left me panting, sighing, wishing, dying, with mighty Love and hope, and after a little time I scal'd my Wall, and return'd unseen to my new Lodging. It was four days after, before I cou'd get any other happiness but that of seeing her at her window which was just against mine from which I never stirr'd, hardly to eat or sleep, and that she saw with joy, for every Morning I had a Billet from her; which we contriv'd that Happy Night shou'd be convey'd me thus—It was a By Street where I lodg'd, and the other side was only the dead wall of her Garden, where early in the morning she us'd to walk, and having the Billet ready, she put it with a Stone into a little Leathern purse, and tost it over the wall, where either my self from the Window or any young friend below waited for it, and that way every Morning and every Evening she receiv'd one from me; but 'tis impossible to tell you the innocent Passion she exprest in them, innocent in that there was no Art, no fain'd, nice folly to express a Virtue that was not in the Soul; but all she spoke confest her hearts soft wishes. At last, (for I am teadious in a relation of what gave me so much pleasure in the injoyment) at last, I say, I receiv'd the happy invitation to come into the Garden as before, and Night advancing for my purpose I need not say that I deliver'd my self upon the place appointed, which was by the Fountain side beneath her Chamber Window, towards which I cast, you may believe, many a longing look: The Clock struck ten, eleven, and then twelve, but no dear Star appear'd to conduct me to my happiness, at last I heard the little Garden door (against the Fountain) open; and saw *Calista* there wrapt in her Night Gown only; I ran like Lightning to her Armes, with all the transports of an eager Lover, and almost smother'd my self in her warm rising Breast, for she taking me in her Arms. Let go her Gown, which falling open left nothing but her Shift, between me and all her Charming Body: But she bid me hear what she had to say before, I proceeded farther, she told me she was forc'd to wait till *Dormina* was a sleep, who lay in her Chamber, and then stealing the Key she came softly down to let me in. *But,* said she, *since I am all undrest, and cannot walk in the Garden with you, will you promise me on Love and Honour, to be obedient to all my Commands, if I carry you to my Chamber, for* Dormina's *sleep is like death it self; however least she chance to awake, and shou'd take an occasion to speak to me, 'twere absolutely necessary, that I were there; for since I serv'd her such a trick the other Night, and let her sleep so long she will not let me walk late.* A very little argument perswaded me to yield to any thing to be with *Calista* any where; so that both returning softly to her Chamber, she put her self into Bed, and left me kneeling on the Carpet: But 'twas not long that I remain'd so; from the dear touches of her hands and breast, we came to kisses, and so equally to a forgetfullness of all we had promis'd and agreed on before, and broke all Rules, and Articles, that were not in the Favour of Love; so that stripping my self by degrees, while she with an unwilling force made some feeble resistance, I got into the Arms of the most Charming Woman that ever Nature made; she was all over perfection: I dare not tell you more; let it suffice she was all that luxurious man cou'd wish, and all that renders woman fine and ravishing. About two hours thus was my Soul in rapture, while sometimes she reproacht me, but so gently, that 'twas to bid me still be false and perjur'd if these were the effects of it; *if disobedience have such wonderous Charms; may I,* said she, *be still Commanding thee, and thou still disobeying:* While thus we lay with equal ravishment, we heard a murmuring noise at distance, which we knew not what to make of, but it grew still louder and louder, but still at distance too; this first Alarm'd us, and I was no sooner perswaded to rise; but I heard a door unlock at the side of the Bed; which was not that by which I enter'd, for that was at the other end of the Chamber towards the Window. *Oh Heavens*, said the fair frighted trembler, *here is the Count of* Clerinau: For he always came up that way, and those Stairs by which I ascended was the back stairs, so that I had just time to grope my way towards the door without so much as taking my Cloaths with me; never was any Amorous adventurer in so lamentable a Condition, I wou'd fain have turn'd upon him, and at once have hinder'd him from entring, with my Sword in my hand, and secur'd him from ever disturbing my pleasure any more, but she implor'd I wou'd not, and in this minutes dispute he came so near me, that he toucht me, as I glided from him; but not being acquainted very well with the Chamber, having never seen my way, I lighted in my passage on *Dormina's* pallate Bed, and threw my self quite over her, to the Chamber door, which made a damnable clattering, and a waking *Dormina* with my Catastrophe, she set up such a bawl as frighted, and Alarm'd the Old Count, who was just taking in a Candle from his Footman, who had lighted it at his Flamboy:[a] So that hearing the noise, and knowing it must be some Body in the Chamber, he lets fall his Candle in the fright, and call'd his Footman in with the Flamboy, draws his Tolledo,[b] which he had in his hand, and wrapt in his Night Gown; with three or four woollen Caps one upon the top of another, ty'd under his tawny Leathern Chops, he made a very pleasant figure, and such an one as had like to have betray'd me by laughing at it; he closely persu'd me, tho' not so close as to see me before him, yet so as not to give me time to ascend the Wall, or to make my escape up or down any Walk, which were straight and long, and not able to conceal any body from pursuers, approacht so near as the Count was to me: What shou'd I do? I was naked, unarm'd and no defence against his jealous rage; and now in danger of my life, I knew not what to resolve on; yet I swear to you *Octavio*, even in that minute (which I thought my last) I had no repentance of the dear sin, or any

---

[a] A torch made of several waxed sticks bound together.
[b] A sword made in the town of Toledo in Spain. The town was renowned for producing weapons of the finest steel.

other fear, but that which possest me for the fair *Calista*; and calling upon *Venus* and her Son for my safety (for I had scarce a thought yet of any other Deity) the Sea born Queen lent me immediate aid, and e're I was aware of it, I toucht the Fountain, and in the same minute threw my self into the Water, which a mighty large Bason or Cistern of white Marble contain'd, of a Compass that forty men might have hid themselves in it, they had pursu'd me so hard, they fancy'd they heard me press the gravel near the Fountain, and with the Torch they search'd round about it, and beat the fringing Flowers that grew pretty high about the bottom of it, while I sometimes div'd, and sometimes peept up to take a view of my busie Coxcomb: Who had like to have made me burst into laughture many times, to see his figure, the dashing of the stream which continually fell from the little Pipes above, into the Bason hinder'd him from hearing the noise I might possibly have made by my swiming in it, after he had surveyed it round without side, he took the Torch in his own hand, and survey'd the Water it self while I div'd, and so long forc'd to remain so, that I believ'd I had escapt his Sword to dye that foolisher way, but just as I was like to expire, he departed muttering, that he was sure some body did go out before him, and now he searched every Walk and Arbour of the Garden, while like a Fish I lay basking in Element still, not daring to adventure out least his hasty return shou'd find me on the Wall, or in my passage over: I thank'd my Stars he had not found the Ladder, so that at last returning to *Calista's* Chamber, after finding no Body, he desir'd (as I heard the next morning) to know what the matter was in her Chamber; but *Calista*, who till now never knew an Art, had before he came laid her Bed in order, and taken up my Cloaths, and put them between her Bed, and Quilt; not forgetting any one thing that belong'd to me, she was laid as fast a sleep as innocence it self, so that *Clarinau* a waking her, she seem'd as surpriz'd and ignorant of all, as if she had indeed been innocent, so that *Dormina* now remain'd the only suspected person, who being ask'd what she cou'd say concerning that uproar she made, she only said, as she thought, that she dream'd his Honour fell out of the Bed upon her, and a waking in a fright, she found 'twas but a Dream, and so she fell a sleep again till he wak'd her, whom she wonder'd to see there at that hour; he told 'em that while they were securely sleeping he was like to have been burn'd in his Bed, a piece of his apartment being burn'd down, which caus'd him to come thither; but he made them both Swear that there was no body in the Chamber of *Calista*, before he wou'd be undeceiv'd, for he vow'd he saw something in the Garden, which to his thinking was all in White, and it vanisht on the sudden behind the Fountain, and we cou'd see no more of it. *Calista* dissembl'd abundance of fear, and said she wou'd never walk out after candle light for fear of that Ghost, and so they past the rest of the Night, while I all wet and cold got me to my Lodging unperceiv'd, for my young friend had left the door open for me.

Thus, dear *Octavio*, I have sent you a Novel,[a] instead of a Letter of my first most happy adventure, of which I must repeat thus much again, that of all the injoyments I ever had, I never was so perfectly well entertain'd for two hours, and I am waiting with infinite impatience a second Encounter. I shall be extreamly glad to hear what progress you have made in your Amour, for I have lost all for *Silvia*, but the affection of a Brother with that Natural pity we have for those we have undone; for my heart, my Soul, and Body are all *Calista*'s, the bright the young, the wity, the Gay, the fondly loveing *Calista*: Only some reserve I have in all for *Octavio*, pardon this long History for 'tis a sort of acting all ones joys again to be telling 'em to a friend so dear as is the Gallant *Octavio* to

Philander.

POSTSCRIPT.

I shou'd for some reasons that concern my safety have quitted this town before, but I am chain'd to't, and have no sense of danger while *Calista* compels, my stay.

---

[a] The term 'novel' derives from the French word *Nouvelles* meaning news. Behn is here using Philander's long narrative letter to refer to the relationship between the early newspapers of the time – often called 'newsletters' – and the first novels which were generally translations or imitations of French short fiction. In particular, Behn is pointing to the 'Secret History' novel genre which had its origins in France and presented the reader with a narrative which was clearly based on actual scandals of the time.

If *Octavio's* Trouble were great before from but his fear of *Calista's* yielding, what must it be now, when he found all his fears confirm'd, the pressures of his Soul were too extream before, and the concern he had for *Silvia* had brought it to the highest tide of Grief; so that this addition o're whelm'd it quite, and left him no room for rage; no, it cou'd not discharge it self so happily, but bow'd and yielded to all the extreams of Love, grief, and sense of Honour? he threw himself upon his Bed, and lay without sense or motion for a whole hour, confus'd with thought, and divided in his concern, half for a Mistress false, and half for a Sister loose and undone; by turns the Sister and the Mistress torture; by turns they break his heart, he had this comfort left before, that if *Calista* were undone, her ruin made way for his Love and happiness with *Silvia*, but now—he had no prospect left, that cou'd afford any ease, he changes from one sad Object to another, from *Silvia* to *Calista*, then back to *Silvia*, but like to feverish men, that toss about here and there, remove for some relief, he shifts but to new pain, where e're he turns he finds the mad man still, in this distraction of thought he remain'd till a Page from *Silvia*, brought him this Letter: Which in midst of all, he started from his Bed with excess of joy and read.

Silvia

Silvia *to* Octavio.

My Lord,
After your last affront by your Page, I believe it will surprise you to receive any thing from *Silvia* but scorn and disdain: But, my Lord, the int'rest you have by a thousand ways been so long making in my heart, cannot so soon be cancell'd by a minutes offence, and every Action of your life has been too generous to make me think you writ what I have receiv'd, at least you are not well in your senses; I have committed a fault against your Love, I must confess, and am not asham'd of the little cheat I put upon you in bringing you to bed to *Antonett* instead of *Silvia*: I was asham'd to be so easily won, and took it ill, your passion was so mercenary, to ask so coursely for the possession

243

of me; too great a pay I thought for so poor a service, as rendering up a Letter, which in Honour you ought before to have shew'd me: I own I gave you hope, in that too I was Criminal, but these are faults that sure deserv'd a kinder punishment than what I last receiv'd——A Whore——A Common Mistress! Death you are a Coward—And even to a Woman dare not say it; when she confronts the Scandaller,——Yet pardon me, I meant not to revile, but gently to reproach, it was unkind—At least allow me that, and much unlike *Octavio*

I think I had not troubl'd you, my Lord, with the least confession of my resentment, but I cou'd not leave the Town, where for the Honour of your Conversation and friendship alone I have remain'd so long without acquitting my self of those Obligations I had to you. I send you therefore the key of my Closet and Cabinet, where you shall find, not only your Letters, but all those presents you have been pleas'd once to think me worthy of: But having taken back your friendship, I render you the less valluable trifles, and will retain no more of *Octavio* than the dear memory of that part of his Life that was so agreeable to the

Unfortunate Silvia.

He finisht this Letter reading with Tears of tender Love; but considering it all over he fancy'd she had put great Constraint upon her natural high Spirit, to write in this Calm manner to him, and through all he found dissembl'd rage, which yet was visible in that one breaking out in the middle of the Letter: He found she was not able to contain at the Word common Mistress, in fine how ever Calm it was, and however design'd, he found at least, he thought he found, the Charming Jilt all over; he fancies from the hint she gave him of the change of *Antonett* for her self in Bed, that it was some new cheat that was to be put upon him, and to bring her self off with Credit: Yet in spight of all this appearing reason, he wishes, and has a secret hope that either she is not in fault, or that she will so cozen[a] him into a belief she is not, that it may serve as well to sooth his willing heart; and now all he fears is, that she will not put so neat a Cheat upon him, but that he shall be able to see through it, and

---

[a] To cheat or defraud.

244

still be oblig'd to retain his ill Opinion of her: But love return'd, she had rous'd the flame a new; and soften'd all his rougher thoughts with this dear Letter, and now in haste he calls for his Cloaths, and suffering himself to be drest with all the advantage of his Sex, he throws himself into his Coach, and goes to *Silvia*, whom he finds just drest *en Chavalier*,[a] (and setting her Hat and Feather in good order, before the Glass) with a design to depart the town, at least so far as shou'd have rais'd a concern in *Octavio*, if yet he had any for her, to have follow'd her; he ran up without asking leave into her Chamber, and e're she was aware of him, threw himself at her Feet, and clasping her knees, to which he fixt his mouth, he remain'd there for a little space without life or motion, and prest her in his Arms as fast as a dying man. She was not offended to see him there, and he appear'd more lovely than ever he yet had been. His grief had added a languishment and paleness to his Face; which sufficiently told her he had not been at ease while absent from her; and on the other side *Silvia* appear'd ten thousand times more Charming than ever; that dress of a Boy adding extreamly to her Beauty, *Oh you are a pretty Lover*, said she, raising him from her knees to her Arms, *to treat a Mistress so for a little innocent raillery.—Come sit and tell me how you came to discover the harmless cheat*; setting him down on the side of her Bed: *Oh name it no more cry'd he, let that damn'd Night be blotted from the year, deceive me, flatter me, say you are innocent, tell me my senses rave, my Eyes were false, deceitful, and my Ears were deaf: Say any thing that may convince my madness, and bring me back to tame adoring Love. What means* Octavio, reply'd *Silvia, sure he is not so nice and squemish a Lover, but a fair young Maid might have been welcome to him coming so prepar'd for Love; tho it was not she whom he expected; it might have serv'd as well i'th' dark at least. Well said,* reply'd *Octavio* forcing a smile—*advance, pursue the dear design, and cheat me still, and to convince my Soul, oh swear it too, for Women want no weapons of defence, Oaths, Vows, and Tears, sighs, imprecations, ravings, are all the tools to fashion mankind Coxcombs, I am an easie fellow fit for use, and long to be initiated Fool, come swear I was not here the other Night. 'Tis granted Sir you were, Why all this passion?* This *Silvia* spoke and took him by the hand, which burnt with raging Fire; and tho he spoke with all the heat of Love, his looks were soft

---

[a] Dressed as a gentleman.

the while as infant Cupids, still he proceeded, *Oh Charming Silvia since you are so unkind to tell me truth, cease, cease to speak at all, and let me only gaze upon those Eyes that can so well deceive: Their looks are innocent, at least they'le flatter me, and tell mine that they lost their faculties that other Night: No*, reply'd *Silvia, I am convinc'd they did not, you saw* Antonett——*Conduct a happy man* (interpreted he) *to* Silvia's *Bed, oh why by your confession must my Soul be tortur'd o're a new!* at this he hung his heap upon his Bosom, and sight, as if each breath wou'd be his last. *Heavens!* cry'd *Silvia, what is't* Octavio *says, Conduct a happy Lover to my Bed; by all that's Sacred I'm abus'd, design'd upon to be betray'd and lost; what said you Sir, a Lover to my Bed!* When he reply'd in a fainting tone, clasping her to his Arms, *now* Silvia, *you are kind, be perfect Woman, and keep to couzening still—Now back it with a very little Oath, and I am as well as e're I saw your falshood, and ne're will lose one thought upon it more. Forbear,* said she, *you'le make me angry: In short what is it you wou'd say, or swear you rave, and then I'le pity what I now despise, if you can think me false.* He only answer'd with a sigh, and she pursu'd, *am I not worth an answer; tell me your Soul and thoughts, as e're you hope for favour from my Love, or to preserve my quiet. If you will promise me to say 'tis false,* reply'd he softly, *I will confess the Errors of my senses. I came the other Night at twelve, the door was open—'Tis true,* said *Silvia — At the Stairs Foot I found a man, and saw him led to you, into your Chamber; sighing as he went, and panting with impatience: Now* Silvia *if you value my Repose, my life, my Reputation, or my services turn it off handsomly and I'm happy*: At that being wholly amaz'd, she told him the whole story, as you heard, of her dressing *Antonett*, and bringing him to her, at which he smil'd, and beg'd her to go on——She fetch the pieces of *Briljards* counterfeit Letters, and shew'd him; this brought him a little to his Wits; and at first sight he was ready to fancy the Letters came indeed from him, he found the Character his, but not the business: And in great amaze reply'd, *Ah Madam, did you know* Octavio's *Soul so well, and cou'd you imagine it capable of a thought like this? A presumption so dareing to the most awful of her Sex: This was unkind indeed: And did you answer 'em? Yes,* reply'd she, *with all kindness I cou'd force my Pen to express*: So that after canvasing the matter, and relating the whole story again with his being taken ill, they concluded from every Circumstance *Briljard* was the man; for *Antonett*

was call'd to Councel, who now recollecting all things in her
mind, and knowing *Briljard* but too well; she confest she verily
believ'd it was he, especially when she told how she stole a
Letter of *Octavio's* for him that day, and how he was ill of the
same disease still. *Octavio* then call'd his Page, and sent him
home for the Note *Briljard* had sent him, and all appear'd as
clear as day: But *Antonett* met with a great many reproaches
for shewing her Ladies Letters, which she excus'd as well as
she cou'd: But never man was so ravisht with joy as *Octavio*
was at the knowledge of *Silvia's* innocence; a thousand times
he kneel'd and beg'd her Pardon, and her figure incouraging
his Caresses; a thousand times he imbrac'd her, he smil'd, and
blusht, and sight with Love and Joy, and knew not how to
express it most effectually: And *Silvia*, who had other business
than Love in her heart and head, suffer'd all the marks of his
eager passion and transport, out of design, for she had a
farther use to make of *Octavio*; tho when she survey'd his
person handsom, young, and adorn'd with all the Graces and
Beauties of his Sex; not at all inferior to *Philander*, if not
exceeding in every Judgement but that of *Silvia*; when she
consider'd his Soul, where Wit, Love and Honour equally
reign'd, when she consults the excellence of his Nature, his
Generosity, Courage, Friendship, and softness, she sight and
cry'd, 'twas pity to impose upon him; and make his Love, for
which she shou'd esteem him, a property to draw him to his
ruin, for so she fancy'd it must be if ever he incounter'd
Philander; and tho good Nature was the least ingredient that
form'd the Soul of this fair Charmer, yet now she found she
had a mixture of it, from her concern for *Octavio*; and that
generous Lover made her so many soft Vows, and tender
protestations of the respect, and awfulness of his passion, that
she was wholly convinc'd he was her Slave, nor cou'd she see
the constant Languisher pouring out his Soul and fortune at
her feet, without suffering some warmth about her heart,
which she had never felt, but for *Philander*; and this day she
exprest her self more obligeingly than ever she had done: And
allows him little freedoms of approaching her with more
softness than hitherto she had; and absolutely Charm'd, he
promises lavishly and without reserve, all she wou'd ask of
him; and in requital she assur'd him all he cou'd wish or hope,
if he wou'd serve her in her revenge against *Philander*: She
recounts to him at large the story of her undoing, her quality,

her Fortune, her nice education, the care and tenderness of her Noble Parents, and charges all her Fate to the evil Conduct of her heedless youth: Sometimes the reflection on her ruin, she looking back upon her former innocence and tranquillity, forces the Tears to flow from her fair Eyes, and makes *Octavio* sigh and weep by simpathy: Sometimes (arriv'd at the Amorous part of her relation, she wou'd sigh and languish with the remembrance of past Joys, in their beginning love;) and sometimes smile at the little unlucky adventures they met with, and their escapes; so that different passions seiz'd her Soul while she spoke, while that of all love fill'd *Octavio's*: He doats, he burns, and every word she utters inflames him still more; he fixes his very Soul upon her Tongue, and darts his very Eyes into her face, and every thing she says raises his vast esteem and passion higher: In fine, having with the Eloquence of sacred Wit, and all the Charms of every differing Passion finisht her moving tale, they both declin'd their Eyes, whose falling showers kept equal time and pace, and for a little time were still as thought: When *Octavio*, opprest with mighty Love! broke the soft silence, and burst into extravagance of passion, says all that men (grown mad with love and wishing) cou'd utter to the Idol of the heart; and to oblige her more recounts his Life in short; where in, in spight of all his modesty, she found all that was great and brave; all that was Noble, Fortunate, and Honest: And having now confirm'd her, he deserv'd her, kneeling implor'd she wou'd accept him not as a Lover for a Term of passion, for dates of Months or years, but for a long Eternity; not as a rifler of her Sacred Honour, but to defend it from the sensuring World; he vow'd he wou'd forget that ever any part of it was lost, nor by a look or Action e're upbraid her with a misfortune past, but still look forward, on Nobler joys to come: And now implores that he may bring a Priest to tie the Solemn knot: In spight of all her Love for *Philander*, she cou'd not chuse but take this offer kindly, and indeed it made a very great impression on her heart, she knew nothing but the height of Love cou'd oblige a man of his quality, and vast fortune, with all the advantages of youth and Beauty, to marry her in so ill Circumstances; and paying him first those acknowledgments that were due on so great an occasion, with all the tenderness in her Voice and Eyes that she cou'd put on; she excus'd her self from receiving the Favour, by telling him she was so unfortunate as to be with Child[a] by the ungrateful man: And falling at that thought into new Tears, she mov'd him to infinite Love; and infinite compassion; in so much that wholly abandoning himself to softness, he assur'd her, if she wou'd secure him all his happiness by marrying him now, that he wou'd wait till she were brought to Bed, before he wou'd demand the glorious recompence he aspir'd to; so that *Silvia* being opprest with Obligation, finding yet in her Soul a violent passion for *Philander*, she knew not how to take, or how to refuse the Blessing offer'd, since *Octavio* was a man, whom in her height of innocence and youth she might have been vain and proud of ingaging to this degree: He saw her pain and irresolution, and being absolutely undone with love, delivers her *Philanders* last Letter to him, with what he had sent her inclos'd; the sight of the very outside of it made her grow pale as Death; and a feebleness seiz'd her all over that made her unable for a moment to open it; all which, confusion *Octavio* saw with pain; which she perceiving recollected her thoughts as well as she cou'd, and open'd it and read it; that to *Octavio* first, as being fondest of the continuation of the History of his falshood, she read and often paus'd to recover her Spirits that were fainting at every period; and having finisht it, she fell down on the Bed, where they sate; *Octavio* caught her in her fall in his Arms, where she remain'd dead some moments; While he, just on the point of being so himself, ravingly call'd for help, and *Antonett* being in the dressing Room ran to 'em, and by degrees *Silvia* recover'd and ask'd *Octavio* a thousand pardons for exposing a weakness to him, which was but the effects of the last blaze of Love: And taking a Cordial which *Antonett* brought her, she rous'd, resolv'd, and

---

[a] Contemporary intelligence reports verify that Henrietta Berkeley had a child in Cleve. One spy noted that

> he saw also ye Lady Hen:Berkeley whom he likewise knew, & believes her to be att least four months gone with child, she looked very thin, & is perfect trallop, in a plaine scarf & black hood

Thomas Chudleigh, the English ambassador to the Hague, visited Cleve incognito and was told by the daughter of the owners of the Hoff van Holland that,

> there is still there ye Ld. Gray & his Lady, who (says she) will be shortly brought to bed & that there are some coming hither from England to waite on her when she lyes in...she told me likewise that she knew that ye d. of Monmouth had writt to ye Ld. Gray to come over to England & that he would make his peace; I ask'd her why he & ye others went not? She could not well answer me in this, only said, that she thought my Lady's being neare her time might be a hinderance in part, &, she knew (said she) that they would all goe over as soon as ye winter was over

took *Octavio* by the hand: *Now,* said she, *shew your self that generous Lover you have profest and give me your Vows of revenge on* Philander, *and after that, by all that's Holy,* kneeling as she spoke, and holding him fast, *by all my injur'd innocence, by all my Noble Fathers wrong, and my dear Mothers grief; by all my Sisters sufferings; I swear! I'le marry you, love you, and give you all!* this she spoke without considering *Antonett* was by, and spoke it with all the rage and blushes in her Face, that injur'd Love and revenge cou'd inspire: And on the other side, the sense of his Sisters Honour lost, and that of the tender passion he had for *Silvia,* made him swear by all that was sacred, and by all the Vows of Eternal Love and Honour he had made to *Silvia,* to go and revenge himself and her on the false Friend and Lover; and confest the second motive; which was his Sisters Fame, *For,* cry'd he, *that foul Adultress, that false* Calista, *is so allied to me*: But still he urg'd that wou'd add to the justness of his cause, if he might depart her Husband as well as Lover; and revenge an Injur'd wife as well as Sister; and now he cou'd ask nothing, she did not easily grant; and because 'twas late in the day they conclude that the Morning shall consumate all his desires: And now she gives him her Letter to read, *For* said she, *I shall esteem my self henceforth so absolutely* Octavio's, *that I will not so much as read a Line from that perjur'd ruiner of my Honour,* he took the Letter with smiles and bows of gratitude, and read it:

Philander,

Philander *to* Silvia.

There are a thousand reasons, dearest *Silvia,* at this time that prevents my writing to you, reasons that will be convincing enough to oblige my pardon; and plead my Cause with her, that Loves me, all which I will lay before you, when I have the happiness to see you; I have met with some affairs since my arrival to this place, that wholly takes up my time, affairs of state whose fatigues have put my heart extreamly out of Tune, and if not carefully manag'd may turn to my perpetual ruin, so that I have not an hour in a day to spare for *Silvia;* which believe me is the greatest affliction of my Life; and I have no prospect of Ease in the endless toyls of Life, but that of reposing in the Arms of

Silvia: Some short intervals: Pardon my hast, for you cannot guess the weighty business that at present, robs you of

Your Philander.

You lie, false Villain—reply'd *Silvia* in mighty rage; *I can guess your business, and can revenge it too, curse on thee Slave; to think me grown as poor in sense, as Honour: To be cajol'd with this— Stuff that wou'd never sham a Chamber Maid: Death am I so forlorn, so despicable, I am not worth the pains of being well dissembl'd with. Confusion overtake him; misery seize him, may I become his plague, while life remains, or publique tortures end him*: This, with all the madness that ever inspired a Lunatick, she utter'd with Tears and Violent Actions: When *Octavio* besought her not to afflict her self, and almost wisht he did not love a temper so contrary to his own: He told her he was sorry, extreamly sorry, to find she still retain'd so violent a passion for a man unworthy of her least concern, when she reply'd——*'Do not mistake my soul, by Heav'n 'tis Pride, disdain, despight and hate——to think he shou'd believe this dull excuse cou'd pass upon my judgment, had the false Traytor told me that he hated me, or that his faithless date of Love was out, I had been tame with all my injuries, but poorly thus to impose my Wit——By Heav'n he shall not bear the affront to hell in Triumph! No more——I've vow'd he shall not,——My soul has fixt, and now will be at ease.——Forgive me, oh Octavio,'* and letting her self fall into his Arms, she soon obtain'd what she ask'd for, one touch of the fair Charmer cou'd calm him into Love, and softness.

Thus after a thousand transports of passion on his side, and all the seeming tenderness on hers the Night being far advanc'd, and new Confirmations given and taken on either side of pursuing the happy Agreement in the Morning, which they had again resolv'd, they appointed that *Silvia* and *Antonett* shou'd go three Miles out of Town to a little Village, where there was a Church, and that Octavio should meet 'em there to be Confirm'd and secur'd of all the happiness he propos'd to himself in this World——*Silvia*, being so wholly bent upon revenge (for the accomplishment of which alone, she accepted of *Octavio*,) that she had lost all remembrance of her former Marriage, with *Briljard*: Or if it ever enter'd into her thought 'twas only consider'd as a sham, nothing design'd but to secure her from being taken from *Philander* by her Parents: And, without any respect to the Sacred tie, to be regarded no more; nor did she design this with *Octavio* from any respect she had to the Holy State of Matrimony, but from a Lust of Vengeance which she wou'd buy at any price; and which she found no Man so well able to satisfie as *Octavio*.

But what wretched changes of Fortune she met with after this, and a miserable Portion of Fate was destined to this unhappy Wanderer, the last Part of *Philander*'s Life, and the Third and Last Part of this History, shall most Faithfully relate.

The End of the Second Part

THE
AMOURS
OF
PHILANDER
AND
SILVIA:

Being the Third and Laſt Part
OF THE
Love-Letters
Between a
NOBLE-MAN
AND HIS
SISTER.

LONDON,
Printed, and are to be Sold by moſt
Book-Sellers, 1687.

LORD SPENCER.[a]

My Lord,

*When a New Book comes into the World, the first thing we consider, is
the Dedication; and according to the Quality and Humour of the
Patron, we are apt to make a Judgment of the following Subject: If to a
States-man we believe it Grave and Politick; if a Gown-man, Law or
Divinity, if to the Young and Gay, Love and Gallantry. By this Rule,
I believe the gentle Reader, who finds your Lordship's Name prefix'd
before this, will make as many various Opinions of it, as they do
Characters of your Lordship, whose youthful Sallies, have been the
business of so much Discourse, and which according to the Relator's
Sence or good Nature, is either aggravated or excused; though the
Womans Quarrel to your Lordship has some more reasonable Foundation, than that of your own Sex; for your Lordship being Form'd with
all the Beauties and Graces of Man-kind, all the Charms of Wit, Youth
and Sweetness of Disposition (derived to you from an Illustrious Race
of Hero's) adapting you to noblest Love and Softness; they cannot but
complain on that mistaken Conduct of Yours, that so lavishly deals out
those agreeable Attractions, Squandering away that Youth and Time
on many, which might be more advantageously dedicated to some one
of the Fair; and by a Liberty (which they call) not being Discreet
enough, robb 'em of all the Hopes of Conquest over that Heart which
they believe can fix no where; they cannot carress you into Tameness,
or if you sometimes appear so, they are still upon their Guard with you;
for like a Young Lyon, you are ever apt to leap into your Natural
Wildness; the Greatness of your Soul disdaining to be confined to lazy
Repose; tho the Delicacy of your Person and Constitution so absolutely
require it; your Lordship not being made for Diversions so rough and
fatigueing, as those your active Mind would impose upon it. Your*

---

[a] Robert, Lord Spencer (1666–88). Lord Spencer led a wild, profligate life of
gambling and duelling. As with Thomas Condon, Behn dedicates her work to a
man whose private life has parallels with Philander's.

Lordship is placed in so Glorious a Station (the Son of so Great a Father)[a] as renders all you do more perspicuous to the World, than the Actions of common Men already; the advantages of your Birth have drawn all Eyes upon you, and yet more on those coming Greatnesses, to which you were born; if Heaven preserves your Lordship amidst the too vigorous Efforts, and too dangerous Adventures, which a too brisk Fire in your Noble Blood, a too forward desire of gaining Fame daily exposes you to; and will, unless some force confine your too impatient Bravery, shorten those Days which Heaven has surely designed for more Glorious Actions; for according to all the Maxims of the Judging Wise, the little Extravagancies of Youth accomplish, and perfect the Riper Years. 'Tis this that makes indulgent Parents permit those Sparks of Fire, that are Gleaming in Young Hearts, to kindle into a Flame, knowing well that the Consideration and Temperament of a few more Years will regulate it to that just degree, where the noble and generous Spirit should fix it self: And for this we have had the Examples of some of the greatest Men that ever adorned History.

My Lord, I presume to lay at your Lordship's Feet, an Illustrious Youth; the unhappy Circumstances of whose Life ought to be Written in lasting Characters of all Languages, for a Precedent to succeeding Ages, of the Misfortune of heedless Love, and a too Early Thirst of Glory; for in him, your Lordship will find the fatal Effects of great Courage without Conduct, Wit without Discretion, and a Greatness of Mind without the steady Vertues of it; so that from a Prince even ador'd by all, by an imprudence, that too often attends the Great and Young, and from the most exhalted Height of Glory, mis-led by false notions of Honour, and falser Friends, fell the most pityed Object, that ever was abandoned by Fortune. I hope no One will imagine I intend this as a Parallel between your Lordship and our mistaken brave Unfortunate, since your Lordship hath an unquestioned and hereditary Loyalty, which nothing can deface, born from a Father, who has given the World so evident Proofs, that no fear of threatned danger can separate his useful Service, and Duties from the Interest of his Royal and God-like Master,[b] which he pursues with an undaunted Fortitude, in disdain of Phanatical Censures, and those that want the Bravery to do a just Action, for fear of future Turns of State. And such indeed is

---

[a] Robert Spencer, the 2nd Earl of Sunderland, was one of James II's most powerful ministers when Behn wrote her preface.

[b] Behn is again alluding to the English king and the belief that he was appointed by God. By the time Part III of *Love-Letters* was published Charles II was dead and James II was on the throne.

your true Man of Honour; *and as such I doubt not but your Lordship will acquit your self in all times, and on all occasions.*

Pardon the Liberty, my Zeal for your Lordship has here presumed to take, since among all those that make Vows and Prayers for your Lordship's Health and Preservation, none offers them more devoutly, than,

My LORD,

Your Lordships,

Most Humble and

Obedient Servant,

A. B.

THE
AMOURS
OF
PHILANDER and *SILVIA*.

Octavio the Brave, the Generous, and the Amorous, having left *Silvia* absolutely resolv'd to give her self to that doting fond Lover, or rather to sacrifice her self to her Revenge, that unconsidering Unfortunate, whose Passion had expos'd him to all the unreasonable Effects of it, return'd to his own House, wholly transported with his happy Success. He thinks on nothing but vast coming Joys: Nor did one kind Thought direct him back to the evil Consequences of what he so hastily pursu'd; he reflects not on her Circumstances, but her Charms; not on the Infamy he should espouse with *Silvia*, but of those ravishing Pleasures she was capable of giving him: he regards not the Reproaches of his Friends; but wholly abandon'd to Love and youthful Imaginations, gives a Loose to young Desire and Fancy, that deludes him with a thousand soft Ideas: He reflects not that his gentle and easy Temper, was most unfit to joyn with that of *Silvia*, which was the most haughty and humorous in Nature; for tho' she had all the Charms of Youth and Beauty, that are conquering in her Sex, all the Wit and Insinuation that even surpasses Youth and Beauty, yet to render her Character impartially, she had also abundance of disagreeing Qualities mixt with her Perfections. She was Imperious and Proud, even to Insolence; Vain and Conceited even to Folly; she knew her Vertues and her Graces too well, and her Vices too little; she was very Opinionated and Obstinate, hard to be convinced of the falsest Argument, but very positive in her fancied Judgment: Abounding in her own Sense, and very critical on that of others: Censorious, and too apt to charge others with those Crimes to which she was her self addicted, or had been guilty of: Amorously inclin'd and indiscreet in the Management of her Amours, and constant

257

rather from Pride and Shame than Inclination; fond of catching
at every trifling Conquest, and lov'd the Triumph tho' she
hated the Slave. Yet she had Vertues too, that balanc'd her
Vices, among which we must allow her to have lov'd *Philander*
with a Passion, that nothing but his Ingratitude could have
decay'd in her Heart, nor was it lessen'd but by a Force that
gave her a thousand Tortures, Racks, and Pangs, which had
almost cost her her less valu'd Life; for being of a Temper nice
in Love, and very fiery, apt to fly into Rages at every Accident
that did but touch that tenderest Part, her Heart; she suffered a
world of Violence and Extremity of Rage and Grief by turns: at
this Affront and Inconstancy of *Philander*. Nevertheless she was
now so discreet, or rather Cunning, to dissemble her Resentment the best she could to her generous Lover, for whom she
had more Inclination than she yet had leisure to perceive, and
which she now attributes wholly to her Revenge; and considering *Octavio* as the most proper Instrument for that, she fancies,
what was indeed a growing Tenderness from the sense of his
Merit, to be the Effects of that Revenge she so much desired and
thirsted after; and tho' without she dissembled a Calm; within
she was all Fury and Disorder, all Storm and Distraction: She
went to Bed rack'd with a thousand thoughts of dispairing
Love; sometimes all the Softness of *Philander* in their happy
Enjoyments came in view, and made her sometimes weep, and
sometimes faint with the dear lov'd Remembrance; sometimes
his late Enjoyments with *Calista*, and then she rav'd and burnt
with frantick Rage: But oh! at last she found her Hope was gon,
and wisely fell to argue with her Soul. She knew Love would
not long subsist on the thin Diet of Dispair, and resolving he
was never to be retriev'd who once had ceas'd to Love, she
strove to bend her Soul to useful Reason, and thinks on all
Octavio's Obligations, his Vows, his Assiduity, his Beauty, his
Youth, his Fortune, and his generous Offer, and with the Aid of
Pride resolves to unfix her Heart, and give it better Treatment in
his Bosom: To cease at least to love the false *Philander*, if she
could never force her Soul to hate him: And tho' this was not so
soon done as thought on, in a Heart so pre-possest as that of
Silvia's, yet there is some Hope of Recovery, when a Woman in
that Extremity will but think of listening to Love from any new
Adorer; and having once resolv'd to pursue the Fugitive no
more with the natural Artillery of their Sighs and Tears, Reproaches and Complaints, they have Recourse to every thing

that may soonest chase from the Heart those Thoughts that oppress it: For Nature is not inclin'd to hurt it self, and there are but very few who find it necessary to die of the Disease of Love. Of this sort was our *Silvia*, tho' to give her her due, never any Person who did not indeed die, ever languished under the Torments of Love, as did that charming and afflicted Maid.

While *Silvia* remain'd in these eternal Inquietudes, *Antonett* having quitted her Chamber, takes this Opportunity to go to that of *Brilljard* whom she had not visited in two days before, being extreamly troubled at his Design which she now found he had on her Lady; she had a mind to vent her Spleen, and as the Proverb says, *call W——re first*.[a] *Brilljard* long'd as much to see her, to rail at her for being privy to *Octavio*'s Approach to *Silvia*'s Bed, as he thought (she imagin'd) and not giving him an account of it, as she us'd to do, of all the Secrets of her Lady. She finds him alone in his Chamber, recover'd from all but the Torments of his unhappy Disappointment. She approach'd him with all the Anger her sort of Passion could inspire (for Love in a mean unthinking Soul, is not that glorious thing it is in the Brave) however she had enough to serve her Pleasure, for *Brilljard* was young and handsome, and both being bent on Railing, without knowing each others Intentions, they both equally flew into high Words; he upbraiding her with her Infidelity, and she him with his. *Are not you,* said he (growing more calm) *the falsest of your Tribe, to keep a Secret from me that so much concern'd me? is it for this I have refus'd the Addresses of Burgomasters Wives and Daughters, where I could have made my Fortune and my Satisfaction, to keep myself intirely for a thing that betrays me, and keeps every Secret of her Heart from me? false and forsworn, I will be Fool no more.* 'Tis well Sir (reply'd *Antonett*) *that you having been the most perfidious Man alive, should accuse me who am Innocent; Come, come Sir, you have not carried Matters so swimingly but I could easily dive into the other Nights Intrigue and Secret. What Secret, thou false one? Thou art all over secret; a very hopeful Bawd at eighteen——go I hate ye——*At this she wept, and he pursu'd his Railing to out-noyse her, *You thought because your Deeds were done in Darkness, they were conceal'd from a Lovers Eyes; no thou young Viper, I saw, I heard, and felt, and satisfi'd every Sense of this thy Falshood, when* Octavio *was conducted to* Silvia's *Bed by*

---

[a] To accuse someone first, before being accused by them.

thee. But what, said she, *if instead of* Octavio *I conducted the perfidious Traytor to love* Brilljard? *Who then was false and perjur'd?* At this he blush'd extreamly, which was too visible on his fair Face. She being now confirm'd she had the better of him, continued——*Let thy Confusion*, said she with Scorn, *witness the Truth of what I say, and I have been but too well acquainted with that Body of yours*, weeping as she spoke, *to mistake it for that of* Octavio. *Softly dear* Antonett, reply'd he,——*nay now your Tears have calm'd me*; and taking her in his Arms, sought to appease her by all the Arguments of seeming Love and Tenderness; while she yet wholly unsatisfied in that Cheat of his of going to *Silvia*'s Bed, remain'd still pouting and very frumpish. But he that had but one Argument left, that on all Occasions serv'd to convince her, had at last Recourse to that, which put her in good Humour, and hanging on his Neck she kindly chid him for putting such a Trick upon her Lady. He told her, and confirm'd it with an Oath, That he did it but to try how far she was Just to his Friend and Lord, and not any Desire he had for a Beauty that was too much of his own Complexion to charm him, 'twas only the Brunet and the Black, such as her self, that could move him to Desire; thus he shams her into perfect Peace. *And why*, said she, *were you not satisfied that she was False, as well from the Assignation as the Tryal*. Oh no. said he, *you Women have a thousand Arts of Gibing, and no Man ought to believe you, but put you to the Tryal*. Well, said she, *when I had brought you to the Bed, when you found her Arms stretch'd out to receive you, why did you not retire like an honest Man, and leave her to her self?* Oh fy, said he, *that had not been to have acted* Octavio *to the Life, but would have made a Discovery*. Ay, said she, *that was your Aim to have acted* Octavio *to the Life, I believe, and not to discover my Lady's Constancy to your Lord, but I suppose you have been sworn at the But of* Hedleburgh,[a] *never to kiss the Maid when you can kiss the Mistress:* But he renewing his Caresses and Asseverations of Love to her, she suffered herself to be convinc'd of all he had a mind to have her believe. After this she could not contain any Secret from him, but told him she had something to say to him, which if he knew, would convince him she had all the Passion in the World for him: He presses eagerly to know, and she pursues to tell

---

[a] A 'butt' is a wine cask. The Elector of the Palatine, Karl Theodor, had a vast wine cask built in Heidelberg to collect the annual tithe from the region's wine harvest. The cask could hold 220,000 litres of wine.

him, 'tis as much as her Life is worth to discover it, and that she lies under the Obligation of an Oath not to tell it; but Kisses and Rhetorick prevails, and she crys——*What will you say now if my Lady may Marry one of the greatest and most considerable Persons in all this Country? I should not wonder at her Conquests* (reply'd Brilljard) *but I should wonder if she should Marry. Then cease your Wonder*, reply'd she, *for she is to morrow to be married to Count Octavio, whom she is to meet at nine in the Morning to that end, at a little Village a League from this place.* She spoke, and he believes; and finds it true by the raging of his Blood, which he could not conceal from *Antonett*, and for which he feigns a thousand Excuses to the Amorous Maid, and charges his Concern on that for his Lord: At last (after some more Discourse on that Subject) he pretends to grow sleepy, and hastens her to her Chamber, and locking the Door after her, he began to reflect on what she had said, and grew to all the Torment of Rage, Jealousie, and all the Dispairs of a passionate Lover: And tho' his Hope was not Extreme before, yet as Lovers do, he found, or fancy'd a Probability (from his Lords Inconstancy, and his own right of Marriage) that the Necessity she might chance to be in of his Friendship and Assistance in a strange Country, might some happy Moment or other render him the Blessing he so long had waited for from *Silvia*; for he ever design'd, when either his Lord left her, grew cold, or should happen to die, to put in his Claim of Husband. And the soft familiar way, with which she eternally liv'd with him, incourag'd this Hope and Design; nay she had often made him Advances to that happy Expectation. But this fatal Blow had driven him from all his fancy'd Joys, to the most wretched Estate of a desperate Lover. He traverses his Chamber wounded with a thousand different Thoughts, mixt with those of preventing this Union the next Morning. Sometimes he resolves to fight *Octavio*, for his Birth might pretend to it, and he wanted no Courage, but he is afraid of being overcome by that gallant Man, and either loosing his Hopes with his Life, or if he kill *Octavio*, to be forc'd to fly from his Happiness, or die an ignominious Death. Sometimes he resolves to own *Silvia* for his Wife, but then he fears the Rage of that dear Object of his Soul, which he dreads more than Death it self: So that tost from one Extream to another, from one Resolution to a hundred, he was not able to fix upon any thing. In this Perplexity he remain'd till Day appear'd; that Day that must advance with his undoing, while *Silvia* and *Antonett* were preparing for the Design concluded on the last Night. This he heard, and every Minute that approach'd gave him new Torments, so that now he would have given himself to the Prince of Darkness for a kind of Disappointment: He was often ready to go and throw himself at her Feet, and plead against her Enterprize in hand, and to urge the unlawfulness of a double Marriage, ready to make Vows for the Fidelity of *Philander*, tho' before so much against his own Interest, and to tell her all those Letters from him were forg'd: He thought on all things, but nothing remain'd with him, but Dispair of every thing. At last the Devil and his own Subtilty, put him upon a Prevention, tho' base, yet the most likely to succeed in his Opinion.

He knew there were many Factions in *Holland*,[a] and that the States themselves were divided in their Interests, and a thousand Jealousies and Fears were eternally spread amongst the Rable; there were Cabals for every Interest, that of the *French* so prevailing, that of the *English*, and that of the Illustrious *Orange*, and others for the States; so that it was not a Difficulty to move any Mischief, and pass it off among the Crowd for dangerous Consequences. *Brilljard* knew each Division, and which way they were inclin'd, he knew *Octavio* was not so well with the States as not to be easily rendred worse; for he was so intirely a Creature and Favourite of the Prince that they conceiv'd abundance of Jealousies of him which they durst not own. *Brilljard* besides knew a great Man, who having a Pique to *Octavio*, might the sooner be brought to receive any ill Character of him: To this sullen Magistrate he applies himself, and deluding the Credulous busie old Man with a thousand circumstantial Lies, he discovers to him that *Octavio* held a Correspondence with the *French* King to betray the State; and that he Caball'd to that end with some who were look'd upon as *French* Rebels,[b] but indeed were no other than Spies to *France*. This coming from a Man of that Party, and whose Lord was a *French* Rebel, gain'd a perfect Credit with the old Sr. *Politic*; so

---

[a] Holland at the time was the centre of an alliance against Louis XIV and France. The House of Orange's attempts to strengthen its authority in the republic raised opposing factions among the various States of Holland. The considerable number of English rebels in Holland and the Prince of Orange's marital links with the Stuarts also created conflict.

[b] Having discussed the actual political situation in Holland above, Behn now returns to her ploy of substituting France for England. The 'French King' here refers to Charles II and the '*French* rebels' are the supporters of Monmouth and Grey.

that immediately hasting to the State-House he lays this weighty Affair before them, who soon found it reasonable, and if not true, at least they fear'd, and sent out a Warrant for the speedy apprehending him; but coming to his House, tho' early, they found him gone, and being inform'd which way he took, the Messenger pursu'd him, and found his Coach at the Door of a *Caberett*, too Obscure for his Quality; which made them apprehend this was some place of Rendezvouz, where he possibly met with his Trayterous Associators: They send in, and cunningly inquire who he waited for, or who was with him, and they understood he stay'd for some Gentlemen of the *French* Nation, for he had ordered *Silvia* to come in mans Cloaths, that she might not be known; and had given Order below, that if two *French* Gentlemen came they should be brought to him. This Information made the Scandal as clear as Day, and the Messenger no longer doubted of the Reasonableness of his Warrant, tho' he was loath to serve it on a Person whose Father he had serv'd many Years. He waits at some distance from the House unseen, tho' he could take a View of all; he saw *Octavio* come often out into the Balcony and look with longing Eyes towards the Road that leads to the Town; he saw him all rich and gay as a young Bridegroom, lovely and young as the Morning that flattered him with so fair and happy a Day; at last he saw two Gentlemen alight at the Door, and giving their Horses to a Page to walk a while, they ran up into the Chamber where *Octavio* was waiting, who had already sent his Page to prepare the Priest in the Village Church to marry them. You may imagine with what Love and Joy the ravished Youth approach'd the Idol of his Soul, and she who beholds him in more Beauty than ever yet she thought he had appear'd, pleas'd with all things he had on, with the gay Morning, the flowry Field, the Air, the little Journey, and a thousand diverting things, made no Resistance to those fond Imbraces that prest her a thousand times with silent Transport, and falling Tears of eager Love and Pleasure, but even in that moment of Content she forgot *Philander*, and receiv'd all the Satisfaction so soft a Lover could dispence: While they were mutually thus exchanging Looks, and almost Hearts, the Messenger came into the Room, and as civilly as possible told *Octavio* he had a Warrant for him to secure him as a Traytor to the State, and a Spy for *France*. You need not be told the Surprize and Astonishment he was in; however he obey'd: The Messenger turning to *Silvia*, cry'd Sr.

Tho' I can hardly credit this Crime that is charged to my Lord, yet the finding him here with two *French* Gentlemen gives me some more Fears that there may be something in it; and it would do well if you would deliver your selves into my Hands for the farther clearing this Gentleman. The foolish grave Speech of the Messenger had like to have put *Octavio* into a loud Laughter, he addressing himself to two Women, for two Men: But *Silvia* reply'd, Sir, I hope you do not take us for so little Friends to the gallant *Octavio*, to abandon him in his Misfortune; no, we will share it with him, be it what it will. To this the generous Lover, blushing with kind Surprize, bow'd, and kissing her Hand with Transport, calling her his charming Friend; and so all three being guarded back in *Octavio*'s Coach, they return to the Town, and to the House of the Messenger, which made a great Noise all over, that *Octavio* was taken with two *French* Jesuits[a] plotting to fire *Amsterdam*, and a thousand things equally Ridiculous. They were all three lodg'd together in one House, that of the Messenger, which was very fine, and fit to entertain any Persons of Quality; while *Brilljard*, who did not like that part of the Project, bethought him of a thousand ways how to free her from thence; for he design'd as soon as *Octavio* should be taken to have got her to have quitted the Town under pretence of being taken upon Suspicion of holding Correspondence with him, because they were *French*; but her delivering herself up, had not only undone all his Design, but had made it unsafe for him to stay. While he was thus bethinking himself what he should do, *Octavio*'s Uncle, who was one of the States, extreamly affronted at the Indignity put upon his Nephew and his sole Heir, the Darling of his Heart and Eyes, commands that this Informer may be secur'd; and accordingly *Brilljard* was taken into Custody, who giving himself over for a lost Man, revolves to put himself upon *Octavio*'s Mercy, by telling him the Motives that induc'd him to this violent and ungenerous Course. It was some days before the Council thought fit to call for *Octavio*, to hear what he had to say for himself in the mean time, he having not had Permission yet to see *Silvia*; and being extreamly desirous of that Happiness, he bethought himself that the Messenger having been in his Fathers Service, might have so much Respect for the Son as to allow him

---

[a] Members of the Society of Jesus, a Roman Catholic order founded by Ignatius of Loyola in 1534. They were noted for their missionary zeal and their taste for political intrigue.

to speak to that fair Charmer, provided he might be a Witness to what he should say: He sends for him, and demanded of him where those two fair Prisoners were lodg'd who came with him in the Morning; he told him, in a very good Apartment on the same Floor, and that they were very well Accommodated, and seem'd to have no other Trouble but what they suffered for him. I hope my Lord, added he——your Confinement will not be long, for I hear there is a Person taken up, who has confest he did it for a Revenge on you. At this *Octavio* was very well pleased, and asked him who it was; and he told him a *French* Gentleman belonging to the Count *Philander*, who about six Months ago was obliged to quit the Town as an Enemy to France. He soon knew it to be *Brilljard*, and comparing this Action with some others of his lately Committed, he no longer doubts it the Effects of his Jealousie. He ask'd the Messenger if it were impossible to gain so much Favour of him, as to let him visit those two *French* Gentlemen, he being by while he was with them: The Keeper soon granted his Request, and reply'd ——There was no Hazzard, he would not run to serve him; and immediately, putting back the Hangings, with one of those Keys he had in his Hand, he opened a Door in his Chamber that led into a Gallery of fine Pictures, and from thence they past into the Apartment of *Silvia*: As soon as he came in he threw himself at her Feet, and she received him, and took him up into her Arms with all the Transports of Joy a Soul (more than ever possest with Love for him) could conceive; and tho' they all appear'd of the Masculine Sex, the Messenger soon perceiv'd his Error, and beg'd a thousand Pardons. *Octavio* makes hast to tell her his Opinion of the cause of all this Trouble to both; and she easily believ'd, when she heard *Brilljard* was taken, that it was as he imagin'd, for he had been found too often faulty not to be suspected now: This Thought brought a great Calm to both their Spirits, and almost reduc'd them to their first soft Tranquillity, with which they began the day: For he protested his Innocence a thousand times, which was wholly needless, for the generous Maid believed before he spoke, he could not be guilty of the Sin of Treachery. He renews his Vows to her of eternal Love, and that he would perform what they were so unluckily prevented of doing this Morning, and that tho' possibly by this unhappy Adventure his Design might have taken Air, and have arrived to the Knowledge of his Uncle, yet in spite of all Opposition of Friends, or the Malice of *Brilljard*, he would pursue his Glorious Design of marrying her, tho' he were forc'd for it to wander to the farthest parts of the Earth with his lovely Prize. He begs she will not disesteem him for this Scandal on his Fame, for he was all Love, all soft Desire, and had no other Design than that of making himself Master of that greatest Treasure in the World; that of the possessing the most charming, the all ravishing *Silvia*: In return, she paid him all the Vows that could secure an Infidel in Love, she made him all the indearing Advances a Heart could wish, wholly given up to tender Passion, insomuch that he believes, and is the gayest Man that ever was blest by Love. And the Messenger who was present all this while, found that this Caballing with the *French* Spies, was only an innocent Design to give himself away to a fine young Lady: And therefore fully convinc'd he was guilty of no other Crime, he gave them all the Freedom they desired; and which they made use of to the most Advantage Love could direct or Youth inspire. This Suffering with *Octavio* begot a Pity and Compassion in the Heart of *Silvia*, and that grew up to Love, for he had all the Charms that could inspire it; and every Hour was adding new Fire to her Heart, which at last burnt into a Flame, such Power has mighty Obligation on a Heart that has any grateful Sentiments: And yet when she was absent anights from *Octavio*, and thought on *Philander*'s Passion for *Calista*, she would Rage and Rave, and find the Effects of wondrous Love, and wondrous Pride, and be even ready to make Vows against *Octavio*: But those were Fits that seldomer seiz'd her now, and every Fit was like a departing Ague, still weaker than the former, and at the sight of *Octavio* all would vanish, her Blushes would rise and discover the soft Thoughts her Heart conceived for the approaching Lover; and she soon found that vulgar Error of the Impossibility of Loving more than once. It was four days they thus remained without being call'd to the Councel, and every day brought its new Joys along with it: They were never asunder, never interrupted with any Visit, but once for a few Moments in a day by *Octavio*'s Uncle, and then he would go into his own Apartment to receive him: He offered to baile him out; but *Octavio*, who had found more real Joy there than in any part of the Earth besides, evaded the Obligation, by telling his Uncle he would be oblig'd to nothing but his Innocence for his Liberty: So would get rid of the fond old Gentleman, who never knew a Passion but for his darling Nephew, and return with as much Joy to the Lodgings of *Silvia* as if he had been absent a

Week, which is an Age to a Lover; there they sometimes would play at Cards, where he would lose considerable Summs to her, or at Hazard, or be studying what they should do next to pass the Hours most to her Content; not but he had rather have lain eternally at her Feet, gazing, doating, and saying a thousand fond things, which at every View he took were conceived in his Soul: And tho' but this last Minute he had finish'd saying all that Love could Dictate, he found his Heart oppress'd with a vast store of new Softness, which he languish'd to unload in her ravishing Bosom: But she, who was not arrived to his pitch of Loving, diverts his softer Hours with Play sometimes, and otherwhile with making him follow her into the Gallery, which was adorn'd with pleasant Pictures, all of *Hempskerk's*[a] hand, which afforded great Variety of Objects very Drole and Antique, *Octavio* finding something to say of every one that might be of Advantage to his own Heart; for whatever Argument was in dispute, he would be sure to bring it home to the Passion he had for *Silvia*; it should end in Love however remotely begun: So strange an Art has Love to turn all things to the Advantage of a Lover.

'Twas thus they pass'd their time, and nothing was wanting that lavish Expence could procure, and every Minute he advances to new Freedoms, and unspeakable Delights, but still such as might hitherto be allow'd with Honour; he sighs, and wishes, he languishes and dies for more, but dares not utter the Meaning of one Motion of Breath, for he lov'd so very much that every Look from those fair Eyes that charm'd him, aw'd him to a Respect that rob'd him of many happy Moments a bolder Lover would have turn'd to his Advantage, and he treated her as if she had been an unspotted Maid; with Caution of Offending, he had forgot that general Rule, That where the sacred Laws of Honour are once invaded, Love makes the easier Conquest.

All this while you may imagine *Brilljard* indured no little Torment, he could not on the one side determine what the *States* would do with him, when once they should find him a

---

[a] Martin van Heemskerck (1498–1574), a Dutch painter. Van Heemskerck worked in Haarlem and produced portraits, religious alterpieces and paintings of mythological subjects such as *Venus and Cupid*, *Vulcan's Forge* and *The Triumph of Silenus*. His work emphasizes the sensual through his attention to musculature and skin tone and his depiction of heavy, rounded bodies.

false Accuser of so great a Man, and on the other side he suffered a thousand Pains and Jealousies from Love; he knew too well the Charms and Power of *Octavio*, and what Effects Importunity and Opportunity have on the Temper of feeble Woman: He found the *States* did not make so considerable a matter of his being Impeach'd as to confine his strictly, and he dies with the Fears of those happy Moments he might possibly enjoy with *Silvia*, where there might be no Spies about her to give him any kind Intelligence; and all that could afford him any glimps of Consolation, was, That while they were thus confin'd he was out of Fear of their being married. *Octavio*'s Uncle this while was not Idle, but taking it for a high Indignity his Nephew should remain so long without being heard, he mov'd it to the Councel, and accordingly they sent for him to the State-House[a] the next Morning, where *Brilljard* was brought to confront him; whom, as soon as *Octavio* saw, with a scornful Smile, he cry'd——'*Tis well*, Brilljard, *that you who durst not fight me fairly, should find out this nobler way of ridding your self of a Rival; I am glad at least, that I have no more honourable a Witness against me.* *Brilljard*, who never before wanted Assurance, at this Reproach was wholly Confounded; for it was not from any Villainy in his Nature, but the absolute Effects of mad and desperate Passion, which put him on the only Remedy that could relieve him; and looking on *Octavio* with modest Blushes, that half pleaded for him, he cry'd——*Yes my Lord, I am your Accuser, and come to charge your Innocence with the greatest of Crimes, and you ought to thank me for my Accusation; when you shall know 'tis regard to my own Honour, violent Love for Silvia, and extream Respect to your Lordship, has made me thus sawcy with your unspotted Fame. How,* reply'd Octavio, *shall I thank you for accusing me with a Plot upon the State? Yes my Lord,* reply'd *Brilljard; and yet you had a Plot to betray the State, and by so new a way as could be found out by none but so great and brave a Man.*——*Heavens,* reply'd *Octavio* inrag'd, *this is an Impudence, that nothing but a Traytor to his own King, and one bred up in Plots and Mischiefs, could have invented; I betray my own Country?*——*Yes my Lord,* cry'd he (more briskly than before, seeing *Octavio* colour so at him) *to all the Loosness of unthinking Youth, to all the Breach of Laws both Human and Divine, if all the Youth should follow your Example, you would betray Posterity it self;*

---

[a] The States General had its assembly chamber in The Hague.

and only mad Confusion would abound: In short, my Lord, that Lady who was taken with you by the Messenger, was my Wife: And going towards *Silvia*, who was struck as with a Thunderbolt, he seiz'd her Hand, and Cry'd,——while all stood gazing on——*This Lady Sir I mean——she is my Wife, my lawful married Wife.* At this *Silvia* could no longer hold her Patience within it Bounds, but with that other Hand he had left her, she struck him a Box on the Ear, that almost stagger'd him, coming unawares, and as she struck she cry'd aloud, *Thou liest base Villain——and I'll be reveng'd;* and flinging herself out of his Hand, she got on the other side of *Octavio,* while the whole Company remained confounded at what they saw and heard. *How,* cry'd out old *Sebastian, Uncle* to *Octavio, a Woman, this? By my Troth, sweet Lady, if you be one, methought you were a very pretty Fellow:* And turning to *Brilljard,* he cry'd——*Why, what Sir, then it seems all this Noise of betraying the State was but a Cuckold's Dream. Hah! and this wonderful and dangerous Plot, was but one upon your Wife Sir; hah——was it so? Marry Sir, at this rate, I rather think 'tis you have a Design of betraying the State——you cuckoldly Knaves that bring your handsome Wives to seduce our young Senators from their Sobriety and Wits.* Are these the Recompences, reply'd *Brilljard, you give the Injured, and in lieu of restoring me my Right, am I reproach'd with the most scandalous Infamy that can befal a Man.* Well Sir, reply'd *Sebastian, this is all you have to charge this Gentleman with?* At which he bow'd and was silent——and *Sebastian* continu'd—— *If your Wife, Sir, have a mind to my Nephew, or he to her, it should have been your Care to have forbid it, or prevented it, by keeping her under Lock and Key, if no other way to be secured; and Sir, we do not sit here to relieve Fools and Cuckolds; if your Lady will be Civil to my Nephew, what's that to us: Let her speak for herself; What say you Madam?——I say,* reply'd *Silvia, that this Fellow is mad and raves; that he is my Vassal, my Servant, my Slave; but, after this, unworthy of the meanest of these Titles.* This she spoke with a Disdain that sufficiently show'd the Pride and Anger of her Soul——*La you Sir,* reply'd *Sebastian, you are discharg'd your Ladys Service, 'tis a plain case she has more mind to the young Count than the Husband, and we cannot compel People to be honest against their Inclinations.* And coming down from the Seat where he sate, he imbraced *Octavio* a hundred times, and told the Board, he was extreamly glad they found the mighty Plot but a Vagary of Youth, and the Spleen of a Jealous Husband or Lover, or whatsoever other malicious thing; and desired the angry Man might be discharged since he had so just a Provocation as the loss of a Mistress. So all laughing at the Jest, that had made so great a Noise among the Grave and Wise, they freed 'em all: And *Sebastian* advised his Nephew, that the next Cuckold he made, he would make a Friend of him first, that he might hear of no more Complaints against him. But *Octavio* very gravely reply'd: *Sir, you have infinitely mistaken the Character of this Lady, she is a Person of too great Quality for this Raillery; at more Leisure you shall have her Story.* While he was speaking this, and their Discharges were making, *Silvia* confounded with Shame, Indignation, and Anger, goes out, and taking *Octavio's* Coach that stood at the Gate, went directly to his House, for she resolved to go no more where *Brilljard* was. After this *Sebastian* fell seriously to good Advice, and earnestly besought his Darling to leave off those wild Extravagancies that had so long made so great a Discourse all the Province over, where nothing but his splendid Amours, Treats, Balls, and Magnificences of Love, was the Business of the Town, and that he had forborn to tell him of it, and had hitherto justified his Actions, tho they had not deserved it; and he doubted this was the Lady to whom for this six or eight Months he heard he had so intirely dedicated himself: He desires him to quit this Lady, or if he will pursue his Love, to do it discreetly, to love some unmarried Woman, and not injure his Neighbours; to all which he blushed and bowed, and silently seem'd to thank him for his grave Councel. And *Brilljard* having received his Discharge, and Advice how he provoked the Displeasure of the *States* any more, by accusing of great Persons, he was ordered to ask *Octavio's* Pardon, but in lieu of that, he came up to him and challenged him to fight him for the Injustice he had done him, in taking from him his Wife; for he was sure he was undone in her Favour, and that Thought made him mad enough to put himself on this second Extravagancy: However this was not so silently managed but *Sebastian* perceived it, and was so inraged at the young Fellow for this second Insolence, that he was again confined, and sent back to Prison, where he swore he should suffer the utmost of the Law: And the Council breaking up, every one departed to his own Home. But never was Man Ravished with excess of Joy as *Octavio* was, to find *Silvia* meet him with extended Arms on the Stare-Case, whom he did not imagine to have found there, nor knew he how he stood in the Heart of that Charmer of his own, since the Affront she had received in the Court from those that however did not know her for they did not imagine this was that Lady, Sister to *Philander*, of whose Beauty they had heard so much, and her Face being turn'd from the Light, the old Gentlemen did not so much consider or see it. *Silvia* came into his House the back way, through the Stables and Garden, and had the good Fortune to be seen of none of his Family, but the Coach-man who brought her home, whom she conjur'd not to speak of it to the rest of his Servants; and unseen of any body she got into his Apartment, for often she had been there at Treats and Balls with *Philander*. She was all alone, for *Antonett* stay'd to see what became of her false Lover, who, after he was seized again, retired to her Lodging the most disconsolate Woman in the World, for having lost her Hopes of *Brilljard*, to whom she had ingaged all that Honour she had. But when she missed her Lady there, she accused herself with all the Falshood in the World, and fell to repent her Treachery. She sends the Page to inquire at *Octavio*'s House, but no body there cou'd give him any Intelligence, so that the poor amorous Youth returning without Hope, indur'd all the Pain of a hopeless Lover, for *Octavio* had anew charm'd his Coach-man: And calling up an ancient Woman who was his Housekeeper, who had been his Nurse, he acquainted her with the short History of his Passion for *Silvia*, and order'd her to give her attendance on the treasure of his Life; he bid her prepare all things as magnificent as she could in that Apartment he design'd her, which was very rich and gay, and towards a fine Garden: The Hangings and Beds all glorious, and fitter for a Monarch than a Subject; the finest Pictures the World afforded, Flowers in-laid with Silver, and Ivory, guilded Roofs, carved Wainscot, Tables of Plate, with all the rest of the moveables in the Chambers of the same, all of great value, and all was perfumed like an Altar, or the Marriage-Bed of some young King. Here *Silvia* was design'd to lodge, and hither *Octavio* conducted her; and setting her on a Couch while the Supper was getting ready, he sits himself down by her, and his heart being ready to burst with Grief, at the thought of the Claim which was laid to her by *Brilljard*; he silently views her, while Tears were ready to break from his fix'd Eyes,[a] and Sighs stopt what he would fain have spoke: While she wholly confounded with Shame, Guilt, and Disappointment

---

[a] In a stare.

(for she could not imagine that *Brilljard* could have had the Impudence to have claim'd her for a Wife) fix'd her fair Eyes to Earth, and durst not behold the languishing *Octavio*. They remain'd thus a long time silent, she not daring to defend herself from a Crime, of which she knew too well she was guilty, nor he daring to ask her a Question to which the Answer might prove so fatal; he fears to know what he dies to be satisfied in, and she fears to discover too late a Secret which was the only one she had conceal'd from him. *Octavio* runs over in his Mind a thousand Thoughts that perplex'd him, of the Probability of her being married; he considers how often he had found her with that happy young Man, who more freely entertain'd her than Servants use to do: He now considers how he has seen 'em once on a Bed together, when *Silvia* was in the Disorder of a yielding Mistress, and *Brilljard* of a ravish'd Lover; he considers how he has found 'em alone at Cards and Dice, and often entertaining her with Freedoms of a Husband, and how he wholly managed her Affairs, commanded her Servants like their proper Master, and was in full Authority of all. These and a thousand more Circumstances confirms *Octavio* in all his Fears: A thousand times she is about to speak, but either fears to lose *Octavio* by a clear Confession, or to run herself into farther Error by denying the matter of Fact, stops her words, and she only blushes and sighs at what she dares not tell, and if by chance their speaking Eyes meet, they would both decline 'em hastily again, as afraid to find there what their Language could not confess. Sometimes he would press her Hand and sigh—— *Ah* Silvia, *you have undone my Quiet*; to which she would return no Answer but Sigh; and now rising from the Couch she walk'd about the Chamber as sad and silent as Death, attending when he should have advanced in speaking to her, tho' she dreads the Voice she wishes to hear, and he waits for her Reply, tho' the Mouth that he adores should deliver Poyson and Daggers to his Heart. While thus they remained in the most silent and sad Entertainment (that ever was between Lovers that had so much to say) the Page, which *Octavio* only trusts to wait, brought him this Letter.

Brilljard *to* Octavio.

My Lord,
I am too sensible of my many high Offences to your Lordship, and have as much Penitence for my Sin committed towards you as 'tis possible to conceive; but when I implore a Pardon from a Lover, who by his own Passion may guess at the violent Effects of my dispairing Flame, I am yet so vain to hope it. Antonett gave me the Intelligence of your Design, and raised me up to a Madness that hurried me to that Barbarity against your unspotted Honour. I own the baseness of the Fact, but Lovers are not, my Lord, always guided by Rules of Justice and Reason; or if I had, I should have kill'd the fair Adultress that drew you to your Undoing, and who merits more your Hate than your Regard; and who having first violated her marriage Vow to me, with Philander, would sacrifice us both to you, and at the same time betray you to a Marriage that cannot but prove fatal to you, as it is most unlawful in her; so that, my Lord, if I have injured you, I have at the same time saved you from a Sin and Ruin, and humbly implore that you will suffer the Good I have rendered you in the last, to atone for the Ill I did you in the first. If I have accused you of a Design against the State, it was to save you from that of the too subtil and too charming Silvia, which none but myself could have snatcht you from: 'Tis true I might have acted something more worthy of my Birth and Education; but, my Lord, I knew the Power of Silvia, and if I should have sent you the Knowledge of this, when I sent the Warrant for the Security of your Person, the haughty Creature would have prevail'd above all my Truths, with the Eloquence of Love, and you had yielded and been betray'd worse by her, than by the most ungenerous Measures I took to prevent it: Suffer this Reason, my Lord, to plead for me in that Heart where Silvia Reigns, and shews how powerful she is every where. Pardon all the Faults of a most unfortunate Man undone by Love, and by your own guess what his Passion would put him on who aims or wishes at least for the intire Possession of Silvia, tho' it was never absolutely hop'd by

the most unfortunate

Brilljard.

At the beginning of this Letter *Octavio* hoped it contained the Confession of his Fault in claiming *Silvia*; he hop'd he would have own'd it done in order to his Service to his Lord, or his Love to *Silvia*, or any thing but what it really was; but when he read on——and found that he yet confirm'd his Claim, he yielded to all the Grief that could sink a Heart over burthen'd with violent Love; he fell down on the Couch were he was sate, and only calling *Silvia* with a dying Groan, he held out his Hand in which the Letter remain'd, and look'd on her with Eyes that languished with Death, Love, and Dispair; while she who already feared from whom it came, received it with Disdain, Shame, and Confusion: And *Octavio* recovering a little—— Cry'd in a faint Voice——*See Charming, Cruel, Fair*——*see how much my Soul adores you, when even this*——*cannot extinguish one spark of that Flame you have kindled in my Soul:* At this she blush'd and bow'd with a graceful modesty that was like to have given the lie to all the Accusations against her: She reads the Letter, while he greedily fixes his Eyes upon her Face as she read, observing with curious Search every Motion there, all killing and adorable. He saw her Blushes sometimes rise, then sink again to their proper Fountain, her Heart; there swell and rise, and beat against her Breast that had no other Covering than a thin Shirt, for all her Bosom was open, and betray'd the nimble Motions of her Heart. Her Eyes sometimes would sparkle with Disdain, and glow upon the fatal tell-tale Lines; and sometimes languish with excess of Grief: But having concluded the Letter, she laid it on the Table and began again to traverse the Room, her Head declined, and her Arms across her Bosom. *Octavio* made too true an Interpretation of this Silence, and Calm in *Silvia*, and no longer doubted his Fate. He fixes his Eyes eternally upon her, while she considers what she shall say to that afflicted Lover; she find's *Philander* lost, or if he ever return, 'tis not to Love, so that he was for ever gone; for too well she knew no Arts, Obligations, or Industry, could retrieve a flying *Cupid*: She found if even that, could return, his whole Fortune was so exhausted he could not support her; and that she was of a Nature so haughty and impatient of Injuries, that she could never forgive him those Affronts he had done her Honour first, and now her Love, she resolves no Law or Force shall submit her to *Brilljard*; she finds this Fallacy she has put on *Octavio*, has ruined her Credit in his Esteem, at least she justly fears it; so that believing herself abandoned by all in a strange Country, she fell to weeping her Fate, and the Tears wet the Floor as she walk'd: At which Sight so melting, *Octavio* starts from the Couch, and catching her in his trembling Arms, he cry'd, *be false, be cruel, and deceitful; yet still I must, I am compell'd to Adore you*—— This being spoken in so hearty and resolved a Tone, from a Man, of whose Heart she was so sure, and knew to be so generous, gave her a little Courage——and like sinking Men she catches at all that presents her any Hope of escaping. She resolves by discovering the whole Truth to save that last Stake, his Heart, tho' she could pretend to no more; and taking the fainting Lover by the Hand, she leads him to the Couch: *Well*, said she, Octavio, *you are too generous to be impos'd on in any thing; and therefore I will tell you my Heart without Reserve as absolutely as to Heaven it self, if I were interceeding my last Peace there*. She begg'd a thousand Pardons of him for having conceal'd any part of her Story from him, but she could no longer be guilty of that Crime, to a Man for whom she had so perfect a Passion; and as she spoke she imbraced him with an unresistable Softness that wholly charm'd him: She reconciles him with every Touch, and sighs on his Bosom a thousand grateful Vows and Excuses for her Fault, while he weeps with Love, and almost Expires in her Arms; she is not able to see his Passion and his Grief, and tells him she will do all things for his Repose. *Ah* Silvia, sigh'd he, *talk not of my Repose, when you confess your self Wife to one, and Mistress to another, in either of which I have alass no part: Ah, what is reserv'd for the Unfortunate* Octavio, *when two happy Lovers divide the Treasure of his Soul! Yet tell me Truth, because it will look like Love; shew me that excellent Vertue, so rarely found in all your fickle Sex. Oh! tell me Truth, and let me know how much my Heart can bear before it break with Love; and yet perhaps to hear thee speak to me, with that insinuating dear Voice of thine, may save me from the Terror of thy Words; and tho' each make a Wound, their very Accents have a Balm to heal! Oh, quickly pour it then into my listening Soul, and I'll be silent, as o'er ravished Lovers, whom Joys have charm'd to tender Sighs and Pantings*. At this, imbracing her anew, he let fall a Shower of Tears upon her Bosom, and sighing Cry'd——*Now I attend thy Story*: She then began anew the Repetition of the Loves between herself and *Philander*; which she slightly ran over, because he had already heard every Circumstance of it, both from herself and *Philander*; till she arriv'd to that part of it where she left *Belfont*, her Fathers House: *Thus far*, said she, *you have had a faithful Relation: And I was no sooner miss'd by my Parent, but you may imagine the diligent Search that would be made, both by* Foscario, *whom I was to have married the next day, and my tender* Parents; *but all Search, all Hu-an-Crys were vain; at last they put me into the weekly* Gazette,[a] *describing me to the very Features of my Face, my Hair, my Breast, my Stature, Youth and Beauty, omitting nothing that might render me apparent to all that should see me, offering vast Sums to any that should give Intelligence of such a lost Maid of Quality.* Philander, *who understood too well the Nature of the common People, and that they would betray their very Fathers for such a proferr'd Sum, durst trust me no longer to their Mercy: His Affairs were so involved with those of* Cæsario, *he could not leave* Paris; *for they every Moment expected the People should rise against their King,[b] and these Glorious Chiefs of the Faction were obliged to wait and watch the Motions of the dirty Croud.[c] Nor durst be trust me in any place from him, for he could not live a Day without me.* At that Thought she sign'd, and then went on: *so that I was oblig'd to remain obscurely lodged in* Paris, *where now I durst no longer trust myself, tho' disguis'd in as many Shapes as I was obliged to have Lodgings. At last we were betray'd, and had only the short Notice given us to yield or secure our selves from the hand of Justice by the next Morning, when they design'd to surprize us: To escape we found almost impossible, and very hazardous to attempt it; so that* Philander, *who was raving with his Fear, call'd myself and this young Gentleman,* Brilljard, *(then Master of his Horse) and one that had serv'd us faithfully through the whole Course of our Loves) to Councel: Many things were in vain debated, but at last this hard Shift was found out, of marrying me to* Brilljard,[d] *for to* Philander *it was impossible; so that no Authority of a Father could take me from the Husband. I was*

---

[a] At the end of September, 1682 an advertisement was placed in *The London Gazette* by Lord Berkeley stating that 'the Lady Henrietta Berkeley has been absent from her father's house since 20 August last past and is not known where she is or whether she is alive or dead.' A reward of £200 was offered to anyone who could return her to her family. The advertisement also described her a 'a young lady of a fair complexion, fair haired, full-breasted and indifferent tall'.

[b] Monmouth and his supporters had been preparing a rebellion at the end of 1682 before Grey and others were arrested for treason.

[c] Silvia echoes Behn's attitude to the mob as expressed in her state verse such as *A Poem to Sir Roger L'Estrange, On his Third Part of the History of the Times*: 'The Inspir'd Rabble, now wou'd Monarchs Rule, / And Government was turn'd to Ridicule;' [*Works of Aphra Behn*, Vol. 1, no. 82, ll.28–29]

[d] In October *The London Gazette* reported that 'Whereas in Benskin's *Domestic Intelligence* published on Monday 2nd it is said that the Lady Henrietta Berkeley hath in a letter to her father given an account of her departure and that she is married etc. It is thought fit to give notice that this is a false report and in all probability spread on purpose to hinder the discovery of her'.

at first extreamly unwilling, but when Philander *told me it was to be only a mock-Marriage, to secure me to himself, I was reconcil'd to it, and more, when I found the infinite Submission of the young Man, who vow'd he would never look up to me with the Eyes of a Lover or Husband, but in Obedience to his Lord did it to preserve me intirely for him: Nay further, to secure my future Fear, he confest to me he was already privately married to a Gentlewoman,[a] by whom he had two Children. Oh——tell me true my* Silvia, *Was he married to another?* Cry'd out the over-joy'd Lover. *Yes, on my Life,* reply'd *Silvia; for when it was proved in Court that I was married to* Brilljard, *(as at last I was, and innocently Beded) this Lady came and brought her Children to me, and falling at my Feet, wept and implor'd I would not own her Husband, for only she had right to him; we all were forced to discover to her the truth of the Matter, and that he had only married me to secure me from the Rage of my Parents; that if he were her Husband, she was still as intirely possest of him as ever, and that he had advanc'd her Fortune in what he had done, for she should have him restored with those Advantages that should make her Life, and that of her Children more Comfortable; and* Philander *making both her and the children considerable Presents, sent her away very well satisfied. After this, before People, we used him to a thousand Freedoms, but when alone, he retain'd his Respect intire; however this us'd him to something more Familiarity than formerly, and he grew to be more a Companion than a Servant, as indeed we desired he should; and of late have found him more presumptious than usual: And thus much more I must confess, I have reason to believe him a most passionate Lover, and have lately found he had Designs upon me, as you well know.*

Judge now, oh dear Octavio, *how unfortunate I am; yet judge too, whether I ought to esteem this a Marriage, or him a Husband: No,* reply'd *Octavio,* more briskly than before, *nor can he by the Laws of God or Man, pretend to such a Blessing, and you may be divorc'd.* Pleas'd with this Thought, he soon assum'd his native Temper of Joy and Softness, and making a thousand new Vows that he would perform all he had sworn on his part; and imploring and pressing her to renew those she had made to him, she obeys him; she makes a thousand grateful Returns, and they pass the Evening the most happily that ever Lovers did. By this time Supper was served up, noble and handsome; and after Supper

---

[a] When Henrietta Berkeley declared in court that she was married to William Turner he was immediately accused of being already married. Cf. Appendix I.

he led her to his Closet, where he presented her with Jewels and other Rareties of great Value, and omitted nothing that might oblige an Avaritious designing Woman, if *Silvia* had been such; nor any thing that might beget Love and Gratitude in the most insensible Heart: And all he did and all he gave was with a peculiar Grace, in which there lies as great an Obligation, as in the Gift it self: The handsom way of giving being an Art so rarely known, even to the most Generous. In these happy and glorious Moments of Love, wherein the Lover omitted nothing that could please, *Philander* was almost forgotten, for 'tis natural for Love to beget Love, and Inconstancy its Likeness, or Disdain: And we must conclude *Silvia* a Maid wholly insensible, if she had not been touch'd with Tenderness, and even Love it self, at all these extravagant marks of Passion in *Octavio*; and it must be confess'd, she was of a Nature soft and apt for Impression; she was, in a word, a Woman. She had her Vanities, and her little Fevibleses, and lov'd to see Adorers at her Feet, especially those in whom all things, all Graces, Charms of Youth, Wit and Fortune agreed to form for Love and Conquest: She naturally lov'd Power and Dominion; and it was her Maxim, That never any Woman was displeased to find she could beget Desire.

'Twas thus they liv'd with uninterrupted Joys, no Spies to pry upon their Actions, no false Friends to censure their real Pleasures, no Rivals to poyson their true Content, no Parents to give Bounds or grave Rules to the distruction of nobler lavish Love; but all the Day was past in new Delights, and every Day produc'd a thousand Pleasures; and even the Thoughts of Revenge were no more remembred on either side; it lessen'd in *Silvia*'s Heart, as Love advanced there, and her Resentment against *Philander* was lost in her growing Passion for *Octavio*: And sure if any Woman had Excuses for Loving and Inconstancy, the most Wise and Prudent must allow 'em now to *Silvia*; and if she had Reason for Loving, 'twas now, for what she paid the most deserving of his Sex, and whom she managed with that Art of Loving (if there be Art in Love) that she gain'd every Minute upon his Heart, and he became more and more her Slave, the more he found he was belov'd: In spight of all *Brilljard*'s Pretention he would have married her, but durst not do it while he remain'd in *Holland*, because of the Noise *Brilljard*'s Claim had made; and he fear'd the Displeasure of his Uncle, but waited for a more happy time, when he could settle his Affairs so as to remove her into *Flanders*,[a] tho' he could not tell how to accomplish that without ruining his Interest: These Thoughts alone took up his time whenever he was absent from *Silvia*, and would often give him abundance of Trouble, for he was given over to his Wish of possessing *Silvia*, and could not live without her; he lov'd too much, and thought and consider'd too little. These were his eternal Entertainments, when from the lovely Object of his Desire, which was as seldom as possible, for they were both unwilling to part; tho' Decency and Rest required it, a thousand soft things would hinder him, and make her willing to retain him; and tho' they were to meet again next Morning, they grudge themselves the parting Hours, and the Repose of Nature. He longs and languishes for the blessed Moment that shall give him to the Arms of the ravishing *Silvia*, and she finds but too much yielding on her part, in some of those silent lone Hours, when Love was most prevailing, and feeble Mortals most apt to be overcome by that insinuating God; so that tho' *Octavio* could not ask what he sigh'd and dy'd for; tho' he resolv'd he would not press her, tho' for the Safety of his Life, for any Favours; and tho', on the other side, *Silvia* resolv'd she would not grant, no, tho' mutual Vows had passed, tho' Love within pleaded, and almost unresistible Beauties and Inducements without, tho all the Powers of Love, of Silence, Night, and Opportunity, tho' on the very Point a thousand times of yielding, she had resisted all: But oh! one Night; let it not rise up in Judgment against her, you bashful modest Maids, who never yet try'd any powerful Minute; nor you chast Wives, who give no Opportunities: One night——they lost themselves in Dalliance, forgot how very near they were to yielding, and with imperfect Transports found themselves half dead with Love, clasp'd in each others Arms, betray'd by soft Degrees of Joy, to all they wished. 'Twould be too Amorous to tell you more; to tell you all that Night, that happy Night produc'd; let it suffice that *Silvia* yielded all, and made *Octavio* happier than a God. At first he found her weeping in his Arms, raving on what she had unconsideringly done; and with her soft Reproaches chiding her ravished Lover, who lay sighing by, unable to reply any other way, he held her fast in those Arms that trembled, yet with Love and new-past Joy; he found a Pleasure even in her

---

[a] Flanders lay to the south of the States of Holland and was under Spanish rule.

Railing, with a Tenderness that spoke more Love than any other Language Love could speak. Betwixt his Sighs he pleads his Rights of Love, and the Authority of his solemn Vows; he tells her that the Marriage Ceremony was but contrived to satisfy the Ignorant, and to proclaim his Title to the Crowd, but Vows and Contracts were the same to Heaven: He speaks—— and she believes; and well she might, for all he spoke was honourable Truth. He knew no Guile, but uttered all his Soul, and all that Soul was Honest, Just, and Brave; thus by degrees he brought her to a Calm.

In this soft Rancounter he had discovered a thousand new Charms in *Silvia*; and contrary to those Men, whose end of Love is Lust (which extinguish together) *Octavio* found increase of Tenderness from every Bliss she gave; and grew at last so fond——so doating on the still more charming Maid, that he neglected all his Interest, his Business in the State, and what he ow'd his Uncle, and his Friends, and became the common Theam over all the United Provinces, for his Wantonness and Luxury, as they were pleased to call it; and living so contrary to the Humour of those more sordid and slovenly Men of Quality, which make up the Nobility of that parcel of the World. For while thus he lived retired, scarce visiting any one, or permitting any to visit him, they charge him with a thousand Crimes of having given himself over to Effeminacy; as indeed he grew too Lazy in her Arms; neglecting Glory, Arms, and Power, for the more real Joys of Life; while she even Rifles him with Extravagancy; and grows so bold and hardy, that regarding not the Humours of the stingy censorious Nation, his Interest, or her own Fame, she is seen every day in his Coaches going to take the Air out of Town; puts him upon Balls, and vast expensive Treats; devises new Projects and ways of Diversion, till some of the more busie Impertinents of the Town made a publick Complaint to his Uncle, and the rest of the *States*, urging he was a Scandal to the Reverend and Honourable Society. On which it was decreed that he should either lose that Honour, or take up, and live more according to the Gravity and Authority of a Senator: This Incenses *Sebastian*, both against the States and his Nephew; for tho' he had often reproved and counselled him, yet he scorn'd his Darling should be school'd by his Equals in Power. So that resolving either to discard him, or draw him from the Love of this Woman; he one Morning goes to his Nephews House, and sending him up word by his

Page he would speak to him, he was conducted to his Chamber, where he found him in his Night-Gown: He began to upbraid him, first with his want of Respect and Duty to him, and next, of his Affairs, neglecting to give his Attendance on the Publick: He tells him he is become a Scandal to the Common-Wealth, and that he liv'd a lude Life with another Man's Wife: He tells him he has all her Story, and she was not only a Wife, but a scandalous Mistress too to *Philander. She boasts,* says he, *of Honourable Birth, but what's that, when her Conduct is Infamous? In short, Sir,* continued he, *your Life is obnoxious to the whole Province: Why, what Sir —— cannot honest Men's Daughters* (cry'd he, more angerly) *serve your turn, but you must crack a Commandment? Why, this is flat Adultery: A little Fornication in a civil way, might have been allow'd, but this is stark naught. In fine Sir, quit me this Woman, and quit her me presently; or, in the first place, I renounce thee, cast thee from me as a Stranger, and will leave thee to Ruine, and the incensed States. A little Pleasure——a little Recreation, I can allow: A Layer of Love, and a Layer of Business——But to neglect the Nation for a Wench, is flat Treason against the State; and I wish there were a Law against all such unreasonable Whore-Masters——that are States-Men —— for the rest 'tis no great matter. Therefore in a Word, Sir, leave me off this Mistress of yours, or we will secure her yet for a French Spy, that comes to debauch our Common-Wealths-Men ——· The States can do it Sir, they can*——Hitherto *Octavio* received all with Blush and Bow, in sign of Obedience; but when his Uncle told him the *States* would send away his Mistress; no longer able to contain his Rage, he broke out into all the Violence imaginable against them, and swore he would not now forego *Silvia* to be Monarch over all the nasty Provinces, and 'twas a greater Glory to be a Slave at her Feet. *Go, tell your States,* cry'd he——*They are a company of Cynical Fops, born to moyl on in sordid Business, who never were worthy to understand so great a Happiness of Life, as that of Nobler Love. Tell 'em, I scorn the dull Gravity of those Asses of the Common-Wealth, fit only to bear the dirty Load of State-Affairs, and die old busie Fools.* The Uncle, who little expected such a Return from him who used to be all Obedience, began more gently to perswade him with more solid Reason, but could get no other Answer from him, than that what he commanded he should find it Difficult to disobey; and so for that time they parted. Some days after (he never coming so much as near their Councils) they sent for him, to answer the Contempt: He came and received abundance of hard Reproaches, and finding they were resolved to Degrade him, he presently rallied them in Answer to all they said; nor could all the Cautions of his Friends perswade him to any Submission, after receiving so rough and ill-bred a Treatment as they gave him: And impatient to return to *Silvia*, where all his Joys were Centered, he was with much a-do perswaded to stay and hear the Resolution of the Council, which was to take from him those Honours he held amongst them; at which he cock'd and smil'd, and told 'em he receiv'd what he was much more proud of than of those useless Trifles they call'd Honours; and wishes they might treat all that served them at that ungrateful Rate: For he that had received a hundred Wounds, and lost a Stream of Blood for their Security, shall, if he kiss their Wives against their Wills, be banish'd like a Coward. So hasting from the Council, he got into his Coach, and went to *Silvia*. This incensed the old Gentlemen to a high Degree, and they carried it against the younger Party (because more in Number) That this *French* Lady, who was for high-Treason, as they call'd it, forc'd to fly *France*, should be no longer protected in *Holland*: And in order to her Removal, or rather their Revenge on *Octavio*, they sent out their Warrant to Apprehend her; and either to send her as an Enemy to *France*, or force her to some other part of the World. For a day or two *Sebastian*'s Interest prevailed for the stoping the Warrant; believing he should be able to bring his Nephew to some Submission, which when he found in vain, he betook himself to his Chamber, and refused any Visits or Diversions: By this time *Octavio*'s rallying the *States* was become the Jest of the Town, and all the Sparks laugh'd at them as they past, and Lampoon'd 'em to damnable *Dutch* Tunes, which so highly incens'd 'em that they sent immediately and serv'd the Warrant on *Silvia*, whom they surpriz'd in *Octavio*'s Coach, as she was coming from taking the Air. You may imagine what an Agony of Trouble and Grief our generous and surpriz'd Lover was in: It was in vain to make Resistance, and he who before would not have submitted to have sav'd his Life, to the *States*, now for the Preservation of one moments Consent to *Silvia*, he was ready to go and fall at their Feet, kiss their Shoes, and implore their Pity. He first accompanies her to the House of the Messenger, where he only is permitted to behold her with Eyes of dying Love, and unable to say any thing to her, left her with such Gifts, and Charge, to the Messengers Care, as might oblige him to treat her well; While *Silvia*, less surprized, bid him, at going from her, not to afflict himself for any thing she suffered; she found it was the Malice of the pevish old Magistrates, and that the most they could do to her, was to send her from him: This last she spoke with a Sigh, that pierced his Heart more sensibly than ever any thing yet had done; and he only reply'd (with a Sigh) *No* Silvia, *no rigid Power on Earth shall ever be able to deprive you of my eternal Adoration, or to separate me one Moment from* Silvia, *after she is compell'd to leave this ungrateful Place, and whose Departure I will hasten all that I can, since the Land is not worthy of so great a Blessing.* So leaving her for a little Space, he hasted to his Uncle, whom he found very much discontented: He throws himself at his Feet, and assails him with all the moving Eloquence of Sighs and Tears; in vain was all, in vain alas he pleads. From this he flies to Rage——and says all a distracted Lover could power forth to ease a tortured Heart; what Divinity did he not provoke? Wholly regardless even of Heaven and Man, he made a publick Confession of his Passion, deny'd her being married to *Brilljard*, and weeps as he protests her Innocence: He kneels again, implores and begs anew, and made the movingest Moan that ever touched a Heart, but could receive no other Return but Threats and Frowns: The old Gentleman had never been in Love since he was born, no not enough to marry, but bore an unaccountable Hate to the whole Sex, and therefore was pityless to all he could say on the Score of Love; tho' he endeavours to soften him by a thousand things more dear to him. *For my Sake, Sir,* said he, *if ever my soft Plea were grateful to you, when all your Joy was in the young* Octavio; *release, release, the charming* Silvia; *regard her tender Youth, her blooming Beauty, her timorous helpless Sex, her noble Quality, and save her from the rude Assaults of Power—— Oh save the Lovely Maid!* This he uttered with interrupting Sighs and Tears, which fell upon the Floor as he pursu'd the Obdurate on his Knees: At last Pity touch'd his Heart, and he said——*Spare, Sir, the Character of your inchanting* Circe;[a] *for I have heard too much of her, and what Mischiefs she has bred in* France; *abandoning her Honour, betraying a vertuous Sister, defaming her Noble Parents, and ruining an Illustrious young Noble Man, who was both her Brother and her Lover.* This

---

[a] Circe, the enchantress, used her magical powers to transform men into animals. In Homer's *Odyssey*, she transformed Odysseus's crew into swine, though he himself escaped with the help of Hermes. Circe was then forced to remove her spell from his men and she later became Odysseus's mistress, bearing him a son.

Sir, in short, is the Character of your Beauteous Innocent. Alas Sir,
reply'd *Octavio, you never saw this Maid! or if you had, you would
not be so cruel. Go to, Sir,* reply'd the old Gentleman, *I am not so
soon softened at the sight of Beauty. But do but see her, Sir,* reply'd
*Octavio, and then perhaps you will be charm'd like me—— You are a
Fop, Sir,* reply'd *Sebastian, and if you would have me allow any
Favor to your inchanting Lady, you must promise me first to abandon
her, and marry the Widow of Monsieur —— who is vastly Rich, and
whom I have so often recommended to you, she loves you too; and tho'
she be not fair, she has the best Fortune of any Lady in the* Netherlands. *On these Terms, Sir, I am for a Reconciliation with you, and
will immediately go and deliver the fair Prisoner, and she shall have
her Liberty to go or stay, or do what she please——and now, Sir, you
know my Will and Pleasure——Octavio* found it vain to pursue
him any further with his Petitions; only reply'd it was wonderous hard and cruel. To which the old one reply'd; *'Tis what
must be done, I have resolved it, or my Estate, in value, above two
hundred thousand Pounds, shall be disposed of to your Sister, the
Countess of* Clarinau: And this he ended with an Execration on
himself if he did not do; and he was a Man that always was
just to his Word.

Much more to this ungrateful effect he spoke, and *Octavio*
had Recourse to all the Dissimulation his generous Soul was
capable of; and 'twas the first base thing, and sure the last, that
ever he was guilty of. He promises his Uncle to obey all his
Commands and Injunctions, since he would have it so; and
only beg'd he might be permitted but one Visit, to take his last
Leave of her: This was at first refused, but at last, provided he
might hear what he said to her, he would suffer him to go: *For,*
said the crafty old Man (who knew too well the Cunning of
Youth) *I will have no Tricks put upon me; I will not be outwitted by a
young Knave:* This was the worst part of all; he knew, if he alone
could speak with her, they might have contriv'd, by handsome
agreeing Flattery, to have accomplish'd their Design, which
was; *first,* by the Authority of the old Gentleman to have freed
her from Confinement; and next, to have settled his Affairs in
the best Posture he could; and without valuing his Uncle's
Fortune, his own being greater, he resolv'd to go with her into
Flanders or *Italy*; but his going with him to visit her would
prevent whatever they might resolve: But since the Liberty of
Silvia was first to be considered, he resolves—— since it must be
so, and leaves the rest to Time and his good Fortune. *Well then,*

Sir, said *Octavio*, *since you have resolv'd your self, to be a Witness of those melancholy things, I shall possibly say to her, let us haste to end the great Affair——Hang it,* cry'd *Sebastian, if I go I shall abuse the young Hussie,*[a] *or commit some Indecency that will not be suitable to good Manners——I hope you will, not Sir——* reply'd *Octavio—— Whip 'em, whip 'em,* reply'd the Uncle, *I hate the young cozening Baggages,*[b] *that wander about the World undoing young extravagant Coxcombes; gots so, they are naught, stark-naught——Be sure you dispatch as soon as you can, and——do you hear—— le's have no Whineing. Octavio* overjoy'd he should have her released to Night, promised lavishly all he was urged to; and his own Coach being at the Gate, they both went immediately to the House of the Messenger; and all the way the old Gentleman did nothing but rail against the Vices of the Age, and the Sins of Villainous Youth; the Snares of Beauty, and the Danger of witty Women; and of how ill Consequences these were to a Common-Wealth. He said, if he were to make Laws, he would confine all young Women to Monasteries, where they should never see Man till Forty, and then come out and marry for Generation sake, no more: For his part he had never seen that Beauty yet that could inspire him with that silly thing call'd Love; and wonder'd what the Devil ail'd all the young Fellows of this Age, that they talk'd of nothing else: At this rate they discoursed till they arrrived at the Prison, and calling for the Messenger, he conducted them both to the Chamber of the fair Prisoner, who was laid on a Couch, near which stood a Table with two Candles, which gave a great Light to that part of the Room, and made *Silvia* appear more fair than ever, if possible. She had not that day been dress'd but in a rich Night-Gown, and Cornets[c] of the most advantageous Fashion: At his Approach she blush'd (with a secret Joy, which never had possessed her Soul for him before) and spread a thousand Beauties round her fair Face: She was leaping with a transported Pleasure to his Arms, when she perceived an old Grave Person follow him into the Room: At which she reassum'd a Strangeness, a melancholy Languish-ment, which charm'd no less than her Gayety. She approaches 'em with a modest Grace in her beautiful Eyes; and by the Reception *Octavio* gave her, she found that reverend Person

---

[a] A worthless, impertinent girl.

[b] Saucy women.

[c] Bell-shaped cuffs on sleeves.

was his Uncle, or at least some body of Authority; and therefore
assuming a Gravity unusual, she received 'em with all the
Ceremony due to their Quality: And first she address'd herself
to the old Gentleman, who stood gazing at her, without Mo-
tion; at which she was a little out of Countenance. When *Octavio*
perceiving it, approach'd his Uncle, and cry'd, *Sir, This is the
Lady*——*Sebastian* starting as from a Dream, cry'd——*Pardon me,
Madam, I am a Fellow whom Age hath rendered less Ceremonious than
Youth: I have never yet been so happy as to have been used to a fair
Lady; Women never took up one Minute of my more precious time, but
I have been a Satyr*[a] *upon the whole Sex: And if my Treatment of you
be rougher than your Birth and Beauty Merits, I beseech you*——*fair
Creature, pardon it, since I am come in order to do you Service. Sir,*
reply'd *Silvia* (blushing with Anger at the Presence of a Man
who had contributed to the having brought her to that place) *I
cannot but wonder at this sudden Change of Goodness, in a Person to
whom I am indebted for part of my Misfortune, and which I shall no
longer esteem as such, since it has occasioned me a Happiness, and an
Honour, to which I could no other way have arrived.* This last she
spoke with usual insinuating Charms; the little Affectation of
the Voice sweeten'd to all the Tenderness it was possible to put
on, and so easy and natural to *Silvia*: And if before the old
Gentleman were seized with some unusual Pleasure, which
before he never felt about his icy and insensible Heart, and
which now began to thaw at the Fire of her Eyes——I say, if
before he were surprized with looking, what was he when she
spoke——with a Voice so soft, and an Air so bewitching? He
was all Eyes and Ears, and had use of no other Sense but what
inform'd those: He gazes upon her, as if he waited and listen'd
what she would farther say; and she stood waiting for his
Reply, till asham'd, she turn'd her Eyes into her Bosom, and
knew not how to proceed. *Octavio* views both by turns, and
knows not how to begin the Discourse again, it being his
Uncle's Cue to speak: But finding him altogether mute——he
steps to him, and gently pull'd him by the Sleeve——but finds
no Motion in him; he speaks to him but in vain, for he could
hear nothing but *Silvia*'s charming Voice; nor saw nothing but
her lovely Face, nor attended any thing but when she would
speak again, and look that way. At this *Octavio* smil'd, and

---

[a] Satire.

taking his Adorable by the Hand, he led her nearer her admiring Adversary, whom she approach'd with Modesty and Sweetness in her Eyes, that the old Fellow having never before beheld the like Vision was wholly vanquish'd, and his old Heart burnt in the Socket, which being his last Blaze made the greater Fire. *Fine Lady*, cry'd he——*or rather fine Angel, how is it I shall expiate for a Barbarity that nothing could be guilty of but the Brute, who had not learn'd Humanity from your Eyes: What Atonement can I make for my Sin; and how shall I be punished?* Sir, reply'd *Silvia, if I can merit your Esteem and Assistance, to deliver me from this cruel Confinement, I shall think of what's past as a Joy, since it renders me worthy of your Pity and Compassion. To answer you, Madam, were to hold you under this unworthy Roof too long; therefore let me convince you of my Service, by leading you to a Place more fit for so fair a Person.* And calling for the Messenger, he ask'd him if he would take his Bail for his fair Prisoner; who reply'd, *Your Lordship may Command all things:* So throwing him a little Purse, about thirty Pounds in Gold, he bid him drink the Ladies Health; and without more Ceremony or talk, led her to the Coach; and never so much as asking her whether she would go, insensibly carries her, where he had a mind to have her, to his own House: This was a little Affliction to *Octavio*, who nevertheless durst not say any thing to his Uncle, nor so much as to ask him the Reason why: But being arrived all thither, he conducts her into a very fair Apartment, and bade her there command that World he could command for her: He gave her there a very magnificent Supper, and all three supp'd together, *Octavio* and *Silvia* still wondering what would be the Issue of this Business; for *Octavio* could not imagine that his Uncle, who was a single Man, and a grave Senator, one fam'd for a Woman Hater, a great Railer at the Vices of young Men, should keep a fair young single Woman in his House. But it growing late, and no Preparation for her Departing, she took the Courage to say——*Sir, I am so extreamly Obliged to you, and have received so great a Favour from you, that I cannot flatter myself 'tis for any Vertue in me, or meerly out of Compassion to my Sex, that you have done this; but for somebody's Sake to whom I am more enjaged than I am aware of; and when you pass'd your Parole for my Liberty, I am not so vain to think it was for my Sake; therefore pray inform me, Sir, how can I pay this Debt, and to whom, and who it is you require should be bound for me, to save you harmless.* Madam cry'd *Sebastian, tho' there need no greater Security than your own Innocence, yet least that Innocence should not be sufficient to guard you from the Outrage of a People approaching to Savages. I begg, for your own Security, not mine, that you will make this House your Sanctuary; my Power can save you from impending Harms, and all that I call mine, you shall command.* At this she blushing bow'd, but durst not make Reply to contradict him: She knew at least that there she was safe, and well, free from Fear of the Tyranny of the rest, or any other Apprehension: 'Tis true she found by the Shyness of *Octavio* towards her before his Uncle, that she was to manage her Amour with him by stealth, till they could contrive matters more to their Advantage: She therefore finding she should want nothing, but as much of *Octavio*'s Conversation as she desired; she begg'd he would give her Leave to write a Note to her Page, who was a faithful sober Youth, to bring her Jewels, and what things she had of Value, to her, which she did, and received those of her Servants together, who found a perfect Welcome to the old Lover; but *Antonett* had like to have lost her Place, but that *Octavio* pleaded for her, and she herself confessing 'twas Love to the false *Brilljard*, that made her do that foolish thing (in which she vow'd she thought no harm, tho' it was like to have cost so dear) she was again received into Favour: So that for some Days *Silvia* found herself very much at her Ease with the old Gentleman, and had no want of any thing but *Octavio*'s Company: But she had the Pleasure to find by his Eyes and Sighs he wanted hers more: He dy'd every day, and his fair Face faded like falling Roses: Still she was gay; for if she had it not about her, she assumed it to keep him in Heart: she was not displeased to see the old Man on Fire too, and fancied some Diversion from the Intrigue: But he concealed his Passion all he could, both to hide it from his Nephew, and because he knew not what he ail'd: A strange change he found, a wonderous Disorder in Nature, but could not give a Name to it, nor Sigh aloud for fear he should be heard, and lose his Reputation; especially for this Woman, on whom he had rail'd so lavishly. One day therefore, after a Night of Torment very incommode to his Age, he takes *Octavio* into the Garden alone, telling him he had a great Secret to impart to him. *Octavio* guessing what it might be, put his Heart in as good order as he could to receive it: He at least knew the worst was but for him at last to steal *Silvia* from him, if he should be weak enough to doat on the young Charmer, and therefore resolv'd to hear with patience. But if he were prepared to attend, the other was not prepared to begin, and so both walked many silent Turns about the Garden. *Sebastian* had a-mind to ask a thousand Questions of his Nephew, who he found, maugre of his Vows of deserting *Silvia*, had no power of doing it: He had a-mind to urge him to marry the Widow, but durst not now press it, tho' he used to do so, least he should take it for Jealousy in him; nor durst he now forbid him seeing her, least he should betray the Secrets of his Soul: He began every Moment to love him less, as he loved *Silvia* more, and beholds him as an Enimy to his Repose, nay his very Life. At last the old Man (who thought if he brought his Nephew forth under pretence of a Secret, and said nothing to him, it would have look'd ill) began to speak. *Octavio*, said he, *I have hitherto found you so just in all you have said, that 'twere a Sin to doubt you, in what relates to* Silvia. *You have told me she is nobly Born; and you have with infinite Imprecations convinced me she is Vertuous; and lastly, you have sworn she was not Married*——At this he sigh'd and paus'd, and left *Octavio* trembling with Fear of the Result: A thousand times he was like to have denyed all, but durst not defame the most sacred Idol of his Soul: Sometimes he thought his Uncle would be generous, and think it fit to give him *Silvia*; but that Thought was too Seraphick[a] to remain a Moment in his Heart. *Sir*, reply'd *Octavio*, *I own I said so of* Silvia, *and hope no Action she has committed since she had a Protection under your Roof has contradicted any thing I said*, No, said *Sebastian*, sighing——and pausing, as loath to speak more: *Sir*, said *Octavio, I suppose this is not the Secret you had to impart to me, for which you separate me to this lonely Walk; fear not to trust me with it, whatever it be, for I am so intirely your own, that I will grant, submit, prostrate myself, and give up all my Will, Power, and Faculties to your Interest or Designs.* This incouraged the old Lover, who reply'd —— *Tell me on Truth,* Octavio, *which I require of you, and I will desire no more*—— *Have not you had the Possession of this fair Maid?* You apprehend me: Now it was that he fear'd what Design the Amorous old Gentleman had in his Head and Heart; and was at a loss what to say, whether to give him some Jealousy that he had known and possess'd her, and so prevent his Designs on her; or by saying he had not, to leave her Defenceless to his Love. But on second Thoughts, he could not resolve to say any thing to the Disadvantage of *Silvia*, tho' to save his own Life;

---

[a] A Seraph was a celestial being associated with love, illumination and purity.

and therefore assured his Uncle he never durst assume the Boldness to ask so rude a Question of a Woman of her Quality: And much more he spoke to that purpose to convince him. That 'tis true he wou'd have Marry'd her, if he cou'd have gain'd his consent; maugre all the Scandal that the malicious World had thrown upon her. But since he was positive in his command for the Widow, he wou'd bend his Mind to Obedience. *In that, replied Sebastian, you are Wise, and I am glad all your Youthful Fires are blown over; and having once fixt you in the World as I design, I have resolved on an Affair* —— At this again he paused —— *I am, says he, in Love,* —— *I think it is Love, or that which you call so: I cannot eat nor sleep, nor even pray, but this fair Stranger interposes; or if by chance I slumber, all my Dreams are of her; I see her, I touch her, I imbrace her, and find a Pleasure even then that all my waking Thoughts cou'd never procure me. If I go to the State House I mind nothing there, my Heart's at home with the Young Gentlewoman, on the* Change *or wheresoever I go, my restless Thoughts present her still before me: And prethee tell me, is not this Love,* Octavio? *It may arrive to Love,* replied the blushing Youth, *if you shou'd fondly give way to it: But you are Wise and Grave, and hate all Women, Sir, till about Forty, and then for Generation only: You are above the Follies of vain Youth. And let me tell you, Sir, without Offending, Already you are charged with a Thousand little Vanities unsuitable to your Years, and the Character you have had, and the Figure you have made in the World. I heard a Lampoon on you the other day,* —— *Pardon my Freedom, Sir, for keeping a Beauty in your House, who they are pleased to say was my Mistress before.* And pulling out a Lampoon, which his Page had before given him, he gave it his Uncle. But instead of making him resolve to quit *Silvia*, it only serv'd to incense him against *Octavio*; he rail'd at all Wits, and swore there was not a more dangerous Enemy to a civil, sober Commonwealth: That a Poet was to be banish'd as a Spy, or hang'd as a Traytor: That it ought to be as much against the Law to let 'em live, as to Shoot with white Powder,[a] and that to write Lampoons should be put into the Statue against Stabbing. And cou'd he find the Rogue that had the Wit to write that, he wou'd make him a warning to all the Race of that Damnable Vermin; what to abuse a Magistrate, one of the States, a very Monarch of the Commonwealth! —— 'twas Abominable and not to be born, —— and

---

[a] A type of gunpowder which was meant to explode without making any noise.

looking on his Nephew, —— and considering his Face awhile,
he cry'd, —— *I Fancy, Sir, by your Physiognomy, that you your self
have a hand in this Libel:* At which *Octavio* blush'd, which he
taking for guilt, flew out into terrible Anger against him, not
suffering him to speak for himself, or clear his Innocence. And
as he was going in this Rage from him, having forbidden him
ever to set his Foot within his Doors, he told him,——*If,* said
he, *the scandalous Town, from your Instructions, have such Thoughts
of me, I will convince it by Marrying this fair Stranger the first thing I
do: I cannot doubt but to find a welcom since she is a Banish'd Woman,
without Friend or Protection; and especially when she shall see how
civilly you have handled her here, in your Dogerel Ballad: I'll teach you
to be a Wit, Sir; and so your Humble Servant.* —— And leaving him
almost wild with his Fears, he went directly to *Silvia,* where he
told her, his Nephew was going to make up the Match between
himself and Madam the Widow of —— and that he had made a
scandalous Lampoon on her Fair self. He forgot nothing that
might make her hate the Amiable young Nobleman, whom she
knew too well to believe that any thing of this was other than
the effects of his own growing Passion for her. For tho' she saw
Octavio every day, in this time she had remain'd at his Uncles,
yet the Old Lover so watch'd their very Looks, that 'twas
impossible almost to tell one anothers Heart by any Glance
there. But *Octavio* had once in this time convey'd a Letter to her,
which having Opportunity to do he put it into her Comb-box,
when he was with his Uncle one day in her Dressing-room; for
he durst not trust her Page, and less *Antonett,* who had before
betray'd 'em: And having for *Silvia*'s release so solemnly Sworn
to his Uncle, (to which Vows he took Religious care to keep
him.) He had so perfect an awe upon his Spirits from every
Look and Command of his Uncles, he took infinitely heed how
he gave him any Umbrage by any Action of his; and the rather
because he hoped when time shou'd serve to bring about his
Business of stealing *Silvia* from him, for she was kept and
guarded like a mighty Heiress; so that by this prudent Management on both sides, they heighten'd the growing Love in every
Heart. In that Billet which he dropt in her Comb-box, he did not
only made Ten thousand Vows of Eternal Passion and Faith,
and beg the same assurance of her again; but told her he was
secur'd (so well he thought of her) from fears of his Uncles
Addresses to her, and beg'd she wou'd not let 'em perplex her,
but rather serve her for her diversion; that she should from time

to time write him all he said to her, and how he treated her when alone; and that since the Old Lover was so watchful, she should not trust her Letters with any body; but as she walk'd out into the Garden, she shou'd in passing throw the Hall, put her Letter in at the broken Glass of an Old Sedan[a] that stood there, and had stood for several Years; and that his own Page, whom he could trust, shou'd, when he came with him to his Uncles, take it from thence. —— Thus every Day they writ, and received the dearest returns in the World; where all the Satisfaction, that Vows oft repeated cou'd give, was rendred each other; with an account from *Silvia* that was very pleasant, of all the Passion of the Doating Old *Sebastian*, the Presents he made her, the Fantastick Youth he would assume, and the unusual manner of his Love, which was a great diversion to both; and this Difficulty of speaking to *Silvia*, and entertaining her with Love, tho' it had its Pains, had its infinite Pleasures too; it increas'd their Love on both sides, and all their Wishes. But now by this last Banishment from the House where she was, to lose that only Pleasure of beholding the Adorable Maid, gave him all the Pains without the hope of one Pleasure; and he began to fear he should have a World of Difficulty to secure the dear Object of his continual Thoughts: He found no way to send to her, and dreads all his Malicious Uncle and Rival may say to his disadvantage: He dreads even that infinite Tenderness and Esteem he had for the good Old Man, who had been so fond a Parent to him; least even that should make him unwilling to use that Extremity against him in the regaining *Silvia*, which he would use to any other Man. Oh, how he Curses the fatal hour that ever he implored his Aid for her Release; and having overcome all Difficulties, even that of his Fears of *Philander*, (from whom they had received no Letter in Two Months) and that of *Silvia*'s Disdain, and had Establish'd himself in her Soul and her Arms; he should, by employing his Uncle's Authority for *Silvia*'s Service, be so Unfortunate to involve 'em into new Dangers and Difficulties, of which he could foresee no other end, than that which must be fatal to some of 'em. But he believed half his Torture would be eased, could he but write to *Silvia*, for see her he could not hope: He bethought himself of a way at last.

---

[a] A vehicle consisting of an enclosed seat carried by two chairmen with poles.

His Uncle had belonging to his House the most fine Garden of any in that Province, where those things are not much esteem'd, in which the Old Gentleman took wonderful Delight, and kept a Gardener and his Family in a little House at the farther end of the Garden, on purpose to look to it and dress it. This Man had a very great Veneration for *Octavio*, whom he call'd his Young Lord. Sure of the Fidelity of this Gardener, when it was dark enough to conceal him, he wrapt himself in his Cloak and got him thither by a back-way, where with Presents he soon won those to his Interest, who would before have been Commanded by him in any Service. He had a little clean Room, and some little *French* Novels[a] which he brought; and there he was as well conceal'd as if he had been at the *Indies;*[b] he left word at home that he was gone out of Town. He knew well enough that *Silvia*'s Lodgings look'd that way. And when it was dark enough he walk'd under her Window, till he saw a Candle lighted in *Silvia*'s Bed-Chamber, which was as great a Joy to him as the Star that Guides the Traveller, or wandring Seaman, or the Lamp at *Sestos*,[c] that Guided the Ravish'd Lover o'er the *Hellespont*. And by that time he could imagine all in Bed, he made a little noise with a Key on the Pummel of his Sword;[d] but whether *Silvia* heard it or not I cannot tell, but she anon came to the Window, and putting up the Shash, leaned on her Arms and look'd into the Garden. Oh! who but he himself that Lov'd so well as *Octavio*, can express the Transports he was in at the Sight? which more from the Sight within than that without, he saw was the lovely *Silvia*; whom calling softly by her Name, answered him as if she knew the welcome Voice, and cry'd, —— *Whose there, Octavio?* She was soon Answer'd you may imagine. And they began the most indearing Conversation that ever Love could dictate. He complains on his Fate that sets 'em at that distance, and she pities him. He makes a Thousand Doubts, and she undeceives 'em all. He Fears, and she convinces his Error, and is impatient at his Suspicions. She will not

---

[a] In the 1680s the English novel was in its infancy. Its origins lay partly in short French and Spanish picaresque novels which were available in translation in London at this time.

[b] The West Indies.

[c] A small town on the banks of the Hellespont in Thrace and the home of Hero. Her lover, Leander, swam across the Hellespont each night to visit her, guided by a lamp burning in her tower. After Leander drowned in a storm one night, Hero threw herself into the sea.

[d] A pummel is a large knob on the end of a sword-hilt.

indure him to question a Heart that has given him so many proofs of its Tenderness and Gratitude: She tells him her own Wishes, how soft and fervent they are; and assures him, he is extreamly oblig'd to her —— *Since for you* ——*my Charming Friend*, said she to Octavio, *I have refus'd this Night to Marry your Uncle; have a care*, said she, Smiling, *how you treat me, least I revenge my self on you; become your Aunt, and bring Heirs to the Estate you have a Right to: The Writings of all which I have now in my Chamber, and which were but just now laid at my Feet, and which I cannot yet get him to receive back. And to oblige me to a compliance, has told me, how you have deceived me, by giving your self to another, and exposing me in Lampoons.* —— To this *Octavio* would have replied, but she assured him she needed no Argument to convince her of the Falsehood of all. He Sighs, and told her all she said, tho' Dear and Charming was not sufficient to ease his Heart, for he foresaw a World of hazzard to get her from thence, and mischiefs if she remained; insomuch that he caus'd the Tears to flow from the fair Eyes of *Silvia*, with the Reflections on her rigid Fortune. And she cry'd, *Oh, my* Octavio! *what strange Fate or Stars rul'd my Birth, that I shou'd be born the ruine of what I Love, or of those that Love me?* At this rate they past the Night, sometimes more soft, sometimes incouraging one another; but the last result was to contrive the means of escaping. He fancy'd she might easily do it by the Garden from that Window: But that he was not sure he could trust the Gardener so far, who in all things would serve him, in which his Lord and Master was not Injured; and he amongst the rest of the Servants, had Order not to suffer *Silvia* out of the Garden, for which reason he kept a strict Guard on that back-Door. Some way must be found out which yet was not, and left to time. He told her where he was, and that he wou'd not stir from thence, till he were secur'd of her flight: And Day coming on, tho' loath, yet for fear of Eyes and Ears that might Spy upon 'em, he retired to his little Lodging and *Silvia* to Bed; after giving and receiving a Thousand Vows and Farewels. The next Night he came to the same place, but instead of entertaining her——he only saw her softly put up the Shash a little, and throw something white out of the Window and retire. He was wondring at the meaning, but taking up what was thrown down, he found and smelt it was *Silvia's* Handkerchief, in which was ty'd up a *Billet*: He went to his little Lodging and read it.

Silvia *to* Octavio.

Go from my Window my adorable Friend, and be not afflicted that I do not entertain you, as I had the Joy to do last Night, for both our Voices were heard by some one that Lodges below, and tho' your Uncle could not tell me any part of our Conversation, yet he heard I talk'd to somebody: I have perswaded him the Fellow dream'd, who gave him this Intelligence, and he is almost satisfied he did so; however hazard not thy dear self any more so, but let me lose for a while the greatest Happiness this Earth can afford me (in the Circumstances of our Fortunes) rather than expose what is dearer to me than Life or Honour: Pity the Fate I was born to, and expect all things from

Your Silvia.

I will wait at the Window for your Answer, and let you down a Ribband, by which I will draw it up: But as you love me do not speak.

He had no sooner read this, but he went to write an Answer, which was this.

Octavio *to* Silvia.

Complain not, thou Goddess of my Vows, on the Fate thou wert born to procure to all Mankind: but thank Heaven for having received ten thousand Charms that can recompence all the Injuries you so unwillingly do us: And who would not implore his Ruine from all the angry Powers, if in return they would give him so glorious a Reward? Who would not be undone to all the trifling Honours of the mistaken World; to find himself in lieu of all, possess'd of the Ravishing Silvia*? But oh! where is that presumptious Man, that can at the price of all, lay claim to so vast a Blessing? Alas my* Silvia*, even while I dare call you mine, I am not that hoping Slave, no not after all the valued dear things you*

have said and vow'd to me last Night in the Garden, welcome to my
Soul as Life after a Sentence of Death, or Heaven after Life is ended.
But, oh Silvia! all this, even all you uttered from your dear Mouth is
not sufficient to support me: Alas I die for Silvia; I am not able to bear
the cruel Absence longer, therefore without Delay assist me to contrive
your Escape, or I shall die and leave you to the Ravage of his Love who
holds thee from me; the very Thoughts of that is worse than Death. I
die, alas I die, for an intire Possession of thee: Oh let me grasp my
Treasure, let me ingross it all, here in my longing Arms. I can no
longer languish at this Distance from my eternal Joy, my Life, my
Soul! But oh I Rave! and while I should be speaking a thousand useful
things, I am telling you my Pain, a Pain that you may guess; and
confounding myself between those and their Remedies, am able to fix on
nothing: Help me to think, oh my dear charming Creature, help me to
think how I shall bear thee off! Take your own Measures, flatter him
with Love; sooth him to Faith and Confidence, and then——oh pardon
me if there be Baseness in the Action —— then——Cozen him——
Deceive him——any thing——for he deserves it all, that thinks that
lovely Body was form'd for his Imbraces, whom Age has rendered fitter
for a Grave. Form any Plots, use every Stratagem to save the Life of

Your Octavio.

He writ this in Hast and Disorder, as you may plainly see by
the Stile, and went to the Window with it, where he found
Silvia leaning expecting him: The Shashes were up, and he
toss'd it in the Handkerchief into her Window: She read it, and
writ an Answer back as soft as Love could form, to send him
pleased to Bed; wherein she commanded him to hope all things
from her Wit and industrious Love.

This had partly the Effects she wished, and after kissing his
Hand, and throwing it up towards *Silvia*, they parted as silent
as the Night from Day, which was now just dividing——so long
they stay'd, tho' but to look at each other; so that all the Morning was pass'd in Bed to make the Day seem shorter, which was
too tedious to both: This Pleasure he had after Noon, towards
the Evening, that when *Silvia* walked, as she alwaies did in the
Garden, he could see her thorow the Glass of his Window, but
durst not open it; for the old Gentleman was ever with her. In
this time *Octavio* fail'd not however to essay the good Nature of
the Gardener in order to *Silvia*'s Flight, but found there was no

dealing with him in this Affair; and therefore durst not come right down to the Point: The next Night he came under the Beloved Window again, and found the sacred Object of his Wishes leaning in the Window expecting him: To whom, as soon as she heard his Tread on the Gravel, she threw down a Handkerchief again, which he took up, and toss'd his own with a soft complaining Letter to entertain her till his Return; for he hasted to read hers, and swep'd the Garden as he pass'd as swift as Wind; so impatient he was to see the Inside——which he found thus.

Silvia *to* Octavio.

I Beg, my charming Friend, you will be assur'd of all I have promised you; and to believe that, but for the Pleasure of those dear Billets I receive from you, I could as little support this cruel Confinement as you my Absence. I have but one Game to play, and I beseech you not to be surpriz'd at it; 'tis to promise to marry Sebastian: He is eternally at my Feet, and either I must give him my Vow to become his Wife, or give him hope of other Favours. I am so intirely yours, that I will be guided by you which I shall Flatter him in, to gain my Liberty, for if I grant either he has proposed to carry me to his Country-House, two Leagues from the Town, and there Consummate whatever I design to bless him with; and this is it that has wrought my Consent, that we being to go alone, only my own Servants, you may easily take me thence by Force upon the Road, or after our Arrival, where he will not guard me perhaps so strictly as he does here: For that, I leave it to your Conduct, and expect your Answer to

Your Impatient

Silvia.

He immediately sate down and writ this.

Octavio *to* Silvia.

Have a Care, my Charming Fair, how you play with Vows; and
however you are forc'd for that Religious End of saving your Honour,
to deceive the poor old Lover, whom, by Heaven, I pity; yet rather let
me die than know you can be guilty of Vow-Breach, tho' made in jest. I
am well pleased at the Glimpse of Hope you give me, that I shall see you
at his Villa; and doubt not but to find a way to secure you to myself:
Say any thing, promise to sacrifice all to his Desire; but oh, do not give
away thy dear, thy precious self by Vow, to any but the Languishing

Octavio.

After he had writ this he hast'd and throws it into her Window, and return'd to Bed without seeing her, which was no small Affliction to his Soul: He had an ill Night of it, and fancied a thousand tormenting things; That the old Gentleman might then be with her; and if alone, what might he not perswade by force of rich Presents, of which his Uncle was well stored: And so he guess'd, and as he guess'd it proved, as by his next Nights Letter he was inform'd, that the old Lover no sooner saw *Silvia* retire, but having a mind to try his Fortune in some Critical Minute——for such a Minute he had heard there was that favoured Lovers; but he goes to his Closet, and taking out some Jewels of great Value, to make himself the more welcome, he goes directly to *Silvia*'s Chamber, and entered just as she had taken up *Octavio*'s Letter, and clap'd it in her Bosom as she heard some body at the Door; but was not in a little Confusion when she saw who it was; which she excused, by telling him she was surpriz'd to find herself with a Man in her Chamber: That there he fell to pleading his cause of Love; and offered her again to settle his Estate upon her, and implor'd she would be his Wife. After a thousand faint Denials, she told him she could not possibly receive that Honour, but it she could, she would have look'd upon it as a great Favour from Heaven; at that he was Thunder-struck, and look'd as gastly as if his Mothers Ghost had frighten'd him; and after much Debate, Love and

Grief on his side, Design and Dissimulation on hers, she gave him Hopes that Aton'd for all she had before said; insomuch that before they parted an absolute Bargain was struck up, and he was to settle part of his Estate upon her, as also that *Villa*, to which he had resolved in two days to carry her; in earnest to this he presents her a Necklace of Pearls of good Value, and other Jewels, which was the best Rhetorick he had yet spoke to her; and now she appear'd the most Complaisant Lady in the World, she suffers him to talk wantonly to her, nay even to kiss her, and rub his grizly Beard on her divine Face, grasp her Hands, and touch her Breast; a Blessing he had never before arriv'd to with any body above the Quality of his own Servant-Maid. To all which she makes the best Resistance she can, under the Circumstances of one who was to deceive well; and while she loaths she seems well pleas'd, while the gay Jewels sparkled in her Eyes and *Octavio* in her Heart; so fond is Youth of Vanities, and to purchase an addition of Beauty at any Price. Thus with her pretty Flatteries she wrought upon his Soul, and smil'd and look'd him into Faith; loth to depart she sends him pleas'd away, and having her Heart the more inclin'd to *Octavio* by being Persecuted with his Uncles Love (for by Comparison she finds the mighty Difference) she sets herself to write him the Account of what I have related; this Nights Adventure and Agreement between his Uncle and herself. She tells him that to Morrow, for now 'twas almost Day, she had promised him to go to his *Villa*: She tells him at what rate she has purchased the Blessing expected; and lastly, leaves the management of the rest to him, who needs not be instructed. This Letter he receiv'd the next Night, at the old place, and *Silvia* with it lets down a Velvet Night Bag, which contain'd all the Jewels and things of Value she had receiv'd of himself, his Uncle, or any other: After which he retired, and was pretty well at ease, with the imagination he should ere long be made Happy in the Possession of *Silvia*: In order to it the next Morning he was early up, and dressing himself in a great course Campagne-Coat[a] of the Gardeners, putting up his Hair, as well as he could, under a Country-Hat, he got on a Horse that suited his Habit, and rides to the *Villa*, whither they were to come, and which he knew perfectly well every Room of; for there our Hero was born. He went to a little

---

[a] A soldier's greatcoat.

Caberet[a] in the Village, from whence he could survey all the great House, and see every Body that pass'd in and out: He remain'd fix'd at the Window, fill'd with a thousand Agitations; this he had resolv'd, not to set upon the good old Man as a Thief or Robber; nor could he find in his Heart or Nature to injure him, tho' but in a little afrighting him, who had given him so many anxious Hours, and who had been so unjust to desire that Blessing himself, he would not allow him; and to believe that a Vertue in himself, which he exclaim'd against as so great a Vice in his Nephew; nevertheless he resolv'd to deceive him, to save his own Life. And he wanted that nice part of Generosity, as to satisfy a little unnecessary Lust in an old Man, to ruin the eternal Content of a young one, so nearly allied to his Soul, as was his own dear proper Person. While he was thus considering he saw his Uncle's Coach coming, and *Silvia* with that doting Lover in it, who was that day dressed in all the Fopperies of Youth, and everything was young and gay about him but his Person, that was Winter it self, disguised in artificial Spring; and he was altogether a meer Contradiction: But who can guess the Disorders and Paintings of *Octavio*'s Heart at the Sight; and tho' he had resolved before he would not to save his Life lay violent Hands on his old Parent; yet at their Approach, at their presenting themselves together before his Eyes, as two Lovers going to betray him to all the Miseries, Pangs, and Confusions of Love, going to possess——her, the dear Object and certain Life of his Soul, and she the Parent of him, to whom she had disposed of herself so intirely already, he was provok'd to break from all his Resolutions, and with one of those two Pistols he had in his Pockets, to have sent unerring Death to his old amorous Heart: But that Thought was no sooner born than stifled in his Soul, where it met with all the Sence of Gratitude that ever could present the tender Love and dear Care of a Parent there; and the Coach passing into the Gate put him upon new Designs, and before they were finished he saw *Silvia*'s Page coming from the House, after seeing his Lady to her Apartment, and being show'd his own, where he laid his Vallice[b] and Riding-things, and was now come out to look about a Country where he had never been before. *Octavio* goes down and meets him, and ventures to make himself known to

---

[a] A drinking house or tavern.
[b] Valise or carrying case.

him: And so infinitely glad was the Youth to have an Opportunity to serve him, that he vow'd he would not only do it with his Life, on Occasion, but believ'd he could do it effectually, since the old Gentleman had no sort of Jealousie now; especially since they had so prudently manag'd Matters in this time of his Ladies remaining at *Sebastian's* House. *So that, Sir, it will not be difficult,* says the generous Boy, *for me to convey you to my Lodging when it is dark.* He told him his Lady cast many a longing Look out towards the Road as she pass'd, *for you, I am sure my Lord——for she had told both myself and* Antonett *of her Design before, least our Surprize or Resistance should prevent any Force you might use on the Road, to take her from my Lord* Sebastian: *She sigh'd and look'd on me as she alighted, with Eyes, my Lord, that told me her Grief for your Disappointment.* You may easily imagine how transported the poor *Octavio* was; he kiss'd and imbrac'd the Amiable Boy a thousand times; and taking a Ring from his Finger of considerable Value, gave it the dear Reviver of his Hopes. *Octavio* already knew the Strength of the House, which consisted but of a Gardener, whose Wife was House-keeper, and their Son, who was his Fathers Servant in the Garden, and their Daughter, who was a sort of Maid-servant: And they had brought only the Coach-man, and one Foot-man, who were likely to be mirrily imploy'd in the Kitchin at Night when all got to Supper together. I say, *Octavio* already knew this, and there was now nothing that opposed his Wishes: So that dismissing the dear Boy he remained the rest of the tedious Day at the *Caberet,* the most impatient of Night of any Man on Earth: And when the Boy appear'd it was like the Approach of an Angel. He told him his Lady was the most Melancholy Creature that ever Eyes beheld, and that to conceal the Cause, she had feigned herself Ill, and had not stir'd from her Chamber all the day: That the old Lover was perpetually with her, and the most concern'd Doatard that ever *Cupid* inslav'd: That he had so wholly taken up his Lady with his disagreeable Entertainment, that it was impossible either by a Look or Note to inform her of his being so near her, whom she considered as her present Defender, and her future Happiness. *But this Evening,* continued the Youth, *as I was waiting on her at Supper, she spy'd the Ring on my Finger, which, my Lord, your Bounty made me Master of this Morning. She blush'd a Thousand times and fix'd her Eyes upon it, for she knew it, and was Impatient to have ask'd me some Questions, but contain'd her Words. And after that I saw a Joy dance in her lovely Eyes, that told me, She devin'd you were not far from thence. Therefore I beseech your Lordship let us haste.* So both went out together, and the Page Conducted him into a Chamber he better knew than the Boy, while every Moment he receives Intelligence how Affairs went in that of *Silvia's*, by the Page, who leaving *Octavio* there went out as a Spy for him. In fine, with much ado, *Silvia* perswaded her Old Lover to urge her for no Favours that Night, for she was indispos'd and unfit for Love; yet she perswades with such an Air, so Smiling and Insinuating, that she increases the Fire she endeavour'd to allay: but he, who was all Obedience as well as New Desire, resolves to humour her, and shew the perfect Gallantry of his Love; he promises her she shall command: And after that never was the Old Gentleman seen in so excellent a Humour before, in the whole Course of his Life; a certain Lightening against a Storm, that must be fatal to him. He was no sooner gone from her, with a promise to go to Bed and Sleep, that he might be the earlier up, to show her the fine Gardens which she lov'd, but she sends *Antonett* to call the Page, from whom she long'd to know something of *Octavio*, and was sure he cou'd inform her. But she was undressing while she spoke, and got into her Bed before she left her: But *Antonett*, instead of bringing the Sighing Youth, brought the Transported and Ravish'd *Octavio*, who had by this time pull'd off his Course Campaign and put down his Hair. He fell breathless with Joy on her Bed side; when *Antonett*, who knew that Love desired no lookers on, retired and left *Octavio* almost dead with Joy, in the Clasping Arms of the Trembling Maid, the lovely *Silvia*. Oh, who can guess their satisfaction? Who can guess their Sighs and Love? their tender Words half stifled in Kisses; Lovers! fond Lovers! only can imagine; to all besides this Tale will be Insipid. He now forgets where he is, that not far off lay his Amorous Uncle, that to be found there was Death and something worse; but wholly Ravish'd with the Languishing Beauty, taking his Pistols out of either Pocket, he lays them on a Dressing Table near the Bed side, and in a Moment throws off his Cloths, and gives himself up to all the Heaven of Love that lay ready to receive him there, without thinking of any thing but the vast Power of eithers Charms. They lay and forgot the hasty Hours, but old *Sebastian* did not. They were all counted by him, with the Impatience of a Lover: He Burnt, he Rag'd with fierce Desire, and tost from side to side and found no ease; *Silvia* was present in Imagination, and he like

Tantalus[a] reaches at the Food, which tho' in view, is not within his reach: He wou'd have Pray'd, but he had no Devotion for any Deity but *Silvia*; he rose and walk'd, and went to Bed again, and found himself uneasie every way. A Thousand times he was about to go, and try what Opportunity would do in the dark silent Night——but fears her Rage——he fears she'll chide at least; then he resolves and unresolves as fast: Unhappy Lover —— thus to blow the Fire when there were no Materials to supply it; at last overcome with fierce Desire, too Violent to be withstood, or rather Fate wou'd have it so ordained, he ventures all, and steals to *Silvia*'s Chamber, believing when she found him in her Arms she could not be displeased; or if she were, that was the surest place of Reconciliation: So that only putting his Night Gown about him, he went softly to her Chamber for fear of waking her: The unthinking Lovers had left open the Door, so that it was hardly put to. And the first Alarm was *Octavio*'s Hand being seiz'd, which was Clasping his Treasure. He starts from the frighted Arms of *Silvia*, and leaping from the Bed wou'd have escap'd, for he knew too well the touch of that Old Hand; but *Sebastian* wholly surpriz'd at so robust a repulse, took most unfortunately a stronger hold, and laying both his Hands roughly upon him, with a Resolution to know who he was, for he felt his Hair; and *Octavio* struggling at the same Minute to get from him, they both fell against the Dressing Table, threw down the pistols; in their fall one of which going off, shot the unfortunate Old Lover into the Head, so that he never spoke word more: At the going off of the Pistol, *Silvia*, who had not minded those *Octavio* laid on the Table, cry'd out —— *Oh my* Octavio ! —— *My dearest Charmer*, reply'd he, *I'm well* —— And feeling on the Dead Body, which he wonder'd had no longer Motion, he felt Blood flowing around it, and Sighing cry'd *Ah*, *Silvia! I'm undone* —— *My Uncle* ——*Oh my Parent* —— *Speak, Dear Sir! Oh! what unlucky Accident has done this fatal Deed? Silvia*, who was very soft by Nature, was extreamly surpriz'd, and frightned at the News of a Dead Man in

---

[a] Tantalus, king of Phrygia. Wanting to test the gods, Tantalus invited them to a feast and served them the dismembered corpse of Pelops. All of the gods refused the dish except Demeter. When the trick was discovered, Pelops was restored to life and given an ivory shoulder-bone to replace the portion eaten by Demeter. Tantalus' punishment was to suffer from perpetual hunger and thirst in Hades, surrounded by water which receded when he attempted to drink it and by fruit-trees always just out of his reach.

her Chamber, so that she was ready to run Mad with the Apprehension of it: She rav'd and tore her self, and exprest her Fright in Cries and Distraction; so that *Octavio* was compelled from one charitable Grief to another. He goes to her and Comforts her, and tells, since 'tis by no design of either of them, their Innocence will be their Guardian Angel. He tells her all their fault was Love, which made him so heedlessly fond of Joys with her, he staid to reap those when he should have secur'd 'em by Flight. He tells her this is now no place to stay in, and that he would put on her Clothes and fly with her to some secure part of the World; *For who,* said he, *that finds this poor Unfortunate here, will not charge his Death on me or thee.* —— *Haste then, my dearest Maid, haste, haste, and let us fly*——So dressing her he led her into *Antonett*'s Chamber, and conjured her to say nothing of the Accident, while he went to see which way they could get out. So locking the Chamber door where the dead Body lay, which by this time was stiff and cold; he lock'd that also of his Uncle's Chamber, and calling the Page they all got themselves ready; and putting Two Horses in the Coach, they unseen and unperceived got themselves all out: The Servants having drunk hard at their meeting in the Country last Night, were all too sound a sleep to understand any thing of what past. It being now about the Break of Day, *Octavio* was the Coachman, and the Page Riding by the Coach-side, while *Silvia* and *Antonett* were in it, they in an hours time reach'd the Town, where *Octavio* pack'd up all that was carriageable; took his own Coach and Six Horses; left his Affairs to the Management of a Kinsman that dwelt with him; took Bills to the Value of Two Thousand Pounds, and immediately left the Town, after receiving some Letters that came last Night by the Post, one of which was from *Philander*; and indeed this new Grief upon *Octavio*'s Soul, made him the most Dejected and Melancholy Man in the World, insomuch that he, who never wept for any thing but for Love, was often found with Tears rowling down his Cheeks, at the remembrance of an Accident so deplorable, and of which he and his unhappy Passion was the Cause, tho' Innocently: Yet could not the dire Reflection of that, nor the loss of so tender a Parent, as was *Sebastian*, lessen one Spark of that Fire for *Silvia*, whose unfortunate Flame had been so Fatal. While they were safe out of danger, the Servants of *Sebastian* admired when Ten, Eleven and Twelve a Clock was come, they saw neither the Old Lord nor any of the New Guests. But when the Coachman mist his Coach and Horses he was in a greater maze, and thought some Body had stollen 'em, and accusing himself of Sluggishness and Debauchery, that made him not able to hear when the Coach went out, he forswore all Drinking. But when the Housekeeper and he met and discoursed about the Lady and the rest, they concluded that the old Gentleman and she were agreed upon the matter, and being got to Bed together had quite forgot themselves; and made a Thousand Roguish remarks upon 'em. They believed the Maid and the Page too were as well imploy'd, since they saw neither. But when Dinner was ready she went up to the Maids Chamber and found it empty, as also that of the Page; her Heart then presaging something, she ventures to knock at her Lord's Chamber door, but finding it Lock'd and none Answer, they broke it open; and after doing the same by that of *Silvia*, they found the Poor *Sebastian* stretch'd on the Floor, and Shot in the Head, the *Toylet* pull'd almost down, and the Lock of the Pistol hanging in the point of the *Toylet* intangled, and the Muzzle of it just against the Wound. At first when they saw him they fancy'd *Silvia* might kill him, for either offering to come to Bed to her in the Night, or for some other Malicious end. But when they saw how the Pistol lay they fancy'd it Accident in the Dark; *For*, said the Woman ——*I and my Daughter have been up ever since Day-break, and, I'm sure no such thing happen'd then, nor could they since escape:* And it being natural in *Holland* to cry, *Lope Schellum*, that is, Run Rogue, to him that is alive, and who has kill'd another; and for every Man to set a helping Hand to bear him out of Danger, thinking it too much that one's already dead: I say, this being the Nature of the People, they never pursu'd the Murderers or fled Persons, but suffered *Sebastian* to lie till the Coroner sat upon him, who found it, or at least thought it, Accident; and there was all for that time. But this, with all the reasonable Circumstances, did not satisfie the *States*. Here is one of their High and Mighties killed, a fair Lady fled, and upon inquiry a fine Young Fellow too, the Nephew: All knew they were Rivals in this fair Lady; all knew there were Animosities between 'em; all knew *Octavio* was absconded some Days before; so that, upon Consideration, they concluded he was Murder'd by Compact; and the rather, because they wish'd it so in spight to *Octavio*; and because both he and *Silvia* were fled like Guilty Persons. Upon this they make a Seizure of both his and his Uncle's Estate, to the use of the *States*. Thus the best and most glorious Man that ever grac'd that part of the World was undone by Love. While *Silvia* with Sighs and Tears would often say, *That sure she was born the Fate of all that Ador'd her, and no Man ever thriv'd that had a Design upon her, or a Pretension to her.*

Thus between excess of Grief and excess of Love, which indeed lay veil'd in the first, they arriv'd at *Bruxells;*[a] where *Octavio*, having News of the proceedings of the *States* against him, resolving rather to lose his Life, than tamely to surrender his Right, he went forth in order to take some Care about it: And in these extreams of a troubled Mind he had forgot to read *Philander*'s Letters, but gave 'em to *Silvia* to peruse, till he return'd, beseeching and conjuring her, by all the Charms of Love, not to suffer herself to be afflicted, but now to consider she was wholly his; and she could not, and ought not to rob him of a Sigh or Tear for any other Man. For they had concluded to marry as soon as *Silvia* should be delivered from that part of *Philander* of which she was possess'd. Therefore beholding her intirely his own, of whom he was so fondly tender, he could not indure the Wind should blow on her, and kiss her lovely Face: Jealous of even the Air she breath'd, he was ever putting her in mind of whose and what she was; and she ever giving him new Assurances that she was only *Octavio*'s. The last part of his ill News he conceal'd from her; that of the Usage of the *States*. He was so intirely careful of her Fame, that he had two Lodgings, one, most magnificent, for her, another for himself; and only visited her all the live-long Day. And being now retired from her, she, whose Love and Curiosity grew less every day for the false *Philander*, open'd his Letter with a Sigh of departed Love, and read this.

Philander *to* Octavio.

Sure of your Friendship, my dear Octavio, *I venture to lay before you the History of my Misfortunes, as well as those of my Joys; equally Extream.*

In my last I gave you an Account how triumphing a Lover I was in

---

[a] Brussels. By 1685 many of the rebels had converged on Brussels to pay court to Monmouth.

the Possession of the adorable Calista; *and how very near I was being surpriz'd in the Fountain, where I had hid myself from the Rage of old* Clarinau; *and escaped wet and cold to my Lodging: And tho' indeed I escaped, it was not without giving the old Husband a Jealousy, which put him upon an Inquiry after a stricter manner, as I heard the next day from* Calista; *but with as ill Success as the Night before; notwithstanding it appears by what after happened that he still retain'd his Jealousy, and that of me, from a thousand little Inquiries I had from time to time made, from my being now absent, and most of all from my being (as now he fancied) that Vision which* Calista *saw in the Garden. All these Circumstances wrought a thousand* Canundrums *in his* Spanish *politick Noddle: And he resolves that* Calista's *Actions should be more narrowly watch'd. This I can only guess from what insu'd. I am not able to say by what good Fortune I escap'd several happy Nights after the first, but 'tis certain I did so; for the old Man carrying all things fair to the lovely Countess, she thought herself secure in her Joys hitherto, as to any Discovery: However I never went on this dear Adventure but I was well arm'd against any Mishaps of Poniard,[a] Sword, and Pistol, that Garb of a right* Spaniard.[b] Calista *had been married above two years before I beheld her, and had never been with Child: But it so chanced, that she conceived the very first Night of our Happiness; since which time not all her Flatteries and Charms could prevail for one Night with the old Count: For, whether from her seeming Fondness he imagined the Cause, or what other Reason he had to withstand her Desire and Caresses, I know not: But still he found or feigned some Excuses to put her off; so that* Calista's *Fears and Love increased with her growing Belly. And tho' almost every Night I had the fair young Charmer in Bed with me (without the least Suspicion on* Dormina's *side) or else in the Arbours, or on flowery Banks in the Garden: Till I am confident there was not a Walk, a Grove, an Arbour, or Bed or Sweets, that was not conscious of our stollen Delights. Nay we grew so very bold in Love, that we often suffered the Day to break upon us; and still escaped his Spyes, who by either watching at the wrong Door, or part of the vast Garden; or by Sleepiness and Carelessness still let us pass their View. Four happy Months, thus bless'd and thus secur'd, we liv'd, when* Calista *could no longer conceal her growing Shame from the Jealous* Clarinau *or* Dormina. *She fear'd with too much Reason that 'twas Jealousy which made*

---

[a] A dagger.

[b] In seventeenth-century England the Spanish had a reputation for treachery because they had so often been enemies in war.

*him refrain her Bed, tho' he dissembled well all Day: And one Night,
weeping in my Bosom, with all the tenderness of Love, she said,* That
if I loved her, as she hoped I did, I should be shortly very
miserable: For oh, *cry'd she,* I can no longer hide this—— dear
Effect of my stollen Happiness——and *Clarinau* will no sooner
perceive my Condition, but he will use his utmost Rigour
against me. I know his jealous Nature, and find I am undone—
—*With that she told me how he had killed his first Wife; for which he
was obliged to fly from the Court and Country of* Spain: *And that she
found from all his Severity he was not chang'd from his Nature. In fine,
she said and lov'd so much, that I was wholly charm'd and vow'd
myself her Slave, or Sacrifice, either to follow what she could propose,
or fall a Victim with her to my Love. After which 'twas concluded
(neither having a mind to leave the World, when we both knew so well
how to make our selves happy in it) that the next Night I should bring
her a Suit of Mans Cloths; and she would in that Disguise fly with me
to any part of the World. For she vow'd if this unlucky Force of Flying
had not happened to her, she had not been longer able to have indured
his Tyranny and Slavery: But had resolved to break her Chain, and put
herself upon any Fortune. So that after the usual Indearments on both
sides, I left her resolved to follow my Fortune, and she me, to sacrifice
all to her Repose. That Night, and all next Day, she was not idle; but
put up all her Jewels, of which she had the richest of any Lady in all
those Parts, for in that the old Count was over lavish: And the next
Night I brought her a Suit, which I had made that day on purpose; as
gay as could be made in so short a time; and scaling my Wall well
arm'd, I found her ready at the Door to receive me; and going into an
Arbour, by the aid of a Dark-Lanthorn I carried, she dress'd her in a
lac'd Shirt of mine, and this Suit I had brought her, of blew Velvet,
trim'd with rich Loops and Buttons of Gold; a white Hat and white
Feather; a fair Peruke,*[a]* and scarlet Breeches, the rest suitable. And I
must confess to you, my dear* Octavio, *that never any thing appear'd
so Ravishing, and yet I have seen* Silvia! *But even she a Baby to this
more noble Figure.* Calista *is tall, and fashioned the most divinely——
the most proper for that Dress of any of her Sex: And I own I never saw
any thing so Beautiful all over, from Head to Foot: And viewing her
thus (carrying my Lanthorn all about her, but more especially her Face,
her wondrous Charming Face——(Pardon me if I say, what does but
look like Flattery)——I never saw any thing more resembling my dear*

---

[a] A wig.

Octavio, *than the lovely* Calista. *Your every Feature, your very Smile and Air; so that, if possible, that increas'd my Adoration and Esteem for her: Thus compleated, I Armed her and buckl'd on her Sword, and she would needs have one of my Pistols too, that stuck in my Belt; and now she appeared all lovely Man.* 'Twas so late by that time we had done, that the Moon which began to shine very Bright, gave us a Thousand little Fears, and disposing her Jewels all about us safe, we began our Adventure, with a Thousand dreadful Apprehensions on Calista's *side. And going up the Walk towards the place where we were to mount the Wall; just at the end of it, turning a Corner we encounter'd Two Men, who were too near us to be prevented.* Oh, *cry'd* Calista *to me, who saw 'em first.*——My dear Philander we are undone! *I look'd and saw 'em and replied,* My Charmer do not fear, they are but two to two who e're they be; for Love, and I, shall be of force enough to Encounter 'em. No, my Philander, *replied she briskly,* 'tis I will be your Second in this Rancounter. *At this approaching 'em more near (for they hasted to us, nor could we fly from them,) we soon found by his hobbling, that old* Clarinau *was one, and the other a Tall Spaniard, his Nephew. I clapt my Hair under my Hat, and both of us making a stand, we resolv'd if they durst not venture on us to let 'em pass*——but Clarinau, *who was on that side which faced* Calista, *cry'd,* Ah Villain, have I caught thee! *and at the same instant with a Poniard stabbed her into the Arm; for with a sudden turn she evaded it from her Heart, to which it was designed. At which repaying his Complement, she shot of her Pistol, and down he fell, crying out for a Priest; while I at the same time laid my Tall Boy at his Feet. I caught my dear Virago in my Arms, and hasted through the Garden with her, and was very hasty in mounting my Ladder, putting my fair Second before me, without so much as daring yet to ask her if she were wounded, least it should have hinder'd our flight if I had found her hurt: Nor knew I she was so, till I felt her warm precious Blood streaming on my Face, as I lifted her over the Wall; but I soon conveyed her into my new Lodgings; yet not soon enough to secure her from those that pursu'd us: For with their bauling they alarm'd some of the Servants, who looking narrowly for the Murderers, track'd us by* Calista's *Blood, which they saw with their Flambeaus*[a] *from the place where* Clarinau *and his Nephew lay, to the very Wall; and thinking from our Wounds we could not escape far, they searching the Houses, found me dressing* Calista's *Wound, which I kist a Thousand times.*

---

[a] Torches made of several waxed sticks bound together.

But the matchless Courage of the fair Virago! the Magnanimity of Calista's Soul! nothing of foolish Woman harbour'd there, nothing but softest Love; for while I was raving mad, tearing my Hair and cursing my Fate in vain, she had no concern but for me; no pain but that of her fear of being taken from me and being delivered to Old Clarinau, *whom I fear'd was not dead; nor could the very seizing her daunt her Spirits, but with an unmatch'd Fortitude she bore it all; she only wish'd she could have escaped without Bloodshed. We were both led to Prison, but none knew who we were, for those that seized us had by chance never seen me, and* Calista's *Habit secur'd the discovery. While we both remained there, we had this Comfort of being well Lodg'd together; for they did not go about to part us, being in for one Crime. And all the satisfaction she had, was, that she should, she hop'd, die concealed, if she must die for the Crime; and that was much a greater Joy than to think she should be render'd back to* Clarinau, *who in a few days we heard was upon his Recovery; this gave her new fears; but I confess to you I was not afflicted at it; nor did I think it hard for me to bribe* Calista *off; for the Master of the Prison was very Civil and Poor, so that with the help of some few of* Calista's *Jewels, he was wrought upon to let her escape, I offering to remain and bear all the brunt of the Business, and to pay whatever he could be Fined for it. These Reasons with the ready Jewels mollified the needy Rascal; and tho' loath she were to leave me; yet she being assured that all they could do was but to fine me; and her stay she knew was her inevitable Ruine, she at last submitted, leaving me sufficient in Jewels to satisfie for all that could happen, which were the value of a Hundred thousand Crowns. She is fled to* Bruxells, *to a Nunnery of* Augustin's,[a] *where the Lady Abbess is her Aunt, and where for a little time she is secure, till I can follow her.*

I beg of you, my dear Octavio, *write to me, and write me a Letter of Recommendation to the Magistrates here, who all being concern'd when any one of 'em is a Cuckold, are very severe upon Criminals in those Cases. I tire you with my Melancholy Adventure —— but 'tis some ease in the Extreams of Grief to receive the tender Pity of a Friend, and that I'm sure* Octavio *will afford his unhappy*

Philander.

---

[a] The Orders of the Augustinian Canons and the Augustinian Hermits founded in the Middle Ages. The orders follow the Rule of St Augustine of Hippo.

As cold and as unconcern'd as *Silvia* imagin'd she had found her Heart to *Philander's* Memory, at the reading of this Letter, in spight of all the Tenderness she had for *Octavio*, she was possest with all those pains of Love and Jealousie, which heretofore tormented her when Love was Young, and *Philander* appeared with all those Charms with which he first Conquer'd; she found the Fire was but hid under those Embers, which every little blast blows off and makes it Flame a new. 'Twas now that she forgetting all the past Obligations of *Octavio*, all his vast Presents, his Vows, his Sufferings, his Passion and his Youth, abandon'd herself wholly to her Tenderness for *Philander*, and drowns her fair Cheeks in a Shower of Tears. And having eas'd her Heart a little by this natural Relief of her Sex, she opened the Letter that was design'd for her self, and read this.

To Silvia.

I know, my lovely Silvia, *I am accused of a Thousand Barbarities, for unkindly detaining your Lover, who long ere this ought to have thrown himself at your Feet, imploring a Thousand Pardons for his tedious Six Months absence, tho' the affliction of it is all my own, and I am affraid all the Punishment; but when, my dearest* Silvia, *I reflect again, it is in order to our future Tranquillity, I depend on your Love and Reason for my Excuse. I know my absence has procur'd me a Thousand Rivals, and you as many Adorers, and fear* Philander *appears grown Old in Love, and worn out with Sorrow and Care, unfit for the soft Play of the Young and Delicate* Silvia; *new Lovers have new Vows and new Presents, and your fickle Sex stoop to the lavish Prostrate. Ill luck—— unkind Fate has rifl'd me, and of a shining Fortune left me even to the Charity of the stingy World; and I have no new Compliment to maintain the esteem in so great a Soul as that of* Silvia, *but that old repeated one of telling her my dull, my trifling Heart is still her own: But, oh! I want the presenting Eloquence that so perswades and charms the Fair, and am reduced to that fatal Torment of a generous Mind, rather to ask and take than to bestow. Yet out of my contemptible stock, I have sent my* Silvia *something towards that dangerous unavoidable hour, which will declare me, however, a happy Father of what my* Silvia *bears about her; 'tis a Bill for a Thousand Patacoons. I am at present under an easie restraint, about a little Dispute between a Man of Quality here and my self, I had else been at Bruxells to have provided all things for your coming Illness, but every day expect my Liberty, and then without delay I will take Post and bring Philander to your Arms.*

I have News that Cæsario is arrived at Bruxells.[a] I am at present a Stranger to all that passes, and having a double Obligation to haste, you need not fear but I shall do so.

This Letter raised in her a different Sentiment from that of the Story of his Misfortune; and that taught her to know that this he had writ to her was all false and dissembl'd: Which made her in concluding the Letter, cry out with a vehement Scorn and Indignation —— *Oh how I hate thee Traytor! who hast the Impudence to continue thus to impose upon me, as if I wanted common Sense to see thy Baseness: For what can be more Base and Cowardly than Lyes, that poor Plebeian Shift; contemn'd by Men of Honour or of Wit.* This she spoke without reminding that this most contemptible Quality she herself was equally guilty of, tho' infinitely more excusable in her Sex, there being a thousand little Actions of their Lives liable to Censure and Reproach, which they would willingly excuse and colour over with little Falsities; but in a Man, whose most inconstant Actions pass oftentimes for innocent Gallantries, and to whom 'tis no Infamy to own a thousand Amours, but rather a Glory to his Fame and Merit: I say, in him (whom Custom has favoured with an Allowance to commit any Vice and boast it) 'tis not so brave. And this Fault of *Philander's* cur'd *Silvia* of her Disease of Love; and chaced from her Heart all that Softness which once had so much favoured him. Nevertheless she was fill'd with Thoughts that fail'd not to make her extreamly Melancholy: And 'twas in this Humour *Octavio* found her; who forgetting all his own Griefs, to lessen hers (for his Love was arrived to a degree of Madness) he caresses her with all the Eloquence his Passion could pour out; he falls at her Feet, and pleads with such a Look and Voice as could not be resisted; nor ceas'd he till he had talk'd her into Ease, till he had look'd and lov'd her into a perfect Calm: 'Twas then he urg'd her to a new Confirmation of her Heart to him, and took hold of every yielding Softness in her to improve his

[a] In *The Secret History of the Rye House Plot*, Ford Grey recalls that 'Some time after ye discourse with Mr. Ferguson, the duke of Monmouth came publicly to Brussels, which, as near as I can remember, was about the time of Luxembourg's being beseiged'.

Advantage. He press'd her to all he wish'd, but by such tender Degrees, by Arts so fond and indearing that she could deny nothing. In this Humour she makes a thousand Vows against *Philander*; to hate him as a Man that has first ruined her Honour, and then abandon'd her to all the Ills that attend ungoverned Youth, and unguarded Beauty: She makes *Octavio* swear as often to be reveng'd on him, for the Dishonour of his Sister: Which being performed, they re-assum'd all the Satisfactions, which had seem'd almost destroy'd by adverse Fate, and for a little space liv'd in great Tranquillity; or if *Octavio* had Sentiments that represented past Unhappinesses and a future Prospect of ill Consequences, he strove with all the Power of Love to hide 'em from *Silvia*. In this time they often sent to the Nunnery of the *Augustins*, to inquire of the Countess of *Clarinau*; and at last hearing she was arrived, no force of Perswasion or Reason could hinder *Silvia* from going to make her a Visit: *Octavio* pleads in vain the overthrow of all his Revenge, by his Sisters knowledge that her Intrigue was found out: But in an Undress——for her Condition permitted no other, she is carried to the Monastery, and asks for the Mother Prioress, who came to the Grate: Where after the first Complement's over, she tells her she is a Relation to that Lady who such a day came to the House. *Silvia* by her Habit and Equipage appearing of Quality; was answered, that tho' the Lady were very much indispos'd, and unfit to appear at the Grate, she would nevertheless indeavour to serve her, since she was so earnest; and commanding one of the Nuns to call down Madam the Countess, she immediately came; but tho' in a Dress all negligent, and Face where Languishment appeared, she at first sight surprized our Fair One; with a certain Majesty in her Mein and Motion, and an Air of Greatness in her Face, which resembled that of *Octavio*: So that not being able to sustain herself on her trembling Supporters, she was ready to faint at a Sight so charming, and a Form Angelick. She saw her all that *Philander* had describ'd; nor could the Partiality of his Passion render her more lovely than she appear'd this Instant to *Silvia*. She came to reproach her— —but she found a Majesty in her Looks above all Censure, that aw'd the jealous Upbraider, and almost put her out of Countenance; and with a rising Blush she seem'd asham'd of her Errand. At this Silence the lovely *Calista*, a little surpriz'd, demanded of an attending Nun if that Lady would speak with her? This awaked *Silvia* into an Address, and she reply'd; *Yes*,

Madam, I am the Unfortunate, who am compell'd by my hard Fate to complain of the most charming Woman that ever Nature made: I thought in coming hither I should have had no other Business but to have told you how false, how perjured a Lover I had had; but at a Sight so wonderous I blame him no more (whom I find now compell'd to love) but you, who have taken from me, by your Charms, the only Blessing Heaven had lent me. This she ended with a Sigh, and Madam the Countess, who from the beginning of her speaking guess'd, from a certain trembling at her Heart, who it was she spoke of, resolv'd to show no Signs of a womanish Fear or Jealousy, but with an unalterable Air and Courage, reply'd, *Madam, if my Charms were so powerful, as you are pleased to tell me they are, they sure have attracted too many Lovers for me to understand which of 'em it is I have been so unhappy to rob you of. If he be a gallant Man, I shall neither deny him nor repent my Loving him the more, for his having been a Lover before.* To which, *Silvia,* who expected not so brisk an Answer, reply'd. *She that makes such a Confession with so much Generosity, I know cannot be insensible of the Injuries she does, but will have a Consideration and Pity for those Wretches at least, who are undone to establish her Satisfaction.* Madam, reply'd the Countess (a little touch'd with the Tenderness and Sadness with which she spoke) *you have so just a Character of my Soul, that I assure you, I would not, for any Pleasure in the World, do an Action should render it less worthy of your good Thoughts. Name me the Man——and if I find him such as I may return you with Honour, he shall find my Friendship no more. Ah Madam, 'tis impossible,* cry'd *Silvia, that he can ever be mine, that has once had the Glory of being conquered by you; and what's yet more, of having conquered you.* Nay, *Madam,* reply'd *Calista, if your Loss be irrecoverable, I have no more to do, but to sigh with you, and joyn our hard Fates; but I am not so vain of my own Beauty, nor have so little Admiration for that of yours, to imagine I can retain any thing you have a Claim to; for me, I am not fond of Admirers, if Heaven be pleased to give me one, I ask no more. I'll leave the World to you, so it allow me my* Philander. This she spoke with a little Malice, which call'd up all the Blushes in the fair Face of *Silvia;* who a little netled at the word *Philander,* reply'd. *Go, take the perjured Man, and see how long you can maintain your Empire over his fickle Heart, who has already betray'd you to all the Reproach an incensed Rival and an injured Brother can load you with: See where he has exposed you to* Octavio; *and after that tell me what you can hope from such a perjured Villain*——At these Words she gave her the Letter *Philander* had writ to *Octavio,* with that he had writ to herself——and without taking Leave or speaking any more, she left her thoughtful Rival: Who after pausing a Moment on what should be writ there, and what the angry Lady meant, she silently passed on to her Chamber. But if she were surprized with her Visitor, she was much more when opening the Letters, she found one to her Brother, filled with the History of her Infamy, and what pressed her Soul more sensibly, the other fill'd with Passion and Softness to a Mistress. She had scarcely read them out but a young Nun, her Kinswoman, came into her Chamber; whom I have since heard protest she scarce saw in that Moment any Alteration in her, but that she rose and received her with her wonted Grace and Sweetness; and but for some Answers that she made *mal a propo*,[a] and Sighs that against her Will broke from her Heart, she should not have found an Alteration; but this being unusual made her Inquisitive; and the faint Denial she met with made her importune, and that so earnestly and with so many Vows of Fidelity and Secrecy, that *Calista*'s Heart, even breaking within poured it self for Ease into the Faithful Bosom of this young Devotee; and having told her all the Story of her Misfortune, she began with so much Courage and bravery of Mind, to make Vows against the charming Betrayer of her Fame, and with him all Mankind; and this with such Consideration and Repentance as left no room for Reproach or Perswasion; and from this Moment resolved never to quit the Solitude of the Cloysters. She had all her Life before her Marriage lived in one, and wished now she never had seen the World, or departed from a Life so pure and Innocent. She looked upon this fatal Accident now a Blessing, to bring her back to a Life of Devotion and Tranquillity; and indeed is a Miracle of Piety. Sometime after this she was brought to Bed, but commanded the Child should be removed where she might never see it, which accordingly was done; after which, in due time, she took the Habit; and remains a rare Example of Repentance, and Holy-living. This new Penitent became the News of the whole Town; and it was not without some Pleasure that *Octavio* heard it, as the only Action she could do that could reconcile him to her; the knowledg of which, and a few soft Days with *Silvia*, made him chase away all those Shiverings that had seized him upon several Occasions:

---

[a] *Mal à propos*, meaning 'awkwardly said'.

But *Silvia* was all Sweetness, all Love and good Humour, and made his Days easy, and his Nights intirely Happy. While on the other side there was no Satisfaction, no Pleasure, that the fond lavish Lover did not at any Price purchase for her Repose; for it was the whole Business of his Life to study what would charm and please her: And being assured by so many Vows of her Heart, there was nothing rested to make him perfectly Happy, but her being delivered of what belong'd to his Rival, and in which he had no part, he was at perfect Ease. This she wishes with an Impatience equal to his; whose Love and Fondness for *Octavio* appeared to be arrived to the highest Degree, and she every Minute expected to be freed from the only thing that hinder'd her from giving herself intirely to her impatient Lover.

In the midst of this Serenity of Affairs, *Silvia's* Page one day brings 'em News his Lord was arriv'd, and that he saw him in the Park walking with some *French* Gentlemen, and undiscovered to him came to give her Notice, that she might take her measures accordingly, in spight of all her Love to *Octavio*: Her Blushes flew to her Cheeks at the News, and her Heart panted with unusual Motion; she wonders at her self and Fears, and doubts her own Resolution; she till now believ'd him wholly indifferent to her, but she knows not what Construction this new Disorder will bear; and what confounded and perplext her more, was, That *Octavio* beheld all these Emotions, with unconceivable resentment, he swells with Pride and Anger, and even bursts with Grief, and not able longer to contain his complaint, he reproaches her in the softest Language that every Love and Grief invented; while she weeps with Shame and divided Love, and demands of him a Thousand Pardons; she deals thus kindly at least with him to confess this Truth; that 'twas impossible, but at the approach of a Man who taught her first to love, and for which Knowledge she had paid so infinitely dear, she could not but feel unusual Motions, that that Tenderness and Infant Flame he once inspired could not but have left some warmth about her Heart, and that *Philander*, the once charming dear *Philander*, could never be absolutely to her as a common Man, and beg'd that he would give some grains of allowance to a Maid, so soft by Nature, and who had once lov'd so well to be undone for the dear Object; and tho' every kind word she gave his Rival was a Dagger at his Heart, nevertheless, he found, or would think he found some reason in what she said; at least he seem'd more appeased, while she on the other side dissembled all the ease and repose of Mind, that could flatter him to Calmness.

You must know that for *Silvia*'s Honour, she had Lodgings by her self, and *Octavio* had his in another House, at an Aunts of his, a Widow, and a Woman of great Quality; and *Silvia* being near her Lying-in, had provided all things with the greatest Magnificence imaginable, and past for a Young Widow whose Husband died at the Siege of——[a] *Octavio* only visited her daily, and all the Nights she had to her self. For he treated her as one whom he design'd to make his Wife, and one whose Honour was his own; but that Night the News of *Philander*'s Arrival was told her, she was more than ordinary impatient to have him gone, pretending Illness, and yet seem'd loth to let him go, and Lovers (the greatest Cullies in Nature, and the aptest to be deceived, tho' the most quick-sighted) ——do the soonest believe; and finding it the more necessary he should depart, the more ill she feign'd to be, he took his Leave, and left her to her Repose, after taking all care necessary for one in her Circumstances. But she, to make his Absence more sure, and fearing least he should suspect something of her Design, being herself Guilty, she orders him to be call'd back, and Caresses him anew, tells him she was never more unwilling to part with him, and all the while is complaining and wishing to be in Bed: And says he must not stir till he sees her laid. This obliges and cajoles him anew, and he will not suffer her Women to undress her, but does the grateful Business himself, and reaps some dear Recompence by every Service, and pleases his Eyes and Lips with the ravishing Beauties of the loose unguarded suffering Fair one. She permits him any thing to have him gone, which was not till he saw her laid as if to her Rest: But he was no sooner got into his Coach, but she rose and slip'd on her Night-Gown and some other loose things, and got into a Chair, commanding her Page to conduct the Chair-men to all the great *Cabarets:* Where she believed it most likely to find *Philander*; which was accordingly done; and the Page entering, enquires for such a *Cavalier*, describing his Person and fine remarkable black Hair of his own: But the first he entered into he saw *Brilljard* bespeaking Supper: For you must know that that

---

[a] Possibly the siege of Luxembourg which was taking place at this time.

Husband-Lover being left, as I have said, in Prison in *Holland*, for the Accusation of *Octavio*; the unhappy young Noble Man was no sooner fled upon the unlucky Death of his Uncle, but the States set *Brilljard* at Liberty; who took his Journey immediately to *Philander*, whom he found just released from his troublesome Affair, and design'd for *Bruxells*, where they arriv'd that very Morning. Where the first thing he did was to go to the Nunnery of St *Austin*, to inquire for the fair *Calista*; but instead of encountering the kind, the impatient, the brave *Calista*, he was addressed to by the old Lady Abbess in so rough a manner, that he no longer doubted upon what Terms he stood there, tho' he wondered how they should know his Story with *Calista*: When to put him out of Doubt, she assured him he should never more behold the Face of her injured Neece; for whose Revenge she left him to Heaven. It was in vain he kneel'd and implored; he was confirm'd again and again she should never come from out the Confines of those Walls; and that her whole remaining Life spent in Penitence was too little to wash away her Sins with him: And giving him the Letter he sent to *Octavio* (which *Silvia* had given *Calista*, and she the Lady Abbess, with a full Confession of her Fault) she cry'd; *See there, Sir, the Treachery you have committed against a Woman of Quality—— whom your Criminal Love has rendred the most Miserable of her Sex.* At the ending of which, she drew the Curtain over the Grate and left him, wholly amazed and confounded, finding it to be the same he had writ to *Octavio*, and in it that he had writ to *Silvia*: By the sight of which he no longer doubted but that Confident had betrayed him every way. He rails on his false Friendship, curses the Lady Abbess, himself, his Fortune and his Birth; but finds it all in vain: Nor was he so infinitely afflicted with the thought of the eternal Loss of *Calista* (because he had possessed her) as he was to find himself betray'd to her, and doubtless to *Silvia* by *Octavio*; and nothing but *Calista*'s being confin'd from him (tho' she were very dear and charming to his Thoughts) could have made him rave so extreamly for a Sight of her: He loves her the more by how much more it was impossible for him to see her; and that Difficulty and his Dispair increased his Flame. In this Humour he went to his Lodging, the most undone Extravagant that ever rag'd with Love. He considers her in a place where no Art or force of Love, or humane Wit can retrieve her; no nor so much as send her a Letter. This added to his Fury, and in his first wild Imaginations he resolves nothing less than firing the Monastery, that in that Confusion he might Seize his right of Love; and do a Deed that would render his Name as famous as the *Athenian* Youth,[a] who to get a Fame, tho' an Inglorious one, fired the Temple of their Gods. But his Rage abating by Consideration, that Impiety dwelt not long with him: And he ran over a number more, till from one to another he reduced himself to a degree of Moderation, which presented him with some flattering Hope, that gave him a little Ease: 'Twas then that *Chivalier Tomaso*,[b] and another *French* Gentleman of *Cesario*'s Faction (who were newly arrived in *Bruxells*) came to pay him their Respects: And after a while carried him into the Park to walk, where *Silvia*'s Page had seen him; and from whence they sent *Brilljard* to bespeak Supper at this *Cabaret*, where *Silvia*'s Chair and herself waited, and where the Page found *Brilljard*, of whom he asked for his Lord; but understanding he would not possibly come in some Hours, being design'd for Court that Evening, whither he was obliged to go and kiss the Governours Hands, he went to the Lady, who was almost dead with Impatience, and told her what he had learn'd: Upon which she ordered her Chairmen to carry her back to her Lodgings, for she would not be perswaded to ask any Questions of *Brilljard*, for whom she had a mortal Hate: However she resolved to send the Page back with a Billet to wait *Philander*'s coming; which was not long; for having sooner dispatched their Complement at Court than they believed they should, they went all to Supper together, where *Brilljard* had bespoke it: Where being impatient to learn all the Adventures of *Cesario*[c] since his Departure from him, and of which no Person

---

[a] Herostratus burnt down the temple of Ephesus in 356 BC in order to win immortality.

[b] Chivalier Tomaso is a conflation of two of Monmouth's supporters – Sir Thomas Armstrong and Anthony Ashley Cooper, the Earl of Shaftesbury. Both were dead by the time Monmouth took refuge in Brussels; Shaftesbury had died in Amsterdam in 1682 and Sir Thomas Armstrong had been seized in Leyden in June, 1684, when he was taken back to England and executed. Armstrong, like Shaftesbury was the butt of Tory lampoons such as the following:

A——ng is not to be found either in *Church* or *Conventicle*; but (if you look close) you may find him with a Common Whore at *Stratfords*, or a holy Sister at *Wapping* preaching *Liberty of conscience* to the *Saints*, if his *Politicks* has not spoil'd his *Letching*. *The Hue and Cry after J——Duke of M——, Lord G——y, and Sir Tho. A——g.* Printed for B. A. anno Domini, 1683.

[c] With the discovery of the Rye-House Plot in 1683, a warrant had been issued for the arrest of the Monmouth. The Duke had recently fallen in love with Henrietta Wentworth and, when the warrant was issued, he took refuge at her home in Toddington in Bedfordshire.

could give so good an Account as *Chivalier Tomaso, Philander* gave order that no body whomsoever should disturb them, and sate himself down to listen to the Fortune of the Prince.

You know, my Lord, said *Tomaso*, the state of Things at your Departure; and that all our glorious Designs for the Liberty of all *France* were discovered and betray'd by some of those little Rascals, that great Men are obliged to make use of in the greatest Designs: Upon whose Confession you were proscrib'd, myself, this Gentleman, and several others: It was our good Fortunes to escape untaken, and yours to fall first into the Messenger's Hands, and carried to the *Bastile*, even from whence you had the Luck to escape: But it was not so with *Cesario. Heavens*, cry'd *Philander*, *the Prince I hope is not taken?* Not so neither, reply'd *Tomaso*, nor should you wonder you have receiv'd no News of him in a long time, since forty thousand Crowns[a] being offered for his Head, or to any that could discover him, it would have exposed him to have written to any body, he being beset on all sides with Spies from the King;[b] so that it 'twas impossible to venture a Letter without very great Hazzard of his Life. Besides all these Hindrances, *Cesario*, who, you know, was ever a great admirer of the fair Sex, happen'd in this his Retreat to fall most desperately in Love: Nor could the fears of Death, which alarm'd him on all sides, deterr him from this new Amour: Which because it has Revelation to some part of his Adventures, I cannot omit, especially to your Lordship, his Friend, to whom every Circumstance of that Princes Fate and Fortune will be of Concern.

You must imagin, my Lord, that your Seizure and Escape was enough to alarm the whole Party; and there was not a Man of the League who did not think it high time to look about him, when one, so considerable as your Lordship, was surpriz'd. Nor did the Prince himself any longer believe himself safe; but retired himself under the darkness of the following Night: He went only accompanied with his Page, to a Ladies House, a Widow of Quality in *Paris*, that populous City; being as he conceived, the securest Place to conceal himself in. This Lady

---

[a] The proclamation offered £500 for the apprehension of Monmouth, Grey, Armstrong or Robert Ferguson.

[b] A spy quickly informed the government of Monmouth's presence at Toddington adding that "Tis of that vastness and intricacy that without a most diligent search 'tis impossible to discover all the lurking holes in it, there being several trap-doors in the leads and in closets into places to which there is not other access.'

was Madam the Countess of——[a] who had, as you know, my Lord, one only Daughter, *Madamoiselle Hermione,*[b] the Heiress of her Family. The Prince knew this young Lady had a Tenderness for him ever since they were both very young, which first took beginning in a Mask at Court, where she then acted *Mercury,*[c] and danced so exceedingly finely, that she gave our young Hero new Desire, if not absolute Love; and charm'd him at least into Wishes. She was then old enough to perceive she conquered, as well as to make a Conquest: And she was capable of receiving Impressions, as well as to give 'em: And it was believed by some who were very near the Prince, and knew all his Secrets then, that since this young Lady pitied the Sighs of the Royal Lover, and even then rewarded 'em: And tho' this were mostly credibly whispered, yet methinks it seems impossible he should then have been happy, and after so many Years, after the Possession of so many Beauties, should return to her again, and find all the Passions and Pains of a beginning Flame. But there is nothing to be wondered at in the Contradictions and Humours of Man's human Nature. But however inconstant and wavering he had been, *Hermione* retain'd her first Passion for him; and that I less wonder at, since you know the Prince has the most charming Person in the World, and is the most perfectly Beautiful of all his Sex: To this his Youth and Quality adds no little Lustre; and I should not wonder if all the softer Sex should languish for him, nor that any one should love on—— who hath once been touch'd with Love for him. 'Twas this last Assurance the Prince so absolutely depended on, that (notwithstanding she was far from the Opinion of his Party) made him resolve to take Sanctuary in those Arms he was sure would receive him in any Condition and Circumstances. But now he makes her new Vows, which possibly at first his Safety obliged

---

[a] Lady Philadelphia Wentworth.

[b] Lady Henrietta Wentworth (1657?–86). Her affair with the Duke of Monmouth was first made public in 1680 when her mother withdrew her from the court, only to be followed by the Duke to Toddington. When Monmouth was forced to flee to Brussels, Henrietta joined him there and remained his mistress until his death. Both she and her mother offered their jewels as security for the funds needed for the 1685 rebellion. Henrietta remained in Holland during Monmouth's ill-fated campaign, though she returned to England in 1686 where she died shortly afterwards.

[c] In December Henrietta Wentworth took the part of Jupiter in a masque at the court by John Crowne called *Calisto, or the chaste Nymph.* The Duke of Monmouth also danced in this masque and it is believed that he and Henrietta, then aged seventeen, first became lovers at about this time.

him to, while she return'd 'em with all the Passion of Love. He made a thousand Submissions to Madam the Countess,[a] who he knew was fond of her Daughter to that degree, that for her Repose she was even willing to behold the Sacrifice of her Honour to this Prince, whom she knew *Hermione* loved even to Death; so fond, so blindly fond is Nature: And indeed after a little time that he lay there conceal'd, he reap'd all the Satisfaction that Love could give him, or his Youth could wish, with all the Freedom imaginable. He only made Vows of renouncing all other Women, what Ties or Obligations soever he had upon him; and to resign himself intirely up to *Hermione*. I know not what new Charms he had found by frequent Conversation with her, and being uninterrupted by the sight of any other Ladies; but 'tis most certain, my Lord, he grew to that excess of Love, or rather Doatage (if Love in one so young, can be call'd so) that he languishes for her,[b] even while he possessed her all: He dy'd, if oblig'd by Company to retire from her an Hour, at the end of which, being again brought to her, he would fall at her Feet, and sigh, and weep, and make pitious Moan that ever Love inspir'd. He would complain upon the Cruelty of a Moments Absence, and vow he could not live where she was not. All that disturbed his Happiness, he reproach'd as Enemies to his Repose, and at last made her feign an Illness, that no Visits might be made her, and that he might possess all her Hours. Nor did *Hermione* perceive all this without making her Advantages of so glorious an Opportunity; but with the usual Cunning of her Sex, improved every Minute she gave him: She now found herself sure of the Heart of the finest Man in the World; and of one she believed would prove the greatest, being the Head of a

---

[a] Lady Philadelphia Wentworth encouraged the liaison between Monmouth and her daughter. Her decision to accompany the lovers to Holland shocked her contemporaries. Sir Bevil Skelton, an English minister at The Hague and a family relation, commented on the three exiles that he was

very much concerned to hear that Lady Hen. Wentworth is so dangerously sick, but much more concerned that the Duke of Monmouth takes such care of her, and think it better that she should die than bring a scandal upon herself. I approve not of her conduct, and much less of her mother's, who humours her in it.

[b] It was commonly known that Monmouth and Henrietta Wentworth were devoted to each other. A contemporary noted that

They were both as infatuated, and imagined themselves man and wife…The poor duke alleged a pretence, very airy and absurd, that he was married so very young that he did not know what he was doing, and that my poor Lady Henrietta he regarded as his wife before God, and she was a visionary on her side.

most powerful Faction, who were resolved the first Opportunity to order Affairs so as to come to an open Rebellion, and to
make him a King. All these things, how unlikely soever in
Reason, her Love and Ambition suggested to her; so that she
believed she had but one Game more to play to establish herself
the greatest and most happy Woman in the World. She consults
in this weighty Affair with her Mother, who had a share of
Cunning that could carry on a Design as well as any of her Sex.
They found but one Obstacle to all *Hermione*'s rising Greatness;
and that was the Prince's being married; and that to a Lady of so
considerable Birth and Fortune, so eminent for her Vertue, and
all Perfections of Woman-kind; and withal so excellent for Wit
and Beauty, that 'twas impossible to find any Cause of a Separation between 'em. So that finding it improbable to remove that
Lett to her Glories, she grew very Melancholy; which was soon
perceived by the too Amorous Prince, who pleads, and sighs,
and weeps on her Bosom Day and Night to find the Cause: But
she, who found she had a difficult Game to play, and that she
had need of all her little Aids, pretends a thousand little frivil-
lous Reasons before she discovers the true one; which serv'd
but to oblige him to ask anew, as she design'd he should——At
last, one Morning, finding him in the softest fit in the World,
and ready to give her whatever she could ask in return for the
Secret of her Disquiet, she told him with a Sigh, how Unhappy
she was in loving so violently a Man who could never be any
thing to her more than the Robber of her Honour: And at last
with abundance of Sighs and Tears bewail'd his Marriage ——
He taking her with all the Joy imaginable in his Arms, thank'd
her for speaking of the only thing he had a thousand times been
going to offer to her, but durst not for fear she should Reproach
him. He told her he look'd upon himself as married to no
Woman but herself, to whom, by a thousand solemn Vows he
had contracted himself, and that he would never own any other
while he liv'd, let Fortune do what she pleas'd with him. *Hermione* thriving hitherto so well, urged his easy Heart yet farther,
and told him, Tho' she had left no Doubt remaining in her of his

---

[a] In 1662, Charles II agreed that his illegitimate son, James Crofts, then only 13,
should be married to Anne, Duchess of Monmouth and Countess of Buccleugh. She
too was twelve years old and a wealthy heiress with the largest fortune in Scotland.
With the marriage, the Duke of Monmouth took his wife's family name, Scott, as his
own.

Love and Vertue, no suspicion of his Vows, yet the World would still esteem the Princess his Wife, and herself only as a Prostitute to his Youthful Pleasure; and as she conceiv'd her Birth and Fortune not to be much inferior to that of the Princess, she should die with Indignation and Shame, to bear all the Reproach of his Wantonness, while his now Wife would live esteem'd and pitied as an injured Innocent. To all which he reply'd, as mad in Love, That the Princess, he confess'd, was a Lady to whom he had Obligations, but that he esteem'd her no more his Wife, since he was married to her at the Age of twelve Years; an Age wherein he was not capacitated to chuse Good or Evil, or to answer for himself, or his Inclinations: And tho' she were a Lady of absolute Vertue, of Youth, Wit and Beauty; yet Fate had so ordain'd it, that he had reserv'd his Heart to this Moment intirely for herself; and that he renounc'd all Pretenders to him except herself; that he had now possess'd the Princess for the space of twenty Years; that Youth had a long Race to run, and could not take up at those Years with one single Beauty: That hitherto Ravage and Destruction of Hearts had been his Province and Glory, and that he thought he had never lost time but when he was a little while Constant: But now he was fix'd to all he would ever possess whilst he had Breath; and that she was both his Mistress and his Wife; his eternal Happiness, and the end of all his Loving. 'Tis there he said he would remain as in his first state of Innocence: That hitherto his Ambition had been above his Passion, but that now his Heart was so intirely subdu'd to this fair Charmer (for so he call'd and thought her) that he could be content to live and die in the Glory of being hers alone, without wishing for Liberty or Empire, but to render her more Glorious. A thousand things tender and fond he said to this purpose, and the result of all ended in most solemn Vows, That if ever Fortune favoured him with a Crown, he would fix it on her Head, and make her in spight of all former Ties and Obligations Queen of *France*. This was sufficient to appease her Sighs and Tears, and she remain'd intirely satisfied of his Vows, which were exchanged before Madam the Countess, and confirm'd by all the binding Obligations Love on his side could invent, and Ambition and Subtilty on hers. When I came at any time to visit him, which by stealth a-nights I sometimes did, to take Orders from him how I should act in all things (tho' I lay conceal'd like himself) he would tell me all that had passed between him and *Hermione*. I suppose, not so much for the reposing the Secret in my Breast, as out of a fond Pleasure to be relating Passages of his Doatage, and repeating her Name, which was ever in his Mouth: I saw she had reduc'd him to a great degree of Slavery, and could not look tamely on while a Hero so young, so gay, so great, and so hopeful, lay idling away his precious Time, without doing any thing, either in order for his own Safety or Ambition. 'Twas, my Lord, a great pity to see how his noble Resolution was changed, and how he was perfectly effeminated into soft Woman. I indeavoured at last to rouse him from this Lethargy of Love; and argued with him the little Reason, that in my Opinion he had to be so charm'd. I told him *Hermione*, of all the Beauties of France, was esteemed one of the meanest, and that if ever she had gain'd a Conquest (as many she was infamously fam'd for) it was purely the force of her Youth and Quality; but that now that Bloom was past, and she was one of those, which in less quality, we call'd Old. At these Reproaches of his Judgment, I often perceiv'd him to blush, but more with Anger than Shame. Yet because, according to the Vogue of the Town, he found there was Reason in what I said, and which he could only contradict by saying however she was, she appeared all otherwise to him. He blam'd me a little kindly for my hard Words against her, and began to swear to me he thought her all over Charm. He vow'd there was absolute Fascination in her Eyes and Tongue. 'Tis confess'd, said he, *she has not much of Youth, nor of that which we agree to call Beauty; but she has a Grace so Masculine, an Air so Ravishing, a Wit and Humour so absolutely made to charm, that they all together sufficiently recompense for her want of Delicacy in Complexion and Feature: And in a word, my* Tomaso, cry's he imbracing me; *she is, tho' I know not what, or how, a Maid that compels me to adore her; she has a natural Power to please above the rest of her dull Sex; and I can abate her a Face and Shape, and yet vie her for Beauty with any of the celebrated ones of* France.

I found by the manner of his saying this, that he was really charm'd, and past all Retrieve; bewitch'd to this Lady. I found it vain therefore to press him to a Separation, or to lessen his Passion; but on the contrary told him there was a time for all things; if Fate had so ordain'd it that he must love. But I besought him with all the Eloquence of perfect Duty and Friendship not to suffer his Passion to surmount his Ambition and his Reason, so far as to neglect his Interest and Safety; and for a little Pleasure with a Woman, suffer all his Friends to perish that had woven their Fortunes with his, and must stand or fall as he thriv'd: I implor'd him not to cast away the *Good Cause*[a] which was so far advanc'd, and that yet, notwithstanding this Discourse, might all be retrieved by his Conduct and good Management. That I knew, however the King appeared in outward shew to be offended, that it was yet in his Power to calm the greatest Tempest this Discovery had raised: That 'twas but casting himself at his Majesty's Feet, and begging his Mercy, by a Confession of the Truth of some part of the Matter; and that it was impossible he could fail of a Pardon from so indulgent a Monarch as he had offended: That there was no Action could wholly raze out of the Kings Heart that Tenderness and Passion he had ever expressed towards him; and his Peace might be made with all the Facility imaginable. To this he urged a very great Reluctancy, and cry'd he would sooner die, than by a Confession expose the Lives of his Friends, and let the World see their whole Design before they had power to effect it: And not only so, but put it past all their Industry ever to bring so hopeful a Plot about again. At this I smil'd, and asking his Highness Pardon, told him I was of another Opinion, as most of the Heads of the *Hugonots* were, That what he said to his Majesty in Private could never possibly be made Publick: That his Majesty would content himself with the Knowledge of the Truth, without caring to satisfy the World, so greatly to the Prejudice of a Prince of the Blood, and a Man so very dear to him as himself: He urg'd the Fears this would give those of the Reformed Religion,[b] and alarm 'em with a thousand Apprehensions, that it would discover every Man of 'em, by unraveling the Intrigue. To this I reply'd, that their Fears would be very short liv'd; for as soon as he had by his Submission and Confession gained his Pardon, he had no more to do but to renounce all he had said, leave the Court, and put himself into the Protection of his Friends, who were ready to receive him. That he need but appear abroad a little time, and he would see himself address'd to again by all of the *Hugonot* Party, who would quickly put him into a Condition of fearing nothing.

---

[a] The phrase echoes the commonwealthmen's 'Good Old Cause', a term they used to describe their continuing struggle to strengthen parliament and weaken, or remove, royal authority.

[b] Protestantism. Whig support ranged from Anglicans and Presbyterians to Independent sectarians. They were united by a common belief in constitutional rule of the state.

My Councel, with the same Perswasion from all of Quality of the Party, who came to see him, was at last approved of by him, and he began to say a thousand things to assure me of his Fidelity to his Friends and the Faction, which he vow'd never to forsake for any other Interest, but to stand or fall in its Defence; and that he was resolved to be a King or Nothing; and that he would put in Practice all the Arts and Stratagems of Cunning, as well as Force, to attain to this Glorious End, however crooked and indirect they might appear to Fools. However he conceived the first necessary Step to this, was the getting his Pardon, to gain a little time to manage things anew, to the best Advantage: That at present all things were at a stand without Life or Motion, wanting the sight of himself who was the very Life and Soul of Motion; the Axel-tree[a] that could turn the Wheel of Fortune[b] round again.

And now he had talk'd himself into Sense again; he cry'd—— *Oh my* Tomaso! *I long to be in Action, my Soul is on the Wing, and ready to take its Flight through any Hazzard.*——But sighing, on a suddain again he cry'd: *But oh my Friend, my Wings are impt by Love,[c] I cannot mount the Regions of the Air and thence survey the World; but still as I would rise to mightier Glory, they flag to humble Love, and fix me there. Here I am charm'd to lazy soft Repose, here 'tis I smile and play, and love away my Hours: But I will rouse, I will, my dear* Tomaso; *nor shall the winged Boy hold me inslav'd: Believe me Friend he shall not* —— He sent me away pleased with this, and I left him to his Repose.

Supper being ready to come upon the Table, tho' *Philander* were impatient to hear the Story out, yet he would not press *Tomaso*, till after Supper; in which time they discoursed of nothing but the Miracle of *Cesario's* Love to *Hermione*. He could not but wonder a Prince so young, so amorous, and so gay, should return again, after almost fifteen Years, to an old Mistress;[d] and who had never been in her Youth a celebrated

---

[a] Rod on which a wheel revolves.

[b] One of the attributes of the goddess of luck, Fortuna. The wheel could stand alone as an image of Fortune and, as such, it evolved into the lottery wheel.

[c] 'Imping' was a process used to strengthen a bird's wings, improving flight but here Behn uses it to refer to clipping a bird's wings, impeding flight.

[d] Henrietta Wentworth was now approximately twenty-eight years old. After their earlier affair, both Monmouth and Henrietta had become involved with other lovers. Monmouth had many mistresses including Lady Grey, Ford Grey's wife and sister to Henrietta Berkeley. Henrietta Wentworth also had several lovers and it was rumoured that she would marry the Earl of Thanet, though the match fell through.

Beauty: One, whom it was imagined, the King, several after him at Court, had made a Gallantry with[a] —— On this he paused for some time, and reflected on his Passion for *Silvia*; and this fantastick Intrigue of the Prince's inspired him with a kind of Curiosity to try, whether fleeting Love would carry him back again to this abandoned Maid. In these Thoughts, and such Discourse, they passed away the time during Supper; which ended, and a fresh Bottle brought to the Table, with a new Command that none should interrupt 'em: The impatient *Philander* obliged *Tomaso* to give him a farther Account of the Princes Proceedings; which he did in this manner:

My Lord, having left my Prince, as I imagined, very well resolved, I spoke of it to as many of our Party as I could conveniently meet with, to prepare 'em for the Discovery I believed the Prince would pretend to make, that they should not by being alarm'd at the first News of it, put themselves into Fears that might indeed discover 'em: Nor would I suffer *Cesario* to rest, but daily saw him, or rather nightly stole to him, to keep up his Resolution: And indeed, in spight of Love, to which he had made himself so intire a Slave, I brought him to his own House, to visit Madam his Wife,[b] who was very well at Court, maugre[c] her Husbands ill Conduct, as they call'd it. The King being, as you know, my Lord, extreamly kind to that deserving Lady, often made her Visits, and would without very great Impatiency hear her plead for her Husband, the Prince; and possibly it was not ungrateful to him: All this we daily learn'd from a Page, who secretly brought Intelligence from Madam the Princess: So that we conceived it wholly necessary for the Interest of the Prince, that he should live in a good Understanding with this prudent Lady. To this end he feigned more Respect than usual to her, and as soon as it was dark, every Evening made her his Visits. One Evening among the rest, he happened to be there, just as the Proclamation came forth of four thousand Crowns[d] to any that could discover him; and within half an Hour after came the King to visit the Princess, as every

---

[a] Courted and seduced.

[b] The Duchess of Monmouth did remain in the favour of Charles II. After Monmouth had been siezed at Toddington in 1683, his wife was instrumental in helping to bring about a reconciliation with his father.

[c] Archaic: despite.

[d] The text is inconsistent here as the earlier figure quoted was 'forty thousand crowns'.

Night he did; her Lodging being in the Court: The King came
without giving any Notice, and with a very slender Train that
Night: so that he was almost in the Princess's Bed-chamber
before any body inform'd her he was there; so that the Prince had
no time to retire but into Madam the Princess's *Cabaret*, the Door
of which, she immediately locking, made such a Noise and
Bustle that it was heard by his Majesty, who nevertheless had
passed it by, if her Confusion and Blushes had not farther
betray'd her, with the unusual Address she made to the King:
Who therefore asked her who she had conceal'd in her Closet.
She endeavoured to put him off with some feign'd Replies, but
'twould not do; the more her Confusion, the more the King was
inquisitive, and urged her to give him the Key of her *Cabaret*: But
she, who knew the Life of the Prince would be in very great
Danger, should he be taken so, and knew on the other side, that
to deny it would betray the Truth as much as his Discovery
would, and cause him either to force the Key or the Door, fell
down at his Feet, and wetting his Shoes with her Tears, and
grasping his Knees in her trembling Arms, implor'd that Mercy
and Pity for the Prince her Husband, whom her Vertue had
rendered dear to her, however Criminal he appear'd to his
Majesty: She told him his Majesty had more peculiarly the
Attributes of a God than any other Monarch upon Earth, and
never heard the Wretched or the Innocent plead in vain. She told
him that herself and her Children, who were dearer to her than
Life, should all be as Hostages for the good Conduct and Duty of
the Prince's future Life and Actions: And they would all be
obliged to suffer any Death, tho' never so ignominious, upon the
least breaking out of her Lord: That he should utterly abandon
those of the *reformed Religion*, and yield to what Articles his
Majesty would graciously be pleased to impose, quitting all his
false and unreasonable Pretensions to the Crown, which was
only the Effects of the Flattery of the *Hugonot Party*, and the *Male-
Contents*.[a] Thus with the Vertue and Goodness of an Angel, she
pleaded with such moving Eloquence, mix'd with Tears, from
beautiful Eyes, that she fail'd not to soften the royal Heart, who
knew not how to be deaf when Beauty pleaded: Yet he would not
seem to yield so suddenly, least it should be imagined he had too
light a Sense of his Treasons, which, in any other great Man,

---

[a] The Protestant Whigs who feared an extension of popery and arbitrary government with the succession of the Catholic James, Duke of York.

would have been punished with no less than Death: Yet, as she pleaded, he grew calmer, and suffered it without Interruption, till she waited for his Reply; and obliged him by her Silence to speak. He numbers up the Obligations he had heaped on her Husband; how he had, by putting all Places of great Command and Interest into his Hands, made him the greatest Prince and Favourite, of a Subject, in the World; and infinitely happier than a Monarch: That he had all the Glory and Power of one, and wanted but the Care: All the Sweets of Empire, while all that was disagreeable and toilsom, remain'd with the Title alone. He therefore upbraided him with infinite Ingratitude, and want of Honour; with all the Folly of ambitious Youth: And left nothing unsaid that might make the Princess sensible it was too late to hide any of his Treasons from him, since they were all but too apparent to his Majesty. 'Twas therefore that she urged nothing but his Royal Mercy and Forgiveness, without indeavouring to lessen his Guilt, or inlarge on his Innocency. In fine, my Lord, so well she spoke, that at last she had the Joy to perceive the happy Effects of her Wit and Goodness, which had mov'd Tears of Pity and Compassion from his Majesty's Eyes; which was *Cesario's* Cue to come forth, as immediately he did (having heard all that had pass'd) and threw himself at his Majesty's Feet: And this was the critical Minute he was to snatch for the gaining his Point, and of which he made a most admirable use. He call'd up all the Force of necessary Dissimulation, Tenderness to his Voice, Tears to his Eyes, and Trembling to his Hands, that stay'd the too willing and melting Monarch by his Robe, till he had heard him implore, and granted him his Pity: Nor did he quit his Hold, till the King cry'd with a soft Voice—— Rise—— at which he was assured of what he asked. He refused however to rise, till the Pardon was pronounced. He own'd himself the greatest Criminal in Nature; that he was drawn from his Allegiance by the most subtile Artifices of his Enemies, who under false Friendships had allur'd his Hopes with gilded Promises;[a] and which he now too plainly

---

[a] Monmouth wrote two letters of confession to Charles II, with the help of the Earl of Halifax. In the second he said,

> I confess, sir, I have been in fault, misled, and insensibly engaged in things of which the consequence was not enough understood by me...I humbly beg, sir, to be admitted to your feet, and to be disposed of as you direct, not only now but for the remainder of my life...I am so sensible how ill a guide my own will hath been to me, that I am reolved for the future to put it entirely into your Majesty's hands, that I may by that means never commit a fault but for want of your directions or your commands.

saw were Designs to propagate their own private Interests, and not his Glory. He humbly besought his Majesty to make some gracious Allowances for his Vanities of Youth, and to believe now he had so dearly bought Discretion, at almost the price of his Majesty's eternal Displeasure, that he would reform, and lead so good a Life, so absolutely from any appearance of Ambition, that his Majesty should see he had not a more faithful Subject than himself. In fine, he found himself, by this Acknowledgment he had begun with, to advance yet farther: Nor would his Majesty be satisfied without the whole Scene of the Matter; and how they were to have surprized and seized him; where, and by what Numbers. All which he was forc'd to give an Account of; since now to have fallen back, when he was in their Hands, had been his infallible Ruine. All which he perform'd with as much Tenderness and Respect to his Friends concern'd, as if his own Life had been depending: And tho' he were extreamly prest to discover some of the great ones of the Party, he would never give his consent to an Action so mean, as to be an Evidence.[a] All that could be got from him farther, was, to promise his Majesty to give under his Hand, what he had in private confess'd to him; with which the King remained very well satisfy'd, and order'd him to come to Court the next day. Thus for that Night they parted, with infinite Caresses on the King's part, and no little Joy on his. His Majesty was no sooner gone, but he gave immediate order to the Secretaries of State,[b] to draw up his Pardon, which was done, with good Speed, that he had it in his own Hands the next day. When he came to Court 'tis not to be imagined the Surprize it was to all to behold the Man, in the greatest State imaginable, who but Yesterday was to have been Crucified at any Price: And those, who most exclaim'd against him, were the first who paid him Homage, and caress'd him at the highest rate; only the most Wise and Judicious, prophesied his Glories were not of a long Continuation.

---

[a] After receiving Monmouth's second letter, the king ordered that 'if he desired to render himself capable of mercy, he must place himself in the custody of the secretary, and resolve to disclose whatever he knew, resigning himself entirely to the royal pleasure.' The duke agreed and was placed under arrest. On November 25, 1682, he made a full confession of his knowledge of the conspiracy in an interview with Charles II and James, Duke of York. He named many of the main conspirators and convinced the king that he knew nothing of the assassination plot.

[b] In the Restoration period, a secretary of state acted as a minister for foreign and domestic affairs. The two principal secretaries at this time were Sir Leoline Jenkins and the Earl of Sunderland.

The King made no Visits where the Prince did not publickly appear: He told all People, with infinite Joy, that the Prince had confessed the whole Plot, and that he would give it under his Hand and Seal, in order to having it published thro'out all *France*,[a] for the Satisfaction of all those who had been deluded and deceived by our specious Pretences; and for the Terror of those, who had any ways adhered to so pernicious a Villainy: So that he met with nothing but Reproaches from those of our own Party at Court: For there were many, who, hitherto were unsuspected, and who now, out of fear of being betray'd by the Prince, were ready to fall at the Kings Feet and confess all: Others there were, that left the Court and Town upon it. In fine, the face of things seem'd extreamly altered, while the Prince bore himself like a Person who had the Misfortune justly to lie beneath the Exclamations of a disobliged Multitude, as they at least imagined, and bore all, as if their Fears had been true, without so much as offering at his Justification, to confirm his Majesty's good Opinion of him: He added to his Pardon a Present of twenty thousand Crowns;[b] half of it being paid the next day after his coming to Court. And in short, my Lord, his Majesty grew so fond of the Prince, he could not indure to suffer him out of his Presence; and was never satisfied with seeing him: He carried him the next day to the publick *Theatre* with him, to show the World he was reconcil'd. But by this time he had all confirm'd, and grew impatient to declare himself to his Friends, whom he would not have remain long in their ill Opinion of him. It happened, the third day of his coming to Court (in returning some of those Visits he had received from all the great Persons) he went to wait upon the Dutchess of——[c] a Lady who had ever had a tender Respect for the Prince: In the

---

[a] On November 26th, 1682 Charles II ordered that Monmouth's confession be published in the *Gazette* which was done. Monmouth, reading the *Gazette* at his dining table, announced to his guests – a Mr Hazzard and Dr. Chamberlain – that 'it was all false; that he had been with the King about it, and that it should be altered in the Gazette of the Thursday.' When the Duke of York learnt of Monmouth's denial of his confession he brought several witnesses to the king to testify to these actions.

[b] After the Duke of Monmouth's confession, the king granted him a full pardon and sent him £6000.

[c] The Duchess of Portsmouth, Louise de Kéroualle. The duchess was the king's mistress and had once allied herself with the Duke of Monmouth to prevent accusations of being a spy for the French. Her servant, Mistress Wall, was persuaded to begin rumours of the duchess's attempts to further the Duke of Monmouth's cause. This ploy was eventually discovered and lampoons appeared in the guise of 'intercepted letters' from the duchess to Monmouth.

time of this Visit, a young Lady of Quality happen'd to come in; one whom your Lordship knows a great Wit, and much esteemed at Court, *Madamoisell Mariana*:[a] By this Lady he found himself welcom'd to Court with all the Demonstration of Joy; as also by the old Dutchess, who had divers times heretofore perswaded the Prince to leave the *Hugonots*, and return to the King and Court: She used to tell him he was a handsome Youth, and she loved his Mother well; that he danc'd finely, and she had rather see him in a Ball at Court, than in Rebellion in the Field; and often to this purpose her Love would rally him; and now shew'd no less concern of Joy for his Reconciliation; and looking on him, as a true Convert, fell a-railing, with all the Malice and Wit she could invent, at those publick spirited Knaves who had seduced him. She rail'd me, and cursed those Politicks which had betray'd him, to almost Ruine it self. The Prince heard her, with all the Patience he could, for some time, but when he found her touch him so tenderly, and name his Friends, as if he had own'd any such ill Councellors, his Colour came into his Face, and he could not forbear defending us with all the Force of Friendship.[b] He told her he knew of no such Seducers, no Villains of the Party, nor of any traylerous Design, that either himself, or any Man in *France*, had ever harboured: At which, she growing to upbraid him, in a manner too passionate, he thought it decent to end his Visit, and left her very abuptly. At his going out he met with the Duke of——[c] Brother to the Dutchess, going to visit her: *En passant*[d] a very indifferent Ceremony pass'd on both sides, for this Duke never had entertain'd a Friendship, or scarce Respect for *Cesario* but going into his Sister's, the Dutchess her Chamber, he found her all in a Rage at the Princes so publick Defence of the *Hugonots*, and their Allies; and the Duke entering, they told him what had pass'd. This was a very great Pleasure to him, who had a mortal Hate at this time to the Prince. He made his Visit very short, hastens to Court, and went directly to the King, and told him

---

[a] Possibly Mistress Wall, the Duchess of Portsmouth's confidante.

[b] In order to dispel any uncertainty about the Duke of Monmouth's confession and repentance, the king commanded his son to present a new, more general letter to a committee which was assembled at the Duchess of Portsmouth's lodgings. Monmouth acquiesed but the committee demanded certain changes and after argument he reluctantly signed a modified version of the letter.

[c] James, Duke of York, the king's brother.

[d] *French*: in passing.

how infinitely he found his Majesty mistaken in the imagined Penitence of the Prince; and then told him what he had said at the Dutchess of—— Lodgings, and had disown'd he ever confess'd any treasonable Design against his Majesty, and gave 'em the Lye, who durst charge him with any such Villainy. The King, who was unwilling to credit what he wished not true, plainly told the Duke, he could not believe it, but that it was the Malice of his Enemies who had forg'd this; the Duke reply'd, he would bring those to his Majesty, that heard the Words: Immediately thereupon dispatched away his Page, to begg the Dutchess would come to Court, with *Madamoisell Mariana*. The Dutchess suspecting the truth of the Business, and unwilling to do the Prince an ill Office, excused herself, by sending word she was ill of the Colick. But *Mariana*, who lov'd the King's Interest, and found the Ingratitude, as she call'd it, of the prime, hasted in her Chair to Court, and justified all the Duke had said; who being a Woman of great Wit and Honour, found that Credit which the Duke fail'd of, as an open Enemy to the Prince. About an hour after the Prince appeared at Court, and found the face of Things changed extreamly; and those, who before had kiss'd his Hand, and were proud of every smile from him: Now beheld him with coldness, and scarce made way as he past. However, he went on to the Presence and found the King, whose looks were also verȳ much changed; who taking him into the Bed-Chamber, show'd him his whole Confession, drawn up ready for him to sign, as he had promis'd, tho' he never intended any such thing; and now resolv'd to die rather than do it: He took it in his Hand, while the King cry'd, —— *Here keep your Word, and Sign your Narrative.* ——*Stay, Sir*, replied the Prince, *I have the Council of my Friends to ask first, in so weighty an Affair.*[a] The King confirm'd in all he had heard, no longer doubted but he had been too cunning for him; and going out in a very great discontent, he only cry'd, ——*Sir, if you have any better Friends than my self, I leave you to 'em;*——and with this left him. The Prince was very glad he had got the Confession-Paper, hoping it would never come to light again; the King was

---

[a] After leaving his written confession with the king and committee at the Duchess of Portsmouth's lodgings, Monmouth went to dine with Hampden and Trenchard, two of the conspirators he had implicated by his letter. The following morning he approached the king and asked him to return the confession, saying he would never appear in council to confirm it. The king returned the letter and banished Monmouth from the court.

the only person to whom he had made the Confession, and he was but one Accuser; and him he thought the Party could at any time be too powerful to oppose, all being easily believed on their side, and nothing on that of the Court. After this, in the Evening, the King going to visit Madam the Dutchess of —— for whom he had a very great Esteem, and whither every Day the whole Court followed him: The Prince, with all the assurance imaginable, made his Court there also; but he was no sooner come into the Presence, but he perceived Anger in the Eyes of that Monarch, who had indeed a peculiar Greatness and Firceness there when angry: A Minute after he sent Monsieur —— to the Prince, with a command to leave the Court; and without much Ceremony he accordingly departed, and went directly to *Hermione*, who with all the impatience of Love expected him; nor was much surprized to find him Banisht the Court: For he made her acquainted with his most Secret Designs; who having made all his Interests her own, Espoused whatever related to him, and was capable of retaining all with great Fidelity: Nor had he quitted her one Night, since his coming to Court; and he hath often, with rapture, told me, *Hermione* was a Friend as well as a Mistress, and one with whom, when the First Play was ended, he could Discourse with of useful things of State, as well as Love; and improve in both the Noble Mysteries, by her Charming Conversation. The Night of this second Disgrace, I went to *Hermione*'s to visit him, where we Discours'd what was next to be done. He did not think his Pardon was sufficient to secure him, and he was not willing to trust a King who might be convinced, that that Tenderness he had for him, was absolutely against the Peace and Quiet of all *France*. I was of this Opinion, so that upon farther debate, we thought it absolutely necessary to quit *France*,[a] till the Courts heat should be a little abated, and that the King might imagine himself, by his absence, in more Tranquillity than he really is. In order to this, he made me take my Flight into *Flanders*, here to provide all things necessary against his coming, and I received his command to seek you out, and beg you would attend his coming hither. I expect him

---

[a] After being forbidden to enter the court, Monmouth returned to his country seat, Moore Park, near Rickmansworth. Early in 1684 he was served with a subpoena to give evidence in the trial of John Hampden. Caught between the government and betrayal of his own supporters, the duke fled to Holland to live with Henrietta Wentworth.

every Day. He told me at parting he long'd to consult with you how next to play this mighty Game, on which so many Kingdoms are staked, and which he is resolv'd to win or be nothing. An imperfect Relation, replied *Philander*, we had of this Affair, but I never could learn by what Artifice the Prince brought about his good Fortune at Court; but of your own Escape, I have heard nothing, pray oblige me with the Relation of it: *Sir*, said Thomaso, *there is so little worthy the trouble you will take in hearing it, that you may spare your self the Curiosity. Sir*, reply'd Philander, *I alway had too great a share in what concern'd you not to be Curious of the Story. In which*, reply'd Thomaso, *tho' there be nothing Novel, I will satisfie you.*

Be pleas'd to know, my Lord, that about a Week before our design was fully discovered by some of our own under-Rogues, I had taken a great House in *Fabour St. Jermins*,[a] for my Mistress,[b] whom you know, my Lord, I had liv'd with for the space of a Year. She was gone to drink the Waters of *Bourbon*,[c] for some indisposition, and I had promised her all things should be fitted against her return, agreeable to her Humour and Desire; and indeed I spared no cost to make her Apartment Magnificent: And I believe few Women of Quality could purchace one so rich; for I lov'd the Young Woman, who had Beauty and Discretion enough to charm, tho' the *Parisians* of the Royal Party call'd her *Nicky Nacky*,[d] which was given her in derision to me, not to her, for whom every body, for her own sake, had a considerable Esteem. Besides, my Lord, I had taken up Money out of the Orphans and Widows Bank[e] from the Chamber of

---

[a] Faubourg St-Germain, a wealthy district in the centre of Paris. Behn is probably referring to Charing Cross, a wealthy area of London at that time.

[b] In a December 1681 issue of the *Observator* L'Estrange suggested that the notorious brothel-keeper, Madam Creswell, was the mistress of the Earl of Shaftesbury.

[c] It was fashionable to travel to the spa of Montpellier for the Waters of Bourbon at this time. The phrase also had connotations of political exile as it was the refuge of Clarendon after his fall from power.

[d] In Thomas Otway's *Venice Preserv'd* (1682) the caricature of Shaftesbury – Antonio – has a mistress called Aquilina or 'Nicky Nacky'. Behn also refers to such a mistress in her poem 'The Cabal at Nickey Nackeys'. [Cf. *Works of Aphra Behn*, Vol. 1, no. 48.]

[e] The Earl of Shaftesbury had been a member of the Treasury Board in 1672 when the 'Stop of the Exchequer' Act was passed. Under this act, the government stopped all repayment of state debts to banks and were therefore able to use incoming tax revenue for current expenditure. Shaftesbury opposed the act, telling Charles II that it would 'ruin thousands [including] a multitude of poor widows and orphans'. However, it was said that Shaftesbury had used his advance knowledge of the Act to withdraw his own deposits from the banks before the Stop. His accounts for this period show that he did call in his short term loans in 1671 and that he bought land in Cranborne Chase with these funds.

Paris, and could very well afford to be Lavish when I spent upon the publick Stock. While I was thus ordering all things, my *Vallet*[a] came running out of Breath to tell me, that being at the *Loovre*,[b] he saw several persons carried to the Secretaries Office, with Messengers; and that inquiring who they might be, he found they were two *Parisians*, who had offered themselves to the Messengers, to be carried to be Examined about a Plot, the Prince *Cesario* and those of the *Reformed Religion* had to surprize his Majesty, kill Monsieur[c] his Brother, and set all *Paris* in a Flame: And as to what particularly related to my self; he said, That I was named as the person design'd to seize upon the King's Guards, and dispatch Monsieur. This my own Conscience told me was too true for me to make any doubt, but I was discovered; I therefore left a Servant in the House, and in an Hackney-Coach took my Flight. I drove a little out of *Paris* till Night and then returned again, as the surest part of the World where I could conceal my self: I was not long in studying who I should trust with my Life and safety, but went directly to the Palace of Madam the Countess of——[d] who you know, my Lord, was a Widow, and a Woman who had had, for a year past, a most violent Passion for me; but she being a Lady who had made many such Gallantries, and past her Youth, I had had only a very great Respect and Acknowledgment for her and her Quality, and being obliged to her for the Effects of her Tenderness, shown upon several Occasions, I could not but acquit my self like a *Cavalier* to her, whenever I could possible; and which, tho' I have a thousand times feigned great Business to prevent, yet I could not always be ungrateful; and when I paid her my Services; 'twas ever extreamly well received; and because of her Quality, and setting up for a second Marriage, she always took care to make my Approaches to her in as conceal'd a manner as possible; and only her Porter, one Page, and one Woman, knew this secret Amour; and for the better carrying it on, I ever went

---

[a] Valet.

[b] The Louvre in Paris was one of the French king's palaces. Here it stands for Whitehall Palace in London.

[c] Behn is referring to James, Duke of York.

[d] When the Rye-House Plot was made known to Charles II, Shaftesbury went into hiding at the house of a merchant called Watson in Wood Street. He later stayed with Robert Ferguson and shortly before fleeing to Holland he was at a sea-captain's house in Wapping.

in a Hackney-Coach, least my Livery should be seen at her Gate: And as it was my Custom at other times, so I now sent the Porter (whom, by my Bounty and his Ladies, was intirely my own Creature) for the Page, to come to me, who immediately did, and I desired him to let his Lady know, I waited her Commands; That was the Word: He immediately brought me Answer, that by good Fortune his Lady was all alone, and infinitely wishing she knew where to send him for me: and I immediately, at that good News, ran up to her Chamber; where I was no sooner come, but desiring me to sit, she ordered her Porter to be call'd, and gave him Orders, upon pain of Life, not to tell of my being in the House, whatever Enquiry should be made after me; and having given the same Command to her Page, she dismiss'd 'em, and came to me, with all the Fear and Trembling imaginable. *Ah Monsieur*, cry'd she, falling on my Neck, *we are undone*—— I not imagining she had heard the News already; cry'd, *Why, is my Passion discovered? Ah*, reply'd she in Tears, *I would to Heaven it were no worse! would all the Earth had discovered that, which I should esteem my Glory*—— *But 'tis, my charming Monsieur*, continued she, *Your Treasons and not Amour, whose discovery will be so fatal to me*. At this I seemed amaz'd, and beg'd her to let me understand her: She told me what I have said before; and moreover, That the Council had that very Evening issued out Warrants for me, and she admired how I escaped. After a little Discourse of this kind, I asked her what she would advise me to do? for I was very well assured the violent hate the King had particularly for me, would make him never consent I should live on any terms: And therefore 'twas determined I should not surrender my self; and she resolved to run the risk of concealing me; which in fine she did Three Days furnishing me with Money and Necessaries for my Flight. In this time a Proclamation[a] came forth and offered five hundred Crowns for my Head, or to Seize me alive or dead. This Sum so wrought with the slavish Minds of Men, that no Art was left unessay'd to take me: They searcht all Houses, all Hackney-Coaches that pass'd by Night; and did all that Avarice could inspire to take me, but all in vain: At last this glorious Sum so dazled the Mind of Madam the Countess's Porter, that he went

---

[a] A Proclamation in 1683 offered £500 for the capture of Sir Thomas Armstrong or his associates including Monmouth, Grey and Robert Ferguson.

to a Captain of the Musquetiers,[a] and assured him, if the King would give him the aforesaid Sum, he would betray me, and bring him the following Night to surprize me without any Resistance: The Captain, who thought, if the Porter should have all the Sum, he should get none; and every one hoping to be the happy Man that should take me and win the Prize, could not indure another should have the Glory of both, and so never told the King of the Offer the Porter had made. But however Secret one may imagine an Amour to be kept, yet in so busie a place as *Paris*, and the Apartments of the Court Coquets, this of ours had been discoursed, and the Intrigue more than suspected: Whether this, or the Captain before nam'd, imagined to find me at the House of the Countess, because her Porter had made such an Offer; I say, however it was, the next Morning, upon a *Sunday*, the Guards broke into several Chambers, and missing me, had the Insolence to come to the Door of that of the Countess; and she had only time to slip on her Night-Gown, and running to the Door, besought them to have Respect to her Sex and Quality, while I started from my Bed, which was the same from whence the Countess rose; and not knowing where to hide, or what to do, concealing my Clothes between the Sheets, I mounted from the Table to a great silver Sconce that was fastened to the Wall by the Bed-side, and from thence made but one Spring up to the Tester of the Bed; which being one of those, raised with strong wood-work, and Japan,[b] I could easily do; or rather it was by Miracle I did it; and laid myself along on the top, while my Back touched the Ceiling of the Chamber; by this time, when no Intreaties could prevail, they had burst open the Chamber Door, and running directly to the Bed, they could not believe their Eyes: They saw no Person there, but the plain print of two, with the Pillows for two Persons. This gave them the Curiosity to search farther, which they did, with their Swords, under the Bed, in every Corner, behind every Curtain, up the Chimney, felt all about the Wainscot and Hangings for false Doors, or Closets; survey'd the Floor for a Trap-door: At last, they found my fringed Gloves in the Window, and the Shash a little up, and then they concluded I had made my Escape out at that Window: This Thought they seem'd confirm'd in, and therefore ran to the Garden, where

---

[a] Guards.
[b] A hard varnish, originally from Japan.

they thought I had descended, and with my Gloves, which they bore away, as the Trophies of their almost gained Victory, they searched every Hedge and Bush, Arbour, Grotto, and Tree; but not being able to find what they sought, they concluded me gone, and told all the Town how very near they were to seizing me. After this, the very Porter and Page believed me escaped out at that Window, and there was no farther Search made after me: But the Countess was amazed, as much as any of the Souldiers, to find which way I had convey'd myself, when I came down and undeceiv'd her; but when she saw from whence I came, she wondered more than before, how I could get up so high; when trying the trick again, I could not do it, if I might have won never so considerable a Wager upon it, without pulling down the Sconce and the Teaster also.

After this, I remain'd there undiscovered the whole time the Prince was at *Hermione*'s till his coming to Court, when I verily believed he would have gained me my Pardon, with his own; but the King had sworn my final Destruction, if he ever got me in his Power; and proclaiming me a Traytor, seiz'd all they could find of mine. 'Twas then that I believed it high time to take my Flight; which, as soon as I heard the Prince again in Disgrace, I did, and got safely into *Holland*, where I have remained about six Weeks. But, oh! what is Woman? The first News I heard, and that was while I remain'd at the Countess's, that my Mistriss, for whom I had taken such Care, and who had professed to love me above all things, no sooner heard I was fled and proscrib'd, but retiring to a Friends House (for her own was seized for mine) and the Officers imagining me there too, they came to search; and a young *Cavalier*, of a noble Aspect, great Wit and Courage, and indeed a very fine Gentleman, was the Officer that entered her Chamber to search for me; who, being at first sight, surprized with her Beauty, and melted with her Tears, fell most desperately in Love with her, and after hearing how she had lost all her Money, Plate and Jewels, and rich Furniture, offered her his Service to retrieve 'em, and did do it; and from one Favour to another, continued so to oblige the fair fickle Creature, that he won, with that and his handsom Mien, a Possession of her Heart, and she yielded in a weeks time to my most mortal Enemy. And the Countess, who, at my going from her, swounded, and bathed me all in Tears, making a thousand Vows of Fidelity, and never to favour Mankind more: This very Woman, Sir, as soon as my Back was turn'd, made new Advances to a young Lord, who, believing her to be none of the most Faithful, would not trust her under Matrimony: He being a Man of no great Fortune, and she a Mistress of a very considerable one, his standing off on these Terms, inflames her the more; and I have Advice that she is very much in Love with him, and 'tis believed will do what he desires of her: So that I was no sooner abandoned by Fortune, but fickle Woman followed her Example, and fled me too. Thus, my Lord, you have the History of my double Unhappiness: And I am waiting here a Fate which no Human Wit can guess at: The Arrival of the Prince will give a little Life to our Affair; and I yet have Hope to see him in *Paris*, at the Head of forty thousand *Hugonots*, to revenge all the Insolences we have suffered.

After discoursing of several things, and of the Fate of several Persons, it was Bed-time, and they taking Leave, each Man departed to his Chamber.

Philander, while he was undressing, being alone with *Brilljard*, began to discourse of *Silvia*, and to take some care of letting her know he was arrived at *Bruxells*; and for her Convoy thither, *Brilljard*, who even yet retained some unaccountable Hope, as Lovers do, of one day being happy with that fair one; and believing he could not be so, with so much Facility, while she was in the Hands of *Octavio*, as those of *Philander*, would never tell his Lord his Sentiments of her Conduct, nor of her Love to *Octavio*, and those other Passages that had occur'd in *Holland*: He only cry'd, he believ'd she might be overcome, being left to herself, and by the Merits and good Fashion of *Octavio*; but would not give his Master an absolute Fear, or any account of Truth; that he might live with her again if possible, as before; and that she might hold herself so obliged to him for his Silence in these Affairs, as might one day render him happy. These were the unweighed Reasons he gave for deluding his Lord into a kind Opinion of the fickle Maid: But ever when he named *Silvia*, *Philander* could perceive his Blushes rise, and from 'em, believ'd there was something behind in his Thought, which he had a mind to know: He therefore pressed him to the last degree,——and cry'd——*Come*—— *confess to me*, Brilljard, *the reason of your Blushes: I know you are a Lover, and I was content to suffer you my Rival, knowing your Respect to me.* This, tho' he spoke smiling, raised a greater Confusion in *Brilljard*'s Heart. *I own, my Lord,* said he, *that I have, in spight of that Respect, and all the force of my Soul, had the daring to love her whom you lov'd; but*

still the consideration of my Obligations to your Lordship surmounted
that sawcy Flame, notwithstanding all the Incouragement of
your
Inconstancy, and the Advantage of the Rage it put Silvia *in
against
you*. How, cry'd *Philander, does* Silvia *know then of my Falsness, and
is it certain that* Octavio *has betray'd me to her?* With that *Brilljard*
was forc'd to advance, and with a design of some Revenge
upon *Octavio* (whom, he hoped, would be challenged by his
Lord, where one or both might fall in the Rancounter, and leave
him Master of his Hopes) he told him all that had passed
between 'em, all but real Possession, which he only imagined,
but laid the whole Weight on *Octavio,* making *Silvia* act but as an
incensed Woman, purely out of high Revenge and Resentment
of so great an Injury as was done her Love. He farther told him,
how in the Extravagancy of her Rage she had resolv'd to marry
Octavio, and how he prevented it by making a publick Declaration she was his Wife already; and for which *Octavio* procured
the *States* to put him in Prison; but by an Accident that happened to the Uncle of *Octavio,* for which he was forced to fly,
the *States* released him, when he came to his Lord: *How,* cry'd
Philander, and is the Traytor, Octavio, *fled from* Holland, *and from
the reach of my Chastisement? Yes,* reply'd *Brilljard; and not to hold
you longer from the Truth, has forced* Silvia *away with him.* At this
Philander grew into a violent Rage, sometimes against *Octavio,*
for his Treasons against Friendship; sometimes he felt the old
Flame revive, rais'd and blown by Jealousy, and was raving to
imagine any other should possess the lovely *Silvia.* He now
beholds her with all those Charms that first fired him, and
thinks, if she be Criminal, 'twas only the Effects of the greatest
Love, which always hurries Women on to the highest Revenges. In vain he seeks to extinguish his returning Flame by
the Thought of *Calista;* yet at that Thought he starts like one
awakened from a Dream of Honour, to fall asleep again, and
dream of Love. Before 'twas Rage and Pride, but now it was
Tenderness and Grief, softer Passions, and more insupportable.
New Wounds smart most, but old ones are most dangerous.
While he was thus rageing, walking, pausing, and loving, one
knock'd at his Chamber-Door. It was *Silvia's* Page, who had
waited all the Evening to speak to him, and could not till now
be admitted. *Brilljard* was just going to tell him he was there

before, when he arrived now again: *Philander* was all unbutton'd, his Stockings down, and his Hair under his Cap, when the Page, being let in by *Brilljard*, ran to his Lord, who knew him and imbraced him: And 'twas a pretty while they thus caressed each other, without the Power of speaking; he of asking a Question, and the Boy of delivering his Message; at last he gave him *Silvia*'s Billet; which was thus——

To Philander.

False and perjured as you are, I languish for a Sight of you, and conjure you to give it me as soon as this comes to your Hands. Imagine not that I have prepared those Instruments of Revenge that are so justly due to your Perfidy; but rather, that I have yet too tender Sentiments for you, in spight of the Outrages you have done my Heart; and that for all the Ruine you have made, I still adore you: And tho' I know you now anothers Slave, yet I beg you would vouchsafe to behold the Spoils you have made, and allow me this Recompence for all, to say—— Here was the Beauty I once esteem'd, tho' now she is no more Philander's.

Silvia.

How! cry'd he out, *No more* Philander's Silvia? *By Heaven, I had rather be no more* Philander! And at that word, without considering whether he were in order for a Visit or not, he advancing his joyful Voice, cry'd out to the Page; Lead on, my faithful Boy, lead on to *Silvia*. In vain *Brilljard* beseeches him to put himself into a better Equipage, in vain he urges to him the indecency of making a Visit in that Posture; he thought of nothing but *Silvia*; however he ran after him with his Hat, Cloak, and Comb, and as he was in the Chair dress'd his Hair, and suffered the Page to conduct him where he pleas'd: Which being to *Silvia*'s Lodgings, he ran up Stairs, and into her Chamber, as by Instinct of Love, and found her laid on her Bed, to which he made but one step from the Door; and catching her in his Arms, as he kneeled upon the Carpet, they both remain'd unable to utter any thing but Sighs: And surely *Silvia* never appear'd more charming; she had for a Month or two liv'd at her Ease, and had besides all the

Advantage of fine Dressing, which she had purposly put on, in
the most tempting Fashion, on purpose to ingage him, or
rather, to make him see how fine a Creature his Perfidy had lost
him: She first broke Silence, and with a thousand violent Reproaches, seem'd as if she would fain break from those Arms,
which she wish'd might be too strong for her Force; while he
endeavours to appease her by swearing and lying, as Lovers
do, protesting a thousand times that there was nothing in that
History of his Amour with *Calista*, but Revenge on *Octavio*, who
he knew was making an Interest in her Heart, contrary to all the
Laws of Honour and Friendship (for he had learn'd by the
Reproaches of the Lady Abbess, that *Calista* was Sister to *Octavio*) he has had the daring to confess to me his Passion, said he,
for you, and could I do less in Revenge than tell him I had one
for his Sister? I knew by the violent Reproaches I ever met with
in your Letters, tho' they were not plainly confess'd, that he
had play'd me foul, and discover'd my feign'd Intrigue to you;
and even this I suffered, to see how far you could be prevail'd
with against me. I knew *Octavio* had Charms of Youth and Wit,
and that you had too much the Ascendant over him, to be
deny'd any Secret you had a mind to draw from him; I knew
your Nature too curious, and your Love too inquisitive, not to
press him to a sight of my Letters, which seen, must incense
you; and this Tryal I designedly made of your Faith, and as a
Return to *Octavio*. Thus he flatters, and she believes, because
she has a mind to believe; and thus by degrees he softens the
listening *Silvia*: Swears his Faith with Sighs, and confirms it
with his Tears, which bedew'd her fair Bosom, as they fell from
his bright dissembling Eyes; and yet so well he dissembled, that
he scarce knew himself that he did so: And such Effects it
wrought on *Silvia*, that in spight of all her Honour and Vows
engaged to *Octavio*, and horrid Protestations, never to receive
again the Fugitive to her Arms, she suffers all he ask's, gives
herself up again to Love, and is a second time undone. She
regards him as one to whom she had a peculiar Right as the first
Lover: She was married to his Love, to his Heart, and *Octavio*
appeared the intruding Gallant, that would, and ought to be
content with the Gleanings of the Harvest, *Philander*, should
give him the opportunity to take up: And tho', if she had at this
very time been put to her sober Choice, which she would have
abandoned, it would have been *Philander*, as not in so good
Circumstances at that time to gratify all her Extravagancies of

Expence; but she could not indure to think of loosing either: She was for two Reasons covetous of both, and swore Fidelity to both, protesting each the only Man; and she was now contriving in her Thoughts how to play the Jilt most Artificially; a Help meet, tho' natural enough to her Sex, she had not yet much essay'd, and never to this purpose: She knew well she should have need of all her Cunning in this Affair, for she had to do with Men of Quality and Honour, and too much Wit to be grosly imposed upon. She knew *Octavio* lov'd so well, it would either make her lose him by Death or resenting Pride, if she should ever be discovered to him to be untrue; and she knew she should lose *Philander* to some new Mistress, if he once perceived her false. He asked her a thousand Questions concerning *Octavio*, and she seem'd to lavish every Secret of her Soul to her Lover; but like a right Woman, so ordered her Discourse, as all that made for her Advantage, she declared, and all the rest she conceal'd. She told him that those Hopes which her Revenge had made her give *Octavio*, had obliged him to present her with such and such fine Jewels, such Plate, such Summs; and in fine, made him understand that all her Trophies from the believing Lover, should be laid at his Feet, who had conquered her Heart: And that now, having inriched herself, she would abandon him wholly to Dispair. This did not so well satisfy *Philander*, but that he needed some greater Proofs of her Fidelity, fearing all these rich Presents were not for a little Hope alone; and she fail'd not giving what Protestations he desired.

Thus the Night pass'd away, and in the Morning, she knowing he was not very well furnished with Money, gave him the Key of her Cabinet, where she bid him furnish himself with all he wanted; which he did, and left her, to go take Orders about his Horses and other Affairs, not so absolutely satisfied of her Vertue, but he fear'd himself put upon, which the Advantage he was likely to reap by the Deceit, made him less consider than he would perhaps otherwise have done. He had all the Night a full Possession of *Silvia*, and found in the Morning he was not so violently concern'd as he was overnight: It was but a Repetition of what he had been feasted with before; 'twas no new Treat, but like Matrimony, went dully down: And now he found his Heart warm a little more for *Calista*, with which little Impatience he left *Silvia*.

That Morning a Lady having sent to *Octavio*, to give her an Assignation in the Park; tho' he were not curious after Beauty;

yet believing there might be something more in it than meerly a Lady, he dress'd himself and went, which was the reason he made not his Visit that Morning, as he used to do, to *Silvia*, and so was yet ignorant of her Ingratitude: while she, on the other side, finding herself more possess'd with Vanity than Love; for having gain'd her end as imagined, and got a second Victory over his Heart, in spight of all *Calista*'s Charms, she did not so much consider him as before; nor was he so dear to her as she fancied he would have been, before she believed it possible to get him any more to her Arms; and she found it was Pride and Revenge to *Calista*, that made her so fond of indearing him, and that she should thereby triumph over that haughty Rival, who pretended to be so sure of the Heart of her Hero: And having satisfied her Ambition in that Point, she was more pleased than she imagined she should be, and could now return her Thoughts again to *Octavio*, whose Charms, whose Indearments, and lavish Obligations, came anew to her Memory, and made him appear the most agreeable to her Genius and Humour, which now lean'd to Interest more than Love; and now she fancies she found *Philander* duller in her Arms than *Octavio*, that he tasted of *Calista*, while *Octavio* was all her own intirely, adoring and ever presenting; two Excellencies, of which *Philander* now had but part of one. She found *Philander* now in a Condition to be ever taking from her, while *Octavio*'s was still to be giving; which was a great Weight in the scale of Love, when a fair vain Woman guides the Balance: And now she begins to distrust all that *Philander* had said of his Innocence, from what she now remembers she heard from *Calista* herself, and reproaches her own Weakness for believing: While her penitent Thoughts were thus wandering in favour of *Octavio*, that Lover arriv'd, and approach'd her with all the Joy in his Soul and Eyes that either could express. *'Tis now, my fair Charmer,* said he, *that I am come to offer you, what alone can make me more worthy of you*— — And pulling from his Pocket the Writings and Inventories of all his own and his Uncles Estate—— *See here,* said he, *what those mighty Powers that favour Love, have done for* Silvia? *It is not,* continued he, *the Trifle of a Million of Money (which these amount to) that has pleased me, but because I am now able to lay it without Controul at your Feet.* If she were before inclined to receive him well, what was she now, when a million of Money rendered him so charming: She imbrac'd his Neck with her snowy Arms, lays her Cheek to his ravish'd Face, and kiss'd him a thousand

Welcomes; so well she knew how to make herself Mistriss of all this vast Fortune: And I suppose he never appear'd so fine as at this Moment. While she thus caressed him, he could not forbear sighing, as if there were yet something behind to compleat his Happiness: For tho' *Octavio* were extreamly blinded with Love, he had abundance of Wit, and a great many Doubts (which were augmented by the Arrival of *Philander*) and he was too wise and too haughty to be imposed upon, at least as he believed: And yet he had so very good an Opinion of *Silvia's* Honour and Vows, which she had engaged to him, that he durst hardly name his Fears, when by his Sighs she found them: And willing to leave no Obstacle unremov'd, that might hinder her possessing this Fortune; she told him; *My dear* Octavio——*I am sensible these Sighs proceed from some Fears you have of* Philander's *being in* Bruxells, *and consequently that I will see him as heretofore; but be assured that that false Man shall no more dare to pretend to me; but on the contrary, I will behold him as my mortal Enemy, the Murderer of my Fame and Innocence, and as the most ungrateful and perfidious Man that ever liv'd.* This she confirm'd with Oaths and Tears, and a thousand indearing Expressions. So that establishing his Heart in a perfect Tranquillity, and he leaving his Writings and Accounts with her, he told her he was obliged to dine with the *Advocates*,[a] who had acted for him in *Holland*, and could not stay to dine with her.

You must know, that as soon as the Noise of old *Sebastian, Octavio's* Uncle's Death was noised about, and that he was thereupon fled, they seized all the Estates, both that of the Uncle, and that of *Octavio*, as belonging to him by right of Law; but looking upon him as his Uncle's Murderer, they were forfeited to the *States.* This part of ill News *Octavio* kept from *Silvia*, but took order that there should be such a Process began in his Name with the *States*, that might retrieve it; and sent word, if it could not be carried on by Attornies (for he was not, he said, in Health) that nevertheless he would come into *Holland* himself. But they being not able to prove by the Witness of any of *Octavio's* or *Sebastian's* Servants, that *Octavio* had any hand in his Death; but, on the contrary, all Circumstances, and the Coroner's Verdict, brought it in as a thing done by Accident, and through his own Fault, they were obliged to release to

---

[a] Lawyers.

Octavio all his Fortune, with that of his Uncle, which was this day brought to him, by those he was obliged to dine and make up some Accompts withal: He therefore told her he fear'd he should be absent all that Afternoon; which she was the more pleased at; because, if *Philander* should return before she had ordered the Method of their Visit, so as not to meet with each other, (which was her only Contrivance now) she should be sure he would not see or be seen by *Octavio;* who had no sooner taken his Leave, but *Philander* returns; who being now fully bent upon some Adventure to see *Calista* if possible, and which Intrigue would take up his whole Time, to excuse his Absence to the jealous *Silvia,* he feign'd that he was sent to by Cesario, to meet him upon the Frontiers of *France,* and conduct him into *Flanders,* and that he should be absent some Days. This was as *Silvia* could have wished; and after forcing herself to take as kind a Leave of him as she could, whose Head was wholly possess'd with a Million of Gold, she sent him away, both Parties being very well pleased with the Artifices with which they gilted each other. At *Philander*'s going into his Chair, he was seen by the old Count of *Clarinau,* who cur'd perfectly of his Wound, was come thither to seek *Philander,* in order to take the Revenge of a Man of Honour, as he call'd it; which in *Spanish,* is the private Stab, for private Injuries;[a] and indeed, more reasonable than base *French* Duelling, where the Injured is as likely to suffer as the Injurer: But *Clarinau* durst not attack him by Day-light in the open Street, nor durst he indeed appear in his own Figure in the King of *Spain*'s Dominions,[b] standing already there convicted of the Murder of his first Wife; but in a Disguise came to *Bruxells.* The Chair with *Philander* was no sooner gone from the Lodgings, but he inquired of some of the House who lodged there, that that Gentleman came to visit? and they told him, A great Bellied Lady, who was a Woman of Quality, and a Stranger: This was sufficient, you may believe, for him to think it Madam the Countess of *Clarinau.* With this Assurance he repairs to his Lodging, which was but hard by, and sets a Footman that attended him, to watch the Return of *Philander* to those Lodgings, which he believed would not be long: The Footman, who had not seen *Philander,* only asked a

---

[a] Personal revenge, a matter of honour.

[a] Flanders and Brabant, including Brussels, were controlled by the Spanish at this time and were often referred to as the Spanish Netherlands.

Discription of him; he told him he was a pretty tall Man, in black Clothes (for the Court was then in Mourning) with a long black Hair, fine black Eyes, very handsome, and well made: This was enough for the Lad; he thought he should know him from a thousand by these Marks and Tokens. Away goes the Footman, and waited till the shutting in of the Evening, and then running to his Lord, told him *Philander* was come to those Lodgings; that he saw him alight out of the Chair, and took perfect Notice of him; that he was sure it was that *Philander* he look'd for: *Clarinau*, overjoy'd that his Revenge was at hand, took his Dagger, Sword, and Pistol, and hasted to *Silvia*'s Lodgings, where he found the Chair still waiting, and the Doors all open; he made no more ado, but goes in and ascends the Stairs, and passes on, without any Opposition, to the very Chamber where they sate, *Silvia* in the Arms of her Lover, not *Philander*, but *Octavio*, who being also in black, tall, long brown Hair, and handsome, and by a Sight that might very well deceive; he made no more to do, not doubting but it was *Philander* and *Calista*, but steps to him, and offering to stab him, was prevented by his starting at the suddenness of his Approach; however the Dagger did not absolutely miss him, but wounded him in the left Arm; but *Octavio*'s Youth, too nimble for *Clainau*'s Age, snatching at the Dagger as it wounded him, at once prevented the Hurt being much, and return'd a home Blow at *Clarinau*, so that he fell at *Silvia*'s Feet, whose Shreeks alarm'd the House to their Aid, where they found, by the light of a Candle that was brought, that the Man was not dead, but lay gazing on *Octavio*, who said to him; *Tell me, thou unfortunate Wretch, what miserable Fate brought thee to this place, to disturb the Repose of those who neither know thee, nor had done thee Injury? Ah, Sir,* reply'd *Clarinau, you have Reason for what you say, and I ask Heaven, that unknown Lady, and your self, a thousand Pardons for my Mistake and Crime: Too late I see my Error, pity and forgive me; and let me have a priest, for I believe I am a dead Man.* *Octavio* was extreamly mov'd with Compassion at these Words, and immediately sent his Page, who was alarm'd up in the Crowd, for a Father and a Surgeon; and he declar'd before the rest that he forgave that Stranger, meaning *Octavio*, since he had, by a Mistake of his Footman, pull'd on his own Death, and had deserved it: And thereupon, as well as he could, he told them for whom he had mistaken *Octavio*, who having injured his Honour, he had vow'd Revenge upon; and that he took the fair

Lady, meaning *Silvia*, for a faithless Wife of his, who had been the Authoress of all this. *Octavio* soon divin'd this to be his Brother-in-Law *Clarinau*, whom yet he had never seen; and stooping down to him, he cry'd; *'Tis I, Sir, that ought to demand a thousand Pardons of you, for letting the Revenge of* Calista's *Honour alone so long.* Clarinau wondered who he should be that named *Calista*, and asking him his Name, he told him he was the unhappy Brother to that fair Wanton, whose Story was but too well known to him. This while *Clarinau* viewing his Face, found him the very Picture of that false Charmer; while *Octavio* went on and assured him, if it were his Unhappiness to die, that he would revenge the Honour of him and his Sister on the Betrayer of both. By this time the Surgeon came, who found not his Wound to be mortal, as was feared, and ventured to remove him to his own Lodgings, whither *Octavio* would accompany him; and leaving *Silvia* inclin'd, after her Fright, to be repos'd, he took his Leave of her for that Evening, not daring, out of Respect to her, to visit her any more that Night: He was no sooner gone, but *Philander*, who never us'd to go without two very good pocket Pistols about him, having left 'em under his Pillow last Night at *Silvia*'s Lodgings; and being upon Love Adventures, he knew not what Occasion he might have for 'em, return'd back to her Lodgings: When he came she was a little surprized at first to see him, but after reflecting on what Revenge was threatened him, she exposed *Octavio*'s Secret to him, and told him the whole Adventure, and how she had got his Writings, which would be all her own, if she might be suffered to manage the fond Believer. But he, whose thought ran on the Revenge was threaten'd him, cry'd out—— *He has kindly awaken'd me to my Duty by what he threatens, 'tis I that ought to be reveng'd on his Perfidy of shewing you my Letters; and to that end, by Heaven, I will defer all the Business in the World to meet him, and pay his Courtesy——If I had injoy'd his Sister, he might suppose I knew her not to be so; and what Man of Wit or Youth would refuse a lovely Woman, that presents a Heart laden with Love, and a Person all over Charms, to his Bosom. I were to be esteem'd unworthy the Friendship of a Man of Honour, if I should: But he has basely betray'd me every way, makes Love to my celebrated Mistress, whom he knows I love, and getting Secrets, unravels 'em to make his Court and his Access the easier,* She foresaw the dangerous Consequence of a Quarrel of this nature, and had no sooner blown the Fire (which she did, to the end that *Philander* should avoid her Lodgings, and all places where he might meet *Octavio*) but she hinders all her Designs; and fixing him there, he was resolv'd to expect him at the first place he thought most likely to find him in: She indeavoured, by a thousand Intreaties, to get him gone, urging it all for his Safety; but that made him but the more resolv'd; and all she could do could not hinder him from staying Supper, and after that, from going to Bed: So that she was forced to hide a thousand Terrors and Fears by feigned Caresses, the sooner to get him to meet *Cesario* in the Morning, as he said he was to do: And tho' she could not help flattering both while by, yet she ever lov'd the absent best; and now repented a thousand times that she had told him any thing.

Early the next Morning, as was his Custom, *Octavio* came to inquire of *Silvia*'s Health; and tho' he had oftentimes only inquired and no more (taking Excuse of ill Nights, or Commands that none should come to her till she call'd) and had departed satisfied, and came again: Yet now, when he went into *Antonett*'s Chamber, he found she was in a great Consternation, and her Looks, and flattering Excuses made him know, there was more than usual in his being to day deny'd; he therefore pressed it the more, and she grew to greater Confusion by his pressing her: At last he demanded the Key of her Lady's Chamber, he having, he said, Business of great Importance to communicate to her; she told him she had as great a Reason not to deliver it, —— *That is*, said she (fearing she had said too much) *my Lady's Commands*; and finding no Perswasion would prevail, and rather venturing *Silvia*'s eternal Displeasure, than not to be satisfied in the Jealousies she had raised; especially reflecting on *Philander*'s being in Town, he took *Antonett* in his Arms and forced the Key from her, who was willing to be forced; for she admired *Octavio*'s Bounty, and car'd not for *Philander*. *Octavio* being Master of the Key, flies to *Silvia*'s Door like Lightening, or a jealous Lover, mad to discover, what seen, would kill him: He opens the Chamber-door, and goes softly to the Bed-side, as if he now fear'd to find what he sought, and wished to Heaven he might be mistaken; he opened the Curtains, and found *Silvia* sleeping with *Philander* in her Arms. I need make no Discription of his Confusion and Surprize; the Character I have given of that gallant, honest and generous Lover, is sufficient to make you imagine his Heart, when indeed he could believe his Eyes: Before he thought —— he was about to draw his Sword, and run 'em both through, and revenge at once his injured Honour, his Love, and that of his Sister; but that little Reason he had left check'd that Barbarity, and he was readier, from his own natural sweetness of Disposition to run himself upon his own Sword: And there the *Christian* pleaded—— and yet he found his Heart breaking, his whole Body trembling, his Mind all Agony, his Cheeks cold and pale, his Eyes languishing, his Tongue refusing to give Utterance to his Pressure, and his Leggs to support his Body; and much ado he had to reel into *Antonett*'s Chamber, where he found the Maid dying with Grief for her Concern for him. He was no sooner got to her Bed-side, but he fell dead upon it; while she, who was afraid to alarm her Lady and *Philander*, least *Octavio* being found there, had accused her with betraying 'em; but shutting the Door close (for yet no body had seen him but herself) she indeavoured all she could to bring him to Life again, and it was a great while before she could do so: As soon as he was recovered he lay a good while without speaking, reflecting on his Fate; but after appearing as if he had assum'd all his manly Spirits together, he rose up, and conjured *Antonett* to say nothing of what had happen'd, and that she should not repent the Service she would do him by it. *Antonett*, who was his absolute devoted Slave, promised him all he desired; and he had the Courage to go once again, to confirm himself in the Lewdness of this undone fair one, whose Perjuries had rendered her even odious now to him, and he beheld her with Scorn and Disdain: And that she might know how indifferently he did so (when she should come to know it) he took *Philander*'s Sword, that lay on her *Toylet*,[a] and left his own in the place, and went out pleased; at least in this, that he had commanded his Passion in the midst of the most powerful Occasion for Madness and Revenge that ever was.

They lay, thus secur'd in each others Arms, till nine a-Clock in the Morning, when *Philander* received a Note from *Brilljard*, who was managing his Lords Design of getting a Billet delivered to *Calista* by the way of a Nun, whom *Brilljard* had made some Address to to that end, and sent to beg, his Lord would come to the Grate and speak to the young Nun, who had undertaken for any innocent Message. This Note made him rise and hast to go out, when he received another from an unknown Hand; which was thus:

---

[a] A dressing-room table.

To Philander.

*My Lord, I have important Business with you, and beg I may speak
with you at three of the Clock; I will wait you by the Fountain in the
Park:*

Yours

Silvia, who was impatient to have him gone, never asked to
see either of these Notes, least it should have deterr'd him; and
she knew *Octavio* would visit her early, tho' she knew withal
she could refuse him Enterance with any slight Excuse, so good
an Opinion he had of her Vertue, and so absolute an Ascendant
she had over him. —— She had given Orders, if he came, to be
refused her Chamber; and she was glad to know he had not yet
been at her Lodgings. A hundred times she was about to make
use of the lessen'd Love *Philander* had for her, and to have
proposed to him the suffering *Octavio* to share her Embraces for
so good an Interest, since no Returns could be had from *France*,
nor any Signs of an Amendment of their Fortunes any other
way: But still she fear'd he had too much Honour to permit such
a Cheat in Love, to be put even upon an Enemy. This Fear
deferred her speaking of it, or offering to sacrifice *Octavio* as a
Cully[a] to their Interest, tho' she wished it; nor knew she long
how to deceive both; the Business was to put *Philander* off
handsomly, if possible, since she fail'd of all other Hopes.
These were her Thoughts while *Philander* was dressing, and
rais'd by his asking for some more Pistols[b] from her Cabinet,
which she found would quickly be at an end, if one Lover
diminished daily, and the other was hindered from increasing:
But *Philander* was no sooner dress'd but he left her to her
Repose; and *Octavio* (who had a *Grison*[c] attending the Motions
of *Philander* all that Morning, and had brought him word he was

---

[a] A dupe.
[b] Gold coins.
[c] A servant without livery, employed to deliver secret messages.

gone from *Silvia*) went to visit her, and entered her Chamber, all changed from what he was before, and Death sate in his Face and Eyes, maugre all his Resolves and art of Dissembling. She not at first perceiving it as she lay, she stretch'd out her Arms to receive him with her wonted Caresses, but he gently put her off, and sighing cry'd——*No* Silvia, *I leave those Joys for happier Lovers.* She was a little surpriz'd at that——but not imagining he had known her Guilt, reply'd; *Then those Caresses were only meant for him; for if* Silvia *could make him happy, he was sure of being the Man;* and by force compell'd him to suffer her Kisses and Imbraces, while his Heart was bursting, without any sense of the Pleasure of her Touches. *Ah* Silvia, says he, —— *I can never think myself Secure or Happy while* Philander *is so near you; every absent Moment alarms me with ten thousand Fears; in Sleep I dream thou art false, and gives thy Honour up all my absent Nights, and all day thy Vows:* And that he was sure, she should she again suffer herself to see *Philander*, he should be abandoned; and perhaps she again undone. *For since I parted with you,* continued he, *I heard from* Clarinau, *that he saw* Philander *yesterday come out of your Lodgings. How can I bear this, when you have vow'd, not to see him, with Imprecations that must damn thee,* Silvia, *without severe Repentance?*——At this she offered to swear again, ——but he stop'd her, and begg'd her not to swear till she had well considered; then she confess'd he made her a Visit, but that she us'd him with that Pride and Scorn that if he were a Man of Honour, he could never bear; and she was sure he would trouble her no more: In fine, she flattered, fawn'd, and gilted so, as no Woman common in the Trade of sinful Love, could be so great a Mistress of the Art. He suffered her to go on in all that could confirm him she thought him an errant Coxcomb; and all that could render her the most contemptible of her Sex. He was pleas'd, because it made him dispise her; and that was easier than adoring her; yet tho' he heard her with Scorn, he heard her with too much Love. When she was even Breathless with eager Protestation——he cry'd, *Ah Indiscreet and Unadvised* Silvia, *how I pity thee. Ah,* said she—— observing him speaking this with a scornful Smile—— *it is possible you should indeed be offended for a simple Visit! which neither was by my Invitation or Wish: Can you be angry if I treat* Philander *with the Civility of a Brother? Or rather, that I suffer him to see me to receive my Reproaches?* ——*Stop here,* said he, *thou fair deluding Flatterer, or thou art for ever ruin'd. Do not charge thy Soul yet farther;* —— *do not delude me on*—— *all yet I*

*can forgive, as I am dying, but should I live, I could not promise thee.
Add not new Crimes by cozening me anew, for I shall find out Truth,
tho' it lie hid even in the bottom of* Philander's *Heart.* This he spoke
with an Air of Fierceness—— which seeing her grow pale upon,
he sunk again to Compassion, and in a soft Voice cry'd——
*Whatever Injuries thou hast done thy Honour, thy Word, and Faith to
me, and my poor Heart, I can perhaps forgive when you dare utter
Truth: There is some Honesty in that——* She once more embracing
him, fell a-new to protesting her ill Treatment of *Philander,* how
she gave him back his Vows, and assur'd him she would never
be reconcil'd to him. *And did you part so Silvia?* reply'd the dying
Octavio. Upon my Honour, said she, *just so.* — *Did you not kiss at
parting?* said he faintly,——*Just kiss'd, as Friends, no more, by all
thy Love.* At this he bursts into Tears, and cry'd——*Oh! why,
when I repos'd my Heart with thee, and lavished out my very Soul in
Love, could I not merit this poor Recompence, of being fairly dealt
with? Behold this Sword——I took it from your* Toylet; *view it, it is*
Philander's; *myself this Morning took it from your Table: No more——
since you may guess the fatal rest: I am undone, and I am satisfied.——
I had a thousand Warnings of my Fate, but still the Beauty charmed,
and too good Nature yielded: Oft you have cozen'd me, and oft I saw it,
and still Love made me willing to forgive; the foolish Passion hung
upon my Soul, and sooth'd me into Peace.* Silvia, quite confounded,
(not so much with the Knowledge he had of the unlucky
Adventure, as at her so earnest denying and for-swearing any
Love had pass'd between 'em) lay still to consider how to
retrieve this lost Game, and gave him leisure to go on. ——
Now, said he, *thou art silent—— would thou had'st still been so: Ah
hapless Maid, who hast this Fate attending thee, To ruin all that love
thee! Be dumb, be dumb for ever; let the false Charm that dwells upon
thy Tongue be ended with my Life: Let it no more undo believing Man;
least amongst the Number some one may conquer thee, and deaf to all
thy Wit, and blind to Beauty, in some mad Passion think of all thy
Cozenings, should fall upon thee and forget thy Sex, and by thy Death
revenge the lost* Octavio. At these Words he would have rose
from her Arms, but she detain'd him, and with a pitious Voice
implor'd his Pardon; but he calmly reply'd; *Yes,* Silvia, *I will
pardon thee, and wish that Heaven may do so; to whom apply thy early
Rhetorick and Penitence, for it can never, never, charm me more: My
Fortune, if thou ever want'st Support, to keep thee Chast and Vertuous, shall still be commanded by thee, with that usual Frankness it
has hitherto served thee; but for* Octavio, *he is resolved to go where he*

will never more be seen by Woman——*or hear the name of Love to ought but Heaven.*——*Farewel*——*one parting kiss, and then a long Farewel.*——As he bow'd to kiss her she caught him fast in her Arms, while a Flood of Tears bathe his Face, nor could he prevent his from mixing with hers: While thus they lay, *Philander* came into the Room, and finding them so closely intwin'd, he was as much surpriz'd almost as *Octavio* was before; and drawing his Sword, was about to have kill'd him; but his Honour overcame his Passion; and he would not take him at such Disadvantage, but with the Flat of his Sword striking him on the Back as he lay, he cry'd, *Rise Traytor, and turn to thy mortal Enemy. Octavio*, not at all surpriz'd, turn'd his Head, and his Eyes bedew'd in Tears, towards his Rival. *If thou beest an Enemy*, said he, *thou never could'st have taken me in a better Humour of dying. Finish*, Philander, *that Life then, which if you spare, it will possibly never leave thine in Repose; the Injuries you have done me, being too great to be forgiven. And is it thus*, reply'd *Philander*,—— *thus with my Mistress, that you would revenge 'em? Is it in the Arms of* Silvia *that you would repay me the Favours I did your Sister* Calista? *You have by that Word*, said *Octavio, handsomly reproach'd my Sloath.* And leaping briskly from the Bed he took out his Sword, and cry'd: *Come then,*——*let us go where we may repair both our Losses, since Ladies Chambers are not fit places to adjust Debts of this nature in.* At these Words they both went down Stairs; and 'twas in vain *Silvia* call'd and cry'd out to conjure them to come back; her Power of Commanding she had in one unlucky Day lost over both those gallant Lovers: And both left her with Pity; to say no worse of the Effect of her ill Conduct.

Octavio went directly to the Park, to the Place whither he before had challenged *Philander*, who lost no time but followed him: As soon as he was come to the Fountain he drew, and told *Philander* that was the place whither he invited him in his Billet that Morning; however, if he liked not the Ground, he was ready to remove to any other: *Philander* was a little surpriz'd to find that Invitation was a Challenge, and that *Octavio* should be beforehand with him upon the Score of Revenge; and reply'd; *Sir, if the Billet came from you, it was a Favour I thank you for, since it kindly put me in mind of that Revenge I ought so justly to take of you for betraying the Secrets of Friendship I reposed in you, and making base Advantages of 'em, to recommend your self to a Woman, you knew I lov'd, and who hates you, in spight of all the ungenerous ways you have taken to gain her.* Sir, reply'd *Octavio, I confess with a Blush*

*and infinite Shame the Error with which you accuse me, and have
nothing to defend so great a Perfidy. To tell you I was wrought out of
it by the greatest Cunning imaginable, and that I must have seen* Silvia
*dy at my Feet if I had refus'd 'em, is not Excuse enough for the Breach
of that Friendship. No, tho' I were exasperated with the Relation there
of my Sister's Dishonour; I must therefore adjust that Debt with you as
well as I can; and if I dy in the juster Quarrel of my Sister's Honour, I
shall believe it the Vengeance of Heaven upon me for that one Breach of
Friendship. Sir,* reply'd Philander, *you have given me so great a
Satisfaction in this Confession; and have made so good and gallant an
Atonement by this Acknowledgement, that 'tis with Reluctancy I go to
punish you for other Injuries, of which I am assured you cannot so well
acquit your self. Tho' I would not justify a Baseness,* reply'd Octavio,
*for which there ought to be no Excuse; yet I will not accuse myself, or
acknowledge other Injuries, but leave you something to maintain the
Quarrel on——— and render it a little just on your side; not go to wipe
off the Outrage you pretend I have done your Love, by adoring the fair
Person who at least has been dear to you, by the Wrongs you have done
my Sister. Come, Sir, we shall not by disputing quit Scores,* cry'd
Philander *a little impatiently, what I have so lately seen, has made
my Rage too brisk for long Parly.*[a] At that they both advanced, and
made above twenty Passes before either received any Wound;
the first that bled was *Octavio,* who received a Wound in his
Breast, which he returned on *Philander;* and after that many
were given and taken; so that the Track their Feet made in
following and advancing as they fought, was marked out by
their Blood: In this Condition (still fighting) *Silvia* (who had
call'd 'em back in vain, and only in her Night-Gown in a Chair
pursued 'em that Minute they quitted her Chamber) found 'em
thus imployed, and without any fear she threw herself between
them: *Octavio,* out of Respect to her, ceased; but *Philander,* as if
he had not regarded her, would still have been striving for
Victory, when she stay'd his Hand, and beg'd him to hear her;
he then set the Point of his Sword to the Ground, and breathless and fainting almost, attended what she had to say: She
conjur'd him to cease the Quarrel, and told him if *Octavio* had
injured him in her Heart, he ought to remember he had injured
Octavio as much in that of his Sister: She conjured him by all the
Friendship both she and himself had received at *Octavio's*

---

[a] Discussion or debate.

Hands; and concluded with saying so many fine things of that *Cavalier* that in lieu of appeasing, it but the more exasperated the jealous *Philander*, who took new Courage with new Breath, and passed at *Octavio*. She then addressed to *Octavio*, and cry'd: *Hold, oh hold, or make your way through me, for here I will defend Vertue and Honour!* and put herself before *Octavio*: She spoke with so pitious a Voice, and pleaded with so much Tenderness, that *Octavio* laying his Sword at her Feet, bid her dispose—— false as she was, of his Honour. *For oh,* said he, *my Life is already fallen a Victim to your Perjuries!* He could say no more, but falling where he laid his Sword, left *Philander* master of the Field. By this time some Gentlemen that had been walking came up to 'em, and found a Man ly dead, and a Lady imploring another to fly: They look'd on *Octavio*, and found he had yet Life; and immediately sent for Surgeons, who carried him to his Lodgings, with very little Hope: *Philander*, as well as his Wounds would give him leave, got into a Chair, telling the Gentlemen that looked on him, he would be responsible for *Octavio*'s Life, if he had had the ill Fortune to take it; that his Quarrel was too just to suffer him to fly.——So being carried to the *Cabarett*, with an absolute Command to *Silvia* not to follow him, or visit him: For fear of hurting him by disobeying, she suffered herself to be carried to her Lodgings, where she threw herself on the Bed, and drowned her fair Eyes in a Showre of Tears: She advises with *Antonett* and her Page what to do in this Extremity; she fears she has by her ill Management lost both her Lovers, and she was in a Condition of needing every Aid. They who knew the excellent Temper of *Octavio*, and knew him to be the most considerable Lover of the two, besought her, as the best Expedient she could have Recourse to, to visit *Octavio*, who could not but take it kindly; and they did not doubt but she had so absolute a Power over him, that with a very little Complaisance towards him, she would retrieve that Heart her ill Luck had this Morning forfeited; and which, they protested, they knew nothing of, nor how he got into her Chamber. This Advice she took; but because *Octavio* was carried away dead, she feared (and swounded with the Fear) that he was no longer in the World, or at least, that he would not long be so: However she assum'd her Courage again at the Thought, that, if he did dy, she had an absolute Possession of all his Fortune, which was to her the most considerable part of the Man, or at least, what rendered him so very agreeable to her: However she thought fit to send her Page, which she did in an hour after he was carried home, to see how he did, who brought her word that he was reviv'd to Life, and had commanded his Gentleman to receive no Messages from her. This was all she could learn, and what put her into the greatest Extremity of Grief. She after sent to *Philander*, and found him much the better of the two, but most infinitely incensed against *Silvia*: This also added to her Dispair; yet since she found she had not a Heart that any Love or loss of Honour, or Fortune could break; but on the contrary, a Rest of Youth and Beauty, that might oblige her, with some Reason, to look forward on new Lovers, if the old must depart: The next thing she resolv'd, was, to do her utmost Indeavour to retrieve *Octavio*, which if unattainable, she would make the best of her Youth. She sent therefore (notwithstanding his Commands to suffer none of her People to come and see him) to inquire of his Health; and in four Days (finding he received other Visits) she dress'd herself, with all the Advantages of her Sex, and in a Chair was carried to his Aunt's, where he lay. The good Lady not knowing but she might be that Person of Quality whom she knew to be extreamly in Love with her Nephew, and who liv'd at the Court of *Bruxells*, and was Neece to the Governour, carried her to his Chamber, where she left her, as not willing to be a Witness of a Visit, she knew must be supposed *Incognito*: It was Evening, and *Octavio* was in Bed, and at first sight of her his Blood grew disordered in his Veins, flush'd in his pale Face, and burnt all over his Body, and he was near to swounding as he lay: She approach'd his Bed with a Face all set for Languishment, Love and Shame in her Eyes, and Sighs, that without speaking seem'd to tell her Grief at his Disaster; she sate, or rather, fell on his Bed, as unable to support the sight of him in that Condition; she in a soft manner seiz'd his burning Hand, grasp'd it and sigh'd, then put it to her Mouth, and suffered a Tear or two to fall upon it; and when she would have spoke she made her Sobs resist her Words; and left nothing unacted that might move the tender Hearted *Octavio* to that degree of Passion she wished. A hundred times fain he would have spoke, but still his rising Passion choak'd his Words; and still he feared they would prove either too soft and kind for the Injuries he had received, or too rough and cold for so delicate and charming a Creature, and one who, in spight of all those Injuries, he still adored: She appear'd before him with those Attractions that never fail'd to conquer him; with that Submission and

Pleading in her modest bashful Eyes, that even gave his the
Lye, who had seen her Perfidy. Oh! what should he do to
keep that Fire from breaking forth with Violence, which she
had so throughly kindled in his Heart; how should that excellent good Nature assume an unwonted Sullenness, only to
appear what it could not by Nature be? He was all Soft and
Sweet, and if he had Pride, he knew also how to make his
Pleasure; and his Youth lov'd Love above all the other little
Vanities that attend it, and was the most proper to it. Fain he
would palliate her Crime, and considers in the Condition she
was, she could not but have some Tenderness for *Philander*; that
it was no more than what before past; 'twas no new Lover that
came to kindle new Passions, or to approach her with a new
Flame; but a Decliner, who came and was received with the
Dregs of Love, with all the cold Indifference imaginable: This he
would have perswaded himself, but dares not till he hear her
speak; and yet fears she should not speak his Sense; and this
Fear makes him sighing break Silence, and he cry'd in a soft
Tone; *Ah! why, too lovely Fair, why do you come to trouble the Repose
of my dying Hours? Will you, cruel Maid, pursue me to my Grave,
shall I not have one lone Hour to ask Forgiveness of Heaven, for my Sin
of loving thee? The greatest that ever loaded my Youth——and yet
alas,——the least repented yet. Be kind, and trouble not my Solitude;
depart with all the Trophies of my Ruine, and if they add any Glory to
thy future Life, boast 'em all over the Universe, and tell, what a
deluded Youth thou hast undone. Take, take fair Deceiver, all my
Industry, my right of Birth, my thriving Parents have been so long a
getting to make me happy with; take the useless Trifle, and lavish it on
Pleasure to make thee gay and fit for luckier Lovers: Take that best part
of me, and let this worst alone; 'twas that first won the dear Confession
from thee, that drew my Ruin on——for which I hate it ——and wish
myself born a poor Cottage Boor, where I might never have seen thy
tempting Beauty, but liv'd for ever bless'd in Ignorance.* At this the
Tears ran from his Eyes, with which the soften'd *Silvia* mixed
her welcome Stream, and as soon as she could speak, she
reply'd (with half Cunning and half Love, for still there was too
much of the first mingled with the last) *Oh my* Octavio, *to what
Extremities are you resolved to drive a poor Unfortunate, who, even in
the height of Youth, and some small stock of Beauty, am reduced to all
the Miseries of the Wretched? Far from my noble Parents, lost to
Honour, and abandoned by my Friends; a helpless Wanderer in a
strange Land, exposed to Want, and perishing, and had no Sanctuary*

but thyself, thy dear, thy precious self, whom Heaven had sent, in Mercy, to my Aid; and thou at last, by a mistaken turn of miserable Fate, hast taken that dear Aid away. At this she fell weeping on his panting Bosom; nevertheless he got the Courage to reply once again, before he yielded himself a shameful Victim to her Flattery, and said; *Ah cruel Silvia, is it possible that you can charge the Levity on me! Is it I have taken this poor Aid, as you are pleased to call it, from you? Oh! rather blame your own unhappy Easiness, that after having sworn me Faith and Love, could violate 'em both; both where there was no need. 'Twould better have become thy Pride and Quality, to have resented Injuries receiv'd, than brought again that scorn'd abandon'd Person (fine as it was, and shining still with Youth) to his forgetful Arms.* Alas, said she, *I will not justify my hateful Crime; a Crime I loath to think of, it was a Fault beyond a Prostitution; there might have possibly been new Joy in such a Sin, but here 'twas pall'd and gone——fled to Eternity away:——And but for the dear Cause I did commit it, there were no Expiation for my Fault; no penitent Tears could wash away my Crime.* Alas, said he,—— *if there were any Cause, if there be any possible Excuse for such a breach of Love, give it my Heart; make me believe it, and I yet may live; and tho' I cannot think thee Innocent, to be compell'd by any frivolous Reason, 'twould greatly satisfy my longing Soul. But have a care, do not delude me on——for if thou dost perswade me into Pardon, and to return to all my native Fondness, and then again should'st play me fast and loose; by Heaven—— by all my sacred Passion to thee, by all that Men call Holy, I will pursue thee with my utmost Hate; forsake thee with my Fortune and my Heart, and leave thee wretched to the scorning Crowd. Pardon these rude Expressions of a Love that can hardly forgive the Words it utters: I blush with Shame while I pronounce 'em true.* When she reply'd; *May all you have pronounced, and all your injured Love can yet invent, fall on me, when I ever more deceive you: believe me now, and but forgive what is past, and trust my Love and Honour for the future.* At this she told him, that in the first Visit *Philander* made her, she using him so reproachfully, and upbraiding him with his Inconstancy, made him understand that he was betray'd by *Octavio*, and that the whole Intrigue with *Calista*, confessed by him, was discovered to *Silvia*; Which, he said, put him into so violent a Rage against *Octavio*, that he vow'd that Minute to find him out and kill him. Nor could all the Perswasions of Reason serve to hinder him; so that she (who as she said) lov'd *Octavio* to Death, finding so powerful an Enemy, as her Fears made her fancy *Philander* was, ready to have snatch'd from her,

in one furious Moment, all she ador'd; she had recourse to all
the Flattery of Love to withhold him from an Attempt so dangerous: And 'twas with much ado, with all those Aids, that he
was obliged to stay; which she had forced him to do, to get time
to give him Notice in the Morning for his approaching Danger:
Not that she feared *Octavio*'s Life, had *Philander* attacked it
fairly; but he look'd on himself as a Person injured by close
private ways, and would take a like Revenge, and have hurt
him when he as little dream'd of it, as *Philander* did of the
Discovery he made of his Letter to her. To this she swore, she
weep'd, she imbraced, and still protested it true; adding withal
a thousand Protestations of her future Detestation of him; and
that since the worst was past, and that they had fought, and he
was come off, tho' with so many Wounds, yet with Life, she
was resolv'd utterly to defy *Philander*, as the most perfidious of
his Sex; and assured him that nothing in the World was so
indifferent as she in his Arms. In fine, after having omitted
nothing that might gain a Credit, and assure him of her Love
and Heart, and possess him with a Belief, for the future, of her
lasting Vows: He wholly convinc'd and overcome, snatches her
in his Arms, and bursting into a Shower of Tears, cry'd——
*Take,——take all my Soul, thou lovely Charmer of it, and dispose of
the Destiny of* Octavio. And smothering her with Kisses and
Imbraces, made a perfect Reconciliation. When the Surgeons,
who came to visit him, finding him in the disorder of a Fever,
tho' more Joy was triumphing in his Face than before, they
imagined this Lady, the fair Person, for whom this Quarrel was;
for it had made a great Noise, you may believe; and finding it
hurtful for his Wounds, either to be transported with too much
Rage, Grief or Love, besought him he would not talk too much,
or suffer any Visits that might prejudice his Health: And indeed, with what had been past, he found himself after his
Transport very ill and feverish, so that *Silvia* promised the
Doctors she would visit him no more in a day or two, tho' she
knew not well how to be from him so long; but would content
herself with sending her Page to inquire of his Health. To this
Octavio made very great Opposition, but his Aunt, and the rest
of the Learned, were of Opinion it ought for his Health to be so,
and he was obliged to be satisfied with her Absence: At parting
she came to him, and again besought him to believe her Vows
to be well, and that she would depart somewhere with him far
from *Philander*, who she knew was obliged to attend the Motions

of *Cesario* at *Bruxels*, whom again she imprecated never to see more. This satisfied our impatient Lover, and he suffered her to go and leave him to what Rest he could get. She was no sooner got home, and retired to her Chamber, but finding herself alone, which now she did not care to be, and being assured she should not see *Octavio*; instead of triumphing for her new gain'd Victory, she sent her Page to inquire again of *Philander's* Health, and to intreat that she might visit him: At first, before she sent, she check'd this Thought as base, as against all Honour, and all her Vows and Promises to the brave *Octavio*; but finding an Inclination to it, and proposing a Pleasure and Satisfaction in it; she was of a Nature not to lose a Pleasure for a little Punctilio[a] of Honour; and without considering what would be the event of such a Folly, she sent her Page, tho' he had been repulsed before, and forbid coming with any Messages from his Lady. The Page found no better Success than hitherto he had done; but being with much Intreaty brought to *Philander's* Chamber, he found him sitting in his Night-Gown, to whom addressing himself——he had no sooner named his Lady—— but *Philander* bid him be gone, for he would hear nothing from that false Woman: The Boy would have reply'd, but he grew more inraged; and reviling her with all the Railings of incensed Lovers, he put himself into his Closet without speaking any more, or suffering any Answer. This Message being delivered to the expecting Lady, put her into a very great Rage —— which ended in as deep a Concern: Her great Pride fortified by her Looking-glass, made her highly resent the Affront; and she believed it more to the Glory of her Beauty to have quitted a hundred Lovers than to be abandoned by one. 'Twas this that made her rave and tear, and talk high; and after all, to use her Cunning to retrieve, what it had been most happy for her, should have been for ever lost; and she ought to have blessed the Occasion. But her malicious Star had design'd other Fortune for her: She writ to him several Letters, that were sent back sealed: She railed, she upbraided, and then fell to Submission. At last he was perswaded to open one, but returned such Answers as gave her no Satisfaction, but incouraged her with a little Hope that she should draw him on to a Reconciliation: Between whiles she fail'd not to send *Octavio* the kindest impatient

---

[a] A delicate point of honour or ceremony.

Letters in the World, and received the softest Replies that the Tongue of Man could utter, for he could not write yet. At last, *Philander* having reduced *Silvia* to the very brink of Dispair, and finding by her passionate Importunity, that he could make his Peace with her on any term of Advantage to himself; resolved to draw such Articles of Agreement, as should wholly subdue her to him, or to stand it out to the last: The Conditions were, That he being a Person, by no means, of a Humour to be imposed upon; if he were dear to her, she should give herself intirely to his Possession, and quit the very Conversation of all those he had but an Apprehension would disturb his Repose: That she should remove out of the way of his troublesom Rivals, and suffer herself to be conducted whither he thought good to carry her. These Conditions she liked, all but going away; she could not tell what sort of Confinement that might amount. He flies off wholly, and denies all Treaty upon her least Scruple, and will not be ask'd the Explanation of what he has proposed, so that she bends like a Slave for a little Empire over him; and to purchase the Vanity of retaining him, suffers herself to be absolutely undone. She submits; and that very Day she had leave from the Doctors to visit *Octavio*, and that all ravish'd Lover lay panting in expectation of the blessed Sight, believing every Minute an Age; his Apartment dressed and perfum'd, and all things ready to receive the Darling of his Soul, *Philander* came in a Coach and six Horses (and making her pack up all her Jewels and fine Things, and what they could not carry in the Coach put up to come after them) and hurries her to a little Town in *Luke-Land*,[a] a place between *Flanders* and *Germany*, without giving her time to write, or letting her know whither she was going. While she was putting up her things (I know she has since confessed) her Heart trembled, and foreboaded the Ill that was to come; that is, that she was hasting to Ruin: But she had chanced to say so much to him of her Passion, to retrieve him, that she was ashamed to own the Contrary so soon; but suffered that Force upon her Inclinations to do the most dishonorable and disinterested thing in the World. She had not been

---

[a] Cleve, a principality bordering on Holland. Controlled by the Elector of Brandenburg, Cleve was tolerant and had a mixed religious population. It was a useful place of refuge for the rebels as it was relatively immune from government pressure to evict them. Although Grey and Henrietta Berkeley went to Cleve a month after their arrival on the Continent, Behn has purposely kept the action of her novel in Holland up to this point.

there a Week, and her Trunks of Plate and fine Things were arrived, but she fell in Labour, and was brought to Bed, tho' she show'd very little of her Condition all the time she went. This great Affair being well over, she considers herself a new Woman, and began, or rather continued, to consider the Advantage she had lost in *Octavio*: She regrets extreamly her Conduct, and from one Degree to another she looks on herself as lost to him; she every day saw what she had decay'd, her Jewels sold one by one, and at last her Necessaries. *Philander*, whose Head was running on *Calista*, grudg'd every Moment he was not about that Affair, grew as peevish as shee; she recovers to new Beauty, but he grows colder and colder by Possession; Love decay'd, and ill Humour increased: They grew uneasy on both sides, and not a Day passed wherein they did not break into open and violent Quarrels, upbraiding each other with those Faults, which both wished that either would again commit, that they might be fairly rid of one another: It grew at last to that height, that they were never well but when they were absent from one another; he making a hundred little Intrigues and Gallantries with all the pretty Women, and those of any Quality in the Town or neighbouring *Villa's*. She saw this with Grief, Shame, and Disdain, and could not tell which way to relieve herself: She was not permitted the Privilege of Visits, unless to some grave Ladies, or to Monasteries; a Man was a Rarety she had hardly seen in two Months, which was the time she had been there; so that she had leasure to think of her Folly, bemoan the Effects of her Injustice, and contrive, if she could, to remedy her disagreeable Life, which now was reduced, not only to scurrilous Quarrels, and hard Words; but often in her Fury, she flying upon him, and with the Courage, or Indiscretion of her Sex, would provoke him to Indecencies, that render Life insupportable on both sides. While they liv'd at this rate, both contriving how handsomly to get quit of each other, *Brilljard*, who was left in *Bruxells*, to take care of his Lord's Affairs there, and that as soon as he had heard of *Cesario*'s Arrival, he should come with all speed, and give him notice, thought every Minute an Hour till he could see again the Charmer of his Soul, for whom he suffered continual Fevers of Love. He studies nothing but how first to get her Pardon, and then to compass his Designs of possessing her: He had not seen her, nor durst pretend to it, since she left *Holland*. He believed she would have the Discretion to conceal some of his Faults, least he should

365

discover, in Revenge, some of her's; and fancied she would imagine so of his Conduct: He had met with no Reproaches yet from his Lord, and believed himself Safe. With this Imagination he omitted nothing that might render him acceptable to her, nor to gain any Secret he believed might be of use to him: Knowing therefore that she had not dealt very generously with *Octavio*, by this Flight with *Philander*, and believing that that exasperated Lover, would in Revenge declare any thing to the Prejudice of the fair Fugitive, he (under pretence of throwing himself at his Feet, and asking his Pardon for his ill treating him in *Holland*) design'd before he went into *Luke-Land* to pay *Octavio* a Visit, and accordingly went; he met first with his Page, who being very well acquainted with *Brilljard*, discoursed with him before he carried him to his Lord: He told him, That his Lord that day that *Silvia* departed, being in impatient Expectation of her, and that she came not according to Appointment, sent him to her Lodgings, to know if any Accident had prevented her coming; but that when he came, tho' he had been with her but an Hour before, she was gone away with *Philander*, never more to return. The Youth, not being able to carry this sad news to his Lord, when he came home, offered at a hundred things to conceal the right; but the impatient Lover would not be so answered, but all inraged, commanded him to tell that Truth which he found already but too apparently in his Eyes. The Lad, so commanded, could no longer defer telling him *Silvia* was gone, and being asked again and again, what he meant, with a Face and Voice, that every Moment altered to dying; the Page assured him she was gone out of *Bruxells* with *Philander*, never more to return; which was no sooner told him, but he sunk on the Couch where he lay, and fainted: He farther told him how long it was, and with what Difficulty he was recovered to Life; and that after he was so, he refused to speak or see any Visitors; could for a long time be neither perswaded to eat nor sleep, but that he had spoke to no body ever since, and did now believe he could not procure him the Favour he beg'd: That nevertheless he would go and see what the very Name of any that had but a relation to the Family of *Silvia* would produce in him, whether a storm of Passion, or a calm of Grief: Either would be better than a Dulness, all silent and sad, in which there was no understanding what he meant by it: Whoever spoke, he only made a short sign, and turn'd away, as much as to say, Speak no more to me: But now, resolv'd to try his

Temper, hasted to his Lord, and told him that *Brilljard*, full of Penitence for his past Fault, and Grief, for the ill Condition he heard he was in, was come to pay his humble Respects to him, and gain his Pardon, before he went to his Lord and *Silvia*; without which he had, nor could have any peace of Mind, he being too sensible of the baseness of the Injury he had done him. At the Name of *Philander* and *Silvia*, *Octavio* show'd some signs of listening, but to the rest no regard; and starting from the Bed where he was laid: *Ah! what hast thou said*, cry'd he? The Page then repeated the Message, and was commanded to bring him up; who, accordingly, with all the signs of Submission, cast himself at his Feet and Mercy; and tho' he were an Enemy, the very thought that he belonged to *Silvia* made *Octavio* caress him, as the dearest of Friends: He kept him with him two or three days, and would not suffer him to stir from him; but all their Discourse was of the faithless *Silvia*; of whom, the deceived Lover spoke the softest unheard tender things, that ever Passion utter'd: He made the amorous *Brilljard* weep a hundred times a-day; and ever when he would have sooth'd his Heart with Hopes of seeing her, and one day injoying her intirely to himself, he would with so much peace of Mind renounce her, as *Brilljard* no longer doubted but he would indeed no more trust her fickle Sex. At last the News arrived that *Cesario* was in *Bruxells*, and *Brilljard* was obliged the next Morning to take Horse, and to go to his Lord: And to make himself the more acceptable to *Silvia*, he humbly besought *Octavio* to write some part of his Resentment to her, that he might oblige her to a Reason for what she had so inhumanly done: This flattered him a little, and he was not long before he was overcome by *Brilljard*'s Intreaties; who, having his Ends in every thing, believed this Letter might contain at least something to assist in his Design, by giving him Authority over her by so great a Secret: The next Morning, before he took Horse, he waited on *Octavio* for his Letter, and promised him an Answer at his Return, which would be in a few days. The Letter was open, and *Octavio* suffered *Brilljard* to read it, making him an absolute Confident in his Amour; which having done, he besought him to add one thing more to it; and that was, to beg her to forgive *Brilljard*, which for his sake he knew she would do: He told him, he was obliged as a good *Christian*, and a dying Man, one resolved for Heaven, to do that good Office, and accordingly did. *Brilljard*, taking Post immediately, arrived to *Philander*, where he found every thing as he wished, all out of Humour, still on the Fret, and ever peevish. He had not seen *Silvia*, as I said, since she went from *Holland*, and now knew not which way to approach her: *Philander* was abroad on some of his usual Gallantries, when *Brilljard* arrived; and having discoursed a while on the Affairs of his Lord and *Silvia*, he told *Antonett* he had a great desire to speak with that dissatisfied fair one, assuring her he believed his Visit would be welcome, from what he had to say to her concerning *Octavio*: She told him (with infinite Joy) that she did not doubt of his Pardon from her Lady if he brought any News from that gallant injured Man; and in all hast, tho' her Lady saw no body, but refused to rise from her Couch, she ran to her, and besought her to see *Brilljard*, for he came with a Message from *Octavio*, the Person who was the Subject of their Discourse Night and Day, when alone. She immediately sent for *Brilljard*, who approach'd his Goddess with a trembling Devotion; he kneel'd before her, and humbly besought her Pardon for all that was past: But she, who with the very Thought that he had something to say from *Octavio*, forgot all but that, and hastily bid him rise, and take all he ask'd, and hope for what he wished: In this Transport she imbraced his Head, and kiss'd his Cheek, and took him up. *That, Madam,* said Brilljard, *which your divine Bounty alone has given me, without any Merit in me, I durst not have had the Confidente to have hop'd without my Credential from a nobler Hand.——This, Madam,* said he,—— And gives her a Letter from *Octavio*: The dear hand she knew and kiss'd a hundred times as she opened it; and having intreated *Brilljard* to withdraw for a Moment, that he might not see her Concern at the reading it, she sate her down and found it this.

Octavio *to* Silvia.

I Confess, oh faithless Silvia, *that I shall appear in writing to you, to show a Weakness even below that of your Infidelity; nor durst I have trusted myself to have spoken so many sad soft things as I shall do in this Letter, had I not try'd the Strength of my Heart, and found I could upbraid you without talking myself out of that Resolution I have taken——but because I would dy in perfect Charity with thee as with all the World, I should be glad to know I could forgive thee, for yet thy Sins appear too black for Mercy. Ah! why charming Ingrate, have you left me no one Excuse for all your Ills to me? Why have you injured me to that degree, that I, with all the mighty stock of Love I had hoarded up together in my Heart, must dy reproaching thee to my last Gasp of Life; which had'st thou been so merciful to have ended, by all the Love that's breaking off my Heart, that yet, even yet is soft and charming to me, I swear with my last Breath, I had bless'd thee, Silvia: But thus to use me; thus to leave my Love, distracted raving Love, and no one Hope or Prospect of Relief, either from Reason, Time, or faithless Silvia, was but to stretch the Wretch upon the Rack, and screw him up to all degrees of Pain; yet such, as do not end in kinder Death. Oh thou unhappy Ruiner of my Repose! Oh fair Unfortunate! if yet my Agony would give me leave to argue, I am so miserably lost, to ask thee yet this woful Satisfaction; to tell me why thou hast undone me thus? Why thou shouldest chuse out me from all the Croud of fond admiring Fools, to make the World's Reproach, and turn to ridicule? How could'st thou use that soft good Nature so, that had not one ungrateful sullen Humour in it, for thy Revenge and Pride to work upon? No Baseness in my Love, no dull Severity for Malice to be busie with; but all was gay and kind, all lavish Fondness, and all that Woman vain, with Youth and Beauty, could wish in her Adorer: What could'st thou ask but Empire, which I gave not? My Love, my Soul, my Life, my very Honour, all was resign'd to thee; that Youth that might have gain'd me Fame abroad was dedicated to thy eternal Service, laid at thy Feet, and idly past in Love. Oh charming Maid, whom Heaven has form'd for the Punishment of all, whose Flames are Criminal! why could'st not thou have made some kind distinction between those common Passions and my Flame? I gave thee all my Vows, my honest Vows, before I asked a Recompence for Love. I made thee mine before the sacred Powers, that witness every secret solemn Vow, and fix 'em in the eternal Book of Fate; if thou had'st given thy Faith to any other, as, oh, too sure thou hast, what Fault was this in me, who knew it not, why should I bear that sin? I took thee to me as a Virgin Treasure, sent from the Gods to charm the Ills of Life, to make the tedious Journey short and joyful; I came to make atonement for thy Sin, and to redeem thy Fame; not add to the detested Number. I came to guild thy Stains of Honour over; and set so high a Price upon thy Name, that all Reproaches for thy past Offences, should have been lost in future Crowds of Glory: I came to lead thee from a world of Shame, approaching Ills, and future Miseries; from noisy Flatterers that would sacrifice thee, first to dull Lust, and more unthinking Wit; possess thee, then traduce thee. By Heaven, I swear, it was not for myself alone, I took such pains to gain thee, and set thee free from all those Circumstances that might perhaps debauch thy worthier Nature, and I believed it was with pain you yielded to every buying Lover: No, 'twas for thy Sake, in pity to thy Youth, Heaven had inspired me with Religious Flame; and when I aim'd at Silvia 'twas alone I might attain to Heaven the surest way, by such a pious Conquest: Why hast thou ruin'd a Design so glorious, as saving both our Souls? Perhaps thou vainly thinkest that while I am pleading thus—— I am arguing still for Love; or think this way to move thee into Pity; No, by my hopes of Death to ease my Pain, Love is a Passion not to be compell'd by any force of Reason's Arguments: 'Tis an unthinking Motion of the Soul, that comes and goes as unaccountably as changing Moons, or Ebbs and Flows of Rivers, only with far less certainty. It is not that my Soul is all over Love, that can beget its Likeness in your Heart: Had Heaven and Nature added to that Love all the Perfections that adorn our Sex, it had avail'd me nothing in your Soul: There is a Chance in Love as well as Life, and oft the most unworthy are preferred; and from a Lottery I might win the Prize from all the venturing Throng with as much Reason, as think my Chance should favour me with Silvia; it might perhaps have been, but 'twas a wonderous Odds against me. Beauty is more uncertain than the Dice; and tho' I ventured like a forward Gamester,[a] I was not yet so vain to hope to win, nor had I once complain'd upon my Fate, if I had never hop'd; but when I had fairly won, to have it basely snatch'd from my Possession, and like a bafled Cully, see it seiz'd by a false Gamester, and look tamely on, has show'd me such a Picture of myself; has given me such Idea's of the Fool, I scorn to look into my easy Heart, and loath the Figure you have made me there. Oh Silvia! what an Angel thou had'st been, had'st thou not sooth'd me thus to my Undoing. Alas, it had been no Crime in thee to hate me, it was not thy Fault I was not Aimable; if thy soft Eyes could meet no Charms to please 'em, those soft, those charming Eyes were not in Fault; nor that they Sense, too delicate and nice, could meet no proper Subject for thy Wit, thy Heart, thy tender Heart, was not in fault, because it took not in my tale of Love, and sent soft Wishes back: Oh! no, my Silvia, this tho' I had dy'd, had caused you no Reproach; but first, to fan my Fire by all the Arts that ever Subtle Beauty could prevent; to give me Hope; nay, to dissemble Love; yes, and so very well dissemble too, that not one tender Sigh was breath'd in vain: All that my love-sick Soul was panting for,*

---

[a] Gambler.

the subtle Charmer gave; so well, so very well, she could dissemble: Oh! what more Proofs could I expect from Love, what greater Earnest of eternal Victory? Oh! thou had'st raised me to the height of Heaven, to make my Fall to Hell the more precipitate. Like a fallen Angel now I howl and roar, and curse that Pride that taught me first Ambition; 'tis a poor Satisfaction now, to know (if thou could'st yet tell Truth) what Motive first seduced thee to my Ruin? Had it been Interest——by Heaven, I would have bought my wanton Pleasures at as high Rates as I would gratify my real Passions; at least when Silvia *set a price on Pleasure; nay, higher yet, for Love when 'tis repaid with equal Love, it saves the Chafferer a great Expence: Or were it wantonness of Youth in thee, alas you might have made me understood it, and I had met you with an equal Ardor, and never thought of loving, but quench'd the short liv'd Blaze as soon as kindled; and hoping for no more, had never let my hasty Flame arrive any higher than that powerful Minutes Cure. But oh! in vain I seek for Reasons from thee; perhaps thy own fantastick fickle Humour cannot inform thee why thou hast betray'd me; but thou hast done it* Silvia, *and may it never rise in Judgment on thee, nor fix a Brand upon thy Name for ever, greater than all thy other Guilts can load thee with: Live fair Deceiver, live, and charm* Philander, *to all the Heights of his beginning Flame; maist thou be gaining Power upon his Heart, and bring it to Repentance for Inconstancy; may all thy Beauty still maintain its Lustre, and all thy Charms of Wit be new and gay; maist thou be chast and true; and since it was thy Fate to be undone, let this at least excuse the hapless Maid; 'twas Love alone betray'd her to that Ruin, and it was* Philander *only had that Power: If thou hud'st sinn'd with me, as Heaven's my Witness, after I had plighted thee my sacred Vows, I do not think thou did'st; may all the Powers above forgive thee,* Silvia; *and those thou hast committed since those Vows, will need a world of Tears to wash away: 'Tis I will weep for both, 'tis I will go and be a Sacrifice to atone for all our Sins; 'tis I will be the pressing Penitent, and watch, and pray, and weep, till Heaven have Mercy; and may my Penance be accepted for thee; —— Farewel. ——I have but one Request to make thee, which is, that thou wilt for* Octavio's *Sake forgive the faithful Slave that brings thee this from thy*

Octavio.

Silvia, whose Absence and ill Treatment of *Octavio*, had but served to raise her Flame to a much greater degree, had no sooner read this Letter, but she suffered herself to be distracted, with all the different Passions that possess dispairing Lovers; sometimes raveing, and sometimes sighing and weeping: 'Twas a good while she continued in these Disorders, still thinking on what she had to do next, that might redeem all: Being a little come to herself, she thought good to consult with *Brilljard* in this Affair, between whom and *Octavio* she found there was a very good Understanding: And resolving absolutely to quit *Philander*, she no longer had any Scruples or Doubt what Course to take, nor car'd she what Price she paid for a Reconciliation with *Octavio*, if any Price would purchase it: In order to this Resolve, fix'd in her Heart, she sends for *Brilljard*, whom she caresses anew, with all the Fondness and Familiarity of a Woman, who was resolv'd to make him her Confident, or rather indeed her next Gallant. I have already said he was very handsome, and very well made, and you may believe he took all the care he could in dressing, which he understood very well: He had a good deal of Wit, and was very well fashion'd and bred: ——With all these Accomplishments, and the addition of Love and Youth, he could not be imagined to appear wholly indifferent in the Eyes of any body, tho' hitherto he had in those of *Silvia*, whose Heart was doating on *Philander*; but now, that that Passion was wholly extinguished, and that their eternal Quarrels had made almost a perpetual Separation, she being alone, without the Conversation of Men, which she lov'd, and was used to, and in her Inclination naturally addicted to love, she found *Brilljard* more agreeable than he used to be; which, together with the Designs she had upon him, made her take such a Freedom with him, as wholly transported this almost hopeless Lover: She discourses with him concerning *Octavio* and his Condition, and he failed not to answer, so as to please her, right or wrong; she tells him how uneasy she was with *Philander*, who every day grew more and more insupportable to her; she tells him she had a very great Inclination for *Octavio*, and more for his Fortune, that was able to support her, than his Person; she knew she had a great Power over him, and however it might seem now to be diminished by her unlucky Flight with *Philander*, she doubted not but to reduce him to all that Love he once profess'd to her, by telling him she was forc'd away, and without her Knowledge, being carried only to take the Air, was compell'd to the fatal Place where she now was. *Brilljard* sooths and flatters her in all her Hope, and offers her his Service in her Flight, which he might easily assist, unknown to *Philander*. It was now about six a Clock at Night, and she commanded a Supper to be provided and brought to her Chamber, where *Brilljard* and she supp'd together, and talk'd of nothing but the new Design; the hope of effecting which put her into so good Humour, that she frankly drank her Bottle, and show'd more signs of Mirth than she had done in many Months before: In this good Humour *Brilljard* look'd more amiable than ever, she smiles upon him, she caresses him with all the assurance of Friendship imaginable; she tells him she shall behold him as her dearest Friend, and spoke so many kind things, that he was imbolden'd, and approach'd her by degrees more near; he makes Advances; and the greatest Incouragement was, the Secret he had of her intended Flight: He tells her, He hop'd she would be pleased to consider (that while he was serving her in a new Amour, and assisting to render her into the Arms of another, he was wounding his own Heart which languished for her; that he should not have taken the Presumption to have told her this at such a time as he offered his Life to serve her, but that it was already no Secret to her, and that a Man who lov'd at his rate, and yet would contrive to make his Mistriss happy with another, ought in Justice to receive some Recompence of a Flame so constant and so submissive. While he spake he found he was not regarded with the Looks of Scorn or Disdain; he knew her haughty Temper, and finding it calm, he pressed on to new Submissions; he fell at her Feet, and pleaded so well, where no Opposers were, that *Silvia* no longer resisted, or if she did, it was very feebly, and with a sort of Wish, that he would pursue his Boldness yet farther; which at last he did, from one degree of Softness and gentle Force to another, and made himself the happiest Man in the World; tho' she was very much disordered at the Apprehension of what she had suffered from a Man of his Character, as she imagined so infinitely below her; but he redoubled his Submissions in so cunning a manner, that he soon brought her to her good Humour; and after that he used the kind of Authority of a Husband whenever he had an Opportunity, and found her not displeased at his Services. She considered he had a Secret from her, which if reveal'd, would not only prevent her Design, but ruin her for ever; she found too late she had discovered too much to him, to keep him at the Distance of a Servant, and that she had no other way to attach him eternally to her Interest, but by this means. He now every day appear'd more fine, and well

373

dressed, and omitted nothing that might make him, if possible, an absolute Master of her Heart, which he vow'd he would defend with his Life, from even *Philander* himself; and that he would pretend no other Empire over her, nor presume or pretend to ingross that fair and charming Person which ought to be universally adored. In fine, he fail'd not to please both her Desire and her Vanity, and every day she loved *Philander* less, who sometimes in two or three together came not home to visit her. At this time it so happened, he being in Love with the young Daughter of an Advocate, about a League from his own Lodgings, and he is always eager on the first Address, till he has compleated the Conquest; so that she had not only time to please and revenge herself with *Brilljard*, but fully resolve their Affair, and to provide all things against their Flight, which they had absolutely done before *Philander*'s Return; who, coming home, received *Brilljard* very kindly, and the News which he brought, and which made him understand, he should not have any long time to finish his new Amour in; but as he was very Conquering both in Wit and Beauty, he left not the Village without leaving some Ruins behind of Beauty, which ever after bewail'd his Charms; and since his departure was so necessary, and that in four or five days he was oblig'd to go, they deferr'd their flight till he was gone; which time they had wholly to themselves, and made as good use of it as they could; at least she thought so, and you may be sure, he also, whose Love increas'd with his possession. But *Silvia* longs for Liberty, and those necessary Gallantries, which every day diminish'd; she lov'd rich Cloths, gay Coaches, and to be lavish; and now she was stinted to good Housewifery, a Penury she hated.

The time of *Philander*'s departure being come, he took a very careless leave of *Silvia*, telling her he would see what Commands the Prince had for him, and return in Ten or Twelve days. *Brilljard* pretended some little Indisposition, and beg'd he might be permitted to follow him, which was granted, and the next day, tho *Brilljard* pleaded infinitely for a continuation of his happiness two or three days more, she would not grant it, but oblig'd him, by a thousand kind promises of it for the future, to get Horses ready for her Page, and Woman, and her Coach for her self; which accordingly was done, and they left the Village, whose Name I cannot now call to mind, taking with her what of value she had left. They were three days on their journey; *Brilljard* under pretence of care of her Health, the weather being

Hot, and for fear of overtaking *Philander* by some accident on the Road, delay'd the time as much as was possible, to be as happy as he could all the while; and indeed *Silvia* was never seen in a Humour more Gay. She found this short time of hope and pleasure, had brought all her banish'd Beauties back, that Care, Sickness and Grief, had extreamly tarnisht, only her Shape was a little more inclining to be Fat, which did not at all however yet impare her fineness; and she was indeed too Charming without, for the deformity of her indiscretion within; but she had broke the bounds of Honour, and now stuck at nothing that might carry on an Interest, which she resolved should be the business of her future life.

She at last arriv'd at *Bruxells*, and caus'd a Lodging to be taken for her in the remotest part of the Town; as soon as she came she oblig'd *Brilljard* to visit *Octavio*; but going to his Aunt's, to enquire for him, he was told that he was no longer in the World; he stood amaz'd a while, believing he had been dead, when Madam, the Aunt, told him he was retir'd to the Monastery of the Order of St. *Bernard*,[a] and would in a day or two without the Probationary Year, take Holy Orders. This did not so much surprize him as the other, knowing that he discours'd to him, when he saw him last, as if some such retirement he meant to resolve upon; with this News, which he was not altogether displeas'd at, *Brilljard* return'd to *Silvia*, which soon chang'd all her good Humour to Tears and Melancholy: She inquir'd at what place he was, and believ'd she shou'd have power to withdraw him from a resolution so fatal to her, and so contradictive to his Youth and Fortune; and having consulted the matter with *Brilljard*, he had promised her to go to him, and use all means possible to withdraw him. This resolv'd, she writ a most insinuating Letter to him, wherein she excus'd her flight by a surprize of *Philander*'s, and urg'd her condition, as it then was, for the excuse of her long silence; and that as soon as her Health would give her leave, she came to put her self eternally into his Arms; never to depart more from thence. These Arguments and Reasons, accompanied with all the indearing tenderness her artful Fancy was capable of framing, she sent, with a full assurance it would prevail to perswade him to the World,

---

[a] The Cistercian order of Roman Catholic monks, founded in 1098. One branch of the order, known as the Trappists, had a code of strict silence, manual labour and a vegetarian diet.

and her fair Arms again. While she was preparing this to go, *Philander*, who had heard at his arrival, what made so much noise, that he had been the occasion of the Worlds loss of two of the finest Persons in it, the Sister *Calista* by Debauching her, and the Brother by Ravishing his Mistriss from him, both which were entring without all possibility of prevention, into Holy Orders. He took so great a Melancholy at it, as made him keep his Chamber for two Days, maugre[a] all the urgent affairs that ought to have invited him from thence; he was consulting by what power to prevent the Misfortune; he now ran back to all the Obligations he had to *Octavio*, and pardons him all the injuries he did him; he loves him more by loving *Silvia* less, and remembered how that generous Friend, after he knew he had dishonoured his Sister, had notwithstanding sent him Letters of Credit, to the Majestrates of *Cologne*, and Bills of Exchange to save him from the Murder of his Brother-in-Law, as was likely to have been. He now charges all his little faults to those of Love, and hearing that old *Clarinau* was dead of the wound *Octavio* had given him by mistake, which increased in him new hope of *Calista*, cou'd she be retriev'd from the Monastery, he resolv'd in order to this to make *Octavio* a Visit, to beg his Pardon, and beg his Friendship, and his Continuation in the World. He came accordingly to the Monastery, and was extream civilly received by *Octavio*, who yet had not the Habit on. *Philander* told him, he heard he was leaving the World, and could not suffer him to do so, without indeavouring to gain his Pardon of him, for all the injuries he had done him; that as to what related to his Sister the Countess, he protested upon his Honour, if he had but imagined she had been so, he wou'd have suffer'd death sooner than his Passion to have approach'd her indiscreetly; and that for *Silvia*, if he were assur'd her possession could make him happy, and call him to the World again, he assur'd him he wou'd quit her to him, were she Ten times dearer to him than she was. This he confirm'd with so many protestations of Friendship, that *Octavio* oblig'd to the last degree, believ'd and return'd him this Answer, *Sir, I must confess you have found out the only way to disarm me of my resentment against you, if I were not oblig'd by those Vows I am going to take, to pardon and be at peace with all the World. However these Vows*

---

[a] Archaic: despite.

376

cannot hinder me from conserving intirely that Friendship in my Heart, which your good qualities and beauties at first sight ingag'd there, and from esteeming you more than perhaps I ought to do: the Man whom I must yet own my Rival, and the undoer of my Sisters Honour. But Oh——no more of that, a Friend's above a Sister, or a Mistress. At this he hung down his Eyes and sigh'd —— *Philander* told him he was too much concern'd in him, not to be extreamly afflicted at the resolution he had taken, and besought him to quit a design so injurious to his Youth, and the glorious things that Heaven had destin'd him to; he urg'd all that could be said to diswade him, and after all, could not believe he would quit the World at this Age, when it would be sufficient. Forty Years hence so to do. *Octavio* only answer'd with a Smile; but when he saw *Philander* still persist, he endeavoured to convince him by speaking, and lifting up his Eyes to Heaven; he Vow'd by all the Holy Powers there, he never would look down to Earth again; nor more consider fickle, faithless Beauty; *All the Gay Vanities of Youth,* said he, *for ever I renounce, and leave 'em all to those that find a Pleasure or a Constancy in 'em: for the fair faithless Maid, that has undone me, I leave to you the Empire of her Heart; but have a care,* said he, (and Sighing laid his Arms about his Neck) *for even you with all that stock of Charms, she will at last betray: I wish her well —— so well as to repent of all her Wrongs to me—— 'Tis all I have to say,* What *Philander* could urge, being impossible to prevail with him: And begging his Pardon and Friendship (which was granted by *Octavio,* and implor'd on his side from *Philander*) he took a ring of great value from his Finger, and presented it to *Philander,* and beg'd him to keep it for his Sake; and to remember him while he did so: They Kist, and Sighing parted.

Philander was no sooner gone, but *Brilljard* came to wait on *Octavio,* whom he found at his Devotion, and beg'd his Pardon for disturbing him: He receiv'd him with a very good Grace, and a chearful Countenance, imbracing him, and after some Discourse of the Condition he was going to reduce himself to, and his Admiration, that one so young should think of Devoting himself so early to Heaven, and things of that nature as the time and occasion requir'd, he told him the extream Affliction *Silvia* was seiz'd with, at the News of the Resolution he had taken, and deliver'd him her Letter, which he read without any Emotions in his Heart or Face, as at other times us'd to be visible at the very mention of her Name, or approach of her

Letters. At the finishing of which he only smiling Cry'd; *Alas, I pity her*, and gave him back the Letter. *Brilljard* ask'd if he would not please to write her some Answer, or condescend to see her; *No*, replyed Octavio, *I have done with all the gilded Vanities of Life, now I shall think of* Silvia *but as some Heavenly thing, fit for Diviner Contemplations, but never with the Youthful thoughts of Love. What he should send her now*, he said, *would have a different Stile to those she us'd to receive from him; it would be Pious Counsel, Grave Advice, unfit for Ladies so Young and Gay as* Silvia, *and would scarce find a welcome: He wish'd he could convert her from the World---and save her from the dangers that pursu'd her.* To this purpose was all he said of her, and all that could be got from him by the earnest Solliciter of Love, who perhaps was glad his Negotiation succeeded no better, and took his leave of him, with a promise to visit him often; which *Octavio* besought him to do, and told him he would take some care, that for the good of *Silvia*'s better part, she should not be reduced by want of Necessaries for her Life, and little Equipage, to prostitute her self to vile inconstant Man; he yet had so much respect for her---and besought *Brilljard* to come and take care of it with him, and to intreat *Silvia* to accept of it from him; and if it contributed to her future happiness he should be more pleas'd than to have possest her intirely.

You may imagine how this News pleas'd *Silvia*; who trembling with fear at every Moment, had expected *Brilljard*'s coming, and found no other Benefit by his Negotiation, but she must bear what she cannot avoid; but 'twas rather with the Fury of a Bacchanal, than a Woman of common Sense, and Prudence; all about her pleaded some days in vain, and she hated *Brilljard* for not doing impossibilities; and it was sometime before he could bring her to permit him to speak to her or visit her.

Philander having left *Octavio*, went immediately to wait on *Cesario*, who was extreamly pleas'd to meet him there; and they exchang'd their Souls to each other, and all the Secrets of 'em. After they had discours'd of all that they had a mind to hear and know on both sides, *Cesario* inquir'd of him of *Silvia*'s Health; and *Philander* gave him an account of the uneasiness of her Temper, and the occasions of their Quarrels, in which *Octavio* had his part, as being the subject of some of 'em: From this he falls to give a Character of that Rival, and came to this part of it, where he had put himself into the Orders of the *Bernardines*, resolving to leave the World, and all its Charms and Temptations. As they were speaking, some Gentlemen, who came to make their Court to the Prince, finding 'em speaking of *Octavio*, told them that to morrow he was to be initiated, without the Years Tryal; the Prince would needs go and see the Ceremony, having heard so much of the Man; and accordingly next day, accompanied with the Governour,[a] *Philander, Thomaso*, and abundance of Persons of Quality and Officers he went to the great Church; where were present all the Ladies of the Court, and all that were in the Town. The Noise of it was so great, that *Silvia*, all languishing, and ill as she was, would not be perswaded from going, but so muffl'd in her Hoods, as she was not to be known by any.

Never was any thing so magnificent as this Ceremony,[b] the Church was on no occasion so richly adorn'd; *Silvia* chanc'd to be seated near the Prince of *Michlenburgh*,[c] who was then in *Bruxells* and at the Ceremony; sad as she was, while the soft Musick was playing, she discours'd to him, tho' she knew him not, of the business of the day: He told her she was to see a Sight, that ought to make her Sex less cruel; a Man extreamly Beautiful and Young, whose Fortune could command almost all the pleasures of the World; yet for the Love of the most Amiable Creature in the World, who has treated him with Rigor, he abandons this Youth and Beauty to all the Severities of rigid Devotion: This relation, with a great deal he said of *Octavio*'s Vertues and Bravery, had like to have discovered her by putting her into a Swoon: and she had much ado to support her self in her Seat. I my self[d] went among the rest to this Ceremony,

---

[a] Marquis de Grana, a Spanish nobleman and ruler of the Spanish Netherlands.

[b] Behn may be drawing on accounts of particular ceremonies that took place in Brussels at this time. One envoy describes a January celebration:

On Wednesday the Annual Feast of St Anthony was solemnized here in the Augustin Cloyster by all the Contraternity where his ExLL was with the Generals and...Nobility of the Country, & Publick Ministers, the Entertagnment given by M. Agourlo (the Prevost) was very magnificent, & all was done with great Order the Prince La Tour was chosen Provost for this year

[c] Mecklenburg is a region of Northeastern Germany. Again in January 1685, a ceremony took place which may have required the presence of the prince. An envoy reports that

the Ceremony of the Golden Fleece took place in order to induct the Prince de Ligne into the fraternity. The ceremony took place in the Court chapel and was performed by the Prince de Nassau, seated under a rich canopy of state near the alter. Many other important nobles from the Low Countries were present in their capacity as Knights of the Order and after the ceremony they all paraded through the Court in fine robes.

[d] Behn often claims to have been an eye-witness to events described in her narratives. Cf. *Works of Aphra Behn*, Vol. 4 – *Oronooko* and *The Fair Jilt*.

having in all the time I lived in *Flanders*, never been so curious
to see any such thing: The Order of St. *Bernard* is one of the
neatest of any of 'em, and there is a Monastery of that Order,
which are oblig'd to be all Noble Mens Sons; of which I have
seen fifteen hundred at a time in one House; all handsome, and
most of 'em Young; their Habit adds a Grace to their Person, for
of all the Religious, that is the most becoming: Long white Vests
of fine Cloth, ty'd about with White Silk Sashes, or Cord of
White Silk; over this a long Cloak without a Cape, of the same
fine white Broad-Cloth; their Hair of a pretty Length, as that of
our Parsons in *England*, and a White Beaver;[a] they have very
fine Apartments, fit for their quality, and above all, every one
his Library; They have Attendance and Equipage according to
their Rank, and have nothing of the Inconveniences and Sloven-
liness of some of the Religious, but served in as good order as can
be, and they have nothing of the Monastick ——but the Name,
the Vow of Chastity, and the Opportunity of gaining Heaven,
by the sweetest Retreat in the World, fine House, excellent Air,
and delicate Gardens, Grotto's and Groves. 'Twas this Order
that *Octavio* had chosen, as too delicate to undertake the Auster-
ity of any other; and in my opinion 'tis here a Man may hope to
become a Saint, sooner than in any other, more perplext with
Want, Cold, and all the necessaries of Life, which takes the
thought too much from Heaven, and afflicts it with the Cares of
this World, with Pain and too much Abstinence: and I rather
think 'tis Necessity than Choice that makes a Man a Cordelier,[b]
that may be a *Jesuit* or a *Bernardine*, two the best of the *Holy
Orders*. But to return, 'twas upon a *Thursday* this Ceremony
began; and as I said there was never any thing beheld so fine as
the Church that day was, and all the Fathers that officiated at
the High-Altar; behind which a most magnificent Scene of
Glory was opened, with Clouds most rarely and Artificially set
off, behind which appear'd new ones more bright and dazling,
till from one degree to another, their lustre was hardly able to
be look'd on; and in which sat an hundred little Angels so rarely
dress'd, such shining Robes, such Charming Faces, such flowing bright Hair, Crown'd with Roses of White and Red, with
such Artificial Wings, as one would have said they had born the

---

[a] A hat made from the fur of a beaver.
[b] A Franciscan friar of the strict rule. Their name is derived from the knotted cord
they wear around the waist.

Body up in the Splendid Sky: and these, to soft Musick, Tun'd their soft Voices with such sweetness of Harmony, that for my part, I confess, I thought my self no longer on Earth; and sure there is nothing gives us an Idea of real Heaven, like a Church all adorn'd with rare Pictures, and the other Ornaments of it, with what ever can Charm the Eyes; and Musick, and Voices to Ravish the Ear; both which inspire the Soul with unresistable Devotion; and I can Swear for my own part, in those Moments a thousand times I have wish'd to Die; so absolutely I have forgot the World, and all its Vanities, and fixt my thoughts on Heaven. While this Musick continued, and the Anthems were Singing, Fifty Boys all in White, bearing Silver Censers, cast Incense all round, and perfum'd the Place with the richest and most agreeable Smells, while two hundred Silver Lamps were burning about the Altar, to give a greater Glory to the open'd Scene, while other Boys strow'd Flowers upon the inlaid Pavement, where the gay Victim was to tread; for no Crowd of Gazers fill'd the empty Space, but those that were Spectators, were so placed as rather served to adorn than disorder the awful Ceremony, where all were silent, and as still as Death; as awful as Mourners, that attend the Hearse of some lov'd Monarch. While we were thus listening, the soft Musick playing, and the Angels singing, the whole Fraternity of the Order of St. *Bernard* came in, two by two, in very graceful Order; and going up to the shining Altar, whose Furniture, that day, was Embroidered with Diamonds, Pearls, and Stones of great Value; they bow'd and retired to their Places, into little gilded Stalls, like our Knights of the Garter[a] at *Windsor:* After them fifty Boys sang, approach in order to the Altar, bow'd, and divided on each side; they were dressed in white Cloth of Silver, with golden Wings and rosy Chaplets: After these, the Bishop in his pontifick Robes, set with Diamonds of great Price, and his Mitre richly adorn'd, ascended the Altar; where, after a short Anthem, he turn'd to receive the young Devotee, who was just entered the Church, while all Eyes were fixed on him: He was led, or rather, on each side attended, with two young Noblemen, his Relations; and I never saw any thing more rich in Dress, but that of *Octavio* exceeded all Imagination, for the gayety and fineness of the Work: It was white Cloth of Silver

---

[a] Members of the Order of the Garter, an English order of knighthood, founded in 1348. The order's chapel is St George's Chapel, Windsor.

embroidered with Gold, and Buttons of Diamonds; lin'd with rich Cloth of Gold and Silver Flowers, his Breeches of the same, trim'd with a pale Pinck Garniture;[a] rich Linen, and a white Plume in his white Hat: His Hair, which was long and black, was that day in the finest order that could be imagined; but for his Face and Eyes, I am not able to describe the Charms that adorn'd 'em; no Fancy, no Imagination can paint the Beauties there: He look'd indeed as if he were maid for Heaven; no Mortal ever had such Grace: He look'd, methought, as if the Gods of Love had met in Council to dress him up that day for everlasting Conquest; for to his usual Beauties he seem'd to have the Addition of a thousand more; he bore new Lustre in his Face and Eyes, Smiles on his Cheeks, and Dimples on his Lips: He moved, he trode with nobler Motions, as if some supernatural Influence had took a peculiar Care of him: Ten thousand Sighs, from all sides, were sent to him, as he passed along, which, mix'd with the soft Musick, made such a murmuring as gentle Breezes moving yielding Boughs: I am assured he won that day more Hearts, without Design, than ever he had gain'd with all his Toils of Love and Youth before, when Industry assisted him to conquer. In his Approach to the Altar, he made three Bows; where, at the Foot of it on the lower Step, he kneel'd, and then High-Mass began; in which were all sorts of different Musick, and that so excellent, that wholly ravished with what I saw and heard, I fancied myself no longer on Earth, but absolutely ascended up to the Regions of the Sky. All I could see around me, all I heard, was ravishing and heavenly; the Scene of Glory, and the dazling Altar; the noble Paintings, and the numerous Lamps; the Awfulness, the Musick, and the Order, made me conceive myself above the Stars, and I had no part of mortal Thought about me. After the Holy Ceremony was performed, the Bishop turn'd and bless'd him; and while an Anthem was singing, *Octavio*, who was still kneeling, submitted his Head to the Hands of a Father, who with a pair of Sissors cut off his delicate Hair; at which a soft Murmur of Pity and Grief, fill'd the Place: Those fine Locks, with which *Silvia* had a thousand times play'd, and wound the Curles about her snowy Finger, she now had the dying Grief, for her Sake, for her Infidelity, to behold sacrificed to her Cruelty, and distributed

---

[a] Trimmings.

382

amongst the Ladies, who at any Price would purchase a Curl: After this they took off his Linen, and his Coat, under which he had a white Sattin Wastcoat, and under his Breeches Drawers of the same. Then the Bishop took his Robes, which lay consecrated on the Altar, and put them on, and invested him with the Holy Robe: The Singing continuing to the end of the Ceremony; where, after an Anthem was sung (while he prostrated himself before the Altar) he arose, and instead of the two noble Men that attended him to the Altar, two *Bernardines* approach'd and conducted him from it, to the Seats of every one of the Order, whom he kissed, and imbraced, as they came forth to welcome him to the Society. It was with abundance of Tears that every one beheld this Transformation; but *Silvia* swounded several times during the Ceremony, yet would not suffer herself to be carried out; but *Antonett* and another young Lady of the House where she lodged, that accompanied her, did what they could to conceal her from the publick View. For my part, I swear I was never so affected in my Life, with any thing, as I was at this Ceremony, nor ever found my Heart so oppressed with Tenderness; and was myself ready to sink where I sate, when he came near me, to be welcom'd by a Father that sate next me: After this he was led by two of the eldest Fathers, to his Apartment, and left a thousand sighing Hearts behind him. Had he dy'd, there had not been half that Lamentation; so foolish is the mistaken World, to grieve at our happiest Fortune, either when we go to Heaven, or retreat from this World, which has nothing in it that can really charm, without a thousand Fatigues to attend it: And in this Retreat, I am sure, he himself was the only Person that was not infinitely concerned; who quitted the World with so modest a Bravery, so intire a Joy, as no young Conqueror ever perform'd his Triumphs with more.

The Ceremony being ended, *Antonett* got *Silvia* to her Chair, concern'd even to Death; and she vow'd afterwards, she had much ado to withhold herself from running and seizing him at the Altar, and preventing his Fortune and Design, but that she believed *Philander* would have resented it to the last degree, and possibly have made it fatal to both herself and *Octavio*. It was a great while before she could recover from the Indisposition which this fatal and unexpected Accident had reduced her: But as I have said, she was not of a Nature to dy for Love; and charming and brave as *Octavio* was, it was perhaps her Interest, and the loss of his considerable Fortune, that gave her the greatest Cause of Grief. Sometimes she vainly fancied that yet her Power was such, that with the Expence of one Visit, and some of her usual Arts, which rarely fail, she had power to withdraw his Thoughts from Heaven, and fix 'em all on herself again, and to make him fly those Inclosures to her more agreeable Arms: But again she wisely considered, tho' he might be retriev'd, his Fortune was disposed of to Holy Uses, and could never be so. This last Thought more prevailed upon her, and had more convincing Reason in it, than all that could besides oppose her Flame; for she had this wretched Prudence, even in the highest Flights and Passions of her Love, to have a wise Regard to Interest; insomuch that it is most certain, she refused to give herself up intirely even to *Philander*; him, whom one would have thought nothing but perfect Love, soft irresistable Love could have compell'd her to have transgress'd withal, when so many Reasons contradicted her Passion: How much more then ought we to believe that Interest was the greatest Motive of all her after Passions? However, this powerful Motive fail'd not to beget in her all the Pains and Melancholies that the most violent of Passions could do: But *Brilljard*, who lov'd to a greater Degree than ever, strove all he could to divert the Thoughts of a Grief, for which there was no Remedy; and believed if he could get her out of *Bruxells*, retir'd to the little Town, or rather Village, where he was first made happy, and where *Philander* still believed her to be, he should again reassume that Power over her Heart he had before: In this melancholy Fit of hers he proposed it, urging the Danger he should be in for obeying her, should *Philander* once come to know that she was in *Bruxells*; and that possibly she would not find so civil a Treatment as he ought to pay her, if he should come to the knowledge of it: Besides these Reasons, he said, he had some of greater Importance, which he must not discover till she were withdrawn from *Bruxells*: But there needed not much to perswade her to retire, in the Humour she then was; and with no Opposition on her side, she told him she was ready to go where he thought fit; and accordingly the next day they departed the Town, and in three more arrived to the Village. In all this Journey *Brilljard* never approach'd her but with all the Respect imaginable, but withal with abundance of silent Passion; which manner of Carriage, obliged *Silvia* very often to take Notice of it, with great Satisfaction and Signs of Favour; and as he saw her Melancholy abate, he increased in sighing and Lovers

Boldnesses: Yet with all this he could not oblige her to those Returns he wished: When, after ten days stay, *Philander* writ to him, to inquire of his Health, and of *Silvia*, to whom he sent a very kind good natured Letter, but no more of the Lover than if there had never been such a Joy between 'em: He beg'd her to take care of herself, and told her he would be with her in ten or fifteen days; and desired her to send him *Brilljard*, if he were not wholly necessary to her Service, for he had urgent Affairs to imploy him in: So that *Brilljard*, not being able longer, with any colour to defend his Stay, writ him word he would wait on him in two days: which short time he wholly imploy'd in utmost Indeavour to gain *Silvia's* Favour; but she, whose Thoughts were roving on new Designs, which she thought fit to conceal from a Lover, still put him off with pretended Illness, and thoughtfulness on the late melancholy Object and loss of *Octavio*: But assur'd him as soon as she was recovered of that Pressure, she would receive him with the same Joy she had before, and which his Person and his Services merited from her; 'twas thus she sooth'd the hoping Lover, who went away with all the Satisfaction imaginable; bearing a Letter from *Silvia* to *Philander*, written with all the Art of Flattery. *Brilljard* was no sooner gone, but *Silvia*, whose Head ran on new Adventures, resolv'd to try her Chance; and being, whenever she pleased, of a Humour very Gay, she resolv'd upon a Design, in which she could trust no body but her Page, who lov'd his Lady to the last Degree of Passion, tho he never durst show it, even in his Looks or Sighs; and yet the cunning *Silvia* had by chance found his Flame, and would often take Delight to torture the poor Youth, to laugh at him: She knew he would dy to serve her, and she durst trust him with the most important Business of her Life: She therefore the next Morning sends for him to her Chamber, which she often did, and told him her Design; which was, in Man's Cloths to go back to *Bruxells*, and see if they could find any Adventures by the way that might be worth the Journey, and divert 'em: She told him she would trust him with all her Secrets; and he vow'd Fidelity. She bid him bring her a Suit of those Cloths she used to wear at her first Arrival at *Holland*; and he look'd out one very fine, and which she had worn that day she went to have been married to *Octavio*, when the *States* Messengers took her for a *French* Spy, a Suit *Philander* had never seen: She equips herself, and leaving in charge with *Antonett* what to say in her Absence; and telling her she was going upon a Frolick to divert

herself a day or two, she, accompanied by her Page only, took
Horse, and made away towards *Bruxells*: You must know that
the half-way Stage is a very small Village, in which there is most
lamentable Accommodation, and may vie with any part of *Spain*
for bad Inns. *Silvia*, not used much to riding, as a Man, was
pretty well tired by that time she got to one of those *Hotels*;[a] and
as soon as she alighted she went to her Chamber, to refresh and
cool herself; and while the Page was gone to the Kitchen, to see
what there was to eat, she was leaning out of the Window, and
looking on the Passengers that rode along, many of which took
up in the same House. Among them that alighted, there was a
very handsom young Gentleman, appearing of Quality,
attended only by his Page: She considered this Person a little
more than the rest, and finding him so unaccompanied, had a
Curiosity, natural to her, to know who he was: She ran to
another Window, that look'd into the Yard, a kind of Balcony,
and saw him alight, and look at her; and Saluted her in passing
into the Kitchin, seeing her look like a Youth of Quality: Coming in he saw her Page, and ask'd if he belong'd to that Young
Cavalier in the Gallery; the Page told him he did: And being
ask'd Who he was, he told him he was a young Noble Man of
France; a Stranger to all those parts, and made an escape from
his Tutors, to ramble for his Fancy and his Pleasure; and said he
was of a Humour, never to be out of his way; all places being
alike to him in those little Adventures. So leaving him (with yet
a greater Curiosity) he ran to *Silvia*, and told her what had past
between the young Stranger and him: While she, who was
possest with the same Inquisitive Humour, bid him inquire
who he was, when the Master of the *Hotel* coming in the interim
up to usher in her Supper, she inquir'd of him who that Young
Stranger was; he told her, one of the greatest Persons in *Flanders*; that he was Nephew to the Governour, and who had a
very great Equipage at other times; but that now he was *Incognito*, being on an Intrigue: This Intrigue gave *Silvia* new Curiosity; and hoping the Master would tell him again, she fell into
great praises of his Beauty and his Mein; which for several
reasons pleas'd the Man of the Inn, who departed with the
good News, and told every Word of it to the Young Cavalier:
The good Man having, besides the pleasing him with the grateful

---

[a] At this time the term 'hotel' described a hostelry or inn and stables.

Complements, a farther design in the Relation; for his House being very full of Persons of all sorts, he had no Lodging for the Governour's Nephew, unless he could recommend him to our Young Cavalier. The Gay unknown, extreamly pleas'd with the Character he had given him, by so beautiful a Gentleman, and one who appear'd of so much quality, being alone, and knowing he was so also, sent a *Spanish* Page, and spoke very good *French*, and had a handsome Address, and quick Wit, to make his Complement to the Young *Mounsieur*; which was to beg to be admitted to Sup with him; who readily accepted the Honour, as she call'd it; and the Young Governour, whom we must call *Alonzo*, for a reason or two, immediately after enter'd her Chamber, with an admirable Address, appearing much handsomer near, than at distance; tho' even then he drew *Silvia*'s Eyes with admiration on him; there were a thousand Young Graces in his Person, Sweetnesses in his Face, Love and Fire in his Eyes, and Wit on his Tongue: His Stature was neither Tall nor Low, very well made, and fashion'd; a Light brown Hair, Hazle Eyes, and a very soft and amorous Air; about twenty Years of Age: He spoke very good *French*; and after the first Complements on either side were over, as on such occasions are necessary; in which on both sides were nothing but great Expressions of Esteem, *Silvia* began so very well to be pleas'd with the fair Stranger, that she had like to have forgot the part she was to act, and have made Discoveries of her Sex, by Addressing herself with the Modesty and Blushes of a Woman: But *Alonzo* who had no such apprehension; tho' she appear'd with much more Beauty, than he fansied ever to have seen in a Man, nevertheless admir'd without suspecting, and took all those Signs of Effeminacy to unassur'd Youth, and first Address; and he was absolutely deceiv'd in her. *Alonzo*'s Supper being brought up, which was the best the bad Inn afforded, they sat down, and all Supper time talk'd of a thousand pleasant things, and most of Love and Women, where both exprest, abundance of Gallantry for the fair Sex. *Alonzo* related many short and pleasant accidents, and amours he had had with women. Tho' the Stranger were by Birth a *Spaniard*; yet while they discours'd, the Glass was not Idle, but went as briskly about, as if *Silvia* had been an absolute good Fellow. *Alonzo* Drinks his, and his Mistresses Health, and *Silvia* return'd the Civility, and so on till three Bottles were Sacrific'd to Love and good Humour, while she at the expence of a little Modesty, declared herself so much of the opinion of *Don Alonzo*, for Gay Inconstancy, and the Blessing of Variety, that he was wholly Charm'd with a Conversation so agreeable to his own. I have heard her Page say, from whom I have had a great part of the Truths of her Life, that he never saw *Silvia* in so pleasant a Humour all his life before, nor seem'd so well pleas'd, which gave him, her Lover, a Jealousie, that perplext him above any thing he had ever felt from Love; tho' he durst not own it. But *Alonzo* finding his Young Companion altogether so Charming (and in his own way too) could not forbear very often from falling upon his Neck, and Kissing the fair disguis'd, with as hearty an Ardour, as ever he did one of an other Sex: He told her he Ador'd her; she was directly of his Principle, all gay, inconstant, galiard and roving, and with such a Gusto he commended the Joys of fickle Youth, that *Silvia* would often say, she was then Jealous of him, and Envious of those who possess him, tho' she knew not whom. The more she lookt on him, and heard him speak, the more she fansied him: and Wine that warm'd her Head, made her give him a thousand Demonstrations of Love, that warm'd her Heart; which he mistoke for Friendship, having mistaken her Sex. In this fit of beginning Love (which is always the best) and Jealousie, she bethought her to ask him on what Adventure he had now been; for he being without his Equipage, she believ'd, she said, he was upon some affair of Love: He told her there was a Lady, within an Hours riding of that place, of quality, and handsome, very much Courted: Amongst those that were of the number of her Adorers, he said, was a Young Man of Quality of *France*, who call'd himself *Philander*: This *Philander* had been about eight Days very happy in her Favour, and had hap'ned to boast his good Fortune the next Night at the Governours Table, where he Din'd with the Prince *Cesario*. I told him, continued *Alonzo*, That the Person he so boasted of, had so soon granted him the Favour, that I believ'd she was of a Humour to suffer none to die at her Feet: but this, said he, *Philander* thought an Indignity to his good parts, and told me, he believ'd he was the only Man happy in her Favour, and that could be so: On this I ventur'd a Wager, at which he colour'd extreamly, and the Company laugh'd, which Incens'd him more; the Prince urg'd the Wager, which was a pair of *Spanish* Horses, the best in the Court, on my side, against a Discretion on his: This odds offer'd by me Incens'd him yet more; but urg'd to lay, we ended the Dispute with the Wager, the best Conclusion of all Controversies. He would have known what measures I would take; I refus'd to satisfie him in that; I only swore him upon Honour, that he should not discover the Wager or the dispute to the Lady. The next day I went to pay her a visit, from my Aunt, the Governours Lady, and she receiv'd me with all the civility in the World, I seem'd surpriz'd at her Beauty, and could talk of nothing but the Adoration I had for her, and found her extreamly pleas'd, and vain, of which Feeble Resistance I made so good advantage, that before we parted, being all alone, I receiv'd from her all the Freedoms that I could with any good Manners be allow'd, the first time, she fireing me with Kisses, and suffering my closest Embraces. Having prosper'd so well, I left her for that time, and two days after I made my visit again; she was a Married Lady, and her Husband was a *Dutch Count*, and gone to a little Government he held under my Uncle, so that again I found a free Admittance; I told her 'twas my Aunt's Complement I brought before, but that now 'twas my own I brought, which was that of an impatient Heart, that Burnt with a World of Fire and Flame, and Non-sense. In fine, so eager I was, and so pressing for something more than Dull Kissing, that she began to retire as fast as she advanc'd, and told me, after abundance of pressing her to it, that she had set a price upon her Beauty, and unless I understood how to purchase her, it was not her fault, if I were not happy: At first I so little expected it had been Money, that I reiterated my Vows, and fansied it was the assurance of my Heart she meant; but she very frankly replyed, Sir, you may spare your Pains, and five hundred Pistols will ease you of a great deal of trouble, and be the best Argument of your Love. This generous Consciencious Humour of hers, of suffering none to Die that had five hundred Pistols to present for a Cure, was very good News to me, and I found I was not at all oblig'd to my Youth or Beauty, but that a Man with half a Nose, or a single Eye, or that stunk like an old *Spaniard*, that had Din'd on Rotten Cheese and Garlick, should have been equally as welcome for the aforesaid Sum, to this Charming Insensible. I must confess, I do not love to chaffer for my pleasure, it takes off the best part of it, and were I left to my own Judgment of its worth, I should hardly have offer'd so sneaking a Sum; but that sort of bargaining was her Humour, and to enjoy her mine, tho' she had strangely pall'd me by this management of the Master: all I had now to do, was to appoint

my Night, and bring my Money; now was a very proper time
for it, her Husband being absent: I took my leave of her, infinitely well pleas'd to have gain'd my point on any Terms, with
a promise to deliver my self there the next Night: but she told
me she had a Brother to come to morrow, whom she would not
have see me, and for what reason, (being however not willing
to delay the receiving her Pistoles) she desired I would wait at
this very House, till a Foot-man should give me notice when to
come; accordingly I came, and sent her a Billet, that I waited
prepar'd at all points; and she return'd me a Billet to this
purpose: *That her Brother with some Relations being arriv'd, as she
expected, she beg'd for her Honour's sake, that I would wait till she
sent, which should be as soon as they were gone to their Chambers; and
they having rid a long Journey, would early retire; that she was
impatient of the Blessing, and should be as well prepar'd as himself,
and that she would leave her Woman* Leticia *to give me Admittance.*---
This satisfy'd me very well; and as I attended her, some of my
aquaintance chanced to arrive; with whom I Supp'd, and took
so many Glasses, to her Health, as it past down, that I was
arriv'd at a very handsome pitch, and to say Truth was as full of
Bacchus[a] as *Venus*. However as soon as her Foot-man arriv'd, I
stole away, and took Horse, and by that time it was quite dark
arriv'd at her House, where I was let in by a Young Maid,
whose Habit was very neat and clean, and she herself appear'd
to my Eyes, then dazling with Wine, the most beautiful Young
Creature I had ever seen, as in truth she was; she seemed all
Modesty, and blushing Innocence; so that conducting me into a
low Parlour, while she went to tell her Lady I was come, who
lay ready drest in all the Magnificence of Night-dress to receive
me, I sate contemplating on this fair Young Maid, and no more
thought of her Lady, than of *Bethlehem Gabor*.[b] The Maid soon
return'd, and Curtsying, told me with Blushes on her Face, that
her Lady expected me; the House was still as Sleep, and no
Noise heard, but the little Winds that rush'd among the *Jesamin*

---

[a] The wine had made him both drunk and lustful.

[b] Bethlehem Gabor (d. 1630). Gabor, Prince of Transylvania, fought for the Elector of Brandenburg against the Emperor Ferdinand in return for the Elector's sister,
Catherine, in marriage. The allusion here is to Ben Jonson's play *The Staple of News*
(1631) III.ii in which Gabor is briefly mentioned during a general account of current
European news. The play satirizes the public's growing thirst for news and the
emerging breed of journalists who were willing to supply both factual and apoc-
ryphal stories to satisfy the demand.

that grew at the Window; now whether at that moment, the false Light in the Room, or the true Wine deceived me, I know not; but I beheld this Maid as an Angel for Beauty; and indeed I think she had all the temptations of Nature. I began to kiss her, and she to tremble and blush; yet not so much out of Fear, as Surprize and Shame at my Addresses. I found her pleased with my Vows, and melting at my Kisses; I sigh'd in her Bosom, which panted me a welcome there; that Bosom whiter than Snow, sweeter than the Nosegay she had Planted there. She urg'd me faintly to go to her Lady, who expected me, and I swore it was for her Sake I came (whom I never saw) and that I scorn'd all other Beauties: She kindl'd at this, and her Cheeks glow'd with Love. I press'd her to all I wish'd, but she replyed, she was a Maid, and should be undone. I told her I would Marry her, and swore it with a thousand Oaths; she believed, and grew prettily Fond —— In fine, at last she, yielded to all I ask'd of her, which we had scarce recover'd when her Lady rung. I could not stir, but she who fear'd a Surprize, ran to her, and told her I was gone into the Garden, and would come immediately; she, hastens down again to me, Fires me anew, and pleas'd me anew; 'twas thus I taught a longing Maid the first Lesson of Sin, at the price of Fifty Pistoles, which I presented her; nor could I yet part from this young Charmer, but stayed so long that her Lady rung a Silver Bell again; but my new Prize was so wholly taken up with the pleasure of this new Amour, and the good Fortune arriv'd to her, she heard not the Bell, so that the fair deceiv'd, put on her Night-gown and Slippers, and came softly down Stairs, and found my new Love, and I closely imbracing with all the passion and fondness imaginable. I know not what she saw in me in that kind moment to her Woman, or whether the disappointment gave her a greater desire, but 'tis most certain she fell most desperately in Love with me, and scorning to take notice of the Indignity I put upon her, she unseen stole to her Chamber: Where after a most afflicting Night, she next Morning called her Woman to her (whom I left towards Morning,) better pleased with my Fifty Pistoles worth of Beauty, than I should have been with that of five hundred: the Maid whose Guilt made her very much unassur'd, approach'd her Lady with such tremblings, as she no longer doubted, but she was guilty, but durst not examine her about it, least she, who had her Honour in keeping, should by the discovery she found she had made of her Levity, expose that of her Lady. She therefore, dissembled as well as she could, and examined her about my stay; to which the Maid answer'd, I had fallen asleep, and 'twas impossible to wake me till day appear'd; when for fear of discovery, I posted away. This, tho' the Lady knew was false, she was forc'd to take for currant Excuse, and more raging with Love, than ever, she immediately dispatch'd away her Foot-man, with a Letter to me, upbraiding me extreamly; but at the same time, inviting me with all the passion imaginable; and because I should not again see my young Mistress, who was dying in Love with me, she appointed me to meet her at a little House she had, a Bow-shot from her own, where was a fine Decoy, and a great number of Wild-fowl kept, which her Husband took great delight in; there I was to wait her coming, where liv'd only a Man, and his old Wife, her Servants: I was very glad of this Invitation, and went; she came adorn'd with all her Charms. I consider'd her a new Woman, and one whom I had a Wager to win upon, the conquest of one I had inclination to, till by the discovery of the Jilt in her I began to dispise the Beauty; however, as I said, she was new, and now perhaps easie to be brought to my Terms, as indeed it hap'ned; she caress'd me with all imaginable fondness; was ready to Eat my Lips, instead of Kissing them, and much more forward than I wish'd, who do not love an over easie Conquest; however she pleas'd me for three days together, all which time she detained me there, coming to me early, and staying the latest Hour; and I have no reason to repent my time; for besides that I have past it very well, she at my coming away presented me this Jewel in my Hat, and this Ring on my Finger, and I have sav'd my five hundred Pistoles, my heart, and my credit in the Encounter, and am going to *Bruxells* to triumph over the haughty conceited *Philander*, who set so great a value on his own Beauty, and yet for all his fine Person has paid the Pistoles before he could purchase the Blessing, as she swore to me, who have made a Convert of her, and reduced her to the thing she never yet was, a Lover; insomuch that she has promised me to renounce *Philander*. I have promised to visit her again; but if I do, 'twill be more for the Vanity to please than be pleas'd, for I never repeat any thing with pleasure: All the while he spoke, *Silvia* fix'd her Eyes, and all her soft desires upon him; she envies the happy Countess, but much more the happy Maid, with whom his perfect liking made him happy; she fansies him in her Arms, and wishes him there;

she is ready a thousand times to tell him she is a Woman; but when she reflects on his inconstancy, she fears. When he had ended his Story, she Cry'd sighing: *And you are just come from this fair Lady?* He answered her, he was, *Sound and Heart-hole:* She reply'd, *'Tis very well you are so, but all the young do not thus escape from Beauty, and you may some time or other be Intrapt. Oh,* cry'd he! *I defy the power of one, while Heaven has distributed Variety to all. Were you never in Love,* replyed Silvia? *Never,* said he, *that they call Love: I have burnt and rav'd an Hour or two, or so; pursu'd, and gaz'd, and laid Sieges, till I had overcome; but what's this to Love? Did I ever make a second visit, unless upon Necessity or Gratitude? And yet*——and there he sigh'd; *and yet,* said he, *I saw a Beauty once upon the Tour,*[a] *that has ever since given me Torment. At* Bruxells, said Silvia? *There,* replyed he; *she was the fairest Creature Heaven e're made, such White and Red by Nature, such a Hair, such Eyes, and such a Mouth!* ——*all Youth and ravishing sweetness,* —— *I pursu'd her to her Lodgings, and all I could get, was, that she belonged to a young Noble Man, who since has taken Orders. From the Night I saw her, I never left her Window, but had Spies of all sorts, who brought me in intelligence, and a little after I found she had quitted the place with a new Lover, which made me love and rave for her ten times more, when I knew assuredly she was a Whore*——*and how fine a one I had mist:* This call'd all the blood to *Silvia*'s Face, and so confounded her, she could not answer; she knew it was her self, of whom he spoke; and that course word tho' innocently spoken, or rather gayly express'd, put her quite out of Countenance; however she recover'd again, when she considered they were not meant as rudenesses to her. She lov'd him, and was easie to pardon: With such discourse they past the Evening, till towards Bed-time, and the young *Spaniard,* who had took but little rest in three Nights before, was for some repose; and calling for his Chamber, the Host besought him, since they had the happiness (the young *French* Gentleman and himself) to be so good Friends, that they would share a Bed together;[b] for intruth, said he, Sir, you must sit up all Night else: he replyed, with all his Soul, it was the most grateful proposal, had been ever made him; and Addressing himself to *Silvia,* asked him if he would allow him that Blessing: She blush'd extreamly at the

---

[a] On a walk through a town.

[b] It was common for travellers of the same sex to share a bed at this time.

question, and hung down her Eyes, and he laugh'd to see it: *Sir*, said Silvia, *I will give you my Bed, for 'tis all one to me, to lye on a Bed, or on the Chairs*. Why, *Sir*, said Alonzo, *I am too passionate an adorer of the Female Sex, to incommode any of my own with Addresses; nor am I so Nice, but I can suffer a Man to lye by me, especially so dear a Youth as your self*: at which he Embraced him in his Arms, which did but the more raise *Silvia*'s Blushes, who wish'd for what she dreaded: With you, *Sir*, said she, *I could methinks be content to do what I do not use to do*; and fearing to betray her Sex, forced a consent; for either one or the other she was compell'd to do; and with the assurance that he thought her what she seemed, she chose to give her consent, and they both went to Bed together: to add to her deceit (she being forced in her Sickness to cut off her Hair) when she put off her Perriwig, she discovered nothing of the Woman; nor feared she any thing but her Breasts,[a] which were the roundest and whitest in the World; but she was long in undressing, which to colour the Matter, she suffered her Page to do, who, poor Lad, was never in so trembling a condition, as in that manner to be obliged to serve her, where she discovered so many Charms he never before had seen, but all such as might be seen with Modesty: By that time she came to Bed, *Alonzo* was fast asleep, being so long kept waking, and never so much as dreamt he had a Woman with him; but she whose fears kept her waking, had a thousand Agitations and Wishes, so natural it is when Virtue has broke the bounds of Modesty, to plunge in past all retreat; and I believe there are very few who retire after the first Sin. She considers her condition in a strange Country, her Splendor declining, her Love for *Philander* quite reduced to Friendship, or hardly that; she was young, and eat and drank well; had a World of Vanity, that Food of desire, that Fuel to Vice: She saw this the Beautifullest Youth she imagin'd ever to have seen, of Quality and Fortune able to serve her; all these made her rave with a desire to gain him for a Lover, and she imagined as all the vain and young do, that tho no Charms had yet been able to hold him, she alone had those that would; her Glass had a thousand times told her so; she compares him to *Octavio*, and

---

[a] Behn is here alluding to the description of Henrietta Berkeley in the *London Gazette* as 'full breasted'. The term, which appeared in the first advertisement of her disappearance, was removed from subsequent printings which suggests it was considered too colourful.

finds him in her opinion handsomer; she was possest with some
Love for *Philander*, when he first Address'd to her, and *Octavio*
shar'd at best but half a Heart; but now, that she had lost all for
Philander and *Octavio*, and had a Heart to cast away, or give to a
new Lover; it was like her Money, she hated to keep to it, and
lavish'd it on any Trifle, rather than hoard it, or let it lie by: 'Twas
a loss of time her Youth could not spare: she after reflection
resolved, and when she had resolved, she believ'd it done. By a
Candle she had by her to read a little Novel, she had brought, she
Surveyed him often, as curiously as *Psyche* did her *Cupid*,[a] and
tho he slept like a meer Mortal, he appeared as Charming to her
Eyes as the wing'd God himself; and 'tis believed she wish'd he
would awake and find by her Curiosity, her Sex: For this I know,
she durst no longer trust her self a Bed with him, but got up, and
all the last part of the Night walk'd about the Room: her Page lay
in the Room with her, by her order, on the Table, with a little
Vallice under his Head, which he carryed *Silvia*'s Linen in; she
waked him and told him all her fears in a pleasant manner. In the
Morning *Alonzo* awakes, and wonders to find her up so soon,
and reproach'd her for the unkindness; new Protestations on
both sides passing of eternal Friendship, they both resolved for
Bruxells; but lest she should incounter *Philander* on the way, who
possible might be on visiting his *Dutch* Countess, she desired
him to ride on before, and to suffer him to lose the happiness of
his Company, till they met in *Bruxells:* With much ado he
consents, and taking the Ring the Countess gave him from of his
Finger; Sir, said he, be pleas'd to wear this, and if ever you need
my Fortune or my Sword, send it, and in what part of the World
soever I am, I will fly to your Service. *Silvia* returned him a little
Ring set round with Diamonds, that *Philander* in his wooing time
had given her amongst a thousand of finer value: His Name and
hers was Ingraven, instead of a Poesie in it; which was only
Philander and *Silvia*, and which he took no notice of, and parted
from each other in the tenderest manner, that two young Gentlemen could possible be imagin'd to do, tho it were more than so
on her side; for she was madly in Love with him.

---

[a] Venus, jealous of the beauty of Psyche, asked Cupid to make her fall in love
with someone undesirable. Cupid however, on seeing Psyche, fell in love with her
himself and they were married. Psyche was not permitted to see her husband or to
know his identity and he visited her only at night. Informed that she was married
to Cupid by her sisters, she took a lamp and saw him sleeping. On waking, Cupid
left immediately and Psyche was punished for her curiosity by Venus.

As soon as *Silvia* came to *Bruxells*, she sent in the Evening to search out *Brilljard*, for she had considered, if he should come to the knowledge of her being in Town, and she should not send to him, he would take it so very ill, that he might prevent all her designs and rambles, the now Joy of her Heart; she knew she could make him her Slave, her Pimp, her any thing, for Love, and the hope of her Favour; and his interest might defend her; and she should know all *Philander's* motions, whom now, tho she lov'd no more, she fear'd. She found him, and he took her Lodgings, infinitely pleas'd at the trust she reposed in him; the only means by which he could arrive to happiness. She continues her Mans Habit, and he supplyed the place of *Valet*, dress'd her and undress'd her, shifted her Linen every day; nor did he take all these Freedoms, without advancing a little farther upon occasion and opportunity, which was the hire she gave him to serve her in more Lucky Amours; the Fine she paid to live free, and at ease. She tells him her adventure, which tho it were Daggers to his Heart, was however the only way to keep her his own; for he knew her Spirit was too violent to be restrained by any means. At last she told him her design upon a certain young Man of quality, which she told him was the same she Incountered. She assures him 'twas not Love or Liking, but perfectly Interest that made her design upon him, and that if he would assist her, she would be very kind to him, as a Man that had gain'd very greatly upon her Heart. This Flattery she urg'd with infinite fondness and art, and he over-joy'd believed every word as Gospel; so that he promised her the next day to carry a Billet to the young *Don*: In the mean time she caus'd him to Sup with her, purposly to give her an account of *Philander*, *Cesario* and *Hermione*, whom she heard was come to *Bruxells*, and liv'd publickly with the Prince. He told her it was very true, and that he saw them every day, nay, every moment together; for he verily believed they could not live asunder. That *Philander* was every Evening Caballing[a] there, where all the male contents of the Reformed Religion had taken Sanctuary, and where the Grand Council was every Night held; for some great things were in Agitation, and debating how to trouble the repose of all *France* again with new Broils; he told her, that all the World made their Court to *Hermione*, that if any

---

[a] The plans for the invasion of England were drawn up by the Duke of Monmouth, Lord Grey, Robert Ferguson and the Earl of Argyll in Brussels.

Body had any Petitions, or Addresses to make to the Prince, 'twas by her sole Interest; she sate in their closest Councils, and heard their gravest debates; and she was the Oracle of the Board: The Prince paying her a perfect Adoration, while she, whose Charms of Youth were ended, being turned of thirty, fortifyed her decays with all the Arts her Wit and Sex were capable of, and kept her Illustrious Lover, as perfectly her Slave as if she had ingag'd him by all those types that Fetter the most circumspect, and totally subdued him to her Will, who was without Exception the most lovely Person upon Earth: and tho, Madam, you know him so perfectly well; yet I must tell you my opinion of him; He is all the softer Sex can wish, and ours admire; he is form'd for Love and War; and as he is the most amorous and wanton in Courts, he is also the most fierce and brave in Field: His Birth the most elevated, his Age arriv'd to full blown Man, adorn'd with all the spreading Glories that Charm the Fair, and ingage the World; and I have often heard some of our Party say, his Person gain'd him more numbers to his side, than his Cause or Quality; for he understood all the useful Arts of Popularity, the gracious smile and bow, and all those cheap Favours that so gain upon Hearts; and without the expence of any thing but Ceremony, has made the Nation mad for his Interest, who never otherwise oblig'd 'em; and sure nothing is more necessary in the great, than Affability; nor shows greater marks of Grandure, or shall more etternize them, than bowing to the Crowd. As the Maiden Queen[a] I have read of in *England*, who made herself idoliz'd by that sole Piece of politick Cunning, understanding well the stubborn yet good Nature of the People; and gained more upon 'em by those little Arts, than if she had parted with all the Prerogatives of her Crown. Ah! Madam, you cannot imagine what little Slights govern'd the whole Universe, and how easie 'tis for Monarchs to oblige. This *Cesario* was made to know, and there is none so poor an Object, who may not have Access to him, and whom he does not send away well pleased, tho' he do not grant what they ask. He dispatches quickly, which is a grateful Vertue in great Men; and none ever espoused his Interest, that did not find a Reward and a Protection: 'Tis true, these are all the Tools he is to work with, and he stops at nothing that leads to his

---

[a] Queen Elizabeth I, known as the 'Virgin Queen'.

Ambition; nor has he done all that lies in the Power of Man only, to set all *France* yet in a Flame, but he calls up the very Devils from Hell to his Aid, and there is no Man fam'd for Negromancy,[a] to whom he does not apply himself; which, indeed is done by the Advice of *Hermione* who is very much affected with those sort of People, and puts a very great Trust and Confidence in 'em. She sent, at great Expence, for a *German* Conjurer, who arrived the other Day, and who is perpetually consulting with another of the same sort, a *Scot* by Birth, called *Fergusano*.[b] He was once in Holy Orders, and still is so, but all his Practice is the black Art; and excellent in it he is reported to be. *Hermione* undertakes nothing without his Advice; and as he is absolutely her Creature, so his Art governs her, and she the Prince: She holds her Mid-night Conferences with him; and as she is very superstitious, so she is very learned, and studies this Art, taught by this great Master *Fergusano*: and so far is this glorious Hero bewitched with these Sorcerers, that he puts his whole Trust in these Conjurations and Charms; and so far they have imposed on him, that with an inchanted Oyntment which they have prepared for him, he shall be invulnerable, tho' he face the very Mouth of a Cannon: They have, at the earnest Request of *Hermione*,[c] calculated his Nativity, and find him born to be a King; and that before twenty Moons expire he shall be crown'd in *France*: And flattering his easie Youth with all the Vanities of Ambition, they have made themselves absolutely useful to him. This *Scot*, being a most inveterate Enemy to *France*, lets the Prince rest neither Night nor Day, but is still inspiring him with new Hopes of a Crown, and laying him down all the false Arguments imaginable, to spur the active Spirit: My Lord is not of the Opinion, yet seems to comply with them in Council; he laughs at all the Fopperies of Charms and Incantations; insomuch, that he many times angers the Prince, and is in eternal little Feuds with *Hermione*. The *German*, would often in these Disputes say, he found by his Art, That the Stop

---

[a] The Duke of Monmouth and Henrietta Wentworth shared a strong interest in the occult. After the rebellion, Monmouth's captors found he was carrying a manuscript book of spells and charms for use against death in battle and for opening prison-doors.

[b] Robert Ferguson (d.1714). Originally a Presbyterian minister, Ferguson became an Independent preacher in London. As Shaftesbury's secretary he was a target for Tory satirists and he became notorious for his involvement in plots and conspiracies.

[c] Henrietta Wentworth's interest in astrology was also well known at this time.

to the Princes Glory would be his Love. This so incensed *Hermione*, and consequently the Prince, that they had like to have broke with him, but durst not for fear; he knowing too much to be disobliged: On the other side, *Fergusano* is most wonderfully charmed with the Wit and masculine Spirit of *Hermione*, her Courage, and manliness of her Mind; and understanding what way she would be served, resolved to obey her, finding she had an absolute Ascendant over the Prince, whom, by this means, he knew he should get into his sole Management. *Hermione*, tho' she seemed to be possess'd so intirely of *Cesario*'s Heart, found she had great and powerful Opposers, who believ'd the Prince lay idling in her Arms, and that possibly she might eclipse his Fame by living at that rate with a Woman he had no other Pretensions to but Love; and many other Motives were urged daily to him by the Admirers of his great Actions: And she feared, with reason, that some time or other Ambition might get the Ascendant of Love: She therefore, in her Midnight Conferences with *Fergusano*, often urged him to show her that piece of his Art, to make a Philtre[a] to retain fleeting Love; and not only keep a Passion alive, but even revive it from the dead. She tells him of her Contract with him, she urges his forced Marriage, as she was pleased to call it, in his Youth; and that he being so young, she believed he might find it lawful to marry himself a second time; that possibly his Princess was for the Interest of the King; and Men of his elivated Fortune, ought not to be ty'd to those Strictnesses of common Men, but for the good of the Publick, sometimes act beyond the musty Rules of Law and Equity, those politick Bands to confine the *Mobile*.[b] At this unreasonable rate she pleads her Right to *Cesario*, and he harkens with all Attention, and approves so well all she says, that he resolves, not only to attach the Prince to her by all the force of the black Art, but that of necessary Marriage also: This pleased her to the last degree; and she left him, after he had promised her to bring her the Philtre by the Morning, for it was that she most urged, the other requiring time to argue with him, and work him by degrees to it. Accordingly the next Morning he brings her a Tooth-pick-case[c] of Gold of rare infernal

---

[a] A drink that is meant to stimulate desire in anyone who consumes it.
[b] The mob.
[c] Monmouth is reputed to have bequeathed an object resembling a tooth-pick case to Henrietta Wentworth just before his execution.

Workmanship, wrought with a thousand Charms, of that Force, that every time the Prince should touch it, and while he but wore it about him, his Fondness should not only continue, but increase, and he should hate all Womankind besides, at least in the way of Love; and have no power to possess another Woman, tho' she had all the Attractions of Nature. He tells her the Prince could never suspect so familiar a Present, and for the fineness of the Work, it was a Present for a Prince, *For*, said he, *no human Art could frame so rare a piece of Workmanship, that Nine Nights the most delicate of the Infernals were mixing the Metal with the most powerful of Charms, and watch'd the critical Minutes of the Stars, in which to form the mystick Figures, every one being a Spell upon the Heart of that unerring Magick, no mortal Power could ever dissolve, undo, or conquer.* The only Art now was in giving it, so as to oblige him never to part with it; and she, who had all the Cunning of her Sex, undertook for that part: She dismissed her infernal Confident, and went to her *Toilet* to dress her, knowing well that the Prince would not be long before he came to her: She laid the Tooth-pick-Case down so as he could not avoid seeing it: The Prince came immediately after in, as he ever used to do Night and Morning, to see her dress her; he saw this gay Thing on her Table, and took it in his Hand, admiring the Work of it, as he was the most curious Person in the World: She told him there was not a finer wrought thing in the World, and that she had a very great Esteem for it, it being made by the *Sybils*;[a] and bade him mind the Antiqueness of the Work: The more she commended it, the more he liked it, and told her she must let him call it his: She told him he would give it away to the next Commender: He vow'd he would not: She told him, then he should not only call it his, but it should in reality be so; and he vow'd it should be the last thing he would part with in the World.

From that time forward she found, or thought she found, a more impatient Fondness in him than she had seen before; however it was, she rul'd and govern'd him as she pleased; and indeed, never was so great a Slave to Beauty as, in my Opinion, he was to none at all; for she is far from having any natural Charms; yet it was not long, since it was absolutely believed by all, that he had been resolved to give himself wholly up to her

---

[a] Prophetesses in Greek and Roman mythology.

Arms; to have sought no other Glory than to have retired to a Corner of the World with her, and changed all his Crowns of Laurel for those of Roses:[a] But some stirring Spirits have roused him anew, and awakened Ambition in him, and they are on great Designs, which possibly ere long, may make all *France* to tremble; yet still *Hermione* is oppressed with Love, and the Effects of dayly increasing Passion. He has perpetual Correspondence with the Party[b] in *Paris*, and Advice of all things that pass; they let him know they are ready to receive him whenever he can bring a Force into *France*; nor needs he any considerable Number, he having already there in every place, through which he shall pass, all, or the most part of the Hearts and Hands at his Devotion; and they want but Arms, and they shall gather as they go: They desire he will land himself in some part of the Kingdom, and it would be Incouragement enough to all the joyful People, who will from all parts flock together. In fine, he is offered all Assistance and Money; and least all the Forces of *France* should be bent against him, he has Friends of great Quality and Interest, that are resolved to rise in several places of the Kingdom, in *Languedoc* and *Guinny*,[c] whether the King must be obliged to send his Forces, or a great part of 'em; so that all this side of *France* will be left defenceless. I myself, Madam, have some Share in this great Design,[d] and possibly you will one day see me a Person of a Quality sufficient to merit those Favours I am now blessed with. *Pray*, reply'd *Silvia*, smiling with a little Scorn, *what part are you to play, to arrive at this good Fortune? I am*, said he, *trusted to provide all the Ammunition and Arms, and to hire a Vessel to transport them to some Sea-port Town in* France,[e] *which the Council shall think most proper to receive us. Silvia*

---

[a] The crown of laurel is a traditional emblem of martial victory, while roses imply love and retreat from the world.

[b] Monmouth was constantly gauging the level of support for his plans through the agency of a messenger, Robert Cragg, who travelled back and forth between Brussels and England.

[c] Languedoc and Guyenne, two Southern provinces in seventeenth-century France.

[d] William Turner, Grey's servant, did recruit new officers for Monmouth such as the Scottish Captain Bruce, formerly in the service of the Elector of Brandenburg. It was Nathaniel Wade, however, who was given the task of buying arms. The ship he purchased was the *Helderenburg*, a vessel which was so expensive that there was not enough money left to buy arms for any English supporters who might join the rebellion.

[e] Monmouth decided that his forces would land at Lyme Regis in the South-West of England, where support for his cause was strong.

laughed, and said she prophesied another End of this high Design than they imagined; but desperate Fortunes must take their Chance. *What,* continued she, *does not* Hermione *speak of me, and inquire of me? Yes,* reply'd *Brilljard, but in such a way, as if she look'd on you as a lost Creature, and one of such a Reputation, she would not receive a Visit from for all the World.* At this *Silvia* laughed extreamly, and cry'd, Hermione *would be very well content to be so mean a Sinner as myself, to be so young and so handsome an one. However,* said she, *to be serious, I would be glad to know what real Probability there is in advancing and succeeding in this Design, for I would take my Measures accordingly, and keep* Philander, *whose wavering, or rather lost Fortune, is the greatest Motive of my Resolves to part with him, and that have made me so uneasy to him. Brilljard* told her he was very confident of the Design, and that it was almost impossible to miscarry in the Discontent all *France* was in at this Juncture;[a] and they feared nothing but the Prince's Relapsing, who, now, most certainly preferred Love to Glory. He farther told her, that as they were in Council, one deputed from the *Parisians,* arrived with new Offers, and to know the last Result of the Prince, whether he would not espouse their Interest or not, as they were with Life and Fortune ready to espouse his Glory: They sent him word, it was from him they expected Liberty, and him whom they look'd upon as their titular Deity. Old *Fergusano* was then in Council, that *High-land Wizard,* that manages all, and who is ever at hand to awaken Mischief, alarm'd the Prince to new Glories, reproaching his scandalous Life, withal telling him there were Measures to be taken to reconcile Love and Fame; and which he was to discourse to him about in his Closet only; but as things were, he bade him look into the Story of *Armida* and *Renaldo,*[b] and compare his own with it, and he doubted not but he would return blushing at his Remissness and Sloath: Not that he would exempt his Youth from the Pleasures of Love, but he would not have Love hinder his Glory: This bold Speech before *Hermione,* had like to have begot an ill understanding; but she was as much for the Prince's Glory as *Fergusano,* and therefore

---

[a] Charles II was now dead and James II, his brother and an acknowledged Catholic, was about to be crowned king of England.

[b] Central characters in Tasso's epic romance, *Jerusalem Delivered.* Armida, who lures Christian knights away from the siege of Jerusalem, falls in love with one of her victims, the virtuous Rinaldo. In the climactic battle of the poem, Rinaldo rejects Armida and she attempts to kill him.

could not be angry, when she considered the Elevation of the
Prince, would be her own also. At this necessary reproach, the
Prince blush'd; the Board seconding the wizard, had this good
effect to draw this assurance from him, That they should see he
was not so attach'd to Love, but he could for sometime give a
Cessation to his Heart, and that the Envoy from the *Parisians*,[a]
might return assur'd, that he would as soon as he could put his
affairs in order, to come to their relief, and bring Arms for those
that had none, with such Friends as he could get together; he
could not promise Numbers, least by leading so many here,
their design should take Air, but would wholly trust to Fortune,
and their good resolutions: He demanded a Sum of money[b] of
'em, for the buying these Arms, and they have promised him all
Aids. This is the last result of Council, which broke immediately
up; and the Prince retired to his Closet; where he was no sooner
come, but reflecting on the necessity of leaving *Hermione*, he fell
into the most profound Melancholy and Muzing, that could
seize a Man; while he sat thus, *Hermione* (who had school'd
Fergusano for his rough Speech in Council, and desired he
would now take the opportunity to repair that want of respect,
while the Prince was to be spoken to alone) sent him into the
Closet to him; where he found him walking with his Arms
across, not minding the Bard who stood gazing on him, and at
last called to him; and finding no reply, he advanced, and
pulling him gently by the Arm, cry'd——*Awake, Royal young
Man, awake! and look up to coming Greatness —— I was reflecting*,
replyed Cesario, *on all various Fortunes I have pass'd from the time
of my Birth, to this present hapless day, and would be glad to know if
any supernatural means can tell me, what future Event will befal me?
If I believed I should not gain a Crown by this great Enterprize I am
undertaking, here I would lay me down in silent Ease, give up my Toils
and restless Soul to Love, and never think on vain Ambition more. Ease
thou my troubled Mind, if thou hast any Friend among the Infernals,
and they dare utter Truth; My gracious Prince*, replyed the fawning
Wizard, *this Night, if you dare loose your self from Love, and come
unattended to my Apartment, I'll undertake to show you all the future
Fortune you are to run, the Hazards, Dangers, and Escapes, that*

---

[a] Probably Robert Cragg, Monmouth's messenger to England.
[b] Monmouth's funds for the invasion eventually came from Dutch supporters
(primarily an Anabaptist widow, Madam Smith), and from several loans secured by
the plate and jewelry of Henrietta Wentworth, her mother and himself.

attend your mighty Race of Life: I'll lay the Adamantin Book[a] *before you, where all the Destinies of Princes are Hieroglifick'd.*[b] *I'll show you more, if Hell can furnish Objects, and you dare stand untrembling at the Terrour of 'em.* Enough, replied Cesario; *Name me the Hour.* *'Twixt Twelve and One,* said he; *for that's the sacred dismal time of Night for Fiends to come, for Tombs to open, and let loose their Dead,—— we shall have use of both.——No more,* reply'd Cesario, *I'll attend 'em:* The Prince was going out, when *Fergusano* recalled him, and cry'd, *one thing, Sir, I must caution you, That from this minute to that, wherin I shall show you your Destiny, you commit nothing unlawful with Women-kind: Away,* replyed the Prince, smiling, *and leave your Canting.* The Wizard putting on a more grave Countenance, replyed ——*By all the Infernals, Sir, if you commit unlawful Things, I cannot serve you. If your devils,* replyed the Prince, Laughing, *be so nice, I doubt I shall find 'em too honest for my Purpose. Sir,* said the subtle old Fiend, *such Conscientious Devils your Highness is to converse with to Night; and if you discover the Secret, it will not prove so Lucky. Since they are so Humourous,* cry'd Cesario, *I will give 'em way for once*: And going out of the Room, he went directly to *Hermione*'s apartment; where it being late, she is preparing for Bed, and with a thousand Kisses, and hanging on his Neck, she ask'd him, why he is so slow, and why he suffers not himself to be undress'd? He feigns a thousand excuses, at which she seems extreamly amaz'd; she complains, reproaches and commands —— He tells her he was to wait on the Governour, about his most urgent affairs, and was (late as it was) to consult with him: She ask'd him what affairs he was to negotiate, of which she was not to bear her part? he refuses to tell her; and she replyed she had sense and courage for any Enterprize, and should resent it very ill, if she were not made acquainted with it: But he swore to her, she should know all the whole truth, as soon as he returned: This pacifyed her in some measure, and at the hour appointed, she

---

[a] In the literal sense a book of stone. It suggests a magical book of wisdom or, perhaps, an alchemical text. Tory propaganda frequently linked rebellion and witchcraft, as in these lines satirizing Ferguson's escape to the Continent after Monmouth's defeat: 'So fiends, Associate-wizards still forsake... / He smells Whig-Babel's fall, and parting seems to say / 'Perish ye, with your cause, so I be out o'the way.' *Iter Boreale,* or Esq. Sparepenny's departure to the north, July 3rd, 1682.

[b] On the 22nd of May 1685 an 'Endytement of High Treason' was produced against Robert Ferguson and several others who, it was claimed, 'did frequently meet with Mr. Robert Ferguson, sometime chaplain to the Earl of Shaftesburrie,' and corresponded 'in hieroglyphics and figures, and obscure and mystical terms.'

suffered him to go; and in a Chair was carryed to a little House *Fergusano* had taken without the Town, to which belong'd a large Garden, at the farther end of which was a Thicket of unordered Trees, that surrounded a Grotto; which pass'd a good way under the ground. It had had some rareties of Water-work formerly belonging to it, but now they were decay'd; only here and there a broken Rock let out a little Stream, that murmur'd and dash'd upon the Earth below, and ran away in a little Rivolet; which served to add a Melancholy to the dismal place: Into this the Prince was conducted by the old *German*, who assisted in the Charm; they had only one Torch to light the way, which at the entrance of the Cave, they put out, and within was only one Glimmering Lamp, that rather served to add to the horror of the Vault, discovering its hollowness and ruins. At his entrance he was saluted with a noise like the rushing of Wind, which whiz'd and whistled in the mighty Concave. Anon a more silent whispering surrounded him, without being able to behold any Creature, save the old *German*. Anon came in *Fergusano*, who rowling a great Stone that lay at one corner of the Cave, he desired the Prince to place himself on it, and not be surpriz'd at any thing he should behold, nor to stir from that inchanted Ground: he nodding, assented to obey, while *Fergusano* and the *German*, with each a Wand in their Hands, struck against the unformed Rocks, that finish'd the end of the Cave, Muttering a thousand Incantations; with Voices dreadful, and motions Antick; and after a mighty stroke of Thunder that shook the Earth, the rude Rock divided, and opened a space that discovered a most magnificent Apartment; in which was presented a young *Hero*, attended with Military Officers; his Pages dressing him for the Field, all in gilded Armour. The Prince began to doubt himself, and to swear in his thought, that the Apparition was himself, so very like he was to himself, as if he had seen his proper Figure in a Glass. After this, several Persons seemed to address to this great Man, of all sorts and conditions, from the Prince to the Peasant, with whom he seemed to discourse with great confidence and affability; they offered him the League,[a] which he took and Signed, and gave them back; they attend him to the Door with great Joy and

---

[a] The English throne. Behn may be alluding to Dryden's work, *The History of the League* (1684) in which he compares the Whig plot with the sixteenth-century French League.

respect; but as soon as he was gone, they laugh'd and pointed after him; at which the Prince infinitely incens'd rose, and cryed out, *What means all this, s'Death, am I become the Scorn and Mockery of the Crowd?* *Fergusano* besought him to sit and have patience, and he obey'd, and check'd himself. The Scene of the Apartment being changed to an Arbour of Flowers, and the prospect of a noble and ravishing Garden; the *Hero* is presented Arm'd as he was, only without his Plume-Head-peece, kneeling at the Feet of a fair Woman, in loose Robes and Hair, and attended with abundance of little Loves, who disarm him by degrees, of those Ornaments of War. While she Caresses him with all the signs of Love, the *Cupid's* make Garlands of Flowers, and wreath around his Arms and Neck, Crowning his Head, and fettering him all over in these sweet soft Chains. They Curle his Hair, and adorn him with all Effeminacy; while he lies smiling and pleas'd —— the wanton Boys disposing of his Instruments of War, as they think fit, putting them to ridiculous uses, and Laughing at 'em. While thus he lay, there enters to him a great many States-men and Politicians; grave-Men in Furs and Chains, attended by the common Crowd: and opening a Scene farther off in prospect, show him Crowns, Scepters, Globes, Ensigns, Arms, and Trophies; promiscuously shuffel'd together, with heaps of Gold, Jewels, Parchments, Records, Charters and Seals; at which sight he starts from the Arms of the fair *Medea*,[a] and strove to have approach'd those who waited for him, but she held him fast, and with abundance of Tears and signs of moving Flattery, brought him back to her Arms again, and all dissatisfy'd the promiscuous Crowd depart, some looking back with Scorn, others with signs of Rage, and all the Scene of Glory, of Arms and Crowns, disappear'd with the Crowd, *Cesario* wholly forgeting, cryed out again, *Ha lost! all for a Trifling Woman lost; all those Trophies of thy Conquest for a Mistress! By Heaven I'll shake the Charmer from my Soul, if both I cannot have.* When *Fergusano* advancing to him, cryed——See, Sir, how Supinely the young *Hero*'s laid upon her downy Breast, and smil'd as he spoke, which angered the Prince, who replyed with Scorn, *Now by my Life, a Plot upon my Love*; but they

---

[a] Medea, daughter of the king of Colchis, married Jason and helped him to steal the golden fleece in her father's care. To delay her father's pursuit of them, she scattered the dismembered limbs of her brother on the sea. Later, deserted by Jason, she killed his new wife and her own two sons.

protested it was not so, and beg'd he would be silent; while thus the *Hero* lay regardless of his Glory, all deck'd with Flowers and Bracelets, the Drums beat, and the Trumpets were heard, or seemed to be heard to sound, and a vast opening space was fill'd with armed Wariers, who offer him their Swords, and seem to point at Crowns, that were born behind them; a while they plead in vain, and point to Crowns in vain, at which he only casts a scornful smile, and lays him down in the soft Arms of Love. They urge again, but with one amorous look the *Circe*[a] more prevails, than all their reasonings. At last by force, they divested him of his Rosy-Garlands, in which there lay a Charm, and he assumes new life, while others bore the Inchantress out of his sight; and then he suffering himself to be conducted where they pleas'd, who lead him forth, showing him all the way a prospect of Crowns. At this *Cesario* sigh'd, and the Ceremony continued.

The Scene chang'd, discovering a Sea-shore, where the *Hero* is represented Landed, but with a very Melancholy Air; attended with several Officers and Gentlemen; the Earth seems to ring with Joy, and loud Acclamations at his approach; vast Multitudes thronging to behold him, and striving who first should kiss his Hand; and bearing him aloft in the Air, carry him out of sight with Peals of Welcome and Joy.

He is represented next in Council, and deep debate; and so disappears: Then soft Musick is heard, and he enters in the royal Robe, with a Crown presented him on the Knee; which he receives, and bows to all the Rabble and the Numbers, to give them thanks: He having in his Hand blew Garters, with the order of St. *Espéret*,[b] which he distributes to several persons on either Hand; throwing Ducal Crowns and Coronets, among the Rabble, who scuffle and strive to catch at them: after a great shout of Joy, Thunder and Lightning again shook the Earth, at which they seemed all amaz'd, when a thick black Cloud descended and, covered the whole Scene, and the Rock clos'd again, and *Fergusano* let fall his Wand.

The Prince seeing the Ceremony end here, rises in a rage, and crys out, *I charge ye to go on —— remove the Veil, and let the Sun*

---

[a] An enchantress in Homer's *Odyssey* who transformed men into swine.

[b] Behn is referring here to the French Order of the Holy Ghost (St Esprit), the equivalent of the British Order of the Garter. The French knights wore a blue ribbon called the 'Cordon Bleu'.

appear; advance your mystick Wand, and show what follows next. I cannot, Sir, replyed the trembling Wizard; *the Fates have clos'd the everlasting Book forbiding farther search, Then damn your scanted Art*, replyed the Prince, *a petty Juggler could have done as much, Is't not enough*, replyed the *German* Rabbi, *that we have show'd you Crown'd, and Crown'd in* France *it self? I find the Infernals themselves are bounded here, and can declare no more. Oh, they are pretty Powers that can be Bounded*, replyed the Prince with scorn. They strove with all their Art to reconcile him, laying the fault on some mistake of theirs, in the ingredients of the Charm, which at another time they'd strive to prevent: they sooth him with all the hope in the World, that what was left unreveal'd, must needs be as glorious and fortunate to him, as what he had seen already, which was absolutely to be depended on: thus they brought him to the open Garden again, where they continued their Instructions to him, telling him that now was the time to arrive to all the Glories he had seen; they presented to him the State of Affairs in *France*, and how much a greater interest he had in the Hearts of the People, than their proper Monarch, arguing a thousand Fallacies to the deluded *Hero*, who blind and mad with his Dreams of Glory; his Visions, and Prospects, listen'd with reverence and attention, to all their false perswasions. I call 'em false, Madam, for I never had Faith in these sort of People, and am sorry so many great Men and Ladies of our times, are so bewitch'd to their Prophecies. They there presented him with a List of all the considerable of the Reformed Religion in *Paris*,[a] who had assured him Aids of Men and Money in this Expedition, Merchants, rich Trades-men, Magistrates and Gown-men[b] of the reformed Church, and the Law. Next to this, another of the Contribution of pious Ladies; all which Sums being named, amounted to a considerable supply; so that they assur'd him Hell it self could not with these Aids obstruct his Glory; but on the contrary, should be compell'd to render him assistance, by the help of Charms, to make him invincible: so that wholly o'er-come by them, he has given order, that all Preparations be forthwith made for the most secret and speedy conveyance of himself and Friends to some Sea-port in *France*; he had order'd abundance of Letters to be

---

[a] The Whig supporters of Monmouth. In the end they failed to materialize in the numbers needed to defeat the government, particularly in London.
[b] Clergymen.

writ to those of the *Hugonot* Party[a] into all parts of *France*: all which will be ready to assist him at his Landing. *Fergusano* undertakes for the management of the whole affair,[b] to write, to speak, and to perswade; and you know, Madam, he is the most subtle and insinuating of all his Non-conforming Race, and the most malignant of all our Party, and sainted by 'em for the most pious, and industrious Labourer in the *Cause*; all that he says is Oracle to the Crowd, and all he say's Authentick; and 'tis he alone is the great Engin, that sets the great Work a turning. *Yes, replyed Silvia, and makes the giddy World Mad with his damnable Notions. Pernicious as he is, replyed Brilljard, he has the sole management of affairs under* Hermione; *he has power to treat, to advise, to raise Money, to make and name Officers, and lastly, to draw out a Scene of fair Pretences for* Cesario *to the Crown of* France, *and the lawfulness of his Claim: for let the Conquest be never so sure, the People require it, and the Conquerer is oblig'd to give some better reason, than that of the strength of his Sword, for his Dominion over them. This Pretension is a Declaration,[c] or rather a most scandalous, pernicious, and treasonable Libel, if I may say so, who have so great an Interest in it, pen'd with all the Malice Envy can invent; the most unbred, rude piece of Stuff, as makes it apparent, the Author had neither Wit or common good Manners; besides the hellish Principles he has made evident there. My Lord would have no hand in the Approbation of this gross piece of Villainous Scandal, which has more unfasten'd him from their interest, than any of their other designs, and from which he daily more and more declines, or seems disgusted with, tho he does not wholly intend to quit the Interest. Having no other probable means to make good that fortune, which has been so evidently and wholly destroy'd by it. I am extream glad, said Silvia, that* Philander's *Sentiments are so Generous, and am at nothing so much amaz'd, as to hear the Prince could suffer so gross a thing to pass in his Name. I must, said Brilljard, do the Prince right in this point, to assure you, when the thing was first in the rough draught[d] show'd him, he told* Fergusano, *that those accusations of a Crown'd Head, were too*

---

[a] Behn is referring to the Whig Protestants in England.

[b] Ferguson was central to the negotiations between the Dutch authorities, the Scots and the English rebels as they prepared for the invasion of England.

[c] Monmouth issued a Declaration in Lyme Regis which had been written by Ferguson. The Declaration accused James II of having contrived the Great Fire of London and the poisoning of his brother Charles II.

[d] An earlier draft of the Declaration does exist in manuscript form. The considerable number of emendations to the document confirm doubts about its implications.

Villainous for the thoughts of a Gentleman; and giving it him again, cry'd,——*No*——*let it never be said, that the Royal Blood, that runs in my Veins, could dictate to me no more noble ways for its defence and pretensions, than the mean Cowardice of Lyes; and that to attain to Empire, I should have recourse to the most detestable of all shifts. No, no, my too zealous Friend,* continued he, *I will, with only my Sword in my Hand at the head of my Army, proclaim my right, and demand a Crown,*[a] *which if I win, is mine; if not, 'tis his, whose Sword is better or Lucklier; and tho the future World may call this unjust, at least they'll say it was brave.* At this the Wizard smil'd and reply'd; *Alas, Sir, had we hitherto acted by rules of Generosity only, we had not brought so great advantages to our Interest. You tell me, Sir, of a Speech you'll make, with your Sword in your Hand; that will do very well at the head of an Army, and a handsome Declaration would be proper for men of Sense; but this is not to the Wise, but to the Fools; on whom nothing will pass, but what is pen'd to their Capacity, and who will not be able to hear the Speeches you shall make to an Army: this is to rouse 'em, and find 'em wherever they are; how far remote soever from you, that at once they may be incited to assist you, and espouse your Interest: This is the sort of Gospel they believe; all other is too fine: believe me, Sir, 'tis by these gross devices, you are to perswade those Sons of Earth, whose Spirits never mounted above the Dunghill, whence they grew like o're-ripe Pumpkins. Lyes are the Spirit that inspires 'em, they are the very Brandy*[b] *that make 'em Valiant; and you may as soon beat Sense into their Brains, as the very appearance of Truth; 'tis the very Language of the scarlet Beast*[c] *to 'em. They understand no other than their own, and he that does, knows to what ends we aim. No matter, Sir, what Tools you work withal, so the finisht piece be fine at last. Look forward to the Goal, a Crown attend it! and never mind the dirty Road that leads to't.*

With such false Arguments as these, he wrought upon the easie Nature of the Prince, who ordered some thousands of 'em to be Printed ready for their being disperst all over *France*, as soon as they should be Landed: Especially among the *Parisians*,

---

[a] In the Declaration Monmouth's claim to the throne of England is cautious. Rather than insist on his 'Title', he 'leaves the Determination thereof to the Wisdom, Justice, and Authority of a Parliament legally chosen, and acting with Freedom.'

[b] It was believed at this time that the vapours from wines and spirits rose to the brain, hence Behn's use of the verb 'inspire', meaning literally 'to breathe in'.

[c] In The Book of Revelation 17:2–3 the Whore of Babylon rides upon a scarlet coloured beast and 'the kings of the earth have committed fornication, and the inhabitants of the earth have been made drunk with the wine of her fornication'.

too apt to take any impressions that bore the stamp and pretence of Religion and Liberty.

While these and all other things necessary were preparing, *Cesario* wholly given over to Love, being urg'd by *Hermione*, to know the occasion of his last Nights absence, unravels all the secret, and told my Lord, and she one Night at Supper, the whole Scene of the *Grotto*; so that *Hermione*, more than ever being puft up with Ambitious thoughts, hast'ned to have the Prince press'd to marry her; and consulting with the Councillour of her closest secrets, sets him anew to work; swearing violently, that if he did not bring that design about, she should be able by her Ascendant o're *Cesario*, to ruin all those they had undertaken, and yet turn the Prince from the Enterprize; and that it was more to satisfy her Ambition (to which they were oblig'd for all the Prince had promised) that he had undertaken to Head an Army, and puts himself again into the Hands of the *Hugonots*, and forsake all the soft repose of Love and Life, than for any Inclination or Ambition of his own; and that she who had power to animate him one way, he might be assur'd had the same power another. This she ended in very high Language, with a look too fierce and fiery to leave him any doubt of; and he promised all things should be done as she desired, and that he would overcome the Prince, and bring him absolutely under her power: Not, said she, with a scornful look, that I need your aid in this affair, or want power of my own to command it; but I will not have him look upon it as my Act alone, or a thing of my seeking, but by your advice shall be made to understand it is for the good of the Publick; that having to do with a sort of People of the Reformed Religion, whose pretences were more Nice, than Wise; more seemingly zealous than reasonable or just; they might look upon the Life she lead with the Prince, as scandalous, that was not justifyed by form, tho never so unlawful. A thousand things she urg'd to him, who needed no instruction how to make that appear authentick and just, however contrary to religion and Sense: But so inform'd, he parted from her, and told her the Event should declare his zeal for her Service; and so it did, for he no sooner spoke of it to the Prince, but he took the Hint as a divine Voice; his very Soul flush'd in his lovely Cheeks, and all the Fire of Love was dancing in his Eyes: Yet as if he had fear'd what he wish'd could not handsomely and lawfully be brought to pass; he ask'd a thousand questions concerning it, all which the subtle Wizard so well resolv'd, at least in his judgment, who easily was convinced of what he wish'd, that he no longer deferr'd his happiness; but that very Night in the visit he made *Hermione*, fell at her Feet, and implores her consent of what he had told her *Fergusano* had fully convinced him was necessary for his Interest and Glory, neither of which he could injoy or regard, if she was not the partner of 'em; and that when he should go to *France*, and put himself in the Field to demand a Crown, he should do it with absolute Vigor and Resolution, if she were to be seated as Queen on the same Throne with him, without whom a Cottage would be more pleasant; and he could relish no Joys that were not as intirely and immediately hers as his own: He pleaded impatiently for what she long'd, and would have made her Petition for, and all the while she makes a thousand doubts and scruples only to be convinced and confirmed by him; and after seeming fully satisfied, he leads her into a Chamber (where *Fergusano* waited, and only her Woman, and his faithful confident *Tomaso*,) and Married her:[a] since which, she has wholly managed him with greater power than before; takes abundance of State; is extreamly elevated, I will not say Insolent; and tho they do not make publick Declaration of this; yet she owns it to all her Intimates; and is ever reproaching my Lord with his lewd course of Life; wholly forgetting her own; crying out upon infamous Women, as if she had been all the course of her Life an innocent.

By this time Dinner was ended, and *Silvia* urg'd *Brilljard* to depart with her Letter; but he was extreamly surpriz'd to find it to be to the Governours Nephew, *Don Alonzo*, who was his Lords Friend; and who would doubtless give him an account of all, if he did not show him the Billet, all these reasons could not disswade this fickle wanderer, whose Heart was at that time set on this young inconstant, at least her inclinations. He tells her that her Life would be really in danger, if *Philander* comes to the knowledge of such an Intrigue, which could not possibly be carry'd on in that Town without noise: She tells him she is resolved to quit that false injurer of her Fame and Beauty; who had basely abandoned her for other Women of less merit, even since she had pardoned him the Crimes of Love he committed at *Cologne*; that while he was in the Country with her, during

---

[a] Monmouth often declared that Henrietta Wentworth was his true wife in the eyes of God.

the time of her Lying in, he had given himself to all that would receive him there; that since he came away, he had left no Beauty unattempted; and could he possibly imagine her of a Spirit to bow beneath such injuries? No, she would on to all revenges her Youth and Beauty were capable of taking, and stick at nothing that led to that interest; and that if he did not joyn with her in her noble design, she would abandon him, and put herself wholly out of his Protection: Thus she spoke with a fierceness, that made the Lover tremble with fear of losing her; he therefore told her she had reason; and that since she was resolved, he would confess to her that *Philander* was the most perfidious Creature in the World; and that *Hermione*, the haughty *Hermione*, who hated naughty Women, invited and treated all the handsome Ladies of the Court to Balls, and to the Basset Table,[a] and made very great entertainment, only to draw to her Interest all the brave and the young men; and that she daily gain'd abundance, by these Arts, to *Cesario*, and above all strove by these amusements to engage *Philander*; whom she perceiv'd to grow cold in the great concern; daily treating him with Variety of Beauty; so that there was no Gaity, no Gallantry, or Play, but at *Hermione's*; whither all the Youth of both Qualities repaired; and 'twas there the Governours Nephew was every Evening to be found. Possibly, Madam, I had not told you this, if the Princes Bounty had not taken me totally off from *Philander*; so that I have no other dependance on him, but that of my Respect and Duty, out of perfect Gratitude. After this to gain *Brilljard* intirely, she assur'd him if his Fortune were suitable to her Quality, and her way of Life, she believed she should devote herself to him; and tho what she said were the least of her thoughts, it fail'd not to flatter him agreeably, and he sigh'd with Grief, that he could not ingage her; all he could get was little enough to support him fine, which he was always as any Person of quality at Court, and appear'd as Graceful, and might have had some happy Minutes with very fine Ladies, who thought well of him. To salve this defect of want of Fortune, he told her he had received a command from *Octavio*, to come to him about settling of a very considerable Pension upon her, and that he had at his investing put Money into his Aunt's Hands, who was a Woman of considerable quality; to be

---

[a] Basset was a popular card game of the time.

dispos'd of to that Charitable Use, and that if she pleas'd to maintain her rest of Fame, and live without receiving Love Visits from Men, she might now command that, which would be a much better and nobler support than that from a Lover, which would be Transitory, and last but as long as her Beauty, or a less time, his Love. To this she knew not what to answer, but ready money being the joy of her Heart, and the support of her Vanity, she seems to yield to this, having said so much before; and she considering she wanted a thousand things to adorn her Beauty, being very expensive; she was impatient till this were performed, and deferr'd the sending to *Don Alonzo*, tho her thoughts were perpetually on him. She by the advice of *Brilljard*, writes a Letter to *Octavio*; which was not like those she had before written, but as an humble Penitent would write to a Ghostly Father, treating him with all the respect that was possible: and if ever she mention'd love, it was as if her Heart had, violently and against her will, burst out into softness, as still she retain'd there; and then she would take up again, and ask pardon for that Transgression; she told him it was a passion, which tho she could never Extinguish for him, yet that it should never warm her for another, but she would leave *Philander* to the World, and retire where she was not known, and try to make up her broken Fortunes; with abundance of things to this purpose; which he carried to *Octavio*: he said he could have wish'd she would have retir'd to a Monastery, as all the first part of her Letter had given him hope; and resolved, and retir'd as he was, he could not read this without extream confusion and change of Countenance. He ask'd *Brilljard* a thousand times whether he believ'd he might trust her, or if she would abandon those ways of shame, that at last lose all: He answered, he verily believ'd she would. However said *Octavio*, 'tis not my business to Capitulate, but to believe and act all things for the interest and satisfaction of her, whom I yet adore; and without farther delay writ to his Aunt, to present *Silvia* with those Sums he had left for her; and which had been sufficient to have made her happy all the rest of her Life, if her Sins of Love had not obstructed it. However she no sooner found herself Mistriss of so considerable a Sum, but in lieu of retiring, and ordering her affairs so as to render it for ever serviceable to her, the first thing she does, is to furnish herself with new Coach and Equipage, and to lavish out in Cloth, and Jewels, a great part of it immediately; and was impatient to be seen on the *Toure*, and in

414

all publick Places; nor could *Brilljard* perswade the contrary, but against all good Manners and Reason, she flew into most violent passions with him, till he had resolved to give her way; it hap'ned that the first day she show'd on the *Toure*, neither *Philander*, *Cesario*, nor *Hermione* chanc'd to be there; so that at Supper it was all the news, how glorious a young Creature was seen only with one Lady, which was *Antonett* very well drest in the Coach with her: every Body that made their Court that Night to *Hermione*, spoke of this new Vision, as the most extraordinary Charmer that had ever been seen; all were that day undone with Love, and none could learn who this fair destroyer was; for all the time of *Silvia*'s being at *Bruxells* before, her being big with Child had kept her from appearing in all publick places; so that she was wholly a new Face to all that saw her; and it is easie to be imagined what Charms that delicate Person appear'd with to all, when dress'd to such advantage, who naturally was the most beautiful Creature in the World; with all the Bloom of Youth that could add to Beauty. Among the rest that day that lost their Hearts, was the Governour's Nephew; who came into the presence that Night wholly Transported, and told *Hermione* he dy'd for the lovely Charmer, he had that day seen; so that she, who was the most curious to gain all the Beauties to her side, that the men might be so too, indeavour'd all she could to find out where this Beauty dwelt. *Philander*, now grown the most Amorous and Gallant in the World, grew passionately in love with the very description of her, not imagining it had been *Silvia*, because of her Equipage: He knew she lov'd him, at least he thought she lov'd him too well to conceal herself from him, or be in *Bruxells*, and not let him know it; so that wholly ravish'd with the Description of the imagined new fair One, he burnt with desire of seeing her; and all this Night was pass'd in discourse of this Stranger alone; the next day her Livery being discrib'd to *Hermione*, she sent two Pages all about the Town, to see if they could discover a Livery so remarkable; and that if they did, they should enquire of them who they belonged to, and where that Persons Lodging was. This was not a very difficult matter to perform: *Bruxells* is not a large place, and it was soon survey'd from one end to the other: At last they met with two of her Foot-men, whom they saluted, and taking notice of their Livery, ask'd them who they belong'd to? these Lads were strangers to the Lady they serv'd, and newly taken; and *Silvia* at her first coming resolv'd to change her Name, and was called Madam *De* —— a Name very considerable in *France*; which they told the Pages, and that she liv'd at such a place: This news *Hermione* no sooner heard, but sends a Gentleman in the Name of the Prince and herself to complement her, and tell her she had the Honour to know some great Persons of that name in *France*, and did not doubt but she was related to them: She therefore sent to offer her her Friendship; which possibly in a strange place might not be unserviceable to her, and that she should be extream glad to see her at Court, that is, at *Cesario*'s Palace. The Gentleman who deliver'd this message, being surpriz'd at the dazling Beauty of the fair Stranger, was almost unassur'd in his Address, and the manner of it surpriz'd *Silvia* no less, to be invited as a strange Lady, by one that hated her; she could not tell whether it were real, or a Plot upon her; however she made answer, and bad him tell Madam, the Princess, which Title she gave her, that she receiv'd her Complement as the greatest Honour that could arrive to her, and that she would wait upon her Highness, and let her know from her own Mouth the Sense she had of the Obligation. The Gentleman returned and delivered his message to *Hermione*; but so altered in his Look, so sad and unusual, that she took notice of it, and ask'd him how he liked the new Beauty: He blushed and bow'd and told her, she was a Wonder —— This made *Hermione*'s Colour rise, it being spoke before *Cesario*; for tho' she were assured of the Hero's Heart, she hated he should believe there was a greater Beauty in the World, and one universally Adored. She knew not how so great a Miracle might work upon him, and began to repent she had invited her to Court.

In the mean time, *Silvia*, after debating what to do in this Affair, whether to visit *Hermione* and discover her self, or to remove from *Bruxells*, resolved rather upon the last; but she had fixed her Design as to *Don Alonzo*, and would not depart the Town. To her former beginning Flame, for him was added more Fuel; she had seen him the Day before on the *Toure*; she had seen him gaze at her with all the impatience of Love, with madness of Passion in his Eyes, ready to fling himself out of the Coach every time she past by; and if he appeared Beautiful before, when in his Riding dress, and harass'd for Four Nights together with Love and want of Sleep. What did he now appear to her Amorous Eyes and Heart? She had wholly forgot *Octavio*, *Philander*, and all, and made a Sacrifice of both to this new young Lover: She saw him with all the advantages of Dress, magnificent as Youth and Fortune could invent; and above all, his Beauty and his Quality warmed her Heart a new; and what advanced her Flame yet farther, was a Vanity she had of fixing the dear Wanderer, and making him find there was a Beauty yet in the World, that could put an end to his Inconstancy, and make him languish at her Feet as long as she pleased. Resolv'd on this design, she defers it no longer, but as soon as the Persons of Quality, who used to walk every Evening in the Park, were got together, she accompanied with *Antonett*, and Three or Four strange Pages and Foot-men, went into the Park, Mask'd, drest in perfect Glory. She had not walked long there before she saw *Don Alonzo*, richer than ever in his Habit, and more Beautiful to her Eyes than any thing she had ever seen; he was gotten among the Young and Fair, caressing, laughing, playing, and acting all the little Wantonnesses of Youth. *Silvia*'s Blood grew disordered at this, and she found she loved by her Jealousie, and longs more than ever to have the glory of vanquishing that Heart, that so boasted of never having yet been conquer'd. She therefore uses all her Art to get him to look at her; she passed by him often, and as often as she did so he view'd her with Pleasure; her Shape, her Air, her Mien, had something so Charming, as without the Assistance of her Face, she gained that Evening a Thousand Conquests; but those were not the Trophies she aimed at, it was *Alonzo* was the mark'd out Victim, that she destin'd for the Sacrifice of Love. She found him so ingag'd with Women of great Quality, she almost dispair'd to get to speak to him; her Equipage, who stood at the Entrance of the Park, not being by her, he did not imagine this fine Lady to be her he saw on the *Toure* last Night; yet he look'd at her so much as gave occasion to those he was with to rally him extreamly, and tell him he was in Love with what he had not seen, and who might, notwithstanding all that delicate appearance, be ugly when her Mask was off. *Silvia*, however, still past on with abundance of sighing Lovers after her, some daring to speak, others only languishing; to all she would vouchsafe no word but made signs, as if she were a stranger and understood 'em not; at last, *Alonzo* wholly impatient, breaks from these Ralliers, and gets into the Crowd that pursued this lovely unknown: her Heart leapt when he approach'd her, and the first thing she did was to pull off her Glove, and not only show the fairest Hand that ever Nature made, but that Ring on her Finger *Alonzo* gave her when they parted at the

Village. The Hand alone was enough to invite all Eyes with Pleasure to look that way; but *Alonzo* had a double Motive, he saw the Hand with Love, and the Ring with Jealousie and Surprize; and as 'tis natural in such Cases, the very first Thought that possest him, was, that the young *Bellumere* (for so *Silvia* had call'd herself at the Village) was a Lover of this Lady, and had presented her this Ring. And after his Sighings and little Pantings, that seized him at this thought, would give him leave, he bowing and blushing cry'd,——*Madam, the whole piece must sure be Excellent, when the Pattern is so very fine.* And humbly begging the Favour of a nearer view, he took her Hand and kiss'd it with a passionate Eagerness, which possibly did not so well please *Silvia*, because she did not think he took her for the same person, to whom he show'd such signs of Love last Night. In taking her Hand he survey'd the Ring, and cry'd,——*Madam, would to Heaven I could lay so good a claim to this fair Hand, as I think I once could to this Ring, which this Hand Adorns and Honours. How, Sir* replied Silvia, *I hope you will not charge me with Fellony? I am afraid I shall,* reply'd he, sighing, *for you have attack'd me on the King's High-way and have robbed me of a Heart: I could never have robbed a Person,* said Silvia, *who could more easily have parted with that Trifle; the next fair Object will redeem it, and it will be very little the worse for my using. Ah, Madam,* reply'd he, sighing, *that will be according as you will treat it; for I find already, you have done it more damage than it ever sustained in all the Rancounters it has had with Love and Beauty. You complain too soon,* reply'd *Silvia*, smiling, *and you ought to make a tryal of my good Nature before you reproach me with harming you. I know not,* reply'd *Alonzo*, sighing, *what I may venture to hope from that; but I am afraid, from your Inclinations, I ought to hope for nothing, since a Thousand reasonable Jealousies already possess me, from the sight of that Ring; and I more than doubt I have a powerful Rival, a Youth of the most divine Form I ever met with of his Sex; if from him you received it, I guess my Fate. I perceive, Stranger,* said Silvia, *you begin to be inconstant already, and find excuses to complain on your Fate before you have tried your Fortune. I perswade myself that fine Person you speak of, and to whom you gave this Ring, has so great a value for you, that to leave you no Excuse, I assure you, he will not be displeas'd to find you a Rival, provided you prove a very constant Lover. I confess,* said Alonzo, *Constancy is an imposition I never yet had the Confidence and ill Nature to impose on the Fair; and indeed I never found that Woman yet, of Youth and Beauty, that ever set so small a value on her own*

Charms, to be much in Love with that dull Vertue, or require it of my Heart; but upon occasion, Madam, if such an unreasonable fair one be found —— I am extreamly sorry (interrupted Silvia) *to find you have no better way of recommending yourself; this will be no great incouragement to a person of my Humour to receive your Addresses. Madam, I do not tell you that I am not in my nature wondrous constant, reply'd he; I tell you only what has hitherto happen'd to me, not what will, that I have yet never been so, is no fault of mine, but power, or truth in those Beauties to whom I have given my Heart, rather believe they wanted Charms to hold me, than that I (where Wit and Beauty ingag'd me) should prove so false to my own Pleasure. I am very much afraid, Madam, if I find my Eyes as agreeably entertained when I shall have the Honour to see your Face, as my Ears are with your excellent Wit, I shall be reduced to that very whining, sighing Coxcomb, you like so well in a Lover, and be ever dying at your Feet. I have but one hope left to preserve myself from this wretched thing, you Women love; that is, that I shall not find you so all over Charming, as what I have hitherto found presents it self to be. You have already created Love enough in me for any reasonable Woman, but I find you are not to be approached with the common Devotions we pay your Sex; but like your Beauty, the Passion too must be great; and you are not content unless you see your Lovers die; this is that fatal proof alone that can satisfie you of their Passion. And tho' you laugh to see a Sir* Courtly Nice,[a] *a fop in Fashion acted on the Stage, in your Hearts that foolish thing, that fine neat Pasquel[b] is your Darling, your fine Gentleman, your Well-bred Person.*

Thus sometimes in Jest and sometimes in Earnest, they recommended themselves to each other, and to so great a degree, that it was impossible for them to be more Charm'd on either side, which lasted till it was time to depart; but he besought her not to do so till she had informed him where he might wait on her, and most passionately solicits what she as passionately desired: *To tell you Truth,* said she, *I cannot permit you that freedom without you ask it of* Bellumere. He reply'd, *Next to waiting on her, he should be the most over-joy'd in the World, to pay his Respects to that young Gentleman.* However, to name him, gave him a Thousand Fears; which when he would have urg'd, she bid him

---

[a] The eponymous hero of John Crowne's comedy *Sir Courtly Nice,* 1685. Behn herself favoured such typical names; she wrote a play called *Sir Patient Fancy* and *The City Heiress* was subtitled *Sir Timothy Treat-all.*

[b] Lampoon or caricature.

trust to the generosity of that Man, who was of Quality, and loved him; she then told him his Lodgings (which were her own:) *Alonzo* infinitely over-joyed, resolv'd to lose no time, but promis'd that Evening to visit him: And at their parting he treated her with so much passionate Respect, that she was vext to see it paid to one he yet knew not. However she verily believed her Conquest was certain: He having seen her three times, and all those times for a several Person, and yet was still in Love with her: And she doubted not when all three were joyn'd in one, he would be much more in Love than yet he had been; with this assurance they parted.

Silvia was no sooner got home but she revolved to receive *Alonzo*, who she was assured would come: She hasted to dress herself in a very rich Suit of Man's Cloths, to receive him as the young *French* Gentleman. She believed *Brilljard* would not come till late as was his use, now being at Play at *Hermione's*. She look'd extream pretty when she was drest, and had all the Charms that Heaven could adorn a Face and Shape withal: Her Apartment was very magnificent, and all look'd very great. She was no sooner drest but the young Lover came. *Silvia* received him on the Stair-case with open Arms, and all the signs of Joy that could be exprest, and leads him to a rich drawing Room, where she began to entertain him with that happy Nights adventure, when they both lay together at the Village, while *Alonzo* makes imperfect replies; wholly charmed with the look of the young Cavalier, which so resembled what he had seen the day before in another Garb on the *Toure*. He is wholly ravish'd with his Voice, it being absolutely the same that had charmed him that Day in the Park; the more he gaz'd and listen'd, the more he was confirm'd in his Opinion, that he was the same, and he had the Musick of that dear accent still in his Ears, and could not be deceived. A Thousand times he is about to kneel before her and ask her Pardon, but still is check'd by Doubt: He sees, he hears, this is the same lovely Youth who lay in Bed with him at the Village *Caberett*; and then no longer thinks her Woman: He hears and sees it is the same Face, and Voice, and Hands he saw on the *Toure*, and in the Park, and then believes her Woman: While he is in these perplexities, *Silvia*, who with Vanity and Pride perceiv'd his disorder, taking him in her Arms, cry'd, *Come my* Alonzo, *that you shall no longer doubt but I am perfectly your Friend, I will shew you a Sister of mine, whom you will say is a Beauty, or I am too partial, and I will have your judgment of her.* With that he call'd to *Antonett* to beg her Lady would permit him to bring a young Stranger to kiss her hand. The Maid, instructed, retires, and *Alonzo* stood gazing on *Silvia* as one confounded and amaz'd, not knowing yet how to determine; he now begins to think himself mistaken in the fair Youth, and is ready to ask his Pardon for a Fault but imagin'd, suffering by his silence, the little Pratler to discourse and laugh at him at his pleasure. *Come,* said *Silvia,* smiling, *I find the naming a Beauty to you has made you Melancholy; possibly when you see her she will not appear so to you; we do not always agree in one Object.* Your Judgment, reply'd Alonzo, *is too good to leave me any hope of Liberty at the sight of a fine Woman; if she be like your self I read my destiny in your charming Face.* Silvia answered only with a Smile —— and calling again for *Antonett,* he ask'd if his Sister were in a condition of being seen; she told him she was not, but all undrest and in her Night-clothes; *Nay, then,* said Silvia, *I must use my Authority with her:* And leaving *Alonzo* trembling with Expectation, she ran to her dressing Room where all things were ready, and slipping off her Coat put on a rich Night-Gown, and instead of her Peruke[a] fine Night-Clothes, and came forth to the Charm'd *Alonzo,* who was not able to approach her, she look'd with such a Majesty and so much dazling Beauty; he knew her to be the same he had seen in the *Toure.* She (seeing he only gazed without Life or Motion) approaching him gave him her Hand, and cryed ——*Sir, possibly this is a more old acquaintance of yours than my Face.* At which he blush'd and bow'd, but could not speak: At last *Silvia* laughing out-right, cryed —— Here Antonett *bring me again my Peruke, for I find I shall never be acquainted with* Don Alonzo *in Peticoats.* At this he blush'd a Thousand times more than before, and no longer doubting but this Charmer, and the lovely Youth were one; he fell at her Feet, and told her he was undone, for she had made him give her so undisputable Proofs of his Dulness, he could never hope she should allow him capable of eternally adoring her. *Rise,* cry'd Silvia, smiling, *and believe you have not committed so great an Errour, as you imagine; the mistake has been often made, and Persons of a great deal of Wit have been deceiv'd. You may say what you please,* replyed Alonzo, *to put me in my Countenance; but I shall never forgive my self the Stupidity of that happy Night, that laid*

---

[a] A wig.

me by the most glorious Beauty of the World, and yet afforded me no
kind Instinct to inform my Soul how much I was blest: Oh pity a
wretchedness, Divine Maid, that has no other excuse but that of
Infatuation; a thousand times, my greedy ravish'd Eyes wander'd o're
the dazling brightness of yours; a thousand times I wish'd that Heaven
had made you Woman! and when I look'd, I burnt; but when I Kiss'd
those soft, those lovely Lips, I durst not trust my Heart; for every touch
begot wild Thoughts about it; which yet the Course of all my Fiery
Youth, through all the wild Debauches I had wandered, had never yet
betray'd me to: and going to Bed with all this love and fear about me, I
made a solemn Oath not to approach you, least so much Beauty had
o'er-come my Vertue. But by this new discovery, you have given me a
Flame I have no power nor virtue to oppose: 'tis just, 'tis natural to
adore you; and not to do it, were yet a crime greater than my Sin of
Dulness: and since you have made me lose a Charming Friend; it is but
just I find a Mistriss; give me but your permission to Love, and I will
give you all my life in Services, and wait the rest: I'll watch and pray
for coming happiness; which I will buy at any price of Life or Fortune.
Well, Sir, replyed our easie fair One; *If you believe me worth a*
Conquest o're you, convince me you can love; for I'm no common
Beauty to be won with pretty suddain Services; and could you lay an
Empire at my Feet, I should dispise it where the Heart were wanting.
You may believe the Amorous Youth left no Argument to convince her in that point unsaid; and 'tis most certain they came to
so good an understanding, that he was not seen in *Bruxells* for
eight days and nights after, nor this rare Beauty, for so long a
time, seen on the *Toure* or any publick Place. *Brilljard* came
every day to visit her, and receive her commands, as he us'd to
do, but was answer'd still that *Silvia* was Ill, and kept her
Chamber, not suffering even her Domesticks to approach her:
This did not so well satisfy the Jealous Lover, but he soon
imagined the cause, and was very much displeas'd at the ill
Treatment; if such a design had been carried on, he desired to
have the management of it, and was angry that *Silvia* had not
only deceived him in the promise he had made for her to
Octavio; but had done her own business without him; he spoke
some hard words; so that to undeceive him, she was forced to
oblige *Alonzo* to appear at Court again; which she had much ado
to incline him to, so absolutely she had Charm'd him; however
he went, and she suffered *Brilljard* to visit her, perswading that
easie Lover (as all Lovers are easie) that it was only indisposition that hindered her of the happiness of seeing him, and after

having perfectly reconcil'd herself to him, she ask'd him the news at *Hermione's*, to whom, I had forgot to tell you, she sent every day a Page with a Complement, and to let her know she was Ill, or she would have waited on her: She every day received the Complement from her again, as an unknown Lady. *Brilljard* told her that all things were now prepar'd, and in a very short time, they should go for *France*; but that whatever the matter was, *Philander* almost publickly disown'd the Prince's Interest, and to some very considerable of the Party, has given out, he does not like the Proceedings, and that he verily believed they would find themselves all mistaken; and that instead of a Throne the Prince would meet a Scaffold; so bold and open he has been. Something of it has arriv'd to the Prince's Ear, who was far from believing it, that he could hardly be perswaded to speak of it to him; and when he did, it was with an assurance before hand, that he did not credit such reports. So that he gives him not the pain to deny them: For my part, I am infinitely afraid he will disoblige the Prince one day, for last night, when the Prince desired him to get his Equipage ready, and to make such Provision for you as was necessary; he coldly told him, he had a mind to go to *Hungary*, which at that time was besieg'd by *Solyman* the Magnificent,[a] and that he had no inclination of returning to *France*. This surpriz'd and angered the Prince; but they parted good Friends at last, and he has promised him all things: So that I am very well assur'd he will send me where he supposes you still are, and how shall we manage that affair?

Silvia who had more cunning and subtlety, than all the rest of her Sex; thought it best to see *Philander*, and part with him on as good terms as she could, and that it was better he should think he yet had the absolute possession of her, than that he should return to *France* with an ill opinion of her Vertue, as yet he had known no guilt of that kind, nor did he ever more than fear it, with *Octavio*; so that it would be easie for her to cajole him yet a little longer, and when he was gone, she should have the World to range in, and possess this new Lover, to whom she had

---

[a] Suleiman the Magnificent (?1494–1566), the Ottoman Sultan annexed large areas of Hungary in 1526 and went on to beseige Vienna in 1529. Philander's flippancy was apparently an echo of Lord Grey's wit. In his confession after the Rebellion, Grey also states that he was reluctant to join Monmouth and only did so because of his financial circumstances.

promised all things, and received from him all assurances imaginable of inviolable Love: In order to this then she consulted with *Brilljard*; and they resolved she should for a few days leave *Antonett* with her Equipage, at that House where she was, and retire herself to the Village, where *Philander* had left her, and where he still imagined she was: She desired *Brilljard* to give her a days time for this preparation, and it should be so. He left her, and going to *Hermione*'s, meets *Philander*, who immediately gave him order to go to *Silvia* the next Morning, and let her know how all things went, and to tell her he would be with her in two days. In the mean time *Silvia* sent for *Alonzo*, who was but that Evening gone from her. He flies on the Wings of Love, and she tells him, she is oblig'd to go to a place six or seven days Journey off, whither he could not conduct her for reasons she would tell him at her return: whatever he could plead with all the force of love to the contrary, she gets his consent, with a promise wholly to devote herself to him at her return, and pleas'd she sent him from her, when *Brilljard* returning, told her the commands he had; and 'twas concluded they should both depart next Morning, accompanied only by her Page. I am well assur'd she was very kind to *Brilljard* all that Journey, and which was but too visible to the amorous Youth, who attended them, so absolutely had she deprav'd her reason from one degree of Sin and Shame to another; and he was happy above any imagination, while even her Heart was given to another, and when she could propose no other interest in this looseness, but security, that *Philander* should not know how ill she had treated him. In four days *Philander* came, and finding *Silvia* more fair than ever was anew pleas'd; for she pretended to receive him with all the joy imaginable, and the deceived Lover believed, and express'd abundance of Grief, at the being obliged to part from her; a great many Vows and Tears were lost on both sides, and both believed true: But the Grief of *Brilljard* was not to be conceived; he could not perswade himself he could live, when absent from her: Some Bills *Philander* left her, and was so plain with her, and open-hearted, he told her that he went indeed with *Cesario*, but it was in order to serve the King; that he was weary of their Actions, and foresaw nothing but ruin would attend 'em; that he never repented him of any thing so much, as his being drawn into that Faction; in which he found himself so greatly involved, he could not retire with any credit, but since Self-Preservation was the first principle to

Nature, he had resolved to make that his aim, and rather prove false to a party who had no Justice and Honour on their Side, than to a King whom all the Laws of Heaven and Earth obliged him to serve; however he was so far in the power of these People, that he could not disingage himself, without utter ruin to himself; but that as soon as he was got into *France*, he would abandon their Interest: Let the censuring World say what it would, who never had right notions of things, or ever made true Judgments of mens Actions.

He lived five or six days with *Silvia* there; in which time she fail'd not to assure him of her constant Fidelity a thousand ways, especially by Vows that left no doubt upon his Heart, and it was now that they both indeed found there was a very great Friendship still remaining at the bottom of their Hearts for each other, nor did they part without manifest proofs of it. *Brilljard* took a sad and melancholy leave of her, and had not the freedom to tell it aloud; but obliged to depart with his Lord, they left *Silvia* and posted to *Bruxells*, where they found the Prince ready to depart, having left *Hermione* to her Women more than half dead. I have heard there never was so sad a parting between Two Lovers; a Hundred times they swounded with the apprehension of the separation in each other's Arms, and at last the Prince was forced from her while he left her dead, and was little better himself: He would have returned, but the Officers and People about him, who had espous'd his Quarrel, would by no means suffer him: And he has a Thousand times told a person very near him, That he had rather have forfeited all his hop'd for Glory, than have left that Charmer of his Soul. After he had taken all care imaginable for *Hermione*, for that name so dear to him, was scarce ever out of his Mouth, he suffer'd himself with a heavy Heart and Pace, to be conducted to the Vessel: And I have heard, he was hardly seen to smile all that little Voyage, or his whole Life after, or do any thing but sigh and sometimes weep, which was a very great discouragement to all that followed him; they were a great while at Sea, tost to and fro by stress of Weather,[a] and often driven back to the Shore where they first took Shipping; and not being able to Land where they first designed, they got a-shore in a little Harbour, where no Ship of any bigness could Anchor; so that

---

[a] Because of bad weather, Monmouth's voyage from the Texel in Holland to Lyme took twelve days.

with much ado, getting all their Arms and Men on shore they sunk the Ship, both to secure any from flying, and that it might not fall into the Hands of the *French*. *Cesario* was no sooner on the *French* shore, but numbers came to him of the *Hugonot* Party, for whom he had Arms, and who wanted them he furnish'd as far as he could, and immediately Proclaimed himself King of *France* and *Navarr*,[a] while the dirty Croud, rang him Peals of Joy. But tho' the under World came in great Crowds to his Aid, he wanted still the main supporters of his Cause, the men of more substantial Quality: If the Ladies could have compos'd an Army, he would not have wanted one, for his Beauty had got them all on his side; and he Charm'd the fair wheresoever he rode.——

He march'd from Town to Town without any opposition, Proclaiming himself a King in all the places he came to; still gathering as he march'd, till he had compos'd a very formidable Army. He made Officers of the Kingdom —— *Fergusano* was to have been a Cardinal, and several Lords and Dukes were nominated; and he found no opposition in all his prosperous Course——in the mean time the Royal Army was not Idle, which was composed of Men very well Disciplined, and conducted by several Princes, and Men of great Quality and Conduct. But as it is not the Business of this little History to treat of War, but altogether Love; leaving those rougher Relations to the Chronicles and Historiographers of those Times, I will only hint on such things in this Enterprize as are most proper for my purpose, and tell you that *Cesario* omitted nothing for the carrying on his great Design; he dispersed his Scandals[b] all over *France*, tho' they met with an obstruction at *Paris*, and were immediately suppress'd, it being proclaim'd Death for any person to keep one in their Houses; and if any should by chance come to their Hands, they were on this Penalty, to carry them to the Secretary of State; and after the Punishment had past on Two or Three Offenders, it deterred the rest from medling with those edge Tools: I must tell you also, that the title of King, which *Cesario* had taken so early upon him, was much against his Inclinations; and he desired to see himself at the Head of a

---

[a] Navarre, the southernmost region of France. Navarre is divided into both French and Spanish territories.

[b] Monmouth's Declaration.

more satisfiable Army, before he would take on him a Title he found (in the condition he was in) he should not defend; but those about him insinuated into him, that it was the Title that would not only make him more Venerable, but would make his Cause appear more just and awful; and beget him a perfect Adoration with those People who liv'd remote from Courts, and had never seen that glorious thing called a King. So that believing it would give Nerves to the Cause, he unhappily took upon him that which ruined him; for he had often sworn to the greatest part of those of any Quality of his interest, That his design was Liberty only, and that his end was the publick good, so infinitely above his own private interest, that he desired only the Honour of being the Champion for the opprest *Parisians* and People of *France*; that if they would allow him to lead their Armies, to fight and spend his dearest Blood for them, 'twas all the Glory he aim'd at. 'Twas this pretended Humility in a person of his high rank that first cajol'd the *Mobile*, who look on him as their God, their Deliverer, and all that was sacred and dear to them; but the wiser sort regarded him only as one that had most power and pretension to turn the whole Affairs of *France*, which they disliking were willing at any Price, to reduce to their own conditions and to what they desired; not imagining he would have laid a claim to the Crown, which many of them fancy'd themselves as capable of as himself, rather that he would perhaps have set up the King of *Navarr*. This *Cesario* knew; and understanding their Sentiments, was unwilling to hinder their joyning him, by such a Declaration which he knew would be a means to turn abundance of Hearts against him, as indeed it fell out; and he found himself Master of some few Towns,[a] only with an Army of Fifteen or Sixteen thousand Peasants, ill Armed, unus'd to War, Watchings, and very ill Logding in the Field, very badly Victuall'd, and worse Paid. For, from *Paris* no Aids of any kind could be brought him; the Roads all along being so well guarded and secured by the Royal Forces, and wanting some great Persons to espouse his Quarrel, made him not only dispair of Success, but highly resent it of those who had given him so large promises of Aid. Many, as I said, and most were disgusted with his Title of King; but some

---

[a] Lyme, Taunton and Bridgewater were the only true centres of support for the rebels.

427

waited the success of his first Battle, which was every day
expected, tho' *Cesario* kept himself as clear of the Royal Army as
he could a long time, marching away as soon as they drew near,
hoping by these means, not only to tire them out, but watch an
advantage when to engage, but gather still more Numbers. So
that the greatest mischief he did was teazing the Royal Army,
who could never tell where to have him, so dexterous he was in
marching off. They often came so near, as to have Skirmishes
with one another by small Parties, where some few Men would
fall on both sides: And to say truth, *Cesario* in this Expedition
show'd much more of a Souldier than the Politician: His Skill
was great, his Conduct good, expert in Advantages, and indefatigable in Toils. And I have heard it from the Mouth of a
Gentleman, who in all that undertaking never was from him;
that in Seven or Eight Weeks that he was in Arms he never
absolutely undrest himself, and hardly slept an Hour in the
Four and twenty; and that sometimes was on his Horse's-back,
in a Chariot, or on the ground, suffering even with the meanest
of his Souldiers all the fatigues of the Enterprize: This Gentleman told me he would, in those Hours he should sleep, and
wherein he was not taking Measures and Councils (which were
always held in the Night) that he would be eternally speaking to
him of *Hermione*; and that with the softest concern 'twas possible for Love and tenderest Passion to express. That he being the
only Friend he could repose so great a weakness in, and who
sooth'd him to the degree he wish'd, the Prince was so well
pleas'd with him, as to establish him a Collonel of Horse, for no
other merit than that of having once served *Hermione*, and now
would flatter his disease agreeably: And tho' he did so, he
protested he was ashamed to hear how Poor this fond concern
render'd this great Man, and he has often pity'd what should
have been else admir'd; but who can tell the force of Love,
back'd by Charms supernatural? and who is it that will not sigh
at the Fate of so Illustrious a Young-man, whom Love had
render'd the most miserable of all those numbers he led?

But now the Royal Army, as if they had purposly suffered
him to take his Toore about the Country, to Ensnare him with
the more Facility; had at last, by new Forces that came to their
assistance daily, so incompass'd him, that it was impossible for
him to avoid any longer giving them Battle; however he had the
benefit of Posting himself the most advantageously, that he
could wish; he had the rising Grounds to place his Cannon, and

all things concur'd to give him success. His Numbers exceeding those of the Royal Army; not but he would have avoided a set Battle, if it had been possible, till he had made himself Master of some places of stronger hold; for yet as I said, he had only subdued some inconsiderable places, which were not able to make defence; and which as soon as he was march'd out, surrender'd again to their lawful Prince; and pulling down his Proclamation; put up those of the King: but he was on all sides so embarass'd, he could not come even to parly with any Town of Note; so that as I said, at last, being as it were block'd up, tho' the Royal Army did not offer him Battle: Three Nights they lay thus in view of each other; the first night, the Prince sent out his Scouts, who brought in intelligence, that the Enemy was not so well prepar'd for Battle, as they fear'd they might be if they imagined the Prince would engage 'em, but he had so often given them the slip, that they believed he had no mind to put the Fortune of the Day to the push: And they were glad of these delays, that new forces might advance; when the Scouts returned with this news, the Prince was impatient to fall upon the Enemy; but *Fergusano*, who was continually taking Council of his Charms, and looking into his black Book of Fate, for every sally and step they made, perswaded his Highness to have yet a little patience; positively assuring him his Fortune depended on a Critical Minute, which was not yet come; and that if he offered to give Battle before the Change of the Moon, he was inevitably lost, and that the attendance of that fortunate moment would be the beginning of those of his whole Life: with such like positive perswasions, he gain'd upon the Prince, and overcame his impatience of engageing for that Night, all which he past in Council without being perswaded to take any rest, often blaming the Nicety of their Art and his Stars; and often asking if they lost that opportunity that Fortune had now given 'em, whether all their Art, or Stars, or Devils, could retrieve it? and nothing would that Night appease him, or dispossess'd the Sorcerers of this opinion.

The next day they received certain intelligence, that a considerable supply would re-inforce the Royal Army, under the Conduct of a Prince of the Blood;[a] which were every moment

---

[a] Lieutenant-General Lord Feversham was commander of the regular troops and militia in the West and Lord John Churchill directed the forces in the field. Christopher Monk, the second Duke of Albemarle, commanded the Devon militia.

expected; This news made the Prince rave, and he broke out
into all the rage imaginable against the Wizards, who defended
themselves with all the reasons of their Art; but it was all in
vain, and he vow'd he would that Night engage the Enemy; if
he could find but one faithful Friend to second him; tho he dyed
in the attempt; that he was worn out with the Toils he had
undergone; harass'd almost to death, and would wait no longer
the approach of his lazy Fate, but boldly advancing, meet it
what Face so 'ere it bore. They besought him on their Knees, he
would not overthrow the Glorious Design so long in bringing to
perfection, just in the very Minute of happy projection; but to
wait those certain Fates, that would bring him Glory and Honour on their Wings, and who if slighted, would abandon him to
distruction; it was but some few Hours more, and then they
were his own, to be commanded by him: 'twas thus they drill'd
and delay'd him on till Night; when again he sent out his Scouts
to discover the Posture of the Enemy; and himself in the mean
time went to Council. *Philander* fail'd not to be sent for thither,
who sometimes feign'd Excuses to keep away, and when he did
come, he sate unconcern'd neither giving or receiving any
advice. This was taken notice of by all, but *Cesario*, who look'd
upon it as his being over-watch'd, and fatigu'd with the Toils of
the day: his Sullenness did not pass so in the opinion of the rest;
they saw, or at least thought they saw some other marks of
discontent in his fine Eyes, which Love so much better became.
One of the Princes Officers and Captain of his Guard, who was
an old Hereditary Rogue, and whose Father had suffer'd in a
Rebellion before; a Fellow rough and daring, comes boldly to
the Prince when the Council rose, and ask'd him if he were
resolved to Engage? He told him he was. *Then*, said he, *give me
leave to shoot* Philander *in the Head*:[a] This blunt proposition given
without any manner of reason or Circumstance, made the
Prince start back a step or two, and ask him his meaning of
what he said. *Sir*, replyed the Captain, *if you will be safe*, Philander *must Die; for however it appear to your Highness, to all the Camp
he shows the Traytor, and 'tis more than doubted he, and the King of*

---

[a] During an attack on Bridport, Grey turned his cavalry away from the battle and
returned to Lyme. Among the rebel troops he was now perceived as a coward.
Before the Battle of Sedgemoor, an officer called Matthews asked for the cavalry to
be divided rather than left under the sole command of Lord Grey but Monmouth
refused the request.

France *understand one another but too well: Therefore if you would be Victor, let him be dispatch'd, and I my self will undertake it: Hold,* said the Prince, *if I could believe what you say to be true, I should not take so base a revenge; I would Fight like a Souldier, and he should be treated like a man of Honour: Sir,* said Vaneur,[a] for that was the Captains name; *do not in the Circumstances we now are in talk of treating (with those that would betray us) like men of Honour; we cannot stand upon decency in killing, who have so many to dispatch; we came not into* France *to fight Duels, and stand on nice Punctillios: I say, we must make quick work, and I have a good Pistol charged with two handsome Bullets, that shall as soon as he appears amongst us on Horse-back, do his business as gentilely as can be, and rid you of one of the most powerful of your Enemies.* To this, the Prince would by no means agree; not believing one syllable of the Accusation. *Vaneur* swore then, that he would not draw a Sword for his Service, while *Philander* was suffered to live; and he was as good as his word: He said in going out, that he would obey the Prince, but he beg'd his pardon, if he did not lift a Hand on his side; and in an Hour after sent him his Commission, and waited on him, and was with him almost till the last, in all the danger, but would not Fight, having made a solemn Vow. Several others were of *Vaneur*'s opinion, but the Prince believ'd nothing of it, *Philander* being indeed, as he said, weary of the design and party, and regarded them as his Ruiners, who with fair pretences, drew him into a bad Cause; which his Youth had not then considered, and from which he could not untangle himself.

By this time the Scout was come back, who inform'd the Prince that now was the best time in the World to Attack the Enemy,[b] who all lay supinely in their Tents and did not expect a Surprize; that the very outguards were slender, and that it would not be hard to put 'em to a great deal of Confusion. The Prince who was enough impatient before, now was all Fire and Spirit, and 'twas not in the Power of Magick to withhold him; but hasting immediately to Horse, with as much speed as possible, he got at the Head of his Men; and marching on directly

---

[a] Lieutenant-Colonel Venner, an old Cromwellian and one of Monmouth's most important military advisers. Venner was leading the attack on Bridport when Grey retreated from the battle.

[b] Monmouth's rebels attacked the royal forces on the night of the 5th July, 1685. Again, Grey mishandled his cavalry and left Monmouth's infantry unprotected as his men fled the field. The rebels were completely routed.

to the Enemy put them into so great a surprize, that it may be admired how they got themselves into a condition of defence; and to make short of a business that was not long in acting, I may avow nothing but the immediate hand of the Almighty (who favours the juster side, and is always ready for the support of those who approach so near their own Divinity, sacred and anointed Heads) could have turned the Fortune of the Battle to the Royal side; it was prodigious to consider the unequal numbers, and the advantage all on the Princes part; it was miraculous to behold the order on his side, and surprize on the other, which of it self had been sufficient to have confounded them; yet notwithstanding all this unpreparedness on this side, and the watchfulness and care on the other; so well the General and Officers of the Royal Army managed their scanted Time; so bravely disciplin'd, and experienced the Souldiers were, so resolute and brave, and all so well mounted and armed, that as I said to a Miracle they fought; and 'twas a Miracle they won the Field: tho that fatal Night, *Cesario* did in his own Person wonders, and when his Horse was kill'd under him, he took a *Partizan* and as a common Souldier, at the head of his Foot acted the *Hero*, with as much courage and bravery, as ever *Cæsar* himself could Boast. Yet all this avail'd him nothing, he saw himself abandoned on all sides, and then under the Covert of the Night, he retired from the Battle, with his Sword in his hand, with only one Page, who fought by his side: A thousand times he was about to fall on his own Sword, and like *Brutus*[a] have finish'd a life he could no longer sustain with Glory: But Love, that coward of the Mind, and the Image of Divine *Hermione*, as he esteemed her, still gave him Love to life; and while he could remember she yet lived to charm him, he could even look with contempt on the loss of all his Glory; at which if he repin'd, it was for her sake, who expected to behold him return cover'd o'er with Laurels; in these sad thoughts he wandered as long as his wearied Legs would bear him into a low Forest, far from the Camp; where over-prest with Toil, all over pain, and a Royal Heart even breaking with Anxiety, he laid him down under the shelter of a Tree, and found but his length of Earth left to support him now, who not many hours before beheld

---

[a] At the end of Shakespeare's *Julius Caesar* Brutus falls on his own sword rather than be taken prisoner, saying: 'Think not, thou noble Roman, / That ever Brutus will go bound to Rome'. [V.i.110–111]

himself the greatest Monarch as he imagined in the World. Oh who, that had seen him thus; which of his most mortal Enemies, that had view'd the Royal Youth, adorn'd with all the Charms of Beauty, Heaven ever distributed to Man; Born great, and but now ador'd by all the crowding World with Hat and Knee; now abandon by all, but one kind trembling Boy weeping by his side, while the Illustrious *Hero* lay Gazing with melancholy weeping Eyes, at those Stars that had lately been so cruel to him: Sighing out his great Soul to the Winds that whistled round his uncovered head; breathing his Griefs as silently as the sad fatal Night past away. Where nothing in nature seemed to pity him, but the poor wretched Youth that kneeled by him, and the sighing Air; I say, who that beheld this, would not have scorn'd the World, and all its fickle Worshipers? have curst the Flatteries of vain Ambition, and priz'd a Cottage far above a Throne? a Garland wreath'd by some fair innocent hand, before the restless Glories of a Crown?

Some Authors in the Relation of this Battle affirm, That *Philander* quitted his Post[a] as soon as the Charge was given, and sheer'd off from that Wing he commanded; but all Historians agree in this Point, that if he did, it was not for want of Courage; for in a Thousand Incounters he has given sufficient proofs of as much Bravery as a Man can be capable of: But he disliked the Cause, disapproved of all their Pretensions, and look'd upon the whole Affair and Proceeding to be most unjust and ungenerous: And all the fault his greatest Enemies could charge him with, was, That he did not deal so gratefully with a Prince that loved him and trusted him; and that he ought frankly to have told him, he would not serve him in this Design; and that it had been more Gallant to have quited him that way, than this; but there are so many Reasons to be given for this more Politick and safe Deceit, than are needful in this place, and 'tis most certain as it is the most justifiable to Heaven and Man, to one born a Subject of *France*, and having Sworn Allegiance to his proper King, to abandon any other Interest; so let the Enemies of this great Man say what they please, if a Man be oblig'd to be false to this or that Interest, I think no body of common Honesty, Sense and

---

[a] Many historians have condemned Grey's cowardice. Gilbert Burnet wrote that 'The duke of Monmouth was struck with this, when he found that the person on whom he depended most, and for whom he designed the command of the horse, had already made himself infamous by his cowardice.'

Honour, will dispute which he ought to abandon; and this is most certain, that he did not forsake him because Fortune did so, as this one Instance may make appear. When *Cesario* was first Proclaimed King, and had all the Reason in the World to believe that Fortune would have been wholly partial to him, he offer'd *Philander* his choice of any Principality and Government in *France*, and to have made him of the Order of *Sanct Esprèet*; all which he refused, tho' he knew his great Fortune was lost and already distributed to Favourites at Court, and himself Proscribed and Convicted as a Traytor to *France*. Yet all these refusals did not open the Eyes of this credulous great young Man, who still believed it the sullenness and Generosity of his Temper. No sooner did the day discover to the World the horrid Business of the preceding Night, but a diligent search was made among the infinite number of dead, that covered the Face of the Earth, for the Body of the Prince, or New King, as they called him: But when they could not find him among the dead, they sent out Parties all ways to search the Woods, the Forests, and the Plains; nor was it long they sought in vain, for he who had laid himself, as I said, under the shelter of a Tree, had not for any consideration removed him; but finding himself seiz'd by a common Hand, suffered himself, without Resistance, to be detained by one single Man[a] till more advanced, when he could as easily have kill'd the Rustick as speak or move; an Action so below the Character of this truly brave Man, that there is no reason to be given to excuse this easie submission but this, That he was Stupified with long Watching, Grief, and the Fatigues of his daily Toyl for so many Weeks before: For 'tis not to be imagin'd it was carelessness, or little regard for Life; for if it had been so he would doubtless have lost it Nobly with the Victory, and never have retreated while there had been one Sword left advanced against him; or if he had disdained the Enemy should have had the Advantage and Glory of so great a Conquest, at least when his Sword had been yet left him, he should have died like a *Roman*,[b] and have scorn'd to have added to the Triumph of the Enemy. But Love had unman'd his great Soul,

---

[a] On the 8th July Monmouth was taken prisoner by a soldier called Henry Parkin who found the exhausted duke hiding in a ditch under an ash tree, covered with fern and bracken.

[b] It was dishonourable for Romans to be taken prisoner rather than die on the battlefield.

and *Hermione* pleaded within for Life at any Price, even that of all his Glory; the thought of her alone blacken'd this last Scene of his Life, and for which all his past Triumphs could never atone nor excuse.

Thus taken, he suffered himself to be led away tamely by common Hands without resistance: A Victim now even fallen to the pity of the *Mobile* as he past, and so little imagined by the better Sort who saw him not, they would not give a credit to it, every one affirming and laying Wagers he would die like a *Hero*, and never surrender with Life to the Conqueror. But his submission was but too true for the repose of all his Abettors; nor was his mean surrender all, but he shew'd a dejection all the way they were bringing him to *Paris*, so extreamly unworthy of his Character, that 'tis hardly to be credited so great a change could have been possible. And to show that he had lost all his Spirit and Courage with the Victory, and that the great strings of his Heart were broke, the Captain who had the charge of him, and commanded that little Squadron that conducted him to *Paris*, related to me this remarkable Passage in their Journey; he said, That they Lodged in an Inn, where he believed both the Master, and a great many Strangers who that Night Lodg'd there, were *Hugonots*, and great lovers of the Prince; which the Captain did not know, till after the Lodgings were taken: However he ordered a File of Musqueteers to guard the Door; and himself only remained in the Chamber with the Prince, while Supper was getting ready: The Captain being extreamly weary with Watching and Toyling, for a long time together, laid himself down on a Bench behind a great long Table, that was fast'ned to the Floor, and had unadvisedly laid his Pistols on the Table, and tho he durst not Sleep, he thought there to stretch himself into a little ease; who had not quited his Horseback in a great while: The Prince who was walking with his Arms across about the Room, musing in a very dejected posture; often casting his Eyes to the door; at last advances to the Table, and takes up the Captains Pistols; the while He who——saw him advance, fear'd in that moment, what the Prince was going to do; he thought, if he should rise and snatch at the Pistols, and miss of 'em, it would express so great a distrust of the Prince, it might provoke him to do, what by his generous submitting of 'em, might make him escape; and therefore since it was too late, he suffered the Prince to arm himself with two Pistols; who before was disarmed of even his little Pen-knife

He was, he said, a thousand times about to call out to the Guards; but then he thought before they could enter to his relief, he was sure to be shot Dead, and it was possible the Prince might make his party good with four or five common Souldiers, who perhaps lov'd the Prince as well as any, and might rather assist than hinder his flight; all this he thought in an instant, and at the same time seeing the Prince stand still, in a kind of consideration what to do, looking, turning, and viewing of the Pistols, he doubted not but his thought would determine with his Life; and tho he had been in the heat of all the Battle, and had look'd Death in the Face, when he appeared most horrid, he protested he knew not how to fear till this moment, and that now he trembled with the apprehension of unavoidable Ruin, he curst a thousand times his unadvisedness, now it was too late; he saw the Prince after he had viewed, and reviewed the Pistols walk in a great thoughtfulness again about the Chamber, and at last, as if he had determined what to do, came back and laid them again on the Table; at which the Captain snatch'd 'em up, resolving never to commit so great an over-sight more. He did not doubt, he said, but the Prince in taking them up, had some design of making his escape; and most certainly if he had but had Courage to have attempted it, it had not been hard to have been accomplish'd: At worst he could but have dy'd; but there is a Fate that over-rules the most lucky minutes of the greatest men in the World, and turns even all advantages offered to misfortunes, when it designs their ruin.

While they were on their way to *Paris*, he gave some more signs, that misfortune he had suffered, had lessened his Heart and Courage: He writ several the most submissive Letters in the World,[a] to the King, and to the Queen Mother of *France*; wherein he strove to mitigate his Treason, with the poorest Arguments imaginable; and, as if his good Sense had declined with his Fortune, his Stile was alter'd and debased to that of a common Man, or rather a School-Boy, filled with Tautologies and Stuff of no Coherence; in which he neither showed the Majesty of a Prince, nor Sense of a Gentleman; as I could make appear by exposing those Copies, which I leave to History; all which must

---

[a] After his capture, Monmouth wrote two letters to James and one to the queen dowager in which he begs for mercy and suggests that troops be sent to apprehend rebels in Cheshire. In his first letter to the king he states:

> my misfortun was such, as to meet with some horrid people that made me believe things of your majesty, and gave me soe many false arguments that I was fully led away to belive, that it was a shame and a sin before God not to doe it

be imputed to the disorder his Head and Heart were in, for want of that natural rest he never after found. When he came to *Paris*, he fell at the Feet of his Majesty, to whom they brought him; and with a Showre of Tears bedewing his Shoes, as he lay prostrate, besought his Pardon, and ask'd his Life; perhaps one of his greatest weaknesses to imagine, he could hope for mercy after so many Pardons for the same fault; and which if he had had but one grain of that Bravery left him, he was wont to be Master of, he could not have expected; nor have had the confidence to have implor'd; and he was a poor Spectacle of pity to all that once adored him; to see how he petitioned in vain for Life; which if it had been granted, had been of no other use to him, but to have past in some corner of the Earth with *Hermione*, dispis'd by all the rest: and tho he fetch'd Tears of Pity from the Eyes of the best and, most merciful of Kings, he could not gain on his first resolution; which was never to forgive him that Scurilous Declaration he had dispersed at his first Landing in *France*; that he took upon him the Title of King, he could forgive; that he had been the cause of so much Blood-shed, he could forgive, but never that unworthy Scandal on his unspoted Fame; of which he was much more nice, than of his Crown or Life; and left him (as he told him this) prostrate on the Earth, when the Guards took him up and conveyed him to the *Bastile:* As he came out of the *Louvre*,[a] 'tis said he look'd with his wonted Grace, only a Languishment sat there in greater Beauty, than possible all his gayer looks ever put on, at least in his Circumstances; all that beheld him imagined so; all the *Parisians* were crowded in vast numbers to see him: And oh, see what Fortune is, those that had vow'd him Allegiance in their Hearts, and were upon all occasions ready to rise in Mutiny for his least Interest, now saw him, and suffered him to be carried to the *Bastile* with a small Company of Guards, and never offer'd to rescue the Royal Unfortunate from the Hands of Justice, while he view'd 'em all around with scorning dying Eyes.

While he remained in the *Bastile*, he was visited by several of the Ministers of State,[b] and Cardinals, and Men of the Church,

---

[a] Whitehall Palace.
[a] After his capture Monmouth had interviews with James II, the secretaries of state Lord Sunderland and Lord Middleton, Lord Clarendon, and Lord Arundel of Wardour. When Monmouth's execution was announced, the king sent the Bishop of Ely and the Bishop of Bath and Wells to prepare the duke for his death.

who urged him to some Discoveries, but could not prevail with him: He spoke, he thought, he dreamt of nothing but *Hermione*; and when they talk'd of Heaven, he ran on some Discourse of that Beauty, something of her Praise; and so continued to his last Moment, even on the Scaffold, where he was urged to excuse, as a good Christian ought, his Invasion, his Bloodshed and his unnatural War; he set himself to justifie his Passion to *Hermione*,[a] endeavouring to render the Life he had lead with her, Innocent and Blameless in the sight of Heaven; and all the Churchmen could perswade, could make him speak of very little else. Just before he laid himself down on the Block he called to one of the Gentlemen of his Chamber, and taking out the Inchanted Tooth-pick-case,[b] he whisper'd him in the Ear, and commanded him to bear it from him to *Hermione*; and laying himself down suffer'd the Justice of the Law, and died more pitied than lamented; so that it became a Proverb, If I have an Enemy I wish he may live like —— and die like *Cesario*: So ended the Race of this glorious Youth, who was in his time the greatest Man of a Subject in the World, and the greatest Favourite of his Prince, happy indeed above a Monarch, if Ambition and the Inspiration of Knaves and Fools had not led him to Destruction, and from a Glorious Life brought him to a Shameful Death.

This deplorable News[c] was not long in coming to *Hermione*, who must receive this due, That when she heard her *Hero* was dead, (and with him all her dearer greatness gone,) she betook her self to her Bed, and made a Vow she would never rise nor eat more; and she was as good as her word, she lay in that melancholy Estate about Ten Days, making the most pitious Moan for her dead Lover that e'er was heard, drowning her Pillow in

---

[a] An account of his execution notes that on the scaffold he declared,
I have had a Scandal raised upon me about...Lady Henrietta Wentworth. I declare, That she is a very Vertuous and Godly Woman. I have committed no Sin with her; and that which hath passed betwixt us was very Honest and Innocent in the sight of God....
The account goes on to show that he refused to acknowledge the sin of rebellion.

[b] On the scaffold, Monmouth produced several mementoes to be passed on to Henrietta Wentworth. A contemporary account of his execution also notes that he gave his servant 'something like a Toothpick-case' saying 'give this to the Person to whom you are to deliver the other things.' Accounts of his capture record a gold snuff-box full of gold coins which he dropped while being pursued by royalist forces.

[c] Monmouth's execution was particularly gruesome. The executioner failed to sever the duke's head after five blows of the axe and was forced to cut off the remaining part of the neck with a long knife. Henrietta Wentworth returned to England and died within a year of Monmouth.

Tears, and sighing out her Soul. She called on him in vain as long as she could speak, at last she fell into a Lethargy and dreamed of him, till she could dream no more; an everlasting sleep closed her fair Eyes, and the last word she sigh'd was *Cesario*.

Brilljard had the good Fortune the Night of the Battle to get away under the covert of the Night, and posted into *Flanders*, where he found *Silvia*[a] in the Arms of the young *Spaniard*, and of whom they made so considerable Advantages, that in a short time they ruin'd the Fortune of that young Nobleman, and became the Talk of the Town, insomuch that the Governour not permitting her stay there, she was forced to remove for new Prey, and daily makes considerable Conquests where e'er she shows the Charmer. *Fergusano* escap'd,[b] which was to the last Moment of the Princes Life the greatest Affliction of his Mind; and he would often say in great Rage, That if that Villian had been brought to *Paris*, and that he could have had the satisfaction of seeing him broken on a Wheel before he had died, he should have resign'd his Life with Joy. But his time was not yet come.

Philander lay sometime in the *Bastile*, visited by all the Persons of great Quality about the Court; he behaved himself very Gallantly all the way he came, after his being taken, and to the last Minute of his Imprisonment; and was at last pardoned, kiss'd the King's Hand, and came to Court in as much Splendour as ever,[c] being very well understood by all good Men.

FINIS.

[a] William Turner escaped royalist forces after the Battle of Sedgemoor and made his way back to Holland. Intelligence reports indicate that many of the surviving rebels took refuge in Cleve again and it is possible that Turner and Henrietta Berkeley were among them. In 1686, Turner was pardoned and he returned to England. Henrietta Berkeley may have accompanied him as her will indicates that she died in England in 1702.

[b] After the Rebellion there was an intense search for Ferguson by royalist forces but he eluded them, making his way back to Holland.

[c] Ford Lord Grey was imprisoned in the Tower after the Battle of Sedgemoor. There he wrote a confession which was published in 1754 as *The Secret History of the Rye House Plot*. James II spared his life making it a condition that he paid a bond of £40,000 to the Lord Treasurer and appeared as a witness against in the trials of his former conspirators Lord Brandon and Lord Delamere. In 1688 Grey supported William of Orange's claim to the English throne. He quickly established a political career, becoming Earl of Tankerville in 1695, the Lord Treasurer in 1699 and Lord Privy Seal in 1700.

Appendices

APPENDIX I

Lord Grey was tried before the King's Bench on the 23rd November, 1682 for the abduction of Lady Henrietta Berkeley. Five accomplices were also tried and all but one were found guilty as charged. The scandal created great public interest at the time and shortly after the trial a transcript of the proceedings were published.

The extracts reprinted from the trial in this appendix are those which most clearly seem to have provided facts or embryonic scenes for Behn's imagination in the writing of Part I of *Love Letters between a Nobleman and his Sister*.

EXTRACTS FROM *THE TRIAL OF FORD LORD GREY OF WERK*

Surrey ss. Sir Robert Sawyer, Kt. his majesty's attorney general, has exhibited an Information in this Court, against the right honourable Ford lord Grey of Werk; Robert Charnock, late of the parish of St Botolph, Aldgate, London, gent. Anne Charnock, wife of the said Robert Charnock; David Jones, of the parish of St Martin-in-the-Fields, in the county of Middlesex, milliner; Frances Jones, wife of the said David; and Rebecca Jones, of the same, widow; for that they (with divers other evil-disposed persons, to the said attorney general yet unknown) the 20th day of August, in the 34th year of the reign of our sovereign lord the king that now is, and divers other days and times, as well before as after, at the parish of Epsom in the county of Surrey, falsely, unlawfully, unjustly, and wickedly, by unlawful and impure ways and means, conspiring, contriving, practising, and intending the final ruin and destruction of the lady Henrietta Berkeley, then a virgin unmarried, within the age of 18 years, and one of the daughters of the right honourable George earl of Berkeley (the said lady Henrietta Berkeley, then and there being under the custody, government and education of the aforesaid right honourable George earl of

443

Berkeley her father) they the said Ford lord Grey, Robert Charnock, Anne Charnock, David Jones, Frances Jones, and Rebecca
Jones, and divers other persons unknown, then and there
falsely, unlawfully, and devilishly, to fulfil, perfect, and bring
to effect, their most wicked, impious, and devilish intentions
aforesaid; the said lady Henrietta Berkeley, to desert the aforesaid right honourable George earl of Berkeley, father of the
aforesaid lady Henrietta; and to commit whoredom, fornication, and adultery, and in whoredom, fornication, and adultery, to live with the aforesaid Ford lord Grey (the said Ford
lord Grey, then and long before, and yet, being the husband of
the lady Mary, another daughter of the said right honourable
George earl of Berkeley, and sister of the said lady Henrietta)
against all laws, as well divine as human, impiously, wickedly,
impurely, and scandalously, to live and cohabit, did tempt,
invite, and solicit, and every of them, then and there, did
tempt, invite, and solicit.

[About this time the lady Henrietta came into the court, and
was set by the table at the judges feet.]

Earl of *Berkeley*. My lord, my daughter is here in court, I
desire she may be restored to me.

Serj. *Jeff*. Pray, my lord Berkeley, give us leave to go on, it will
be time enough to move that anon. Swear my lady Berkeley;
(which was done, but she seemed not able to speak).

Sol. Gen. I perceive my lady is much moved at the sight of her
daughter. Swear my lady Arabella her daughter. (Which was
done).

Serj. *Jeff*. Pray, madam, will you acquaint my lords the
judges, and jury, what you know concerning the letter you
discovered, and how you came by that discovery?

Lady *Arabella*. In July last, some time then, my mother came
into my lady Harriett's chamber, and seeing a pen wet with ink,
she examined her who she had been writing to. She, in great
confusion told her, she had been writing her accompts, but my
mother was not satisfied with that answer. The sight of my lord
Grey doth put me quite out of countenance and patience. –
[Here she stopped again.]

[My lord Grey was then by the clerks under the bar, and
stood looking very stedfastly upon her.]

L.C.J. Pray, my lord Grey, sit down (which he did). It is not a
very extraordinary thing, for a witness, in such a cause, to be
dashed out of countenance.

E. of *Berkeley*. He would not, if he were not a very impudent barbarous man, look so confidently and impudently upon her.

Serj. *Jeff*. My lord, I would be very loth to deal otherwise than becomes me, with a person of your quality, but indeed this is not so handsome, and we must desire you to sit down. Pray go on, madam.

Lady *Arabella*. After this, my mother commanded me to search my lady Harriett's room; her maid being then in the room, I thought it not so much for her honour to do it then. I followed my mother down to prayers. After prayers were done, my mother commanded my lady Harriett to give me the keys of her cabinet and of her closet, and when she gave me the keys, she put a note into my hand, which was to my lord Grey; and that was to this effect: 'My sister Bell did not suspect our being together last night, for she did not hear any noise: pray come again Sunday or Monday, if the last I shall be very impatient.' I suppose my lady Harriett gave my lord Grey intelligence of this, for he sent a servant to tell me he desired to speak with me. Upon his first coming in, my lady Harriett fell upon the ground like a dead creature, and my lord Grey took her up, and said, 'Now you see how far it is gone between us: I love nothing upon earth but her; I mean dear lady Hen,' said he to me; 'and if you do expose her, I will be revenged upon you and all the family, for I have no consideration for any thing but her.' After that I told him, We defied him, he could do us no injury; and for my own particular, I defied him, and the Devil and all his works, and would not have any thing to do with such a correspondence. After this, I told my lady Harriett, I was much troubled and amazed, that she should sit by and hear my lord Grey, her brother-in-law, say he had no consideration for any thing on earth but her. 'For my part,' said I, 'Madam, it stabs me to the heart, to hear this said against my poor sister Grey.' I told her, I suspected my woman had an hand in this affair, and therefore I would put her away. Afterwards, the same day my lady Harriett ran away, this woman came to me; and I then told her, 'You have ruined her,' and asked her, 'Why would you send letters between my lord Grey and my lady Harriett?' She denied it, and swore she never did it, but when we came to London, the porter of St John's came and accused her 'of conveying letters to Charnock, my lord Grey's gentleman, formerly his coachman. I then asked her again about it; she then acknowledged to me she had done it. 'But, madam,' said she, 'how could I think there could be any prejudice or ill between a brother-in-law and a sister-in-law?' Said I, 'Were you not my servant? Why did you not tell me? Besides, you know we have all reason to hate Charnock for a great many things'. This is all I have to say that is material, all else is to the same effect.

Serj. *Jeff*. Now this matter being thus discovered to the countess of Berkeley, this unfortunate young lady's mother; she sent for my lord Grey, and we shall tell you what happened to be discoursed between them two, and between the lady and her mother, and what promises of amendment he made. My lady Berkeley, pray will you tell what you know. – [She seemed unable to do it.] She is very much discomposed, the sight of her daughter doth put her out of order.

Lady *Arabella*. I have something more to say, that is, I told my lady Harriett, after my lord Grey had made his declaration of his love to my sister, to me, that if ever he had the impudence to name her name to me, I would immediately go to my father, and tell him all.

[Then the Countess leaned forward, with her hood much over her face.]

Att. Gen. Pray, my lady Berkeley, compose yourself, and speak as loud as you can.

Lady *Berkeley*. When I first discovered this unhappy business, how my son-in-law, my lord Grey, was in love with his sister, I sent to speak with him, and I told him he had done barbarously and basely, and falsely with me, in having an intrigue with his sister-in-law. That I looked upon him, next my own son, as one that was engaged to stand up for the honour of my family, and instead of that, he had endeavoured the ruin of my daughter, and had done worse than if he had murdered her, to hold an intrigue with her of criminal love. He said, he did confess he had been false, and base, and unworthy to me, but he desired me to consider (and then he shed a great many tears) what it was that made him guilty, and that made him do it. I bid him speak. He said he was ashamed to tell me, but I might easily guess. I then said, what? Are you indeed in love with your sister-in-law? He fell a weeping and said, he was unfortunate; But if I made this business public, and let it to take air (he did not say this to threaten me, he would not have me to mistake him) but if I told my lord her father, and his wife of it, it might make him desperate, and it might put such thoughts into his wife's head, that might be an occasion of parting them; and that he being desperate, he did not know what he might do, he might neither consider family, nor relation. I told him this would make him very black in story, though it were her ruin. He said that was true, but he could not help it; he was miserable, and if I knew how miserable, I would pity him: He had the confidence to tell me that. And then he desired, though he said I had no reason to hear him, or take any counsel he gave me (and all this with a great many tears) as if he were my son Dursley, that I would keep his secret. 'For my lord, if he heard it, would be in a great passion, and possibly, he might not be able to contain himself, but let it break out into the world. He may call me rogue and rascal perhaps in his passion, said he, and I should be sorry for it, but that would be all I could do, and what the evil consequence might be, he knew not, and therefore it were best to conceal it.' And after many words to pacify me, though nothing indeed could be sufficient for the injury he had done me; he gave it me as his advice, that I would let my daughter Harriett go abroad into public places with myself, and promised, if I did, he would always avoid them. For a young lady to sit always at home, he said it would not easily get her out of such a thing as this. And upon this he said again, he was to go out of town with the D. of M. in a few days, and being he had been frequently in the family before, it would be looked upon as a very strange thing, that he went away, and did not appear there to take his leave. He promised me, that if for the world's sake, and for his wife's sake (that no one might take notice of it) I would let him come there, and sup before he went into the country, he would not offer anything, by way of letter or otherwise, that might give me any offence. Upon which I did let him come, and he came in at nine o'clock at night, and said, I might very well look ill upon him, as my daughter also did (his sister Bell) for none else in all the family knew any thing of the matter but she and I. After supper he went away, and the next night he sent his page (I think it was) with a letter to me, he gave it to my woman, and she brought it to me; where he says that he would not go out of town. – If your Lordship please I will give you the letter – But he said, he feared my apprehensions of him would continue. – There is the letter.

L.C.J. Show it to my lord Grey, let us see is he owns or denies it.

Lord *Grey*. Yes, pray do, I deny nothing that I have done.

Mr Just. *Dolben*. Be pleased, madam, to put it into the court.

Att. Gen. It is only about his keeping away.

L.C.J. Shew it my lord Grey.

Serj. Jeff. With submission, my lord, it is fully proved without that.

L.C.J. Then let the clerk read it, brother.

Cl. of Crown. There is no direction, that I see, upon it. It is subscribed Grey. – [Reads.]

'Madam;

After I had waited on your ladyship last night, sir Thomas Armstrong came from the D. of M. to acquaint me that he could not possibly go into Sussex; so that journey is at an end. But your ladyship's apprehensions of me I fear will continue: therefore I send this to assure you, that my short stay in town shall no way disturb your ladyship; if I can contribute to your quiet, by avoiding all places where I may possibly see the lady. I hope your ladyship will remember the promise you made to divert her, and pardon me for minding you of it, since it is to no other end that I do so, but that she may not suffer upon my account; I am sure if she doth not in your opinion, she never shall any other way. I wish your ladyship all the ease that you can desire, and more quiet than ever I expect to have. I am with great devotion, Your ladyship's most humble, and obedient servant,

GREY.'

Att. Gen. Madam, will you please to go on with your evidence.

Lady *Arabella*. I have one thing more to say: After this, three or four days after this ugly business was found out, I told my lady Harriett, she was to go to my sister Dursley's. She was in a great anger and passion about it, which made my mother so exasperated against her, that I was a great while before I got my mother to go near her again.

Serj. Jeff. My lady Berkeley, please to go on?

Lady *Berkeley*. When I came to my daughter, (my wretched unkind daughter, I have been so kind a mother to her, and would have died rather, upon the oath I have taken, than have done this, if there had been any other way to reclaim her, and would have done any thing to have hid her faults, and died ten times over, rather than this, dishonour should have come upon my family.) This child of mine, when I came up to her, fell into a great many tears, and begged my pardon for what she had done, and said, she would never continue any conversation with her brother-in-law any more, if I would forgive her; and she said all the things that would make a tender mother believe her. I told her, I did not think it was safe for her to continue at my house, for fear the world should discover it, by my lord Grey's not coming to our house as he used to do; and therefore I would send her to my son's wife, her sister Dursley, for my lord Grey did seldom or never visit there, and the world would not take notice of it. And I thought it better and safer for her to be there with her sister, than at home with me. Upon which this ungracious child wept so bitterly, and begged so heartily of me that I would not send her away to her sister's, and told me, it would not be safe for her to be out of the house from me. She told me, she would obey me in any thing; and said, she would now confess to me, though she had denied it before, that she had writ my lord Grey word that they were discovered, which was the reason he did not come to me upon the first letter that I sent him to come and speak with me. And she said so many tender things, that I believed her penitent, and forgave her, and had compassion upon her, and told her (though she had not deserved so much from me) she might be quiet (seeing her so much concerned) I would not tell her sister Dursley her faults, nor send her thither, till I had spoken with her again. Upon which, she, as I thought, continuing penitent, I kissed her in the bed when she was sick, and hoped that all this ugly business was over, and I should have no more affliction with her, especially if my lord removed his family to Durdants, which he did. When we came there, she came into my chamber one Sunday morning before I was awake, and threw herself upon her knees, and kissed my hand, and cried out, Oh, madam! I have offended you, I have done ill, I will be a good child, and will never do so again; I will break off all correspondence with him, I will do what you please, any thing that you do desire. Then, said I, I hope you will be happy, and I forgive you. Oh; do not tell my father (she said) let him not know my faults. No, said I, I will not tell him; but if you will make a friend of me, I desire you will have no correspondence with your brother-in-law; and though you have done all this to offend me, I will treat you as a sister, more than as a daughter, if you will but use this wicked brother-in-law as he deserves. I tell you that youth, and virtue, and honour, is too much to sacrifice for a base brother-in-law. When she had done this, she came another day into my closet, and there wept very much, and cry'd out, Oh, madam! it is he, he is the villain that has undone me, that has ruined me.

Why? said I, What has he done? Oh! said she, he hath seduced me to this. Oh! said I, fear nothing, you have done nothing, I hope, that is ill, but only harkening to his love. Then I took her about the neck and kissed her, and endeavoured to comfort her. Oh, madam! said she, I have not deserved this kindness from you; but it is he, he is the villain that hath undone me: but I will do any thing that you will command me to do; if he ever send me any letter, I will bring it to you unopened; but pray do not tell my father of my faults. I promised her I would not, so she would break off all correspondence with him –

[Here she swooned, and soon after recovered and went on.]

The trial continued with an account of Henrietta Berkeley's hiding-places in London after she had left Durdans.

Serj. *Jeff.* Now, my lord, we will bring it down to be this very lady. My Lady Arabella, Pray, madam, what clothes did my lady Harriett go away in?

Lady *Arabella*. My lady Harriett had such clothes as they speak of, I cannot say she went away in her night gown, but here is one that can: But there was a striped night-gown, of many colours, green, and blue, and red.

L.C.J. She does remember she had such a one, but she cannot say she went away in it.

Serj. *Jeff.* Was there not a chequered petticoat red and white?

Lady *Arabella*. She had such a petticoat, but I cannot say she went away in it; she had also a white quilted petticoat.

Serj. *Jeff.* Then swear Mrs Doney (Which was done.) My lord, we call this gentlewoman to give an account what habit she went away in; for she lay with her always.

Att. Gen. Did you lie with my lady Harriett Berkeley, when she stole away?

Mrs *Doney.* Yes, indeed, Sir, I did lie in the chamber that night, and she went away with her morning clothes, which lay ready for her there, against she did rise in the morning. It was a striped night-gown of many colours, and a petticoat of white and red, and a quilted petticoat.

Att. Gen. Was she so habited, that came to the house, Mrs Hilton?

L.C.J. She has said so already.

Serj. *Jeff.* Now you are pleased to observe, that besides the circumstances of the clothes, there is mention made of a note;

Mrs Hilton says she received a letter and gave it to Mrs Charnock; and that soon after they went to Patten's house in Wild-
street. We shall call the people of that house, to give an account
what gentlewoman it was that came to their house. Pray swear
Mr Patten. [Which was done.]

Sol. Gen. Pray, will you tell my lord and the jury, whether Mr
Charnock and his wife came to your house, and with whom,
and about what?

Mr *Patten.* My lord, about the latter end of July, or the beginning of August, Mr Charnock and his wife came to my house
when we were just removed, to take some lodgings for a person
of quality; but they did not say who. Said I then, We have no
lodgings now ready; said they, We shall not want them yet, till
towards the middle of September. Says my wife, I suppose by
that time our house will be ready; and if it will do you any
kindness you may have it. About the 20th of August being
Sunday, Mrs Hilton brings a gentlewoman with Mrs Charnock
to my house; and when they were come, they called me up, and
seeing them all three there, I told Mrs Charnock, We have no
lodgings fit for any body of any quality, at present. Says Mrs
Hilton, Let's see the candle, and runs up stairs into a room
where there was a bed, but no hangings; when they came in,
they locked themselves into the room. My wife's daughter
being in the house, I desired her to send for my wife, who was
then abroad; which she did. They desired my wife's daughter to
lodge with the gentlewoman that they brought thither, and
they were making the bed ready. I sent them up word, That I
desired they would walk into the dining-room for the present;
they sent me word down again, They did not desire to do that,
for they were afraid the light would be seen into the street, and
withal, if any body came to enquire for Mrs Charnock, or Mrs
Hilton, I should say there was no body there. Presently after, I
think (or before I cannot justly say which) a letter was carried
up stairs to them, upon which they came down stairs, and away
they went up the street, and when they were gone a little way
on foot, Mrs Charnock desired them to turn back again, for she
hoped to get a coach, and she did so, and went away.

Att. Gen. So they did not lodge there?

Mr *Patten.* No, they did not.

Serj. *Jeff.* Did they say any thing of care that was to be taken,
how they passed by my lady Northumberland's?

Mr *Patten.* My lord, I do not well remember that: But the

next day Mrs Hilton comes again to our house, and she runs up stairs into the same room, and sits her down upon the bed-side. Said I to her, Mrs Hilton, What gentlewoman was that that was here last night? Say she, I cannot tell, but I believe she is some person of quality, for Mrs Charnock brought her to our house at 7 o'clock in the morning. But whoever she is, she is much troubled, we could get her to eat nothing, but her eyes were very red with crying, and we came away to your house at night; because hearing some noise of people in the street, she was afraid some of her father's servants were come, but it was only some people that were gathered about to observe the blazing star. So we whipped out of the door, and so came to your house, for we had never a back-door out of our own.

Att. Gen. Pray give us an account what habit the gentlewoman was in that came to your house.

Mr *Patten.* She had a striped flowered gown, very much sullied, it was flung about her, just as if she had newly come out of bed. I did see her face, but when I had just looked upon her, she clapped her hood together over it presently.

Serj. *Jeff.* Do you think you should know her again if you see her?

Mr *Patten.* I believe I might.

Serj. *Jeff.* Pray, madam, stand up again, and lift up your hood. [Which she did.]

Mr *Patten.* This is the lady. I saw her face twice, once as I told you, and then when she went away, I dropped down, and peeped up, and looked her in the face again, though she hid it as much as she could.

Att. Gen. Thus we have proved it upon Charnock and his wife.

Serj. *Jeff.* He gives an account of the 20th of August, which was the day after she went from her father's house. Pray call Mrs Fletcher.

Att. Gen. We shall now prove that they went from thence to one Mr Jones's; that my lord Grey came there to take lodgings, and after she was brought, came thither again, and though he changed his hair into a perriwig, yet he was known for all his disguise.

Sol. Gen. My lord, you see that it is proved upon three of the defendants, my lord Grey, and Charnock, and his wife; now we shall prove it upon the other two, the Jones's. Swear Mary Fletcher. [Which was done.]

Serj. *Jeff*. Sweetheart, pray tell the court where you lived, and when my lord Grey came to your house; tell the time as near as you can, and the day of the week.

Fletcher. Sir, he came to David Jones's on the Tuesday after my lady Berkeley was missing.

L.C.J. Where does David Jones live?

Fletcher. At Charing-cross just over against the Statue. And living there, my lord Grey came there in a hackney coach, first on the Monday without a perriwig, or any thing of that, and desired Mr Jones to come to the coach side, which he did, and after a little discourse with Mr Jones, they both came into the house, and went up two pair of stairs to look upon lodgings. After that, I had order to make ready the room for some lodgers who were expected to come that night, but did not till the next day. About Tuesday at nine of the clock, my lord Grey comes again in a coach to the door, and threw his cloak over his face, he was then without his perriwig too, and desired to speak with Mr Jones: I and my fellow servant standing at the door, he desired to speak with my master. I went to him, and told him, he came up, and after he had been at the coach side, he bid us go down, and keep down in the kitchen, and would not let us come up any more. And afterwards my fellow servant and I were bid to go to bed, and my mistress shut up the shop-windows herself.

Serj. *Jeff*. Well, go on, what happened after that?

Maid. Afterwards there was the warming-pan, and the candlestick, and other things were carried up into the chamber by my mistress's sister. Says my fellow servant, there is some great stranger sure, come to lodge here, that we must not know of. Ay, said I, this is some great intrigue or other. After a while came in some company that stayed all night. I know not who they were, or how they came.

Serj. *Jeff*. Well, what was done the next morning?

Maid. I was never admitted into the room: while they were there, but through the opening of the door I did see one lady in bed, but I cannot say who she was, nor what she was.

Att. Gen. Do you know her if you see her again? Look at that lady; is that she?

Maid. No, I do not know her; I cannot say that is she: My mistress, and my mistress's sister stood both before me, when I just peeped into the room, and when she perceived that, I did see her pull the clothes over her face.

Sol. Gen. How long did she stay there?
Maid. Nine nights.
Serj. *Jeff.* Do you know my lord Grey well?
Maid. Yes, I have seen him often.
Serj. *Jeff.* Did you know him notwithstanding his disguise? –
Maid. Yes.
Serj. *Jeff.* What did Mrs Jones say to you about my lord Grey?
Maid. She said to us, what fools were we, to say this was my lord Grey, it was a country gentleman.
Serj. *Jeff.* But you are sure it was my lord Grey?
Maid. Yes, I am sure it was he.

The prosecuter later questioned a Mr Smith who had been instructed by Lord Berkeley to offer Grey money for the safe return of his daughter.

Att. Gen. Then swear Mr Smith here, who married one of my lord Berkeley's daughters.

[Which was done.]

Mr *Smith.* Before my lord Berkeley made this affair public, he used all means possible to know where my lady Harriett was; and after it was known to him what concern my lord Grey had in it, there were all means used to make it up: and discoursing with my lady Berkeley about it, it was proposed that she should be married, but that would cost a great deal of money; that my lord did not stick at, nor my lady; if any divine of the church of England did think it proper to treat with any parson about it, after such secret correspondence between her and my lord Grey. And my lord said, If my lord Grey would not prosecute her with any more visits, he would give a sum of money to marry her. Said I, then, my lord, will you give me leave to wait upon my lord Grey in it? He answered, Yes. So I went to him, and offered him that my lord Berkeley would give 6,000*l.* with her, if he would place her in a third hand, where it might be convenient to treat with any one about it. He talked with me as if he knew

Mr Craven then gave his account of his visit to Lord Grey. Craven had been openly sent as a spy by Lord Berkeley and Grey agreed to let him

*remain in order to prove he had no contact with Henrietta Berkeley at
that time.*

One day when we went out a shooting, as we did several
days together; Mr Craven, says he, I will tell you the whole
intrigue between my lady Harriett and I. I have had a great
affection for her ever since she was a child, and have always
been taking great delight in her company; and keeping her
company so often till she grew up, my passion grew to that
height, that I could stifle it no longer, but I was forced to tell her
of it, and then I could not speak to her of it, but writ. But withal
I begged her to take no notice of it to any body, for if she did, it
would ruin us both. She was very angry to hear of it, and
neither by writing nor speaking could I perceive she had any
affection for me again, till the parliament sat at Oxford; and
then I did pursue my love and my amours, and at last, she one
day told me. said she, I have now considered of it, and if you do
not leave writing or speaking of me of this matter, the very first
time you write or speak to me again, I will tell my father and
mother of it. That struck him so, he said, that he did not know
almost what to say or what to do, and he walked up and down
just like a ghost; but he hid it as well as he could, that it should
not be perceived by others. But that parliament being quickly
dissolved, he did intend to go down to Sussex to his house
there, being he found she was resolved against admitting his
affection, and he would stay there several years, till he had
weaned himself of his passion, and by that time she would be
disposed of otherwise, and he might be at ease. And he hiding
his trouble as much as he could from my lord Berkeley and my
lady, forbore to speak to her, but only when he saw her he
could not forbear looking earnestly upon her, and being troubled. My lord Berkeley, not knowing any thing of it, asked him
to go to London with us and not to Sussex? he was very much
persuaded by my lord and my lady to it: and at last, my lady
Harriett Berkeley came to him, and told him, said she, you are
very much persuaded by my father and mother to go to London
and not to Up-Park, why do not you go with them? Madam,
says he, you have stopped my journey to London, you have
hindered my going with them, for I will rather suffer any thing
than render you any disturbance, and if I go to London with
you, I shall not be able to contain myself; but if I go to Sussex, I
alone shall have the trouble of it. But one day, when my lord of

Aylesbury was leading my lady Berkeley, and my lord Grey was leading my lady Harriett, she took my lord Grey's hand and squeezed it against her breast, and there was the first time he perceived she loved him again; and then she told him he should go to London with them; and he did go, and from that time, for a twelve-month before she went away, he did see her frequently, almost every night, pursuing his amour in writing, and speaking to her as often as he could have opportunity. And though my lady Berkeley put a French woman to lie with her, yet she did use to rise from the French woman, and he did use to see her. And one day, says he, do not you remember you came to the chamber door, and she was angry at your coming, and that the door was not bolted, and if you had come in you had found me there?

Serj. *Jeff.* Do you remember any such thing?

Mr *Craven.* I do not unless it were at Durdants. And, says he, you cannot imagine what I have suffered to come to see her. I have been two days locked up in her closet without meat or drink, but only some sweetmeats.

After further interrogation of Grey's accomplices, Henrietta Berkeley was invited to take the stand.

Mr *Williams.* If she be sworn, my lord, we would ask her a question or two. Madam, we would desire your ladyship to answer whether my lord Grey had any hand in your escape?

Lady *Henrietta.* No, Sir.

Just. *Dolben.* You are upon your oath, Madam; have a care what you say; consider with yourself.

Lady *Henrietta.* Yes, I know I am upon my oath, and I do upon my oath say it.

Mr *Williams.* Did my lord Grey advise you to it?

Lady *Henrietta.* No, I had no advice from him, nor any body about him, nor did he know any thing of it, it was all my own design.

Serj. *Jefferies.* Madam, I would ask you this question, and pray consider well before you answer it. Did you see my lord Grey on the Sunday after you went away from your father's? –

Lady *Henrietta.* No, I did not.

Serj. *Jefferies.* Did you see him on Monday?

Lady *Henriètta.* No.

Serj. *Jefferies*. Did you on Tuesday?

Lady *Henrietta*. No.

Serj. *Jefferies*. Did you on Wednesday?

Lady *Henrietta*. No.

Serj. *Jefferies*. Good God! Pray, Madam, how long afterwards was it that you saw him?

Lady *Henrietta*. Sir, it was a great while after.

Mr *Williams*. How many days or weeks after was it?

Lady *Henrietta*. Sir, I cannot tell.

Serj. *Jefferies*. As near as you can, Madam, when was it?

Lady *Henrietta*. I can remember the first place that I saw him at after, but the time exactly I cannot.

Mr *Williams*. Where was that, Madam?

Lady *Henrietta*. It was in a hackney-coach.

Mr *Williams*. That was the time, I suppose, that you sent for him out of the coffee house in Covent-Garden?

Lady *Henrietta*. Yes, I did so.

Mr *Williams*. Pray, Madam, did you write any letter to my lord Grey after your going away?

Lady *Henrietta*. Yes, I did by the next post.

Mr *Williams*. When did you write that letter, Madam?

Lady *Henrietta*. I did write it upon the Tuesday after I came away. I hope that is no offence.

L.C.J. No? Is it not? You should have writ to somebody else sure.

Lady *Henrietta*. I thought him the fittest person for me to write to, and I did not imagine it would be any ways scandalous for him, he being the nearest relation I had in the world, except my own brother, that could protect me.

Mr *Williams*. Had you any answer from my lord Grey to that matter, Madam?

Lady *Henrietta*. Yes; and a very harsh letter it was.

Mr *Williams*. Did you write him any other letter?

Lady *Henrietta*. Yes; but I received no answer of it at all.

Mr *Thompson*. Pray, Madam, did my lord Grey, at any time, persuade you to return to your father's?

Lady *Henrietta*. Yes, he did so several times.

Serj. *Jefferies*. Pray, Madam, do you know Charnock, that was my lord Grey's gentleman?

Lady *Henrietta*. Yes, I do.

Serj. *Jefferies*. Upon your oath, did not he carry you away from Durdants?

Lady *Henrietta*. No.

Serj. *Jefferies*. Nor did not his wife assist you in it? –

Lady *Henrietta*. No.

Serj. *Jefferies*. Nor was she not with you on the Sunday morning?

Lady *Henrietta*. No, nor was not with me.

Att. Gen. Were you not at Mrs Hilton's then, Madam? –

Lady *Henrietta*. No.

Att. Gen. Were you at Pattens?

Lady *Henrietta*. No.

Sol. Gen. Nor at Jones's?

Lady *Henrietta*. No, nor at Jones's upon my oath.

Att. Gen. Pray, who did come with you from Durdants?

Lady *Henrietta*. I shall not give any account of that, for I will not betray any body for their kindness to me.

Mr *Wallop*. If it be no body in the information, she is not bound to tell who it was.

Lady *Henrietta*. If I have vowed to them before, not to discover, I will not break my vow to them.

Just. *Dolben*. If they ask you of any body in the information, you have heard their names, you must tell if it were any of them, but you are not bound to tell if it were any one else.

Lady *Henrietta*. No, it was none of them, I went away upon another account.

L.C.J. If you have no further questions to ask her, pray, Madam, sit down again.

Lady *Henrietta*. Will you not give me leave to tell the reason why I left my father's house?

Just. *Dolben*. If they will ask you it they may. You are their witness.

Mr *Williams*. No, my lord, we do not think fit to ask her any such question; she acquits us, and that is enough.

Lady *Henrietta*. But I desire to tell it myself.

L.C.J. Truly, I see no reason to permit it, except we saw you were a more indifferent person to give evidence than we find you.

Lady *Henrietta*. Will you not give me leave to speak for myself?

Just. *Dolben*. My lord; let her speak what she has a mind to, the jury are gentlemen of discretion enough, to regard it no more than they ought. But, madam, for God's sake consider you are upon your oath; and do not add wilful perjury to your other faults.

Lady *Henrietta*. I have been very much reflected upon here to-day, and my reputation suffers much by the censure of the world, and therefore –

L.C.J. You have injured your own reputation, and prostituted both your body and your honour, and are not to be believed.

The trial ended in uproar when Lady Henrietta declared that she was married to William Turner. There was immediate confusion in the court as it was believed her husband was the son of a Sir William Turner described as an 'advocate'. Lady Henrietta's husband was, in fact, Lord Grey's servant and the marriage was simply one of convenience.

[Then the jury began the withdraw.]

Earl of *Berkeley*. My lord chief justice, I desire I may have my daughter delivered to me again.

L.C.J. My lord Berkeley must have his daughter again.

Lady *Henrietta*. I will not go to my father again.

Just. *Dolben*. My lord, she being now in court, and there being a Homine replegiando against my lord Grey, for her, upon which he was committed, we must now examine her. Are you under any custody or restraint, Madam?

Lady *Henrietta*. No, my lord; I am not.

L.C.J. Then we cannot deny my lord Berkeley the custody of his own daughter.

Lady *Henrietta*. My lord, I am married.

L.C.J. To whom?

Lady *Henrietta*. To Mr Turner.

L.C.J. What Turner? Where is he?

Lady *Henrietta*. He is here in court.

[He being among the crowd, way was made for him to come in, and he stood by the lady and the judges.]

L.C.J. Let's see him that has married you. Are you married to this lady?

Mr *Turner*. Yes, I am so, my lord.

L.C.J. What are you?

Mr *Turner*. I am a gentleman.

L.C.J. Where do you live?

Mr *Turner*. Sometimes in town, sometimes in the country.

L.C.J. Where do you live when you are in the country?

Mr *Turner*. Sometimes in Somersetshire.

Just. *Dolben*. He is, I believe, the son of sir William Turner that was the advocate, he is a little like him.

Serj. *Jefferies*. Ay, we all know Mr Turner well enough. And to satisfy you this is all a part of the same design, and one of the foulest practices that ever was used, we shall prove he was married to another person before, that is now alive, and has children by him.

Mr *Turner*. Ay, do, sir George, if you can, for there never was any such thing.

Serj. *Jefferies*. Pray, Sir, did not you live at Bromley with a woman as man and wife, and had divers children, and living so intimately were you not questioned for it, and you and she owned yourselves to be man and wife?

Mr *Turner*. My lord, there is no such thing; but this is my wife I do acknowledge.

Att. Gen. We pray, my lord, that he may have his oath.

Mr *Turner*. My lord, here are the witnesses ready to prove that were by.

Earl of *Berkeley*. Truly as to that, to examine this matter by witnesses, I conceive this Court, though it be a great Court, yet has not the cognizance of marriages: and though here be a pretence of a marriage, yet I know you will not determine it, how ready soever he be to make it out by witnesses, but I desire she may be delivered up to me, her father, and let him take his remedy.

L.C.J. I see no reason but my lord may take his daughter.

Earl of *Berkeley*. I desire the Court will deliver her to me.

Just. *Dolben*. My lord, we cannot dispose of any other man's wife, and they say they are married. We have nothing to do in it.

L.C.J. My lord Berkeley, your daughter is free for you to take her; as for Mr Turner, if he thinks he has any right to the lady, let him take his course. Are you at liberty and under no restraint?

Lady *Henrietta*. I will go with my husband.

Earl of *Berkeley*. Hussey, you shall go with me home.

Lady *Henrietta*. I will go with my husband.

Earl of *Berkeley*. Hussey, you shall go with me, I say.

Lady *Henrietta*. I will go with my husband.

Then the Court broke up, and passing through the hall there was a great scuffle about the lady, and swords drawn on both sides, but my lord chief justice coming by, ordered the tipstaff that attended him (who had formerly a warrant to search for her and take her into custody) to take charge of her, and carry her over to the King's-bench; and Mr Turner asking if he should be committed too, the chief justice told him, he might go with her if he would, which he did, and as it is reported, they lay together that night in the Marshal's-house, and she was released out of prison, by order of the Court, the last day of the term.

On the morning after the trial, being Friday the 24th November, the jury that tried the cause, having (as is usual in all cases not capital tried at the bar, where the Court do not sit long enough to take the verdict) given in a private verdict the evening before, at a judge's chamber, and being now called over, all appeared, and being asked if they did abide by the verdict that they gave the night before, they answered, yes; which was read by the clerk of the crown to be, that all defendants were guilty of the matters charged in the information, except Rebecca Jones, who was not guilty; which verdict being recorded, was commended by the Court and the king's counsel, and the jury discharged.

But in the next vacation the matter was compromised, and so no judgment was ever prayed, or entered upon record, but Mr Attorney General was pleased, before the next Hilary-Term, to enter a Noli Prosequi as to all the defendants.

APPENDIX II

By 1682 many satires had already appeared on Lord Grey, Monmouth, and Sir Thomas Armstrong. One of the most successful broadsides on the subject of the conspirators was *Lady Grey's Ghost: A True Relation of a Strange Apparition*. After the scandal of Henrietta Berkeley's elopement with Lord Grey, the following satire was published containing particular echoes of Aphra Behn's work:

A NEW VISION OF THE LADY GR——S,
CONCERNING HER SISTER, THE LADY HENRIETTA BERKELEY.
IN A LETTER TO MADAM FAN——————

Madam,
Let Miracles be ceas'd, Heav'n has still preserv'd a way to Reveal its mysteries to the Faithful. Let Divines and Phylosophers say what they will of Oracles and witches, they shall ever beat out of my Brains the Doctrine of Spirits and Visions. Was not Willmore[a] Convicted for a Kidnapper? and was not my own Sister but Spirited away t'other Day? Either you must allow there are Spirits, or a Transmigration, which is more absur'd, and that her Soul is transform'd into some other Beast or Foul, for in her own likeness she is not to be found. I have had (Madam) so many Visions upon this occasion, that I protest I cannot tell which to begin with.

T'other Day coming from the *Spanish Fryar*, as soon as I lay me down, I dream't, that the Amourous Collonel was my Husband, and out of meer kindness, because he cou'd never have enough of me, ran away with my own Sister; but this being an Idea of what had been represented, working upon my Fancy, I took no more notice of it.

---

[a] The central character in Aphra Behn's play *The Rover*. Probably an allusion to the Earl of Rochester, who kidnapped the woman he later married.

I had scarce fall'n into another Slumber, but going through a vast Forest, I saw methought another Vision, and Lo! there appeared unto me a young Dow catch'd in the Toils in a Thicket, where none cou'd find her out, and the Keeper a Prisoner in the Lodge for Decoying her from the Herd, and singling her out for his own use. I made hast to get her out, when behold the Vision vanish'd, and no Track or Resemblance of her left behind. This startled me the more, and made me give more Credit to the Vision, who waking, I found my Sister was to be found no where, and my Husband in a Gaol.

The next Night coming from an Entertainment in the Land of Promise, which the Tories call Whigland, I had no sooner laid me down upon my Pillow, but straight (methought) my Genius appear'd, nay, tho' I were dead asleep, this Prophet by laying Mouth to Mouth, Brest to Brest, Thigh to Thigh, and Foot to Foot, wou'd even raise me to new Life.

This was once the Guardian Genius of the Kingdom, that Inspir'd the Court as well as the Country, but now he has taken up with the Mobile, filling them with strange Notions, Whimsies and Chimeras, and now and then takes a Sally amongst his Petticoat Friends, where (in spite of all Lineal Right, or Succession to the Throne of Love, or the Nation,) he Reigns Absolute Monarch, and no doubt his Soveraignty would be boundless, if he were not govern'd by another Armstrong, or rather Head-strong, Genius, that leads him about as the Vinegar-man does his Ass, by the Nose, crying Liberty Three Pence a Pint, and like the Dog in the Fable,[b] makes him drop his Substance for the Shadow.

This Genius of a Genius, but to me my better Angel, finding the Anguish of my heart, who had often div'd into the bottom of it; come, said he, (my Dear) I know thy Trouble, follow me and I will shew thee thy Sister. Being overjoy'd, (methought) I rose and follow'd him, being led by a Star, which like a Dark-Lanthorn he always carry'd before him. After he had led me through several green Midows, Orchards and Inclosures, we came at last to a deep Cave, which was inaccessible by any Mortal, for no man cou'd yet find the way to it.

Here appeared unto me another Vision, A Red Cow, and a Gray Bull, of the delicatest shape, and the finest stateliest Horns

---

[b] Behn's translation of La Fontaine's Fable LXXX reads 'The wishing Curr growne covetous of all,/To catch the Shadow letts the Substance fall.' See *Works of Aphra Behn*, Vol. 1, p. 258.

as ever adorn'd Brow. Bless me! (said I) wha't here? Jupiter and Io? No said my Genius, 'tis your Sister, and a Friend of yours. My Sister! said I, with that I made up to them, and though I love red Cows Milk naturally, I had a greater Longing to stroak the Bull, but she had been there before, and now making up nearer, the better to discern them, they unanimously fell upon me on either side, Goreing me with their Horns, with the Fright of which I awaked. But Reading the Story of Europa and the Bull, the Day before, in *Sandys's Metamorphosis*, I minded it no further.

The Third Night coming from a friendly Meeting in the same Place, inspir'd with Love and an Evening Lecture, I return'd home, my kind Genius being still at my Elbow, I had much adoe to forbear sleeping in my Coach. I had no sooner got to Bed, but my nimble *Mercury*, my ingenious Genius who was always Gentleman-Usher to my Fancy, had got there before me, cutting Capers over my Pillow, and Charming me as before, to a new Life, methought I found my self in a new World of Pleasure, and indeed so it was, for methought I was in *Fairy*-Land and saw a new Vision, my Sister with Oberon sitting, like Queen Mabb, in a Tulip-stalk, with a Glo-worm for their Foot-stool, feeding on Philters and Love Powders. Bless me! said I , what is my Sister turn'd Queen of the *Fairies* ? yes, said my Genius, and *Oberon* had put the Changeling upon your Husband, for whoever has her in keeping, he must find her out. So I awaked.

London, Printed for J. Smith. 1682.

APPENDIX III

In an attempt to persuade his daughter to abandon Ford Grey, Lord Berkeley persuaded Dr John Tillotson, later to be the Archbishop of Canterbury, to write to her. A copy of the letter has been preserved in the British Library among the papers of Thomas Birch.

A COPPY OF A LETTER WRIT BY DR TILLOTSON TO MY LADY H. BERKELEY UPON HER LEAVING THE FAMILY

Though I have found by experience good councill is for the most part cast away upon those who have plunged themselves so deep into a bad course, as to my great greif & amazement I understand your Ladyship. has done, yet the concernment I have alwaies had for you, whom I look upon as one of the greatest objects of pitty in this world, will not suffer me to leave any means untry'd that may conduce to yr recovery out of ye wicked & wretched condition in wch you are. And therefore I beg of you for Gods sake & your own to give me leave plainly to represent to you ye heinousness of yr fault with the certain dismal consequences of yr continuance in it. And tis of that heinous nature as to be for ought I know without example in this or any other christian nation & hath in it all possible aggravations of guilt towards God, of dishonour to yr self, of a most outragious injury & affront to yr sister of reproach & stain to yr family, of most cruel ingratitude to as kind & indulgent parents as any child ever had, of wch I am a witness, as I have since been of ye deep wound & affliction you have given them to that degree as would grieve the heart of a stranger, & ought surely to make a much deeper impression upon you their child, who have been the cause of it. Consider of it as you will answer it at the judgment of ye Great Day, & now you have done wt you can to ruine your reputation, think of saving yr soul, & do not to please yr self or any body else for a little while venture to be

miserable for ever, as you will most certainly be if you goe on in this course; nay I doubt not but you will be very miserable in this world, not only from the severe relections of yr own mind, but from the distresse you will be reduced too when after a while you will in all probability be dispised & hated & foreseaken by him for whose sake you have made your self odious to all the world. Before this happen, think of reconciling yr self to God & to your best friends under him yr parents of whose kindness & tenderness you have had ye experience, yt you have little reason to fear their cruelty & rigour. Despise not this advice wch is now tendered to you out of great charity & good will & I pray God it may be effectual to bring you to repentance & a better mind. I have but one thing more to beg of you that you would be pleased by a line of two to let me understand that you have read & considered this letter from
Madam
Yr Ladyships. most Faithfull &
Humble Servant
Jo. Tillotson.

VARIANTS

LOVE-LETTERS   PART I

The copy-text is taken from University Microfilms Early English Books 1641–1700, 82:10: (Beinecke copies Ij B395: 6841: 1–3). Variants for *Love-Letters* Part I are taken from the alternative text in the University of Texas (Aj B396: 6841). In the list of variants below the Beinecke text is followed by a semi-colon and the Texas text is prefaced by a T. In the list of emendations, the copy text is followed by a semi-colon and the editor's emendations are prefaced by an E.

3.1: *Paris*; T *Paris*,
5.1: and; T &
5.9: Torism; T Toryism
5.11: hopeful; T hopefull
5.17: solid,; T solid
5.21: only; T onely
5.28: do; T doe
6.2: Age; T age
6.5: beautiful; T beautifull
6.6: amorous; T amarous
6.12: cry; T crie
6.13: did'st; T didst
6.15: Whigg; T Whig
6.17: opini-on to pall; T opioni-ontopaul
6.29: charms; T charmes
7.2: only; T onely
7.5: only; T onely
7.9: do; T doe
7.12: only; T onely
7.15: do; T doe
7.20: o're; T o'er
7.24: preserv'd; T prefer'd
7.25: and,; T and
9.3: *Caesario*; T *Cesario*
9.13: *made*,; T *made*
9.14: *and*; T *and*,
9.16: *Arms*; T *Armes*
9.20: Caesario; T Cesario

10.4: Caesario; T Cesario
10.4: *whatever*; T *mhetever*
10.20: only; T onely
10.24: suffice,; T suffice
10.29: this flight; T their flight
11.18: justifie; T justify
12.1: Maid,; T Maid
12.10: born,; T born
12.11: nonsense. A fit of Honour!; T nonsence. A fit, oh Honour!
12.12: represent; T respreent
12.28: obstinately; T obstinatly
13.8: least my; T leastmy
13.14: distinctions,; T distinctions
13.17: The; T the
13.17: Poppy;; T Poppy:
13.21: powerfull; T powerful
14.12: Arms; T Armes
14.16: God!; T God
14.16-17: Married; T Marryed
14.22: now; T and now
14.34: *Bellfont*; T *Belfont*
15.5: Maid: In; T Maid; in
15.9: Wings; which; T Wings: Which
15.9: interrupted; T interupted
15.10: attoneing; T atoneing

467

15.20: its; T it's
15.20: Beauties;; T Beauties,
15.25: heart--; T heart? -
16.13-14: Husband's careless; T
    Husband, carlless
17.7: Hero; T Heroe
17.13: *Hero*; T *Heroe*
17.20: longer hide; T longerhide
17.22: eyes; T eyes,
17.25: *Silvia;;* T *Silvia,*
18.4: feeble; T feable
18.12: desparing; T dsepairing
18.28: her,; T her;
18.28: i'll; T i'le
18.30: nobles; T nobly
18.31: owns; T ownes
20.3: it's; T 'ts
20.3-4: for ever; T forever
20.5: Arms; T Armes
20.25: words,; T words
20.35: burns; T burnes
21.1: *Silvia's*; T *Silvias*
21.5: Goddess; T Godess
21.9: or'e; T o're
21.10: flowers; T flowres
22.5: with a dread; T with dread
22.14: Brother; T Brother,
22.21: oh!; T oh
22.25: informs; T informes
22.27: unkind!; T unkind;
22.39: eternal; T etternal
23.14: thus it was won; T thus
    was it won
23.19: dy; T dye
23.24: Caesario; T Cesaro
23.26: Rebels; T Rebells
24.5: false,; T false;
24.10: and; T and
24.10: quiet,; T quiet:
24.20: then!; T then:
24.28: I dy; T Idy
25.6: Damons; T Demons
25.7: tranquility; T tranquillity
25.10: mutiners; T mutiniers
25.10: mighty; T mightier
25.25: unspotted; T unspoted
26.2: *Caesario*; T *Cesario*
26.9: passion; T Passion

26.10: *Mertilla,;* T *Mertilla;*
26.14: eccho; T echo
26.15: hers; T her's
26.15: Prize;; T Prize,
26.21: did,; T did;
26.24: I'll; T I'le
26.25: beau-tiful; T beau.tyful
26.30: Nose,; T Nose;
26.31: even,; T even;
26.32: beauti-; T beau
26.37: *Caesario*; T *Cesario*
27.2: *Caesario*; T *Cesario*
27.20: frivolous; T frivollous
28.8: six; T Six
28.26: eyes; T ey's
28.27: Angels; T Angells
28.30: passion; T Passion
28.32: 'twill; T 'twil
29.1: Caesario; T Cesario
29.5: desires?; T desires:
29.11: prejudical; T prejudicial
29.18: easily; T easely
29.19: whither; T whether
29.22: *Dorillus*; T *Dorilluus*
29.26: obscurity; T onscurdity
29.31: Beauties; T Beauty's
29.31: Charms; T Charmes
29.36: I'll; T I'le
29.36: I'll; T I'le
30.1: I'll T I'le
30.5: it:; T it;
30.5: look,; T look;
30.7: opportunity,; T
    opportunity;
30.7: lest; T least
30.15: 'twill; T 'twil
30.15: be an Age; T be a an
    Age
30.18: 'tis pitiful sometimes; T
    oh 'tis pitiful sometimes
30.18: me,; T me;
30.22: Charms; T Charmes
30.28: reproaches;; T
    reproaches:
30.30: passion; T Passion
30.34: dictates; T dictats
30.36: *Bellfont*; T *Belfont*
31.5: faint; T aint

31.6: Clock,; T Clock;
31.11: Faith; T faith
31.11: much,; T much;
31.15: oblig'd if Passion; T oblig'd; if Passion
31.18: pains; T paines
31.19: desires,; T desires;
31.23: Arms; T Armes
31.27: Arms; T Armes
31.28: Glories; T Glor's
32.3: greediness; T greedyness
32.9: grew,; T grew;
32.12: Strawberries; T Strawberies
32.20: Jessamine; T Jesamine
32.24: floor; T floore
32.27: Life; T life
32.30: over-whelm'd; T over whelm'd
32.36: thought,; T thought;
32.37: slackens; T slackens,
32.37: hand,; T hand;
33.5: new,; T new;
33.6: Lover,; T Lover;
33.8: dull:; T dull;
33.9: Rhetorick; T Rethorick
33.10: Sighs,; T Sighs;
33.11: hand,; T hand;
33.14: away,; T away;
33.24: to ruine; T toruine
33.26–7: Apartment,; T Apartment;
33.30: me,; T me;
33.33: strength,; T strength;
33.36: stealth,; T stealth;
34.3: me,; T me;
34.3: fast,; T fast;
34.7: complection; T complexion
34.15: me:; T me;
34.16: sigh'd,; T sigh'd;
34.19: *Bellfont*; T *Belfont*
34.26: wildness; T wileness
34.28: hours?; T hours
34.32: Cabals; T Caballs
34.33: Groves,; T Groves;
35.1: Swains; T Swaines
35.1: homely; T homly
35.3: Streams; T Streames

35.10: turns; T turnes
35.16: troublesome; T toublesome
35.24: Ceremony; T Ce-rimony
35.25: Arms; T Armes
35.35: Bruits; T Bruites
36.7: *Dorillus*; T *Dorilus*
36.9: much difficulty; T muchdifficulty
36.13: happiness; T happyness
36.21: off; T of
37.1: busie; T bussie
38.12: answer me?; T answer me;
38.14: Arms; T Armes
38.15: Bosome; T Bosom
38.16: slow-pac'd; T slow pac'd
38.36: pursuit; T persute
39.7: and give me; T and give, me
39.34: with me; T with with me
39.40: Beauty,; T Beauty;
39.40: mind,; T of mind;
40.21: Murder; T Murder!
40.32: o'reflow; T O'reflow
41.21: Thieves; T Theives
41.29: t'other; T 'tother
42.21: Philander!; T Philander
42.25: gratitude,; T gratitude;
43.5: infamy; T infamie
43.15: *Cassandria*; T *Cassandra*
44.10: at present; T a present
44.28: Charms; T Charmes
45.3: Charms; T Charmes
45.16: 'twill; T 'twil
45.18: 'twill; T 'twil
45.33: must; T mnst
47.10: Charms; T Charmes
48.18: *and then*; T *and then and then*
48.18: *hinkwere*; T *to think where*
48.19: *twaiting*; T *waiting*
49.9: Cermonious; T Cerimonious
49.21: jealous; T jealouse
49.30: *Mertila's*; T *Mertilla's*
49.31: *Philander* T *Phillander*
50.5: *Mertila*; T *Mertilla*

51.4: *Mertila*; T *Mertilla*
52.2: Lorships; T Lordships
53.22: gone; T gon
53.27: I'll T I'le
54.15: taring; T tearing
54.25: restrain me,; T restrain,
  me
54.30: mee; T me
54.34: unhapy; T unhappy
55.27: easie; T easy
56.28: Counterscarps; T
  Counterscraps
57.23: Lovers;; T Lover.
57.24: What! my *Silvia!*; T What
  my *Silvia,*
57.34: conceated; T conceited
63.4: hast; T haste
64.26: Savages; T Sal-vages
65.18: remains; T remains;
66.11: fortune; T fortunate
67.4: to well; T too well
67.18: *Mertilla*; T *Myrtilla*
68.15: easie; T easy
68.22: Awful; T Awfull
69.1: thy; T thou
69.12: and you!; T and you?
69.17: Arms; T Armes
70.2: arms; T armes
70.13–14: before:; T before?
70.16: do; T doe
70.28: arms; T armes
71.2: alas!; T alas,
71.33: bosted; T boasted
72.11: only; T onely
72.12: breath; T breathe
72.17: undo; T undoe
72.18: *Silvia*; T *Silvia,*
72.26: roul; T roll
72.33: *Dorillus*; T *Dorilus*
73.3: controul; T controll
73.8: ne'r; T ne'er
73.10: only; T onely
73.12: *do*; T *doe*
73.25: arms; T armes
73.27: gone,; T gone;
74.17: bloud; T blood
77.6: pursue; T persue
77.26: only; T onely

79.5: only; T onely
79.20: o'recome; T o'ercome
79.26: o're; T o'er
79.29: e're; T e'er
79.39: doe; T doe
80.1: dy; T die
80.4: Arms; T Armes
80.11: where e're T wheree'r
80.19: undo; T undoe
80.28: to have; T to've
81.5: o're; T o'er
81.6: only; T onely
81.14: ne're; T Ne'er
81.20: inventions; neglected; T
  inventions neglected
81.23: *Dorillus*; T *Dorilus*
81.24: arms; T armes
81.26: dy; T die
81.33: arms; T armes
81.41: only; T onely
82.1: only; T onely
82.8: dy; T die
82.11: o're; T o'er
82.31: do't; T doe't
83.21: pursue; T persue
84.10: she; T shee
84.26: whene'r; T whene'er
85.17: o're; T o'er
86.11: glittering; T glitering
86.16: recompense; T
  recompence
86.18: Loves-secrets; T Love-
  Secrets
86.21: Arms; T Armes
86.31: o'rejoy'd; T o'erjoy'd
87.11: e're; T e'er
87.23: happier; T happyer
87.25: Arms; T Armes
88.12: stomack; T stomach
88.12: amorous; T amarous
88.16: armed; T arm'd
88.20: dy; T; T die
88.21: only; T onely
88.27: my poor; T my my poor
88.42: doting; T doating
89.5–6: transcend transcendst
89.8: touches; beside; T touches
  beside

89.17: only; T onely
89.23: when e're; T whene'er
89.24: whate're; T whate'er
89.26: ruine; T ruin
89.33: e're; T e'er
89.33: break'st; T breakst
89.33: e're; T e'er
89.35: dy; T die
89.38: dy; T die
90.6: e're; T e'er
90.20: only; T onely
90.30: shower; T showre
90.32: read; T reade
91.37: *Dorillus*; T *Dorilus*
92.18: Sister.; T Sister;
92.29: arms; T armes
92.30: dy; T die
92.31: sad confusion; T sad a
   confusion
93.1: objects,; T objects
93.34: amorous; T amarous
93.37: fledg'd; T fletch'd
94.11: may'st; T mayst
94.12: string, by which; T string
   by which
94.25: charms; T charmes
95.3: ne're; T ne'er
95.3: dy; T die
95.3: *Mertilla*; T *Mertila*
95.7: may'st; T mayst
95.11: may'st T ne'er
95.16: dy; T die
95.20: do; T doe
96.2: only; T onely
96.7: dy; T die
96.8: *Dorillus*; T *Dorilus*
96.18: do; T doe
96.20: send'st; T sendst
96.21: call'st; T callst
97.2: *Dorillus*; T *Dorilus*
97.6: *Dorillus*; T *Dorilus*
97.12: Arms; T Armes
97.15: can'st; T canst
97.25: ruin; T ruine
97.26: rack; T wrak
98.1: did'st; T didst
98.2: arms; T armes
98.4: swor'st; T sworst

98.10: blessed'st; T blessedst
98.12: arms; T armes
98.20: e're; T e'er
98.21: e're; T e'er
98.22: e're; T e'er
98.23: did'st; T didst
98.25–26: only I, poor I; T onely
   I; poor I
98.42: arms; T armes
99.2: showers; T showrs
99.11: e're; T e'er
99.12: e're; T e'er
99.13: e're; T e'er
100.9: *Dorillus*; T *Dorilus*
100.24: only; T onely
101.1: undo; T undoe
101.3: suffice; T suffize
101.8: arms; T armes
101.19: do; T doe
101.22: dy; T die
101.24: whene're; T when-eer
102.11: do; T doe
102.12: *Guard*; T *Gaurd*
102.17: pursuit; T persuit
102.32: think'st; T thinkst
102.33: think'st; T thinkst
102.33: pursue; T persue
103.2: think'st; T thinkst
103.10: do; T doe
103.23: *Madam*; T Madam
104.4: dy; T die
104.31: feaver; T fever
105.9: e're; T e'er
105.13: might'st; T mightst
105.15: Coach-man; T
   Coachman
105.19-20: my own repose, I
   imagin'd the; T my own
   repose, imagin the
105.27: fern; T ferne
105.36: e're; T e'er
105.37: alighted; T allighted
105.40: arms; T armes
106.13: arms; T armes
106.15: do; T doe
107.1: that a trivial; T that trivial
107.6: uneasie; T shagrine
107.6: arms; T armes

107.18: dy; T die
108.15: hazards; T hazzards
108.25: dy; T die
109.7: e'er; T e're
109.15: dy; T die
109.21: Fauxburgh S. Germans;
    T Fabour St Jer-mins
109.22: Chevalier; T Chievalier
110.16: only; T onely
110.22: joyn; T join
110.31: only; T onely
111.8: blood; T bloud
111.17: *Antonio*; T *Antoyne*

112.11: do; T doe
112.14: He is my Husband; T He
    my Husband
113.3: arms; T armes
113.7: do; T doe
113.8: only; T onely
113.12: only; T onely
113.15: only; T onely
113.19: do't; T doe't
114.111: do; T doe
114.17: only; T onely
115.4: do; T doe
116.6: whene're; T whene'er

EMENDATIONS

18.22: Apetite; E Appetite
18.28: whistler off; E whistle her
    off
18.30: nobles; E nobly
28.6: sigh't; E sighed
37.8: Cerimony; E Ceremony
38.34: carier; E career
42.7: nncertain; E uncertain
51.12: VVorld; E World
53.4: VVell; E Well
61.2: adoe; E ado
71.33: bosted; E boasted
74.25: Leudly; E lewdly
101.30: hapned; E happened
111.8: bloud; E blood
123.29: alied; E allied
126.25: hid; E hide
128.10: tha; E that
128.19: rsentment; E resentment
128.21: if; E of
129.34: fram; E from
130.21: howsa fe; E how safe
133.33: silent; E silence
134.23: infinitey; E infinitely
137.20: leavign; E leaving
139.11: reecive; E receive
145.2: veiw; E view
145.19: where; E were
141.28: greif; E grief

145.2: veiw'd; E view'd
147.8: Philadner; E Philander
147.40: Fortunetellers; E Fortune
    tellers
149.31: lovethose; E love those
161.6: along; E a long
161.11: ayoung; E a young
165.20: Fiers; E Fires
166.18: VVomen; E Women
166.25: ou'd; E cou'd
167.32: oftenimes; E * oftentimes
171.35: femal; E female
176.15: beckning; E beckoning
176.27: VVind; E Wind
176.39: the the thickest; E the
    thickest
176.40: VValks; E Walks
187.28: tooo; E too
187.30: off; E of
191.13: Leter; E Letter
193.29: erxteamly; E extreamly
1948.28: alay; E allay
217.17: youug; E young
219.17: vvich; E which
219.23: vvhen; E when
221.8: soothsit; E sooths it
228.29: Fend; E Fiend
238.29: vvhich; E which
241.22: search; E searched

242.2: Svvear; E Swear
242.2: vvas; E was
242.3: vvou; E wou
250.12: alljed; E allied
250.30: tomy; E to my
274.6: yeilded; E yielded
274.34: flying a Cupid; E flying
  Cupid
282.37: Shooes; E Shoes
285.1: *Witneß*; E *Witness*
286.16: *Goodneß*; E *Goodness*
286.18: *Happineß*; E *Happiness*
289.33: it it was; E it was
290.17: *restleß*; E *restless*
290.27: *Mistreß*; E *Mistress*
292.39: atlast; E at last
294.14: Falsehood; E Falshhood
295.19: *Goddeß*; E *Goddess*
296.17: *Baseneß*; E *Baseness*
297.22: *Bleß*; E *Bless*
304.27: managent; E
  management
304.38: oft hat; E of that
307.9: *form*; E *from*
307.13: *gueß*; E *guess*
307.22: *happineß*; E *happiness*
307.24: *Fondneß*; E *Fondness*
307.35: *Sleepineß*; E *Sleepiness*
307.35: *Carelessneß*; E *Carelessness*
307.35: *paß*; E *pass*
308.2: *tenderneß*; E *tenderness*

308.26: *scaleing*; E *scaling*
308.32: *confeß*; E *confess*
308.35: *Dreß*; E *Dress*
309.21: *paß*; E *pass*
310.1: *matchleß*; E *matchless*
310.16: *confeß*; E *confess*
310.21: *Busineß*; E *Business*
312.2: *Illneß*; E *Illness*
312.13: *Baseneß*; E *Baseness*
329.18: Shooes; E Shoes
339.27: Cieling; E Ceiling
349.7: runing; E running
355.29: *hapleß*; E *hapless*
356.2: *Kiß*; E *Kiss*
356.42: *confeß*; E *confess*
360.41: *helpleß*; E *helpless*
361.8: *Easineß*; E *Easiness*
368.32: *Confeß*; E *Confess*
368.33: *Weakneß*; E *Weakness*
369.10: *faithleß*; E *faithless*
369.42: *posseß*; E *possess*
370.13: *leß*; E *less*
371.27: *Witneß*; E *Witness*
395.23–4: she desired himt o; E
  she desired him to
418.31: *posseß*; E *possess*
418.33: *gueß*; E *guess*
418.39: *confeß*; E *confess*
428.12–13: indfatigable; E
  indefatigable
437.4: Shooes; E A Shoes

READ MORE IN PENGUIN

In every corner of the world, on every subject under the sun, Penguin represents quality and variety – the very best in publishing today.

For complete information about books available from Penguin – including Puffins, Penguin Classics and Arkana – and how to order them, write to us at the appropriate address below. Please note that for copyright reasons the selection of books varies from country to country.

In the United Kingdom: Please write to Dept. EP, Penguin Books Ltd, Bath Road, Harmondsworth, West Drayton, Middlesex UB7 ODA

In the United States: Please write to Consumer Sales, Penguin USA, P.O. Box 999, Dept. 17109, Bergenfield, New Jersey 07621-0120. VISA and MasterCard holders call 1-800-253-6476 to order Penguin titles

In Canada: Please write to Penguin Books Canada Ltd, 10 Alcorn Avenue, Suite 300, Toronto, Ontario M4V 3B2

In Australia: Please write to Penguin Books Australia Ltd, P.O. Box 257, Ringwood, Victoria 3134

In New Zealand: Please write to Penguin Books (NZ) Ltd, Private Bag 102902, North Shore Mail Centre, Auckland 10

In India: Please write to Penguin Books India Pvt Ltd, 706 Eros Apartments, 56 Nehru Place, New Delhi 110 019

In the Netherlands: Please write to Penguin Books Netherlands bv, Postbus 3507, NL-1001 AH Amsterdam

In Germany: Please write to Penguin Books Deutschland GmbH, Metzlerstrasse 26, 60594 Frankfurt am Main

In Spain: Please write to Penguin Books S. A., Bravo Murillo 19, 1° B, 28015 Madrid

In Italy: Please write to Penguin Italia s.r.l., Via Felice Casati 20, I–20124 Milano

In France: Please write to Penguin France S. A., 17 rue Lejeune, F 31000 Toulouse

In Japan: Please write to Penguin Books Japan, Ishikiribashi Building, 2 5–4, Suido, Bunkyo-ku, Tokyo 112

In Greece: Please write to Penguin Hellas Ltd, Dimocritou 3, GR 106 71 Athens

In South Africa: Please write to Longman Penguin Southern Africa (Pty) Ltd, Private Bag X08, Bertsham 2013

PENGUIN AUDIOBOOKS

A Quality of Writing that Speaks for Itself

Penguin Books has always led the field in quality publishing. Now you can listen at leisure to your favourite books, read to you by familiar voices from radio, stage and screen. Penguin Audiobooks are ideal as gifts, for when you are travelling or simply to enjoy at home. They are produced to an excellent standard, and abridgements are always faithful to the original texts. From thrillers to classic literature, biography to humour, with a wealth of titles in between, Penguin Audiobooks offer you quality, entertainment and the chance to rediscover the pleasure of listening.

You can order Penguin Audiobooks through Penguin Direct by telephoning (0181) 899 4036. The lines are open 24 hours every day. Ask for Penguin Direct, quoting your credit card details.

Published or forthcoming:

Emma by Jane Austen, read by Fiona Shaw

Persuasion by Jane Austen, read by Joanna David

Pride and Prejudice by Jane Austen, read by Geraldine McEwan

The Tenant of Wildfell Hall by Anne Brontë, read by Juliet Stevenson

Jane Eyre by Charlotte Brontë, read by Juliet Stevenson

Villette by Charlotte Brontë, read by Juliet Stevenson

Wuthering Heights by Emily Brontë, read by Juliet Stevenson

The Woman in White by Wilkie Collins, read by Nigel Anthony and Susan Jameson

Heart of Darkness by Joseph Conrad, read by David Threlfall

Tales from the One Thousand and One Nights, read by Souad Faress and Raad Rawi

Moll Flanders by Daniel Defoe, read by Frances Barber

Great Expectations by Charles Dickens, read by Hugh Laurie

Hard Times by Charles Dickens, read by Michael Pennington

Martin Chuzzlewit by Charles Dickens, read by John Wells

The Old Curiosity Shop by Charles Dickens, read by Alec McCowen

PENGUIN AUDIOBOOKS

Crime and Punishment by Fyodor Dostoyevsky, read by Alex Jennings

Middlemarch by George Eliot, read by Harriet Walter

Silas Marner by George Eliot, read by Tim Pigott-Smith

The Great Gatsby by F. Scott Fitzgerald, read by Marcus D'Amico

Madame Bovary by Gustave Flaubert, read by Claire Bloom

Jude the Obscure by Thomas Hardy, read by Samuel West

The Return of the Native by Thomas Hardy, read by Steven Pacey

Tess of the D'Urbervilles by Thomas Hardy, read by Eleanor Bron

The Iliad by Homer, read by Derek Jacobi

Dubliners by James Joyce, read by Gerard McSorley

The Dead and Other Stories by James Joyce, read by Gerard McSorley

On the Road by Jack Kerouac, read by David Carradine

Sons and Lovers by D. H. Lawrence, read by Paul Copley

The Fall of the House of Usher by Edgar Allan Poe, read by Andrew Sachs

Wide Sargasso Sea by Jean Rhys, read by Jane Lapotaire and Michael Kitchen

The Little Prince by Antoine de Saint-Exupéry, read by Michael Maloney

Frankenstein by Mary Shelley, read by Richard Pasco

Of Mice and Men by John Steinbeck, read by Gary Sinise

Travels with Charley by John Steinbeck, read by Gary Sinise

The Pearl by John Steinbeck, read by Hector Elizondo

Dr Jekyll and Mr Hyde by Robert Louis Stevenson, read by Jonathan Hyde

Kidnapped by Robert Louis Stevenson, read by Robbie Coltrane

The Age of Innocence by Edith Wharton, read by Kerry Shale

The Buccaneers by Edith Wharton, read by Dana Ivey

Mrs Dalloway by Virginia Woolf, read by Eileen Atkins

READ MORE IN PENGUIN

A CHOICE OF CLASSICS

The Brothers Karamazov Fyodor Dostoyevsky

A drama of parricide and intense family rivalry, *The Brothers Karamazov* is Dostoyevsky's acknowledged masterpiece. It tells the story of the murder of a depraved landowner and the ensuing investigation and trial.

Selections from the Carmina Burana
A verse translation by David Parlett

The famous songs from the *Carmina Burana* (made into an oratorio by Carl Orff) tell of lecherous monks and corrupt clerics, drinkers and gamblers, and the fleeting pleasures of youth.

Fear and Trembling Søren Kierkegaard

A profound meditation on the nature of faith and submission to God's will, which examines with startling originality the story of Abraham and Isaac.

Selected Prose Charles Lamb

Lamb's famous essays (under the strange pseudonym of Elia) on anything and everything have long been celebrated for their apparently innocent charm. This major new edition allows readers to discover the darker and more interesting aspects of Lamb.

The Picture of Dorian Gray Oscar Wilde

Wilde's superb and macabre novel, one of his supreme works, is reprinted here with a masterly Introduction and valuable Notes by Peter Ackroyd.

Frankenstein Mary Shelley

In recounting this chilling tragedy Mary Shelley demonstrates both the corruption of an innocent creature by an immoral society and the dangers of playing God with science.

READ MORE IN PENGUIN

A CHOICE OF CLASSICS

Evelina Frances Burney

Subtitled *The History of a Young Lady's Entrance into the World*, the novel records in letters its young heroine's encounters with society, both high and low, in London and at fashionable watering places. It is acutely observant of the social laws regarding power, authority and authorship, which the author herself partly had to subvert.

The Republic Plato

The best-known of Plato's dialogues, *The Republic* is also one of the supreme masterpieces of Western philosophy, whose influence cannot be overestimated.

Brigitta and Other Tales Adalbert Stifter

Each of these four stories is set in a recognizable world depicted with measured realism. But once the reader has learned to look beneath the calm, apparently seamless surface of the narrative, and, in Stifter's words, 'to see with the heart', strange tensions are revealed.

The Poems of Exile Ovid

Exiled from Rome for his scandalous erotic verse and a mysterious (probably political) misdemeanour, Ovid spent his declining years in the remote Black Sea port of Tunis, trying to use poetry to win a reprieve.

The Birth of Tragedy Friedrich Nietzsche

Dedicated to Richard Wagner, *The Birth of Tragedy* created a furore on its first publication in 1871; it has since become one of the seminal books of European culture.

Madame Bovary Gustave Flaubert

With *Madame Bovary* Flaubert established the realistic novel in France while his central character of Emma Bovary, the bored wife of a provincial doctor, remains one of the great creations of modern literature.

READ MORE IN PENGUIN

A CHOICE OF CLASSICS

St Anselm	**The Prayers and Meditations**
St Augustine	**Confessions**
Bede	**Ecclesiastical History of the English People**
Geoffrey Chaucer	**The Canterbury Tales**
	Love Visions
	Troilus and Criseyde
Marie de France	**The Lais of Marie de France**
Jean Froissart	**The Chronicles**
Geoffrey of Monmouth	**The History of the Kings of Britain**
Gerald of Wales	**History and Topography of Ireland**
	The Journey through Wales and **The Description of Wales**
Gregory of Tours	**The History of the Franks**
Robert Henryson	**The Testament of Cresseid and Other Poems**
Walter Hilton	**The Ladder of Perfection**
Julian of Norwich	**Revelations of Divine Love**
Thomas à Kempis	**The Imitation of Christ**
William Langland	**Piers the Ploughman**
Sir John Mandeville	**The Travels of Sir John Mandeville**
Marguerite de Navarre	**The Heptameron**
Christine de Pisan	**The Treasure of the City of Ladies**
Chrétien de Troyes	**Arthurian Romances**
Marco Polo	**The Travels**
Richard Rolle	**The Fire of Love**
François Villon	**Selected Poems**

READ MORE IN PENGUIN

A CHOICE OF CLASSICS

ANTHOLOGIES AND ANONYMOUS WORKS

The Age of Bede
Alfred the Great
Beowulf
A Celtic Miscellany
The Cloud of Unknowing and Other Works
The Death of King Arthur
The Earliest English Poems
Early Irish Myths and Sagas
Egil's Saga
English Mystery Plays
Eyrbyggja Saga
Hrafnkel's Saga
The Letters of Abelard and Heloise
Medieval English Verse
Njal's Saga
Roman Poets of the Early Empire
Seven Viking Romances
Sir Gawain and the Green Knight

READ MORE IN PENGUIN

A CHOICE OF CLASSICS

Francis Bacon	**The Essays**
George Berkeley	**Principles of Human Knowledge/Three Dialogues between Hylas and Philonous**
James Boswell	**The Life of Samuel Johnson**
Sir Thomas Browne	**The Major Works**
John Bunyan	**The Pilgrim's Progress**
Edmund Burke	**Reflections on the Revolution in France**
Frances Burney	**Evelina**
Margaret Cavendish	**The Blazing World and Other Writings**
William Cobbett	**Rural Rides**
William Congreve	**Comedies**
Thomas de Quincey	**Confessions of an English Opium Eater**
	Recollections of the Lakes and the Lake Poets
Daniel Defoe	**A Journal of the Plague Year**
	Moll Flanders
	Robinson Crusoe
	Roxana
	A Tour through the Whole Island of Great Britain
Henry Fielding	**Amelia**
	Jonathan Wild
	Joseph Andrews
	Tom Jones
John Gay	**The Beggar's Opera**
Oliver Goldsmith	**The Vicar of Wakefield**

READ MORE IN PENGUIN

A CHOICE OF CLASSICS

William Hazlitt	**Selected Writings**
George Herbert	**The Complete English Poems**
Thomas Hobbes	**Leviathan**
Samuel Johnson/	
James Boswell	**A Journey to the Western Islands of Scotland and The Journal of a Tour of the Hebrides**
Charles Lamb	**Selected Prose**
George Meredith	**The Egoist**
Thomas Middleton	**Five Plays**
John Milton	**Paradise Lost**
Samuel Richardson	**Clarissa**
	Pamela
Earl of Rochester	**Complete Works**
Richard Brinsley	
Sheridan	**The School for Scandal and Other Plays**
Sir Philip Sidney	**Selected Poems**
Christopher Smart	**Selected Poems**
Adam Smith	**The Wealth of Nations**
Tobias Smollett	**The Adventures of Ferdinand Count Fathom**
	Humphrey Clinker
Laurence Sterne	**The Life and Opinions of Tristram Shandy**
	A Sentimental Journey Through France and Italy
Jonathan Swift	**Gulliver's Travels**
	Selected Poems
Thomas Traherne	**Selected Poems and Prose**
Sir John Vanbrugh	**Four Comedies**

READ MORE IN PENGUIN

A CHOICE OF CLASSICS

Matthew Arnold	**Selected Prose**
Jane Austen	**Emma**
	Lady Susan/The Watsons/Sanditon
	Mansfield Park
	Northanger Abbey
	Persuasion
	Pride and Prejudice
	Sense and Sensibility
William Barnes	**Selected Poems**
Anne Brontë	**Agnes Grey**
	The Tenant of Wildfell Hall
Charlotte Brontë	**Jane Eyre**
	Shirley
	Villette
Emily Brontë	**Wuthering Heights**
Samuel Butler	**Erewhon**
	The Way of All Flesh
Thomas Carlyle	**Selected Writings**
Arthur Hugh Clough	**Selected Poems**
Wilkie Collins	**The Moonstone**
	The Woman in White
Charles Darwin	**The Origin of Species**
	The Voyage of the _Beagle_
Benjamin Disraeli	**Sybil**
George Eliot	**Adam Bede**
	Daniel Deronda
	Felix Holt
	Middlemarch
	The Mill on the Floss
	Romola
	Scenes of Clerical Life
	Silas Marner
Elizabeth Gaskell	**Cranford/Cousin Phillis**
	The Life of Charlotte Brontë
	Mary Barton
	North and South
	Wives and Daughters

READ MORE IN PENGUIN

A CHOICE OF CLASSICS

A CHOICE OF CLASSICS

Lord Macaulay	**The History of England**
Henry Mayhew	**London Labour and the London Poor**
John Stuart Mill	**The Autobiography**
	On Liberty
William Morris	**News from Nowhere** and **Selected Writings and Designs**
John Henry Newman	**Apologia Pro Vita Sua**
Robert Owen	**A New View of Society and Other Writings**
Walter Pater	**Marius the Epicurean**
John Ruskin	**'Unto This Last' and Other Writings**
Walter Scott	**Ivanhoe**
	Heart of Midlothian
Robert Louis Stevenson	**Kidnapped**
	Dr Jekyll and Mr Hyde and Other Stories
William Makepeace Thackeray	**The History of Henry Esmond**
	The History of Pendennis
	Vanity Fair
Anthony Trollope	**Barchester Towers**
	Can You Forgive Her?
	The Eustace Diamonds
	Framley Parsonage
	He Knew He Was Right
	The Last Chronicle of Barset
	Phineas Finn
	The Prime Minister
	The Small House at Allington
	The Warden
	The Way We Live Now
Oscar Wilde	**Complete Short Fiction**
Mary Wollstonecraft	**A Vindication of the Rights of Woman**
	Mary and Maria
	Matilda
Dorothy and William Wordsworth	**Home at Grasmere**